W9-AEC-810

WITHDRAWN
NDSU

THE DIVINE FIRE

BY

MAY SINCLAIR

NEW YORK
HENRY HOLT AND COMPANY
1906

CONTENTS

BOOK I

DISJECTA MEMBRA POETÆ

CHAPTER I

HORACE JEWDWINE had made the most remarkable of his many remarkable discoveries. At least he thought he had. He could not be quite sure, which was his excuse for referring it to his cousin Lucia, whose instinct (he would not call it judgment) in these matters was infallible. Strangely infallible for so young a girl. What, he wondered, would she say to Savage Keith Rickman?

On Saturday, when he first came down into Devonshire, he would have been glad to know. But to-day, which was a Tuesday, he was not interested in Rickman. To eat strawberries all morning; to lie out in the hammock all afternoon under the beech-tree on the lawn of Court House; to let the peace of the old green garden sink into him; to look at Lucia and forget, utterly forget, about his work (the making of discoveries), that was what he wanted. But Lucia wanted to talk, and to talk about Rickman earnestly as if he were a burning question, when, even lying in the hammock, Jewdwine was so hot that it bothered him to talk at all.

He was beginning to be sorry that he had introduced him —the exciting topic, that is to say, not the man; for Rickman you could scarcely introduce, not at any rate to Lucia Harden.

"Well, Lucia." He pronounced her name in the Italian manner, "Loo-chee-a," with a languid stress on the vowels, and his tone conveyed a certain weary but polite forbearance.

Lucia herself, he noticed, had an ardent look, as if a particularly interesting idea had just occurred to her. He wished it hadn't. An idea of Lucia's would commit him to an opinion of his own; and at the moment Jewdwine was not prepared to abandon himself to anything so definite and irretrievable. He had not yet made up his mind about Rickman, and did not want to make it up now. Certainty was impossible, owing to his somewhat embarrassing acquaintance with the man. That, again, was where Lucia had come in. Her vision of him would be free and undisturbed by any suggestion of his bodily presence.

Meanwhile, Rickman's poem, or rather the first two Acts of his neo-classic drama, *Helen in Leuce,* lay on Lucia's lap. Jewdwine had obtained it under protest and with much secrecy. He had promised Rickman, solemnly, not to show it to a soul; but he had shown it to Lucia. It was all right, he said, so long as he refrained from disclosing the name of the person who had written it. Not that she would have been any the wiser if he had.

"And it was you who discovered him?" Her voice lingered with a peculiarly tender and agreeable vibration on the "you." He closed his eyes and let that, too, sink into him.

"Yes," he murmured, "nobody else has had a hand in it —as yet."

"And what are you going to do with him now you have discovered him?"

He opened his eyes, startled by the uncomfortable suggestion. It had not yet occurred to him that the discovery of Rickman could entail any responsibility whatever.

"I don't know that I'm going to do anything with him. Unless some day I use him for an article."

"Oh, Horace, is that the way you treat your friends?"

He smiled. "Yes, Lucy, sometimes, when they deserve it."

"You haven't told me your friend's name?"

"No. I betrayed his innocent confidence sufficiently in showing you his play. I can't tell you his name."

"After all, his name doesn't matter."

"No, it doesn't matter. Very likely you'll hear enough of it some day. You haven't told me what you think of him."

" I don't know what I think—But then, I don't know him."

" No," he said, roused to interest by her hesitation, " you don't know him. That's the beauty of it."

She gave the manuscript back into his hands. " Take him away. He makes me feel uncomfortable."

" To tell the truth, Lucy, he makes me feel uncomfortable, too."

" Why? "

" Well, when you think you've got hold of a genius, and you take him up and stake your reputation on him—and all the time you can't be sure whether it's a spark of the divine fire or a mere flash in the pan. It happens over and over again. The burnt critic dreads the divine fire."

His eyes were fixed on the title page as if fascinated by the words, *Helen in Leuce*.

" But this is not bad—it's *not* bad for two and twenty."

" Only two and twenty? "

" That's all. It looks as if he were made for immortality."

She turned to him that ardent gaze which made the hot day hotter.

" Dear Horace, you're going to do great things for him."

The worst of having a cousin who adores you is that magnificence is expected of you, regularly and as a matter of course. He was not even sure that Lucia did not credit him with power to work miracles. The idea was flattering but also somewhat inconvenient.

" I don't know about great things. I should like to do something. The question is what. He's a little unfortunate in—in his surroundings, and he's been ill, poor fellow. If one could give him a change. If one were only rich and could afford to send him abroad for a year. I *had* thought of asking him down to Oxford."

" And why didn't you? "

" Well, you know, one gets rather crowded up with things in term time."

Lucia looked thoughtfully at the refined, luxurious figure in the hammock. Horace was entitled to the hammock, for he had been ill. He was entitled also to the ministrations of his cousin Lucia. Lucia spent her time in planning and doing kind things, and, from the sudden luminous sweetness of her face, he gathered that something of the sort was in preparation now.

It was. "Horace," she said, "would you like to ask him here?"

"No, Lucy, I wouldn't. I don't think it would do."

"But why not—if he's your friend?"

"If he's my friend?"

"You *said* he was your friend. You did, you know." (Another awkward consequence of a cousin's adoration; she is apt to remember and attach importance to your most trivial utterances.)

"Pardon me, I said he was my find."

"Where did you find him?"

"I found him in the City—in a shop."

She smiled at the rhythmic utterance. The tragedy of the revelation was such that it could be expressed only in blank verse.

"The shop doesn't matter."

"No, but he does. You couldn't stand him, Lucia. You see, for one thing, he sometimes drops his aitches."

"Well, if he does,—he'll be out all day, and there's the open country to drop them in. I really don't mind if you'd like to ask him. Do you think he'd like to be asked?"

"There's no possible doubt about that."

"Then ask him. Ask him now. You can't do it when father's not at home."

Jewdwine repressed a smile. Even now from the windows of the east wing there burst, suddenly, the sound of fiddling, a masterly fiddling, inspired by infernal passion, controlled by divine technique. It was his uncle, Sir Frederick, and he wished him at the devil. If all accounts were true, Sir Frederick, when not actually fiddling, was going there with a celerity that left nothing to be desired; he was, if you came to think of it, a rather amazing sort of chaperone.

And yet, but for that fleeting and tumultuous presence, Horace himself would not be staying at Court House. Really, he reflected, Lucia ought to get some lady to live with her. It was the correct thing and therefore it was not a little surprising that Lucia did not do it. An expression of disapproval passed over his pale, fastidious face.

"Father won't mind," she said.

"No, but I should." He said it in a tone which was meant to settle the question.

She sat still, turning over the pages of the manuscript which she had again taken on her lap.

" I suppose he is very dreadful. Still, I think we ought to do something for him."

" And what would you propose to do? "

There was an irritating smile on her cousin's face. He was thinking, " So she wants to patronize him, does she? "

He did not say what he thought; with Lucia that was unnecessary, for she always knew. He only said, " I don't exactly see you playing Beatrice to his Dante."

Lucia coloured, and Horace felt that he had been right. The Hardens had always been patronizing; his mother and sister were the most superbly patronizing women he knew. And Rickman might or might not be a great man, but Lucia, even at three and twenty, was a great lady in her way. Why shouldn't she patronize him, if she liked? And he smiled again more irritatingly than ever. Nobody could be more irritating than this Oxford don when he gave his mind to it.

" Lucy—if you only knew him, I don't think you'd suggest my bringing him down here."

He was smiling still, while his imagination dallied with the monstrous vision.

" I wouldn't have suggested it," she said coldly, " if I hadn't thought you'd like it."

Horace felt a little ashamed of himself. He knew he had only to think about Lucia in her presence to change the colour on her cheeks, and his last thought had left a stain there like the mark of a blow. Never had he known any woman so sensitive as his cousin Lucia.

" So I should like it, dear, if it were possible, or rather if *he* were not impossible. His manners have not that repose which distinguishes his *Helen*. Really, for two and twenty, he is marvellously restrained."

" Restrained? Do you think so? "

" Certainly," he said, his thought gaining precision in opposition to her vagueness, " his *Helen* is pure Vere de Vere. You might read me some of it."

She read, and in the golden afternoon her voice built up the cold, polished marble of the verse. She had not been able to tell him what she thought of Rickman; but her voice, in its profound vibrations, made apparent that which she, and she only, had discerned in him, the troubled pulse of youth, the passion of the imprisoned and tumultuous soul, the soul which Horace had assured her inhabited the body of an aitchless shopman. Lucia might not have the intuition of genius, but she had the genius of intuition; she had seen what the great Oxford critic had not been able to see.

The sound of the fiddling ceased as suddenly as it had begun; and over the grey house and the green garden was the peace of heaven and of the enfolding hills.

Jewdwine breathed a sigh of contentment at the close of the great chorus in the second Act. After all, Rickman was the best antidote to Rickman.

But Lucia was looking ardent again, as if she were about to speak.

"Don't, Lucy," he murmured.

"Don't what?"

"Don't talk any more about him now. It's too hot. Wait till the cool of the evening."

"I thought you wanted me to play to you then."

Jewdwine looked at her; he noted the purity of her face, the beautiful pose of her body, stretched in the deck-chair, her fine white hands and arms that hung there, slender, inert, and frail. He admired these things so much that he failed to see that they expressed, not only beauty, but a certain delicacy of physique, and that her languor which appealed to him was not the languor of fatigue.

"You might play to me now," he said.

She looked at him again, a lingering, meditative look, a look in which, if adoration was quiescent, there was no criticism and no reproach, only a melancholy wonder. And he, too, wondered; wondered what she was thinking of.

She was thinking a dreadful thought. "Is Horace selfish? Is Horace selfish?" a little voice kept calling at the back of her brain and would not be quiet. At last she answered it to her own satisfaction. "No, he is not selfish, he is only ill."

And presently, as if on mature consideration, she rose and went into the house.

His eyes followed, well pleased, the delicate undulations of her figure.

Horace Jewdwine was the most exacting, the most fastidious of men. His entire nature was dominated by the critical faculty in him, and Lucia satisfied its most difficult demands. Try as he would, there was really nothing in her which he could take exception to, barring her absurd adoration of his uncle Frederick; and even that, when you came to think of it, flowed from the innocence which was more than half her charm. He could not say positively wherein her beauty consisted, therefore he was always tempted to look at her in the hope of finding out. There was nothing insistent and nothing obvious about it. Some women, for instance, irritated your admiration by the capricious prettiness of one or two features, or fatigued it by the monotonous regularity of all. The beauty of others was vulgarized by the flamboyance of some irrelevant detail, such as hair. Lucia's hair was merely dark, and it made, as hair should make, the simplest adornment for her head, the most perfect setting for her face. As for her features (though it was impossible to think of them, or anything about her as incorrect) they eluded while they fascinated him by their subtlety. Lucia's beauty, in short, appealed to him because it did not commit him to any irretrievable opinion.

But nothing, not even her beauty, pleased him better than the way in which she managed her intellect, divining by some infallible instinct how much of it was wanted by any given listener at a given time. She had none of the nasty tricks that clever women have, always on the lookout to go one better, and to catch you tripping. Her lucidity was remarkable; but it served to show up other people's strong points rather than her own. Lucia did not impress you as being clever, and Jewdwine, who had a clever man's natural distaste for clever women, admired his cousin's intellect, as well he might, for it was he who had taught her how to use it. Her sense of humour, too (for Lucia was dangerously gifted), that sense which more than any of her senses can wreck a woman—he would have liked her just as well if she had had none; but some, no doubt, she needed, if only to save her from the situations to which her kindness and her innocence exposed her; and she had just the right amount and no more. Heavens! Supposing, without it, she had met Keith Rickman and had yielded to the temptation to be kind to him! Even in the heat Jewdwine shivered at the thought.

He put it from him, he put Rickman altogether from his

mind. It was not to think about Rickman that he came
down to Court House. On a day as hot as this, he wanted
nothing but to keep cool. The gentle oscillation of the
hammock, in the green shadows of the beech-tree, symbol-
ized his attitude towards Rickman and all other ardent
questions.

Still, it was not disagreeable to know that if he could
only make up his mind to something very definite and irretrievable indeed, Court House would one day be his. It was
the only house in England that came up to his idea of what
a country house should be. A square Tudor building with
two short, gable-ended wings, thrown out at right angles to
its front; three friendly grey walls, enclosing a little courtyard made golden all day long with sunshine from the south.
Court House was older than anything near it, except Harmouth Bridge and the Parish Church. Standing apart in
its own green lands, it looked older than the young red earth
beneath it, a mass upheaved from the grey foundations of
the hills. Its face, turned seawards, was rough and pitted
with the salt air; thousands upon thousands of lichens gave
it a greenish bloom, with here and there a rusty patch on
groin and gable. It contained the Harden Library, *the* Harden Library, one of the finest private collections in the country. It contained also his cousin Lucia.

He had always loved Court House, but not always his
cousin Lucia. The scholarly descendant of a long line of
scholars, Jewdwine knew that he had been a favourite with
his grandfather, Sir Joseph Harden, the Master of Lazarus,
he was convinced (erroneously) that he was a Harden by
blood and by temperament, and of course if he had only
been a Harden by name, and not a Jewdwine, Court House
and the great Harden Library would have been his instead
of his cousin Lucia's. He knew that his grandfather had
wished them to be his. Lucia's mother was dead long ago;
and when his uncle Sir Frederick definitely renounced the
domestic life, Lucia, and Lucia alone, stood between him and
the inheritance that should have been his. This hardly constituted a reason for being fond of Lucia.

His grandfather had wished him to be fond of her. But
not until Jewdwine was five and twenty, and began to feel
the primordial manhood stirring in his scholarly blood, did
he perceive that his cousin Lucia was not a hindrance, but

a way. The way was so obvious that it was no wonder that he did not see it all at once. He did not really see it till Sir Joseph sent for him on his death-bed.

" There's been some mistake, Horace," Sir Joseph had then said. " Your mother should have been the boy and your uncle Frederick the girl. Then Lucia would have been a Jewdwine, and you a Harden."

And Horace had said, " I'm afraid I can't be a Harden, sir; but is there any reason why Lucia——? "

" I was coming to that," said Sir Joseph. But he never came to it. Horace, however, was in some way aware that the same idea had occurred to both of them. Whatever it was, the old man had died happy in it.

There was no engagement, only a something altogether intangible and vague, understood to be an understanding. And Lucia adored him. If she had not adored him he might have been urged to something irretrievable and definite. As it was, there was no need, and nothing could have been more soothing than the golden concord of that understanding.

Needless to say, if Lucia had been anybody but Lucia, such a solution would have been impossible. He was fastidious. He would not have married a woman simply because his grandfather wished it; and he could not have married a woman simply because she inherited property that ought to have been his. And he could not have married any woman who would have suspected him of such brutality. He could only marry a woman who was consummately suitable to him, in whom nothing jarred, nothing offended; and his cousin Lucia was such a woman. The very fact that she was his cousin was an assurance of her rightness. It followed that, love being the expression of that perfect and predestined harmony, he could only marry for love. Not for a great estate, for Court House and the Harden Library. No, to do him justice, his seeking of Lucia was independent of his reflection that these things would be added unto him. Still, once married to Lucia, there was only Sir Frederick and his infernal fiddle between him and ultimate, inviolable possession; and Sir Frederick, to use his own phrase, had "about played himself out." From what a stage and to what mad music!

From the east wing came the sound, not of his uncle's

fiddle, but of the music he desired, the tremendous and difficult music that, on a hot July afternoon, taxed the delicate player's strength to its utmost. Lucia began with Scarlatti and Bach; wandered off through Schumann into Chopin, a moonlit enchanted wilderness of sound; paused, and wound up superbly with Beethoven, the "Sonata Appassionata."

And, as she came back to him over the green lawn, she seemed to Jewdwine to be trailing tumultuous echoes of her music; the splendour and the passion of her playing hung about her like a luminous cloud. He rose and went to meet her, and in his eyes there was a light, a light of wonder and worship.

" I think," she said, " you do look a little happier."

" I am tolerably happy, thanks."

" So am I."

" Yes, but *you* don't look it. What are you thinking of? "

She turned, and they walked together towards the house.

" I was thinking—it's quite cool, now, Horace—of what you said—about that friend of yours."

" Lucy! Was I rude? Did I make you unhappy? "

" Not you. Don't you see that it's just because I'm happy that I want to be kind to him? "

" Just like your sweetness. But, dear child, you can't be kind to everybody. It really doesn't do."

She said no more; she had certainly something else to think about.

That was on a Tuesday, a hot afternoon in July, eighteen ninety-one.

CHAPTER II

IT was Wednesday evening in April, eighteen ninety-two. Spring was coming up on the south wind from the river; spring was in the narrow streets and in the great highway of the Strand, and in a certain bookseller's shop in the Strand. And it was Easter, not to say Bank Holiday, already in the soul of the young man who sat there compiling the Quarterly Catalogue. For it was in the days of his obscurity.

The shop, a corner one, was part of a gigantic modern structure, with a decorated façade in pinkish terra-cotta, and topped by four pinkish cupolas. It was brutally, tyrannously imposing. It towered above its neighbours, dwarfing the long sky-line of the Strand; its flushed cupolas mocked the white and heavenly soaring of St. Mary's. Whether you approached it from the river, or from the City, or from the west, you could see nothing else, so monstrous was it, so flagrant and so new. Though the day was not yet done, the electric light streamed over the pavement from the huge windows of the ground floor; a coronal of dazzling globes hung over the doorway at the corner; there, as you turned, the sombre windows of the second-hand department stretched half way down the side street; here, in the great thoroughfare, the newest of new books stood out, solicitous and alluring, in suits of blazing scarlet and vivid green, of vellum and gilt, of polished leather that shone like amber and malachite and lapis lazuli.

Within, a wall broken by a wide and lofty arch divided the front from the back shop. On the right of the arch was the mahogany pew of the cashier, on the left, a tall pillar stove radiating intolerable heat. Four steps led through the arch into the back shop, the floor of which was raised in a sort of platform. On the platform was a table, and at the table sat the young man compiling the Quarterly Catalogue.

Front shop and back shop reeked with the smells of new mahogany, dust, pillar-stove, gum, hot-pressed paper and Russian leather. He sat in the middle of them, in an atmosphere so thick that it could be seen hanging about him like an aura, luminous in the glare of the electric light. His slender, nervous hands worked rapidly, with a businesslike air of dexterity and dispatch. But every now and then he raised his head and stared for quite a long time at the round, white, foolish face of the clock, and whenever he did this his eyes were the eyes of a young man who has no adequate sense of his surroundings.

The remarkable thing about the new shop was that already, like a bar or a restaurant, it drew to it a certain group of young men, punctually, irresistibly. A small group —you could almost count them on the fingers of one hand —they came from Fleet Street, from the Temple, from the Junior Journalists' Club over the way. They were never seen looking in at the windows or hanging about the counter; they were not the least bit of good to the shop, those customers. But they were evidently some good to the young man. Whatever they did or did not do, they always ended by drifting to the platform, to his table. They sat on it in friendly attitudes and talked to him.

He was so glad to be talked to, so frankly, engagingly, beautifully glad, that the pathos of it would have been too poignant, the obligation it almost forced on you too unbearable, but for his power, his monstrous, mysterious, personal glamour.

It lay partly, no doubt, in his appearance; not, no, not at all, in his make-up. He wore, like a thousand city clerks, a high collar, a speckled tie, a straight, dark blue serge suit. But in spite of the stiffness thus imposed on him, he had, unaccountably, the shy, savage beauty of an animal untamed, uncaught. He belonged to the slender, nervous, fair type; but the colour proper to it had been taken out of him by the shop. His head presented the utmost clearness of line compatible with irregularity of outline; and his face (from its heavy square forehead to its light square jaw) was full of strange harmonies, adjustments, compensations. His chin, rather long in a front view, rather prominent in profile, balanced the powerful proportions of his forehead. His upper lip, in spite of its slender arch, betrayed a youthful eagerness of the senses; but this effect was subtilized by the fineness of his lower lip, and, when they closed, it disappeared in the sudden, serious straightening of the lines. Even his nose (otherwise a firm feature, straight in the bridge and rather broad at the end) became grave or eager as the pose of the head hid or revealed the nostrils. He had queer eyes, of a thick dark blue, large, though deep set, showing a great deal of iris and very little white. Without being good-looking he was good to look at, when you could look long enough to find all these things out. He did not like being looked at. If you tried to hold him that way, his eyes were all over the place, seeking an escape; but they held *you,* whether you liked it or not.

It was uncanny, that fascination. If he had chosen to exert it in the interests of his shop, he could presumably have cleaned those friendly young men out any day. But he never did exert it. Surrounded by wares whose very appearance was a venal solicitation, he never hinted by so much as the turn of a phrase that there was anything about him to be bought. And after what had passed between them, they felt that to hint it themselves—to him—would have been the last indelicacy. If they ever asked the price of a book it was to propitiate the grim grizzled fellow, so like a Methodist parson, who glared at them from the counter.

They kept their discovery to themselves, as if it had been something too precious to be handled, as if its charm, the poetry, the pathos of it must escape under discussion. But any of them who did compare notes agreed that their first idea had been that the shop was absurdly too big for the young man; their next that the young man was too big for the shop, miles, oh, miles too big for it; their final impression being the tragedy of the disproportion, the misfit. Then, sadly, with lowered voices, they admitted that he had one flaw; when the poor fellow got excited, don't you know, he sometimes dropt—no—no, he skipped—his aitches. It didn't happen often, but they felt it terrible that it should happen at all—to him. They touched it tenderly; if it was not exactly part of his poetry it was part of his pathos. The shop was responsible for it. He ought never, never to have been there.

And yet, bad as it was, they felt that he must be consoled, sustained by what he knew about himself, what it was inconceivable that he should not know.

He may, indeed, have reflected with some complacency that in spite of everything, his great classic drama, *Helen in Leuce,* was lying finished in the dressing-table drawer in his bedroom, and that for the last month those very modern poems that he called *Saturnalia* had been careening through the columns of *The Planet.* But at the moment he was mainly supported by the coming of Easter.

CHAPTER III

THE scene of the tragedy, that shop in the Strand, was well-lit and well-appointed. But he, Savage Keith Rickman, had much preferred the dark little second-hand shop in the City where he had laboured as a boy. There was

something soothing in its very obscurity and retirement.
He could sit there for an hour at a time, peacefully reading
his Homer. In that agreeable dusty twilight, outward forms
were dimmed with familiarity and dirt. His dreams took
shape before him, they came and went at will, undisturbed
by any gross collision with reality. There was hardly any
part of it that was not consecrated by some divine visitation.
It was in the corner by the window, standing on a step-
ladder, and fumbling in the darkness for a copy of Demos-
thenes, *De Corona,* that he lit on his first Idea. From his
seat behind the counter, staring as was his custom, into the
recess where the coal-scuttle was, he first saw the immortal
face of Helen in Leuce.

Here, all that beautiful world of thought lay open to the
terrific invasion of things. His dreams refused to stand
out with sufficient distinctness from a background of coloured bindings, plate glass, and mahogany. They were liable
at any moment to be broken by the violent contours of customers. A sight of Helen in Leuce could be obtained only
by dint of much concentrated staring at the clock; and as
often as not Mr. Rickman's eye dropt its visionary freight
on encountering the cashier's eye in its passage from the
clock to the paper.

But (as he reflected with some humour) though Mr. Rickman's ideas so frequently miscarried, owing to that malignant influence, his genius, like Nature irresistible and indestructible, compelled him perpetually to bring forth.
Exposed on his little dais or platform, in hideous publicity,
he suffered the divine labour and agony of creation. He
was the slave of his passion and his hour.

CHAPTER IV

A WAVE of heat broke from the pillar-stove and spread
through the shop, strewing the heavier smells like a
wrack behind it. And through it all, with every swing of
the great mahogany doors, there stole into his young senses
a something delicious and disturbing, faintly discernible as
the Spring.

He thrust his work from him, tilted back his chair at a

dangerous angle, and began reviewing his engagements for the coming Bank Holiday.

He was only three and twenty, and at three and twenty an infinite measure of life can be pressed into the great three days. He saw in fancy the procession of the hours, the flight of the dreams, of all the gorgeous intellectual pageants that move through the pages of *Saturnalia*. For in ninety-two Savage Keith Rickman was a little poet about town, a Cockney poet, the poet not only of neo-classic drama, but of green suburban Saturday noons, and flaming Saturday nights, and of a great many things besides. He had made his plans long beforehand, and was prepared to consign to instant perdition the person or thing that should interfere with them. Good Friday morning, an hour's cycling before breakfast in Regent's Park, by way of pumping some air into his lungs; then, ten hours at least of high Parnassian leisure, of dalliance in Academic shades; he saw himself wooing some reluctant classic, or, far more likely, flirting with his own capricious and bewildering muse. (In a world of prose it is only by such divine snatches that poets are made.) Friday evening, dinner at his club, the Junior Journalists. Saturday morning, recovery from dinner at the Junior Journalists. Saturday afternoon, to Hampstead or the Hippodrome with Flossie Walker, the little clerk, who lived in his boarding-house and never had any fun to speak of. Saturday night, supper with—well, with Miss Poppy Grace of the Jubilee Variety Theatre. He had a sudden vision of Poppy, as he was wont to meet her in delightful intimacy, instantaneously followed by her image that flaunted on the posters out there in the Strand, Poppy as she appeared behind the footlights, in red silk skirts and black silk stockings, skimming, whirling, swaying, and deftly shaking her foot at him. Midnight and morning merging into one. Sunday, to Richmond, probably, with Poppy, and some others. Monday, up the river with Himself. Not for worlds, that is to say, not for any amount of Poppies, would he have broken his appointment with that brilliant and yet inscrutable companion who is so eternally fascinating at twenty-three. Monday was indistinct but luminous, a restless, shimmering background for ideas. Ideas! They swarmed like motes in the blue air; they loomed, they floated, vague, and somewhat

supernaturaliy large, all made out of Mr. Rickman's brain.
And in the midst of the ideas a figure insanely whirled, till
it became a mere wheel of flying skirts and tossing limbs.

At this point Mr. Rickman caught the cashier's eye looking
at him over the little mahogany rails of his pew, and he
began wondering how on earth the cashier would behave
when they loosed him out for the Bank Holiday. Then he
set to and wrote hard at the Quarterly Catalogue. In all
London there was not a more prolific or versatile writer
than Savage Keith Rickman. But if, in ninety-two, you
had asked him for his master-piece, his *magnum opus,* his
life-work, he would mention nothing that he had written,
but refer you, soberly and benignly, to that colossal performance, the Quarterly Catalogue.

"Vandam: Amours of Great Men (a little soiled). Rare.
30s." He was in the middle of the Vs now and within
measurable distance of the end. Business being slack in
the front shop, he finished earlier than usual, and actually
found himself with nearly a whole hour upon his hands
before dinner. He had half a mind to spend it at his club,
the Junior Journalists, in the side street over the way.

Only half a mind; for Mr. Rickman entertained the most
innocent beliefs with regard to that club of his. He was
not yet sure whether it belonged to him or he to it; but in
going to the Junior Journalists he conceived himself to be
going into society. So extreme was his illusion.

Mr. Rickman's place was in the shop and his home was
in the boarding-house and for years he had thought of
belonging to that club; but quite hopelessly, as of a thing
beyond attainment. It had never occurred to him that
anything could come of those invasions of the friendly young
men. Yet this was what had come of them. He was friends,
under the rose, that is to say, over the counter, with Horace
Jewdwine of Lazarus College, Oxford. Jewdwine had proposed him on his own merits, somebody else had seconded
him (he supposed) on Jewdwine's, and between them they
had smuggled him in. This would be his first appearance
as a Junior Journalist. And he might well feel a little diffident about it; for, though some of the members knew him,
he could not honestly say he knew any of them, except
Rankin (of *The Planet*), who possibly mightn't, and Jewdwine, who certainly wouldn't, be there. But the plunge

had to be made some time; he might as well make it
now.

From the threshold of the Junior Journalists he looked
back across the side street, as across a gulf, at the place he
had just left. His eyes moved from the jutting signboard
at the corner, announcing *Gentlemen's Libraries Purchased,*
to the legend that ran above the window, blazoned in letters
of gold:

Isaac Rickman: New & Second-Hand Bookseller.

His connection with it was by no means casual and temporary. It was his father's shop.

CHAPTER V

THE little booksellers of the Strand, in their death struggle against Rickman's, never cursed that house more
heartily than did the Junior Journalists, in their friendly,
shabby little den, smelling of old leather and tobacco and
the town. They complained that it cut off two-thirds of
the light from the front windows of the reading-room. Not
that any of them were ever known to read in it. They used
it chiefly as a place to talk in, for which purpose little illumination was required.

To-night one of the windows in question was occupied
by a small group of talkers isolated from the rest. There
was Mackinnon, of *The Literary Observer.* There were the
three wild young spirits of *The Planet,* Stables, who had
launched it with frightful impetus into space (having
borrowed a sum sufficient for the purpose), Maddox, who
controlled its course, and Rankin, whose brilliance made
it twinkle so brightly in the firmament. With them, but
emphatically not of them, was Horace Jewdwine, of Lazarus, who had come up from Oxford to join the staff of
The Museion.

Jewdwine and Mackinnon, both secure of a position and
a salary, looked solemn and a little anxious; but the men
of *The Planet,* having formed themselves into a sort of
unlimited liability company, and started a brand new
" weekly " of their own (upon no sort of security beyond

their bare brains) were as persons without a single care, worry, or responsibility. They were exchanging ideas in an off-hand and light-hearted manner, the only stipulation being that the ideas must be new; for, by some unwritten law of the club, the conversational currency was liable at any moment to be called in.

This evening, however, they had hit on a topic almost virgin from the mint.

"S. K. R.? *Who* is he? *What* is he?" said Mackinnon.

"I can't tell you what he *is;* but I can pretty soon tell you what he's not," said Stables. He was a very young man with a white face and red eyelids, who looked as if he sat up all night and went to bed in the day-time, as indeed he generally did.

"*Omnis negatio est determinatio,*" murmured Jewdwine, without looking up from the letter he was trying to write.

"What has he done?" persisted Mackinnon.

"He has done a great many remarkable things," said Rankin; "things almost as remarkable as himself."

"Who unearthed him?"

"I did," said Rankin, so complacently that the deep lines relaxed round the five copper-coloured bosses that were his chin and cheeks and brow. (The rest of Rankin's face was spectacles and moustache.)

"Oh, did you?" said Maddox. Maddox was a short man with large shoulders; heavy browed, heavy jowled, heavy moustached. Maddox's appearance belied him; he looked British when he was half Celt; he struck you as over-bearing when he was only top-heavy; he spoke as if he was angry when he was only in fun, as you could see by his eyes. Little babyish blue eyes they were with curly corners, a gay light in the sombre truculence of his face. They looked cautiously round.

"I can tell you a little tale about S. K. R. You know the last time Smythe was ill——?"

"You mean drunk."

"Well—temporarily extinguished. S. K. R., who knows his music-halls, was offered Smythe's berth. We delicately intimated to him that if he liked at any time to devote a little paragraph to Miss Poppy Grace, he was at perfect liberty to do so."

"A liberty he interpreted as poetic licence."

" Nothing of the sort. He absolutely declined the job."

" Why? "

" Well—the marvellous boy informed me that he was too intimate with the lady to write about her. At any rate with that noble impartiality which distinguishes the utterances of *The Planet.*"

" He told ye? " said Mackinnon.

" I didn't say he *told* me, I said he informed me."

" And whar's the differ'nce? I don't see it at all."

" Trepan him, trepan him."

Stables took out his pen-knife and indicated by dumb show a surgical operation on Mackinnon's dome-like head.

" I gathered it," continued Maddox suavely, " from his manner. I culled his young thought like a flower."

" Perhaps," Rankin suggested, " he was afraid of compromising Poppy."

" He might have left that subtle consideration to Pilkington."

" That was it," continued Maddox. " He scented Dicky's hand in it, and wasn't particularly anxious to oblige him. The point of the joke is that he happens to owe Dicky a great deal more than he can conveniently pay. That'll give you some faint notion of the magnificence of his cheek."

Stables was impressed. He wondered what sort of young man it could be who had the moral courage to oppose Dicky Pilkington at such a moment. He could not have done it himself. Dicky Pilkington was the great and mysterious power at the back of *The Planet.*

" But this isn't the end of it. I told him, for his future guidance and encouragement, that he had mistaken cause and effect—that little variety *artistes,* like other people, are not popular because they are written about, but written about because they are popular—that *The Planet* is the organ of public opinion, not of private opinions; in short, that he wasn't in it, at all. I thought I'd sat on him till he was about flat—and the very next week he comes bounding in with his *Saturnalia,* as he calls them."

" That was your moment. Why didn't you rise up in your majesty and r-r-reject them? "

" Couldn't. They were too damned good." Maddox smiled at the reminiscence. " I wasn't going to let him sign them, but he took the wind out of my sails by stating

beforehand that he didn't want to—that if I didn't mind—
mind, if you please—he'd very much rather not. It's only
the last week (when the *Saturnalia* were getting better and
better) that he graciously permitted his initials to appear.
S. K. R.—Savage Keith Rickman."

"Good Lord!" said Rankin; "what must he be like?"

"Ask Jewdwine," said Stables, "he's Jewdwine's man."

"Excuse *me,*" said Maddox, "he is *mine.* I say, Jewdwine, what *is* he like?"

Jewdwine did not respond very eagerly; he wanted to
get on with his letter. But the club had another unwritten
law as to writing. If a majority of members desired to
write, silence was vigorously insisted on. Any number
short of a majority wrote as best they could. For this
unforunate scribe there could be no concession; he was in
a minority of one.

"If,"—said he, "you can imagine the soul of a young
Sophocles, battling with that of a—of a junior journalist,
in the body of a dissipated little Cockney——"

"Can't," said Stables. "Haven't got enough imagination."

"The child of 'Ellas and of 'Ollywell Street—innocent of
—er—the rough breathing," suggested Maddox.

As it was now seven o'clock, and the Junior Journalists
were dropping off one by one to the dining-room below,
the young men of *The Planet* began to stretch their legs,
and raise their voices, and behave like young men who
believe their privacy to be inviolable and complete. They
soon had the place to themselves, except for one person
whose entrance had been covered by the outgoing stream;
and he had delicately turned his back on them, and taken a
seat in the farthest window, where his unobtrusive presence could be no possible hindrance to conversation.

"I've seen him after supper," said Maddox. He was
obliged to speak rather loudly, because of the noise that
came up from the overcrowded dining-room.

"Well, then, how did he strike you?"

Maddox's eyes curled with limpid, infantile deviltry.

"Well, I dare say he might be a bit of a bounder when he's
sober, but he's a perfect little gentleman when he's drunk.
Softens him down somehow."

"*In vino veritas*—a true gentleman at heart."

" One of Nature's gentlemen. *I* know 'em," said Stables.

" One of Art's gentlemen," interposed Jewdwine severely,
" and a very fine gentleman, too, if you take him that
way."

Jewdwine raised his head from his letter and looked
round uneasily. Personalities were not altogether to his
taste; besides, he was really anxious to finish that letter.
He caught sight of a back at the other window.

" I think," said he quietly, " this conversation had better
cease."

The owner of the back had moved, a little ostentatiously.
He now got up and crossed the room. The back was still
towards the group of talkers. Jewdwine followed its passage. He was fascinated. He gasped.

He could have sworn to that back anywhere, with its
square but slender shoulders, its defiant swing from the
straight hips, the head tossed a little backwards, as if to
correct the student's tendency to stoop. He looked from
the back to Maddox. Maddox could not see what he saw,
but his face reflected the horror of Jewdwine's.

Their voices were inaudible enough now.

" Do you know who it is?"

" I should think I did. It's the man himself."

" How truly damnable," said Rankin. After those words
there was a silence which Jewdwine, like the wise man he
was, utilized for his correspondence.

It was Maddox who recovered first. " Call him what
you like," said he, in a wonderfully natural voice, between
two puffs of a cigarette, " I consider him an uncommonly
good sort. A bit of a bounder, but no end of a good sort."

The others were evidently impressed by this bold though
desperate policy. Maddox himself was inclined to think
that it had saved the situation, but he was anxious to make
sure. Edging his chair by slow degrees, he turned discreetly round. With the tail of his eye he could see "the man
himself " standing at the far end of the room. He saw, too,
that his own effort, though supreme, had been unavail-
ing. It had deceived no one, least of all S. K. R. " The
man himself " stood on the very hearth of the club, with
his back to the fireplace. It was the attitude of mastery,
a master the most superb because unconscious. His eyes,
too, were the eyes of a master, twinkling a little as to their

light, but steady as to their direction, being fixed on Maddox. He was smiling.

There was nothing malignant, or bitter, or sardonic about that smile. No deviltry of delight at their confusion. No base abandonment of the whole countenance to mirth, but a curious one-sided smile, implying delicacies, reservations. A slow smile, reminiscent, ruminant, appreciative; it expressed (if so subtle and refined a thing could be said to express anything) a certain exquisite enjoyment of the phrases in which they had defined him.

And seeing it, Maddox said to himself, "He isn't a gentleman. He's something more."

In that moment the Celtic soul of Maddox had recognized its master, and had sworn to him unhesitating allegiance.

CHAPTER VI

IT was not until Rankin and the others had left the room that Jewdwine had courage to raise his head tentatively. He had only seen that young man's back, and he still clung to the hope that it might not be Rickman's, after all.

He looked up as steadily as he dared. Oh, no doubt that it was Rickman's back; no doubt, too, that it was his, Jewdwine's, duty to go up and speak to him. The young man had changed his place; he was at his window again contemplating—as Jewdwine reflected with a pang of sympathy—the shop. So profound, so sacred almost, was his absorption that Jewdwine hesitated in his approach.

"*Is* it Rickman?" he asked, still tentative.

"Mr. Jewdwine!" Rickman's soul leapt to Jewdwine's from the depths; but the "Mister" marked the space it had to travel. "When did you come up?"

"Three hours ago." ("He looks innocent," said Jewdwine to himself.)

"Then you weren't prepared for that?"

Jewdwine followed his fascinated gaze. He smiled faintly.

"You haven't noticed our new departure? We not only purchase Gentlemen's Libraries, but we sell the works of persons who may or may not be gentlemen."

Jewdwine felt profoundly uncomfortable. Rickman's

face preserved its inimitable innocence, but he continued to stare fixedly before him.

"Poor fellow," thought Jewdwine, "he must have heard those imbecilities." He felt horribly responsible, responsible to the Club for the behaviour of Rickman, and responsible to Rickman for the behaviour of the Club. What could he do to make it up to him? Happy thought—he would ask him to dinner at—yes, at his sister's, Miss Jewdwine's, house at Hampstead. That was to say, if his cousin, Lucia Harden, did not happen to be staying there. He was not quite sure how Rickman would strike that most fastidious of young ladies. And Rankin had said he drank.

In the light of Lucia Harden's and his sister's possible criticism, he considered him more carefully than he had done before.

The contrast between the two men was certainly rather marked. A gentleman can be neither more nor less than a gentleman, and Rickman, in a sense not altogether intended by Maddox, was decidedly more. His individuality was too exuberant, too irrepressible. He had the restless, emphatic air of a man who has but little leisure and is too obviously anxious to make the most of what he has. He always seemed to be talking against time; and as he talked his emotions played visibly, too visibly, on his humorous, irregular face. Taking into account his remarkable firmness of physique, it struck you that this transparency must be due to some excessive radiance of soul. A soul (in Jewdwine's opinion) a trifle too demonstrative in its hospitality to vagrant impressions. The Junior Journalists may have been a little hard on him. On the whole, he left you dubious, until the moment when, from pure nervousness, his speech went wild, even suffering that slight elision of the aspirate observed by some of them. But then, he had a voice of such singular musical felicity that it charmed you into forgetfulness of these enormities.

It had charmed Jewdwine from the first, and Jewdwine was hard to charm. There was no room for speculation as to him. Even to the eye his type had none of the uncertainty and complexity of Rickman's. He looked neither more nor less than he was—an Oxford don, developing into a London Journalist. You divined that the process would be slow There was no unseemly haste about Jewdwine;

time had not been spared in the moulding of his body and
his soul. He bore the impress of the ages; the whole man
was clean-cut, aristocratic, finished, defined. You instinctively looked up to him; which was perhaps the reason why
you remembered his conspicuously intellectual forehead
and his pathetically fastidious nose, and forgot the vacil-
lating mouth that dropped under a scanty, colourless moustache, hiding its weakness out of sight.

Rickman had always looked up to him. For Jewdwine,
as Rankin had intimated, was the man who had discovered
S. K. R. He was always discovering him. Not, as he was
careful to inform you, that this argued any sort of intimacy; on the contrary, it meant that he was always losing
sight of him in between. These lapses in their intercourse
might be shorter or longer (they were frequently immense),
but they had this advantage, that each fresh encounter presented Rickman as an entirely new thing, if anything, more
curious and interesting than on the day, three years ago,
when he unearthed him from behind the counter of a dingy
second-hand bookshop in the City. He felt responsible
for that, too.

Rickman was instantly aware that he was under criticism.
But he mistook its nature and its grounds.

"Don't suppose," said he, "I'm ashamed of the shop. It
isn't that. I wasn't ashamed of our other place—that little
rat 'ole in the City."

Jewdwine shuddered through all his being.

"But I *am* ashamed of this gaudy, pink concern. It's
so brutally big. It can't live, you know, without sucking
the life out of the little booksellers. They mayn't have
made a great thing out of it, but they were happy enough
before we came here."

"I never thought of it in that light."

"Haven't you? I have."

It was evident that little Rickman was deeply moved.
His sentiments did him credit, and he deserved to be asked
to dinner. At Hampstead? No—no, not at Hampstead;
here, at the Club. The Club was the proper thing; a public
recognition of him was the *amende honorable*. Besides, after
all, it was the Club, not Jewdwine, that had offended, and
it was right that the Club should expiate its offence.

"What are you doing at Easter?" he asked.

Rickman stroked his upper lip and smiled, as if cherishing a joy as secret and unborn as his moustache. He recited a selection from the tale of his engagements.

" Can you dine with me here on Saturday? You're free, then, didn't you say? "

Rickman hesitated. That was not what he had said. He was anything but free, for was he not engaged for that evening to Miss Poppy Grace? He was pulled two ways, a hard pull. He admired Jewdwine with simple, hero-worshipping fervour; but he also admired Miss Poppy Grace. Again, he shrank from mentioning an engagement of that sort to Jewdwine, while, on the other hand, concealment was equally painful, being foreign to his nature.

So he flushed a little as he replied, " Thanks awfully, I'm afraid I can't. I'm booked that night to Poppy Grace."

The flush deepened. Besides his natural sensitiveness on the subject of Miss Poppy Grace, he suffered tortures not wholly sentimental whenever he had occasion to mention her by her name. Poppy Grace—he felt that somehow it did not give you a very high idea of the lady, and that in this it did her an injustice. He could have avoided it by referring to her loftily as Miss Grace; but this course, besides being unfamiliar, would have savoured somewhat of subterfuge. So he blurted it all out with an air of defiance, as much as to say, that when you had called her Poppy Grace you had said the worst of her.

Jewdwine's face expressed, as Rickman, had anticipated, an exquisite disapproval. His own taste in women was refined almost to nullity. How a poet and a scholar, even if not strictly speaking a gentleman, could care to spend two minutes in the society of Poppy Grace, was incomprehensible to Jewdwine.

" I didn't know you cultivated that sort of person."

" Oh—cultivate her? " His tone implied that the soil was rather too light for *that*.

" How long have you known her? "

" About six months, on and orf."

" Oh, only on and off."

" On and orf the *stage,* I mean. And that's knowledge," said Rickman. " Anybody can know them on; but it's not one man in a thousand knows them orf—really knows them."

" I'm very glad to hear it."

He changed the subject. In Rickman the poet he was deeply interested; but at the moment Rickman the man inspired him with disgust.

Jewdwine had a weak digestion. When he sat at the high table, peering at his sole and chicken, with critical and pathetic twitchings of his fastidious nose, he shuddered at the vigorous animal appetites of the undergraduates in Hall.

Even so he shrank now from the coarse exuberance of Rickman's youth. When it came to women, Rickman *was* impossible.

" And yet," he continued thoughtfully, " the man who wrote *Helen in Leuce* was a poet. Or at least," he added, " one-seventh part of a poet."

" Thanks," said Rickman, " you've got the fraction all right, anyhow. A poet one day out of seven; the other six days a potman in an infernal, stinking, flaring Gin Palace of Art."

As he looked at Rickman's, blazing with all its lights, he felt that he had hit on the satisfying, the defining phrase.

His face expressed a wistful desire to confer further with Jewdwine on this matter; but a certain delicacy restrained him.

Something fine in Jewdwine's nature, something half-human, half-tutorial, responded to the mute appeal that said so plainly, " Won't you hear me? I've so much to ask, so much to say. So many ideas, and you're the only man that can understand them." Jewdwine impressed everybody, himself included, as a person of prodigious understanding.

The question was, having understood Rickman, having discovered in him a neglected genius, having introduced him to the Club and asked him to dinner on the strength of it, how much further was he prepared to go? Why— provided he was sure of the genius, almost any length, short of introducing him to the ladies of his family. But was he sure? Savage Rickman was young, and youth is deceptive. Supposing he—Jewdwine—was deceived? Supposing the genius were to elude him, leaving him saddled with the man? What on earth should he do with him?

Things had been simpler in the earlier days of their acquaintance, when the counter stood between them, and formed a firm natural barrier to closer intercourse. Nobody, not even Jewdwine, knew what that handshake across the counter had meant for Rickman; how his soul had hungered and thirsted for Jewdwine's society; how, in " the little rat 'ole in the City," it had consumed itself with longing. It was his first great passion, a passion that waited upon chance; to be gratified for five minutes, ten minutes at the most. Once Jewdwine had hung about the shop for half an hour talking; the interview being broken by Rickman's incessant calls to the counter. Once, they had taken a walk together down Cheapside, which from that moment became a holy place. Then came the day when, at Jewdwine's invitation, *Helen in Leuce* travelled down from London to Oxford, and from Oxford to Harmouth. Her neo-classic beauty appealed to Jewdwine's taste (and to the taste of Jewdwine's cousin) ; he recognized in Rickman a disciple, and was instantly persuaded of his genius. At one bound Rickman had leapt the barrier of the counter; and here he was, enthusiastic and devoted. To be sure, his devotion was not fed largely upon praise; for, unlike the younger man, Jewdwine admired but sparingly. Neither was it tainted with any thought of material advantage. Jewdwine was very free with his criticism and advice; but, beyond these high intellectual aids, it never occurred to Rickman that he had anything to gain by Jewdwine's friendship. Discipleship is the purest of all human relations.

Jewdwine divined this purity, and was touched by it. He prepared to accept a certain amount of responsibility. He looked at his watch. He could still get to Hampstead by eight o'clock, if he took a cab—say,—twenty minutes. He could spare him another ten. The Junior Journalists were coming back from their dinner and the room would soon be crowded. He took his disciple's arm in a protecting manner and steered him into a near recess. He felt that the ten minutes he was about to give him would be decisive in the young man's career.

" You've still got to find your formula. Not to have found your formula," he said solemnly, " is not to have found yourself."

" Perhaps I haven't been looking in very likely places,"

said Rickman, nobly touched, as he always was by the more personal utterances of the master.

"The Jubilee Variety Theatre, for instance. Do you go there to find the ideal, or in pursuit of the fugitive actuality?"

"Whichever you like to call it. Its name on the programme is Miss Poppy Grace."

"Look here, Rickman," said Jewdwine gently; "when are you going to give up this business?"

"Which business?"

"Well, at the moment, I referred to your situation in the Gin Palace of Art——"

"I can't chuck it just yet. There's my father, you see. It would spoil all his pleasure in that new plate-glass and mahogany devilry. He's excited about it; wants to make it a big thing——"

"So he puts a big man into it?"

"Oh, well, I must see him started."

He spoke simply, as of a thing self-evident and indisputable. Jewdwine admired.

"You're quite right. You *are* handicapped. Heavily handicapped. So, for goodness' sake, don't weigh yourself any more. If you can't drop the Gin Palace, drop Miss Poppy Grace."

"Poppy Grace? She weighs about a feather."

"Drop her, drop her, all the same."

"I can't. She wouldn't drop. She'd float."

"Don't float with her."

As he rose he spoke slowly and impressively. "What you've got to do is to pull yourself together. You can't afford to be dissolute, or even dissipated."

Rickman looked hard at Jewdwine's boots. Irreproachable boots, well made, well polished, unspotted by the world. And the only distinguishable word in Rickman's answer was "Life." And as he said "Life" he blushed, like a girl when for the first time she says "Love," a blush of rapture and of shame, her young blood sensitive to the least hint of apathy in her audience.

Jewdwine's apathy was immense.

"Another name for the fugitive actuality," he said. "Well, I'm afraid I haven't any more time——" He looked round the room a little vaguely, and as he did so he laid

on the young man's shoulder a delicate fastidious hand.
"There are one or two men here I should have liked to
introduce you to, if I'd had time. Another night, perhaps——" He piloted him downstairs and so out into the
Strand.

"Good-night. Good-night. Take my advice and leave
the fugitive actuality alone."

Those were Jewdwine's last words, spoken from the
depths of the hansom. It carried him to the classic heights
of Hampstead, to the haunts of the cultivated, the intellectual, the refined.

Rickman remained a moment. His dreamy gaze was
fixed on the massive pile before him, that rose, solidly soaring, flaunting a brutal challenge to the tender April sky.
It stood for the vast material reality, the whole of that
eternal, implacable Power which is at enmity with dreams;
which may be conquered, propitiated, absorbed, but never
annihilated or denied.

That actuality was not fugitive.

CHAPTER VII

PERHAPS it was not to be wondered at if Mr. Rickman
had not yet found himself. There were, as he sorrowfully reflected, so many Mr. Rickmans.

There was Mr. Rickman of the front shop and second-
hand department, known as "our Mr. Rickman." The
shop was proud of him; his appearance was supposed to
give it a certain *cachet*. He neither strutted nor grovelled;
he moved about from shelf to shelf in an absent-minded
scholarly manner. He served you, not with obsequiousness,
nor yet with condescension, but with a certain remoteness
and abstraction, a noble apathy. Though a bookseller, his
literary conscience remained incorruptible. He would introduce you to his favourite authors with a magnificent take-
it-or-leave-it air, while an almost imperceptible lifting of his
eyebrows as he handed you *your* favourite was a subtle criticism of your taste. This method of conducting business
was called keeping up the tone of the establishment. The
appearance and disappearance of this person was timed and
regulated by circumstances beyond his own control, so that

of necessity all the other Mr. Rickmans were subject to him.

For there was Mr. Rickman the student and recluse, who inhabited the insides of other men's books. Owing to his habitual converse with intellects greater—really greater—than his own, he was an exceedingly humble and reverent person. A high and stainless soul. You would never have suspected his connection with Mr. Rickman the Junior Journalist, the obscure writer of brilliant paragraphs, a fellow destitute of reverence and decency and everything except consummate impudence, a disconcerting humour and a startling style. But he was still more distantly related to Mr. Rickman the young man about town. And that made four. Besides these four there was a fifth, the serene and perfect intelligence, who from some height immeasurably far above them sat in judgment on them all. But for his abnormal sense of humour he would have been a Mr. Rickman of the pure reason, no good at all. As it was, he occasionally offered some reflection which was enjoyed but seldom acted upon.

And underneath these Mr. Rickmans, though inextricably, damnably one with them, was a certain apparently commonplace but amiable young man, who lived in a Bloomsbury boarding-house and dropped his aitches. This young man was tender and chivalrous, full of little innocent civilities to the ladies of his boarding-house; he admired, above all things, modesty in a woman, and somewhere, in the dark and unexplored corners of his nature, he concealed a prejudice in favour of marriage and the sanctities of home.

That made six, and no doubt they would have pulled together well enough; but the bother was that any one of them was liable at any moment to the visitation of the seventh—Mr. Rickman the genius. There was no telling whether he would come in the form of a high god or a demon, a consolation or a torment. Sometimes he would descend upon Mr. Rickman in the second-hand department, and attempt to seduce him from his allegiance to the Quarterly Catalogue. Or he would take up the poor journalist's copy as it lay on a table, and change it so that its own editor wouldn't know it again. And sometimes he would swoop down on the little bookseller as he sat at breakfast on a

Sunday morning, in his nice frock coat and clean collar, and wrap his big flapping wings round him, and carry him off to the place where the divine ideas come from. Leaving a silent and to all appearances idiotic young gentleman in his place. Or he would sit down by that young gentleman's side and shake him out of his little innocences and complacencies, and turn all his little jokes into his own incomprehensible humour. And then the boarding-house would look uncomfortable and say to itself that Mr. Rickman had been drinking.

In short, it was a very confusing state of affairs, and one that made it almost impossible for Mr. Rickman to establish his identity. Seven Rickmans—only think of it! And some reckon an eighth, Mr. Rickman drunk. But this is not altogether fair; for intoxication acted rather on all seven at once, producing in them gentle fusion with each other and the universe. They had ceased to struggle. But Mr. Rickman was not often drunk, or at least not nearly so often as his friends supposed.

So it was all very well for Jewdwine, who was not so bewilderingly constructed, to talk about finding your formula and pulling yourself together. How, Mr. Rickman argued, could you hope to find the formula of a fellow who could only be expressed in fractions, and vulgar fractions, too? How on earth could you pull yourself together when Nature had deliberately cut you into little pieces? Never since poor Orpheus was torn to tatters by the Maenads was there a poet so horribly subdivided. Talk of being dissolute, dissipated! Those adjectives were a poor description of S. K. R. It was more than sowing a mere handful of wild oats, it was a disintegration, a scattering of Rickmans to all the winds of the world.

Find himself, indeed!

Still, he was perfectly willing to try; and to that end (after dining with people who were anything but cultivated, or intellectual, or refined) he turned himself loose into the streets.

The streets—he was never tired of them. After nine or ten hours of sitting in a dusty second-hand bookshop, his soul was dry with thirst for the living world, and the young joy of the world, "the fugitive actuality." And her ways were in the streets.

Being a young poet about town, he turned to the streets as naturally as a young poet in the country turns to the woods and fields. For in the streets, if you know how to listen, you can hear the lyric soul of things as plainly, more plainly perhaps, than in the woods or fields. Only it sings another sort of song. And going into the streets was Rickman's way (the only way open to him as yet) of going into society. The doors were thrown hospitably wide to him; one day was as good as another; the world was always at home.

It was a world where he could pick and choose his acquaintance; where, indeed, out of that multitudinous, never-ending procession of persons, his power of selection was unlimited. He never had any difficulty with them; their methods were so charmingly simple and direct. In the streets the soul is surprised through the lifting of an eyelid, and the secret of the heart sits lightly on the curl of the lip. These passers by never wearied him; they flung him the flower of the mystery and—passed by. The perfection of social intercourse he conceived as a similar succession of radiant intimacies.

To-night he went southwards down Gower Street, drawn by the never-ending, fugitive perspective of the lamps. He went westwards down Shaftesbury Avenue to Piccadilly. The Circus was a gleaming basin filled with grey night clear as water, the floor of it alive with lights. Lights that stood still; lights that wandered from darkness into darkness; that met and parted; darted, wheeling, and crossing in their flight. Long avenues opened out of it, precipitous deep cuttings leading into the night. The steep, shadowy masses of building seemed piled sky-high, like a city of the air; here the gleam of some golden white façade, there some aerial battlement crowned with stars, with clusters, and points, and rings of flame that made a lucid twilight of the dark above them. Over all was an illusion of immensity.

Nine o'clock of an April night—the time when a great city has most power over those that love her; the time when she lowers her voice and subdues her brilliance, intimating that she is not what she seems; when she makes herself unearthly and insubstantial, veiling her grossness in the half-transparent night. Like some consummate temptress, she plays the mystic, clothing herself with light and darkness, skirting the intangible, hinting at the infinities, flinging out the eternal spiritual lure, so that she may better seduce the senses through the soul. And Rickman was too young a poet to distinguish clearly between his senses and his imagination, or his imagination and his soul.

He stood in Piccadilly Circus and regarded the spectacle of the night. He watched the groups gathering at the street corners, the boys that went laughing arm in arm, the young girls smiling into their lovers' eyes; here and there the faces of other women, dubious divinities of the gas-light and the pavement, passing and passing. A very ordinary spectacle. But to Rickman it had an immense significance, a rhythmic, processional resonance and grandeur. It was an unrhymed song out of *Saturnalia,* it was the luminous, passionate nocturne of the streets.

Half-past nine; a young girl met him and stopped. She laughed into his face.

" Pretty well pleased with yourself, aren't you? " said the young girl.

He laughed back again. He was pleased with the world, so of course he was pleased with himself. They were one. The same spirit was in Mr. Rickman that was in the young girl and in the young April night.

They walked together as far as the Strand, conversing innocently.

CHAPTER VIII

AT ten o'clock he found himself in a corridor of the Jubilee Variety Theatre. The young girl had vanished. For a moment he stood debating whether he would go home and work out some ideas he had. Or whether he would pursue the young Joy, the fugitive actuality, to the very threshold of the dawn. Whether, in short, he would make a night of it.

He was aroused by the sound of a box-door opening and shutting; and a shining shirt-front and a shining face darted suddenly into the light. At the same moment a voice hailed him.

" Hello, Razors! That you? "

Voice, face, and shining shirt-front belonged to Mr. Richard Pilkington, Financial Agent, of Shaftesbury Avenue.

"Razors" was the name by which Rickman was known to his intimates, in subtle allusion to his youth. He responded sulkily to the hail. Dicky Pilkington was the last person he desired to meet. For he owed Dicky a certain sum, not large, but larger than he could conveniently pay, and Dicky was objectionable for other reasons. He had mysterious relations with the Management of the Jubilee Theatre, and, consequently, unlimited facilities of access to Miss Poppy Grace. Besides, there was something about him that was deadly to ideas.

Ideas or no ideas, Mr. Pilkington was not to be evaded. He bore down on Rickman, shining genially, and addressed him with an air of banter.

"Couldn't have arranged it better. You're the very fellow I want."

There was a suggestion of a chuckle in his voice which sent Rickman's thoughts flying fearfully to his last I. O. U. The alert mind of Pilkington followed their flight. He was intensely amused. He always was amused when anybody showed a marked distaste for his society.

"Your business, not mine, this time, Rick. I happen to know of a ripping old library for sale down in Devonshire. Shouldn't have thought of it if I hadn't seen you."

"Well?" Rickman's face expressed an utter inability to perceive the connection. Once the iron shutters had closed on Rickman's he felt that he was no more a part of it. Words could not express his abhorrence of the indecent people who insisted on talking shop out of shop hours. And Dick never had any decency.

"Well—it's practically on our hands, d'ye see? And if your people care to take over the whole lot, I can let you have it pretty reasonably."

Rickman's face emptied itself of all expression whatever.

"I say, you are a cool young cuss. Is this the way you generally do business?"

"I'll think it over."

"Wouldn't think too long if I were you. It ought to go by auction, and it might; only private contract's preferred."

" Why preferred? "

" Out of respect for the feelin's of the family."

Rickman's eyes were wandering dreamily from the matter in hand. They had alighted on an enormous photograph of Miss Poppy Grace. For an instant thought, like a cloud, obscured the brilliance of Mr. Pilkington's face.

" Anyhow I've given you the straight tip," said Pilkington.

" Thanks. We'll send a fellow down to overhaul the thing."

" He'd better hurry up then. It *may* have to go by auction after all. But if you'd like the refusal of it, now's your chance."

But Rickman betrayed no enthusiasm.

" You'd better see the guv'nor about it," said he.

Mr. Pilkington looked Rickman up and down, and encountered an immovable determination in his gaze.

" Right you are. I'll send him word to-night. Ta-ta! " He turned again in the moment of departing. " I say, he must send a good man down, you know. It'll take an expert. There's a lot of old things—Greek and Latin—that's something in *your* line, isn't it? "

But Rickman's line at present was the line of least resistance. It was ten past ten, and Poppy Grace was " on " from ten fifteen to ten forty.

CHAPTER IX

SHE was only an ordinary little variety actress, and he knew her little programme pretty well by heart. But her fascinations were independent of the glamour of the footlights. It was off the stage that he had first come to know her, really know her, a thing that at the first blush of it seems impossible; for the great goddess Diana is not more divinely secret and secluded than (to a young bookseller) a popular Dance and Song Artiste in private life. Poppy's rooms were next door to the boarding-house balcony, and it was the balcony that did it.

Now, in the matter of balconies, if you choose to regard the receding wooden partition as a partition, and sit very far back behind it, you will have your balcony all to yourself, that is to say, you will see nothing, neither will you be seen. If, however, you prefer, as Mr. Rickman preferred, to lean forward over the railings and observe things passing in the street below, you can hardly help establishing some sort of communication with the next-door neighbour who happens to be doing the same thing. At first this communication was purely in the region of the mind, without so much as the movement of an eyelid on either side, and that made it all the more intimate and intense. But to sit there Sunday evening after Sunday evening, when the other boarders were at church, both looking at the same plane-tree opposite, or the same tail-end of a sunset flung across the chimney pots, without uttering a syllable or a sound, was at last seen by both in its true light, as a thing not only painful, but absurd. So one evening the deep, full-hearted silence burst and flowered into speech. In common courtesy Mr. Rickman had to open his lips to ask her whether she objected to his smoking. (She did not.) Then it came to acknowledging each other in the streets; after that, to Poppy's coming out and looking over the balcony about the time when Mr. Rickman would be looking to see if Poppy was looking; and so on, to that wonderful night when he saw her home from the Jubilee Theatre. The stars were out; not that Poppy cared a rap about the stars.

Her first appearance to-night was in the character of a coster-girl, a part well suited to her audacity and impertinent prettiness. Poppy was the tiniest dancer that ever whirled across a stage, a circumstance that somewhat diminished the vulgarity of her impersonation, while it gave it a very engaging character of its own. Her small Cockney face, with its impudent laughing nose, its curling mouth (none too small), its big, twinkling blue eyes, was framed in a golden fringe and side curls. She wore a purple velveteen skirt, a purple velveteen jacket with a large lace collar, and a still larger purple velveteen hat with white ostrich feathers that swayed madly from the perpendicular.

The secret of Poppy's popularity lay in this, that you could always depend on her; she always played the same part in the same manner; but her manner was her own. To come on the stage quietly; to look, in spite of her coster costume, the picture of suburban innocence and pink and white propriety; to stand facing her audience for a second of time, motionless and in perfect gravity—it was a trick that, though Poppy never varied it, had a more killing effect than the most ingenious impromptu.

"Sh-sh-sh-sh!" A flutter of programmes in the pit was indignantly suppressed by the gallery. There was a movement of Poppy's right eyelid which in a larger woman would have been called a wink; in Poppy it appeared as an exaggerated twinkle. It was greeted with a roar of rapturous applause. Then Poppy, with her hands on her hips, and her head on one side, raised her Cockney voice in a high-pitched song, executing between each verse a slow, swinging chassée to the stage Humourist with the concertina.

> "Oh, she's my fancy girl,
>   With 'er 'air all outer curl,
> 'Ooks orf, eyes orf, petticoats all awry.
>   For then she isn't shy;
>   She gives 'er bangs a twirl,
> And it's—'Kiss me quick!'—and—'That's the Trick!'
>   —and—(*dim*)—'*Wouldn't* yer like to try?'"

When the stage Humourist with the concertina stopped chasséeing, and put his finger to his nose, and observed, "That's wot you might call a dim innuender," Rickman could have kicked him.

> (*cresc.*),   "But got up fit ter kill,
>   In 'er velverteen an' frill,
> It's—'Ands orf!'—'Heyes orf!'—'Fetch yer one in
>   the heye!'—
> A strollin' down the 'Igh,
>   With 'Enery, Alf an' Bill,
> It's—'None er that!'—and 'Mind my 'at!'—and
> (*fortissimo*)—'WOULDN'T yer like to try!'"

"To try! To try!" Her chassée quickened ever so little, doubled on itself, and became a tortuous thing. Poppy's feet beat out the measure that is danced on East End pavements to the music of the concertina. In the very abandonment of burlesque Poppy remained an artist, and her dance preserved the gravity of the original ballet, designed for performance on a flagstone. Now it unfolded; it burst its bounds; it was a rhythmic stampede. Louder and louder, her clicking heels beat the furious time; higher and higher her dexterous toes flew to her feathers that bowed to meet them, and when her last superhuman kick sent her hat

flying, and the Humourist caught it on his head, they had
brought the house down.

Rickman went out to the bar, where he found Dicky
Pilkington, and at Dicky's suggestion he endeavoured to
quench with brandy and soda his inextinguishable thirst.

He returned to the storm and glare of the ballet, the last
appearance of that small, incarnate genius of Folly. There
were other dancers, but he saw none but her. He knew
every pose and movement of her body, from her first tentative, preluding pirouette, to her last moon-struck dance,
when she tossed her tall grenadier's cap to the back of the
stage, and still spinning, shook out her hair, and flung herself
backwards, till it streamed and eddied with the whirlwind
of her dance. In her fantastic dress (she wore her colours,
the red and black) her very womanhood had vanished, she
was a mere insignificant morsel of flesh and blood, inspired
by the dizzy, reckless Fury of the footlights.

There was a noise of many boots beating the floor of the
house; it grew into a thick, solid body of sound, torn at
intervals by a screaming whistle from the galleries. Someone up there shouted her name—" Poppy—Poppy Grace! "
and Rickman shivered.

To Rickman's mind the name was an outrage; it reeked
of popularity; it suggested—absurdly and abominably—
a certain cheap drink of sudden and ephemeral efferves-
cence. He never let his mind dwell on those dreadful
syllables any longer than he could help; he never thought
of her as Poppy Grace at all. He thought of her in undefined, extraordinary ways; now as some nameless aerial
spirit, unaccountably wandering about in a world too gross
for it; and now as the Young Joy, the fugitive actuality.
To-night, after brandy and soda, his imagination possessed
itself of Poppy, and wove round her the glory and gloom
of the world. It saw in her, not the incarnation of the rosy
moment, but the eternal sacrifice of woman, the tragedy
of her abasement, her obedience to the world. Which, when
he came to think of it, was really very clever of his imagination.

Meanwhile Poppy was behaving, as she had behaved for
the last fifty nights, like a lunatic humming top. Now it
had steadied itself in the intensity of its speed; the little
humming-top was sleeping. Poppy, as the span, seemed

to be standing, her feet rooted, her body swaying delicately from the hips, like a flower rocked by the wind, the light of her flickering flamewise. There was a stir, a wave, as if the heart of the house had heaved. Pit and gallery breathed hard. Rickman leaned forward with clouded eyes and troubled forehead, while the young shop-men—the other young shop-men—thrilled with familiar and delicious emotion. Now she curtsied, as she had curtsied for the last fifty nights, bowing lower and lower till her hair fell over her face and swept the stage; and now she shook her head till the great golden whirl of hair seemed the only part of her left spinning; then Poppy folded her arms and sank, sank till she sat on her heels, herself invisible, curtained in modest and mystic fashion by her hair.

"Bravo! Bravo!" "That's the trick!"—"Encore!"— "Oh, *she's* my fancy girl!"—"Encore-ore-ore-ore-ore!"

It was all over.

CHAPTER X

HE hurried back to Bloomsbury, in the wake of her hansom, to the house of the balcony opposite the plane-trees. The plane-tree was half-withdrawn into the night, but the balcony hung out black in the yellow light from its three long windows. Poppy was not in the balcony.

He went up into the room where the light was, a room that had been once an ordinary Bloomsbury drawing-room, the drawing-room of Propriety. Now it was Poppy's drawing-room.

You came straight out of a desert of dreary and obscure respectability, and it burst, it blossomed into Poppy before your eyes. Portraits of Poppy on the walls, in every conceivable and inconceivable attitude. Poppy's canary in the window, in a cage hung with yellow gauze. Poppy's mandoline in an easy chair by itself. Poppy's hat on the grand piano, tumbling head over heels among a litter of coffee cups. On the tea-table a pair of shoes that could have belonged to nobody but Poppy, they were so diminutive. In the waste paper basket a bouquet that must have been Poppy's too, it was so enormous. And on the table in the window a Japanese flower-bowl that served as a handy

receptacle for cigarette ash and spent vestas. Two immense mirrors facing each other reflected these objects and
Poppy, when she was there, for ever and ever, in diminishing perspective. But Poppy was not there.

Passing through this brilliant scene into the back room
beyond, he found her finishing her supper.

Poppy was not at all surprised to see him. She addressed
him as " Rickets," and invited him under that name to sit
down and have some supper, too.

But Rickets did not want any supper. He sat down
at the clear end of the table, and looked on as in a dream.
And when Poppy had finished she came and sat by him
on the clear end of the table, and made cigarettes, and drank
champagne out of a little tumbler.

" Thought you might feel a little lonely over there, Ricky-
ticky," said she.

Poppy was in spirits. If she had yielded to the glad impulse of her heart, she would have stood on one foot and
twirled the other over Ricky-ticky's head. But she restrained herself. Somehow, before Ricky-ticky, Poppy never
played any of those tricks that delighted Mr. Pilkington and
other gentlemen of her acquaintance. She merely sat on
the table. She was in her ballet-dress, and before sitting
on the table she arranged her red skirts over her black legs
with a prodigious air of propriety. Poppy herself did not
know whether this meant that she wanted Ricky-ticky to
think her nice, or whether she wanted to think Ricky-ticky
nice. After all, it came to the same thing; for to Poppy
the peculiar charm of Ricky-ticky was his innocence.

The clock on St. Pancras Church struck half-past eleven;
in his hanging cage in the front room, behind his yellow
gauze curtain, Poppy's canary woke out of his first sleep.
He untucked his head from under his wing and chirruped
drowsily.

" Oh, dicky," said Poppy, " it's time you were in your
little bed ! "

He did not take the hint. He was intent on certain movements of Poppy's fingers and the tip of her tongue concerned
in the making of cigarettes.

He was gazing into her face as if it held for him the secret
of the world. And that look embarrassed her. It had
all the assurance of age and all the wonder of youth in it.

Poppy's eyes were trained to look out for danger signals in the eyes of boys, for Poppy, according to those lights of hers, was honest. If she knew the secret of the world, she would not have told it to Ricky-ticky; he was much too young. Men, in Poppy's code of morality, were different. But this amazing, dreamy, interrogative look was not the sort of thing that Poppy was accustomed to, and for once in her life Poppy felt shy.

"I say, Rickets, there goes a quarter to twelve. *Did* I wake him out of his little sleep?"

Poppy talked as much to the canary as to Rickets, which made it all quite proper. As for Rickman, he talked hardly at all.

"You'll have to go in ten minutes, Rick." And by way of softening this announcement she gave him some champagne.

He had paid no attention to that hint either, being occupied with a curious phenomenon. Though Poppy was, for her, most unusually stationary, he found that it was making him slightly giddy to look at her.

He was arriving at that moment of intoxication when things lose their baldness and immobility, and the world begins to float like an enchanted island in a beautiful blood-warm haze. Nothing could be more agreeable than the first approaches of this blessed state; he encouraged it, anticipating with ecstasy each stage in the mounting of the illusion. For when he was sober he saw Poppy very much as she was; but when he was drunk she became for him a being immaculate, divine. He moved in a region of gross but glorious exaggeration, where his wretched little Cockney passion assumed the proportions of a superb romance. His soul that minute was the home of the purest, most exalted emotions. Yes, he could certainly feel it coming on. Poppy's face was growing bigger and bigger, opening out and blossoming like an enormous flower.

"Nine minutes up. In another minute you go."

It seemed to him that Poppy was measuring time by pouring champagne into little tumblers, and that she gave him champagne to drink. He knew it was no use drinking it, for that thirst of his was unquenchable; but he drank, for the sake of the illusion; and as he drank it seemed to him that, not only was Poppy worthy of all adoration, but that his passion for her was no mere vulgar and earthly passion; it was a glorious and immortal thing.

Poppy looked at him curiously. She was the soul of hospitality, but it struck her that she was being a little too liberal with the champagne.

"No, Razors. No more fizz. If I were to drink a drop more it would spoil my little dance that always fetches the boys."

She turned her tumbler upside down in token of renunciation, and led the way into the front room. He followed her with enchanted feet. He was now moving as in an Arabian Night's dream.

In the front room was a sofa—No, a divan, and on the divan the skin of a Polar bear sprawling. Rickman and Poppy sat on the top of the bear. Such a disreputable, out-of-elbow, cosmopolitan bear! His little eye-holes were screwed up in a wicked wink, a wink that repudiated any connection with his native waters of the Pole.

The house was very still. Behind his yellow gauze curtain the canary stirred in his sleep. "Swe-eet," he murmured plaintively in his dream.

"Swee-eet, dicky!" echoed Poppy. Then, because she had nothing to say, she began to sing. She sang the song of Simpson the tenor, Simpson the master of tears.

> "'Twas on the night our little byby died,
> And Bill, 'e comes, and, Sall,' 'e sez, 'look 'ere,
> I've signed a pledge,' sez 'e, agans the beer.
>   D'ye see?'
>   Sez 'e.
>   'And wot I 'ope te syve
> Will tittervyte 'is bloomin' little gryve.'
> Then—Well—yo' should 'ave 'eard us 'ow we cried—
> Like bloomin' kids—the—night—the byby—died.

"That song," said Poppy, "doesn't exactly suit my style of beauty. You should have heard Simpey sing it. *That* 'd 'ave given you something to 'owl for."

For Rickman looked depressed.

The sound of Poppy's song waked the canary; he fluttered down from his perch and stretched his wings, trailing them on the floor of his cage to brush the sleep out of them.

"Did you ever see such affectation?" said Poppy. "Look at him, striking attitudes up there, all by 'is little self!"

Poppy seemed to cling to the idea of the canary as a symbol of propriety.

"Do you know, Rickets, it's past twelve o'clock?"

No, he didn't know. He had taken no count of time. But he knew that he had drunk a great many little tumblers of champagne, and that his love for Poppy seemed more than ever a supersensuous and immortal thing. He pulled himself together in order to tell her so; but at that moment he was confronted by an insuperable difficulty. In the tender and passionate speech that he was about to make to her, it would be necessary to address her by name. But how—in Heaven's name—could he address a divinity as Poppy? He settled the difficulty by deciding that he would not address her at all. There should be no invocation. He would simply explain.

He got up and walked about the room, and explained in such words as pleased him the distinction between the corruptible and the incorruptible Eros. From time to time he chanted his own poems in the intervals of explaining; for they bore upon the matter in hand.

"Rickets," said Poppy severely, "you've had too much fizz. I can see it in your eyes—most unmistakably. I know it isn't very nice of me to say so, when it's my fizz you've been drinking; but it isn't really mine, it's Dicky Pilkington's—at least he paid for it."

But Rickets did not hear her. His soul, soaring on wings of champagne, was borne far away from Dicky Pilkington.

"Know" (chanted Rickets) "that the Love which is my
    Lord most high,
  He changeth not with seasons and with days,
  His feet are shod with light in all his ways,
And when he followeth none have power to fly.

"He chooseth whom he will, and draweth nigh,
    To them alone whom he himself doth raise
  Unto his perfect service and his praise;
Of such Love's lowliest minister am I."

"If you'd asked me," said Poppy, "I should have said he had a pretty good opinion of himself. What do you say, dicky?"

"Sweet!" sang the canary in one pure, penetrating note, the voice of Innocence itself.

"Isn't he rakish?" But Poppy got no answer from the sonneteer. He had wheeled round from her, carried away in the triumph and rapture of the sestette. His steps marked the beat of the iambics, he turned on his heel at the end of every line. For the moment he was sober, as men count sobriety.

> "For he I serve hath paced Heaven's golden floor,
>   And chanted with the Seraphims' glad choir;
>   Lo! All his wings are plumed with fervent fire;
> He hath twain that bear him upward evermore,
> With twain he veils his holy eyes before
>   The mystery of his own divine desire.

"Does it remind you of anything?" he asked. It struck her as odd that he seemed to realize her presence with difficulty.

"No, I can't say that I ever heard anything like it in my life."

"Well, the idea's bagged from Dante—I mean Dante-gabrier-rossetti. But he doesn't want it as badly as I do. In fac', I don' think he wants it at all where he is now. If he does, he can take any of mine in exchange. You bear me out, Poppy—I invite the gentleman to step down and make's 's own s'lection. Nobody can say I plagiarize anyborry—anyborry but myself."

"All right, don't you worry, old chappy," said Poppy soothingly. "You come here and sit quiet."

He came and sat down beside her, as if the evening had only just begun. He sat down carefully, tenderly, lest he should crush so much as the hem of her fan-like, diaphanous skirts. And then he began to talk to her.

He said there was no woman—no lady—in the world for whom he felt such reverence and admiration; "Pop-oppy," he said, "you're fit to dance before God on the floor of Heaven when they've swept it."

"Oh, come," said Poppy, "can't you go one better?"

He could. He did. He intimated that though he worshipped every hair of Poppy's little head and every inch of Poppy's little body, what held him, at the moment, were the fascinations of her mind, and the positively gorgeous beauty of her soul. Yes; there could be no doubt that the object of his devotion was Poppy's imperishable soul.

" Well," said Poppy, " that tykes the very tip-top macaroon ! "

Then she laughed; she laughed as if she would never have done. She laughed, first with her eyes, then with her throat, then with her whole body, shaking her head and rocking herself backwards and forwards. She laughed till her hair came down, and he took it and smoothed it into two sleek straight bands, and tied them in a loose knot under her chin.

Then she stopped laughing. Her face between the two tight sheaths of hair seemed to close and shrink to a thin sharp bud. It closed and opened again, it grew nearer and bigger, it bent forward and put out its mouth (for it had a mouth, this extraordinary flower) and kissed him.

" I sy, it's nearly one o'clock," said she. " You've got to clear out of this. Come ! "

She rose; she stood before him holding out her hands to help him to get up and go. She laughed again. She laughed wide-mouthed, her head flung back, her face fore-shortened, her white throat swelled and quivering—the abandoned figure of Low Comedy incarnate. But that was not what he saw.

To him it was as if the dark, impenetrable world had suddenly unfolded, had blossomed and flowered in the rose of her mouth; as if all the roses of all the world went to make up the petals of that rose. Her body was nothing but a shining, transparent vessel for the fire of life. It ran over; it leapt from her; the hands she stretched out to him were two shallow lamps that could hardly hold the tall, upward shooting, wind-tortured splendour of the flame.

He rose unsteadily to his feet. The movement, being somewhat complicated, brought him within a yard of his own figure as presented in one of the long mirrors. He stood there, arrested, fascinated, shocked by that person in the mirror. The face he was accustomed to see in mirrors was grave, and not high coloured, and it always kept its mouth shut. This person's face was very red, and his mouth was slightly open, a detail he noticed with a peculiar disgust. He could not get away from it, either. It was held there, illuminated, insisted on, repeated for ever and ever, smaller and smaller, an endless procession of faces, all animated by one frenzy and one flame. He was appalled by this mysterious multiplication of his person, and by the flushed and brilliant infamy of his face. The face was the worst; he thought he had never seen anything so detestable as the face. He sat down and hid it in his hands.

"Poor Rickets," said Poppy softly. She drew his hands from his face by a finger at a time.

"Oh, Ricky-ticky, you are such a rum little fellow. I suppose that's why I like you. But for the life of me I can't think why I kissed you; unless it was to say Good-night."

A kiss more or less was nothing to Poppy. And that one, she felt, had been valedictory. She had kissed, not Ricky-ticky, but his dying Innocence, the boy in him. And she had really wanted him to go.

The house was stiller than ever. The canary had tucked his head under his wing and gone to sleep again. Out of the silence the clock at St. Pancras Church struck one.

And yet he had not gone.

CHAPTER XI

A STEP was heard on the pavement outside; then the click of a latch-key; a step on the stairs, at the threshold, and Mr. Pilkington walked in with the air of being the master of the house and everything in it.

The little laughing mask slipped from Poppy's face, her eyes were two sapphire crescents darting fright under down-dropped lids. There was a look in Dicky's face she did not care for. But Rickman—as Maddox had testified—was a perfect little gentleman when he was drunk, and at the sight of Pilkington, chivalry, immortal chivalry, leapt in his heart.

He became suddenly grave, steady and coherent.

"I was just going, Miss Grace. But—if you want me to stay a little longer, I'll stay."

"You'd better *go*," said Miss Grace.

Her eyes followed him sullenly as he went; so did Pilkington's.

"Well," she said, "I suppose that's what you wanted?"

"Yes, but there's no good overdoing the thing, you know. This," said Pilkington, "is a damned sight too expensive game for him to play."

" He's all right. It wasn't his fault. I let him drink too much champagne."

" What did you do that for? Couldn't you see he'd had enough already? "

" How was I to know? He's nicer when he's drunk than other people are when they're sober."

He looked at her critically. " I know all about him. What I'd like to know is what *you* see in him."

Poppy returned his look with interest. Coarseness in Dicky Pilkington's eyes sat brilliant and unashamed.

"Would you? So would I. P'raps it's wot I don't see in him."

Now subtlety was the last thing Dicky expected from Poppy, and it aroused suspicion.

Whatever Poppy's instructions were she had evidently exceeded them. Poppy read his thoughts with accuracy.

" I only did what you told me. If you don't like it, you can finish the job yourself. I'm tired," said Poppy, wearily coiling up her hair. She was no longer in spirits.

CHAPTER XII

A TINY jet of gas made a glimmer in the fan-light of Mrs. Downey's boarding-house next door. Mrs. Downey kept it burning there for Mr. Rickman.

Guided by this beacon, he reached his door, escaping many dangers. For the curbstone was a rocking precipice, and the street below it a grey and shimmering stream, that rolled, and flowed, and rolled, and never rested. The houses, too, were so drunk as to be dangerous. They bowed over him, swaying hideously from their foundations. They seemed to be attracted, just as he was, by that abominable slimy flow and glister of the asphalt. Another wriggle of the latch-key, and they would be over on the top of him.

He approached his bedroom candle with infinite precaution. He had tried to effect a noiseless entry, but every match, as it spurted and went out, was a little fiendish spit-fire tongue betraying him. From behind a bedroom door, ajar at the dark end of the passage, the voice of Mrs. Downey gently reminded him not to forget to turn the gas out.

There was a bright clear space in his brain which Pilkington's champagne had not penetrated, so intolerably clear and bright that it hurt him to look at it. In that space three figures reeled and whirled; three, yet one and the same; Poppy of the coster-dance, Poppy of the lunatic ballet, and Poppy of the Arabian night. Beyond the bright space and the figures there was a dark place that was somehow curtained off. Something had happened there, he could not see what. And in trying to see he forgot to turn the gas out. He turned it up instead.

He left it blazing away at the rate of a penny an hour, a witness against him in the face of morning. But he did not forget to sit down at the bottom of the stairs and take his boots off, lest he should wake Flossie Walker, the little clerk, who worked so hard, and had to be up so early. He left them on the stairs, where Flossie tripped over them in the morning.

On the first landing a young man in a frowsy sleeping suit stood waiting for him. A fresh, sober, and thoroughly wide-awake young man.

"Gurra bed, Spinks," said Mr. Rickman severely to the young man.

"All right, old man." Mr. Spinks lowered his voice to a discreet whisper. "I say—do you want me to help you find your legs?"

"Wish you'd fin' any par' of me that is n' legs," said Mr. Rickman. And he went on to explain and to demonstrate to Mr. Spinks the resemblance (amounting to identity) between himself and the Manx arms. "Three legs, rampant, on the bend, proper. Amazin', isn't it?"

"It *is* amazin'."

Feigning surprise and interest, Mr. Spinks relieved him of his candle; and under that escort Mr. Rickman managed to attain to the second floor.

Mr. Rickman's room was bared to the glimmer of a lamp in the street below. He plunged and stumbled through a litter of books. The glimmer fell on the books, on many books; books that covered three walls from floor to ceiling; books ranged above and beside the little camp-bed in the corner; books piled on the table and under it. The glimmer fell, too, on the mantel-piece, reflected from the glass above it, right on to the white statuette of the Venus of Milo that supported a photograph of a dancing Poppy—Poppy, who laughed in the face of the goddess with insatiable impudence, and flung to the immortal forehead the flick of her shameless foot. White and austere gleamed the Venus (if Venus she be, for some say she is a Wingless Victory, and Rickman, when sober, inclined to that opinion). White and austere gleamed the little camp-bed in the corner. He ignored Mr. Spinks' discreet suggestion. He wasn't going to undress to please Spinks or anybody. He'd see Spinks in another world first. He wasn't going to bed like a potman; he was going to sit up like a poet and write. That's what he was going to do. This was his study.

With shaking hands he lit the lamp on his study table; the wick sputtered, and the light in his head jigged horribly with the jigging of the flame. It was as if he was being stabbed with little knives of light.

He plunged his head into a basin of cold water, threw open his window, and leaned out into the pure regenerating night. Spinks sat down on a chair and watched him, his fresh, handsome face clouded with anxiety. He adored Rickman sober; but for Rickman drunk he had a curious yearning affection. If anything, he preferred him in that state. It seemed to bring him nearer to him. Spinks had never been drunk in his life; but that was his feeling.

Rickman laid his arms upon the window sill and his head upon his arms.

"'The blessed damozel leaned out,'" he said, (the idea in his mind being that *he* was a blessed damozel).

"'From the gold bar of heaven.'"

("Never knew they had 'em up there," murmured Spinks.)

"'Her eyes were deeper than the depth of water stilled at even——' Oh—my—God!"

A great sigh shook him, and went shuddering into the night, like the passing of a lost soul. He got up and staggered to the table, and grasped it by the edge, nearly upsetting the lamp. The flare in his brain had died down as the lamp burnt steadily. Under its shade a round of light fell on his Euripides, open at the page he had been reading the night before.

ΕΛΕΝΗ

He saw it very black, with the edges a little wavering, a

little blurred, as if it had been burnt by fire into the whiteness of the page. Below, the smaller type of a chorus reeled and shook through all its lines. Set up by an intoxicated compositor.

Under the Euripides was the piled up manuscript of Rickman's great neo-classic drama, *Helen in Leuce*. He implored Spinks to read it. (Spinks was a draper's assistant and uncultured.) He thrust the manuscript into his hands.

" There," he said, " rèa' that. Tha's the sor' o' thing I write when I'm drunk. Couldn' do it now t' save my life. Temp'rance been *my* ruin."

He threw himself on his bed.

" It's allrigh'. At nine o'clock to-morrow morning, no—at a quar'er pas' nine. I mean three quar'ers pas' nine, I shall be drunk. Not disgustingly and ridicklelously, as you are, Spinky, at this minute, but soo-p-p-perbubbly, loominously, divinely drunk! You don't know what I could do if I was only drunk."

" Oh, come, I shouldn't complain, if I was you. You'll do pretty well as you are, I think."

With an almost maternal tenderness and tact Mr. Spinks contrived to separate the poet from his poem. He then undressed him. That is to say, by alternate feats of strength, dexterity, and cunning, he succeeded in disengaging him from the looser portion of his clothing. From his shirt and trousers Rickman refused to part, refused with a shake of the head, slow, gentle, and implacable, and with a smile of great sweetness and gravity and wisdom. He seemed to regard those garments with a peculiar emotion as the symbols of his dignity, and more especially, as the insignia of sobriety.

Spinks sat down and stared at the object of his devotion. " Poor old chappie," he murmured tenderly. He was helpless before that slow melancholy shaking of the head, that mysterious and steadfast smile. He approached tip-toe on deprecating feet. But Rickman would none of him; his whole attitude was eloquent of rebuke. He waved Spinks away with one pathetic hand; with the other he clutched and gathered round him the last remnants of his personal majesty. And thus, in his own time and in his own fashion, he wandered to his bed. Even then he conveyed reproach and reproof by his manner of entering it;

he seemed to vanish subtly, to withdraw himself, as into some sacred and inviolable retreat.

Spinks crept away, saddened by the rebuff. After all, he was no nearer to Rickman drunk than to Rickman sober. Half an hour later, he was asleep in the adjoining room, dreaming a lightsome dream of ladies and *mousselines de laine,* when suddenly the dream turned to a nightmare. It seemed to him that there descended upon him a heavy rolling weight, as of a bale of woollens. He awoke and found that it was Rickman.

The poet lay face downwards across the body of his friend, and was crooning into his ear the great chorus from the third act of *Helen in Leuce*. He said that nobody but Spinky understood it. And Spinky couldn't understand it if he wasn't drunk.

Whereupon Spinks was most curiously uplifted and consoled.

CHAPTER XIII

HE woke tired out, as well as he might be, after spending half the night in the pursuit of young Joy, personified in Miss Poppy Grace, young Joy, who, like that little dancer, is the swiftest of all swift things.

Rickman carried into this adventure a sort of innocence that renewed itself, as by a miracle, every evening. His youth remained virgin because of its incorruptible hope. He almost disarmed criticism by the gaiety, the naïveté of the pursuit. She was always in front of him, that young Joy; but if he did not overtake her by midnight, he was all the more sure that he would find her in the morning, with the dew on her feet and the dawn on her forehead. He was convinced that it was that sweet mystic mouth of hers which would one day tell him the secret of the world. And long before the morning she would pick up her skirts and be off again, swifter than ever, carrying her secret with her.

And so the chase went on.

At the present moment he found himself in the society of Shame, the oldest and most haggard of all the daughters of the night. *She* was in no hurry to leave him. It seemed to him that she sat beside him, formless and immense, that she laid her hands about him, and that the burning on his poor forehead was her brand there; that the scorching in his poor throat was the clutch of her fingers, and the torment in all his miserable body her fine manipulation of his nerves. She knew the secret of the world; and had no sort of hesitation about telling it; it sounded to him uncommonly like something that he had heard before. He recognized her as the form and voice of his own desire, the loathsome familiar body of unuttered thoughts, sordid, virulent, accusing, with a tongue that lashed through the flesh to the obscure spirit inside him. And because he was a poet, and knew himself a poet, because he had sinned chiefly through his imagination, it was through his imagination that he suffered, so that the horror was supreme. For all the while, though Shame was there, his ideas were there too, somewhere, the divine thoughts and the proud beautiful dreams, and the great pure loves, winged and veiled; they stood a long way off and turned away their faces from him, and that was the worst punishment he had to bear.

Which meant that, as Savage Keith Rickman lay in bed the morning after that glorious April night, he knew that he had been making an April fool of himself. He knew it by the pain in his head and other disagreeable signs; also by the remarkable fact that he still wore the shirt and trousers of the day.

And he knew that, in spite of the pain, he would have to get up and go down to breakfast as if nothing had happened; he would have to meet Mr. Spinks' eyes twinkling with malign intelligence, and Flossie's wondering looks, and Mrs. Downey's tender womanly concern, as he turned white over the bacon and the butter. He didn't know which were worse, the knowing eyes or the innocent ones. He had to be at the shop by nine o'clock, too, to force that poor, dizzy, aching head of his to its eight hours' work.

In this unnerved, attenuated state, this mortal paleness of mind and body, it was terrible to have to face the robust reality of "Rickman's." At nine o'clock in the morning it was more real to him than any real thing; it even assumed an abominable personality; it was an all-compelling, all-consuming power that sucked from him his time, his life, his energy, and for six days out of the seven required of him his soul. That at the same time it provided him with the means of bodily subsistence only added to the horror of the thing. It was as if "Rickman's," destroyer and preserver, renewed his life every quarter day that it might draw in, devour, annihilate it as before. There was a diabolical precision in the action of the machine that made and unmade him.

And yet, with its rhythm of days and weeks, it was in its turn part of a vaster system, whose revolutions brought round a longer pause—when for three days his soul would be given back to him. The only thing that kept him up at this moment was the blessed hope of the Bank Holiday.

While young Keith was still lying very sick and miserable in his bed, the elder Rickman, in his villa residence at Ilford in Essex, was up and eager for the day. By the time Keith had got down to breakfast Isaac had caught the early train that landed him in the City at nine. Before half-past he was in the front shop, taking a look round.

And as he looked round and surveyed his possessions, his new stock on the shelves, his plate-glass and his mahogany fittings, his assistants, from the boy in shirt sleeves, now washing down the great front window, to the gentlemanly cashier, high-collared and frock-coated, in his pew, he rubbed his hands softly, and his heart swelled with thankfulness and pride. For Isaac Rickman was a dreamer, too, in his way. There are dreams and dreams, and the incontestible merit and glory of Isaac's dreams was that they had all, or very nearly all, come true. They were of the sort that can be handed over the counter, locked up in a cash-box and lodged in the Bank. His latest dream had been carried out in plate-glass and mahogany; it towered into space and was finished off with a beautiful pink cupola at the top.

There was not much of the father in the son. Keith, presumably, took after his mother, a hectic, pale-haired woman, who had died in the supreme effort of his birth. On her own birth there had been something in the nature of a slur. She had taken it to heart, and exhausted herself in the endeavour to conceal from her very respectable husband the shameful fact that she had once served as barmaid in a City restaurant, and that she was the illegitimate daughter of a village sempstress and a village squire. Isaac,

before he dreamed of greatness, had met her at a Band of
Hope meeting, and had married her because of her sweetness
and pathetic beauty. She left to her boy her fairness, her
expressive face, her own nerves and her mother's passion.
Isaac and he were alike only in a certain slenderness, a
fleshless refinement of physique. Coarseness in grain, usually revealed by the lower half of a man's countenance, had
with the elder Rickman taken up its abode in the superior,
the intellectual region. Isaac's eyes and forehead trafficked
grossly with the world, while the rest of his face preserved
the stern reticences and sanctities of the spirit. Isaac was
a Wesleyan; and his dress (soft black felt hat, smooth black
frock-coat, narrow tie, black but clerical) almost suggested
that he was a minister of that persuasion. His lips were
hidden under an iron grey moustache, the short grizzled
beard was smoothed forward and fined to a point by the
perpetual caress of a meditative hand. Such was Isaac.

Impossible to deny a certain genius to the man who had
raised that mighty pile, the Gin Palace of Art. Those
stately premises, with their clustering lights, their carpeted
floors, their polished fittings, were very different from the
dark little house in Paternoster Row where Keith first
saw what light there was to be seen. When Isaac grew
great and moved further west, the little shop was kept on
and devoted to the sale of Bibles, hymn-books, and Nonconformist literature. For Isaac, life was a compromise between
the pious Wesleyan he was and the successful tradesman
he aspired to be. There were, in fact, two Rickmans:
Rickman's in the City and Rickman's in the Strand. Rickman's in the Strand bore on its fore-front most unmistakably the seal of the world; Rickman's in the City was
sealed with the Lord's seal.

So that now there was not a single need of the great
book-buying, book-loving Public that Rickman's did not
provide for and represent. It pandered to (Isaac said
"catered for") the highest and the lowest, the spirit as
well as the flesh. Only Isaac was wise enough to keep the
two branches of the business separate and distinct. His
right hand professed complete ignorance of the doings of
his left.

It may be that Isaac's heart was in his City shop. But
there was something in him greater than his heart, his

ambition, which was colossal. He meant, he always had meant, to be the founder of a great House, which should make the name of Rickman live after him. He aimed at nothing less than supremacy. He proposed to spread his nets till they had drawn in the greater part of the book trade of London; till Rickman's had reared its gigantic palaces in every district of the capital. In '92 there was some talk of depression in the book trade. Firms had failed. Isaac did not join in the talk, and he had his own theory of the failure. Men went smash for want of will, for want of brains, for want of courage and capital. Above all for want of capital. As if any man need want capital so long as he had the pluck to borrow, that is to say, to buy it. So ran his dream. And Isaac believed in his dream, and what was more, he had made Mr. Richard Pilkington, Financial Agent, of Shaftesbury Avenue, believe in it. "Rickman's," backed by Pilkington, would stand firm, firm as a rock.

Courage and capital are great, but brains are greater. It was not only by shrewdness, energy, and an incomparable audacity that Isaac Rickman had raised himself from those obscure beginnings. Isaac was an artist in his own enormous way, and he had made an exhaustive study of the Public. With incredible versatility he followed every twist and turn of the great mind; the slow, colossal movements which make capital, the fitful balancing, the sudden start and mad rush forward by which, if you can but foresee and keep pace with it, you reap the golden harvest of the hour. He never took his eye off the Public. He laid his finger, as it were, on that mighty pulse and recorded its fluctuations in his ledger.

But there was a region beyond those fluctuations. With new books there was always a pound's worth of risk to a pennyworth of profit; but there was no end of money to be got out of old ones, if only you knew how to set about it. And Isaac did not quite know how. In his front shop it was the Public, in his side shop it was the books that mattered, and knowledge of the one, however exhaustive, was no guide to the other. Isaac by himself cut a somewhat unfortunate figure; he stood fully equipped in the field where there was much danger and but little gain; he was helpless where the price of knowledge ruled immeasurably high. In the second-hand department audacity without education can do nothing. What he still wanted, then, was brains and yet more brains; not the raw material, mind you, he had plenty of that, but the finished product, the trained, cultured intellect. Isaac was a self-made man, a man ignorant of many things, religious, but uneducated.

But he had a son, and the son had a head on his shoulders, a magnificent head that boy had. Mr. Horace Jewdwine had noticed it the first minute he came into the shop. And the magnificence of Keith's head had been pointed out to Isaac long before that, when Keith couldn't have been more than ten—why, nine he was; that was the beginning of it. Isaac could remember how Sir Joseph Harden of Lazarus, the great scholar, who was one of Isaac's best customers, poking round the little dingy shop in Paternoster Row (it was all second-hand in those days), came on the young monkey perched on the step-ladder, reading Homer. Sir Joseph had made him come down and translate for him then and there. And Keith went at it, translating for twenty minutes straight on end. Sir Joseph had said nothing, but he asked him what he was going to be, and the young Turk grinned up at him and said he was going to be a poet, " like 'Omer, that was what he was going to be." Isaac had said that was just like his impudence, but Sir Joseph stood there looking at him and smiling on the side of his face that Keith couldn't see, and he told the little chap to "work hard and mind his rough breathings." Isaac had supposed that was some sort of a joke, for Keith, he tried hard to grin, though his face went red hot all over. Then Sir Joseph had turned round very serious and asked if he, Rickman, had any other sons, because, whatever he did with the rest of them, he must make this one a scholar. Isaac had said No, he hadn't any but that one boy, and he would have to be brought up to the business. He was afraid he couldn't spare the time to make much of a scholar of him. Time, said Isaac, was money. What Sir Joseph said then Isaac had never forgotten. He had said: " True, time *was* money, loose cash in your pockets; but brains were capital." And there wasn't a better investment for them, he had added, than a good sound classical education. Isaac was to send the boy to the City of London, then to the London University, if he couldn't rise to Oxford; but Sir Joseph's advice was Oxford.

Let him try for a scholarship. He added that he would like
to do something for him later on if he lived. Isaac had
never forgotten it; his memory being assisted by the circumstance that Sir Joseph had that very same day bought
one hundred and twenty-five pounds' worth of books for his
great library down in Devonshire.

The boy was sent to an "Academy," then to the City of
London; Isaac had not risen to Oxford. Keith never tried
for a scholarship, and if he had, Isaac would have drawn
the line at a university education, as tending towards an
unholy leisure and the wisdom of this world. Otherwise
he had spared no expense, for he had grasped the fact that
this was an investment, and he looked to have his money
back again with something like fifty per cent. interest. And
the boy, the boy was to come back, too, with a brain as
bright as steel, all its queer little complicated parts in working order; in short, a superb machine; and Isaac would
only have to touch a spring to set it going.

But the question was, what spring? And that, unfortunately, was what old Rickman never could lay his finger on.

Still it went, that machine of his, apparently of its own
accord. It went mysteriously, capriciously, but fairly satis-
factorily on the whole. And Isaac was wise; his very
respect for the thing that had cost him so much prevented
him from tampering with it.

It was in accordance with this policy of caution that they
lived apart. Isaac loved the suburbs; Keith loved the town,
and it was as well for one of them to live in it, near to their
place of business. Isaac had married again, and though he
was proud of his boy and fond of him, he contrived to be
completely happy without him. He loved his little detached
villa residence at Ilford in Essex, with its little flower-garden
showing from the high road, its little stable for the pony
and little paddock for the cow. He loved his large smooth-
faced second wife, with her large balance at the bank and
still larger credit in the Wesleyan circle they lived and
moved in. He loved that Wesleyan circle, the comfortable, safe community that knew only the best, the Sunday
best, of him. And Keith loved none of these things. By
the education he had got and which he, Isaac, had given
him, by the "religion" he hadn't got, and which nothing
would induce him to take, by the obscure barriers of indi-

viduality and temperament, the son was separated from
the father. As for meeting each other half-way, Isaac had
tried it once or twice of a Sunday, when Keith had met him
indeed, but with a directness that shocked Isaac and distressed him. He was made positively uncomfortable by his
son's money-bought superiority; though the boy didn't bring
it out and show it, Isaac felt all the time that it was there.
He was very much happier without the boy. Keith among
other things suggested vividly the thoughts which the Wesleyan desired to put away from Saturday afternoon to Monday morning, thoughts of the present evil world, for which,
on Sundays, he more than half suspected that he might be
imperilling his immortal soul.

Sometimes in the watches of the night, especially of a
Sunday night, it occurred to him that (owing to the domestic arrangement which kept the boy in a place which, when
all was said and done, was a place of temptation) Keith's
soul, no less immortal, might be in jeopardy too. He
thought of him, an innocent lad, thrown on the mercy of
London, as it were. But Isaac had faith in the mercy of
the Lord. Besides, he wasn't the sort, a quiet, studious
young fellow like Keith wasn't. And when Isaac's conscience began to feel a little uncertain upon that point, he
simply laid the case circumstantially before the Lord, who
knew all his difficulties and all his sins, and was infinitely
able and eternally willing to bear them for him. By casting
Keith upon the Lord an immense burden of responsibility
was slipped from his conscience; and by the time Monday
morning came round Isaac was again convinced that he
had made the very best arrangements.

For not only was the state of Keith's soul a reproach
to Isaac's conscience, but the brilliance of Keith's intellect
was a terror to it. Any day that same swift, illuminating
power might be turned on to the dark places in his own
soul, showing up the deplorable discrepancies between his
inner and his outer life. He wanted his son and everybody
else to think well of him, and Keith's lucid sincerity at times
appalled him. He had not yet discovered that his protection was in the very thing he feared. Keith was so recklessly single-minded that it never occurred to him that his
father could lead a double life; he never doubted for an instant that, as in his own case, the Saturday to Monday state

revealed the real man. He, Keith, sat so lightly to the business and with so detached a mind, that he simply could not imagine how any human being could be so wedded to a thing in itself uninteresting as to sacrifice to it any immortal chances. The book trade was not a matter for high spiritual romance; it was simply the way they got their living, as honest a way as any other, taking it all round. The shop was one thing, and his father was another. In fact, so far from identifying them, he was inclined to pity his father as a fellow-victim of the tyranny and malignity of the shop.

But when in his right mind he had no grudge whatever against the shop. He had been born over the shop, nursed behind the shop, and the shop had been his schoolroom ever since he could spell. It was books, found in the shop and studied in the shop, that first opened his eyes to the glory of the world, as he sat on the step-ladder, reading his Shakespeare, or puzzling out his first Greek by the light of a single gas-flare; and for the sake of these things he had a tender recollection of Paternoster Row. It was to Rickman's that he owed his education. Doggedly at first, and afterwards mechanically, abstractedly, he got through the work he had to do. At times he even appreciated with a certain enjoyment the exquisite irony of his fate. Perhaps, when it came to the Gin Palace of Art, he had felt that the thing was getting almost beyond a joke. He had not been prepared for that lurid departure. He did not realize that he was in it, that his father had staked, not only his hopes, but his capital on him. He simply knew that " the guv'nor " was wrapt up in the horrid thing, that he had spent enormous sums on it, and he wasn't going to throw him over at the start.

But he had not the smallest intention of spending his whole life so. As always, long ago, in the darkness of the City shop, he had seen a brilliance of his own spreading around Rickman's and beyond it, shining away into the distance, so he saw it now, flinging out a broad, flaming, unmistakable path that could by no possibility lead back there. He only suffered a certain limited and unimportant part of him to be made into a machine.

Meanwhile it was perhaps in the divine mercy that the workings of this machine were hidden from Isaac. He hadn't even found out that the secret spring was not in the brain, but the heart of it. He would look up a little uneasily as Keith pushed through the big swinging doors and took his seat at the table on the platform, and while he wondered what Keith was thinking of him, ten to one Keith wasn't thinking of him at all.

This morning, however, he *was* thinking of him, as it happened. And when the old man saw him up there, holding his poor bursting head in his hands, and said: " 'Ead achin', my boy, again? That comes of studyin' too 'ard!" he thought, with a touch of compunction, " What would he say if he knew I'd gone drunk to bed last night? And if he knew about Poppy?"

Isaac approached his son gingerly and with a certain fear. The only thing he had discovered about this admirable machine of his was that it went better when you left it alone. It had not been going quite so well lately, though, and this morning it seemed decidedly out of order. He took a seat at the table and busied himself with a catalogue. Presently he rose and touched the boy gently on the shoulder.

"Come into the office a minute, will you?" he said, with a glance at the cashier. And Keith, wondering what on earth he wanted with him, followed into a recess shut off from the shop by a plate-glass and mahogany screen. Isaac hunted among the papers on his writing-table for a letter he could not find.

"You remember your old friend, Sir Joseph Harden, don't you?"

"Yes." Keith was, in fact, devoted to Sir Joseph's memory. He had often wondered what it was, that mysterious "something" which Sir Joseph would have done for him if he had lived, and whether, if he had done it, it would have made a difference.

"Well, I got a letter from his place in Devonshire this morning. They've asked me to send them someone down to catalogue his library. They want an expert, and he must go at once and finish by the twenty-seventh, or it's no use. Dear me, where is that letter?"

Keith goaded his brain to an agonizing activity. It seemed to him that some such proposal had been made to him before. But where or when he couldn't for the life of him remember.

"Pilkington says he told you something about it, last night. I've heard from him this morning, too."

Pilkington—he remembered now. Dicky had bothered him about a library last night; and he had wished Dicky at the devil. He beat his brains till he struck from them an illuminating flash (Lord, how it hurt too!).

"He didn't say it was the Harden Library."

"It is, though." Isaac's coarse forehead flushed with triumph. "He's promised me the refusal of it when it comes into the market."

At any other time Keith would have been interested; but his head ached too much now. Still he was not too far gone to recognize the magnitude of the affair.

"You'll have to go down and look at it," continued Isaac persuasively, "and here's the opportunity. You go on their business, and do mine at the same time, and get well paid for it, too."

"I don't quite like going that way. If the thing's got to be sold why do they want it catalogued?"

"That's their business, not mine."

"It looks like 'their' mistake, whoever they are. Where's the letter?"

"I've mislaid it. That's not my business either. My business is to send you off before they find out their mistake. You can catch the eleven express from Waterloo if you look sharp."

Sharp? Never had he looked less so. Still, with his aching head he dimly perceived that his Easter was being tampered with.

"And supposing they want me to stay?"

"Stay then. The longer the better."

"I'll go after Easter, then. I can't go before. I can't possibly. It's—it's out of the question."

His brain was clear enough on that point. He had suffered many things from the brutality of Rickman's; but hitherto its dealings had always been plain and above board, It had kept him many an evening working overtime, it had even exacted an occasional Saturday afternoon; but it had never before swindled him out of a Bank holiday. The thing was incredible; it could not be. Rickman's had no rights over his Easter; whatever happened, that holy festival was indubitably, incontestably his.

"Don't be afraid. You'll get your holiday, my boy, when you come back. I'll make it worth your while."

"It isn't money—damn my head! It's so confoundedly inconvenient. You see, I'd made no end of engagements."

"It's a foolish thing to make engagements so long beforehand. We never know the day or the hour——"

"I knew both."

"Well, in any case you couldn't be going to any place of amusement on the Sunday."

Isaac and his conscience had agreed together to assume that young Keith walked habitually and of his own fancy in the right way.

"Come," he continued, "you're not going to fling up a chance like this without rhyme or reason."

"I don't know," said Keith, with a queer little one-sided smile, "I'd fling up a good many chances for a really good rhyme."

As for reason, there were at least two reasons why the present chance should not lightly be let go. One was the Harden Library. If the Harden Library was not great, it was almost historic; it contained the Aldine Plato of 1513, the Neapolitan Horace of 1474, and the *Aurea Legenda* of Wynkyn de Worde. The other reason was Dicky Pilkington, the Vandal into whose hands destiny had delivered it. Upon the Harden Library Pilkington was about to descend like Alaric on the treasures of Rome. Rickman's was hand in glove with Pilkington, and since the young barbarian actually offered them the chance of buying it outright for an old song, no time was to be lost. It would not do to trust too long to Dicky's ignorance. At any moment knowledge might enter into him and corrupt his soul.

No; clearly, he would have to go; he didn't see how he was to get out of it.

Isaac became uneasy, for the spirit of imprecation sat visibly on his son's brow. "When I said I'd make it worth your while I meant it."

"I know. It isn't that——"

"Wot is it? Wot is it then? Wot's the matter with you? Wot tomfoolery are you up to? Is it——" (Isaac's gross forehead flushed, his speech came thick through his stern lips.) "Is it a woman?"

He had also been young; though he had denied his youth.
The boy's white face quivered with a little wave of heat
and pain. He clasped his forehead with his hands.
" Let me think."

His fingers tightened their hold, as if to grasp thought
by holding the dizzy, aching head that contained it. He
could think of nothing but Poppy. He had seen his father's
point quite steadily and clearly a minute ago; but when he
thought of Poppy his brain began to turn round and
round again. He gripped his forehead harder still, to
stop it.

His thinking drifted into a kind of moody metaphysics,
instead of concentrating itself on the matter in hand. " It
takes a poet," he said to himself, " to create a world, and
this world would disgrace a Junior Journalist." Was it,
he wondered, the last effort of a cycle of transcendental
decadence, melancholy, sophisticated? Or was it a cruel
young jest, flung off in the barbarous spring-time of creative
energy? Either way it chiefly impressed him with its imbecility. He saw through it. He saw through most things,
Himself included. He knew perfectly well that he had
developed his sudden turn for speculative thought because
he was baulked of an appointment with a little variety actress.
That he should see through the little variety actress was
not to be expected. Poppy was in her nature impenetrable,
woman being the ultimate fact, the inexorable necessity of
thought. Supposing the universe to be nothing more than
a dance of fortuitous atoms, then Poppy, herself a fortuitous atom, led the dance; she was the whirligig centre
towards which all things whirled. No wonder that it made
him giddy to think of her.

Suddenly out of its giddiness his brain conceived and
instantly matured a plan. A practical plan. He would
catch that eleven-thirty express all right. He would go
down into Devonshire, and stay in Devonshire till Saturday.
If necessary, he would sit up with those abominable books
all Thursday night and Friday night. And on Saturday
he would return. At the worst he would only have to go
down again on Monday. He would have missed the Junior
Journalists' dinner, he would be lucky if he saw the ghost
of an idea on this side Whit Sunday, but he would have torn
the heart out of his holiday.

He rose abruptly. " All right. It's a most awful nuisance, as it happens, but I'll go."

" I'm glad you're willing to oblige me. You'll not regret it."

Isaac was really meditating something very handsome in the way of a commission. As he looked benignly into his son's face and saw its deep misery and repugnance, he answered his own question.

" It *is* a woman."

BOOK II

LUCIA'S WAY

CHAPTER XIV

HE wondered how much longer they were going to keep him waiting. His head still ached, and every nerve was irritable. He began to suspect the servant of having failed to report his arrival; he thought of ringing for him and announcing himself a second time. Then he remembered that he was only the man who had come about the books; he was there on the Hardens' business, and their time was his time. And there were worse places to wait in than the library of Court House.

He found himself in a long low room that seemed to him immense. It was lighted by four deep-set windows, one to the south, one (a smaller side lattice) to the east, two to the west, and still the corners were left in gloom. The bookcases that covered the length and height of the walls were of one blackness with the oak floor and ceiling. The scattered blues and crimsons of the carpets (repeated in duller tones in the old morocco bindings), the gilded tracery of the tooling, and here and there a blood-red lettering-piece, gave an effect as of some dim, rich arabesque flung on to the darkness. At this hour the sunlight made the most of all it found there; it washed the faded carpet with a new dye; it licked every jutting angle, every polished surface, every patch of vellum; it streamed out of the great golden white busts on their pedestals in the windows, it lay in pale gleams over the eastern walls till it perished in the marble blackness of the roof and floor, sucked in as by an upper and nether abyss. This blackness intensified the glory of the April world outside, whose luminous greens and blues were held like blazonry in the leaded lozenge panes. The two western windows thrown open looked over the valley to the hills; Castle Hill with its black battlement of pines, and round-topped Core; to Harmouth Gap, the great doorway of the west wind, and the straight, brown flank of Muttersmoor, stretching to the sea. He seated himself by one of these open lattices, looked at the view, one of the loveliest in south Devon, and thought of Miss Poppy Grace. The vision of her that had still attended him on his journey down faded, as if rebuked by the great tranquil presence of the hills. He was left supremely, magically alone.

Now it may have been prescience, it may have been merely the deplorable state of his nerves, but, as he continued to look out upon that unfamiliar landscape, the beauty of it, growing on him, became almost intolerable. It affected him with an indescribable uneasiness, a yearning, a foreboding, a terror. He gave a deep sigh and turned his back on it abruptly.

He picked up a book that lay on the window seat; it was the *History of Harmouth,* and the history of Harmouth was the history of the Hardens of Court House. Court House was older than Harmouth and the Hardens were older than Court House. In early Tudor times, the chronicler informed him, the house was the court of justice for east Devon. Under Elizabeth it and the land for miles around it passed to the Hardens as a reward for their services to the Crown. The first thing they did was to pull down the gibbet on the north side and build their kitchen offices there. Next they threw out a short gable-ended wing to the east, and another to the west, enclosing a pleasant courtyard on the south. The west wing was now thrown into one with the long room that held the Harden Library. Rickman searched carefully for information under this head. He learnt that the Harden Library was the work of ten generations of scholars, beginning with Sir Thomas, a Jacobean maker of madrigals, and ending with Sir Joseph, the Victorian Master of Lazarus; that the founder's date is carved on the oak chimney-piece at the north end, with the Harden motto:

16 INVICTUS 20;

that the late Master of Lazarus bought books by the cartload, and was obliged to break through the south wall and

sacrifice the west wing (his wife's boudoir) to make room
for them. But where he looked for some record of these
treasures he found nothing but an elaborate description
of the Harden arms with all their quarterings. The his-
torian was not useful for Rickman's purposes. He was preoccupied with the Hardens, their antiquity and splendour;
he grovelled before them; every event in their history gave
him an opportunity of observing that their motto was
Invictus. He certainly seemed to have found them so; for
when he wrote of them his style took on the curious contor-
tions and prostrations of his spirit. The poor wretch, in
the pay of the local bookseller, had saturated himself with
heraldry till he saw gules.

To a vision thus inflamed book-collecting was simply a
quaint hereditary freak, and scholarship a distinction wholly
superfluous in a race that owned half the parish, and had
its arms blazoned on the east windows of a church and the
sign-board of a public-house. And with the last generation
the hereditary passion had apparently exhausted itself.
" The present owner, Sir Frederick Harden," said the chronicler, " has made no addition to the library of his ances-
tors." What he had done was not recorded in the history
of the Hardens. It was silent also as to the ladies of
that house, beyond drawing attention to the curious fact
that no woman had ever been permitted to inherit the Harden Library. The inspired pen of the chronicler evoked
the long procession of those Hardens whose motto was
Invictus; cross-legged crusading Hardens, Hardens in trunk
hose, Hardens in ruff and doublet, in ruffles and periwig;
Hardens in powder and patches, in the loosest of stocks and
the tightest of trousers; and never a petticoat among them
all. It was just as well, Rickman reflected, that Poppy's
frivolous little phantom had not danced after him into
the Harden Library; those other phantoms might not have
received it very kindly, unless indeed Sir Thomas, the
maker of madrigals, had spared it a shadowy smile.

He looked round and realized that his separation from
Poppy would be disagreeably prolonged if he was expected
to catalogue and arrange all the books in the Harden
Library. Allowing so much time to so much space (measuring by feet of bookshelf), hours ran rapidly to days, and
days to weeks—why, months might pass and find him still

labouring there. He would be buried in the blackness, forgotten by Poppy and the world. That was assuming that the Harden Library really belonged to the Hardens. And if it was to belong to Dicky Pilkington, what on earth had he been sent for?

"You were sent in answer to my letter, I suppose?"

Rickman's nervous system was still so far under the dominion of Dicky's champagne that he started violently. Double doors and double carpets deadened all sound of coming and going, and the voice seemed to have got into the room by itself. As from its softness he judged it to be still some yards distant, he suffered a further shock on finding a lady standing by his elbow.

It had been growing on him lately, this habit of starting at nothing, this ridiculous spasm of shoulder-blade, eyelids, and mouth. It was a cause of many smiles to the young ladies of his boarding-house; and this lady was smiling, too, though after another fashion. Her smile was remote and delicately poised; it hovered in the fine, long-drawn corners of her mouth and eyes; it sobered suddenly, as a second and less violent movement turned towards her his white and too expressive face. He could not say by what subtle and tender transitions it passed into indifference, nor how in passing it contrived to intimate her regret at having taken him somewhat at disadvantage. It was all done and atoned for in the lifting of an eyelid, before he could take in what she had actually said.

Her letter? He murmured some sort of assent, and entered on a dreamy and protracted search for his pocket handkerchief. He was miserably conscious that she was looking, looking down on him all the time. For this lady was tall, so tall indeed that her gaze seemed to light on his eyelids rather than his eyes. When he had found his courage and his hankerchief he looked up and their eyes met half way. Hers were brown with the tinge of hazel that makes brown eyes clear; they had a liquid surface of light divided from their darkness, and behind the darkness was more light, and the light and darkness were both unfathomable.

These eyes were entirely unembarrassed by the encounter. They still swept him with their long gaze, lucid, meditative, and a little critical.

"You have been very prompt."

" We understood that no time was to be lost."

She hesitated. " Mr. Rickman understood, did he not, that I asked for someone with experience? "

Most certainly Mr. Rickman understood.

" Do you think you will be able to do what I want? "

Her eyes implied that he seemed to her too young to have had any experience at all.

Knowing that a sense of humour was not one of the things required of him, he controlled a smile.

" We understood you wanted an expert, so I came myself."

" You are Mr. Rickman, then? "

" Well—Mr. Rickman's son."

The lady puckered her brows, as if trying to recall something, an idea, a memory that escaped her. She gave it up.

" Have you been waiting long? "

" Not more than half an hour or so."

" I am sorry. Perhaps you had better stay now and see what has to be done."

He was tired, he had eaten nothing all day, his nerves were out of order, and he had an abominable headache, but he intimated that he and his time were at her service. She spoke with authority, and he wondered who she was. Sir Frederick Harden's daughter? Or his sister? Or his wife?

" As you see, the books are fairly well arranged. It will not take very long to sort them."

Oh, wouldn't it, though! His heart sank miserably as he followed her progress round the room.

" They'll have to be catalogued under their subjects— alphabetically, of course."

" Quite so."

She continued with the same swiftness and serenity, mistress of her time and intelligence, as of her own luminous and elaborate plan. " Their size will have to be given, the edition, the place and date of publication, the number of their shelf, and their place on the shelves."

Their place on the shelves indeed! If those books had got into Dicky Pilkington's clutches their place would know them no more. He wondered; did she know nothing about Dicky Pilkington? Her plan implied certainty of possession, the permanence of the Harden Library world without end. He wondered whether he ought not to remind her that it might be about to come into the market, if it were not already as good as sold?

"Besides the cataloguing I want notes on all the rare or remarkable books. I believe some of them are unique."

He wondered more and more, and ended by wondering whether Dicky Pilkington were really so sure of his game?

"I see. You want a catalogue *raisonné.*"

"I want something like this." She opened a drawer and showed him one of Rickman's Special Quarterly Catalogues of a year back. He remembered; it used to be sent regularly to old Sir Joseph Harden, their best customer.

"My grandfather said these catalogues were models of their kind—they could only have been done by a scholar. He wanted the library catalogued on the same lines. It was to have been done in his life-time——"

"I wish it had been. I should have liked to have worked for Sir Joseph 'Arden."

Stirred by the praise, and by a sudden recollection of Sir Joseph, he spoke with a certain emotion, so that an aitch went by the board.

"Are you quite sure," said she, "that you know all about this sort of work?"

Had she noticed that hideous accident? And did it shake her belief in his fitness for the scholarly task?

"This *is* my work. I made that catalogue. I have to make them every quarter, so it keeps my hand in."

"Are you a quick worker?"

"Yes, I can be pretty quick."

"Could you finish my catalogue by the twenty-seventh? That's a little more than three weeks."

"Well—it would depend rather on the number of notes you wanted. Let me see—there must be about fourteen or fifteen thousand books here——"

"There are fifteen thousand."

"It would take three weeks to make an ordinary catalogue; and that would be quick work, even for me. I'm afraid you must give me rather more time."

"I can't. I'm leaving England on the twenty-sixth."

"Couldn't I go on with it in your absence?"

"No, that would hardly do."

"If you could only give me another week——"

"I couldn't possibly. I have to join my father at Cannes on the twenty-seventh."

So she was Sir Frederick Harden's daughter then, not his wife. Her last words were illuminating; they suggested the programme of a family whose affairs were in liquidation. They also revealed Sir Frederick Harden's amazing indifference to the fate of the library, an indifference that argued a certain ignorance of its commercial value. His father, who had a scent keen as a hound's for business, had taken in the situation. And Dicky, you might trust Dicky to be sure of his game. But if this were so, why should the Hardens engage in such a leisurely and expensive undertaking as a catalogue *raisonné?* Was the gay Sir Frederick trying to throw dust in the eyes of his creditors?

"I see," he said, "Sir Frederick Harden is anxious to have the catalogue finished before you leave?"

"No, he isn't anxious about it at all. He doesn't know it's being done. It is entirely my affair."

So Sir Frederick's affairs and his daughter's were separate and distinct; and apparently neither knew what the other was about. Rickman's conscience reproached him for the rather low cunning which had prompted him to force her hand. It also suggested that he ought not to take advantage of her ignorance. Miss Harden was charming, but evidently she was a little rash.

"If I may make the suggestion, it might perhaps be wiser to wait till your return."

"If it isn't done before I go," said Miss Harden, "it may never be done at all."

"And you are very anxious that it should be done?"

"Yes, I am. But if you can't do it, you had better say so at once."

"That would not be strictly true. I could do it, if I worked at it pretty nearly all day and half the night. Say sixteen hours out of the twenty-four."

"You are thinking of one person's work?"

"Yes."

"But if there are two persons?"

"Then, of course, it would take eight hours."

"So, if *I* worked, too——"

"In that case," he replied imperturbably, "it would take twelve hours."

" You said eight just now."

" Assuming that the two persons worked equally hard."

She crossed to a table in the middle of the room, it was littered with papers. She brought and showed him some sheets covered with delicate handwriting; her work, poor lady.

" This is a rough catalogue as far as I've got. I think it will be some help."

" Very great help," he murmured, stung by an indescribable compunction. He had not reckoned on this complication; and it made the ambiguity of his position detestable. It was bad enough to come sneaking into her house as his father's agent and spy, and be doing his business all the while that this adorably innocent lady believed him to be exclusively engaged on hers. But that she should work with him, toiling at a catalogue which would eventually be Rickman's catalogue, there was something in the notion extremely repulsive to his sense of honour. Under its muffling of headache his mind wrestled feebly with the situation. He wished he had not got drunk last night so that he could see the thing clearly all round. As far as he could see at present the only decent course was to back out of it.

" What I have done covers the first five sections up to F."

" I see," he said with a faint interest, " you are keeping the classical and modern sections distinct."

" Yes, I thought that was better."

" Much better."

" I haven't begun the classical section yet. Can I leave that to you ? "

" Certainly." He felt that every assent was committing him to he knew not what.

" You see a great deal of the work is done already. That makes a difference, doesn't it ? "

" Oh, yes; it makes all the difference." And indeed it did.

" In this case you can undertake it ? "

" No. I think that in this case I couldn't undertake it at all."

" But—why not ? " she asked, as well she might.

Why not, indeed ? He walked two or three paces from

her, trying to think it out. If only his head didn't ache so
abominably! To refuse to share the work with her was of
course to lay himself open to a most disgusting suspicion.

He paced back again. Did she suspect him of mercenary
motives? No; she suspected nothing. Her face expressed
disappointment and bewilderment, so far as she allowed it
to express anything. One more turn. Thank goodness,
she was not looking at him; she was giving him time. Only
a second, though. She had seated herself, as much as to
say she was now waiting for an explanation. He mustn't
keep her waiting; he must say something, but what on earth
was he going to say?

And as he looked at the lady so serenely seated, there
rose up before him a sudden impertinent, incongruous vision of Miss Poppy Grace's legs. They reminded him that
certain affairs of his own imperatively called him back to
town. Happy thought—why not say so?

"I ought to have said that in any case I couldn't undertake it. I couldn't make time without giving up some
very important engagements."

"Could you not have thought of that before you came?"

"I did think of it. I thought I could fit everything in
by going up to town from Saturday to Monday. But if I'm
to finish by the twenty-seventh, even—even with your help,
I oughtn't to lose a day, much less three days."

"I see. You are afraid of not being able to finish?"

He wavered, selecting some form of expression that might
shadow forth what was passing in his mind.

"I'm afraid of making any promises I mightn't be able
to keep."

Man's vacillation is Fate's determination, and Miss Harden was as firm at Fate. He felt that the fine long hands
playing with the catalogue were shaping events for him,
while her eyes measured him with their meditative gaze.

"I must risk that," she said. "I should lose more than
three days in finding a substitute, and I think you will do
the work as I want it done."

"And supposing I can't do it in time?"

"Will you do your best—that's all?"

"Certainly; whatever I do, I shall do my best. And
if I fail you——"

Left unfinished, hanging in mid air, the phrase suggested the vague phantasmal contingencies for which he could find no name.

"I am willing to take the risk."

Her phrase, too, was satisfying. Its generous amplitude covered him like a cloak.

"But we haven't arranged anything about terms."

No, they had not. Was it in her adorable simplicity, or in the mere recklessness of her youth, that she engaged him first and talked about terms afterwards? Or did she know an honest man when she saw one? He took his note-book and pencil and made out an estimate with the rapidity of happy inspiration, a fantastic estimate, incredibly and ludicrously small.

"Then," she said, "there will be your expenses."

He had not thought of that difficulty; but he soared above it, still reckless and inspired.

"Expenses? Oh, expenses are included."

She considered the estimate with a pretty pucker of her meditative brows.

"I don't understand these things; but—it seems very little."

"Our usual charge."

So swiftly did the wings of his inspiration carry him into the blue ideal, high above both verbal verity and the gross material fact.

She acquiesced, though with some reluctance. "Well, and when do you think you can begin?"

"Whenever it's most convenient to you. I shall have to take a look round first."

"You can do that at once."

By this time he had forgotten that whatever he might have drunk he had eaten nothing since the dinner of last night. He had ceased to feel faint and headachy and hungry, having reached that stage of faintness, headache, and hunger when the body sheds its weight and seems to walk gloriously upon air, to be possessed of supernatural energy. He went up and down library steps that were ladders, and stood perilously on the tops of them. He walked round and round the walls, making calculations, till the library began to swing slowly round, too, and a thin circle of grey mist swung with it. And all the time he was obscurely aware of a delicate grey-clad figure, going to and fro in the grey mist, or seated intent at the table, doing his work. He felt that her eyes followed him now and then.

Heroism sustained him for an hour. At the end of the hour his progress round the room grew slower; and in passing by the table where she sat, he had to steady himself with one hand. A cold sweat broke on his forehead. He mopped it furtively. He had every reason to believe that his appearance was repulsive; and, in the same painful instant in which this conviction sank into him, she raised her head and he saw that she was beautiful. The upward look revealed her. It was as if some veil, soft but obscuring, had dropped from her face. As her eyes scanned him gently, it occurred to him that she had probably never before had an opportunity of intimately observing a gentleman suffering from the remoter effects of intoxication.

" You look tired," she said. " Or are you ill? "

He stood shame-faced before her; for her eyes were more disconcerting than when he had looked down on him from their height. They were tranquil now, full of kind thought and innocence and candour. Of innocence above all, a luminous innocence, a piercing purity. He was troubled by her presence; but it was not so much her womanhood that troubled him as the deep mystery of her youth.

He could not look at it as it looked at him; for in looking at it he remembered last night and many nights before. Somehow it made him see the things it could not see, his drunkenness, his folly, his passion, the villianous naked body of his sin. And it was for their work, and their marks upon him, that she pitied him.

" Have you had anything to *eat?*" said she.

" Oh, yes, thanks," he answered vaguely.

" When? "

" Well—as far as I can remember it was about eight o'clock last night."

" Oh—how very thoughtless of me. I am so sorry."

" It's my own fault entirely. I wouldn't have mentioned it, except to account for my stupidity."

She crossed the room with a quick movement of distress and rang the bell. With horror he perceived her hospitable intention.

She was actually ordering his dinner and his room. He

heard every word of her soft voice; it was saying that he was to have some soup, and the chicken, and the tart—no, the jelly, and a bottle of burgundy, in the morning-room. He saw the young footman standing almost on tiptoe, winged for service, fired with her enthusiasm and her secrecy.

Coming on that sinister and ambiguous errand, how could he sleep under her roof? How could he eat her chicken, and drink her burgundy, and sit in her morning-room? And how could he explain that he could not? Happily she left him to settle the point with the footman.

With surprise and a little concern Lucia Harden learnt that the rather extraordinary young man, Mr. Savage Keith Rickman, had betaken himself to an hotel. It appeared, that courteously, but with an earnestness that admitted of no contradiction, he had declined all hospitality whatever.

CHAPTER XV

IT was Friday morning, and Mr. Rickman lay in bed, outwardly beholding through the open window the divinity of the sea, inwardly contemplating the phantoms of the mind. For he judged them to be phantoms (alcoholic in their origin), his scruples of last night. Strictly speaking, it was on Wednesday night that he had got drunk; but he felt as if his intoxication had prolonged itself abnormally, as if this were the first moment of indubitable sobriety.

And as he lay there, he prepared himself to act the part of the cold, abstracted, supercilious man of business, the part already too horribly familiar to him as young Mr. Rickman of Rickman's. He reflected how nearly he had wrecked his prospects in that character. He bade himself beware of woman and of drink, the two things most fatal to stability of judgment. He recalled, painfully, the events of last evening. He was not quite sure what he had done, or hadn't done; but he believed he had all but flung up the chance of securing for Rickman's the great Harden Library. And he had quite a vivid and disturbing recollection of the face, the person that had inspired him with that impulse of fantastic folly.

In the candid light of morning this view of his conduct

presented itself as the sane thinking of a regenerated intellect. He realized, as he had not realized before, how colossal was the opportunity he had so narrowly let slip. The great Harden Library would come virgin into the market, undefiled by the touch of commerce, the breath of publicity. It had been the pure and solitary delight of scholar lovers who would have been insulted by the suggestion that they should traffic in its treasures. Everything depended on his keeping its secret inviolate. Heavens! supposing he had backed out of that catalogue, and Miss Harden had called in another expert. At this point he detected in himself a tendency to wander from the matter in hand. He reminded himself that whatever else he was there for, he was there to guard the virginal seclusion of the Aldine Plato, the Neapolitan Horace and the *Aurea Legenda* of Wynkyn de Worde. He tried to shut his eyes against his vivid and disturbing vision of the lady of the library. It suggested that he was allowing that innocent person to pay fifteen pounds for a catalogue which he had some reason to believe would be of no earthly use to her. He sat up in bed, and silenced its suggestions with all the gravity of his official character. If the young lady insisted on having a catalogue made, he might as well make it as any one else; in fact, a great deal better. He tried to make himself believe that he regretted having charged her fifteen pounds when he might have got fifty. It was more than unbusiness-like; it was, even for him, an incredibly idiotic thing to do; he would never have done it if he had not been hopelessly drunk the night before.

He got out of bed with a certain slow dignity and stepped into his cold bath solemnly, as into a font of regeneration. And as he bathed he still rehearsed with brilliance his appointed part. No criticism of the performance was offered by his actual self as revealed to him in the looking-glass. It stared at him with an abstracted air, conspicuous in the helpless pathos of its nakedness. It affected absorption in the intricate evolutions of the bath. Something in its manner inspired him with a vague distrust. He noticed that this morning it soaped itself with a peculiar care, that it displayed more than usual interest in the trivial details of dress. It rejected an otherwise irreproachable shirt because of a minute wine stain on the cuff. It sniffed critically at

its coat and trousers, and flung them to the other end of
the room. It arrayed itself finally in a brand-new suit of
grey flannel, altogether inexpressive of his rôle. He could
not but feel that its behaviour compromised the dignity of
the character he had determined to represent. It is not in
his best coat and trousers that the book-dealer sets out on
the dusty quest of the Aldine Plato, and the Neapolitan
Horace, and the *Aurea Legenda* of Wynkyn de Worde.

He could no longer conceal the fact that he had dressed
himself elaborately for an interview with Miss Harden. But
he endeavored to adjust his mind to a new and less disturbing view of the lady. He had seen her last night through a
flush of emotion that obscured her; he would see her to-day
in the pure and imperturbable light of the morning, and his
nerves should not play the devil with him this time. He
would be cool, calm, incorruptibly impersonal, as became
Rickman the man of business, Rickman of Rickman's.

Unfortunately, though the rôle was rehearsed with ease
in the privacy of his bedroom, it proved impossible to sustain
it under Miss Harden's candid eyes. At the first sight of
them he lost all grasp and memory of his part; he broke
down disgracefully, miserably. The sound of her voice
revived his agony of the previous night. True, the flush
of emotion had subsided, but in the fierce intellectual light
that followed, his doubts and scruples showed plainer than
ever. They even acquired a certain logical order and
cohesion.

He concealed himself behind the projecting wing of a
bookcase, and wrestled with them there. Dispassionately
considered, the situation stood thus. He was possessed of
certain knowledge relating to Sir Frederick Harden's affairs.
That was neither bad nor good. He had allowed Sir Frederick Harden's daughter to engage him in a certain capacity, knowing perfectly well that she would not have done
so had she herself possessed that knowledge. That was
bad—distinctly bad. He was going to take advantage of
that engagement to act in another capacity, not contemplated
by his employer, namely, as valuer of said employer's property and possibly as the agent for its purchase, well knowing that such purchase would be effected without reference
to its intrinsic or even to its market value. That was
worse.

These were the simple data of his problem. The problem (seen with excruciating lucidity) stated itself thus. Assuming, first of all, Miss Harden's ignorance and his own knowledge, what was the correct attitude of his knowledge to her ignorance? In other words, was it his business to enlighten her as to the state of her father's finances?

No; it might be somebody else's business, but most decidedly it was not his. His business, as far as he could see it, was simply to withdraw as gracefully as possible from a position so difficult to occupy with any decency.

He must then make another attempt to back out of it. No doubt it would be an uncommonly awkward thing to do. The lady had already shown a very pretty little will of her own, and supposing she insisted on holding him to his bargain? There was that estimate, too; it seemed to have clinched things, somehow, between him and Miss Harden. He did not exactly know how to deal with that high-handed innocence, but he would ask her to allow him to reconsider it.

He approached her with his head tossed up a little more than usual, his way when he was about to do something disagreeable, to drive a bargain or to ask a favour.

" Miss Harden, may I speak to you one moment? "

She looked up. Her face and figure were radiant in the light from the south window.

" What is it? " she asked.

She was busy at one of the bookcases with a note-book and pencil, cataloguing on an absurd but independent plan of her own. He gave a rueful glance at her.

" I'm not sure that I ought to have let you engage me last night. I wonder if I might ask you——"

" To release you from your engagement? "

" You must think I'm behaving very badly."

She did not contradict him; neither did she assent. She held him for the moment under her long penetrating gaze. Her eyes were not of the detective sort, quick to penetrate disguises. They were (though she did not know it) eyes that possessed the power of spiritual seduction, luring souls to confession. Your falseness might escape them; but if there was any truth in you, she compelled you to be true.

She compelled Rickman to be impulsive.

" I'd give anything to know what I ought to do."

She did not help him out.

"I can't make up my mind about this work."

"Is it the question of time? I thought we had made that clear? You didn't undertake to finish by the twenty-seventh."

"The question is whether I should have undertaken it at all."

"It might have been as well to have answered that question first."

"I couldn't answer it. There were so many things——"

"Do you want a longer time in town?"

"I want a longer time here, to think it over, to make up my mind whether I can go on——"

"And in the meanwhile?"

"The work goes on just the same."

"And if you decide that you can't continue it?"

"I should find a substitute."

"The substitute might not be just the same. For instance, he might not have so scrupulous a conscience."

"You mean he might not be so eager to back out of his engagements."

"I mean what I said. Your position seems to be a little difficult."

"I wish to goodness, Miss Harden, I could explain it."

"I don't suggest that you should explain it. It doesn't seem to be so very clear to yourself."

"It isn't. I really *don't* know what I ought to do."

"No more do I. But I can tell you what you ought to have done. You ought to have made up your mind last night."

"Well, the fact is—last night I—hadn't very much mind left to make up."

"No, I remember. You *were* rather done up. I don't want to bind you by last night, if it's at all unfair to you."

"It isn't in the least unfair to me. But I'm not sure that it mightn't be very unfair to you; and, you see, I want to think it out."

"Very well, think it out, and let me know some time to-night. Will that satisfy you?"

"It ought to."

And for the moment it did satisfy him. He felt that conscience, that stern guardian of his conduct, was off duty for the day. He was free (for the day) to abandon himself to the charm of Miss Harden's society. The experience, he told himself, would be altogether new and delightful.

New it undoubtedly was; but he remained a little uncertain as to the delight; the immediate effect of Miss Harden's presence being an intellectual disturbance amounting almost to aberration. It showed itself, first of all, in a frightful exaltation of the consciousness of self. To Mr. Rickman, striving to be noiseless, it seemed that the sound of his boots, as he crossed the library, reverberated through the immensity of space, while the creaking of his new braces advertised in the most horrible manner his rising up and his sitting down. Things were worse when he sat down; for then his breathing, light but noticeably frequent, made him the unquiet centre of the room. In the surrounding stillness the blowing of his nose became a monstrous and appalling act. And no sooner was his attention abstracted from his nose than it settled in his throat, producing a series of spasmodic contractions which he imagined to be distinctly audible. It was really as if his body had somehow detached itself, and was rioting in a conspicuous and unseemly individuality of its own. He wondered what Miss Harden thought of its behaviour.

This state of things was bad enough when he was separated from her by the entire length of the room; but their work required a certain collaboration, and there were occasions when he was established near her, when deliberately, in cold blood and of his own initiative, he was compelled to speak to her. No language could describe the anguish and difficulty of these approaches. His way was beset by obstacles and perils, by traps and snares; and at every turn there waited for him the shameful pitfall of the aitch. He whose easy courtesy charmed away the shyness of Miss Flossie Walker, whose conversation (when he designed to converse) was the wonder and delight of the ladies of his boarding-house, now blushed to hear himself speak. The tones of his voice were hateful to him; he detected in them some subtle and abominable quality that he had not observed before. How would they appeal to Miss Harden? For this miserable consciousness of himself was pervaded, transcended by his consciousness of her.

Of her beauty he grew every minute more aware. It was

not of the conspicuous and conquering kind; it carried no
flaming banner of triumphant sex; indeed, it demanded a
kindred fineness of perception to discern it, being yet vague
with the softness of her youth. Her hair was mere darkness
without colour or flame, her face mere whiteness without
a flush; all her colour and her light were, where her soul
was, in her mouth and eyes. These showed more vivid for
that toneless setting; they dominated her face. However
he looked at her his gaze was led up to them. For the long
dim lines of her body flowed upwards from her feet like the
curves of a slender flame, mingling, aspiring, vanishing;
the edges of her features were indistinct as the edges of a
flame. This effect of an upward sweep was repeated in the
tilt of her vivid mouth and emphasized by the arch of her
eyebrows, giving a faintly interrogative expression to her
face. All this he noticed. He noticed everything about
her, from the fine curling flame-like edges of her mouth and
the flawless rim of her ears, to her finger-tips and the slope
of her small imperious feet. He caught every inflection of
her voice; without looking at her, he was aware of every
turn of her head, every movement of her eyelids; he watched
with furtive interest her way of touching and handling
things, of rising and sitting, of walking and being still. It
was a new way, unlike Poppy's way, or Flossie's way, or the
way of any woman he had yet seen. What struck him most
was the intense quiet of her presence; it was this that made
his own so noisy and obtrusive.

And yet, she didn't, she really didn't appear to notice it.
She might have been unaware that there was any such
person as Mr. Savage Keith Rickman in the room. He
wondered how on earth she achieved that serene unconsciousness; he came to the conclusion that it was not her
own achievement at all, but the achievement of her race.
Theirs too that something subtly imperious in her bearing,
which seemed not so much the attitude of her mind as the
way her head was set on her shoulders. He could not say
that she betrayed any sense of his social inferiority, unless
it were in a certain courtesy, which he gathered to be rather
more finished than any she would have shown to a man of
her own class.

It was not only finished, it was final. The thing was so
perfect in itself that obviously it could lead no further. She

would say in her exquisite voice, " Would you mind taking
these five volumes back to your shelf?" or, " I'm sorry to
interrupt you, but can you tell me whether this is the original
binding?" Under no circumstances could he imagine himself replying, " I wouldn't mind taking fifty volumes," or,
" I like being interrupted." All this was a complete in-
version of the rules that Keith Rickman was acquainted
with as governing polite intercourse between the sexes, and
he found it extremely disconcerting. It was as if some fine
but untransparent veil had been hung between him and
her, dividing them more effectually than a barricade.

The wonder, which grew with the morning, was not so
much in the things she said as in the things she didn't say.
Her powers of reservation seemed to Rickman little short of
miraculous. Until yesterday he had never met a woman
who did not, by some look or tone or movement of her body,
reveal what she was thinking about him. Whatever Miss
Harden thought about him she kept it to herself. Unfortunately the same high degree of reticence was expected from
him, and to Keith Rickman, when not restrained by excess
of shyness, reticence came hard. It was apt to break down
when a severe strain was put on it, as had been the case that
morning. And it was appointed that the same thing should
happen to him this afternoon.

As far as he could remember it happened in this way. He
was busy getting the Greek dramatists into their places, an
enterprise which frequently took him to her end of the room,
where Sir Joseph had established his classical library. He
was sitting on the top of the steps, when she approached
him carrying six vellum-bound volumes in her arms, Sir
Joseph's edition of Euripides, of which the notes exceeded
the text. He dismounted and took the books from her,
turning very red as he did so.

" You should let me do all the carrying. These books are
too heavy for you."

" Thank you, I think they ought to go with the others, on
this shelf."

He did not answer all at once. He was absorbed in the
Euripides. It was an *édition de luxe,* the Greek text exquisitely printed from a font of semi-uncial type, the special
glory of the Harden Classics.

He exclaimed, " What magnificent type!"

She smiled.

"It's rare, too. I've never seen any other specimen—in modern printing."

"There is no other specimen," said she.

"Yes, there is. One book at least, printed, I think, in Germany."

"Is there? It was set up from a new font specially made for this edition. I always supposed my grandfather invented it."

"Oh, no, he couldn't have done that. He may have adapted it. In fact, he must have adapted it."

This young man had set aside a cherished tradition, as lightly as if he were blowing the dust off the leaves. She was interested.

"How can you tell that?"

"Oh, I know. It's very like a manuscript in the British Museum."

"What manuscript?"

"The Greek text of the Complutensian Polyglot." (He could not help saying to himself, "That ought to fetch her!") "But it doesn't follow that it's the same type. Whatever it is, it's very beautiful."

"It's easier to read, too, than the ordinary kind."

He was still turning over the pages, handling the book as a lover handles the thing he loves. The very touch of the vellum thrilled him with an almost sensual rapture. Here and there a line flashed from a chorus and lured him deeper into the text. His impulse was still to exclaim, but a finer instinct taught him to suppress his scholarly emotion. Looking up as she spoke he saw her eyes fixed on him with a curious sympathy. And as he thought of the possible destiny of the Euripides he felt guilty as of a treachery towards her in loving the same book.

"Do you read Euripides?" he asked with naïve wonder. "Yes."

"And Æschylus and Sophocles and Aristoph——?" Mr. Rickman became embarrassed as he recalled certain curious passages, and in his embarrassment he rushed upon his doom—"and—and 'Omer?"

It was a breakdown unparalleled in his history. Never since his childhood had he neglected the aspirate in Homer. A flush made manifest his agony. He frowned, and gazed at her steadily, as if he defied her to judge him by that lapse.

"Yes," said the lady; but she was not thinking of Homer.

"By Jove," he murmured pensively. His eyes turned from her and devoured the text. He was torn between abject admiration of the lady and of the book.

"Which do you like best?" he asked suddenly. "Æschylus or Sophocles? But it's an absurd question."

"Why absurd?"

"Because they're so different."

"Are they?" To tell the truth she was not thinking of them any more than she had been thinking of Homer.

He became perfectly hectic with excitement. "Rather! Can't you see the difference? Sophocles carved his tragedies. He carved them in ivory, polished them up, back and front, till you can't see the marks of the chisel. And Æschylus jabbed his out of the naked granite where it stood, and left them there with the sea at their feet, and the mist round their heads, and the fire at their hearts."

"But—but he left the edges a little rough."

"He did. God leaves them so sometimes when he's making a big thing."

Something like a faint ripple of light passed over her face under the obscuring veil it wore for him.

"But Sophocles is perfect," said she. She was not thinking of Sophocles one bit; she was thinking that when God made Mr. Rickman he had left the edges rough, and wondering whether it was possible that he had made "a big thing."

"Oh, yes, he's perfect." He began to quote softly and fluently, to her uttermost surprise. His English was at times a thing to shudder at, but his Greek was irreproachable, perfect in its modulation and its flow. Freed from all flaws of accent, the musical quality of his voice declared itself indubitably, marvellously pure.

The veil lifted. Her smile was a flash of intelligence, the sexless, impersonal intelligence of the scholar. This maker of catalogues, with the tripping tongue that Greek made golden, he had touched the electric chain that linked them under the deep, under the social gulf.

"Did you ever hear such a chorus? Pure liquid gold,

every line of it. Still, you can read Sophocles with your hair on. I should have thought most wom—most ladies would like Euripides best?"

"Why? Because they understand him best?"

"No. Because he understood them best."

"Did he understand them? Euripides," said the young lady with decision, "was a decadent."

"Was he? How about the *Bacchæ?* Of course, it's worth all the rest of his plays put together; they're not in the same street with it. It's a thing to dream about, to go mad about."

"My grandfather says it's not Euripidean."

"Good Lord! How do we know it isn't the most Euripidean of the lot?"

"Well, it stands alone, doesn't it?"

"Yes. And he stands with it."

"Does he? My grandfather was judging him by his average."

"His average? Oh, I say, you know, you could reduce some very great poets to mediocrity by striking their average. Wouldn't you allow a man to be at least as great as his greatest achievement?"

"I wonder——"

"Anyhow, those are ripping good notes in that edition."

"They ought to be. They were by a good scholar—his greatest achievement."

He put down the Harden Euripides; and it struck Lucia that if Sir Joseph had been there this truthful young man would not have hesitated to put him down too. She laid her hand on the book with an air of possession and protection, which was a lesson in tact for the truthful young man. He leaned up against the bookcase with his hands in his pockets.

"I say," said he, "I hope you don't mind my talking like this to you?"

No. Why shouldn't you?"

"Well, it isn't exactly what I'm here for."

That exciting conversation had lasted barely fifteen minutes; but it had set him for the time being at his ease. He had at any rate proved himself a scholar, and he was so far happier. He felt that he was beginning to get on with Miss Harden, to see a little way across the gulf, discerning the outlines of the further shore where that high lady walked unveiled.

Then suddenly, owing to a most humiliating incident, the gulf yawned again.

It was five o'clock, and he was left alone in the company of a fascinating little tea-table, laid, as if for a guest, with fine white linen, silk embroidered, with early Georgian silver and old china. It was laid for him, that little tea-table. He had delayed a little before beginning his repast, and it happened that when Miss Harden appeared again she found him holding a tea-cup to his lips with one hand, while the other groped in a dish of cream cakes, abstractedly, and without the guidance of a selective eye. Both eyes indeed were gazing dreamily over the rim of the tea-cup at her empty chair. He was all right; so why, oh, why, did he turn brick-red and dash his cup down and draw back his innocent hand? That was what he had seen the errand boy at Rickman's do, when he caught him eating lunch in a dark passage. He always had compassion on that poor pariah and left him to finish his meal in privacy; and with the same delicacy Miss Harden, perceiving his agony, withdrew. He was aware that the incident had marked him.

He stood exactly where he stood before. Expert knowledge was nothing. Mere conversational dexterity was nothing. He could talk to her about Euripides and Sophocles till all was blue; he could not blow his nose before her, or eat and drink before her, like a gentleman, without shame and fear.

They talked no more that evening.

CHAPTER XVI

AT seven he again refused Miss Harden's hospitality and withdrew to his hotel. He was to return before nine to let her know his decision, and as yet he had done nothing towards thinking it out.

A letter had come for him by the evening post. It had been forwarded from his rooms and ran thus:

"MY DEAR RICKETS:
   "I haven't forgotten about your little supper, so mind you turn

up at our little picnic before Dicky drinks all the champagne. It's going to be awfully select.

"Ever your own and nobody else's,

"POPPY GRACE.

"P. S.—How is your poor head?"

There are many ways of being kind and that was Poppy's way. She wanted to tell him not to be cut up about Wednesday night; that, whatever Dicky Pilkington thought of his pretensions, she still reckoned him in the number of the awfully select. And, lest he should have deeper grounds for uneasiness, her postscript hinted in the most delicate manner possible that she had not taken him seriously, attributing his utterances to their true cause. And yet she was his own and nobody else's. She was a good sort, Poppy, taking her all round.

He tried to think about Poppy and found it difficult. His mind wandered; not into the realms of fancy, but into paths strange and humiliating for a scholar and a poet. He caught himself murmuring, "Harmouth—Harcombe— Homer—Harden." He had got them all right. He never dreamed of—of dropping them when he wasn't excited. It was only in the beaten tracks where his father had gone before him that he was apt to slide. He was triumphant over Harmouth where he might have tripped over Hammersmith. Homer and Hesiod were as safe with him as with Horace Jewdwine. (He couldn't think how he had managed to come to grief over Homer just now. It was nerves, or luck, or pure accident, the sort of thing that might have happened to anybody.) Thank Heaven, his tongue was almost virgin to the aitch in Harden.

Harden—Lucia Harden. He knew her name and how to pronounce it; for he had seen it written in the fly-leaf of a book, and heard it spoken by the footman who called her Miss Loocher. This he took to be a corruption of the Italian form.

Here he again tried to evoke a vivid image of Poppy; but without success. And then he remembered that he had still to think it out.

First of all, then, he would eliminate sentiment. Sentiment apart, he was by no means sure that he would do well to act on the impulse of the morning and decamp. After

all, what *was* he sure of? Was he sure that Sir Frederick
Harden's affairs, including his library, were involved beyond
redemption? Put it that there was an off-chance of Sir
Frederick's financial recovery.

From the bare, uninteresting, financial point of view that
event would entail some regrettable consequences for himself. He had been extremely rash. He had undertaken to
accomplish three weeks' expert work to the value of fifty
pounds for which he had charged fifteen, an estimate that
at Rickman's would have been considered ridiculous for a
man's bare time. He had not so much as mentioned his
fare; he had refused board and lodging; and on the most
sanguine computation his fees would only cover his expenses by about five pounds. The difference between fifteen
pounds and fifty would have to be refunded out of his own
private pocket. When it came to settling accounts with
Rickman's, his position would be, to say the least of it, embarrassing. It was difficult to unravel the mental process
that had led him into it; but it was not the first time that
these luxurious subtleties of conscience had caused him to
run short of ready money. It was only another of those
innumerable occasions when he and his father failed to see
face to face, and when he had had to pay for the pleasure of
supporting a fantastic personal view. Only the view in this
case was so hideously complicated and—and exaggerated.
And this time, in order to clear himself, he would be compelled to borrow again from Dicky Pilkington. There was
no other way. No sooner did Sir Frederick's head appear
rising above water than he saw his own hopelessly sub-
merged.

Nevertheless it was this prospect that he found himself
contemplating with all the ardour of desire. It justified not
only his presence in the Harden Library, but Miss Harden's
presence as his collaborator. With all its unpleasantness
it was infinitely preferable to the other alternative. He let
his mind dwell on it until the off-chance began to look like
an absolute certainty.

Put it then that Sir Frederick recovered. In this case
the Hardens scored. Since he had charged Miss Harden
fifteen where he was entitled to fifty, the best part of his
labour might be considered a free gift to the lady. What
was more, in the matter of commission, he stood to lose a

very considerable sum. Put it that the chances were even, and the whole business resolved itself into a game of pitch and toss. Heads, Miss Harden lost; tails, she won; and he wasn't responsible for the tossing.

But put it that Sir Frederick did not recover. Then, he, Keith Rickman, was in a position most unpleasant for himself; but he could not make things a bit pleasanter for Miss Harden by wriggling out of it. The library would be sold whether he stayed there or not; and by staying he might possibly protect her interests in the sale. It wasn't a nice thing to have to be keeping his eye all the time on the Aldine Plato, and the Neapolitan Horace, and the *Aurea Legenda* of Wynkyn de Worde; but he would only be doing what must be done by somebody in any case. Conclusion: however unpleasant for him to be the agent for the sale, it would be safer for Miss Harden.

And how about those confounded profits, represented by his commission? That was easily settled. He would have nothing to do with the filthy things. He wouldn't touch his commission with the end of the poker. Unfortunately he would never be able to explain all this to her, and Heaven only knew what she would think of him when it all came out in the long-run, as it was bound to come. Well, it wouldn't matter what she thought of him, so long as he knew that his hands were clean. Rickman's hands might not be so presentable, but they were not human hands as his were; they were the iron, irresponsible hands of a machine.

There remained his arrangements for the Bank holiday. They seemed to have been made so long ago that they hardly counted. Still, there was that engagement to Poppy Grace, and he had promised to take poor Flossie to the Hippodrome. Poor Flossie would be disappointed if he did not take her to the Hippodrome. At the moment Flossie's disappointment presented itself as considerably more vital than his own.

To-morrow, then, being Saturday, he would go up to town; and on Monday he would return to his ambiguous post.

He had thought it out.

CHAPTER XVII

"THERE'S a lot of rot," said Mr. Rickman, "talked about Greek tragedy. But really, if you come to think of it, it's only in Sophocles you get the tragedy of Fate. There isn't any such thing in Æschylus, you know."

He had gone up to acquaint Miss Harden with his decision and had been led off into this hopeful track by the seductions that still lurked in the Euripides.

"There's Nemesis, which is the same thing," said she.

"Not at all the same thing. Nemesis is simply the horrid jealousy of the gods; and the responsibility lies with the person who provokes them, whether it's Prometheus, or Agamemnon, or Agamemnon's great-great-grandfather. It's the tragedy of human responsibility, the most brutal tragedy of all. All these people are crumpled up with it, they go about tearing their hair over it, and howling out δράσαντι παθεῖν. There isn't any Fate in that, you know. Is there?"

He did not wait for an answer.

"In Sophocles now, it's all the other way about. His people aren't responsible in the least. They're just a thundering lot of lunatics. They go knocking their poor heads against the divine law, and trying to see which is the hardest, till they end by breaking both. There's no question of paying for the damage. It's pure Fate."

"Well—and Euripides?"

"Oh, Euripides goes on another tack altogether. There aren't any laws to break, yet everybody's miserable all round, and nobody's responsible. It's τῷ παθόντι παθεῖν. They suffer because they suffer, and there's an end of it. And it's the end of Fate in Greek tragedy. I know this isn't the orthodox view of it."

He paused, a little out of breath, for he had talked as usual against time, leaving behind him a luminous trail of ideas struck out furiously as he rushed along. His excitement was of the strong-winged kind that carried him triumphantly over all obstacles, even the barrier of the aitch.

Was she listening?

She was; but as she listened she looked down, and her fingers played with the slender gold chain that went twice round her throat and fell among the laces of her gown. On her mouth there was the same smile he had seen when he first saw her; he took it for a smile of innermost amusement. It didn't lurk; there was nothing underhand about it. It hovered, delicately poised for flight.

"Euripides," she said, "had the deeper insight, then. He knew that character is destiny."

"That character is destiny? Whose character? For all I know your character may be my destiny."

It was one of those unconsidered speeches, flashed out in the heat of argument, which nevertheless, once uttered, are felt to be terrific and momentous. He wondered how Miss Harden would take it. She took it (as she seemed to take most things) calmly.

"No character could have any power over you except through your own."

"Perhaps not. All the same, you are not me, you are something outside. You would be my destiny."

He paused again. Personalities were pitfalls which he must avoid. No such danger existed for the lady; she simply ignored it; her mind never touched those deeper issues of the discussion where his floundered, perilously immersed. Still she was not unwilling to pursue the theme.

"It all depends," said she, "on what you mean by destiny."

"Well, say I mean the end, the end I'm moving towards, the end I ultimately arrive at——"

"Surely that depends on your character, your character, of course, as a whole."

"It may or mayn't. It may depend on what I eat or don't eat for dinner, on the paper I take in or the pattern of my waistcoat. And the end may be utterly repellent to my character as a whole. Say I end by adopting an unsuitable profession. Is that my character or my destiny?"

"Your character, I think, or you wouldn't have adopted it."

"H'm. Supposing it adopts me?"

"It couldn't—against your will."

"No. But my will in this instance might not be the expression of my character as a whole. Why, I may be doing violence to my character as a whole by—by the unique absurdity that dishes me. That's destiny, if you like, but it's not character—not my character, anyhow."

Personalities again. Whither could he flee from their presence? Even the frigid realm of abstractions was shaken by the beating of his own passionate heart. Her eyes had the allurements of the confessional; he hovered, fascinated, round the holy precincts, for ever on the brink of revelation. It was ungovernable, this tendency to talk about himself. In another minute—But no, most decidedly that was not what he was there for.

If it came to that, what *was* he there for? It was so incredible that he should be there at all. And yet there he was going to stay, for three weeks, and more. He had come to tell her so.

Miss Harden received the announcement as if it had been a foregone conclusion.

" It is settled, then? " said she, " you will have no more scruples? "

" None."

" There's only one thing. I must ask you not to give anybody any information about the library. We don't want to be bothered with dealers and collectors. Some of the books are so valuable that we should never have any peace if their whereabouts became known. Can you keep the secret? "

His heart sank as he remembered the Aldine Plato, and the Neapolitan Horace, and the *Aurea Legenda* of Wynkyn de Worde. But he pledged himself to absolute discretion, an inviolable secrecy. Why not? He was a dealer himself and obviously it was his interest to keep other dealers in the dark. It was an entirely sensible and business-like pledge. And yet in giving it he felt that he was committing himself to something unique, something profound, and intimate and irrevocable. He had burnt his ships, severed himself, body and soul, from Rickman's. If it were Miss Harden's interest that he should defend that secret from his own father, he would have to defend it. He had given his word; and for the life of him he could not tell why.

In the same way he felt that in spite of his many ingenious arguments his determination to stay had in it something mysterious and unforeseen. He had said to her, " Your character may be my destiny." And perhaps it was. He felt that tremendous issues hung upon his decision, and that all along he had been forced into it somehow from outside himself, rather than from within. And yet, as he sat there feeling all this, while he worked at the abominable catalogue *raisonné,* he decided further that he would not go away at all.

He would not go back to town to-morrow. He could not afford the time. He must and would finish that catalogue *raisonné* by the twenty-seventh. He had as good as pledged his word to Miss Harden. Supposing the pledge had a purely ideal, even fantastic value, he was none the less bound by it, in fact considerably more. For he and she could only meet in an ideal and fantastic region, and he served her in an ideal and fantastic capacity, on the wholly ideal and fantastic assumption that the library was hers. Such a pledge would, he imagined, be held supreme in the world where honour and Miss Harden met face to face. And on him it was conceivably more binding than the promise to take Flossie to the Hippodrome on Saturday, or to intoxicate himself on Sunday with champagne in the society of Miss Poppy Grace. Its sovereignty cancelled the priority of the more trivial and the grosser claim. His word to Miss Harden was one of those fine immortal things that can only be redeemed at the cost of the actual. To redeem it he was prepared for sacrifice, even the sacrifice of the great three days.

He worked late that night, and she told him of a short cut to the town by the river path at the bottom of the garden. Half-way to the river he stopped and looked back. The beech-tree dreamed, silent on a slope of glimmering lawn. The house loomed in the background, a grey mass with blurred outlines. From a window open in the east wing he could hear the sound of a piano.

He stood still and listened. All around was the tender, indescribable Devonshire night; it hung about him with warm scented breath; he felt its heart beat in the innumerable pulses of the stars. Behind the blue transparent darkness the music throbbed like a dawn; it swayed and sank, piano, pianissimo, and streamed out again into the night, dividing the darkness. It flowed on in a tumult, a tremendous tumult, rhythmic and controlled. What was she playing? If he stayed till midnight he must hear it through. Night sheltered him, and he drew nearer lest he should lose a note. He stretched himself on the lawn, and, with his

head on his arms, he lay under the beech-tree, under the
stars, dreaming, while Lucia Harden played to him the
Sonata Appassionata.

It was good to be there; but he did not know, and the
music did not tell him, why he was there and what he was
there for.

And yet it was the Sonata Appassionata.

CHAPTER XVIII

IT was the afternoon of Saturday, the fourth, that Mr.
Rickman, looking up from his table, saw a brilliant apparition coming across the lawn. He dreaded afternoon
callers, he dreaded the post, he dreaded every person and
every thing which reminded him that Lucia Harden had a
life that he knew not and that knew not him.

"Lucia—Lucia!" Mr. Rickman looked up and saw the
brilliant apparition standing in the south window. "Lu-
chee-a!—" it pleaded. "You can't say you're out when I
can see perfectly well that you're in."

"Go away, Kitty, I'm busy."

"You've no business to be busy at five o'clock in the
afternoon."

Miss Kitty Palliser's body was outside the window, but
her head, crowned with a marvellous double-peaked hat of
Parma violets, was already within the room.

"I'm dying of thirst," she said; "take me in and be kind
to me and give me tea."

Lucia rose and went to the window, reluctant but re-
signed. Scraps of their conversation floated down to Mr.
Rickman's end of the room.

"Yes, you may well look at my hat."

"I wasn't looking at it, I was looking through it."

"Well, if you can see through my hat, Lucia, you can
see through me. What do you think of it?"

"Of the hat? Oh, the hat is a poem."

"Isn't it? Did you ever see anything so inspired, so
impassioned?"

"Inspired, but—don't you think—just a little, a little
meaningless?"

"Meaningless? It's *packed* with meaning."

" I should like to know what it means."

" If it means nothing else it means that I've been going to and fro the whole blessed afternoon, paying calls in Harmouth for my sins."

" Poor Kitty."

" The last three times I paid calls in Harmouth," said poor Kitty, " I sported a cycling skirt, the blousiest of blouses, and a tam-o'shanter over my left ear. Of course everybody was in. So I thought if I went like this—brand new frock—swagger hat—white gloves—that everybody would be out."

" And were they? "

" No. Just like my luck—they were all—all in! "

" And yet you have the audacity to come here and ask for tea? "

" For goodness' sake, don't talk of tea."

" I thought your were so thirsty."

" So I am. I thirst for amusement."

" Kitty! You've been amusing yourself all afternoon— at other people's expense."

" Yes. It's cheap—awfully cheap, but fatiguing. I don't want to amuse myself; I want to be amused."

Mr. Rickman took a longer look at the brilliant apparition.

Now, at a little distance, Miss Palliser passed as merely an ordinary specimen of a brilliant but conventional type. This effect was an illusion produced by her irreproachably correct attire. As she drew nearer it became apparent that convention could never have had very much to do with her. Tailor and milliner were responsible for the general correctness of Miss Palliser's appearance, Miss Palliser herself for the riot and confusion of the details. Her coat, flung open, displayed a tangle of laces disposed after her own fancy. Her skirts, so flawless and sedate, swept as if inspired by the storm of her long-legged impetuous stride. Under her too, too fashionable hat her brown hair was twisted in a way entirely her own; and fashion had left untouched the wild originality of her face. Bumpy brows, jutting eye-brows, and nose long in the bridge, wide in the nostril, tilted in a gentle gradient; a wide, full-lipped, nervous mouth, and no chin to speak of. A thin face lit by restless greenish eyes; stag-like, dog-like, humorous and alert.

Miss Palliser sent the gaze of those eyes round the room. The hungry, Satanic humour in them roved, seeking what it might devour. It fell upon Mr. Rickman.

" What have you got there? "

Miss Harden's reply was inaudible.

" Let me in. I want to look at it."

" Don't, Kitty." Apparently an explanation followed from Miss Harden. It also was inaudible.

" Lu-*chee*-a! Where is Miss Roots, B. A.? "

" Please, *please,* Kitty. Do go into the morning-room."

This painful scene was cut short by Robert, who announced that tea was served.

" Oh, joy! " said Miss Palliser and disappeared.

Lucia, following, found her examining the tea-tray.

" Only two cups," said Miss Palliser. " Isn't it going to get any tea then? "

" Isn't what going to get any tea? "

" *It.* The man thing you keep in there."

" Yes. But it doesn't get it here."

" I think you might ask it in. It might amuse me."

Lucia ignored the suggestion.

" I haven't talked," said Miss Palliser, " to a man thing for ages."

" It hasn't come to be talked to. It's much too busy."

" Mayn't it come in, just for a treat? "

Lucia shook her head.

" What's it like? Is it nice to look at? "

" No—yes—no."

" What? Haven't you made up your mind yet? "

" I haven't thought about it."

" Lucia, you're a perfect dog in the manger. You don't care a rap about the creature yourself, and yet you refuse to share it with your friend. I put it to you. Here we are, you and I, living in a howling wilderness untrodden by the foot of man, where even curates are at a premium—is it right, is it fair of you, to have a presentable man-thing in the house, and to keep it to yourself? "

" Well—you see, it—it isn't so very presentable."

" Rubbish! I saw it. It looked perfectly all right."

" That," said Lucia, " is illusion. You haven't heard it speak."

" What's wrong with it? "

"Nothing—nothing. Only it isn't exactly what you'd call a gentleman."

"Oh! Well, I think you might have told me that before."

"I've been trying to tell you."

Kitty reflected a moment. "So it's making a catalogue, is it? Whose bright idea is that?"

"It was grandpapa's. It's mine now." She did not mention that it was also Horace Jewdwine's.

"And what will your little papa say?"

"He won't say anything. He never does. The library's mine—mine to do as I like with."

"You've broken the spell. Isn't there some weird legend about women never inheriting it?"

"Well, they never have. I shall be the first."

"I say, if I were you, I should feel a little creepy."

"I do—sometimes. That's one reason why I want to get this thing made in my lifetime, before I go away."

"Good gracious. You're not going away to die."

"I don't know what I'm going away to do. Anyhow, the catalogue will be done. All ready for Horace when he steps into my shoes."

"Unless—happy thought—you marry him. That, I suppose, is *another* pair of shoes?"

There was a pause, during which Miss Palliser gazed thoughtfully at her friend.

"What have you been doing to yourself? You look most awfully tired."

"I've been sitting up rather late the last few nights, cataloguing."

"What on earth did you do that for?"

"Because I want to finish by the twenty-seventh."

There was a pause while Miss Palliser ate tea-cake.

"Is Horace coming down before you go?"

"No. He's too busy. Besides, he never comes when father isn't here."

"Oh, dear, no, he doesn't think it proper. It's odd," said Miss Palliser, looking down at her tea-cake with an air of profound philosophic reflection. "You can't ask your cousin to stay with you, because it's improper; but it isn't improper to sit up making catalogues with young Mr. Thing-um-a-jig till all hours of the night."

"Why should it be improper?"

" For goodness' sake don't ask me. How should *I* know?
Don't you find yourself wishing sometimes that Mr. Thing-
um-a-jig was Mr. Jewdwine? "

" More tea, Kitty? "

" Rather! I'm going into the library to choose a book
when I've finished my tea. I shall take the opportunity
of observing for myself whether Mr.—Mr.—— "

" Mr. Savage Keith Rickman. "

" Good Lord deliver us! Whether Mr. Savage Keith
Rickman is a proper person for you to know. That reminds
me. Dearest, do you know what they talk about in Harmouth? They talk about *you*. Conversation jiggers round
you like a silly moth round a candle. Would you like to
know what Harmouth thinks of you? "

" No. I haven't the smallest curiosity. "

" I shall tell you all the same, because it's good for you
to see yourself as others see you. They say, dear, that you
do put on such a thundering lot of side. They say that attitude is absurd in one so young. They say you ought to
marry, that if you don't marry you can't possibly hope to
keep it up, and they say you never will marry if you continue to be so exclusive. Exclusive was the word. But
before I left they'd married you to Mr. Jewdwine. You see,
dear, you're so exclusive that you're bound to marry into
your own family, no other family being good enough. "

" It's certainly a new light on my character. "

" I ought to tell you that Mrs. Crampton takes a charitable
view. She says she doesn't believe you really mean it, dear,
she thinks that you are only very, *very* shy. She has heard
so much about you, and is *dying* to know you. Don't be
frightened, Lucia, I was most discreet. "

" How did you show your discretion? "

" I told her not to die. I tried to persuade her that she
wouldn't love you so much if she did know you. "

" Kitty, that wasn't very kind. "

" It was the kindest thing I could think of. It must soothe
her to feel that this exclusiveness doesn't imply any reflection on her social position, but merely a weird, unaccountable dislike. How is it that some people can't understand
that your social position is like your digestion, or the nose
on your face, you're never aware of either, unless there's
something wrong with it. "

"Kitty, you're not in a nice mood this afternoon."

"I know I'm not. I've been in Harmouth. Lucy, there are moments when I loathe my fellow-creatures."

"Poor things. Whatever have they been doing now?"

"Oh, I don't know. The same old thing. They make my life a burden to me."

"But how?"

"They're always bothering me, always trying to get at you through me. They're always asking me to tea to meet people in the hope that I'll ask them back to meet you. I'm worn out with keeping them off you. Some day all Harmouth will come bursting into your drawing-room over my prostrate form, flattened out upon the door-mat."

"Never mind."

"I wouldn't, sweetheart, if they really cared about you. But they don't. If you lost your money and your social position to-morrow they wouldn't care a rap. That's why I hate them."

"Why do you visit them if you hate them?"

"Because, as I told you, I hunger and thirst for amusement, and they do amuse me when they don't make me ill."

"Dear Kitty, I'm sure they're nicer than you think. Most people are, you know."

"If you think so, why don't *you* visit them?" snapped Kitty.

"I would, if——"

"If they ceased to be amusing; if they broke their legs or lost their money, or if they got paralytic strokes, or something. You'd visit them in their affliction, but not in the ordinary playful circumstances of life. That's because you're an angel. *I*," said Miss Palliser contentiously, "am not. Why do I always come to you when I feel most hopelessly the other thing?"

Lucia said something that had a very soothing effect; it sounded like "Skittles!" but the word was "Kittikin!"

"Lucy, I shouldn't be such a bad sort if I lived with you. I've been here exactly twenty minutes, and I laid in enough goodness to last me for a week. And now," said Miss Palliser with decision, "I'm going."

Lucia looked up in some trepidation.

"Where are you going?"

"I am going—to choose that book."

" Oh, Kitty, do be careful."

" I am always careful," said Miss Palliser, " in choosing a book."

In about ten minutes' time she returned. Her chastened mood had vanished.

" Lucia," said she, " you have an immense regard for that young man."

" How do you know that I have an immense regard for him? "

" I suppose you expect me to say that I can tell by your manner. I can't. Your manner is perfection. It's by Robert's manner that I judged. Robert's manner is not perfection; for a footman, you know, it's a shade too eager, too emotional."

" That, to my mind, is the charm of Robert."

" Still, there are drawbacks. A footman's face ought not to betray the feelings of his mistress. That's how I knew that Mabel Flosser was cooling off—by the increasing frostiness of Blundell. I shall feel sure of you, Lucia, as long as Robert continues to struggle against his fascinating smile. Take my advice—if you should ever cherish a secret passion, get rid of Robert, for, sure as fate, he'll give you away. Perhaps," she added meditatively, " it *was* a little mean of me."

" Kitty, what have you been up to? "

" It was your fault. You shouldn't be so mysterious. Wishing to ascertain your real opinion of Mr. Savage Keith Rickman, I watched Robert as he was bringing in his tea."

" I hope he was properly attentive."

" Attentive isn't the word for it. He may have felt that my eye was upon him, and so got flustered, but it struck me that he overdid the thing. He waited on Mr. Rickman as if he positively loved him. That won't do, you know. He'll be raising fatal hopes in the bosom of the Savage Keith. Let us hope that Mr. Rickman is not observant."

" He is, as it happens, excessively observant."

" So I found out. I found out all sorts of things."

" What things? "

" Well, in the first place, that he is conscientious. He doesn't waste time. He writes with one hand while he takes his tea with the other; which of course is very clever of him. He's marvellously ambidexterous, so long as he doesn't know you're looking at him. Unfortunately, my eye arrested him in the double act. Lucy, my eye must have some horrible malignant power, for it instantly gave him St. Vitus's dance. Have you ever noticed anything peculiar about my eye?"

"What a shame!"

"Yes. I'm afraid he'll have to do a little re-copying."

"Oh, Kitty, why couldn't you leave the poor thing in peace?"

"There wasn't any peace to leave him in. Really, you'd have thought that taking afternoon tea was an offence within the meaning of the Act. He couldn't have been more excited if I'd caught him in his bath. Mr. Rickman suffers from excess of modesty."

"Mr. Rickman could hardly say the same of you. You might have had the decency to go away."

"There wouldn't have been any decency in going away. Flight would have argued that I shared the theory of his guilt. I stayed where I was for two seconds just to re-assure him; then I went away—to the other end of the room."

"You should have gone away altogether."

"Why? The library is big enough for two. It's so big that you *could* take a bath, or do a murder, at one end without anybody being aware of it at the other. I went away; I wandered round the bookcases; I even hummed a tune, not so much to show that I was at my ease as to set him at his."

"In fact, you behaved as like a dreadful young person as you possibly could."

"I thought that would set him at his ease sooner than anything. I did it on purpose. I am nothing if not subtle. *You* would have crushed him with a delicate and ladylike retreat; *I* left him as happy as he could be, smiling dreamily to himself over the catalogue."

"And then?"

"Then, I admit, I felt it might be time to go. But before I went I made another discovery. You know, Lucia, he really is rather nice to look at. Adieu, my exclusive one."

CHAPTER XIX

THE chronicler who recorded that no woman had ever inherited the Harden Library contented himself with the bare statement of the fact. It was not his business to search into causes, which belonged to the obscurer regions of psychology. Sir Joseph Harden and those book-lovers who went before him had the incurable defects of their qualities. Hereditary instinct, working in them with a force as of some blind fatality, drove too many of them to espouse their opposites. Their wives were not expected to do anything noteworthy, beyond sitting for their portraits to the masters of their day; though, as a matter of fact, many of them contrived to achieve a far less enviable distinction. The portraits have immortalized their faces and their temperaments. Ladies of lax fibre, with shining lips and hazy eyes; ladies of slender build, with small and fragile foreheads, they hang for ever facing their uniformly heavy-browed and serious lords. Looking at those faces, you cannot wonder that those old scholars had but a poor opinion of woman, the irrational and mutable element in things, or that the library had been handed down from father to son, from uncle to nephew, evading the cosmic vanity by devious lines of descent. It was a tradition in the family that its men should be scholars and its women beauties, occasionally frail.

And scholarship, in obedience to the family tradition, ran superbly in the male line for ten generations, when it encountered an insuperable obstacle in the temperament of Sir Frederick. Then came Sir Frederick's daughter, and between them they made short work of the family tradition. Sir Frederick had appropriated the features of one of his great grandmothers, her auburn hair, her side-long eyes, her fawn-like, tilted lip, her perfect ease of manners and of morals. By a still more perverse hereditary freak the Harden intellect, which had lapsed in Sir Frederick, appeared again in his daughter, not in its well-known austere and colourless form, but with a certain brilliance and passion, a touch of purely feminine uncertainty and charm.

The Harden intellect had changed its sex. It was Horace

Jewdwine who had found that out, counting it as the first of his many remarkable discoveries. Being (in spite of his conviction to the contrary) a Jewdwine rather than a Harden, he had felt a certain malignant but voluptuous satisfaction in drawing the attention of the Master of Lazarus to this curious lapse in the family tradition. Now in the opinion of the Master of Lazarus the feminine intellect was simply a contradiction in terms. Having engaged the best masters in the county, whose fees, together with their fares (second class from Exeter to Harmouth), he had himself punctually paid, he had declined to take any further interest in his granddaughter. He had no objection to her taking up music, a study which, being no musician, he was unable to regard as in any sense intellectual. He supported his view by frequent allusions to the brainlessness of song-birds; in fact, he had been always a little bitter on the subject, having before his eyes the flagrant instance of his son Frederick.

Frederick was no scholar. He despised his forefathers as a race of pedants, and boasted that he never opened a book, barring the book of life, in which he flattered himself he could have stood a very stiff examination. He used a certain unbowdlerized edition, which he was careful to conceal from the ladies of his family. Before he was forty Frederick had fiddled away the family tradition, and not only the family tradition, but the family splendour and the family credit. When Lucia at seventeen was studying the classics under Horace Jewdwine, Frederick's debts came rolling in; at about the same period old Sir Joseph's health showed signs of failing, and Frederick took to raising money on his expectations. He had just five years to do it in.

It was then that Lucia first began to notice a change in her grandfather's manner towards her. Sometimes she would catch his eyes fixed on her with a curious, scrutinizing gaze, and once or twice she thought she detected in them a profound sadness. Whenever at these moments they happened to meet her eyes they were immediately averted. Sir Joseph had not been given to betraying emotion, save only on points of scholarship, and it was evident that he had something on his mind.

What he had on his mind was the thought that at the

rate Frederick was living he might at any moment cease
to live, and then what would become of Lucia? And what
would become of the Harden Library? What of the family
tradition? By much pondering on the consequences of
Frederick's decease Sir Joseph had considerably hastened
his own. Lucia knew nothing of all this. She was only
aware that her grandfather had sent for Horace Jewdwine
on his death-bed. What had passed between them remained
known only to Horace. But part of a sum of money left by
Sir Joseph's will towards the founding of a Harden scholarship was transferred by a codicil to Lucia for her education.

The task begun by Horace Jewdwine was continued by a
learned lady, Miss Sophia Roots, B. A.; and Miss Roots
did her work so well that when Sir Frederick assumed his
rightful guardianship of his daughter he pronounced her
the worst educated young woman in Europe. Of all that
Miss Roots had so laboriously imparted to her she retained,
not a smattering, but a masterly selection. And now at
four and twenty she had what is called a beautiful view of
life; with that exciting book which her father kept so sedu-
lously out of her reach she was acquainted as it were through
anthologies and translations. For anything Lucia knew to
the contrary, life might be all bursts of lyric rapture and
noble sequences of selected prose. She was even in danger
of trusting too much to her own inspired version of certain
passages. But anthologies are not always representative, and
nobody knew better than Lucia that the best translations
sometimes fail to give the spirit of the original.

Something of this spirit she caught from her father's
brilliant and disturbing presence. Lucia adored her father.
He brought into her life an element of uncertainty and
freedom that saved it from the tyranny of books. It was a
perpetual coming and going. A dozen times in a year Sir
Frederick hurled himself from Harmouth to London, from
London to the Continent, and from the Continent back again
to Harmouth, to recruit. The very transience of his appearances and Lucia's ignorance of all that lay behind them
preserved her in her attitude of adoration.

Sir Frederick took precious good care that it should not
be disturbed by the familiarity born of frequent intercourse,
that she should see him only in his moods of unnatural
sobriety. And as he left Lucia to the library so much, it

was to be supposed that, in defiance of the family tradition, he would leave the library to Lucia. But after all Sir Frederick had some respect for the family tradition. When it seemed only too likely that a woman would inherit the Harden Library, he stepped in and saved it from that supreme disgrace by the happy expedient of a bill of sale. Otherwise his natural inclination would have been to leave it to his daughter, for whom he had more or less affection, rather than to his nephew, for whom he had none.

As it happened, it was Horace Jewdwine who was responsible for the labour which Lucia had so impetuously undertaken. Lucia was aware that her grandfather's desire had been to rearrange and catalogue the library. When she came of age and found herself mistress of a tiny income (derived from capital left by her mother, carefully tied up to keep it from Sir Frederick, and enlarged by regular accumulations at compound interest), her first idea was to carry out her grandfather's wishes; but it was not until Horace Jewdwine's last visit that her idea became a determination. Horace had been strolling round the library, turning over the books, not exactly with the covetous eye of the heir apparent, but with that peculiar air of appropriation which he affected in all matters of the intellect. In that mood Lucia had found him irritating, and it had appeared that Horace had been irritated, too. He had always felt a little sore about the library; not that he really wanted it himself, but that he hated to see it in the possession of such a rank barbarian as his uncle Frederick. A person who, if his life depended on it, could not have told an Aldine from an Elzevir. A person, incapable not only of appreciating valuable books, but of taking ordinary decent care of them. There were gaps on the shelves, a thing that he hated to see. Lucia, too; Lucia would take books out by tens and twenties at a time and leave them lying all over the house, and they would be stuck in again anywhere and anyhow. No sort of method in their arrangement. No blinds, no glass doors to protect them. He had pointed this out to Lucia, suggesting that it was not a good thing to let too much dust accumulate on the tops of books, neither was it altogether desirable that a strong south-westerly light should play upon them all day long. Had she ever noticed how the bindings were cracking and fading? For all this he seemed to be blaming Lucia; and this, Lucia tried to persuade herself, was no great matter; but when he asked for a catalogue, and she calmly told him that there was none, he become involved in a sentence about a scandal and a Vandal in which his opinion of his uncle Frederick unmistakably appeared. He even forgot himself so far as to reflect on the sanity of the late Master of Lazarus, at which point Lucia had left him to his reflections.

She had not yet forgiven Horace for his interference that day, nor for his remark about the scandal and the Vandal. As for his other observations, they were insufferably true. Hence her desperate efforts to set the library in order before she went abroad; hence the secrecy and haste with which she had applied to Rickman's, without asking Horace's advice, as she naturally would have done; hence, too, her vast delight at the success of her unassisted scheme. Mr. Rickman was turning out splendidly. If she had looked all through London she could not have found a better man.

CHAPTER XX

IT was Easter Sunday and Lucia's heart was glad, for she had had a letter from her father. There never was such a father and there never were such letters as, once in a blue moon and when the fancy seized him, he wrote to his adorable Lucy. Generally speaking, they were all about himself and his fiddle, the fiddle that, when he was at home, he played from morning to night. But this letter was more exciting. It was full of all the foolish and delightful things they were to do together in Cannes, in Venice, and in Florence and in Rome. He was always in one or other of these places, but this was the first time he had proposed that his adorable Lucy should join him. "You're too young to see the world," he used to say. "You wouldn't enjoy it, Lucy, you really wouldn't. The world is simply wasted on any woman under five and thirty." Lucia was not quite five and twenty. She was not very strong, and she felt that if she didn't see the world soon she might not enjoy it very much when she did see it. And it was barely a month now till the twenty-seventh.

Lucia went singing downstairs and into the library to throw all its four windows open to the delicious spring, and there, to her amazement (for it was Sunday), she came upon Mr. Rickman cataloguing hard.

She felt a little pang of self-reproach at the sight of him. There was something pathetic in his attitude, in his bowed head and spread elbows, the whole assiduous and devoted figure. How hard he was working, with what a surprising speed in his slender, nervous hands. She had not meant him to give up the whole of his three days' holiday to her, and she really could not take his Easter Sunday, poor little man. So, with that courtesy which was Mr. Rickman's admiration and despair, she insisted on restoring it to him, and earnestly advised his spending it in the open air. In the evening he could have the library to himself, to read or write or rest in; he would, she thought, be more comfortable there than in the inn. Mr. Rickman admitted that he would like to have a walk to stretch his legs a bit, and as she opened the south window she had a back view of him stretching them across the lawn. He walked as rapidly as he wrote, holding his head very high in the air. He wore a light grey suit and a new straw hat with a dull olive green ribbon on it, poor dear. She was glad that it was a fine day for the hat.

She watched him till the beech-tree hid him from her sight; then she opened the west windows, and the south wind that she had just let in tried to rush out again by them, and in its passage it lifted up the leaves of Mr. Rickman's catalogue and sent them flying. The last of them, escaping playfully from her grasp, careened across the room and hid itself under a window curtain. Stooping to recover it, she came upon a long slip of paper printed on one side. It was signed S. K. R., and Savage Keith Rickman was the name she had seen on Mr. Rickman's card. The headline, *Helen in Leuce*, drew her up with a little shock of recognition. The title was familiar, so was the motto from Euripides,

σὺ Διὸς ἔφυς, ὦ ʽΕλένα θυγάτηρ

and she read,

> The wonder and the curse of friend and foe,
> She watched the ranks of battle cloud and shine,
> And heard, Achilles, that great voice of thine,
> That thundered in the trenches far below.

Tears upon tears, woe upon mortal woe,
  Follow her feet, and funeral fire on fire,
  While she, that phantom of the heart's desire,
Flies thither, where all dreams and phantoms go.

Oh Strength unconquerable, Achilles! Thee
  She follows far into the shadeless land
  Of Leuce, girdled by the gleaming sand,
Amidst the calm of an enchanted sea,
  Where, children of the Immortals, hand in hand,
  Ye share one golden immortality.

It was a voice from the sad, modern world she knew so well,
and, in spite of its form (which was a little too neo-classic
and conventional to please her), she felt it to be a cry from
the heart of a living man. That man she had identified with
the boy her grandfather had found, years ago, in a City
bookshop. There had been no room for doubt on that
point when she saw him in the flush of his intellectual passion, bursting so joyously, so preposterously, into Greek.
He had, therefore, already a certain claim on her attention.
Besides, he seemed to be undergoing some incomprehensible struggle which she conceived to be of a moral nature,
and she had been sorry for him on that account.

But, if he were also—Was it possible that her grandfather's marvellous boy had grown into her cousin's still
more marvellous man? Horace, too, had made his great
discovery in a City shop. *Helen in Leuce* and a City shop—
it hardly amounted to proof; but, if it did, what then? Oh
then, she was still more profoundly sorry for him. For
then he was a modern poet, which in the best of circumstances is to be marked for suffering. And to Mr. Rickman circumstances had not been exactly kind.

A modern poet, was he? One whom the gods torment
with inspired and hopeless passion; a lover of his own
" fugitive and yet eternal bride," the Helen of Homer, of
Æschylus and Euripides, the Helen of Marlowe and Goethe,
the Helen of them all. And for Mr. Rickman, unhappy
Mr. Rickman, perdition lurked darkly in her very name.
What, oh what, must it feel like, to be capable of eliding the
aitch in " Helen " and yet divinely and deliriously in love
with her? Here Lucia was wrong, for Mr. Rickman was
entirely happy with the aitch in Helen.

She was so sorry for him. But she did not see at the

moment what she could do for him besides being sorry. And yet, if he were Horace's friend, she must do more. She was aware that she had been sorry for him chiefly because he was not a gentleman. Well, she had seen men before who were not gentlemen, and she had been very far from feeling any sort of sorrow for them. But she had never in all her life seen anything like this inspired young Cockney, with his musical voice and afflicting accent, a person whose emotions declared themselves publicly and painfully, whose thoughts came and went as transparently as the blood in his cheeks, who yet contrived somehow to remain in the last resort impenetrable.

She could not ignore him. Apart from Horace he had established his claim; and if he *was* Horace's friend he had another and a stronger title to consideration. But was he? She had really no proof.

She wondered whether Mr. Rickman had missed his sonnet. She laid it almost tenderly in a conspicuous place on his table, and put a bronze head of Pallas Athene on it to keep it down. Then she wondered again whether he enjoyed the bookshop, whether he enjoyed making catalogues *raisonnés,* whether he enjoyed himself generally, and she hoped that at any rate he would enjoy his Easter Sunday. Poor little man.

Lucia was so happy herself that she wanted Mr. Rickman to be happy, too.

CHAPTER XXI

MR. RICKMAN was anything but happy as he set out for his walk that glorious April morning.

Outside the gate of Court House he stood and looked about him, uncertain of the way he would go. All ways were open to him, and finally, avoiding the high road, he climbed up a steep and stony lane to the great eastern rampart which is Harcombe Hill. Beneath him lay Harmouth, at the red mouth of the valley where the river Hare trickles into the sea through a barrier of shingle. Two gigantic and flaming cliffs dwarf the little town to the proportions of a hamlet. In any other situation Harmouth might have preserved its elegant Regency air, but, sprawl-

ing on the beach and scattered on the hillsides, it has a
haphazard appearance, as if it had been dropped there when
those two huge arms of the upland stretched out and opened
to the sea.

But Nature on the whole has been kind to Harmouth,
though the first thing that strikes the stranger in that place
is her amazing and apparently capricious versatility.
Nature, round about Harmouth, is never in the same
mood for a mile together. The cliffs change their form
and colour with every dip in the way; now they are red
like blood, and now a soft and powdery pink with violet
shadows in their seams. Inland, it is a medley of fields
and orchards, beech-woods, pine-woods, dark moorland and
sallow down, cut by the deep warm lanes where hardly a
leaf stirs on a windy day. It is not so much a landscape
as the fragments of many landscapes, samples in little of
the things that Nature does elsewhere on a grand scale.
The effect on a stranger is at first alluring, captivating, like
the caprices of a beautiful woman; then it becomes disconcerting, maddening, fatiguing; and a great longing seizes
him for vast level spaces, for sameness, for the infinity
where he may lose himself and rest. Then one day he
climbs to the top of Harcombe or Muttersmoor and finds
the immensity he longed for. As far as his sight can reach,
the shoulders of the hills and the prone backs of the long
ridges are all of one height; the combes and valleys are
mere rifts and dents in a great moor that has no boundary
but the sky. The country has revealed its august, eternal
soul. He is no longer distracted by its many moods; he
loves it the more for them, as a man loves the mutable ways
of the woman whose soul he knows.

Rickman stood upon a vantage ground, looking over the
valley and the bay. To him it was as if the soul of this
land, like the soul of Lucia Harden, had put on a veil. The
hillside beneath him dropped steeply to the valley and the
town. Down there, alone and apart from Harmouth, divided
from the last white Regency villa by half a mile of meadow-
land, stood Court House; and as he looked at it he became
more acutely conscious of his misery. He sat down among
the furze and heather and bracken; he could think of nothing better than to sit there and stare into the face of Nature,
not like a poet whom love makes lyrical, but like a quite

ordinary person whom it makes dumb. And Nature never turned to a poet a lovelier and more appealing face. It had rained in the night. From the enfolding blue, sky blue and sea blue, blue of the aerial hills, the earth flung out her colours, new washed, radiantly, immaculately pure. Bared to the sea, she flamed from rose pink to rose red. Only the greater hills and the dark flank of Muttersmoor waited for their hour, the hour of the ling and the heather; the valleys and the lower slopes were glad with green. There was an art in Nature's way; for, lest a joyousness so brimming and so tender should melt and overflow into mere pathos, it was bounded and restrained by that solemn and tragic line of Muttersmoor drawn straight against the sky.

It was the same scene that had troubled him when he first looked at it, and it troubled him still; not with that thrill of prescient delight and terror, but with a feeling more mysterious and baffling, an exquisite and indefinable reproach. He stared, as if he could hope by staring to capture the meaning of the beautiful, tender face; but beyond that inscrutable reproach it had no meaning for him and no expression. He had come to a land prophetic of inspiration, where, if anywhere, he might have hoped to hear the lyric soul of things; and the lyric soul of things absolutely refused to sing to him. It had sung loud enough in the streets last Wednesday; it had hymned the procession of his dreams and the loud tumultuous orgy of his passions; and why could he not hear it now? For here his senses were satisfied to the full. Never had Nature's material loveliness been more vividly, piercingly present to him. The warm air was like a touch, palpable yet divine. He lay face downwards on the earth and pressed it with his hands, he smelt the good smell of the grass and young bracken, and the sweet almond-scented blossom of the furze. And he suffered all the torment of the lover who possesses the lips and body of his mistress, and knows that her heart is far from him and that her soul is not for him.

He felt himself to be severed from the sources of his inspiration; estranged, profoundly and eternally, from the beauty he desired. And that conviction, melancholy in itself, was followed by an overpowering sense of intellectual dissolution, the corruption and decay of the poetic faculty in him. He was aware, feverishly aware, of a faint flowing measure, the reverberation of dead songs; of ideas, a miserable attenuated procession, trailing feebly in the dark of his brain, which, when he tried to grasp them, would be gone. They were only the ghosts of the ideas that he had brought with him from London, that had died on the journey down. The beauty of this place was devilish and malign. He looked into Harmouth valley as if it had been a graveyard. They were all buried down there, his dead dreams and his dead power, buried without hope of any resurrection. Rickman's genius, the only thing he genuinely trusted, had forsaken him.

It may be that every poet once in his lifetime has to come to this Calvary, to hang through his black hour on the cross, and send out after the faithless deity his Lama Sabachthani. For Rickman no agony could compare with that isolation and emptiness of soul. He could see nothing beyond that hour, for he had never felt anything like it before, not even on waking in the morning after getting drunk. His ideas had always come back again when he was in a fit state to receive them. But this time, though he had not been drinking, he felt that they had gone for ever, and that all his songs were sung. And over his head high up in the sky, a lark, a little fiend of a lark, had chosen that moment for bursting into music. With diabolical ease and maddening ecstasy, he flung out his perfect and incommunicable song. A song of joy and mockery and triumph.

He did not know how old that skylark was, but here was he, Savage Keith Rickman, played out at three and twenty. Was it, he wondered, the result, not of ordinary inebriety, but of the finer excesses of the soul? Was he a precocious genius? Had he taken the immortal drink too early and too hard? Or was it, as Jewdwine had suggested, that there were too many Rickmans, and that this poor seventh part of him had been crushed by the competition of the other six? The horrible thing was that they would live on for years, eating and getting drunk and falling in love and buying suits of clothes, while the poet in him was dead, like Keats, at three and twenty.

Then suddenly, for no reason whatever, a vision of Lucia Harden rose before him like a light and refused to leave him.

It wrought in him, as he contemplated it, a gradual burning illumination. He perceived that it was he himself who was responsible for all this. He perceived the real nature of the things he had pursued so passionately, the thing he called pleasure, the thing he called love, and the thing he called his imagination. His notion of pleasure was getting drunk and making love to Miss Poppy Grace; the love he made was better described by a stronger and coarser monosyllable, and he had used his imagination to glorify it. Oh, yes, because he had imagination, because he was a poet, he had not gone down into the clay-pits and wallowed in the clay; neither had he been content to dabble in it; he had taken it up in his hands and moulded it into the form of a divinity, and then fallen down and worshipped it. Fallen down and worshipped at the feet, the gaily twirling feet, of Miss Poppy Grace.

Poor Poppy, if he could have thought of her at all, he might have felt a sort of pity for her transience, the transience of the feeling she inspired. But he did not think of her; he did not even try to think of her. Her image, once so persistent, had dropped clean out of his mind, which was one reason why it was so empty. It had not been much to boast of, that infatuation for Poppy, and yet somehow, after living so intimately with it, he felt quite lost without it. It was a little odd, if you came to think of it, that the thing he called his genius, and the thing he called his love, should have chosen the same moment to abandon him. Was it—was it possible—that there was some vital connection between them? As the singing of birds in the pairing season, was his genius merely a rather peculiar symptom of the very ordinary condition known as falling in love? So that, failing that source of inspiration—? That no doubt *was* what was the matter with him. His imagination languished because his passion for Poppy was played out, and he had nothing to put in its place.

Well, yes, there was something; something that was not an instinct or a passion, but an acquired taste. To be sure he had acquired it very quickly, it had only taken him three days. In those three days he had developed a preference for the society of ladies (the women of his own class were not ladies, but " young ladies," a distinction he now appreciated for the first time). It was a preference that, as things stood, he would never be able to gratify; there was something about it ruinous and unhappy, like a craze for first editions in an impecunious scholar, for ever limited to the twopenny bundle and the eighteenpenny lot. He could not hope to enjoy Miss Harden's society for more than three weeks at the outside. He only enjoyed it at all through an accident too extraordinary, too fantastic to occur again. Between him and her there stood the barrier of the counter. The barrier itself was not insuperable: he might get over the counter, so might Miss Harden, but there were other things that she never could get over. Though in some ways he was all right, in others, again, he was not— he could see very well that he was not—what Miss Harden would call a gentleman. He was, through that abominable nervousness of his, an impossible person, hopelessly, irredeemably involved in social solecisms. Or if not impossible, he was, at any rate, highly improbable.

Perceiving all this, he was still unable to perceive the meaning of his insight and his misery. He did not know, and there was nobody to tell him, that this emptiness of his was the emptiness created by the forerunners and servants of Love, who sweep and purify the death-chamber where a soul has died and another soul is waiting to be born. For in the house of Love there is only one chamber for birth and for dying; and into that clean, unfurnished place the soul enters unattended and endures its agony alone. There is no Mother-soul to bear for it the birth-pains of the new life.

But Mr. Rickman was young, and youth's healthy instinct urged him to vigorous exercise as the best means of shaking off his misery. He crossed the road that runs along the top of Harcombe Hill, and made for the cliffs in a south-easterly direction across the fields. He then kept along the coast-line, dipping into Harcombe valley, climbing again to Easton Down. Here the coast was upheaved into terraces of grey limestone, topped by a layer of sand riddled with rabbit holes. Before one of these two young hawks were watching, perched on a projecting boulder. So intent was their gaze and they so motionless that the air seemed to stand still and wait for the sweep of their wings. Mr. Rickman, whom youth made reckless, lay flat on his stomach and peered over the edge of the cliff. He was fascinated, breathlessly absorbed. He pressed the turf a little closer in his eagerness, and so loosened a large stone that rolled down, starting a cataract of sand and rubble. He had just time to throw himself back sideways, as the hollow fringe of turf gave way and plunged down the cliff-side. So far from taking his escape with becoming seriousness, he amused himself by trying to feel as he would have felt if he had actually gone over the cliff. He found that his keenest emotion was a thrill of horror, as he imagined Miss Harden a possible spectator of the ridiculous evolutions performed by his person in its passage through the air.

After an hour dipping and climbing he reached a small fishing village. Here he dined and rested, and it was mid-afternoon before he turned again towards Harmouth. There was no chance of missing his way; he had nothing to do but follow the coast-line as he had done before.

There were signs in the valley of the white fog that sometimes, even in April, comes in before sunset; already a veil of liquid air was drawn across the hills, and, when he crossed Easton Down (if it was Easton Down) again, the sea's face was blurred with mist.

As he went on westwards the mist kept pace with him, gradually diminishing the view he had hoped to see. And as it shifted and closed round him, his movements became labyrinthine, then circular.

And now his view was all foreground; he was simply walking through circles of moor, enclosed by walls of fine grey fog. He passed through these walls, like a spirit, into smaller and smaller circles; then, hopelessly bewildered, he stopped, turned, and walked in what he took to be a contrary direction, feeling that the chance of going over the cliff-side lent an agreeable excitement to a pastime that threatened to become monotonous. This was assuming the cliff-side to be somewhere near; and he was beginning to feel that it might be anywhere, under his feet for all he knew, when the fog lifted a little from the high ground, and he saw that he had lost his bearings altogether. He had been going round and round through these circles without returning to the point he started from. He went forward less cautiously in a larger round, and then he suddenly stood still. He was not alone.

His foreground had widened slightly and a figure stood in the middle of it. There was something familiar in the blurred outlines, traced as if by a watery finger on the wall of mist. An idea had taken shape stealthily behind him and flung its shadow there. The idea was Lucia Harden. The fog hung in her hair in drops like rain; it made her grey dress cling close about her straight, fine limbs; it gave its own grandeur and indistinctness to her solitary figure.

She turned, unstartled, but with an air of imperfect recognition. He raised his hat; the hat with the green ribbon on it.

"I beg your pardon, but can you tell me the shortest cut to Harmouth? I think I've lost my way."

She answered absently. "You are all right. Turn to the left, and you'll find the path along the cliff. It will bring you out on to Harmouth beach."

He followed the patch she had pointed out. Still absently she looked after him, a dim figure going down into the fog, and it occurred to her that she had sent him on a dangerous way. There were rabbit wires and pitfalls on that path; places where the cliff was eaten away under its curling edge of turf, and for Mr. Rickman, who didn't know his ground, a single step might mean death.

She could not see him now. She called to him; "Mr. Rickman!" but there was no answer; only the sound of Mr. Rickman going down deeper. She called again, a little imperiously, and yet again. The last time her voice carried well, for there was the vibrating note of terror in it. He turned and saw her coming down the path towards him.

"I forgot," she said, still with the slight tremor of fear in her voice. It seemed to draw out and intensify its sweetness. "That path isn't safe in a fog like this. You had better go round by the road."

"Oh, thanks. You shouldn't have troubled. I should have got on all right." They were climbing up the moor together.

"I'm afraid you wouldn't. I wasn't thinking, or I would never have sent you that way."

"Why not? It was a very good way."

"Yes. But you were going down into the thick of the fog. You might easily have walked over the cliff—and broken your neck."

He laughed as if that was the most delightful humorous idea.

"I don't know," said he, "that it would have mattered very much if I had."

She said nothing. She never did when he made these excursions into the personal. Of course it would not have mattered to Miss Harden if he had gone over the cliff. He had been guilty, not only of an unpardonable social solecism, but of a still more unpardonable platitude.

They had reached the top of the cliff, and Lucia stood still.

"Isn't there another short cut across the valley?" he asked.

"There is; but I don't advise you to try it. And there is a way round by the road—if you can find it."

He smiled. Had he tried to approach her too soon, and was she reminding him that short cuts are dangerous? There was a way round—if he could find it. If indeed!

"Oh, I shall find it all right," said he, inspired by his double meaning.

"I don't think you will, if the fog lasts. I am going that way and I had better show you."

Show him? Was it possible?

She led the way, all too swiftly, yet with a certain leisure in her haste. He followed with a shy delight.

He was familiar enough by this time with her indoor aspect, with her unique and perfect manner of sitting still; now he saw that her beauty was of that rare kind that is most beautiful in movement. He would have liked that walk to last for ever, for the pure pleasure of following, now the delicate poise of her head, now the faint ripple of her shoulders under her thin coat, now the lines of her skirt breaking and flowing with the almost imperceptible swinging of the hips.

Her beauty, as he now reflected, was of the sort that dwells less in the parts than in the whole, it was subtle, pervading, and profound. It rejected all but the finer elements of sex. In those light vanishing curves her womanhood was more suggested than defined; it dawned on him in tender adumbration rather than in light. Such beauty is eloquent and prophetic through its richness of association, its kindred with all forms of loveliness. As Lucia moved she parted with some of that remoter quality that had first fascinated, then estranged him; she took on the grace of the creatures that live free in the sunlight and in the open air.

The mist shut them in with its grey walls. There was nothing to be seen but the patch of grass trodden by her feet, and her moving figure, grey on grey.

The walk was somewhat lacking in incident and conversational openings. Such as occurred seemed, like Kitty Palliser's hat, to be packed with meaning. There was the moment, the dreadful moment, then he lagged behind and lost sight of her. The moment, his opportunity, when an enormous bramble caught and pinned her by the feet and skirt. She tried to tread on it with one foot and walk away from it with the other, a thing manifestly impossible and absurd. Besides, it hurt—horribly. He knelt before her on the wet moor, unconscious of his brand-new trousers, conscious of nothing but the exquisite moment; and, with hands that trembled violently, freed first her delicate feet and then her skirt. He breathed hard, for the operation was intricate and took time. That bramble seemed to have neither beginning nor end, it branched out in all directions and was set with multitudinous and powerful thorns. Lucia stood still, being indeed unable to move, and watched his long, slender fingers adroitly disentangling her.

"I'm afraid you're hurting yourself," said she.

"Not at all," said Mr. Rickman gallantly, though the thorns tortured his hands, drawing drops of blood. His bliss annihilated pain.

"Take care," said she, "you are letting yourself get terribly torn."

He took no notice; but breathed harder than ever. "There, I've got it all off now, I think."

"Thank you very much." She drew her skirt gently from his detaining grasp.

"No—wait—please. There's a great hulking brute of a thorn stuck in the hem."

She waited.

"Confound my clumsiness! I've done it now!"

"Done what?" She looked down; on the dainty hem there appeared three distinct crimson stains. Mr. Rickman's face was crimson, too, with a flush of agony. Whatever he did for her, his clumsiness made wrong.

"I'm awfully sorry, but I've ruined your—your pretty dress, Miss Harden."

For it was a pretty, a very pretty, a charming dress. And

he was making matters worse by rubbing it with his pocket-handkerchief.

"Please—please don't bother," said she, "it doesn't matter." (How different from the behaviour of Miss Walker when Spinks spilt the melted butter on her shoulder!) "You've hurt your own hands more than my dress."

The episode seemed significant of the perils that awaited him in his intercourse with Miss Harden.

She went on. The narrow hill-track ended in the broad bridle-path that goes straight up Harcombe (not Harmouth) valley. He wondered, with quite painful perplexity, whether he ought still to follow at a discreet distance, or whether he might now walk beside her. She settled the question by turning round and waiting for him to come up with her. So they went up the valley together, and together climbed the steep road that leads out of it and back in the direction they had just left. The mist was thinner here at the top of the hill, and Rickman recognized the road he had crossed when he had turned eastwards that morning. He could now have found his way back perfectly well; but he did not say so. A few minutes' walk brought them to the place where he had sat down in his misery and looked over Harmouth valley.

Here they stopped, each struck by the strange landscape now suddenly revealed to them. They stood in clear air above the fog. It had come rolling in from the south, submerging the cliffs, and the town, and the valley; and now it lay smooth and cold and blue-white, like the sea under a winter sky. They might have been looking down on some mysterious world made before man. No land was to be seen save the tops of the hills lashed by the torn edges of the mist. Westward, across the bay, the peaks of the cliffs showed like a low, flat coast, a dull purplish line tormented by a livid surf. The flooded valley had become an arm of that vague sea. And from under the fog, immeasurably far below, there came the muffled sound of the mother sea, as if it were beating on the invisible floor of the world.

"I say, that's rather uncanny, isn't it?" So uncanny did it seem to him that he felt that it called for remark.

She looked at him with that faintly interrogative lifting of the eyebrows, which always seemed familiar to him. He remembered afterwards that Horace Jewdwine had the same trick. But in her, accompanied as it was by a pretty lifting of the corners of her mouth, it expressed friendly interest, in Jewdwine, apathy and a certain insolence. And yet all the time she was wondering how she should break it to him that their ways must now diverge.

"There's a horrible unconsciousness about it," he went on, pursuing as usual his own fancy. "If you *could* get bare nature without spirit, it would look like that."

"It *doesn't* look quite real," she admitted. (After that, there must be no more concessions. They must separate.)

"It hasn't any reality but what we give it."

"Hasn't it?"

(A statement so sweeping challenged contradiction.)

"You think that's only my Cockney view?"

"I think it isn't Nature. It's your own idea."

"It isn't even my own idea; I bagged it from Coleridge. P'raps you'll say he muddled himself with opium till he couldn't tell which was Nature and which was Coleridge; but there was old Wordsworth, as sober as a churchwarden, and he knew. What you call my Cockney view is the view of the modern poets. They don't—they can't distinguish between Nature and the human soul. Talk of getting near to Nature—we wouldn't know Nature if we saw it now. Those everlasting poets have got so near it that they've blocked the view for themselves and everybody else."

"Really, you talk as if they were a set of trippers."

"So they are! Wordsworth was nothing but a tripper, a glorified tripper. Nature's never looked the same since he ran his Excursion-train through the Lake country— special service to Tintern and Yarrow."

"This is slightly profane."

"No—it only means that if you want Nature you mustn't go to the poets of Nature. They've humanized it. I wouldn't mind that, if they hadn't womanized it, too."

"That only means that they loved it," she said softly.

"It means that they've demoralized it; and that now it demoralizes us. Nature is the supreme sentimentalist. It's all their fault. They've been flinging themselves on the bosom of Mother Earth, and sitting and writing Stanzas in Dejection on it, and lying down like a tired child on it, and weeping away their lives of care, that they have borne and yet must bear, on it, till they've saturated it with their beastly pathos. There isn't a dry comfortable place left for anybody else."

"Perhaps that's just the way Nature inspires poets, by giving out the humanity it absorbs."

"Perhaps. I can't say it inspires me."

"Are you a poet?" she asked. She was beginning to think it must be a case of mistaken identity; for this was not what she had expected of him.

He did not answer at first, neither did he look at her. He looked at the beautiful face of Nature (the sentimentalist), and a wave of hot colour rushed again over his own.

"I don't know whether I am or not."

"Let us hope not, since you want to make a clean sweep of them."

"I'd make a clean sweep of myself if I stood in my own light. Anything for a good view. But I'm afraid it's too late." His tone dropped from the extreme of levity to an almost tragic earnest. "We've done our work, and it can't be undone. We've given Nature a human voice, and now we shall never—never hear anything else."

"That's rather dreadful; I wish you hadn't."

"Oh, no, you don't. It's not the human voice you draw the line at—it's the Cockney accent."

Lucia's smile flickered and went out, extinguished by the waves of her blush. She was not prepared to have her thoughts read—and read aloud to her—in his way; and that particular thought was one she would have preferred him not to read.

"I dare say Keats had a cockney accent, if we did but know; and I dare say a good many people never heard anything else."

"I'm afraid you'd have heard it yourself, Miss Harden, if you'd met him."

"Possibly. It isn't what I should have remembered him by, though. That reminds me. I came upon a poem—a sonnet—of yours—if it was yours—this morning. It was lying on the library floor. You will find it under the bronze Pallas on the table."

Mr. Rickman stooped, picked up a sod and examined it carefully.

"Thank you very much. It *was* mine. I was afraid it was lost."

" It would have been a great pity if it had been."

Mr. Rickman dropped his sod.

She answered the question that appeared in his eyes, though not on his tongue. " Yes, I read it. It was printed, you see. I read it before I could make up my mind whether I might or not."

" It was all right. But I wish you hadn't."

To look at Mr. Rickman you would have said that all his mind was concentrated on the heel of his boot, as it slowly but savagely ground the sod to dust. Even so, the action seemed to say, even so could he have destroyed that sonnet.

" What did you think of it?"

He had looked up, when she least expected, with his disarming and ingenuous smile. Lucia felt that he had laid an ambush for her by his abstraction; the question and the smile shot, flashed, out of it, with a directness that made subterfuge impossible.

The seriousness of the question was what made it so awkward for a lady with the pleasure-giving instinct. If Mr. Rickman had merely asked her if she liked his new straw hat with the olive green ribbon (supposing them to be on terms that made such a question possible), she would probably have said " Yes," whether she liked it or not; because she wanted to give pleasure, because she didn't care a straw about his straw hat. But when Mr. Rickman asked her how she liked his sonnet, he was talking about the things that really mattered; and in the things that really mattered Lucia was sincerity itself.

" I thought," said she, " I thought the first dozen lines extremely beautiful."

" In a sonnet *every* line should be beautiful—should be perfect."

" Oh—if you're aiming at perfection."

" Why, what else in Heaven's name should I aim at?"

Lucia was silent; and he mistook her silence for distrust.

" I don't want you to judge me by that sonnet."

" But I shouldn't dream of judging you by that sonnet, any more than I should judge that sonnet by its last two lines. They're not the last you'll ever write."

" They're the last you will ever read."

" Well, it's something to have written one good sonnet."

" One swallow doesn't make a spring."

"No; but it tells us spring is coming, and the other swallows."

"There won't be any other swallows. All my swallows have flown."

"Oh, they'll fly back again, you'll see, if you wait till next spring."

"You weren't serious just now when you asked me if I was a poet. *I* was serious enough when I said I didn't know."

Something passed over Lucia's face, a ripple of shadow and flame, some moving of the under currents of the soul that told him that he was understood, that something had happened there, something that for the moment permitted him to be personal.

"What made you say so?"

"I can't tell you. Not natural modesty. I'm modest about some things, but not about that."

"Yet surely you must know?"

"I did yesterday."

"Yesterday?"

"Yesterday—last night; in fact up to eleven o'clock this morning I firmly believed that I had genius, or something uncommonly like it. I still believe that I *had* it."

He seemed to himself to have become almost grossly personal; but to Lucia he had ceased to be personal at all; he had passed into the region of realities; and in so passing had become intensely interesting. To Lucia, with the blood of ten generations of scholars in her veins, the question of a man's talent was supremely important; the man himself might not matter, but his talent mattered very much; to discuss it with him was entirely natural and proper. So she never once stopped to ask herself why she was standing on Harcombe Hill, holding this really very intimate conversation with Mr. Rickman.

"The things," he continued, "the things I've written prove it. I can say so without the smallest conceit, because I haven't it now, and never shall have it again. I feel as if it had belonged to somebody else."

Mr. Rickman was losing all likeness to his former self. He spoke no longer impulsively, but in the steady deliberate tones of unalterable conviction. And Lucia no longer heard the Cockney accent in this voice that came to her out of a suffering so lucid and so profound. She forgot that it came from the other side of the social gulf. If at any point in that conversation she had thought of dismissing him, she could not have dismissed him now. There was very little use in having saved his neck if she abandoned him to his misery.

Instead of abondoning him she sat down on a rough seat by the roadside to consider Mr. Rickman's case in all its bearings. In doing so she found herself for the first time contemplating his personal appearance as such; and that not altogether with disapproval. Though it was not in the least what she would have expected, he showed to advantage in the open air. She began to perceive the secret of his extravagant and preposterous charm. There was something about him—something that he had no right to have about him, being born a dweller in cities, which none the less he undeniably and inevitably had, something that made him one with this moorland setting, untamed and beautiful and shy. The great natural features of the landscape did him no wrong; for he was natural, too.

Well, she had found his sonnet for him; but could she help him to recover what he had lost now?

"I hope you won't mind my asking, but don't you know any one who can help you?"

"Not any one who can help me out of this."

"I believe it must have been you Sir Joseph Harden used to talk about. I think he saw you once when you were a boy. I know if he were alive he would have been glad to help you."

"He did help me. I owe my education to the advice he gave my father."

"Is that the case? I am very glad."

She paused, exultant; she felt that she was now upon the right track. "You said you had written other things. What have you written?"

"A lyrical drama for one thing. That sonnet was meant for a sort of motto to it."

A lyrical drama? She was right, then; he was Horace Jewdwine's great "find." If so, the subject was fenced around with difficulty. She must on no account give Horace away. Mr. Rickman had seemed annoyed because she had read his sonnet (which was printed); he would be still more annoyed if he knew that she had read his lyrical drama in manuscript. He was inclined to be reticent about his writings.

Lucia was wrong. Mr. Rickman had never been less inclined to reticence in his life. He wished she had read his drama instead of his sonnet. His spring-time was there; the swift unreturning spring-time of his youth. If she had read his drama she would have believed in his pursuit of the intangible perfection. As it was, she never would believe.

"I wonder," she said, feeling her ground carefully, "if my cousin Horace Jewdwine would be any good to you?"

"Mr. Jewdwine?"

"Do you know him?"

"Yes, slightly. That is—he knows—he knows what I can do. I mean what I've done."

"Really?" The chain of evidence was now complete. "Well, what does he say?"

Rickman laughed as he recalled his last conversation with the critic. "He says I'm one-seventh part of a poet."

"Does he? Then you may be very sure you are a great deal more. My cousin is most terribly exacting. I should be glad if I succeeded in satisfying him; but I don't think I should be seriously unhappy if—if I failed. Did he say anything to discourage, to depress you?"

"Not he. I don't think I should have minded if he had. I felt strong enough for anything then. It was this morning. I was sitting out here, looking at all this beautiful inspiring scenery, when it came to me, that notion that I should never do anything again."

"Is it—" her hesitations were delightful to him—"Is it the want of recognition that disheartens you?"

He laughed again, a healthy, honest laugh. "Oh, dear me, no! I don't worry about recognition. That would be all right if I could go on. But I can't go on."

"Have you ever felt like this before?"

"N—no. No, never. And for the life of me I can't think why I should now."

"And yet you've been making catalogues for years, haven't you?"

Lucia had said to herself, "It's that catalogue *raisonné*, I know."

" Do you like making catalogues? "

" Well, under ordinary circumstances it isn't exactly what you'd call exciting. But I'm afraid that hasn't got anything to do with it this time."

" It may have everything to do with it—such a dreadful kind of work."

" No. It isn't the work that's dreadful."

" Then perhaps it's the worry? And I'm afraid I'm responsible for that."

He started, shaken out of his admirable self-possession by that glaring personality. " How could you be? "

" By insisting on engaging you as I did. From what you told me it's very evident that you had something on your mind, and that the work has been very dreadful, very difficult."

" I *have* something on my mind and—it *has* been difficult —all the same——"

" I wouldn't have pressed you if I had really known. I'm very sorry. Is it too late? Would it be any good if I released you now? "

If she released him!

" Miss Harden, you are most awfully good to me."

" *Would* that help you? "

He looked at her. Over her face there ran again that little ripple of thought and sympathy, like shadow and flame. One fear was removed from him. Whatever happened Miss Harden would never misunderstand him. At the same time he realized that any prospect, however calamitous, would be more endurable than the course she now proposed.

" It wouldn't help me. The best thing I can do is to stay where I am and finish."

" Is that the truth? "

" Nothing but the truth."

(" But not the whole truth," thought Lucia.)

" Well," she said, rising, " whatever you do, don't lose heart."

He smiled drearily. It was all very well to say that when his heart was lost already.

" Wait—wait till next spring comes."

He could put what meaning he liked into that graceful little commonplace. But it dismissed at the same time that it reassured him. The very ease and delicacy with which it was done left him no doubt on that point.

He was not going to accept his dismissal then and there. A bold thought leapt in his brain. Could he—might he——? She had read his sonnet; would it do to ask her to read his drama also? To be sure the sonnet had but fourteen lines, while the drama had twice as many hundred. But the drama, the drama, his beautiful *Helen in Leuce,* was his ultimate achievement, the highest, completest expression of his soul. And what he required of Lucia Harden was not her praise, but fuller, more perfect comprehension. He stood in a cruel and false position, and he longed for her to know the finest and the best of him, before she knew (as she must know) the worst.

She was turning away; but there was a closed gate between her and the hill-path that led down into the valley.

" Miss Harden——"

" Yes? "

She turned. His heart beat violently. He was afraid to look up lest his face should betray his emotion; it must seem so disproportioned to its cause. And yet he was going to ask her for leave to put his drama, the fine off-spring of his soul, into her hands.

" May I send you the drama I spoke of? I would like you to see it."

" Nothing would give me greater pleasure."

He tried to stammer out some words of thanks; but they died before utterance.

" You know your way now, don't you? " said she.

" Yes, thanks."

Her hand was on the gate; he opened it to let her pass. He also made a movement as though he would have held out his hand, but thought better of it, raising his hat instead.

He stood uncovered until she had passed.

He walked up and down the road, giving her time to get well out of sight. Then he returned to the place where he had suffered, and stood a long while looking over the valley.

He knew now the meaning of his great misery; and it was misery no longer. The veil was lifted from the face of Nature; and it was a face that he had never yet seen. It had lost that look of mysterious, indefinable reproach. It was is if the beauty of the land, seeking after the heart that should love it, was appeased and reconciled. He could hear the lyric soul of things most clearly and unmistakably, and it was singing a new song. A strange, double-burdened, contradictory song. There was sorrow in it, such sorrow as her children drink from the breast of the tragic earth; and, through it all and over it, the laughter as of some yet virgin and imperishable joy.

For Nature sings to every poet the song of his own soul.

He spent the last of that Easter Sunday in his shabby little bedroom in the Marine Hotel, where, with windows open to the wind and sea, he sat writing long past midnight. And hope rose again in him as he surveyed the first rough draft—that wild battlefield and slaughter-ground of lines, lines shooting and flying in all directions, lines broken and scattered and routed by other lines, over-ridden and trampled down by word upon triumphing word. Above the hideous confusion at least two verses shone luminous and clear; they had come swinging into the pure ether, full-formed and golden from their birth. And over the whole he wrote in legible characters, "*On Harcombe Hill.*"

His doubt had died there; and on Easter Monday he awoke exulting in another blessed day.

CHAPTER XXII

LUCIA had yielded recklessly to her pleasure-giving instinct, and was only half contented. She had given pleasure to her father by writing him a long letter; she was in a fair way of giving pleasure to Horace Jewdwine by undertaking this monstrous labour of the catalogue; and she had given pleasure to herself in giving pleasure to them. But there was one person to whom she had not given pleasure; and that person was Horace Jewdwine's friend. On the contrary, she had robbed the poor man of the one solitary pleasure he had anticipated in his three-days' holiday; with what disastrous results she had just witnessed.

It was impossible for Lucia to do anybody a wrong, however innocently, without making up for it. On that Sunday evening she conceived a great idea. She had deprived Mr.

Rickman of a small opportunity; she would give him a large one. Restitution was to be on a noble scale. Lucia had a small sum left to her by her grandfather, and even when Mr. Rickman was paid for his four weeks' work on the catalogue that sum would only be reduced to £285. On the strength of it she now proposed to offer Mr. Rickman the post of secretary to herself, for one year, at a salary of a hundred, the remainder to be devoted to his travelling and household expenses. As secretary he would assist her in editing Sir Joseph's unpublished works, while she secured him abundant leisure for his own.

For one year he would be free from all sordid demands on his time and energy. He would be free, for one year, from the shop and the Quarterly Catalogue. He would enrich his mind, and improve his manners, with travel, for one year. At the end of that year he would know if there was anything in him.

In other words she would give the little man his chance. The plan had the further advantage that it would have given her grandfather pleasure if he could have known it. It was also to be presumed that it would give pleasure to Horace Jewdwine, since it was the very thing he himself had said he wished to do for Rickman. Of all conceivable ways of spending Sir Joseph's money it was the fittest and most beautiful. In its lesser way it was in line with the best traditions of the family; for the Hardens had been known for generations as the patrons of poor scholars and struggling men of letters. And as Lucia inherited the intellect of her forefathers in a more graceful, capricious, and spontaneous form, so what in them had been heavy patronage, appeared in her as the pleasure-giving instinct. If she had inherited a large fortune along with it she would have been a lady of lavish and indiscreet munificence.

By way of discretion she slept on her programme before finally committing herself to it. In the morning discretion suggested that she had better wait a week. She decided to act on that suggestion; at the same time she stifled the inner voice which kept telling her that the thing she was doing " to please Horace " would not really please him at all.

She had already ignored the advice he had given her on one point; for Horace had long ago told her plainly that there was no use in editing their grandfather's posthumous works; that on any subject other than textual criticism, Sir Joseph was absurd.

Meanwhile, by sympathy perhaps, Rickman also had become discreet. He entered on his new week a new man. As if he had divined that he was on his trial, he redoubled his prodigious efforts, he applied himself to his hideous task with silent and concentrated frenzy. He seemed to live and move and have his being in the catalogue *raisonné*. Whenever Lucia had occasion to look up at him he was assiduous, rapid, absorbed. He never stopped to talk about Æschylus and Euripides. Now and then they exchanged a necessary word, but not more than once or twice in the morning. If Lucia by any chance gave him an opening he ignored it. He maintained a silence that was almost stern.

Mr. Rickman was undergoing a process of regeneration.

He would not have called it by so fine a name. In fact, in its earlier stages, he seemed to himself to be merely pushing to the point of mania a strong predelection for personal cleanliness. He was first of all possessed, recklessly, ruinously, by a passion for immaculate shirts. He had telegraphed to Spinks to send down all of his linen that he could lay his hands on; meanwhile he had supplied deficiencies at the local haberdasher's. At Mrs. Downey's there was a low standard for the more slender particulars of the toilette, and Mr. Rickman had compared favourably with his fellow-boarders. Now he looked back with incredulity and horror on his former self. Since his person had been brought into daily contact with Miss Harden he had begun to bestow on it a solemn, almost religious care. In the matter of the pocket handkerchief he practised an extreme ritual, permitting himself none but the finest lawn, which he changed after the first trivial crumpling. The pocket-handkerchief being thus glorified and exalted in the heirarchy of dress, one source of painful misgiving was removed.

For the first few days he had been merely formal in this cult of the person. Piety was appeased with external rites and symbols, with changes of vestment, excessive lustrations, and the like. Now he had grown earnest, uncompromising, in his religion; and consistency entailed a further step. Clearly his person, the object of such superstitious veneration, must be guarded from all unbecoming and ridiculous accidents; such an accident, for instance, as getting drunk. If you came to think of it, few things could be more compromising to the person than that (Heavens! if Miss Harden had seen it last Wednesday night!). And since any friendship with ladies of doubtful character might be considered equally derogatory from its dignity, he further resolved to eliminate (absolutely) Miss Poppy Grace. He took no credit for these acts of renunciation. They seemed to him no more morally meritorious than the removal of dust from his coat sleeves, or of ink-stains from his hands.

But though he exterminated the devil in him with so light a touch, it was gravely, tragically almost, that he turned to the expulsion of the Cockney. Intoxication was an unlucky casualty; so, if you came to think of it, was a violent infatuation for Miss Poppy Grace; infinitely more disastrous, more humiliating, were the fatal habits of his speech. Take the occasional but terrific destruction of the aitch. It was worse than drink; it wrecked a man more certainly, more utterly beyond redemption and excuse. It was anxiety on this point that partly accounted for his reserve. He simply dared not talk about Æschylus or Euripides, because such topics were exciting, and excitement was apt to induce this lapse.

But most of all he dreaded the supreme agitation of love. For he knew now perfectly well what had happened to him; though he had never known it happen to him in this manner before. It was love, as his heart had imagined it in the days before he became the thrall of Miss Poppy Grace. He had known the feeling, but until now he had not known the woman who could inspire it. It was as if his heart had renewed its primal virginity in preparation for some divine experience.

The night of Sunday beheld the withdrawal of Mr. Rickman into the immensity of his preposterous dream. From this blessed state he emerged on Monday morning, enlightened as to the whole comedy and tragedy of his passion. To approach Lucia Harden required nothing less than a change of spirit; and Mr. Rickman doubted whether he could manage that. He could only change his shirts. And at this point there arose the hideous fear lest love itself might work to hinder and betray him.

As it turned out, love proved his ally, not his enemy. So far from exciting him, it produced a depression that rendered him disinclined for continuous utterance. In this it did him good service. It prevented him from obtruding his presence unduly on Miss Harden. In his seat at the opposite table he had achieved something of her profound detachment, her consummate calm. And Lucia said to herself, " Good. He can keep quiet for a whole day at a time, which is what I doubted."

Six days had passed in this manner, and he had not yet attempted to penetrate the mystery and seclusion of the Aldine Plato, the Neapolitan Horace, and the *Aurea Legenda* of Wynkyn de Worde. He turned away his eyes from that corner of the bookcase where he had good reason to suppose them to be. He would have to look at them some time, meanwhile he shrank from approaching them as from some gross impiety. His father had written to him several times, making special inquiries after the Aldine Plato, the Neapolitan Horace, and the *Aurea Legenda* of Wynkyn de Worde. He replied with generalities in a guarded manner. He was kept very busy, and was as yet unable to send him any more detailed information. He had begun to feel it strange that these questions should be put, to marvel at the assumption that they could in any way concern him. Rickman's had ceased altogether to exist for him.

He was beginning to lose all sense of strangeness in his position. The six days might have been six years and Court House the home of his infancy, Lucia's presence filled it with so warm an atmosphere of kindness and of love. The very servants had learnt something of her gentle, considerate ways. He was at home there as he had never been at home before. He knew every aspect of the library, through all the changes of the light, from the first waking of its blues and crimsons in the early morning to the broad and golden sweep of noonday through the south window; from the quick rushing flame of the sunset to its premature death among the rafters. Then the lamps; a little light on the centre where they sat, and the thick enclosing darkness round about them.

Each of those six days was like a Sunday, and Sunday to Rickman was always a day of beatitude, being the day of dreams. And she, in her sweet, unfamiliar beauty, only half real, though so piercingly present to him, was an incarnate dream. She always sat with her back to the south window, so that her head and shoulders appeared somewhat indistinct against the outer world, a background of flower-beds and green grass and sky, covered with the criss-cross of the leaded lozenge panes and the watery shimmer of the glass. The outline of her head was indicated by a little line of light that threaded her hair and tipped the curve of her small ears. He knew every change of her face, from its serene, faint-tinted morning look, to its flower-like pallor in the dusk. He knew only too well its look under the lamp light after a hard day's work; the look that came with a slight blurring of its soft contours; and a drooping of the tired eyelids over pathetic eyes. He saw what Jewdwine had failed to see, that Lucia was not strong.

Six days, and three days before that, nine days in all; and it was as if he had known that face all his life; he could not conceive a time when he had not known it. As for the things he had known, horrible, curious, and incredible things, such as Rickman's, Mrs. Downey's, St. Pancras Church, and the editor of *The Museion* (whose last letter he had left unanswered), they belonged to an infinitely remote and unimaginable past. It seemed the entirely obvious and natural thing that he should be sitting there alone with Lucia Harden. He was never very far from her. The east window looked across the courtyard to the window of her drawing-room; he could see her there, sitting in the lamp-light; he could hear the music that she made. Her bedroom was above the library; it was pleasant to him to know that when she left him it was to sleep there overhead. The deep quiet of his passion had drawn him again into his dream.

And then, all of a sudden, he woke up and broke the silence. It was ten o'clock on Saturday evening. Lucia had shifted the shade of the lamp. From where he sat her face was in twilight and her body in darkness. He had got up to put a book into its place, when he saw her leaning back and covering her eyes with her hand.

The sight was too much for him. He came up and stood beside her.

" Miss Harden, I don't like this. I—I can't stand it any longer."

She looked up. She had been unaware of Mr. Rickman for the last hour, and certainly did not expect to find him there.

" What is it that you can't stand? "

" To see you working from morning to night. It—it isn't right, you know. You're paying me for this, and doing the half of it yourself."

" I'm not doing a quarter of it. You forget that you're working three times as fast as I can."

" And you forget that you're working three times as hard."

" No. I'm leaving the hard work to you."

" I wish you'd leave it all to me."

" In that case we should never have finished," said the lady.

He smiled. " Perhaps not. At any rate you've worked so hard that I can finish it now myself."

She looked round the room. Undisguised fatigue was in the look. What they had done was nothing to what they had yet to do.

" You can't," she said.

" I can. Easily. I miscalculated the time it would take."

She said nothing, for she knew that he had lied. His miscalculation was all the other way. She bent again over her work. It was all that he could do not to lift her arms, gently but firmly, from the table, to take away her pen and ink, and put out her lamp. He would have liked to have done some violence to the catalogue.

" I say, you know, you'll make yourself ill. You're burning the candle at both ends. May I suggest that the game isn't worth the candle? "

" Have you very much more to do? "

" About two hours' work. Would it be impertinent to say that I could do it better by myself? "

She looked at her watch and ignored his last question. " You can't do two hours' work. It's twenty minutes past your time already."

Past his time, indeed! As if he hadn't been working past his time every night since he came. She had grown mighty particular all of a sudden!

"The presence of these engaging little Elzevirs is a terrible temptation to a second-hand bookseller, still I believe you can trust me with them alone."

From the expression of her face he gathered that this remark was even more impertinent than the other. He had meant it to be.

"I really think," said the lady, "that you had better go."

"Just as you please; I shall only have to sit up two hours later to-morrow night."

He walked to his place with his head thrown farther back and his chin thrust farther forward than ever. He began to sort and arrange his papers preparatory to his departure. It took him five minutes. At the end of the five minutes he was aware that Lucia had risen and was bidding him good-night.

"You were quite right," she was saying. "I *am* tired, and I had better leave off. If you had rather stay and finish, please stay."

At those words Mr. Rickman was filled with a monstrous and amazing courage. He made for the door, crossing without a tremor the whole length of the library. He reached the door before Miss Harden, and opened it. He returned her good-night with a hope that she would be rested in the morning. And as he went back to his solitary labour he smiled softly to himself, a smile of self-congratulation.

He had meant her to go—and she had gone.

Upstairs in her room overhead Lucia communed with her own face in the glass.

"My private secretary?"

The face in the glass looked dubious.

"Of course I would rather have a gentleman for my private secretary. Some people would say he isn't a gentleman." (She had said it herself the other day.)

The face in the glass smiled dimly, between two parted veils of hair.

"What *is* a gentleman?"

The face in the glass suggested that this was indeed a subtle and a difficult question.

"It was not his business if I chose to tire myself. Would it have been his business if he'd been a gentleman?"

The face in the glass offered no opinion.

"I think I like him best when he's impertinent. He is so *very* funny, poor dear, when he tries to be polite."

The face in the glass, framed by two white arms raising a column of hair, was suffused with rosy mirth.

"I wonder what Horace really thinks of him?"

The face, triumphantly crowned with its dark coil, looked grave.

"He *is* a gentleman. At least, he lied like one."

By this time Lucia was in bed, and there was no face in the glass to dispute or corroborate that statement.

CHAPTER XXIII

THE next morning he gave into her hands the manuscript of *Helen in Leuce*. It had arrived two or three days ago, packed by Spinks between his new shirts. She had expected to feel a little guilty as she received the familiar sheets; but as she glanced over them she saw that they were anything but familiar; what she had to deal with was a clean new draft.

She had a fairly clear recollection of the outline of the play.

In Act I Helen lands in the enchanted island of Leuce, and is found watching the ship that brought her sailing away with the dead Menelaus, for he, being altogether mortal, may not follow her there. The Chorus tells the story of Helen, her rape by Theseus, her marriage with Menelaus, her flight with Paris, the tragedy of Troy and her return to Argos. It tells how through all her adventures the godhead in her remained pure, untouched, holding itself apart.

In Act II Helen is asleep, for the soul of Leda still troubles her divinity, and her mortality is heavy upon her. Helen rises out of her sleep; her divinity is seen struggling with her mortality, burning through the beauty of her body. Desire wakens in Achilles, and in Helen terror and anguish, as of one about to enter again into the pain of mortal life. But he may not touch her till he, too, has put on immortality. Helen prays for deliverance from the power of Aphrodite. She rouses in Achilles a great anger against Aphrodite by reminding him of the death of Patroclus; so that he calls down upon the goddess the curses of all the generations of men.

It was this Act that lived in Lucia's memory. Act III she had not yet read, but she had gathered from the argument that Pallas Athene was there to appear to Achilles and divest him of his mortality; that she was to lead him to Helen, whose apotheosis was supposed to be complete; the Act concluding with two choruses, an epithalamium celebrating the wedding of Helen and Achilles, and a Hymn in praise of Athene.

She remembered how when Horace had first told her of the subject, Helen in Leuce, she had looked it up in Lemprière, found a reference in Homer and another in Euripides, had shaken her head and said, " What can he make of that? " Now for the first time she saw what he had made of it. Rickman's Helen was to the Helen of Euripides what Shelley's Prometheus is to the Prometheus of Æschylus. Rickman had done what seemed good in his own eyes. He had made his own metres, his own myth and his own drama. A drama of flesh and blood, a drama of spirit, a drama of dreams. Only a very young poet could have had the courage to charge it with such a weight of symbolism; but he had contrived to breathe into his symbols the breath of life; the phantoms of his brain, a shadowy Helen and Achilles, turned into flesh and blood under his hands. It was as if their bodies, warm, throbbing, full-formed, instinct with irresistible and violent life, had come crashing through the delicate fabric of his dream.

As she read Lucia's mind was troubled, shaken out of its critical serenity. She heard a new music; she felt herself in the grasp of a new power, a new spirit. It was not the classic spirit. There was too much tumult in its harmonies, as if the music of a whole orchestra had been torn from its instruments and flung broadcast, riding triumphantly on the wings of a great wind. There were passages (notably the Hymn to Aphrodite in the second Act) that brought the things of sense and the terrible mysteries of flesh and blood so near to her that she flinched. Rickman had made her share the thrilling triumph, the flushed passion of his youth. And when she was most hurt and bruised under the confusion of it, he lifted her up and carried her away into the regions of spiritual beauty and eternal strength.

It was all over; the tumult of the flesh and the agony of the spirit; over, too, the heaven-piercing singing, the rapture of spirit and of flesh made one. Rickman had ended his amazing drama with the broad majestic music of his Hymn to Athene. Lucia had borne up under the parting of Helen and Menelaus; but she was young, and at that touch of superb and ultimate beauty, two tears, the large and heavy tears of youth, fell upon Rickman's immaculate manuscript, where their marks remain to this day. The sight of them had the happy effect of making her laugh, and then, and not till then, she thought of Rickman—Mr. Rickman. She thought of him living a dreadful life among dreadful people; she thought of him sitting in his father's shop making catalogues *raisonnés;* she thought of him sitting in the library making one at that very moment. And this was the man she had had the impertinence to pity; whom Horace would say she now proposed to patronise. As she stood contemplating the pile of manuscript before her, Miss Lucia Harden felt (for a great lady) quite absurdly small.

In that humble mood she was found by Miss Palliser.

" What's up? " said Kitty.

" Kitty, that little man in there—he's written the most beautiful play. It's so terribly sad."

" What, the play? "

" No, the little man. It's a classic, Kitty—ti'll live."

" Then I'm sure you needn't pity him. Let's have a look at the thing." Miss Palliser dipped into the manuscript, and was lost.

" By Jove," she said, " it does look ripping. Where does the sadness come in? "

" He thinks he'll never write another."

" Well, perhaps he won't."

" He will—think of it—he's a genius, the real thing, this time. Only—he has to stand behind a counter and make catalogues."

Miss Palliser meditated. " Does he—does he by any chance drop his aitches? "

" Kitty, he *does.*"

" Then Lucy, dear child, beware, beware, his flashing eyes, his floating hair——"

" Don't. That little man is on my mind."

"I shouldn't let him stop there too long, if I were you. He might refuse to get off."

"I must do something for him, and I must do it now. What *can* I do?"

"Not much, I imagine."

"I—I think I'll ask him to dinner."

"I wouldn't. You said he drops his aitches. Weave," said Miss Palliser, "a circle round him thrice, and close your eyes with holy dread, but whatever you do, don't ask him to dinner."

"Why not?"

"Because ten to one it would make him most horribly uncomfortable. Not that that matters so much. But wouldn't the faithful Robert think it a little odd?"

"Robert is too faithful to think anything at all."

"I'm not so sure of that. Personally, I wish you *would* ask him to dinner—I seem to foresee a certain amount of amusing incident."

"Well, I don't think I will ask him—to dinner. Perhaps he wouldn't enjoy it. But as I've got to talk over his play with him, I should like to ask him to something."

"Ask him to coffee afterwards."

"Coffee hardly seems enough."

"It depends. Serve it festively—on a table, and pour it out yourself. Offer him strange and bewitching forms of food. Comfort him with—with angel cake—and savoury sandwiches and bread and butter."

"I see—a sort of compromise?"

"Exactly. Society, my child, is based on compromise."

"Very well, then, I'll write him a note."

She wrote it, and sent Robert with it to the library.

"I suppose," said she, "it's about time to dress for dinner?"

"Don't make yourself too pretty, dear."

Lucia looked back through the doorway.

"I shall make myself as pretty as ever I can. He has had nothing but ugly things to look at all his life."

Miss Palliser apostrophized the departing figure of her friend.

"Oh, Lucy, Lucy, what an angelic little fool you *are!*"

CHAPTER XXIV

HALF-PAST SIX, and Miss Harden had not yet appeared in the library. It was the first time that Rickman had passed a whole day without seeing her. He began
to be uneasy, to wonder whether she were really ill. At seven
he was leaving the house as usual for his hotel when Robert
brought him a little three-cornered note.

"DEAR MR. RICKMAN [it said—Dear Mr. Rickman!] : You see I
have taken your advice, and given myself a holiday. I have spent
it very pleasantly—reading *Helen in Leuce*. It would give me
much pleasure if you would come in for coffee this evening, about
eight o'clock. We can then talk it over.
        "Very truly yours,
                "LUCIA HARDEN.
    "You need only send a verbal answer."

A verbal answer? No. That would never do. He
could not trust himself with speech, but in writing he knew
he was impeccable.

"DEAR MISS HARDEN : How very kind of you! But I am sorry
that you did not give yourself a complete rest. I should be sorrier,
if I were not so grateful for the trouble you have taken. It will
give me great pleasure to come in this evening at the time you name.
        "With many thanks, yours very truly,
                "S. K. RICKMAN."

He was not pleased with it; it erred on the side of
redundancy; he had not attained the perfect utterance, the
supreme simplicity. But he was obliged to let it go. Two
hours later Robert announced that coffee was served in
the drawing-room.

It seemed that to reach the drawing-room you had to
cross the whole length of the house from west to east. In
this passage he realized (what his mind had not greatly
dwelt upon) the antiquity of the Hardens, and the march
of their splendid generations. Going from the Tudor
Library into the grim stone hall of the Court House, he
took a cold plunge backward into time. Thence his progress was straightforward, bringing him into the Jacobean
picture gallery that cut the house from north to south. Here
he paused, perceiving that the double line of portraits

began with a Vandyck and a Lely. Robert stood with his hand on the brass rose knob of an oak door; in his eternal attitude of affection, mingled with immobile respect, he waited for the moment when Mr. Rickman should elect to tear himself from the Lely and the Vandyck. The moment came, and Mr. Rickman heard himself announced in a clear high voice as he passed over the threshold.

He found himself in a long oak-panelled room; that room whose west window looked out across the courtyard to the east window of the library. It was almost dark, except for a small fire-lit, lamp-lit square at the far end. Lucia was sitting in a low chair by the fire-place, under the tall shaded lamp, where the light fell full on her shoulders. She was not alone. On a settee by the other side of the open hearth sat the young lady who had intruded on his solitude in the library. The presence of the young lady filled him with anxiety and dismay.

He had to cross a vast, dim space before he reached that lighted region. With what seemed to him a reeling and uncertain gait, he approached over the perilously slippery parquet. Miss Harden rose and came forward, mercifully cutting short that frightful passage from the threshold to her chair.

Lucia had not carried out the intention she had announced to Kitty. She had dressed in haste; but in Rickman's eyes the effect was that which Kitty had seen fit to deprecate. She had made herself very pretty indeed. He could not have given a very clear account of it, could not have said whether the thing she wore, that floating, sweeping, curling, trailing, folding, and caressing garment were made of grey gossamer in white or white in grey, but he was aware that it showed how divinely her slender body carried its flower, her head; showed that her arms, her throat, and the first sweep and swell of her shoulders, were of one tone with the luminous pallor of her face. Something in the dress, in her bearing and manner of approach, gave her the assured charm of womanhood for the unfinished loveliness of youth.

She introduced him to her friend Miss Palliser, whose green eyes smiled in recognition. He bowed with the stiffness of a back unaccustomed to that form of salutation. He hardly knew what happened after that, till he found himself backing, nervously, ridiculously backing into a lonely seat in the middle of the room.

The three were now grouped in a neat geometrical figure, Mr. Rickman, on the chair of his choice, forming the apex of a prolonged triangle, having the hearthrug for its base. He was aware that Miss Harden and Miss Palliser were saying something; but he had no idea of what they said. He sat there wondering whether he ought to be seated at all, whether he ought not rather to be hovering about that little table, ready to wait upon Miss Palliser. He was still wondering when Miss Palliser got up with the evident intention of waiting upon him.

That, he knew, was all wrong; it was not to be permitted for a moment. Inspired by a strange, unnatural courage, he advanced and took his coffee from her hand, retreating with it to his remote and solitary position.

He sat silent, moodily looking at his coffee, stirring it from time to time and wondering whether he would ever be brave enough to drink it. He waited for an opportunity of dispatching it unperceived. The presence of Miss Palliser paralyzed him. He wondered whether he ought to say anything to her or to Miss Harden, or to neither or to both; he tried to think of something suitable to say.

Meanwhile Miss Palliser talked for all three. It seemed that she had dined with her friend on her way to an " at home " in Harmouth.

" Bread and butter? " said she judicially. " N—no, I think not, thanks. I've got to eat jellies and sandwiches and things for two hours straight on end. It sounds horrible, but I shall be driven to it. At the Flossers'," she explained for her friend's benefit, " you must either eat or talk; and if you can't talk scandal you're not expected to talk at all." And still talking Miss Palliser slowly bore down upon Mr. Rickman with a plate of bread and butter.

Mr. Rickman's earnest and chivalrous endeavour to forestall her caused a rug to slide under his feet. It slid, and Mr. Rickman with it, for quite a considerable distance; and though Mr. Rickman, indeed, preserved the erect attitude by a series of complicated movements (a superb triumph of muscular ingenuity, but somewhat curious and fantastic as a spectacle), his coffee cup flung itself violently on its side, and poured out its contents at the lady's feet.

He looked at Miss Harden. She was smiling; for who wouldn't have smiled? But her smile became almost tender in her perception of his distress.

Miss Palliser continued to talk.

"Ah," said Miss Palliser, "I was waiting for that to happen. I've been wondering which of us would do it first. I rather thought it would be me; but for pure, delightful unexpectedness, give me a parquet floor. I wouldn't mop it up with my pocket handkerchief, if I were you."

"No—please—it doesn't matter. It happens every day."

"And it puts a visitor on an agreeable footing at once. You *can't* keep up any stiffness or formality, when what you took for a drawing-room turns itself into a skating rink."

"Quite so," said Rickman, "and if you fall, it breaks the ice." He was entering shyly into her humour. "I'm afraid my be-h-haviour wasn't quite so h-happy and spontaneous as it might have been."

"I assure you it was extremely naïve and natural, as far as it went," said Kitty, laughing.

"I think you were very clever to keep your balance," said Lucia.

"Too clever by half. If you'd been a really genial person, Mr. Rickman, you'd have lost it."

Thus lightly did they cover his confusion, thus adroitly turn the malignant hand of circumstance.

"Kitty," said Lucia, "I don't want to hurry you, but it's past nine, and you'll *have* to hurry if you don't want to be late."

"But I do want to be late. I mean to be late. I can't eat sandwiches for more than two hours."

And Kitty flung herself on her settee again in cross-legged, unpremeditated ease, and there she conversed with Mr. Rickman as if she had known him all her life. Kitty was amused at last.

So was Mr. Rickman. He found himself answering with appropriate light-heartedness; he heard himself laughing in the manner of one infinitely at ease. It was impossible to be anything else in Kitty Palliser's society. He was, in fact, surprised at himself. Though it was only by immense expenditure of thought and effort that he managed to secure the elusive aspirate, still he secured it. Never for a moment did he allow himself to be cheated into the monstrous belief that its absence was, or could, be unperceived.

But though he was grateful to Miss Palliser, he wished all the time that she would go. At last she rose and drew her fur-collared cloak about her with a slow, reluctant air.

" Well, I suppose I must be off. I shall be back before eleven, Lucy. Good-night, Mr. Rickman, if I don't see you again."

He was alone with Lucia Harden.

It was one thing to be alone with Lucia Harden in the library or on Harcombe Moor, and quite another thing to be left with her in the lamp-lit, fire-lit room. The library belonged to her race and to their historic past; the moor to nature and to all time; this room to her and to the burning present. There was no sign or suggestion of another presence.

A kindly room (barring that parquet floor!); a beautiful room; full of warm lights, and broad and pleasing shadows; furnished with an extreme simplicity, such bareness as musicians love. He was struck by that absence of all trivial decoration, all disturbing and irrelevant detail. In such a room, the divinity of the human form was not dwarfed or obscured by excess of furniture. Such a room, he reflected, was also eminently disadvantageous to any figure that was not entirely sure of its divinity. But for two persons who desired to know each other better there couldn't be a better place. It left them so securely, so intimately alone.

For the first time, then, he was alone with Lucia Harden. She had risen and had unlocked a drawer in the writing-table near her, and taken out the thick pile of manuscript. He noticed that she detached from it some loose pencilled sheets and put them back into the drawer. She seated herself in her old place and signed to him to take the low chair beside her.

He approached her (for the first time) without nervousness or embarrassment; for he saw his *Helen* lying on her knees and knew that she held his dreams in her soul. He had made her acquainted with the best and highest in him, and she would judge him by that alone. In her sight his genius would stand apart from all in him that was jarring and obscure. It at least was untouched by the accident of his birth, the baseness of his false position.

"I sent for you," said she, "because I wanted to talk to you about this, while it is all fresh in my mind. I thought we could talk better here."

"Thanks. I want awfully to know what you have to say."

"I can't have anything to say that you don't know already."

"I—I know nothing." (What a hypocrite he felt as he said it!)

"Nor I. As far as knowledge goes I haven't any right to speak. Only—the other evening, you expressed such absolute disbelief in yourself——"

"I was perfectly sincere."

"I know you were. That's what made me believe in you."

(Well, then, if *that* was what made her believe in him he would continue to express disbelief in himself.)

She paused. "It's the little men, isn't it, the men of talent, that are always so self-conscious and so sure? I don't know much about it, but it seems to me that genius isn't bound to be like that. It might be so different from your ordinary self that you couldn't be aware of it in the ordinary way. There would always be a sort of divine uncertainty about it."

"I'm afraid I don't agree with you. All the great geniuses have been not only aware of themselves, but most uncommonly certain."

"Still, their genius may have been the part of themselves they understood least. If they had tried to understand it, they would have doubted too."

"There's something in that. You mean genius understands everything—except itself?"

"I think that's what I meant."

"Yes; but whether genius understands itself or not, whatever it does, you see, it doesn't doubt."

"Doesn't it? Have you read Keats' letters? *He* doubted."

"Only when he was in love with Fanny Brawne."

He paused abruptly. He was seized by an idea, a rushing irresistible idea, that lifted him off his feet and whirled him suddenly into a region of light, tumultuous and profound. Keats was in love when he doubted. Could that be the explanation of his own misgiving?

" That," he said hastily, " that's another thing altogether. Anyway, if you don't believe in yourself, you'll have some difficulty in making other people believe in you."

" And if other people *do* believe in you, before you believed in yourself?"

" Before? It might be done before, but not after. You may make a man conceited, but you can't give him back the conceit he had on Saturday, if he's lost it all by Monday."

" That means that you know you've written a beautiful thing and you only think you'll never write another."

" Perhaps it does." (He had to keep it up for the pleasure of hearing her say she believed in him.)

" Well, I don't suppose you will write another *Helen in Leuce.*"

" I'm afraid not." He went on to tell her that the wonder was how he wrote the thing at all. It had been done anyhow, anywhere, in successive bursts or spasms of creative energy; the circumstances of his life (he referred to them with some diffidence) not being exactly favourable to sustained effort. " How did *you* feel about it?" he inquired.

" I can hardly tell you. I think I felt as you feel about anything beautiful that comes to you for the first time. I don't know what it is you've done. It's as if something had been done to me, as if I'd been given a new sense. It's like hearing Beethoven or Wagner for the first time." As she spoke she saw the swift blood grow hot in his face, she saw the slight trembling of the hand that propped his chin and she thought, " Poor fellow, so much emotion for a little praise?"

" What did you mean by it?" she said.

He considered a moment—as who should say " What the dickens did I mean by it?"

Lucia leaned back now, for the first time, in the breathing space he gave her, attentively watching the man she proposed to make her secretary; and as she watched him she found herself defending him against her own criticism. If he dropped his aitches it was not grossly as the illiterate do; she wouldn't go so far as to say he *dropped* them; he slipped them, slided them; it was no more than a subtle slur, a delicate elision. And that only in the commoner words, the current coin of his world. He was as right as possible, she noticed, in all words whose acquaintance he had made on his own account. And his voice—his voice pleaded against her prejudice with all its lyric modulations. Much may be forgiven to such voices. And there were other points in his favour.

Kitty was right. He was nice to look at. She was beginning to know the changes of his face; she liked it best when, as now, its features became suddenly subtle and serious and straight. At the moment his eyes, almost opaque from the thickness of their blue, were dull under the shadow of the eye-bone. But when he grew excited (as he frequently did) they had a way of clearing suddenly, they flashed first colour at you, then light, then fire. That was what they were doing now; for now he let himself go.

His Helen, he said, was the eternal Beauty, the eternal Dream. Beauty, perpetually desirous of incarnation, perpetually unfaithful to flesh and blood; the Dream that longs for the embrace of reality, that wanders, never satisfied till it finds a reality as immortal as itself. Helen couldn't stay in the house of Theseus, or the house of Menelaus, or the house of Priam. Theseus was a fool if he thought he would take her by force, and Paris was a fool if he thought he could keep her for pleasure; and Menelaus was the biggest fool of all if he expected her to bear him children and to mind his house. They all do violence to the divinity in her, and she vindicates it by eluding them. Her vengeance is the vengeance of an immortal made victim to mortality. Helen of Argos and Troy is the Dream divorced from reality.

"Yes—yes. I see." She leaned back in her chair fascinated, while the wonderful voice went on, covering its own offences with exquisite resonances and overtones.

"This divorce is the cause of all the evil that can happen to men and women. Because of it Helen becomes an instrument in the hands of Aphrodite—Venus Genetrix— do you see? She's the marriage-breaker, the destroyer of men. She brings war and pestilence and death. She is the supreme illusion. But *Helen in Leuce* is the true Helen. In Leuce, you know, she appears as she is, in her divine form, freed from the tyranny of perpetual incarnation. I can't explain it, but that's the idea. Don't you see how the chorus in praise of Aphrodite breaks off into a prayer for deliverance from her? And at the end I make Athene bring Helen to Achilles, who was her enemy in Troy.— That's part of the idea, too."

" And Achilles? "

" Achilles is strength, virility, indestructible *will*."

It seemed that while trivial excitement corrupted, intense feeling purified his speech, and as he pronounced these words every accent was irreproachable. A lyric exaltation seemed to have seized him, as it had seized him in the reading of Sophocles.

" The idea is reconciliation, the wedding of the Dream to reality. I haven't made up my mind whether the last chorus will be the Epithalamium or the Hymn to Pallas Athene."

He paused for reflection, and in reflection the lyric rapture died. He added pensively. " The 'Ymn, I think."

Lucia averted her ardent gaze before the horror in his young blue eyes. They were the eyes of some wild winged creature dashed down from its soaring and frenzied by the fall. Lucia could have wept for him.

" Then this," said she, feigning an uninterrupted absorption in the manuscript, " this is not what my cousin saw? "

" No, h—he only saw the first draft of the two first Acts. It was horribly stiff and cold. He said it was classical; I don't know what he'd say it is now. I began it that way, and it finished itself this way, and then I re-wrote the beginning."

" I see. I see. Something happened to you." As she spoke she still kept her eyes fixed on the manuscript, as if she were only reading what was written there. " You woke up—in the middle of the second Act, wasn't it?— and came to life. You heard the world—the real world— calling to you, and Helen and Achilles and all the rest of them turned to flesh and blood on your hands."

" Yes," he said, " they were only symbols and I'd no notion what they meant till they left off meaning it."

She looked from the manuscript to him. " You know in your heart you *must* be certain of yourself. And yet—I suspect the trouble with you is that *your* dream is divorced from reality."

He stared in amazement at the young girl who thus interpreted him to herself. At this rate he saw no end to her powers of divination. There were depths in his life where her innocence could not penetrate, but she had seized on the essential. It had been as she had said. That first draft was the work of the young scholar poet, the adorer of classic form, the dreamer who found in his dreams escape from the grossness of his own lower nature and from the brutalities of the world he lived in. A great neo-classic drama was to be his protest against modernity and actuality. Then came an interval of a year, in which he learnt many things that are not to be found in books, or adequately expressed through a neo-classic drama; and the thing was finished and re-written at a time when, as she had said, something had happened to him; when that same gross actual world was making its claims felt through all his senses. And he was suffering now the deep melancholy of perspicuous youth, unable to part with its dreams, but aware that its dreams are hopelessly divorced from reality. That was so; but how on earth did she know it?

"It's hardly a divorce," he said, laughing. "I think it's separation by mutual consent."

"That's a pity," said she, "life is so lovable."

"I don't always find it either lovable or loving. But then it's life in a fifth-rate boarding-house in Bloomsbury—if you know what that is."

She did not know what that was, and her silence suggested that she conceived it to be something too unpleasant to discuss with him.

"I work eight hours a day in my father's shop——"

"And when your work is done?"

"I go back to the boarding-house and dine."

"And after dinner?"

Mr. Rickman became visibly embarrassed. "Oh, after dinner, there are the streets, and the theatres, and—and things."

"Nothing else?"

"Nothing. Except a club I belong to."

"That's something, isn't it? You make friends."

"I don't know anybody in it, except Mr. Jewdwine;

and I don't really know him. It's the shop, you know. You forget the shop."

" No I don't forget it; but I wish you would. If only you could get away from it, away from everything. If you could get away from London altogether for a while."

" If—if? I shall never get away."

" Why not? I've been thinking it over. I wonder whether things could not be made a little easier for you? You ought to make your peace with the world, you know. Supposing you could go and live where the world happens to be beautiful, in Rome or Florence or Venice, wouldn't that reconcile you to reality? "

" It might. But I don't see how I'm to go and live there. You see there's the shop. There always is the shop."

" Would it be impossible to leave it for a while? "

" Not impossible, perhaps; but "—he smiled, " well—highly imprudent."

" But if something else were open to you? "

" Nothing else is, at present. Most doors seem closed pretty tight except the one marked Tradesmen's Entrance."

" You can't ' arrive ' by that."

" Not, I admit, with any dignity. My idea was to walk up the steps—there are a great many steps, I know—to the big front door and keep on knocking at it till they let me in."

" I'm afraid the front door isn't always open very early in the day. But there may be side doors."

" I don't know where to find them. And if I did, they would be bolted, too."

" Not the one I am thinking of. Would you like to go abroad, to Italy? "

" There are a great many things I should like to do, and not the remotest chance of doing them."

" Supposing that you got the chance, some way—even if it wasn't quite the best way—would you take it? "

" The chance? I wish I saw one! "

" I think I told you I was going abroad to join my father. We shall be in Italy for some time. When we are settled, in Rome, for the winter, I shall want a secretary. I'm thinking of editing my grandfather's unpublished writings, and I can't do this without a scholar's help. It struck me that if you want to go abroad, and nothing better turns up,

you might care to take this work for a year. For the sake
of seeing Italy."

Seeing Italy? Italy that he had once desired with all
his heart to see. And now it was nothing to him that
he would see Italy; the point was that he would see her.
Talk of open doors! It was dawning on him that the
door of heaven was being opened to him. He could say
nothing. He leaned forward staring at his own loosely
clasped hands.

She mistook his silence for hesitation, and it was her
turn to become diffident and shy. " The salary would not
be very large, I'm afraid——"

The salary? He smiled. She had opened the door of
heaven for him and she actually proposed to pay him for
walking in!

" But there would be no expenses, and you would have
space and time. I should not want your help for more
than three or four hours in the morning. After that you
would be absolutely free."

And still he said nothing. But the fine long nervous
hands tortured each other in their clasp. So this was what
came of keeping up the farce?

" Of course," she said, " you must think it over."

" Miss Harden, I don't know how to thank you. I don't
know what to say."

" Don't say anything. Think."

" I don't know what to think."

But he was thinking hard; trying to realize where he was
and what was being proposed to him. To have entertained
the possibility of such a proposal in the middle of last week
would have argued that he was drunk. And here he was
indubitably, conspicuously sober. Sober? Well, not exactly. He ought never to have taken that little cup of
black coffee! Was there any difference beween drinking
champagne with Miss Poppy Grace and drinking coffee
with Lucia Harden, when the effect was so indistinguishably
the same? Or, rather, for completeness and splendour of
hallucination there was no comparison. He was drunk,
drunk as he had never been drunk before, most luminously,
most divinely intoxicated with that little cup of black coffee.

And yet her scheme was entirely in keeping with that
ideal and fantastic world he lived in; a world which in the

last six days had yet, for him, the illusion of reality. He was aware that it *was* illusion. An illusion which she blindly shared.

He was overcome by the appalling extent of his knowledge and her ignorance. She thought she was rich; he knew that she was in all probability poor. She thought a hundred a year (or thereabouts) an insignificant sum; he knew that before long she might have less than that to live on. She thought herself at the present moment a wise and understanding woman. He knew that she was a child. A child playing with its own beautiful imagination.

He wondered how much of him she understood. Should he tell her that she did not understand him at all; that she was engaging as her private secretary a young man who drank, who was quite shockingly drunk no longer ago than the middle of last week; a young man who was an intimate friend of a lady whom it was impossible to describe accurately in her presence? Or did she understand him better than he understood himself? Had she, with her child's innocence, the divine lucidity of a child? Did she fail to realize his baser possibilities because they were the least real part of him? Or was she, in this, ideal and fantastic too?

Whichever it was, her fascination was so persuasive that he found himself yielding to her proposal as if it were the most natural thing in the world. He accepted it as humbly, as gratefully, as gravely, as if it were a thing actually in her power to bestow. If he could have suspected her of any intention to patronize him, he could not have resented it, knowing as he did its pathetic impotence.

" I know it isn't the best way," she said, " but it *is* a way."

" It's a glorious way."

" I don't know about the glory. But you will see Florence and Venice and Rome, and they are glorious."

Yes, he would see them, if she said so. Why not? In this ideal and fantastic world, could any prospect be more ideal and fantastic than another?

" And you will have plenty of time to yourself. You will be a great deal alone. Too much alone perhaps. You must think of that. It might really be better for you to stay in London where you are beginning to make friends."

Was she trying to break it to him as gently, as delicately

as possible that there would be no intimacy between him and her? That as her private secretary his privacy would be painfully unbroken?

She saw it and corrected herself. "Friends, I mean, who may be able to help you more. You must choose between the two advantages. It will be a complete break with your old life."

"That would be the best thing that could happen to me."

This time she did not see. "Well—don't be in a hurry. There isn't any hurry. Remember, it means a whole year out of your life."

A whole year out of his life? Was that the way she looked at it?

Yes. She was giving him his chance; but she did not conceive herself to be giving him anything more. She understood him sufficiently to trust him; her insight went so far and no farther. She actually believed that there could be a choice for him between seeing her every day for a whole year and never seeing her again. Evidently she had not the remotest conception of his state of mind. He doubted whether it could have occurred to her to allow for the possibility of her private secretary falling in love with her in the innermost privacy of his secretaryship. He saw that hers was not the order of mind that entertains such possibilities on an intimate footing. She was generous, large-sighted; he understood that she would let herself be carried away on the superb sweep of the impersonal, reckless of contingencies. He also understood that with this particular private secretary she would consider herself safe. The social difference was as much her protection as some preposterous incompatibility of age. And as if that were not enough, in their thoughts they were so akin that she might feel herself guarded from him by some law of spiritual consanguinity.

"Oh, my life," he said with a queer laugh that sounded like a sob. "Well, I must be getting back to my work."

"You are *not* going to work again to-night?"

"I must." Yet he did not get up to go. He seemed to be waiting to say something. "I—I haven't thanked you. I don't know how to."

"Don't try. I've done nothing. There is little that one person can do for another."

" There's something that you might do for me—some day
—if I might ask—if you would."

" What is that? "

She followed his gaze as it travelled into the depth of the
room beyond the circle of the lamp-light, where the grand
piano stood. Its keyboard shone in an even band of white,
its massive body merged in the gleaming darkness.

" If you would play to me—some day."

" I will play to you with pleasure." Her voice sounded
as if she were breathing more freely; perhaps she had wondered what on earth he was going to say. " Now, if you
like."

Why not? If she had enjoyed his music, had he not a
right to enjoy hers? Why should she not give him that little
pleasure, he who had so few?

" What shall I play? "

" I should like to hear that thing you were playing the
other night."

" Let me think. Oh, the ' Sonata Appassionata.' "

" Yes, if it isn't too late." The moment he had said it he
reflected that that was a scruple that might have been better
left to the lady.

He watched her grey-white figure departing into the dusk
of the room. He longed to follow, but some fear restrained
him. He remained where he was, leaning back in the deep
chair under the lamp, while she sat down there, in the dusk,
playing to him the Sonata Appassionata.

The space around the lamp grew dim to him; she had
gathered into herself all the whiteness of the flame; the
music was a part of her radiance, it was the singing of her
pulses, the rhythm of her breath.

When she had stopped playing he rose and held out his
hand to say good-night.

" Thank you. I don't think so badly of my life now.
You've given me one perfect moment."

" Are you so fond of music? "

She was about to ring when he prevented her.

" Please don't ring. I can find my way. I'd rather."

She judged that he desired to keep the perfection of his
moment unimpaired. She understood his feeling about it,
for the Sonata Appassionata is a most glorious and moving
composition, and she had played it well.

It was true that he desired to be alone; and he took advantage of his solitude to linger in the picture gallery. He went down the double row of portraits that began with Sir Thomas, the maker of madrigals, and ended with Sir Frederick, the father of Lucia. He paused at each, searching for Lucia's likeness in the likeness of those dead and gone gentlemen and ladies; gentlemen with grave and intellectual faces, some peevish, others proud (rather like Jewdwine), ladies with faces joyous, dreamy, sad, voluptuous, tender, and insipid, faces alike only in their indestructible racial distinction. Lucia had taken nothing from them but what was beautiful and fine; hers was the deep-drawn unconscious beauty of the race; beauty of flesh and blood, purified, spiritualized in its passage through the generations, beauty that gives the illusion of eternity, being both younger and older than the soul. It was as if Nature had become Art in the making of Lucia, forming her by the subtlest processes of selection and rejection.

Having gone the round of the gallery, he paused before the modern portraits which brought him again to the door of the drawing-room. Sir Frederick held him with his joyous satyr-face, for it was curiously, incredibly like his daughter's (to be sure, Sir Frederick had blue eyes and reddish hair, which made a difference). His eye-brows had a far-off hint of her; she lingered in the tilted corners of his mouth and eyes. And, if there could be any likeness between a thing so gross and a thing so spiritual, his upper lip took a sweep that suggested Lucia's with its long-drawn subtle curve.

He was startled out of these reflections by the opening of the door. Lucia stood beside him. She had a lamp in her hand which she raised for an instant, so that the light fell full upon the portrait. Her own face appeared as if illuminated from within by the flaming spirit of love.

"That is my father," she said simply, and passed on.

He looked again at the portrait, but the likeness had vanished. In the frank sensuality of Sir Frederick's crimson smirk he could find no affinity to Lucia's grave and tender smile.

"There are some things," he said to himself, "that she could never see."

CHAPTER XXV

IF Lucia was not, as her father had pronounced her, the worst educated young woman in Europe, there was a sense (not intended by Sir Frederick) in which her education might be called incomplete. She had learnt the things that she liked, and she had left unlearnt the things that she did not like. It was the method of discreet skipping; and it answered so well in the world of books that she had applied it to the world of men and women. She knew the people she liked, and she left unknown those whom she did not like. Here in Harmouth her peculiar art or instinct of selection earned for her, as Kitty Palliser had lately told her, the character of exclusiveness. This, by the way, was family tradition again. From time immemorial there had been a certain well-recognized distance between Court House and the little Georgian town. And when Harmouth was discovered by a stock-broker and became a watering-place, and people began to talk about Harmouth society, Court House remained innocently unaware that anything of the sort existed. Lucia selected her friends elsewhere with such supreme fastidiousness that she could count them on the fingers of one hand, her instinct, like all great natural gifts, being entirely spontaneous and unconscious.

And now it seemed she had added Mr. Savage Keith Rickman to the list. She owned quite frankly that in spite of everything she liked him.

But Rickman was right. Lucia with all her insight had not the remotest conception of his state of mind. The acquaintance had arisen quite naturally out of her desire to please Horace, and if on this there supervened a desire to please Mr. Rickman, there was not a particle of vanity in it. She had no thought of being Mr. Rickman's inspiration; her attitude to his genius was humbly reverent, her attitude to his manhood profoundly unconscious. She had preserved a most formidable innocence. There had been nothing in Horace Jewdwine's slow and well-regulated courtship to stir her senses or give her the smallest inkling of her own power that way. Kitty's suggestion seemed to her preposterous; it was only the Kittishness of Kitty, and could have no possible application to herself.

All this was not humility on her part—nothing of the sort. So far from being humble, Miss Lucia Harden held the superb conviction that any course she adopted was consecrated by her adoption. It was as if she had been aware that her nature was rich, and that she could afford to do what other women couldn't; " there were ways," she would say, " of doing them."

And in Mr. Savage Keith Rickman she had divined a nature no less generously gifted. He could afford to take what she could afford to offer; better still, he would take just so much and no more. With some people certain possibilities were moral miracles; and her instinct told her that this man's mind was incapable of vulgar misconception. She was safe with him. These things she pondered during that brief time when Rickman lingered in the portrait gallery.

He saw her again that night for yet another moment. Lucia was called back into the picture gallery by the voice of Kitty Palliser, whose return coincided with his departure. Kitty from the safe threshold of the drawing-room looked back after his retreating figure.

" Poor darling, he has dressed himself with care."

" He always does. He has broken every literary convention."

Lucia drew Kitty into the room and shut the door.

" Has he been trying any more experiments in diminished friction on polished surfaces? "

" No; there was a good deal more repose about him after you left. The friction was decidedly diminished. What do you think of him? "

" Oh, I rather like the way he drops his aitches. It gives a pathetic piquancy to his conversation."

" Don't, Kitty."

" I won't. But, after all, how do we know that this young man is not a fraud? "

" How do we know anything? "

" Oh, if you're going to be metaphysical, *I'm* off to my little bed."

" Not yet, Kitty. Sit down and toast your toes. I want to talk to you."

" All right, fire away."

But Lucia hesitated; Kitty was in an unpropitious mood.

" What do you think I've done? " she said.

Kitty's green eyes danced merrily; but in spite of their mockery Lucia told her tale.

" It was the best I could do," said she.

Kitty's eyes had left off dancing.

" Lucia, you *can't*. It's impossible. You must *not* go on being so kind to people. Remember, dear, if he is a heaven-born genius, he's not—he really *is* not a gentleman."

" I know. I've thought of that. But if he isn't a gentleman, he isn't the other thing. He's something by himself."

" I admit he's a genius, but—he drops his aitches."

" He doesn't drop half as many as he did. He only does it when he's flustered. And I won't let him be flustered. I shall be very kind to him."

" Oh," groaned Kitty, " there's no possible doubt about that."

" On the whole I think I'm rather glad he isn't a gentleman. He would be much more likely to get in my way if he were. I don't believe this little man would get in my way. He's got eyes at the back of his head, and nerves all over him; he'd see in a minute when I didn't want him. He'd see it before I did, and be off."

" You don't know. You might have to be very unpleasant to him before you said good-bye."

" No, I should never have to be unpleasant to him; because he would know that would be very unpleasant for me."

" All this might mean that he was a gentleman; but I'm afraid it only means that he's a genius."

" Genius of that sort," said Lucia, " comes to very much the same thing." And Kitty reluctantly admitted that it did. She sat silent for some minutes gazing into the fire.

" Lucia, does it never occur to you that in your passion for giving pleasure you may be giving a great deal of pain? "

" It doesn't occur to me that I'm giving either in this case; and it will not occur to him. He knows I'm only giving him his chance. I owe it him. Kitty—when you only think what I've done. I've taken this wonderful, beautiful, delicate thing and set it down to the most abominable drudgery for three weeks. No wonder he was depressed. And I took his Easter from him—Kitty—think—his one happy breathing-time in the whole hateful year."

" Whitsuntide and Christmas yet remain."

" They're not at all the same thing."

" That's you, Lucy, all over; you bagged his Bank holiday, and you think you've got to give him a year in Italy to make up."

" Not altogether to make up."

" Well, I don't know what to say. There's no doubt you can do a great many things other women can't; still, it certainly seems a risky thing to do."

" How risky?"

" I don't want to be coarse, but—I'm not humbugging this time—supposing, merely supposing—he falls in love with you, what then?"

" But he won't."

" How do you know?"

" Because he's in love already, in love with perfection."

" But as he'll be sure to identify perfection with you—— "

" He will see very little of me."

" Then he's all the more likely to."

" Kitty, *am* I the sort of woman who allows that sort of thing to happen—with that sort of man?"

" My dear, you're the sort of woman who treats men as if they were disembodied spirits, and that's the most dangerous sort I know. If I'm not mistaken Mr. Savage Keith Rickman's spirit is very much embodied."

" What *is* the good of trying to make me uncomfortable when it's all settled? I can't go back on my word."

" No, I suppose you've got to stick to it. Unless, of course, your father interferes."

" Father never interferes. Did you ever know him in his life refuse me anything I wanted?"

" I can't say I ever did." Kitty's tone intimated that perhaps it would have been better if he sometimes had. " Still, Sir Frederick objects strongly to people who interfere with him, and he may not care to have the young Savage poet, or poet Savage, hanging about."

" Father? He won't mind a bit. He says he's going to take part of the Palazzo Barberini for six months. It's big enough to hold fifty poets."

" Not big enough to hold one like Mr. Savage Keith

Rickman." Kitty rose to her feet, she stood majestic, for the spirit of prophecy was upon her; she gathered herself together for the deliverance of her soul. "You say he won't be in the way. He will. He'll be most horribly in the way. He'll go sliding and falling all over the place, and dashing cups of coffee on the marble floor of the Palazzo; he'll wind his feet in the tails of your best gowns, not out of any malice, but in sheer nervous panic; he'll do unutterable things with soup—I can see him doing them."

"*I* can't."

"No. I know you can't. I don't say you've no imagination; but I *do* say you're deficient in a certain kind of profane fancy."

CHAPTER XXVI

IT was extraordinary; if he had given himself time to reflect on it he might even have considered it uncanny, the peace that had settled on him with regard to the Harden Library.

It remained absolutely unshaken by the growing agitation of his father's letters. Isaac wrote reproachfully, irritably, frantically, and received only the briefest, most unsatisfactory replies. "I can't tell you anything more than I have. But I wouldn't be in a hurry to make any arrangements with Pilkington, if I were you." Not the smallest reference to the Aldine Plato, the Neapolitan Horace, or the *Aurea Legenda* of Wynkyn de Worde.

Why indeed should he trouble himself? He couldn't understand his father's state of mind. He had now a positive intuition that Sir Frederick would recover in the manner of a gentleman whose motto was *Invictus;* an infinite assurance was conveyed by that titled faun-like smile. He even found himself believing in his own delightful future as Miss Harden's private secretary, so entirely had he submitted to the empire of divine possibility.

Meanwhile he redoubled his attentions to the catalogue. (Could there be anything more unreasonable than that catalogue *raisonné?*) He had frequently got up and worked at it for an hour or two before breakfast, lifted out of bed by the bounding of his heart. But whereas he had been in the habit of leaving it at any time between nine o'clock and midnight, he now sat up with it till the small hours of the morning. This extreme devotion was necessary if he was to finish it by the twenty-seventh. It was now the fifteenth.

He had told Miss Harden that he could work better by himself, and apparently she had taken him at his word; she had left him to finish the catalogue alone. As it happened he didn't work a bit better by himself. What with speculating on the chance of her appearing, listening for her voice and her footsteps on the stairs, or the distant sound of her playing, to say nothing of his desperate efforts not to stare out of the windows when he knew her to be in the garden, Lucia absent was even more disturbing than Lucia on the spot. He tried to console himself with the reflection that she was no longer overworking herself; and herein appeared the great purity and self-abnegation of Mr. Rickman's love. Rather than see her making herself ill, he was actually manœuvring so as not to see her at all. He kept his vigils secret, having a suspicion that if she heard of them she would insist on returning to her hideous task.

To this end he devised an ingenious system of deceit. He left off work for an hour every afternoon, alleging his need of air and exercise. He then asked permission to sit up a little later than usual by way of making good the time thus lost. He knew that by eleven the lights would be out, and Lucia and the servants all in bed. He demanded black coffee to keep him awake and the key of the side door to let himself out. All on the understanding that he would leave the house by half-past eleven or twelve at the latest. He could thus put in a good five hours extra without any one being any the wiser; and four o'clock would find Mr. Rickman stealing back to his hotel over the grey and dewy grass.

For three days and three nights love's miraculous energy sustained him. On the fourth night he was overcome by a slight fatigue, and at one o'clock he lay down on the hearth rug to sleep, registering in his brain his intention to wake punctually at two.

And for three days and three nights Lucia hardly gave a thought to Mr. Rickman. She was busy with preparations for her departure, trying to see as much of Kitty Palliser as possible, and thinking a great deal of that adorable father whom she would meet on the twenty-seventh.

Lucia's room, as Mr. Rickman knew, was in the west wing, over the south-west end of the library, and from her window she could see the pale yellow green shaft of light that Mr. Rickman's lamp flung across the lawn. The clock on the stable belfry struck the hours one by one, and Lucia, fast asleep, never knew that the shaft of light lay there until the dawn.

On the fourth night, the night of Thursday, the fifteenth, Lucia did not sleep so well. She dreamed, but her dreams were too light and transparent to veil the reality that lay on the waking side of them. Three times that night she started on her journey to Cannes, three times she missed her train, and three times she said to herself, " It's only a dream, so of course it doesn't matter." When, after prodigious efforts extending over interminable time, she found herself on Harmouth platform, shuddering in her nightgown before a whole train full of people, she was not in the least disconcerted, because of her perception of that reality behind her dream; no, not even when Mr. Rickman appeared just as she was saying to herself, " It doesn't matter. This is only the fifteenth and I don't really start till the twenty-sixth." His presence was so transparent, so insubstantial, that it didn't seem to matter either. He said, " Miss 'Arden, you've made a miscalculation. You must start this minute if you're to be there in time." His statement seemed to her to be founded on some solid reality; but when she asked him what he was doing there, he spoilt it all by saying that as private secretary he was in charge of the expedition. By that, and by something unnatural and absurd in his appearance, she knew that she was dreaming. Then, for more time than she could measure, she lay watching herself dream, with a curious sense of being able to foretell and control the fantastic procession of events.

And now she was aware of something that moved with their movement, a trouble or a terror, that hovered out there, not on the waking border, but in the region of reality that lay on the other side. Almost discernible behind the transparent insubstantial walls of sleep, it waited to break through them and invade her dream. For refuge from it she plunged deeper into her dream. She came out walking on a terrace of grey grass set with strange clusters of swords, sharp-pointed and double-edged. Tall grey trees shot up into a grey white sky; they were coated with sharp scales, grey and toothed like the scales of a shark's skin; and some bore yet more swords for branches, slender and waving swords; and some, branchless, were topped with heads of curled scimitars, the blades pointing downwards. All these scaley, spiky, two-edged things stood out piercing and distinct against the grey; and she knew that they were aloes and palm-trees, and that she had come to the end of her journey and was walking in the garden of the Villa des Palmes. And the thing she dreaded was still waiting a little way beyond the garden, beyond the insubstantial walls; it was looking for her, crying after her, it stretched out its arms to draw her from her sleep.

A little twilight wind came creeping over the grey grass, it covered her feet like water, it rose higher and higher above the sword points of the aloes, and she sank in it and floated, floated and sank. And now it tossed and rolled and shook the palm-trees till all their blades rattled like steel; and beyond the wind she heard the calling of the thing she feared, the thing that had hunted her from dream to dream. She feared it no longer; she too was looking and crying; all her desire was to find what she had feared; to answer it, to see it face to face. Her body was clasped tight by the arms of the wind; yet her yearning was so strong that she struggled with them and flung them from her, breaking through the bonds and barriers of sleep.

Lucia was awake and accounting for her dream. The weather had changed in the night, and a cold wind was rushing through the open window on to her bed. She had been lying with her feet uncovered, and the bed-clothes heaped on to her chest. She had been waked by the rattling of a loosened lattice in the room below. She got out of bed and looked out of the window. There was a vast movement in the sky, as if the darkness were being visibly upheaved and rolled away westwards by the wind. Over the garden was the dense grey blackness of an obliterated dawn. The trees, not yet detached from the ground of night, showed like monstrous skeletons of the whole immense body of gloom, while the violent rocking of their branches made them one with that dark and wandering tumult of cloud and wind.

The shaft of light no longer lay upon the lawn; Mr.

Rickman's lamp was out; therefore, she argued, Mr. Rickman had gone; having, in the recklessness of his genius, forgotten to close the library windows.

One of the west windows creaked and crashed by turns as it swung heavily in its leaded frame. Lucia put on her dressing gown and slippers, threw a light shawl about her shoulders, and went down to fasten the lattice. A small swinging lamp gave light to the hall and staircase. A gleam followed her into the library; it lay in a pool behind her, its thin stream lost in the blackness of the floor. She could distinguish nothing in the room but the three dim white busts on their dusky pedestals. Behind the lattice-work the window panes were like chequered sheets of liquid twilight let down over the face of the night.

The wind held the open lattice backwards, and she had some difficulty in reaching the hasp. A shallow gust ran over the floor, chilling her half-naked feet. As she leaned out on the sill a great fear came over her, the fear that had always possessed her in childhood at the coming and passing of the night. As she struggled with the lattice, she had a sense of pulling it against some detaining hand. It swung slowly round, and the figure of a man slid with it sidelong, and stood behind it looking in. The figure seemed to lean forward out of the darkness; its face, pressed close against the panes, was vivid, as if seen in a strong daylight. She saw the flame of its red moustache and hair, the flicker of its faun-like tilted smile. Its eyes were fixed piercingly on hers.

It stood so for the space of six heart-beats. The window slipped from her hand and swung back on its hinges. The cloud was heaved from the edges of the world, and face and figure were wiped out by the great grey sweep of the dawn. Lucia (strangely as it seemed to her afterwards) was not startled by the apparition, but by the aspect of the world it had appeared in. She stood motionless, as if afraid of waking her own fear; she caught the lattice, drew it towards her and deliberately secured it by the hasp. She turned with relief from the terrible twilight of the windows to the darkness of the room. She crossed it with slow soft footsteps, lest she should give her terror the signal to pursue.

There was a slight stir on the hearth as a mound of ashes sank and broke asunder, opening its dull red heart.

Lucia turned in the direction of the sound, came forward, and saw that she was not alone.

Stretched on the rug in front of the fireplace with his feet towards her lay Mr. Rickman.

Her first feeling was of relief, protection, deliverance. She stood looking at him, finding comfort in the sheer corporeality of his presence. But as she looked at him that emotion merged in concern for Mr. Rickman himself. He lay on his back in a deep sleep; one arm was flung above his head, the hand brushing back his damp hair; his forehead was beaded with the thick sweat of exhaustion. He must have been lying so for hours, having dropped off to sleep when the night was still warm. He had thrown back his coat and loosened his shirt-collar, and lay undefended from the draught that raked the floor. The window at this end of the room had been left open too, and the fire was almost dead.

Lucia looked doubtfully at the window. She knew its ways; sagged on its hinges and was not to be shut without the grating shriek of iron upon stone. She looked, still more doubtfully, at Mr. Rickman. His face in the strange light showed white and sharp and pathetically refined.

And as she looked her heart was filled with compassion for the helpless sleeper. She moved very softly to the fire-place, where an oak chest stood open stored with wood; she gathered the embers together and laid on them a few light logs. The first log dropped through the ashes to the hearth, and Mr. Rickman heaved a deep sigh and turned on his side.

Lucia knelt there motionless, till his breathing assured her that he still slept. With swift noiseless movements she went on building up the dying fire. The wood crackled; and a little flame leapt up, and Mr. Rickman opened his eyes. For a moment he kept them open, fixed in sleepy wonder on the woman who knelt beside him by the hearth. He was obscurely aware that it was Lucia Harden, but his wonder was free from the more vivid and disturbing element of surprise; for he had been dreaming about her and was still under the enchantment of his dream. Never had she seemed more beautiful to him.

Her head was bowed, her face turned from him and

shaded by her hair; and with her hands she tended a dying flame. Her shawl had slipped from her shoulders, and he saw the delicate curve of her body as she knelt; it was overlaid by her hair that fell to her hips in a loose flat braid. He closed his eyes again, feigning abysmal sleep. He kept guard over his breath, over his eyelids, lest a tremor should startle her into shamefaced flight. Yet he knew that she had risen and that her face was set towards him; that she turned from him and then paused in her going; that she looked at the fire again to make sure of its burning, and at him to make sure of his sleep (so intently that she never noticed the white thing which had slipped from her shoulders as she stood upright); that she stooped to draw his coat more closely over him. He heard the flowing of her gown, and saw, without seeing, her feet shining as she went from him.

And his desire went after her, and the mere bodiless idea of her became a torment to his body as it had been a joy to his soul.

He took up her shawl which lay there by the hearth and looked at it; he stroked it, unfolded it, spread it out and looked at it again; he held it to his face; its whiteness and its tender texture were as flame to his sight and touch, the scarcely perceptible scent of it pierced him like a delicate pain. He gathered it up again in a heap and covered it with kisses. Then, because it made his longing for her insupportable, he flung it back, that innocent little white shawl, as if shaking off her touch and her presence.

He rose to his feet and tramped up and down the room savagely, like a wild animal in a cage. With every thought of Lucia his torment returned upon him. He tried to think of the whiteness and the beauty of her soul, and he could think of nothing but the whiteness of her face and the beauty of her bending body.

He sat down, stretched his arms on the table and laid his miserable head upon them, all among the pages of the catalogue *raisonné*. He had passed from his agony of desire to an agony of contrition. He felt that the very vehemence of his longing was an affront to her white unconsciousness. Up till now he had not admitted that he was " in love " with Lucia; he was indeed hardly aware of it. He imagined his feeling for her to be something altogether immaterial and incorruptible. It now seemed to him that in the last few minutes he had lowered it almost to the level of the emotion inspired by Miss Poppy Grace. It was not, and it never could be, what it had been three weeks ago. Why, he could not even recall his sensations of Easter Sunday, that strange renewal of his heart's virginity, his first vague imperfect vision of the dawn of love, his joy when he discerned its tender and mysterious approach. He knew that it held no rights, or held them only on the most subtle and uncertain tenure, that his soul touched the soul of Lucia Harden by the extreme tips of its wings stretched to the utmost. Still his passion for her had been, so far, satisfied by that difficult and immaterial relationship. He was bound to her by an immaterial, intangible link.

But he had put an end to that relationship; he had broken the immaterial, intangible link. It was as if he had given a body to some delicate and spiritual dream, and destroyed it in a furious embrace. And in destroying it he had destroyed everything.

Then he reflected that though this deed seemed to belong wholly to the present moment, it had in reality been done a long time before, when he first became the slave of that absurd and execrable passion for Miss Poppy Grace. Rickman the poet had believed in Love, the immortal and invincible, the highest of high divinities, and as such had celebrated him in song. But he had been unfortunate in his first actual experience of him. He had found him, not " pacing Heaven's golden floor," but staggering across Miss Grace's drawing-room, a most offensive, fifth-rate, disreputable little god. Of course he knew it wasn't the same thing, it wasn't the same thing at all. But he was bound by the past. He had forged a chain of infamous but irresistible association that degraded love in his eyes, that in his thoughts degraded *her*. Every hour that he had spent in the little dancer's society had its kindred with this hour. In his passion for Lucia Harden there leapt up the passion of that night—that night three weeks ago. It was then—then—that he had sinned against her.

He had not meant—he had not meant to love her—like that. And yet he perceived how all along, unremittingly, imperceptibly, this passion had waylaid him and misled

him and found him out. It was it that had drawn him
every morning across the fields to Court House, that
upheld him on his giddy perch on the library steps, that
chained him to his chair at the library table, and kept him
sweating over that abominable catalogue till four o'clock
in the morning. It had looked at him with so pure and
spiritual a face that he had not recognized it. But how
otherwise could he have stayed here for three weeks, fool-
ing with that unlucky conscience of his; persuading it
one minute that he had nothing to do with Miss Harden,
and that her father's affairs were no business of his, the
next that they were so much his business that he was bound
not to betray them; while as for Miss Harden, he had so
much to do with her that it was his duty to stay where he
was and protect her? He had had absolutely no duty in
the matter except to tell her the truth and clear out.

Telling the truth—it ought to have been easy for him
who was so truthful, so passionately sincere. And yet
almost anything would have been easier: for the next step
to telling the truth was going away. Of course he had
suffered in staying, but he would have suffered anything
rather than go.

It had been so insidious. His feet had been caught in a
net so fine that he had thought it woven of the hairs split by
an exceedingly acute and subtle conscience. He should
have stood still and snapt them one by one; but he had
struggled, until he was so entangled that he could not get
out. And now he perceived that the net which seemed
so fine was the strong net woven by desire. All his subtle
reasonings, his chivalry, his delicacy, his sincerity itself,
could be reduced to this simple and contemptible element.
Positively, his whole character as he now contemplated
it seemed to slip away from him and dissolve in the irresistible stream, primeval, monstrous, indestructible.

The horror of his position returned upon him, the burden
of his knowledge and her ignorance. If only she knew, if
only he could go to her and tell her everything, all that he
knew and all that he guessed. He was still firm in his
conviction that he had no moral right to his knowledge;
it was a thing he almost seemed to have come by dishonestly. If Miss Harden knew nothing of her father's affairs,
it was to be presumed that they had been purposely kept

from her to save her pain. He had no right to tell her. No matter, he would tell her, he would tell her this morning, and having told her, he would go.

He got up and paced to and fro again. He stood before the open window till he had chilled himself through; then he came back and cowered over the fire. A white thing lay by the hearth at his feet, it was Lucia Harden's shawl, lying crumpled where he had thrown it. It was the sign and symbol of her presence there. It was also the proof of it.

How would she feel if she knew that he had been aware of it all the time? The fact remained that she had risked his waking; there was comfort for him in that. She had always been kind to him, and he had never had even a momentary illusion as to the source and the nature of her kindness. He had taken it, as he had taken her extreme courtesy, for the measure of the distance that divided them. It showed her secure in her detachment, her freedom from any intimate thought of him, from any thought of him at all. But in this last act of kindness it could hardly be that she had not taken him into consideration. She could hardly have been pleased if she knew he had been awake, yet she had risked his waking. Before she risked it she must have credited him with something of her own simplicity of soul.

And this was how he repaid her.

He saw her as she had knelt by him, mending the dying fire, as she had stood looking at him, as she had stooped over him to cover him, and as she had turned away; and he saw himself, sinning as he had sinned against her in his heart.

He knew perfectly well that the average man would have felt no compunction whatever upon this head. To the average man his imagination (if he has any) is an unreal thing; to Rickman it was the most real thing about him. It was so young, and in its youth so ungovernably creative, that it flung out its ideas, as it were, alive and kicking. It was only partially true of him that his dream was divorced from reality. For with him the phantoms of the mind (which to the average man are merely phantoms) projected themselves with a bodily vividness and violence. Not only had they the colour and authority of accomplished fact, they were invested with an immortality denied to facts. His imagination was in this so far spiritual that it perceived desire to be the eternal soul of the deed, and the deed to be but the perishing body of desire. From this point of view, conduct may figure as comparatively unimportant; therefore this point of view is very properly avoided by the average man.

Rickman, now reduced to the last degree of humility and contrition, picked up Lucia's shawl very gently and reverently, and folded it with care, smoothing out the horrid creases he had made in it. He took it to the other end of the room and laid it over the back of her chair, so that it might look to Robert as if his mistress had left it there.

Would he see her again that morning? That depended on the amount of work that remained for her to do. He looked over her table; her tray was empty, the slips were pinned together in bundles in the way he had taught her, Section XII, Poetry, was complete. There was nothing now to keep her in the library. And he had only ten days' work to do. He might see her once or twice perhaps on those days; but she would not sit with him, nor work with him, and when the ten days were over she would go away and he would never see her again.

Then he remembered that he had got to tell her and go away himself, at once, this very morning.

Meanwhile he sat down and worked till it was time to go back to his hotel. He worked mechanically, miserably, oppressed alike by his sense of his own villainy and of the futility of his task. He did not know how, when it was ended, he was to take up this kind of work again. He had only been kept up by his joy in her presence, and in her absence by the hope of her return. But he could not bear to look into a future in which she had no part.

CHAPTER XXVII

HE found a letter from Dicky Pilkington waiting for him at the hotel. Dicky's subtlety seemed to have divined his scruples, for he gave him the information he most wanted in terms whose terseness left very little room for uncertainty. "Look sharp," wrote Dicky, " and let me know if you've made up your great mind about that library. If

Freddy Harden doesn't pay up I shall have to put my men in on the twenty-seventh. Between you and me there isn't the ghost of a chance for Freddy. I hear the unlucky devil's just cleaned himself out at Monte Carlo."

The twenty-seventh? It was the day when Miss Harden was to join her father at Cannes. The coincidence of dates was significant; it amounted to proof. It meant that Sir Frederick must have long anticipated the catastrophe, and that he had the decency to spare her the last painful details. She would not have to witness the invasion of the Vandals, the overturning of the household gods, and the defilement of their sacred places.

Well, he thought bitterly, they couldn't be much more defiled than they were already. He saw himself as an abominable object, a thing with a double face and an unclean and aitchless tongue, sitting there from morning to night, spying, calculating, appraising, with a view to fraud. At least that was how she would think of him when she knew; and he had got to tell her.

He was on the rack again; and the wonder was how he had ever left it. It seemed to him that he could never have been long released at any time. He had had moments of comparative ease, when he could lie on it at one end of the room and see Lucia sitting at the other, and the sight of her must have soothed his agony. He had had moments of forgetfulness, of illusion, when he had gone to sleep on the rack, and had dreamed the most delicious dreams, moments even of deliverance, when his conscience, exhausted with the sheer effort of winding, had dropped to sleep too. And then had come the reckless moments, when he had yielded himself wholly to the delight of her presence; and that supreme instant when his love for Lucia seemed to have set him free.

And now it was love itself, furiously accusing, that flung him back upon the torture, and stretched him out further than he had been stretched before.

But Dicky's letter had to be answered at once. He settled Dicky for the present by reminding him that nothing could be done by either of them till the twenty-seventh. But he thought that if Sir Frederick or any of his family were unable to pay up, there ought to be no difficulty in arranging with his father.

To his father he sent a word of warning. " For goodness' sake don't commit yourself with Pilkington until you
see me. I shall probably be back down in town to-morrow
afternoon! "

Having settled Dicky, he breakfasted, bathed, was a
little long over his dressing, taking care that nothing in
his appearance should suggest the dishevelled person of
the dawn. Thus he was rather later than usual in presenting himself at the library. He found Miss Harden
there at his end of the table, with his note-book, busy over
his pile and engaged in finishing his Section—Philosophy.
Her clear and candid eyes greeted him without a shadow
of remembrance. She had always this air of accepting
him provisionally, for the moment only, as if her kindness
had no springs in the past and could promise nothing for the
future. He had always found this manner a little distressing, and it baffled him completely now. Still, in another
minute he would have to tell her, whatever her manner
or her mood.

" Miss Harden," he began, " you've been so awfully good
to me, there's something that I want most awfully to say
to you."

" Well, say it." But there was that in her tone which
warned him not to be too long about it.

" It's something I ought to have said—to have confessed—ages ago——"

" Oh, no, really Mr. Rickman, if it's a confession, you
mustn't do it now. We shall never finish at this rate."

" When may I ? "

" Some time in the afternoon, perhaps." Her smile,
which was exceedingly subtle, disconcerted him inexpressibly. She turned at once to the business of the day. The
question was whether he would begin on a new section, or
finish this one with her, writing at her dictation?

He, too, was calm, business-like, detached. He strangled
a happy smile which suggested that her question was absurd. To start a new section was to work gloomily by
himself, at some distant quarter of the room ; to write to
her dictation was to be near her, soothed by her voice and
made forgetful by her eyes. Hypocritically he feigned a
minute's reflection, as if it were a matter for hesitation and
for choice.

" Wouldn't you find it less tiring if I read and you wrote? "

" No, I had better read. You can write faster than I can."

So he wrote his fastest, while Lucia Harden read out titles to him in the sonorous Latin tongue. She was standing ankle-deep in Gnostics and Neo-Platonists; as for Mr. Rickman, he was, as he observed, out of his depth there altogether.

" Iamblichus, *De Mysteriis Egyptiorum*. Do you know him? "

Mr. Rickman smiled as he admitted that his acquaintance with Iamblichus was of the slightest; Lucia laughed as she confessed an ignorance extending to the very name. He noticed that she always seemed pleased when she had any ignorance to own up to; had she found out that this gave pleasure to other people?

" Is he Philosophy, or is he Religion? " She invariably deferred to Rickman on a question of classification. She handed the book to him. " Can you tell? "

" I really don't know; he seems to be both. I'd better have a look at him." He turned over the pages, glancing at the text. " I say, listen to this."

He hit on a passage at random, and read out the Greek, translating fluently.

" ' If, then, the presence of the divine fire and the unspeakable form of the divine light descend upon a man, wholly filling and dominating him, and encompassing him on every side, so that he can in no way carry on his own affairs, what sense, or understanding, or perception of ordinary matters should he have who has received the divine fire? ' Can he be referring to the business capacity of poets? "

Lucia listened amused. And all the time he was thinking, " If I don't tell her now I shall never tell her. She'll sneak off with Miss Palliser somewhere in the afternoon." Neither noticed that Robert had come in and was standing by with a telegram. Robert gazed at Mr. Rickman with admiration, while he respectfully waited for the end of the paragraph; that, he judged, being the proper moment for attracting his mistress's attention.

Never in all his life would Rickman forget that passage in the *De Mysteriis* which he had not been thinking about.

As Lucia took the telegram she was still looking at Rickman and the smile of amusement was still on her face. Robert respectfully withdrew. Lucia opened the envelope and Rickman looked down, apparently absorbed in Iamblichus. He was now considering in what form of words he would tell her.

Then, without looking up, he knew that something had happened. His first feeling was that it had happened to himself. He could not say how, or why, or what was the precise moment of its happening; he only knew that she had been talking to him, listening to him, smiling at him, and that then something had swept him on one side and carried her away, he did not know where, except that it was beyond his reach.

He looked up, startled by a sudden change in her breathing. She was standing opposite him; she seemed to be keeping herself upright by her hands, pressed palms downwards on the table. The telegram was spread open there before her; and she was not looking at it; she was looking straight at him, but without seeing him. Her mouth was so tightly closed that it might have been the pressure of her lips that drove the blood from them; she breathed heavily through her nostrils, her small thin breast heaving without a sob. In her face there was neither sorrow nor terror, and he could see that there was no thought in her brain, and that all the life in her body was gathered into her swollen, labouring heart. And as he looked at her he was pierced with a great pang of pity.

She stood there so, supporting herself by her hands for about a minute. He was certain that no sense of his presence reached her across the gulf of her unknown and immeasurable anguish.

At last she drew her hands from the table, first one, then the other, slowly, as if she were dragging a weight; her body swayed, and he sprang to his feet with an inarticulate murmur, and held out one arm to steady her. At his touch her perishing will revived and her faintness passed from her. She put him gently aside and went slowly out of the room.

As he turned to the table the five words of her telegram stared him in the face: " Your father died this morning."

It would have been horrible if he had told her.

His first thought was for her; and he thanked Heaven that had tied his tongue. Then, try as he would to realize her suffering, it eluded him; he could only feel that a moment ago she had been with him, standing there and smiling, and that now he was alone. He could still feel her hand pushing against his outstretched arm. There had been nothing to wound him in that gesture of repulse; it was as if she had accepted rather than refused his touch, as if her numbed body took from it the impetus it craved.

There was a sound of hurry and confusion in the house; servants went up and down stairs, or stood about whispering in the passages. He heard footsteps in that room above him which he knew to be her room. A bell rang once; he could feel the vibration of the wire down the wall of the library. It was her bell, and he wondered if she were ill.

Robert rushed in with a wild white face, shaken out of his respectful calm. He was asking Rickman if he had seen this month's Bradshaw. They joined in a frenzied search for it.

She was not ill; she was going away.

A few minutes later he heard the sound of wheels grating on the gravel drive, of the front door being flung open, of her voice, her sweet quiet voice, then the grating of the wheels again, and she was gone. That, of course, ended it.

Now for the first time he realized what Sir Frederick's death meant for himself. In thus snatching her from him in the very crisis of confession it had taken away his chance of redeeming his dishonour.

If he had only told her!

CHAPTER XXVIII

HE did not go back to town on the twenty-seventh. He stayed to finish roughly, brutally almost, with the utmost possible dispatch, the disastrous catalogue which would now be required, whatever happened. Until every book in the library had passed through his hands he was hardly in a position to give a just estimate of its value. His father had written again in some perturbation. It seemed that the old song for which he might obtain the Harden Library went to the tune of one thousand pounds; but Pilkington was asking one thousand two hundred. "It's a large sum," wrote Isaac, "and without more precise information than you've given me yet, I can't tell whether we should be justified in paying it."

That confirmed his worst misgivings. He answered it very precisely indeed. "We shouldn't be morally justified in paying less than four thousand for such a collection; and we should make a pretty big profit at that. But if we can't afford the price we must simply withdraw. In fact I consider that we ought to hold back in any case until we see whether Miss Harden or any of her people are going to come forward. It's only fair to give them the chance. You can expect me on the twentieth."

Beside writing to his father, he had done the only honest and straightforward thing that was left for him to do. He had written to Horace Jewdwine. That was indeed what he ought to have done at the very first. He could see it now, the simple, obvious duty that had been staring him in the face all the time. He hardly cared to think what subtle but atrocious egoism of passion had prevented him from disclosing to Jewdwine the fact of his presence at Court House; even now he said nothing about the two weeks that he had spent working with Jewdwine's cousin. The catalogue *raisonné* was so bound up with the history of his passion that the thing had become a catalogue *raisonné* of its vicissitudes. Some instinct, not wholly selfish, told him that the least said about that the better. He wrote on the assumption that Jewdwine knew (as he might very well have done) the truth about the Harden Library, briefly informing him that they, Rickman's, had been, or rather would be, in treaty with Mr. Pilkington for the purchase; but that he, Savage Keith Rickman, considered it was only fair to suggest that Mr. Jewdwine or some other member of Sir Frederick Harden's family should have the option of buying it, provided it could be so arranged with Mr. Pilkington. As Jewdwine was probably aware, the library represented security for one thousand pounds; whereas Rickman estimated its market value at four or even five times as much. But as Mr. Pilkington was not inclined to let it go for less than one thousand two hundred, Jewdwine had better be prepared to offer a little more than that sum. If Jewdwine felt inclined to act on this suggestion Rickman would be glad if he would let him know within the next ten days; as otherwise his father would be obliged to close with Mr. Pilkington in due form after the twenty-seventh. Would he kindly wire an acknowledgment of the letter?

Jewdwine had wired from London. "Thanks. Letter received, will write." That was on the seventeenth, and it was now the twenty-seventh and Jewdwine had not written. Rickman should have been back in London long before that time; he had allowed himself four days to finish his horrible work; and he had finished it. But as it happened the end of twelve days found him still in Harmouth. Seven of them passed without his being very vividly aware of them, though up till now he had kept a strict account of time. Two weeks once struck off the reckoning, he had come down to calculating by days, by hours, by half hours, to measuring minutes as if they had been drops of some precious liquid slowly evaporating. And now he had let a whole week go by without comment, while he lay in bed in his room at the Marine Hotel, doing nothing, not even sleeping. For seven days Mr. Rickman had been ill. The broad term nervous fever was considered to have sufficiently covered all his symptoms.

They were not improved by the discovery that Jewdwine had failed to give any sign; while the only reply sent by Rickman's was a brief note from his father to the effect that Keith's letter should have his very best consideration, and that by the time he saw him he would no doubt be in a better position to answer it. There was a post-card written on the twenty-first, inquiring the cause of his non-appearance on the twentieth. This had been answered by the doctor. It had been followed by a letter of purely parental solicitude, in which all mention of business was avoided. Avoided; and it was now the twenty-seventh.

Rickman literally flung from his sick-bed a feverish and illegible note to Horace Jewdwine. "For God's sake, wire me what you mean to do," an effort which sent his temperature up considerably. He passed these days of convalescence in an anxious watching for the post. To the chambermaid, to the head waiter, to the landlord and landlady of the Marine Hotel, to the friendly commercial gentleman, who put his head twice a day round the door to inquire "'ow he was gettin' on," Mr. Rickman had, during his seven days' illness,

put the same unvarying question. These persons had adopted
a policy of silence, shaking their heads or twisting their
mouths into the suggestion of a " No," by way of escape
from the poignancy of the situation. But on the afternoon
of the twenty-ninth, Mr. Rickman being for the first time up
and dressed, Tom, the waiter, replied to the accustomed
query with a cheerful " No, sir, no letters ; but a lady was inquiring for you this morning, sir." In Tom's mind a lady
and a letter amounted to very much the same thing.

" Do you know who it was ? "

" Yes, sir, Miss Palliser."

" Miss Parry ? I don't know any Miss Parry," said Rickman wearily.

" I didn't say Miss Parry, sir, I said Miss Palliser, sir.
Wanted to know 'ow you was ; I said you was a trifle better, sir."

" I ? I'm all right. I think I shall go out and take a
walk." The violent excitement of his veins and nerves
gave him the illusion of recovered strength.

His walk extended from the hotel door to a seat on the
sea-front opposite. He repeated it the next morning with
less difficulty, and even succeeded in reaching a further
seat beyond the range of the hotel windows. There he
sat looking at the sea, and watching without interest the
loiterers on the esplanade. At last, by sheer repetition,
three figures forced themselves on his attention ; two ladies,
one young, the other middle-aged, and a clergyman, who
walked incessantly up and down. They were talking as
they passed him ; he caught the man's steep-pitched organ
monotone, " Yes, I shall certainly go up to the house and
see her," and the girl's voice that answered in a hard bright
trill, " You won't see her. She hasn't seen anybody but
Kitty Palliser."

The blood boiled in his brain. She ? She ? Was it possible that they were talking about her ? He sat there debating
this question for ten minutes, when he was aware that he
himself had become an object of intense interest to the
three. The two ladies were, in fact, staring rather hard.
The stare of the younger was so wide that it merely included him as an unregarded detail in the panorama of sea
and sky ; but the stare of the elder, a stout lady in a florid
gown, was concentrated, almost passionate ; it came straight

at him through a double eye-glass elevated on a tortoise-shell stem. The clergyman endeavoured to suggest by his attitude that he took no part in the staring or the talk; he smiled out to sea with an air of beatific union with Nature.

Harmouth beach is a safe place for scandal; for even a steep-pitched organ monotone with a brilliant feminine flourish on the top of it are lost in the accompaniment of the sea. So, happily for him, no word of the dialogue reached Rickman. All the same, to have a pair of blank blue eyes and a tortoise-shell binocular levelled at him in that fashion is a little disturbing to a young man just recovering from a nervous fever; and Rickman got up and dragged himself to the other end of the esplanade out of the reach of the enemy's fire. Therefore he did not see that Miss Palliser, who had been watching the scene from a balcony on the front, had come down and joined the group; neither did he hear her cheerful replies to a volley of inquiries.

"Yes; I've seen her. Nice day, isn't it? What? No, I wouldn't if I were you. I say, what a swagger eye-glass! Jolly, those long stems, aren't they? You can stare for ever without pinching your nose or gouging your next door neighbour's eye out with your elbow—Oh, yes, rather; he's a friend of Horace Jewdwine's. Do observe Tubs bathing; his figure is not adapted—Did you say a gentleman? Yes, no, yes; ask somebody else. It entirely depends on the point of view. He's an awfully good sort. *Really,* Tubs ought to be made to bathe before breakfast, when there's nobody about. Yes, of course she did. She gave him the work to please Mr. Jewdwine, I suppose. He's been ill, poor little beggar; I must go and speak to him."

After having thus first harried, then effectually baffled the enemy, Miss Palliser started with a swinging stride in pursuit of Mr. Rickman. He sat alone in an attitude of extreme dejection, on the stones of an unfinished and forsaken jetty that marked the farthest western limit of the esplanade. Having turned his back on that public rendezvous, he was unaware of Miss Palliser's approach until she stood beside him.

"Glad to see you again," said she.

He sprang to his feet and raised his hat. At the first sight of his face Miss Palliser had a shrewd idea of the cause and nature of his illness.

" Thank you so much for your kind messages. I'm all right again, as you see."

" I see nothing of the sort, as yet." She had meant to tell him that it was Lucia who had sent her to inquire; but she thought better of it.

" Oh, well, I ought to get round in this bracing air."

" Harmouth air," said Kitty, " is not particularly bracing. In fact it's very relaxing. It probably helped you to break down."

" Well, I shall be out of it soon, anyway." He sighed. " Miss Palliser, can you tell me if Miss Harden has come back?"

" She came back the day before yesterday."

" Have you seen her?"

" Yes, I've seen her."

There was a long pause, filled by the insistent clamour of the sea. His next question was less audible to the outer than to the inner ear.

" How is she?"

Miss Palliser was seldom at a loss for a word; but this time she hesitated. " She—she is very plucky."

There was another and a longer pause in which neither had the courage to look at the other.

" Can I—Would it be possible for me to see her?"

Miss Palliser did not answer.

" I wouldn't dream of asking her, except that I've got something on my mind."

" And she—my dear man, she's got everything on her mind."

" I know. I—I want to see her on business."

Miss Palliser's lithe figure grew rigid. She turned on him a look of indignation and contempt. " Everybody wants to see her on business. But some of them have had the grace to wait."

He smiled in the faint, tolerant manner of a man so steeped in the bitterness of the situation that no comment on it can add a further sting.

" I can't wait. My business hasn't much to do with me; but it has a great deal to do with Miss Harden."

She looked at him as she spoke. Something in his face and in his voice, too, made her feel that her judgment of him had been unspeakably, unpardonably coarse.

"I beg your pardon," she said gently.

"Oh, don't. I'm not surprised that you thought that of me."

"I didn't think it. I don't quite know what I'm saying. I've spent the last two days trying to keep fools from worrying her. I hate the people who want to go to her; I hate the people who keep away; I hate them all. But I'm sorry I spoke like that to you. You look horribly ill."

"I'm not ill. But I'm nearly out of my mind about this business."

"What is it? Tell me, has it anything to do with the library?"

"Yes."

"Well; the library's going to be sold."

"I know. That's what I want to speak to her about."

"There's not a bit of good in speaking to her. There are at this moment," said Kitty incisively, "two persons in the house who call themselves the men in possession."

"The brutes——"

"You may as well sit down. You can't turn them out, they're two to one, and their position is, I believe, legally sound."

"I must go to her at once—I knew this would happen— Miss Palliser, is any one with her?"

"I am with her. I'm going back to her in a minute; but I want to talk to you first. Everybody's looking at us, but that can't be helped. Did you say you *knew* this would happen?"

"Yes—Miss Palliser, I'm in the most intolerable position with regard to Miss Harden."

"You knew they were making these arrangements?"

"Oh, yes, I knew it all the time I was working for her. What's more, I'm supposed to be the agent for this sale."

"Well—if it's got to be sold, why not?"

"Well, you see, my father's only an ordinary dealer. I'm about the only person concerned who knows the real value and I know that it's been undervalued. Of course, without the smallest dishonesty on Mr. Pilkington's part."

"Mr. who?" Kitty had not yet heard of Mr. Pilkington.

"Pilkington."

"What's his address?"

He gave it her.

Kitty made a note of the name and address.

"Unfortunately Mr. Pilkington has an absolute right to sell it, and my father has an absolute right to buy it."

"Well, somebody's got to buy it, I suppose?"

"Yes, but it seems to me we oughtn't to do anything till we know whether any of Miss Harden's people will come forward."

"She is the last of her people."

"How about Mr. Jewdwine? He's her cousin."

"On her mother's side."

"Still he's her cousin. I wrote to him ten days ago; and I haven't got any answer as yet."

"What did you say to him?"

"I invited him to step in and buy the library over our heads."

"And how much would he have had to pay for it?"

"Probably more than one thousand two hundred."

"Well—if you think that Mr. Jewdwine is the man to deal so lightly with two hundred pounds, let alone the thousand! Really, that's the quaintest thing you've done yet. May I ask if this is the way you generally do business?"

"No, I can't say that it is."

"Well, well, you were very safe."

"Safe? I don't want to be safe. Don't you see how horrible it is for me? I'd give anything if he or any one else would come in now and walk over us."

"Still, I don't wonder that you got no answer to your very remarkable proposal."

"It seemed to me a very simple and obvious proposal."

"I don't know much about business," said Kitty, "but I can think of a much more simple and obvious one. Why can't your people buy in the library and sell it again for Miss Harden on commission?"

"Do you suppose I haven't thought of that? It would be very simple and obvious if it rested with me, but I'm afraid my father mightn't see it in the same light. You see, the thing doesn't lie between Miss Harden and me, but between my father and Mr. Pilkington."

"I don't understand."

"It's this way. My father won't be buying the library from Miss Harden, but from Mr. Pilkington. And—my father is a man of business."

" And you most certainly are not."

" So he isn't likely to give any more for it than he can help."

" Of course not."

" Well, but—do you know what the library was valued at ? "

Kitty did, and she would have blurted it out had not an inner voice told her to be discreet for once. He took her silence for a confession of ignorance.

" Would you think a thousand pounds an absurdly high valuation ? "

" I don't know."

Kitty tried to banish all expression from her face. She really knew very little about business, and was as yet unaware of the necessary publicity of bills of sale. The suspicion crossed her mind that Rickman, in his father's interests, might be trying to pump her as to the smallest sum that need be offered.

" Because," he added, " it isn't. Miss Harden stands to lose something like three thousand pounds by it."

Kitty's evil surmises vanished utterly. " Good Heavens ! " she exclaimed, " how do you make that out ? "

" It's only the difference between what the library ought to fetch and what will be given for it. Of course no dealer could give the *full* value; still, between one thousand and four thousand there's a considerable difference."

"And who pockets it ? "

" My fa— the dealer, if he succeeds in selling again to the best advantage. He might not, and my father, as it happens, considers that he's taking a great risk. But I know more about it than he does, and I don't agree with him. That's why I don't want him to get hold of those books if I can help it."

Kitty was thoughtful.

" You see," he continued, " I know he'd like to do what he thinks generous under the circumstances, but he isn't interested in Miss Harden, and he *is* interested in the Harden Library. It's a chance that a dealer like him gets only once in a lifetime and I'm afraid it isn't in human nature to let it go."

" But," said Kitty wildly, " he *must* let it go. You must make him. Do you mean to say you're going to sit and look on calmly while Miss Harden loses three thousand pounds?"

"I'm not looking on calmly. On the contrary, I've lost my head."

"What's the good of losing your head, if Miss Harden loses her money? What do you propose to do *besides* losing your head? Lose time, I suppose? As if you hadn't lost enough already."

"I wrote to Mr. Jewdwine as soon as I heard of Sir Frederick Harden's death. Still, you're right, I did lose time; and time was everything. You can't reproach me more than I reproach myself."

"My dear man, I'm not reproaching you. I only want to know what you're going to *do?*"

"Do? Is there anything left for me to do?"

"Not much, that I can see."

"If I'd only spoken straight out in the beginning——"

"Do you mean to her?"

"To her." He whispered the pronoun so softly that it sounded like a sigh.

"Why didn't you?"

"Why didn't I? I can see it was the one honest thing to do. But I thought I'd no business to know about her father's affairs if she didn't; and certainly no business to talk about them."

"No. I don't see how you could have done it."

"All the same I'd made up my mind to do it that morning—when the telegram came. That stopped me."

"You were well out of it. You don't know what an awful thing it would have been to do. She worshipped her father. Is this what you've been making yourself ill about?"

"I suppose so. You know how adorably kind she was to me?"

"I can guess. She is adorably kind to every one," said Kitty, gentle but astute.

"And, you see, I've behaved dishonourably to her."

"No. I don't see that."

"Don't you? Don't you? Why, my father sent me partly as his agent, and all the time she believed I was only working for her."

"Did you behave as your father's agent?"

"No. But I let her slave from morning till night over that catalogue."

"Which she would have done in any case."

"Don't you see that I ought to have backed out of it altogether, in the very beginning?"

"Ah, yes—if everybody did what they ought."

"I tried twice, but it was no good. I suppose I didn't try hard enough."

"What good would you have done by going? If she wanted you to stay?"

"That's how I argued. But the fact is, I stayed because I couldn't go away. Of course, it was an abominable position, but I assure you it felt like heaven when it didn't feel like 'ell."

His anguish, mercifully, was too great for him to feel the horror of his lapse. And Kitty hardly noticed it; at any rate she never felt the smallest inclination to smile, not even in recalling it afterwards.

It was, if you come to think of it, an unusual, a remarkable confession. But she remembered that he had had a nervous fever; it was his nerves, then, and his fever that had cried out, a cry covered, made decent almost, by the clangour of the sea.

She wondered how it came that, when her mind was as full as it could be of Lucia and her affairs, it could give such concentrated attention to him and his. If he had been what the tortoise-shell eyeglass took him for, a common man, it ought to have been easy and natural to dismiss him. But she could not dismiss him. There was some force in him, not consciously exerted, which held her there on that conspicuous seat beside him, under the gage of the tortoise-shell eye glass. Kitty was by no means deficient in what she had called "profane fancy," and she felt to her finger tips that she was making a spectacle of herself at the end of the esplanade. Their backs at this moment she knew must be standing out very clear and bold against the sky-line. But she herself was losing the keen sense she had once had of his inappropriateness to the scenes he moved in. Wherever he was he was natural; he was (she had it in one word) sincere, as few people are sincere nowadays. He was not a common man. That was it. All along it had been the justification of their strange proceedings, this fact

that he was not common, that he was indeed unique.
On that ground Lucia had always met him, and she had
ignored the rest. Kitty was trying to sympathize with
Lucia.

"But," he went on simply, "I can't tell her that."

"No, you can't tell her that, but you can tell her everything else. Look here, supposing that instead of sitting
here tearing your nervous system to tatters you go straight
away and do it."

"What will she think of me?"

"Think of you? If she thinks of you at all, she'll bless
you for having spared her father's memory up to the last
possible minute."

"Has it occurred to you that my motives are open to
the worst construction?"

"Well, frankly, it has. But it won't occur to Miss
Harden. Go to her and tell her everything."

"After all, what am I to tell her?"

"Oh, it doesn't matter much what you tell her now."

"It matters a great deal to me. I don't want her to
think me more dishonourable than I am."

"Oh, she won't do that."

"Perhaps she can't?"

"Well, you see, I don't know how dishonourable you've
been. I only know if I'd done a dishonourable thing—if
I'd done—oh, the most disgraceful thing I can imagine,
a thing I couldn't *possibly* tell to anybody else, I wouldn't
mind telling Lucia Harden. I should *have* to tell her. It
wouldn't matter. She's so perfectly good, that your own
little amateur efforts in that line simply aren't in it; so
when it comes to telling her things, you may as well be hung
for a sheep as a lamb. And wait a minute; you're not likely
to make a lamb of your sheep; but don't go to the other
extreme, and make a full-grown sheep of your lamb."

"I shall not deceive her."

"You couldn't. She's not only a good woman, but a
very clever one, though she doesn't let you see it. Mind
you, you won't find her clever about stupid things. I
doubt if you'll be able to make her understand all this library
affair. But she'll understand *your* business."

They rose, and walked together forgetful of the eagerly
observant group.

"Could she see me to-day, this evening? I'm going to-morrow."

"Yes, I'll tell her you're coming. When you *do* see her, don't be afraid—speak out."

"I'm not afraid of speaking to her—I'm afraid——"

"Of what?"

"Simply of *seeing* her."

"You mean you are afraid of seeing her changed?" She understood him; for it was what she herself had been afraid of.

"Horribly afraid."

"My dear Mr. Rickman, people in great trouble don't change to other people. They only change to themselves."

He raised his hat and turned from her without speaking.

Kitty felt remorseful as she looked after him, for she had not scrupled to sacrifice him to her idea. Kitty's idea was to get as high a price as possible out of Rickman Senior, and Rickman Junior was the only man who could get it. If the object was to shunt Rickman Senior altogether, Rickman Junior could be depended on for that, too. She could see that under the influence of his unhappy passion he had absolutely detached himself from his father's interests and his own. Kitty was profoundly sorry for him, and if she had yielded to her impulses of mercy and pity she would have kept him from Lucia as she would have kept a poor insane moth from the candle. It might be necessary to turn the moth out of doors in order to save it, and—well, she would have turned him out of doors, too, in sheer mercy and pity. But Kitty had a practical mind, and that practical mind perceived the services that might be rendered by a person so suicidally inspired. If she had read him aright, fire and water were nothing to what Mr. Rickman was prepared to go through for Lucia. Therefore she sent him to Lucia. But it was on his own account, for his healing and his consolation, that she advised him to make a clean breast of it.

CHAPTER XXIX

LUCIA was in the library and alone. Everything was as she had left it that morning two weeks ago; she saw the same solid floor and ceiling, the same faded Persian rugs, the same yellow pale busts on their tall pedestals, the same bookshelves, wing after wing and row upon row. The south lattice still showed through its leaded lozenge panes the bright green lawn, the beech-tree and the blue sky; the west lattice held the valley and the hills, with the river, a sinuous band of silver between the emerald and the amethyst. These things were so woven with the tissue of her mind that the sense of them had remained with her during the terrible seven days at Cannes. But now they appeared to her stripped of their air of permanence and familiarity. They were blurred and insubstantial, like things remembered rather than actually seen. All that subdued and tender loveliness belonged only to her young past, and she had been torn from it so violently, it had been flung so far behind her, that it seemed to her at the moment incredible and impossible. Life, that had hitherto dealt with her so gently and so graciously, had in the last two weeks turned hideous and brutal.

She had no very clear idea of how she had got to Cannes. The going was wiped out. She had been driven through the garden of the Villa des Palmes, and had recognized it as the garden of her dream. She had passed (through the doors of the Villa) into a state of stupor in which she had recognized nothing, and thence into a sequence of states which she could now too well recall. There had been a state of waking, in which she had found herself in a little gilt and velvet salon. There was another woman in it, a vast woman in a thin black dress twinkling all over with little black eyes. She had a great white powdered face, and they called her Madame. Then followed a state of hallucination, in which she believed Madame to be an innocent person, the housekeeper; a state of obsession, in which Madame, as she looked at her, seemed to grow vaster, to become immense; a state of imbecility, in which her mind feebly tried to grapple with the details of her father's death as presented brokenly by Madame. Last had come a state of frenzy, in which she had freed herself from Madame. After that something had appeared to her in vivid violent illumination.

So vivid and so violent that it seemed to her even now that she was still sitting in the gilt and velvet salon in the Villa des Palmes; she still saw the thin green light that came slanting through the half-closed shutters; warm southern smells floated in, they mixed with the thick stifling scent of patchouli and orris root wafted from Madame as she went to and fro, and with some other odour, bitter and sickly, that came from the room beyond.

She had made out certain familiar objects in this unfamiliar scene. Her father's travelling rug lay folded on the red velvet sofa; his cap and gloves were there, just as he had flung them down; his violin, dumb in its black coffinlike case, stood propped up against the wall. Everywhere else (only gradually discerned) were things belonging to Madame, evidence of her supreme and intimate occupation of the room.

And outside was the garden of sharp aloes and palms, where, as she believed, her father's spirit had gone looking for her, and had not found her. His body lay in the inner room behind the closed door.

That horrible little gilt and velvet salon! Whenever she thought of it she saw Madame; she saw Madame's little dry eyes blinking in her great white powdered face; she saw the vast heaving of Madame's bust where the little jet sequins shivered and shook; she heard her voice cooing and purring voluptuous condolence; and she felt again her own passion of disgust and fear as she wrenched herself free from the warm scented body, quivering in its thin black sheath.

Then she saw the inner room behind the closed door. Nothing was obscure and secret there. The slats of the shutter let in great shafts of daylight; the coffin stood in the middle of the room, raised on trestles, and covered with a white sheet. A crucifix stood at the head of the coffin, propped against a chest of drawers. Three candles, flickering in their sockets, were set on the table at its foot. On each knob of the two top-drawers hung a wreath of yellow immortelles.

That long coffin, raised high on its trestles, seemed to fill the little room. Lucia saw it now, she saw the face in it turned up to the ceiling, sharp and yellow, the limp red moustache hanging like a curtain over the half-open mouth. No trace of the tilted faun-like smile.

She would never get away from that terrible room. The pattern of its walls (garlands of pink rosebuds between blue stripes) was stamped upon her brain. There too, as in the salon, abode the inextinguishable odour shaken from Madame's dress; it mixed with the hot reek of carbolic and the bitter stabbing odour of the coffin.

On the floor by the trestles lay a glove, a long enormous glove, Madame's glove; it was greyish white, and wrinkled like the cast skin of a snake. The finger of its fellow hung from the chest of drawers beside the crucifix. It pointed downwards at the dead man.

Within the gay garlanded walls, surrounded by those symbols and souvenirs of Madame, he lay with his face turned up to the ceiling, and his mouth half open, as if it still gasped piteously for breath. One more breath to beg for forgiveness, to defend himself, explain; while bit by bit the place he had lived in gave up his secret.

She could not tell whether she forgave him or not. When she stood by him there she could have implored *his* forgiveness for having thus come upon him unawares, for having found what he had taken such pains to hide from her. It seemed somehow cruel and unfair. She did not tax him with hypocrisy, because he had so long contrived to keep himself clean in her sight; she was grateful to him for having spared her this knowledge. But whether she forgave him or not—no, looking back on it at this moment, she could not tell. Lucia was too young for the great forgiveness that comes of understanding.

She walked up and down the library, staring at the books, at the tables piled with papers; she stood at each window in turn and looked out on the garden, the valley and the hills, Harmouth Gap, and the long brown rampart line of Muttersmoor. It was simply impossible for her to realize their once intimate relation to her life.

She was unaware that her mood was chiefly the result of physical and mental exhaustion. It seemed to her rather that she had acquired strange powers of insight, that she had pierced to the back of the illusion. Never had she possessed so luminous a sense of the unreality of things. She found this view consoling, for it is the desire of unhappy youth that there shall be no permanence where there is pain.

·On this unreal and insubstantial background faces came and went all day long, faces solemn and obsequious, faces glazed and feverish with emotion; Robert's face with red-rimmed eyes, hiding Robert's unutterable sympathy under a thin mask of fright; Kitty's face, with an entirely new expression on it; and her own face met them with an incomprehensible and tearless calm. For she was not even sure of that, not even sure of her own sorrow. She had had to do with sorrow once before, when her grandfather died, and she thought she would be sure to know it when it came to her again; but she had no name for this new feeling, and at times it seemed to her that it was not sorrow at all.

Whatever it was, she had determined to bear it as far as possible alone. She was almost sorry that she had not refused Kitty's offer to stay with her; she suffered so from Kitty's inability to conceal the truth. Not that Kitty said anything; it was her unnatural silence that was so terrible. With that extraordinary acuteness that had come upon her now Lucia saw, by the involuntary hardening and flushing of Kitty's face, that in Kitty's mind her father was not only suspected, but condemned. She was afraid lest she herself should in some moment of weakness betray him; and Kitty's strange unusual tenderness inspired her with terror. She shrank even from old Mrs. Palliser, Kitty's mother, with her soft trembling face and clinging hands. Their sympathy was poignant and unnerving, and she needed all her strength for the things she had to do.

She did them, too. While one half of her brain had slackened its grip of the world, the other half retained the most perfect grasp of certain necessary details. She spent the morning with her father's solicitor, while he explained to her the first principles of finance, and the inner meaning of mortgages and bills of sale. She understood clearly that the things which would naturally have come to her on her father's death belonged in a certain sense to Mr. Richard Pilkington of Shaftesbury Avenue. Mr. Schofield, poor man, had approached this branch of his subject gently and gingerly, with every delicacy of phrasing that his fancy could suggest. He leaned back in his chair and looked at her through half-closed eyes, respectfully veiling the shrewdness of his gaze. Lucia had at first displayed so little interest and intelligence that he felt himself compelled to a broader and simpler statement of the facts. With the exception of her own personal possessions, nothing in Court House remained to her, nothing, not a book, not a solitary piece of drawing-room furniture. Mr. Pilkington's bill of sale was, he grieved to say, inclusive of everything, from the Harden Library and the great gallery of portraits, to the glass and china in the pantry, and the blankets on the beds. " Not even," he had said, " that little paper weight that you have in your hand, Miss Harden." And Lucia had examined the paper weight as if she saw it for the first time ; she put it down and smiled. It struck her as incomprehensible, ludicrous almost, that any one could spend so much passion and solemnity on things so unimportant, so irrelevant ; she was not in the least surprised to hear that they did not belong to her ; the inconceivable thing was that they ever had belonged to her.

And as the solicitor looked at her the corners of his mouth twitched with a little spasm of pity ; his eyes lost their veiled shrewdness, and when she smiled they stared in frankest fright. For a moment he supposed that the shock of his announcement had turned her brain. It never occurred to that astute intelligence that she was smiling at his own simplicity.

When he had left she returned to the writing-table ; she sorted and arranged a disordered heap of business letters, letters of condolence and tradesmen's bills. She pushed aside the letters of condolence—Kitty would answer those. She unlocked a drawer and took from it two open envelopes scored with many postmarks and addressed to Harmouth, to Cannes and to Harmouth again ; these she scrutinized anxiously, as if they disclosed some secret guarded by their contents. Then she read the letters carefully all over again.

One was from her cousin Edith Jewdwine. Edith's sympathy covered two sheets ; it flowed from her pen, facile and fluent. Edith had had the influenza, otherwise Edith would have come to Lucia at once. Could not Lucia come to her instead ? Edith could not bear to think of Lucia alone there in her trouble, in that great big house. She was glad that Kitty Palliser was with her. If only she had not been so unfortunate as to catch influenza and so on.

Lucia was sorry that Edith had influenza, but she was not sorry that she had not come. She did not want Edith with her.

The other letter was from Horace. Horace had refined

his expressions of condolence into one faultless phrase. The rest of his letter consisted of apologies and offers of service. These his close cramped handwriting confined to the centre of the sheet, leaving a broad and decent margin to suggest the inexpressible. He had heard of his uncle's death indirectly; why had she not sent for him? If she had wired to him at once he could have made arrangements to meet and take her to Cannes, or he could have joined her there and brought her home. At present he was overwhelmed with business; but he hoped to run down to Harmouth at the end of the week, and travel up to town with her. He understood that she was going to stay with Edith. Busy as he was, he would come now, at any minute, if he could be of any immediate use. She had only to wire if she wanted him.

She laid down that letter, pushed it aside, took it up again, and read it a second time, as if to satisfy herself as to the writer's meaning. She was not sure as to what Horace was or was not willing to do, but there could be no doubt that he was deeply sorry for her. Why had she not sent for him? Why indeed? Her first instinct had been to send for him. She had only to let him know that she was in trouble, and he would have come to her at any inconvenience to himself. And that, of course, was why she had not sent. It would have been so impossible for him to refuse.

And now she was thankful that she had spared him, and that he had not followed her to those terrible rooms in the Villa des Palmes, that he knew nothing of those seven days. She would have endured any suffering, paid any price to obliterate the memory of them. It was horrible to think how nearly Horace had been there. Horace of all people—the fastidious, the immaculate, the merciless. If she had found it hard to judge her dead father tenderly, she knew what Horace's judgment would have been.

She had "only to wire if she wanted him." Oh, no; he was the last person that she wanted now.

Those two letters she answered without more delay. To Horace she wrote in a reassuring manner, so as to absolve him from any sense of obligation he might happen to feel. She would rather he came down a little later than he proposed. Meanwhile he was not to be anxious, for Mr. Schofield was managing her affairs extremely well. She admitted that when those wonderful affairs were settled her income would be but small (she considered that this was a thing Horace ought to be told before—before he wrote any more letters). She added that the library, the pictures, and the furniture would have to be sold. And Court House, too, she was afraid. (That also was a fact that must not be concealed from him for a moment. It seemed to concern Horace so much more than it did her.) These things, which it was her duty to tell him, she told simply and plainly. But she omitted to mention that two men in possession were sitting in the housekeeper's room, in attitudes of more or less constraint. She ended by assuring Horace of her gratitude, with a fervency which suggested that he had some cause to doubt it. And indeed, at the moment, she could hardly tell whether she were more grateful to him for offering to come to her or for having stopped away.

All this necessary business Lucia transacted with one half of her mind; while the other stood far off, possessed by its sense of unreality, of illusion.

Next she went through the tradesmen's bills. There were a great many people to be paid, and unless Court House were sold there would be nothing to pay them with. It was at this point that Robert came in with the announcement that Mr. Rickman had called and wished to see her.

At first (the active intelligence being busy with accounts), her only idea was that she owed Mr. Rickman fifteen pounds and that when all debts were paid fifteen pounds would represent a very solid portion of her income. Then her dreaming self awoke to the memory of something unachieved, an obligation rashly incurred, a promise that could never be fulfilled.

Yes. She would see Mr. Rickman.

CHAPTER XXX

LUCIA had risen and was standing in the embrasure of the south window. She had her back to the door so that she could not see him as he came in.

He wondered how on earth he was going to get over the space between the window and the door. A sudden wave of weakness went through his body; he had horrible sensations of sinking at the middle and of giving way altogether at the knees. He had been afraid of seeing her suffer; now he knew that what he was really afraid of was her fear of seeing him. He expected to see her face set in abhorrence of his sympathy, her body shrink in anticipation of a touch on her pain.

Lucia spared him all the embarrassments of that approach. As if she had divined his feeling, she turned, she came forward to meet him, she held out her hand and smiled as she would have smiled if nothing had happened.

His hand trembled visibly as it dropt from hers. He hid it in his breast pocket where it pretended to be looking for things.

" Miss Palliser said she thought you would see me——"

" Yes, I wanted to see you; I would have sent for you if you had not come. Sit down, please."

She sat down herself, in her old place at the writing-table.

He took the chair beside her and leaned back, resting his arm on the table. She turned so as to face him.

She was not so changed but what his hungry and unhappy eyes could rest on her, appeased and comforted. And yet she *was* changed, too. Her girlhood, with all its innocence of suffering, had died in her. But the touch of that death was masterly, it had redeemed her beauty from the vagueness of its youth. Grief, that drags or sharpens or deforms the faces of older women, had given to hers the precision that it lacked. There was a faint sallow tinge in the whiteness of her skin, and her eyelids drooped as if she were tired to the point of exhaustion. He noticed, too, the pathetic tension that restrained the quivering of her mouth. It was the upper lip that trembled.

" You have been ill? " she said.

And as he answered that, " Oh, it was nothing," he was aware for the first time how very much it had been. She too was aware of it.

She expressed her concern, she hoped that they had looked after him well at the hotel.

Decidedly she had grown older and her manner had grown older too. It suggested that it was she who was the protector; that she wished, as far as possible, to spare him in an interview which must necessarily be painful. It was as if she remembered that he at any rate was young, and that these gloomy circumstances must be highly distasteful to his youth. In that she was the same as ever; every nerve in her shrank from the pain of giving pain.

At least that was his first impression. And then (no consoling view being really open to him) he told himself he was a fool to suppose that in the circumstances she could think of him at all. He had nothing tangible to go upon. He could see through it. He could see perfectly through the smile, the self-possession, even the air of polite and leisurely interest in his illness. She dwelt on him because he was of all themes the one most indifferent to her. She was simply holding herself in, according to the indestructible instincts of her race.

He need not have been afraid of seeing her suffer; that, at any rate, he would not see. To let him see it would have been to her an extreme personal degradation, an offence against the decencies of her class. This sorrow of hers, this invisible, yet implacable sorrow, stood between them, waving him away. It opened up again the impassable gulf. He felt himself not only a stranger, but an inferior, separated from her beyond all possibility of approach. She had not changed. She had simply reverted to her type.

Her eyes waited for him to speak. But they were not the eyes he knew, the eyes that had drawn him to confession. It was borne in upon him that this (though it might be his last moment with her) was not the moment to confess. There was a positive grossness in the idea of unburdening himself in the presence of this incommunicable grief. It was like putting in a claim for consideration as an equal sufferer. He had no right to obtrude himself upon her at all. In her calm-eyed attention there was a hint—a very delicate and gentle one—that he would do well to be impersonal, business-like, and above all, brief.

" It was about the library that I wanted to see you, Miss Harden."

" Was it? I was just going to ask you not to do anything more to the catalogue if you have not finished it."

" I finished it ten days ago—before the twenty-seventh."

She smiled faintly. " Then you kept your promise. It doesn't matter. What I most wanted to speak to you about was the secretaryship I offered you. I'm afraid we must give it up."

" Oh—Miss Harden——" His tone expressed that he had always given it up, that it was not to be thought of for an instant. But evidently she was possessed with the idea that he had a claim upon her.

" I'm very sorry; but as things have turned out I shan't be able to keep a secretary. In fact, as you may have heard, I'm not able to keep anything hardly—not even my promises."

" Please—please don't think of it——"

" There is no use thinking of it. Still, I wanted you to know that I really meant it—I really believed it could be done. Of course I don't know how much you really wanted it."

" Wanted it? I'd 'ave given half my life for a year of it."

Lucia's hand, laid lightly on the table's edge, felt a strong vibration communicated to it from Mr. Rickman's arm. She looked up, in time to see his white face quiver before he hid it with his hand.

" I'm so sorry. Did it mean so much to you? "

He smiled through his agony at the cause assigned to it. " I'm not thinking of that. What it means to me—what it always will mean is your goodness—in thinking of it. In thinking of it now."

It was his nearest approach to a sympathetic allusion. She did not wince (perceptibly), but she ignored the allusion.

" Oh, that is nothing. You would have been of great use to me. If I thought of helping you at all, my idea was simply—how shall I put it?—to make up in some way for the harm I've done you."

" What harm have you ever done me? "

For one moment he thought that she had discovered his preposterous passion, and reproached herself for being a cause of pain. But she explained.

" I ought to say the harm the catalogue did you. I'm afraid it was responsible for your illness."

He protested. But she stuck to it. " And after all I might just as well have let you go. For the library will have to be sold. But I did not know that."

" I knew it, though."

" You knew it? How did you know it? "

" I know Mr. Pilkington, who knows my father. He

practically gave him the refusal of the library. Which is exactly what I want to speak to you about."

He explained the situation to her as he had explained it to Miss Palliser, only at greater length and with considerably greater difficulty. For Lucia did not take it up as Miss Palliser had done, point by point, she laid it down, rather, dismissed it with a statement of her trust in the integrity of Rickman's.

"If," she said, "the library must be sold, I'm very glad that it's your father who is going to buy it."

He tried to make her see (without too deeply incriminating his father) that this was not the destiny most to be desired for it.

It was in approaching this part of his subject that he most diverged from his manner of treating it before Miss Palliser.

Miss Palliser had appreciated the commercial point of view. Her practical mind accepted the assumption that a dealer was but human, and that abnegation on his part in such a matter would amount to nothing less than a moral miracle. But Miss Harden would have a higher conception of human obligation than Miss Palliser; at any rate he could hardly expect her sense of honour to be less delicate than his own, and if *he* considered that his father was morally bound to withdraw from the business she could only think one thing of his remaining in it. Therefore to suggest to Miss Harden that his father might insist upon remaining, constituted a far more terrible exposure of that person than anything he had said to Miss Palliser.

"Why shouldn't he buy it?" she asked.

"Because, I'm afraid, selling it in—in that way, you won't make much money over it."

"Well—it's not a question of making money, it's a question of paying a debt."

"How much you make—or lose—of course, depends on the amount of the debt—what it was valued at."

Lucia, unlike Kitty, was neither suspicious nor discreet. She had the required fact at her fingers' ends and instantly produced it. "It was valued at exactly one thousand pounds."

"And it should have been valued at four. My father can't give anything like that. We ought to be able to find somebody who can. But it might take a considerable time."

"And there is no time. What do you advise me to do then?"

"Well, if we could persuade Mr. Pilkington to sell by auction that would be all right. If we can't, I advise you to buy it back, or a part of it, yourself. Buy back the books that make it valuable. You've got the Aldine Plato, and the Neapolitan Horace, and the *Aurea Legenda* printed by Wynkyn de Worde." (He positively blushed as he consummated this final act of treachery to Rickman's.) "And heaps of others equally valuable; I can give you a list of fifty or so. You can buy them for a pound apiece and sell the lot for three thousand. If Pilkington collars the rest he'll still be paid, and there may be something over."

She considered a moment. "Has Mr. Pilkington any idea of the value of those books?"

"I'm certain he hasn't. Only an expert could have."

"Would it be perfectly fair to him?"

"To *him?* Perfectly fair. You buy them at his own valuation."

"I see. I should like to do that—if—if it can be managed."

"I think it can be managed. My father isn't likely to settle with Mr. Pilkington without consulting me. If he *has* settled we must try and get him to withdraw."

"Oh, surely there would be no difficulty about that?"

He said nothing. It was really terrible the way she took integrity for granted. To be sure his father had a reputation with the family. He remembered how Sir Joseph used to praise him to his face as the only honest dealer in London. But Sir Joseph was in the habit of buying books, not selling them.

He rose and turned away, evading her innocent eyes.

"I hope not. I'll see Mr. Pilkington about it. By the way, here *is* Mr. Pilkington. Did you expect him?"

"No I——" Her voice died away, extinguished in her horror.

CHAPTER XXXI

THERE could be no mistake about it.

Mr. Pilkington was coming by the private way, stepping softly over a fair green lawn. The low golden light before sunset flooded the lawn so that Mr. Pilkington walking in it was strangely and gloriously illuminated. Everything about him shone, from his high silk hat to the tips of his varnished boots. His frock coat and trousers of grey summer suiting clung to his figure like a warm and sunny skin. All over Mr. Pilkington and round about him there hung the atmosphere of the City. Not of the actual murky labyrinth, roofed with fog, but of the City as she stands transfigured before the eyes of the young speculator, in her orient golden mood.

Lucia had seen him. The light died out of her face, her lips straightened. She stood motionless, superb, intent. With such a look and in such an attitude a Roman maiden might have listened to the feet of the Vandal at the gate.

He was coming very swiftly, was Dicky, as if borne by an impetus of conquest. As he caught sight of Miss Harden through the open window, though he kept his head rigidly averted, his eyes slewed round towards her, and at the same moment his fingers rose instinctively to his little fair moustache. It was the gesture of the irresistible male.

"*Must* I see him?" she asked helplessly. She had realized everything in that moment.

"Not unless you like. Shall I deal with him?"

"If you would be so good. But no—it doesn't matter. I shall have to see him later."

She sat down again and waited. The silence was so tense that it seemed to bear the impact of her pulses; it throbbed and quivered with pain. Outside, the sound of the pebbles, crunched under Pilkington's footsteps, became a concert of shrieks.

Rickman did not offer to go as Mr. Pilkington advanced; for, Heaven knew how, in some obscure and subtle way she had managed to convey to him that his presence was a protection.

Mr. Pilkington entered the room with the air of a man completely assured as to his reception. He bowed to Miss

Harden; an extraordinary bow. No words could have conveyed the exquisite intimations of Mr. Pilkington's spine. It was as if he had said to her, "Madam, you needn't be afraid; in your presence I am all deference and chivalry and restraint." But no sooner had Dicky achieved this admirable effect of refinement than he spoilt it all by the glance he levelled at young Rickman. *That* expressed nothing but the crude emotion of the insolent male, baulked of his desire to find himself alone on the field. It insulted her as brutally as any words by its unblushing assumption of the attitude of sex.

"I must introduce myself, Miss 'Arden," he said, ignoring Rickman. "I think I have *not* had the pleasure——" His large mouth closed reluctantly on the unfinished phrase.

He seated himself with circumstance, parting the tails of his coat very carefully. He had chosen a seat opposite the window. As if conscious of the glory of his appearance, he offered himself liberally to the light. He let it play over his figure, a figure that youth subdued to sleekness that would one day be corpulence; it drew out all the yellow in his moustache and hair; it blazed in his gold-rimmed eyeglass; thence it alighted, a pale, watery splendour, on the bridge of his nose. It was a bridge where two nationalities met and contended for mastery. Mr. Pilkington's nose had started with a distinctly Semitic intention, frustrated by the Anglo-Saxon in him, its downward course being docked to the proportion of a snub. Nobody knew better than Mr. Pilkington that it was that snub that saved him. He was proud of it as a proof of his descent from the dominant race. Assisted by his reluctantly closing mouth and double eye-glasses it inspired confidence, giving to Mr. Pilkington's face an expression of extreme openness and candour. He was proud of his eye-glass, too. He considered that it made him look like a man of science or of letters. But it didn't. It did much better for him than that. It took all the subtlety out of his face and endowed it with an earnest and enormous stare. And as that large mouth couldn't and wouldn't close properly, his sentences had a way of dying off in a faint gasp, leaving a great deal to the imagination. All these natural characteristics were invaluable for business purposes.

But if you had asked Mr. Pilkington for the secret of his

success, he would have told you that he owed it to his possession of two qualities, "bounce" and "tact." To both, mind you; for tact without bounce will carry a man neither far nor high; while bounce without tact will elevate him occasionally to his own perdition. Conversationally he was furnished with tentacles sensitive to the lightest touch of an idea; he had the very subtlest discernment of shades within shades. He grasped with airy impact; he moved by a delicate contact and recoil, a process he was pleased to describe as "feelin' his way."

He did not rush brutally into business, as a man of coarser fibre might have done. He removed his gloves, adjusted his eye-glasses, and admired the view. He shrank from the suggestion that he had come to "take possession," but clearly he could not take possession of the view. It was a safe and soothing topic.

"You have a very glorious outlook here, Miss Harden."

Then Mr. Pilkington perceived a shade. Miss Harden's outlook was *not* glorious.

By an almost visible recoil from his own blunder he strove to convey an impression of excessive delicacy.

"Wot very exceptional weather we are enjoying——" Perceiving another and a finer shade (for evidently Miss Harden was not enjoying the weather, or indeed anything else) Mr. Pilkington again shifted his ground. He spoke of books. He noticed with approval the arrangement of the library. He admired the Harden taste in costly bindings, as if he were by no means personally concerned with any of these things. And thus by a delicate and imperceptible transition, he slid into his theme.

"Now, as regards this—this sale, Miss Harden. I hope you understand——"

"I understand that you are my father's chief creditor, and that the sale is necessary."

"Quite so. But I'm most awfully sorry for the necessity. As for time—I don't want you to feel that you're pressed or hurried in any way." Mr. Pilkington's eyes gazed up at her under their great glasses, humid and immense. His lower lip drooped in an uncertain manner. He had a great deal of nice feeling about him, had Dicky.

"I hope those men aren't making a nuisance of themselves. They've had strict orders to keep in the background. I'm orf'ly upset," said Mr. Pilkington in a thick, emotional voice, " about this affair; and I want to consider you, Miss Harden, in every possible way."

" You are very kind. But I would rather you didn't consider me. In any way at all."

As she said this Mr. Rickman looked at her with a grave smile, conveying (behind Mr. Pilkington's back) an unmistakable warning.

Mr. Pilkington smiled too, a large and fluttering smile, as of one indulgent to any little attempt at brilliance on the part of a young lady under a cloud. Lucia swept him and his smile with her long and steady gaze, a gaze which made Dicky exceedingly uncomfortable.

" I think if you have any arrangements to make, you had better see my solicitor."

" I have an appointment," said Dicky, not without a certain dignity, " with Mr. Schofield, to-morrow morning."

" Then I suppose what you want now is to look over the house ? "

The question and the gaze were so direct that Dicky (who had meant to amble delicately round that point for another quarter of an hour) lost his head, dropt his eyeglass, and fairly let himself go.

" Well, perhaps as I *am* here, I'd better 'ave a look round. Of course—if—if it's in any way inconvenient——"

" Not in the least. You can look round at once."

She rang the bell. On her way to it she gathered up some books that were lying out of sight and laid them on the table.

" These," she said to Rickman, " belong to the library. They must go with the rest."

He looked at them. One was an Aldine Dante, he had seen her reading it. He took Pilkington aside and said something to him in a tone which Lucia could not hear. Her hand was on the door when Pilkington sprang forward.

" One moment, Miss Harden. Everything must be sold in the regular way, but if you'll tell me of any books you've a special fancy for, I'll make a note of them and buy them in for you." He paused awaiting the breath of inspiration. It came. " For—for a merely nominal sum."

To do Dicky justice this delicate idea greatly commended itself to his good nature. Business is business, but not willingly did Dicky inflict pain, least of all upon a young and pretty woman. Besides he had an eye to his reputation; he was disposed to do this thing handsomely. Rickman envied him his inspiration, his " merely nominal sum."

" Thank you. The books were not mine," said Lucia in spite of another meaning look from her ally.

" Quite so. But I should disregard that if I were you. Anyhow you can think it over, and if you change your mind you can let me or Mr. Rickman know before the sale."

Lucia looked down at him from her height. " I shall not change my mind. If I want to keep any of the books, I can buy them from Mr. Rickman."

She turned to Rickman in the doorway. " All the same, it was kind of you to think of it." She said it very distinctly, so that Mr. Pilkington could hear.

Rickman followed her out of the room and closed the door behind them. She turned on him eyes positively luminous with trust. It was as if she had abandoned the leading of her intellect and flung the reins on the neck of her intuition.

" I was right, wasn't I? I would so much rather buy them back from you."

" From my father?"

" It's the same thing, isn't it?"

He smiled sadly. " I'm afraid it isn't, quite. Why didn't you accept his offer?"

" I couldn't." She shuddered slightly. Her face expressed her deep and desperate repugnance. " I *can* buy them back from you. He is really arranging with your father, isn't he?"

" Yes." It was the third time that she had appealed from Pilkington to him, and there was a profound humiliation in the thought that at this precise moment the loathsome Dicky might be of more solid use to her than he.

" Well, then," she said almost triumphantly, " I shall be safe. You will do your best for me."

It was a statement, but he met it as if it had been a question.

" I will indeed."

He saw that it was in identifying his father with him that she left it to their honour.

CHAPTER XXXII

DICKY PILKINGTON did not belong to the aristocracy of finance. Indeed, finance had not in any form claimed him at the first.

Under the grey frock-coat and gleaming shirt-front, hidden away behind the unapparent splendours of Dicky Pilkington's attire (his undermost garments were of woven silk), in a corner of his young barbarian heart there lurked an obscure veneration for culture and for art. When his day's work was done, the time that Dicky did not spend in the promenade of the Jubilee Variety Theatre, he spent in reading Karl Pearson and Robert Louis Stevenson, with his feet on the fender. He knew the Greek characters. He *said* he could tell Plato from Aristotle by the look of the text. Dicky had begun life as a Junior Journalist. But before that, long, long before, when he was an innocent schoolboy, Dicky had a pair of wings, dear little cherubic wings, that fluttered uneasily under his little jacket. The wings moulted as Dicky grew older; they shrank (in the course of his evolution) to mere rudimentary appendages, and poor Dicky flopped instead of flying. Finally they dropt off and Dicky was much happier without them. Rickman used to say that if you stripped him you saw the marks of them still quite plainly; and Dicky was always stripping himself and showing them. They proved to these writing fellows what he might have been if he had only chosen. He had begun by being a poet like the best of them, and in his heart of hearts Dicky believed that it was as a poet he should end. His maxim upon this head was: "When I've feathered my nest it will be time enough for me to sing."

Dicky's nest was not long in feathering, and yet Dicky had not begun to sing. Still, at moments, after supper, or on a Sunday afternoon, walking in a green lane, Dicky would unbosom himself. He would tell you touching legends of his boyhood and adolescence. Then he would talk to you of women. And then he would tell you how it was that he came to forsake literature for finance.

He had begun in a small way by financing little tradesmen, little journalists and actresses in temporary difficulties; lending small sums to distressed clergymen, to governesses and the mistresses of boarding-houses. By charging a moderate interest he acquired a character for fairness and straight-forwardness. Now and then he did what he called a really tip-top generous thing. " Character," said Dicky Pilkington, " is capital "; and at thirty he had managed to save enough of it to live on without bothering about earning any more.

Then, by slow degrees, Dicky extended his business. He lent larger sums at correspondingly higher interest. Then he let himself go. He was caught by the glory of the thing, the poetry of finance. He soared to all the heights and sounded all the depths of speculation. He took risks with rapture. He fancied himself lending vast sums at giddy interest. " That," said Dicky to his conscience, " was to " cover his risk." He hadn't forgotten that character is capital. And when it occurred to him as it sometimes did, that he was making rather a large hole in it, he would then achieve some colossal act of generosity which set him on his legs again. So that Dicky Pilkington was always happy in his conscience as in everything else.

He had been prepared to do the handsome thing by Miss Harden, only her manner had somehow " choked him off." He could have afforded it, for he considered this Freddy Harden business as his very largest deal. He held a mortgage on the land, from the river to the top of Harcombe Hill. There was any amount to be got out of the pictures and the furniture. And the library was not altogether to be sneezed at. It had been Fred Harden's last desperate resource (rather poor security in Dicky's opinion); but if the sum advanced had not been prodigious (compared with the sums that had gone before it) the interest had been high. So that, in returning from his tour of inspection, he felt considerably elated.

Rickman, as he went down the High Street that evening, saw Dicky a little way in front of him. He noticed that the financial agent was an object of considerable interest to the people of Harmouth. Men stood at shop doors and street corners, women (according to their social standing) hung out of bedroom windows, or hid behind parlour curtains, to look after him as he went. Here and there Rickman caught sullen and indignant glances, derisive words

and laughter. Evidently the spirit of Harmouth was hostile
to Dicky. A Harden was a Harden, and Sir Frederick's
magnificently complete disaster had moved even the towns-
people, his creditors.

The excitement caused by Dicky concentrated at the windows of the London and Provincial Bank, where Sir
Frederick had had a large balance—overdrawn.

Harmouth High Street is a lane, wide at the top and
narrow at the bottom, which gives on to the esplanade between the Marine Hotel and the Bank. At a certain distance these buildings cut the view into a thin slip of grey
beach and steep blue sea. The form of Dicky was now visible in the centre of that slip, top-hatted, distinct against the
blue. He stood on the edge of the esplanade as on a railway platform, reading the paper and smoking a cigar.
From time to time, looking up with an expression half visionary, half voluptuous, he puffed and spat in dreamy
rhythmic sequence.

"*Cœlum, non animam,*" said Rickman to himself, "they
change their skies, but not their habits." When he came
up with him, he found the soul of Pilkington disporting
itself in its own airy element, exchanging ideas with two
young damsels who frolicked on the beach below. Backwards and forwards flew the light-hearted banter, like balls
of sea-foam, Mr. Pilkington the inspirer and the inspired.
The after-glow of his last triumphant witticism still illuminated his countenance when he turned again to the printed
page.

Now, owing to its peculiar construction, Harmouth High
Street acts as a funnel for the off-shore breezes; they rush
through it as they rush through Windy Gap, that rift in
the coast before which the wary fisherman slackens sail.
Just such an air was careering seawards when Mr. Pilkington was about to perform the difficult feat of folding his
paper backwards. It smote one side of the broadsheet and
tore it from his grasp, making it flutter like a sail escaped
from the lanyard. The breeze dropped; it hovered; it
waited like the wanton that it was; and when Mr. Pilkington's free hand made a clutch at the flying columns, it
seized that moment to lift his hat from his head and dash it
to the ground. Then the demon of the wind entered into
and possessed that high thing; the hat rolled, it curvetted, it

turned brim over crown, it took wings and flew, low and
eager like a cormorant; finally it struck the beach, gathering a frightful impetus from the shock, and bounded seawards, the pebbles beating from it a thin drum-like note.
Never was any created thing so tortured with indecent merriment in the face of doom. The end seemed certain, for
Dicky Pilkington, though he joined in the hysterics of the
crowd, had not compromised his dignity by pursuit; when,
just as the hat touched the foam of perdition, Molly Trick,
the fat bathing woman, interposed the bulwark of her body;
she stopped; she spread her wide skirts, and the maniac
leapt into them as into a haven.

The young men who watched this breezy incident over
the blinds of the London and Provincial Bank were immensely diverted. Even Rickman laughed as Dicky turned
to him his cheerful face buffeted by the wind.

Mr. Pilkington had put up at the same hotel as Rickman, and they found themselves alone at the dinner-table.

"Glori-orious air this," said Mr. Pilkington. "I don't
know how you feel, young 'un, but there's a voice that tells
me I shall dine."

Mr. Pilkington was not deceived by that prophetic voice.
He dined with appetite undiminished by his companion's
gloom. From time to time he rallied him on his coyness
under the fascinations of beef-steak, lager-beer, apricots,
and Devonshire cream.

"Well, Razors," he said at last, "and wot do you think
of the Harden Library?"

Rickman was discreet. "Oh, it isn't bad for a private
show. Sir Frederick doesn't seem to have been much of a
collector."

"Wasn't he though! In his own line he was a pretty
considerable collector, quite a what d'you call 'em—
virtuoso."

"Not very much virtue about him, I imagine."

"Well, whatever there may have been, in ten years that
joker went through his capital as if it had been a paper
hoop. Slap through it and out at the other side, on his feet,
grinning at you."

"How did he manage it?"

"Cards—horses—women—everything you can name,"
said Dicky, "that's amusing, and at the same time expen-

sive. They're precious slow down here in the country; but get 'em up to town, and there's nothing like 'em for going the pace, when they *do* go it."

"His velocity must have been something tremendous, to judge by the smash." Rickman was looking at the financial agent with an expression which some people might have been inclined to resent, but Dicky's gaiety was proof against criticism.

"What did he die of?" Rickman asked slowly.

"What a beastly question to ask at dinner. He died like most people, of his way of living. If Freddy Harden had had opportunities equal to his talents he would have smashed up ten years ago. Talent wasn't the word for it, it was genius."

"I see. And when you come across a poor struggling devil with a gift like that, you long to be kind to him, don't you? To bring him forward, to remove every obstacle to his career?"

"Well, yes, I suppose I did run Harden for all he was worth. Queer fish, Harden. He used to rave like a lunatic about his daughter; but I don't suppose he spent a fiver on her in his life. It's pretty rough on her, this business. But Loocher'll do. She's got cheek enough for half a dozen." Dicky chuckled at the memory of his discomfiture. "I like it. I like a girl with some bounce in her. Trust her to fall on her little tootsies anywhere you drop her."

"I can't say you've made the falling very easy for her."

Dicky's bright face clouded. "Wot the devil has that got to do with me? I've done *my* level best. Why, I could have cleaned them out years ago, if I'd chosen. Now, just to show you what sort of fellow Freddy Harden was—last time I ever saw him, poor chap, he told me that girl of his was a regular musical genius, just a little more technique, you know, and she'd beat Paderewski into a cocked hat. She was wonderful. That's the way he piled it on, and it may have been all true; he could have made a fortune, fiddling, if he hadn't been as proud as Satan and as lazy as a wombat. Well, I said, if that was so, I'd take her up and run her as a pro.—for friendship, mind you. I liked Freddy, and I was orf'ly sorry for him. She could pay me if she pulled it off; if not, she could let it stand over till the day of judgment."

Rickman flushed. "Did you know anything of Miss Harden, then?"

"Not I. Never set eyes on her. She might have been as ugly as sin for all I knew. I risked that."

"What did Sir Frederick say to your generous proposal?"

Dicky's face became luminous at the recollection. "He said he'd see me d——d first. But I meant it. I'd do it to-morrow if she asked me prettily."

"Have you any notion how she'll be left after all this?"

"Yes. There's the house, and her mother's money. Freddy couldn't get at that. When it's all settled up she can't be so badly off, I fancy. Still it's a beastly back-hander in the face, poor girl. By Jove, she does stand up to it in form, too. Too d——d well bred to let you know she's hit. You wouldn't think she'd be plucky, to look at her, would you? It's queer how the breeding comes out in a woman."

Rickman held himself in with difficulty. When pearls are cast before swine you look for depreciation as a matter of course; you would be infinitely more revolted if, instead of trampling them under their feet, the animals insisted on wearing them in their snouts. So Pilkington rooting in Miss Harden's affairs; Pilkington posing as Miss Harden's adviser; Pilkington adorning his obscene conversation with Miss Harden's name, was to Rickman an infinitely more abominable beast than Pilkington behaving according to his nature. But to quarrel with Pilkington on this head would have provoked the vulgarest of comments, and for Miss Harden's sake he restrained himself.

Dicky remained unconscious. "I'm glad you put me up to offering some of those books back. It goes against me to sell them, but what the devil am I to do?"

"*I* can't tell you."

"I shan't collar all this furniture, either. I'll buy in some of it and return it. The decent thing would be to give her back poor Freddy's portrait."

He passed his hand over a bunch of bananas,—he selected one, pinched it, smelt it, put it down and took another.

"It's a pity it's a Watts, that portrait," he murmured dreamily. He seemed to be wrestling with himself; and apparently he overcame. When he had eaten his banana his face was flushed and almost firm.

"I'll not take it. He sticks in my throat, does Freddy."

Rickman left the table. If he had disliked Dicky when he was callous, he loathed him when he was kind.

He threw open the window, and sat on the ledge. The breeze had died down and the heat in the little hotel was stifling. Across the passage glasses clinked in the bar, sounding a suitable accompaniment to the voice of Dicky. From time to time bursts of laughter came from the billiard-room overhead. Outside there, in the night, the sea smothered these jarring human notes with its own majestic tumult. Rickman, giving up his sickened senses to the night and the sea, was fortunate enough to miss a great deal that Pilkington was saying.

For Dicky, still seated at the table, talked on. He had mingled soda with whisky, and as he drank it, the veil of our earthly life lifted for Dicky, and there was revealed to him the underlying verity, the fabric of the world. In other words, Dicky had arrived at the inspired moment of the evening, and was chanting the Hymn of Finance.

"Look," said Dicky, "at the Power it gives you. Now all you writing chaps, you know, you're not in it, you're not in it at all. You're simply 'opping and dodging round the outside—you 'aven't a chance of really seeing the show. Whereas—look at *me*. I go and take my seat plump down in the middle of the stage box. I've got my ear to the heart of 'Umanity and my 'and on its pulse. I've got a grip of realities. You say you want to por-tray life. Very well, por-tray it. When all's said and done you've only got a picture. And wot's a picture, if it's ever so life-like? You 'aven't got a bit nearer to the real thing. I tell you, you aren't in it with me. I'd have been a writer myself if I'd thought it was good enough. I began that way; but as to going back to it, you might just as well expect me to go back to kissing a woman's photo when I can put my arm round her waist."

And Dicky, gracefully descending on the wings of his metaphor, alighted on Miss Poppy Grace. But to Rickman the figure of Poppy, once an obsession, was now as indistinct as the figure of Dicky seen through a cloud of tobacco smoke. He was roused by a more direct appeal, and what seemed to him a violent change of theme.

"Did you notice what rum eyes Miss Harden's got?

They haven't taught her how to use 'em, though. Hi, Ricky! Aren't you going to join us in a drink?"

"No, I'm not." His tone implied that he was not going to join Pilkington in anything.

"You seem a bit cut up on Miss Harden's account."

"If you mean that I think she's been most infernally treated, I do."

"H'm. Well, I will say the wind is not exactly tempered to that shorn lamb. But it's an ill wind that blows nobody any good. Queer how things are mixed up in this world. You wouldn't think there was much connection between Miss Harden and Miss Poppy Grace, would you? Well, wot's Loocher's loss is Popsie's gain; if that's any consolation."

"I certainly don't see the connection."

"No? I say, can't you shut the window? That d——d sea makes such a noise I can't hear myself speak. I was going to say I'd some notion of running Poppy on her own before long. And I think—I *think* I can do it out of this haul, before she signs another contract. Of course, we expect you and your friends to back us."

Dicky's voice came slightly muffled from the depths of his long tumbler.

Rickman turned round. "What did you say about Bacchus?" He had turned in anger, but at the spectacle presented by Pilkington he laughed aloud in the insolence of his youth.

"Shut that window, can't you? I say, if you can get at any of the papers and give them the tip——"

"Well?" Rickman's hand closed fiercely over the top of a soda-water syphon. Pilkington followed the movement with an innocent, but by no means unobservant eye.

Only the other day they had been rivals for the favour of Miss Poppy Grace, which seemed to be very evenly divided between them. If Rickman had her heart, he—Pilkington—held her by the power of the purse. Jealous he might be, but jealousy counted for little in the great mind of Pilkington. Human passions were the stuff he worked in. Where they raged highest it was his to ride on the whirlwind and direct the storm. If in Poppy's case they raged too high, his position as creditor gave him a tight grip of young Rickman. On the other hand, Rickman was now a full-fledged Junior Journalist, and Pilkington, amid the wreck of morals and the crash of creeds, had preserved a simple childlike faith in the omnipotence of the press. So, if it was madness for Rickman to irritate Pilkington, it was not altogether expedient for Pilkington to irritate him.

"Look here, Razors," said he, "you needn't go shying any syphons about. There's nothing behind this show but business. What I do for Miss Grace I do for cold cash. See? Of course, I take an interest in the girl——"

"Interest at something like a hundred and fifty per cent., I suppose?"

"That's about the figure. With your permission, I'll remove that fizz-gig out of your way. What do you think of it—my idea, I mean?"

"I think there's a d——d lot more interest than principle in it."

"You young goat! I'm out of it. Honour bright. So if you feel inclined to slog away and boom the lady, there's no reason why you shouldn't."

"Is there any reason why I should?" inquired Rickman with treacherous severity. So immense was his calm that Dicky was taken in by it and blundered.

"Well, yes," said he, "in that case, we might consider our little account settled."

"Our little account, Dicky, will be run up on the wrong side of the paper if you don't take care."

"Wot d'you mean?"

"I mean that when you've got a particularly filthy job on hand, it's as well to keep away from people who are not fond of dirt. At any rate, I advise you not to come too near me."

Dicky for the first time that evening looked uncomfortable. It occurred to Dicky that whiskey and soda was not the very best drink to talk business on.

"I've noticed, Rickman," said he, "that since you've been living down in the country, you don't seem able to understand a joke."

But Rickman had got his legs on the other side of the window ledge, and as Dicky approached him he slid down on to the esplanade and slipped into the night.

CHAPTER XXXIII

HARDLY knowing how he got there he found himself on the top of Harcombe Hill. His head was bare, and the soles of his thin slippers were cut with the flints of the hillside lane. He had walked, walked, walked, driven by a fury in his body and a fever in his feet.

His first idea had been to get as far away as possible from his companion. He felt that he never could be clean again after his contact with Dicky. How had the thing happened? Yesterday London seemed as far away from Harmouth as Babylon from Arcadia, and Rickman was not more infinitely removed from Lucia than Lucia was from Poppy; yet here they were, all three tangled together in Dicky's complicated draw-net. He held them all, Lucia by her honour, Poppy by her vanity, and him, Rickman, by the lusts and follies of his youth. This was what it had led him to, that superb triumphal progress of the passions. In language as plain as he could put it, he—he—had been offered a bribe to advertise Poppy Grace for the benefit of Dicky, who kept her. To advertise a little painted—he disposed of poor Poppy in a powerful word which would have given her propriety a fit if it could have heard him. That he himself should ever have been infatuated with Poppy seemed to him now incredible, monstrous. In the last three weeks he had not only grown sober, but mature. That youth of his which once seemed immortal, had then ceased to be a part of him. He had cut himself loose from it and put it behind him with all its miseries and tumults and pollutions. But he couldn't get rid of it. Like an unclean spirit cast out of him it seemed to have entered into Dicky as into a convenient herd of swine. And in Dicky's detestable person it rose up against him and pursued him. For Dicky, though sensual as any swine, was cautious. Dicky, even with an unclean spirit in him, was not in the least likely to rush violently down any steep place into the sea and so perish out of his life.

That Dicky should have appeared on his last night here seemed the vilest stroke that fate had ever dealt him. But Dicky could not follow him up Harcombe Hill.

He looked before him. The lights of Harmouth opened

out a thin line to the esplanade, dividing the sea from the
land by fire instead of foam; strewn in the bed of the valley
they revealed, as through some pure and liquid medium,
its darkness and its depth. Above them the great flank of
Muttersmoor stretched like the rampart of the night. Night
itself was twilight against that black and tragic line.

And Rickman, standing bareheaded on the hillside, was
lifted up out of his immense misery and unrest. He remembered how this land that he loved so passionately had
once refused him the inspiration that he sought. And now
it seemed to him that it could refuse him nothing, that
Nature, under cover of the darkness, gave up her inmost
ultimate secret. And if it be true that Nature's innermost
ultimate secret is known only to the pure, it was a sign of
his own cleansing, this sense of comfort and reconciliation,
of unspoiled communion, of profound, immeasurable peace.
In that moment his genius seemed to have passed behind
veils upon veils of separation, to possess that tender and
tragic beauty, to become one with the soul of the divine
illimitable night.

He was not in the least deceived as to the true source
of his inspiration. In all this, if you went back far enough,
his body counted; his body which he had made a house of
shame and hunger and desire, shaken by its own shivering
nerves and leaping, desperate pulses. But what of that
now? What matter, since that tumult of his blood had set
throbbing such subtle, such infinite vibrations in his soul.
That was what counted. He could tell by it the quality
and immensity of his passion, by just that spiritual resonance and response. It was the measure of Lucia's power
to move him, the measure too of his nearness to her no less
than of his separation.

She could not take away what she had given; and among
his sources of inspiration, of the unique and unforgetable
secret that had passed into him with the night, on Harcombe Hill, as he looked towards Muttersmoor, she also
counted. She would be always there, a part of it, a part
of him, whether she would or no. If that was any
consolation.

CHAPTER XXXIV

HE had made no empty promise when he assured her that he would do his best; for there was something that could still be done. He built great hopes on the result of the coming interview with his father. His idea was to go up to town by the early morning train and talk the whole thing over as calmly as might be. He would first of all appeal to his father's better feelings; he would make him see this thing as he saw it, he would rouse in him the spirit of integrity, the spirit of mercy and pity, the spirit of justice and chivalry and honour.

But if all the arts of persuasion failed to touch him, Rickman Junior had in reserve one powerful argument against which Rickman Senior would hardly be able to contend. There would no doubt be inspirations, but as to the main lines of his pleading he was already clear. He felt entirely confident and light-hearted as he rose at five the next morning to catch that early train.

Rickman Senior was not in the shop when Rickman Junior arrived on the scene. He was in a great bare room on an upper floor of the second-hand department. He looked more than ever studious and ascetic, having exchanged his soft felt hat for a velvet skull-cup, and his frock coat for a thin alpaca. He was attended by a charwoman with scrubbing brush and pail, a boy with ladder and broom, and a carpenter with foot-rule, note-book, and pencil. He moved among them with his most solemn, most visionary air, the air, not so much of a Wesleyan minister, as of a priest engaged in some high service of dedication. He was in fact making arrangements for the reception of no less than fifteen thousand volumes, the collection of the late Sir Joseph Harden, of Court House, Harmouth. And as he looked around him his face expressed the smooth and delicately voluptuous satisfaction of the dreamer who has touched his dream.

This look of beatitude faded perceptibly when the message came that Mr. Keith was in the front shop and wished to see him. Mr. Keith, it appeared, had no time to spare. Isaac had, in fact, expressed a slight shock at the earliness of Keith's return. His first thought was that at the last moment there had been some serious hitch with Pilkington. He found Keith sitting before the counter in the attitude of a rather imperious customer; but the warm pressure of his son's hand removed this disagreeable effect of superiority. Keith's face wore signs of worry and agitation that confirmed Isaac's original fear.

"Well," he said a little anxiously, "I didn't expect you back as early as this."

"I haven't come to stop. I've got to catch the twelve-thirty back again. I came up because I wanted to talk to you."

"Come," said Isaac, "into the office."

He laid his hand on Keith's shoulder as they went. He felt very kindly towards him at that moment. His heart was big with trust in the brilliant, impetuous boy. When he touched Keith's hand he had felt that intellectual virtue had gone out of it. He guessed that there was a crisis in the affairs of the House of Rickman, and that Keith had come with warning and with help. He knew his power of swift and effectual action in a crisis. Yes, yes; Keith's wits might go wool-gathering; but he was safe enough when he had gathered his wool.

"Well?" he repeated, lifting grave interrogative eyebrows. He had seated himself; but Keith remained standing, a sign with him of extreme perturbation.

"I thought I could explain things better if I saw you," he began.

"Quite so; quite so. I hope you haven't come to tell me there's been any 'itch."

"Well, I told you as much when I wrote."

"I understand you advised me to withdraw, because you thought Pilkington wanted a big price."

"I didn't know what he wanted; I knew what we ought to give."

"That was settled by looking in the register. You don't mean to say *he's* going to back out of it?"

Keith was so preoccupied that he failed to see the drift of his father's questioning. "You see," he continued, following his own thoughts, "it's not as if we had only ourselves to consider. There's Miss Harden."

"Ah, yes, Pilkington did make some mention of a young lady."

"She was good enough to say she'd rather we bought the library than anybody. I think we're bound to justify her confidence."

"Certainly, most certainly, we are," said Isaac with solemnity. He was agreeably flattered by this tribute to the greatness of his house.

"I thought I did right in promising that we would do our very best for her."

"Of course you were. But that's all settled. Mr. Pilkington knows that I'm prepared to meet his wishes."

"His wishes?"

"He gave me to understand that he was anxious to have a sum to hand over to the young lady. In fact, he wrote me a most touching appeal."

"What d——d impertinence! He had no business to appeal!"

"Well, per'aps it wasn't strictly business-like. But I think, under the circumstances, 'e was morally—*morally*—justified. And I think he will consider I've responded very handsomely."

"You've made him an offer, then?"

"I made it three days ago, provisionally, and he's accepted it," said Isaac, with some heat. "Why, he's got the cheque."

"For how much?"

"For twelve hundred."

"My dear father, you know, really, that won't do."

"Do you think it was foolish to pay the two hundred extra?"

Isaac gazed at him over his fine gold-rimmed spectacles; and as he gazed he kept drawing his beard slowly through one lean and meditative hand. It was thus that he grasped his son's argument and drew it to a point.

"Foolish? It was—don't you see? We—we simply can't do it."

"Why, you said yourself we could go as far as four thousand five, or four thousand at the very least."

Keith looked steadily at his father, who was too deeply and solemnly absorbed to perceive the meaning of the look. "That was not quite what I said. I said—if we were *not* prepared to go so far, it was our duty to withdraw. I thought I had made that clear to you."

" You 'aven't made it clear to me why you're objecting to that two hundred now."

Isaac was beginning to feel that stupidity was now his refuge.

" I'm not objecting to your reckless extravagance, as you seem to think. I'm trying to suggest that twelve hundred is a ridiculously small offer for a collection which can't be worth less than four thousand."

" It may be worth that to a collector. It isn't worth it to me."

" It's worth it to any dealer who knows his business."

" Pretty business, if you have to buy at fancy prices and sell at a risk."

" I allowed for the risk in the valuation—I always do. There's one point where you *are* extravagant, if you like. What's the use of paying me for advice if you won't take it? "

Isaac's stupidity increased.

" 'Ow do you mean—paying you for your advice? "

" Paying a valuer, then, if you won't accept his valuation."

So unwilling was he to admit the sharpness of his father's practice that he tried to persuade himself that they had merely disagreed on a point of connoisseurship. " My advice, if you remember, was to withdraw decently, or pay a decent price."

" I've paid my price, and I'm certainly not going to withdraw."

" Well, but I'm afraid, if you won't withdraw, I must. You haven't paid *my* price, and I can't be responsible."

Isaac caressed his beard gently, and looked at Keith with a gaze so clear that it might have passed for pure. He was saying to himself, as he had said once before, " There's a woman in it."

" Don't you see," Keith broke out, " the atrocious position that I'm in? I promised Miss Harden that we'd do our best for her, and now we're taking advantage of the situation to drive an iniquitous bargain with her."

As Keith made this powerful statement Isaac smiled, puzzled and indulgent, as at some play of diverting but incomprehensible humour. In fact, he never could clearly distinguish between Keith's sense of humour and his sense of honour; both seemed equally removed from the safe, intelligible methods of ordinary men. He wasn't sure but what there was something fine in it, something in keeping with the intellectual extravagance that distinguished his son from other people's sons. There were moments when it amused and interested him, but he did not care to have it obtruded on him in business hours.

" I'm driving no bargain with the lady at all. The books aren't hers, they're Pilkington's. I'm dealing with him."

" And you refuse to consider her interests? "

" How can you say so when I'm paying two hundred more than I need do, on her account alone? You must explain that clearly to her."

" Not I. You can explain it yourself. To me, you see, the whole thing's simply a colossal fraud. I won't have anything to do with it."

" You 'aven't anything to do with it. I made the bargain, and I keep to it."

" Very well, then, you must choose between your bargain and me."

" Wot do you mean, choose between my bargain and you? "

" I mean exactly what I say. I know (if you don't) that that two hundred ought to be three thousand, and if it isn't paid I shall have to shunt the business. I never meant to stay in it for ever, but in this case I shall simply clear out at once, that's all. See? "

" No. I don't see. I don't see myself paying three thousand to a man who's willing to take two hundred."

" See my point, I mean. If the three thousand isn't paid, I go. On the other hand, if it is paid, I stay."

This was one of those inspirations on which he had counted, and it presented itself to him as a " clincher." At the same instant he realized that he was selling himself into slavery for three thousand pounds. No, not for three thousand pounds, for his honour's sake and Lucia Harden's.

Isaac looked graver, alarmed even; it struck him that Keith's peculiar vein of extravagance was becoming dangerous.

" You can calculate the interest at four per cent., and knock a hundred and twenty off my salary, if you like; but I'll stay. It's pretty clear, isn't it? I think, on the whole, it might be as well for you to close with the offer. It seems to me that if I'm worth anything at all, I'm worth three thousand."

" I haven't priced your services yet." Isaac's gaze shifted. He was beginning to feel something of that profound discomfort he had experienced before in the presence of his son. " Now, when you spoke to Miss 'Arden, had she any notion of the value of the library?"

" None whatever, till I told her."

" Do you mean to stand there and say that you were fool enough to tell her?"

" Certainly; I thought it only fair to her."

" And did you think it was fair to me?"

" Why not? If you're not dealing with her what difference could it make?"

He said to himself, " I've got him there!"

Isaac was indeed staggered by the blow, and lost his admirable composure.

" Do you know wot you've done? You've compromised me. You've compromised the honour and the reputation of my 'Ouse. And you've done it for a woman. You can't 'ide it; you're a perfect fool where women are concerned."

" If anybody's compromised, I think it's me. I pledged my word."

" And wot business had you to pledge it?"

" Oh, I thought it safe. I didn't think you'd dishonour my draft on your reputation."

" Draft indeed! That's it. You might just as well 'ave taken my cheque-book out of the drawer there and forged my signature at the bottom. Why, it's moral forgery—that's wot it is. I can see it all. You thought you were acting very generous and grand with this young lady. I say you were mean. You did it on the cheap. You'd no expense, or risk, or responsibility at all. I know you can't see it that way, but that's 'ow it is."

Keith did not defend himself against this view of his conduct, and Isaac preserved his attitude of moral superiority.

" I'm not blaming you, my boy. It's my own fault. I shouldn't 'ave sent you out like that, *with* cart blansh, so to speak, and without it. I should 'ave given you some responsibility."

"Oh, thanks, I couldn't very well have done with more than I had."

"Ah—you don't know the kind of responsibility I mean. You seem very ready to play fast and loose with my business. I daresay, now, you think since you 'aven't much to lose, you 'aven't much to gain?"

"Well, frankly, I can't see that I have—much. But I've got to catch a train in twenty minutes, and I want to know what you're going to do? Am I worth three thousand, or am I not?"

"You're worth a great deal more to me. You've got an education I 'aven't got; you've got brains; you've got tact, when you choose to use it. You've got expert knowledge, and I can't carry on my business without that. I'm not unreasonable. I can see that you can't act to advantage if you're not made responsible, if you haven't any direct interest in the business." He fixed his son with a glance that was nothing if not spiritually fine. Keith found himself struggling against an infamous, an intolerable suspicion.

"And that," said Isaac, "is wot I mean to give you. I've thought it well over, and I believe it's worth my while." He went on, joining his finger-tips, like a man who fits careful thought to careful thought, suggesting the final adjustment of a plan long ago determined and approved, for something in Keith's face made him anxious that this offer should not appear to be born of the subject under discussion.

"It was always my intention to take you into partnership. I didn't mean to do it quite so soon, but rather than 'ear this talk of flinging up the business, I'm prepared to do it now."

"On the same conditions?"

Now that Rickman's should eventually become Rickman and Son was a very natural development, and, in any ordinary circumstances, Isaac could hardly have made a more innocent and suitable proposal. But it was no longer possible for Keith to ignore its significance. It meant that his father was ready to buy his services at any price; to bribe him into silence.

His worst misgivings had never included such a possibility. In fact, before going down to Devonshire he had never had any serious misgivings at all. His position in his father's shop had hitherto presented no difficulties to a sensitive honour. He had not been sure that his honour was particularly sensitive, not more so, he supposed, than other people's. Acting as part of the machinery of Rickman's, he had sometimes made a clever bargain; he had never, so far as he knew, driven a hard one. He was expected to make clever bargains, to buy cheap and sell dear, to watch people's faces, lowering the price by their anxiety to sell, raising it by their eagerness to buy. That was his stern duty in the second-hand department. But there had been so many occasions on which he had never done his duty; times when he was tempted to actual defiance of it, when a wistful calculating look in the eyes of some seedy scholar would knock all the moral fibre out of him, and a two and sixpenny book would go for ninepence or a shilling. And such was his conception of loyalty to Rickman's, that he generally paid for these excesses out of his own pocket, so that conscience was satisfied both ways. Therefore there had been no moral element in his dislike to Rickman's; he had shrunk from it with the half-fantastic aversion of the mind, not with this sickening hatred of the soul. After three weeks of Lucia Harden's society he had perceived how sordid were the beginnings from which his life had sprung. As his boyish dreams had been wrought like a broidery of stars on the floor of the backshop, so honour, an unattainable ideal, had stood out in forlorn splendour against a darker and a dirtier background. He had felt himself obscurely tainted and involved. Now he realized, as he had never realized before, that the foundations of Rickman's were laid in bottomless corruption. It was a House built, not only on every vile and vulgar art known to trade, but on many instances of such a day's work as this. And it was into this pit of infamy that his father was blandly inviting him to descend. He had such an abominably clear vision of it that he writhed and shuddered with shame and disgust; he could hardly have suffered more if he had gone down into it bodily himself. He endured in imagination the emotions that his father should have felt and apparently did not feel.

He came out of his shudderings and writhings unspeakably consoled and clean; knowing that it is with such nausea and pangs that the soul of honour is born.

Their eyes met; and it was the elder Rickman's turn for bitterness. It had come, the moment that he had dreaded. He was afraid to meet his son's eyes, for he knew that they had judged him. He felt that he stood revealed in that sudden illumination of the boy's radiant soul. An instinct of self-preservation now prompted him to belittle Keith's character. He had found amazing comfort in the reflection that Keith was not all that he ought to be. As far as Isaac could make out, he was always running after the women. He was a regular young profligate, an infidel he was. What right had he to sit in judgment?

Shrewd even in anger, he took refuge in an adroit misconstruction of Keith's language. "I lay down *no* conditions. I'm much too anxious about you. I want to see you in a house of your own, settled down and married to some good girl who'll keep you steady and respectable. It's a simple straightforward offer, and you take it or leave it."

"I'll take it on two conditions. First, as I said before, that we either withdraw or pay over that three thousand. Second, that in the future no bargains are made without my knowledge—and consent. That means giving me the entire control of my own department."

"It means reducing me to a mere cypher."

"Such bargains are questions for experts, and should be left to experts."

"If I were to leave them to experts like you I should be bankrupt in a fortnight."

"I'm sorry, but you must choose between your methods and mine. There's ten minutes to do it in."

"It won't take ten minutes to see what will ruin me quickest. As I told you before, I'm not going back on my bargain."

"Nor I on mine."

Isaac spent three minutes in reflection. He reflected first, that Keith had been in the past "a young profligate"; secondly, that he was at the present moment in love; thirdly, that in the future he would infallibly be hungry. He would think very differently when he had forgotten the lady; or if he didn't think differently he would behave differently when his belly pinched him. Isaac was a firm believer in the persuasive power of the primitive appetites.

"Only seven minutes," murmured Keith. "I'm sorry to hurry you, father, but I really must catch that train."

"Wait—steady. Do you know wot you're about? You shan't do anything rash for want of a clear understanding. Mind—as you stand there, you're nothing but a paid shop-assistant; and if you leave the shop, you leave it without a penny to your name."

"Quite so. My name will hardly be any the worse for that. You're sure you've decided? You—really—do *not* —want—to keep me?"

After all, did he want to keep him, to be unsettled in his conscience and ruined in his trade? What, after all, had Keith brought into the business but three alien and terrible spirits, the spirit of superiority, the spirit of criticism, the spirit of tempestuous youth? He would be glad to be rid of him, to be rid of those clear young eyes, of the whole brilliant and insurgent presence. Not that he believed that it would really go. He had a genial vision of the hour of Keith's humiliation and return, a vivid image of Keith crawling back on that empty belly.

At that moment Keith smiled, a smile that had in it all the sweetness of his youth. It softened his father's mood, though it could not change it.

"I'm afraid I can't afford to pay your price, my boy."

He was the first to turn away.

And Keith understood too thoroughly to condemn. That was it. His father couldn't pay his price. The question was, could he afford to pay it himself?

As the great swinging doors closed behind him, he realized that whatever price he had paid for it, he had redeemed his soul. And he had bought his liberty.

CHAPTER XXXV

REALLY, as Miss Harden's solicitor pointed out to her in the presence of Miss Palliser, things looked very black against the young man. It was clear, from the letter Mr. Schofield had received from Mr. Jewdwine that morning, that the library was worth at least three times the amount these Rickmans had paid for it. Barring the fact that sale by private contract was irregular and unsatisfactory, he completely exonerated Mr. Pilkington from all blame in the matter. His valuation had evidently been made in all good faith, if in some ignorance. But the young man, who by Pilkington's account had been acting all along as his father's agent, must have been perfectly aware of the nature of the bargain he had made. There was every reason to suppose that he had known all about the bill of sale before he came down to Harmouth; and there could be no doubt he had made use of his very exceptional opportunities to inform himself precisely of the value of the books he was cataloguing. He must have known that they had been undervalued by Mr. Pilkington, and seen his chance of buying them for a mere song.

So what does he do? He carefully conceals his knowledge from the persons most concerned; obviously, that he and his father may keep the market to themselves. Then at the last moment he comes and pretends to give Miss Harden a chance of forestalling the purchase, knowing well that before she can take a single step the purchase will be concluded. Then he hurries up to town; and the next thing you hear is that he's very sorry, but arrangements have unfortunately already been made with Mr. Pilkington. No doubt, as agent of the sale, that young man would pocket a very substantial commission. Clearly in the face of the evidence, it was impossible to acquit him of dishonesty; but no action could be brought against him, because the matter lay entirely between him and Mr. Pilkington.

Lucia and Kitty had listened attentively to the masterly analysis of Mr. Rickman's motives; and at the end Kitty admitted that appearances were certainly against him; while Lucia protested that he was a poet, and therefore constitutionally incapable of the peculiar sort of cleverness imputed to him. The man of law submitted that because he was a poet it did not follow that he was not an uncommonly knowing young man too. Whereupon Kitty pointed out one or two flaws in the legal argument. In the first place, urged Kitty, the one thing that this knowing young man did not know was the amount of security the library represented.

Mr. Schofield smiled in genial forbearance with a lady's ignorance. He *must* have known, for such information is always published for the benefit of all whom it may concern.

But Kitty went on triumphantly. There was nothing to prove it, nothing to show that this knowing young man knew all the facts when he first undertook to work for Miss Harden. So far from concealing the facts later on, he had, to her certain knowledge, written at once to Mr. Jewdwine advising him to buy in the library, literally over old Rickman's head. That old Rickman's action had not followed on young Rickman's visit to town was sufficiently proved by the dates. The letter to Mr. Pilkington enclosing the cheque for twelve hundred had been written and posted at least twelve hours before his arrival. What the evidence did prove was that he had moved heaven and earth to make his father withdraw from his bargain.

Mr. Schofield coldly replied that the better half of Miss Palliser's arguments rested on the statements of the young man himself, to which he was hardly inclined to attach so much importance as she did. If his main assertion was correct, that he had written to inform Mr. Jewdwine of the facts, it was a little odd, to say the least of it, that Mr. Jewdwine made no mention of having received that letter. And that he had *not* received it might be fairly inferred from the discrepancy between young Rickman's exaggerated account of the value and Mr. Jewdwine's more moderate estimate.

Lucia and Kitty first looked at each other, and then away to opposite corners of the room. And at that moment Kitty was certain, while Lucia doubted; for Kitty went by the logic of the evidence and Lucia by the intuition which was one with her desire. Surely it was more likely that Rickman had never written to Horace than that Horace should have failed her, if he knew? Meanwhile the cold legal voice went on to shatter the last point in Kitty's defence, observing that, if Rickman had not had time to get up to town before his father wrote to Mr. Pilkington, he had plenty of time to telegraph. He added that the young man's moral character need not concern them now. Whatever might be thought of his conduct it was not actionable. And to the legal mind what was not actionable was irrelevant.

But for Lucia, to whom at the moment material things were unrealities, the burning question was the honesty or dishonesty of Rickman; for it involved the loyalty or disloyalty, or rather, the ardour or the indifference of Horace.

If Rickman were cleared of the grosser guilt, her cousin was, on a certain minor count, condemned; and there could be no doubt which of the two she was the more anxious to acquit.

" I suppose you'll see him if he calls?" asked Kitty when they were alone.

" See who?"

" Mr. Savage Keith Rickman." Even in the midst of their misery Kitty could not forbear a smile.

But for once Lucia was inaccessible to the humour of the name.

" Of course I shall see him," she said gravely.

CHAPTER XXXVI

HE called soon after six that evening, coming straight from the station to the house. Miss Palliser was in the library, but his face as he entered bore such unmistakable signs of emotion that Kitty in the kindness of her heart withdrew.

He was alone there, as he had been on that evening of his first coming. He looked round at the place he had loved so well, and knew that he was looking at it now for the last time. At his feet the long shadow from the bust of Sophocles lay dusk upon the dull crimson; the level light from the west streamed over the book-shelves, lying softly on brown Russia leather and milk-white vellum, lighting up the delicate gold of the tooling, glowing in the blood-red splashes of the lettering pieces; it fell slant-wise on the black chimney piece, chiselling afresh the Harden motto: *Invictus*. There was nothing meretricious, nothing flagrantly modern there, as in that place of books he had just left; its bloom was the bloom of time, the beauty of a world already passing away. Yet how he had loved it; how he had given himself up to it; how it had soothed him with its suggestion of immortal things. And now, for this last time, he felt himself surrounded by intelligences, influences; above the voices of his anguish and his shame he heard the stately generations calling; they approved; they upheld him in his resolution.

He turned and saw Lucia standing beside him. She had

come in unheard, as on that evening which seemed now so long ago.

She held out her hand. Not to have shaken hands with the poor fellow would, she felt, have been to condemn him without a hearing.

He did not see the offered hand, nor yet the chair it signed him to take. As if he knew that he was on his trial, he stood rigidly before her. His eyes alone approached her, looking to hers to see if they condemned him.

Lucia's eyes were strictly non-committal. They, too, seemed to stand still, to wait, wide and expectant, for his defence. Her attitude was so far judicial that she was not going to help him by a leading question. She merely relieved the torture of his visible bodily constraint by inviting him to sit down. He dropped into a chair that stood obliquely by the window, and screwed himself round in it so as to face her.

"I saw my father this morning," he began. "I went up by the early train."

"I know."

"Then you know by this time that I was a day too late."

"Mr. Pilkington sent me your father's letter."

"What did you think of it?"

The question, so cool, so sudden, so direct, was not what she felt she had a right to expect from him.

"Well—what did you think of it yourself?"

She looked at him and saw that she had said a cruel thing.

"Can't you imagine what I think of it?"

This again was too sudden; it took her at a disadvantage, compelling her instantly to commit herself to a theory of innocence or complicity.

"If you can't," said he, "of course there's no more to be said." He said it very simply, as if he were not in the least offended, and she looked at him again.

No. There was no wounded dignity about him, there was the tragic, irremediable misery of a man condemned unheard. And could that be her doing—Lucia's? She who used to be so kind and just? Never in all her life had she condemned anybody unheard.

But she had to choose between this man, who a month ago was an utter stranger to her, and Horace, who was of

her own blood, her own class, her own life. Did she really
want Mr. Rickman to be tainted that Horace might be
clean? And she knew he trusted her; he had made his
appeal to the spirit that had once divined him. He might
well say, " could she not imagine what he thought of it?"

"Yes," she said gently, " I think I can. If you had not
told me what the library was worth, of course I should
have thought your father very generous in giving as much
for it as he has done."

"I did tell you I was anxious he—we—should not buy
it; because I knew we couldn't give you a proper price."

"Yes, you told me. And I wanted you to buy it, because I thought you would do your best for me."

"I know. I know. If it wasn't for that—but that's the
horrible part of it."

"Why? You did your best, did you not?"

"Yes. I really thought it would be all right if I went
up and saw him. I felt certain he would see it as I
did——"

"Well?"

He answered with painful hesitation. " Well—he didn't
see it. My father hasn't very much imagination—he
couldn't realize the thing in the same way, because he
wasn't in it as I was. He'd seen nobody but Pilkington,
you see."

Something in her face told him that this line of defence
was distasteful to her, that he had no right to make a personal matter of an abstract question of justice. It was
through those personalities that he had always erred.

"I don't see what that has to do with it," she said.

"He—he thought it was only a question of a bargain
between Pilkington and him."

"What you mean is that he wouldn't admit that I came
into it at all?"

She saw that she was putting him to the torture. He
could not defend himself without exposing his father; but
she meant that he should defend himself, that he should if
possible stand clear.

"Yes. He hadn't seen you. He wouldn't go back on
his bargain, and I couldn't make him. God knows I tried
hard enough!"

"Did you think you could do anything by trying?"

"I thought I could do a good deal. I had a hold on him, you see. I happen to be extremely useful to him in this branch of his business. I was trained for it; in fact, I'm hopelessly mixed up with it. Well, he can't do very much without me, and I told him that if he didn't give up the library I should give him up. It wasn't a nice thing to have to say to your father——"

"And you said it?" Her face expressed both admiration and a certain horror.

"Yes. I told him he must choose between me and his bargain."

"That must have been hard."

"He didn't seem to find it so. Anyhow, he hasn't chosen me."

"I meant hard for you to have to say it."

"I assure you it came uncommonly easy at the moment."

"Don't—don't."

"I'm not going to defend him simply because he happens to be my father. I don't even defend myself."

"You? You didn't know."

"I knew quite enough. I knew he might cheat you without meaning to. I didn't think he'd do it so soon or so infamously, but, to tell the truth, I went up to town on purpose to prevent it."

"I know—I know that was what you went for." She seemed to be answering some incessant voice that accused him, and he perceived that the precipitancy of his action suggested a very different interpretation. His position was odious enough in all conscience, but as yet it had not occurred to him that he could be suspected of complicity in the actual fraud.

"Why didn't I do something to prevent it before?"

"But—didn't you?"

"I did everything I could. I wrote to my father—if that's anything; the result, as you see, was a cheque for the two hundred that should have been three thousand."

"Did it never occur to you to write to anybody else, to Mr. Jewdwine, for instance?"

She brought out the question shrinkingly, as if urged against her will by some intolerable compulsion, and he judged that this time they had touched what was, for her a vital point.

" Of course it occurred to me. Haven't you heard from him? "

" I have. But hardly in time for him to do anything."

He reflected. Jewdwine had written; therefore his intentions had been good. But he had delayed considerably in writing; evidently, then, he had been embarrassed. He had not mentioned that he had heard from him; and why shouldn't he have mentioned it? Oh, well—after all, why should he? At the back of his mind there had crawled a wriggling, worm-like suspicion of Jewdwine. He saw it wriggling and stamped on it instantly.

There were signs of acute anxiety on Miss Harden's face. It was as if she implored him to say something consoling about Jewdwine, something that would make him pure in her troubled sight. A light dawned on him.

" *Did* you write to him? " she asked.

He saw what she wanted him to say, and he said it. " Yes, I wrote. But I suppose I did it too late, like everything else I've done."

He had told the truth, but not the whole truth, which would have been damaging to Jewdwine. To deny altogether that he had written would have been a clumsy and unnecessary falsehood, easily detected. Something more masterly was required of him, and he achieved it without an instant's hesitation, and with his eyes open to the consequences. He knew that he was deliberately suppressing the one detail that proved his own innocence. But as their eyes met he saw that she knew it, too; that she divined him through the web that wrapped him round.

" Well," she said, " if you wrote to Mr. Jewdwine, you did indeed do your best."

The answer, on her part, was not less masterly in its way. He could not help admiring its significant ambiguity. It was both an act of justice, an assurance of her belief in him, and a superb intimation of her trust in Horace Jewdwine. And it was not only superb, it was almost humble in that which it further confessed and implied—her gratitude to him for having made that act of justice consistent with loyalty to her cousin. How clever of her to pack so many meanings into one little phrase!

" I did it too late," he said, emphasizing the point which served for Jewdwine's vindication.

" Never mind that. You did it."

" Miss Harden, is it possible that you still believe in me? " The question was wrung from him; for her belief in him remained incredible.

" Why should it not be possible? "

" Any man of business would tell you that appearances are against me."

" Well, I don't believe in appearances; and I do believe in you. You are not a man of business, you see."

" Thank goodness, I'm not, now."

" You never were, I think."

" No. And yet, I'm so horribly mixed up with this business, that I can never think of myself as an honest man again."

She seemed to be considering whether this outburst was genuine or only part of his sublime pretence.

"And I could never think of you as anything else. I should say, from all I have seen of you, that you are, if anything, *too* honest, too painfully sincere."

(" Yes, yes," her heart cried out, " I believe in him, *because* he didn't tell the truth about that letter to Horace." She could have loved him for that lie.)

He was now at liberty to part with her on that understanding, leaving her to think him all that was disinterested and honourable and fine. But he could not do it. Not in the face of her almost impassioned declaration of belief.

At that moment he was ready rather to fall at her feet in the torture of his shame. And as he looked at her, tears came into his eyes, those tears that cut through the flesh like knives, that are painful to bring forth and terrible to see.

" I've not been an honest man, though. I've no right to let you believe in me."

Her face was sweeter than ever with its piteous, pathetic smile struggling through the white eclipse of grief.

" What have you done? "

" It's not what I have done. It's what I didn't do. I told you that I knew the library was going to be sold. I told you that yesterday, and you naturally thought I only *knew* it yesterday, didn't you? "

" Well, yes, but I don't see——"

She paused, and his confession dropt into the silence with an awful weight.

" I knew—all the time."

She leaned back in her chair, the change of bodily posture emphasizing the spiritual recoil.

"All the time, and you never told me?"

"All the time and I never told you. I'd *almost* forgotten when you offered me that secretaryship, but I knew it when I let you engage me; I knew it before I came down. I never would have come if I had realized what it meant, but when I did know, I stayed all the same."

" What do you think you ought to have done?"

" Of course, I ought to have gone away—since I couldn't be honest and tell you."

"And why," she said it very gently, but with no change in her attitude, " why couldn't you be honest and tell me?"

" I'm not sure that I'd any right to tell you what I hadn't any right to know. I'm only sure of one thing—as I did know, I oughn't to have stayed. But," he reiterated sorrowfully, " I did stay."

" You stayed to help me."

" Yes; with all my dishonesty I wouldn't have done it if I hadn't made myself believe that. As it's turned out, I've helped to ruin you."

" Please—please don't. As far as I'm concerned you've nothing to reproach yourself with. Your position was a very difficult one."

" I ought never to have got into it."

" Still, you did your best."

" My best! You can't say I did what an honourable man would have done; I mean at the beginning."

" No—no. I'm afraid I can't say that."

He did not expect anything but sincerity from her, neither did he desire that her sense of honour should be less fine than his. But he longed for some word of absolution, some look even that should reinstate him in his self-esteem; and it seemed to him that there was none.

" You can't think worse of me than I think of myself," he said, and turned mournfully away.

She sat suddenly upright, with one hand on the arm of her chair, as if ready to rise and cut off his retreat.

"Wait," she said. "Have you any idea what you are going to do?"

The question held him within a foot's length of her chair, where the light fell full on his face.

"I only know I'm not going back to the shop."

"You were in earnest, then? It really has come to that?"

"It couldn't very well come to anything else."

She looked up at him gravely, realizing for the first time, through her own sorrow, the precise nature and the consequences of his action. He had burnt his ships, parted with his means of livelihood, in a quixotic endeavour to serve her interests, and redeem his own honour.

"Forgive my asking, but for the present this leaves you stranded?"

"It leaves me free."

She rose. "I know what that means. You won't mind my paying my debts at once, instead of later?"

He stared stupidly, as if her words had stunned him. She was seated at her writing-table, and had begun filling in a cheque before he completely grasped the horrible significance of what she had said.

"What are you doing?" he asked.

"I'm writing thirty instead of fifteen, because that is what you ought to have asked for in the beginning. You see I am more business-like now than I was then."

He smiled.

"And do you really suppose I am going to take it?"

He meant his smile to be bitter, but somehow it was not. After all, she was so helpless and so young.

"Of course you are going to take it."

"I needn't ask what you think of me."

This time the smile was bitterness itself.

"But it's yours—what I owe you. I'm only paying it to-day instead of some other day."

"But you have not got to pay me anything. What do you think you're paying me for?"

"For your work, for the catalogue, of course."

"That infamous catalogue ought never to have been made—not by me at any rate."

"But you made it. You made it for me. I ordered it."

"You ordered it from my father. In ordinary circum-

stances you would have owed him fifteen pounds. But even
he wouldn't take it now. I think he considers himself quite
sufficiently paid."

"You are mixing up two things that are absolutely
distinct."

"No. I'm only refusing to be mixed up with them."

"But you *are* mixed up with them."

He laughed at that shot, as a brave man laughs at a hurt.

"You needn't remind me of that. I meant—any more
than I can help; though it may seem to you that I haven't
very much lower to sink."

"Believe me, I don't associate you with this wretched
business. I want you to forget it."

"I can't forget it. If I could, it would only be by
refusing to degrade myself further in connection with it."

His words were clumsy and wild, as the hasty, terrified
movements of a naked soul trying to gather round it the
last rags of deceny and honour.

"There *is* no connection," she added, more gently than
ever, seeing how she hurt him. "Don't you see that it lies
between you and me?"

He saw that as she spoke she was curling the cheque into
a convenient form for slipping into his hand in the moment
of leave-taking.

"Indeed—indeed you must," she whispered.

He drew back sharply.

"Miss Harden, won't you leave me a shred of self-
respect?"

"And what about mine?" said she.

It was too much even for chivalry to bear.

"That's not exactly my affair, is it?"

He hardly realized the full significance of his answer,
but he deemed it apt. If, as she had been so careful to point
out to him, her honour and his moved on different planes,
how *could* her self-respect be his affair?

"It ought to be," she murmured in a tone whose sweetness should have been a salve to any wound. But he did
not perceive its meaning any more than he had perceived
his own, being still blinded by what seemed to him the
cruelty and degradation of the final blow.

She had stripped him; then she stabbed.

To hide his shame and his hurt, he turned his face from

her and left her. So strangely and so drunkenly did he go, with such a mist in his eyes, and such anguish and fury in his heart and brain, that on the threshold of the Harden library he stumbled past Miss Palliser without seeing her.

She found Lucia standing where he had left her, looking at a little roll of pale green paper that her fingers curled and uncurled.

" Lucia," she said, " what have you done to him? "

Lucia let the little roll of paper fall from her fingers to the floor.

" I don't know, Kitty. Something horrible, I think."

BOOK III

THE HOUSE OF BONDAGE

CHAPTER XXXVII

MRS. DOWNEY'S boarding-house was the light of Tavistock Place, Bloomsbury. In the brown monotony of the street it stood out splendid, conspicuous. Its door and half its front were painted a beautiful, a remarkable, pea-green, while its door-knob and door-knocker were of polished brass. Mrs. Downey's boarding-house knew nothing of concealment or disguise. Every evening, at the hour of seven, through its ground-floor window it offered to the world a scene of stupefying brilliance. The blinds were up, the curtains half-drawn, revealing the allurements of the interior.

From both sides of the street the entire length of the dinner-table was visible. Above it, a handsome gilt gaselier spread out its branches, and on this gaselier as many as three gas-jets burned furiously at once. In the intense illumination the faces of the boarders could be distinctly seen. They sat, as it were, transfigured, in a nebulous whorl or glory of yellow light. It fell on the high collars, the quite remarkably high collars, of the young gentlemen, and on those gay, those positively hilarious, blouses which the young ladies at Mrs. Downey's wear. Beside the water-bottles and tumblers of red glass it lay like a rosy shadow on the cloth. It gave back their green again to the aspidistras that, rising from a ruche of pink paper, formed the central ornament of the table. It made a luminous body of Mrs. Downey's face. The graver values were not sacrificed to this joyous expenditure of gas-light, for the wall-paper (the design was in chocolate, on a ground of ochre) sustained the note of fundamental melancholy.

If everything around Mrs. Downey was on a liberal scale, so was Mrs. Downey herself. She was expansive in her person, prodigal in sympathy, exuberant in dress. If she had one eye to the main chance, the other smiled at you in pure benignity. On her round face was a festal flush, flooding and effacing the little care-worn lines and wrinkles which appeared on it by day. It wore the colour of the hour which, evening after evening, renewed for her the great drama and spectacle of the Dinner.

Her table was disposed with a view to scenic effect. It was not by accident that Mrs. Downey herself was seated at the obscure or sideboard end, and that she gathered round her there the older and less attractive members of her circle. This arrangement had the further advantage of giving prominence to the young people whose brilliant appearance of an evening was as good as an advertisement for Mrs. Downey's.

First then, at the top of the table, sat two elderly ladies, dishevelled birds of passage, guests of a day and a night, Next, on Mrs. Downey's right, came old Miss Bramble, with old Mr. Partridge opposite on the left. The young gentleman at the extreme bottom or public end of the table was Mr. Spinks. He was almost blatantly visible from the street. At Mr. Spinks' side sat Miss Ada Bishop, the young lady in the fascinating pink blouse; and opposite him, Miss Flossie Walker, in the still more fascinating blue. To the left of Miss Bishop in the very centre of the table was a middle-aged commercial gentleman, Mr. Soper (not specially conspicuous) ; and facing him on Miss Walker's right came Miss Roots, who might be any age you please between thirty and forty. Between them at the present moment, there was an empty chair.

That empty seat was reserved for Mr. Rickman, who was generally late. On his arrival the blinds would be pulled down in deference to his wish for a more perfect privacy. Meanwhile they remained up, so that wandering persons in hansoms, lonely persons having furnished apartments, persons living expensively in hotels or miserably in other boarding-houses, might look in, and long to be received into Mrs. Downey's, to enjoy the luxury, the comfort, the society.

The society—yes; as Mrs. Downey surveyed her table

and its guests, her imagination ignored the base commercial tie; she felt herself to be a social power, having called into existence an assembly so various, so brilliant, and so gay. One thing only interfered with Mrs. Downey's happiness, Mr. Rickman's habit of being late. And to-night Mr. Rickman was later than ever.

Such a habit would not have mattered so much in any of the other boarders, because, remarkable as they were collectively, individually Mrs. Downey seldom thought of them unless they happened to be there, whereas with Mr. Rickman, now, whether he was there or not, she could think of nothing else.

" I'm really beginning to be afraid," said Mrs. Downey, " that he can't be coming."

The middle-aged gentleman, Mr. Soper, was heard muttering something to the effect that he thought they could bear up if he didn't come. Whereupon Mrs. Downey begged Mr. Soper's pardon in a manner which was a challenge to him to repeat his last remark. Therefore he repeated it.

" I say, I 'ope we can manage to bear up."

" Speak for yourself, Mr. Soper." (This from Mr. Spinks, who adored Rickman.)

" Well, really, I can't think how it is you and he don't seem to hit it off together. A young fellow that can make himself so pleasant when he likes."

" Ah-h! When he likes. And when he doesn't like? When he comes into the room like a young lord with his head in the air, and plumps himself down straight in front of you, and looks at you as if you were a sorter ea'wig or a centerpede? Call that pleasant?"

Mr. Spinks chuckled behind his table napkin. " He means a centre piece. Wouldn't he make a handsome one!"

Mr. Soper combined a certain stateliness of carriage with a restless insignificance of feature.

" We all know," said Mrs. Downey, " that Mr. Rickman is a very reserved gentleman. He has his own thoughts."

" Thoughts? I've got my thoughts. But they don't make me disagreeable to everybody."

Mr. Spinks craned forward as far as the height of his collar permitted him. " I wouldn't be too cock-sure if I were you, Mr. Soper."

The young end of the table heaved and quivered with

primeval mirth. Even Flossie Walker was moved to a faint smile. For Mr. Soper, though outwardly taciturn and morose, was possessed inwardly by a perfect fury of sociability, an immortal and insatiable craving to converse. It was an instinct, which, if gratified, would have undermined the whole fabric of the Dinner, being essentially egotistic, destructive, and malign. Mr. Soper resented the rapidity with which Rickman had been accepted by the boarding-house; he himself, after two years' residence, only maintaining a precarious popularity by little offerings of bon-bons to the ladies. Hence the bitterness of his present mood.

"There are thoughts *and* thoughts," said Mrs. Downey severely, for the commercial gentleman had touched her in a very sensitive place. "And when Mr. Rickman is in wot I call 'is vein, there's nobody like him for making a dinner go off."

Here Mr. Soper achieved a sardonic, a really sardonic smile. "Oh, of course, if you're eludin' to the young gentleman's appetite——"

But this was insufferable, it was wounding Mrs. Downey in the tenderest spot of all. The rose of her face became a peony.

"I'm doing no such thing. If any gentleman wishes to pay me a compliment,"—her gay smile took for granted that no gentleman could be so barbarous as not to feel that wish,—"let him show an appetite. As for the ladies, I wish they had an appetite to show. Mr. Partridge, let me give you a little more canary pudding. It's as light as light. No? Oh—come, Mr. Partridge."

Mr. Partridge's gesture of refusal was so vast, so expressive, that it amounted to a solemn personal revelation which implied, not so much that Mr. Partridge rejected canary pudding as that he renounced pleasure, of which canary pudding was but the symbol and the sign.

"Mr. Spinks then? He'll let me give him another slice, *I* know."

"You bet. Tell you wot it is, Mrs. Downey, the canary that pudding was made of must have been an uncommonly fine bird."

There was a swift step on the pavement, the determined click of a latch-key, and the clang of a closing door.

"Why, here *is* Mr. Rickman," said Mrs. Downey, betraying the pre-occupation of her soul.

Rickman's entrance produced a certain vibration down both sides of the table, a movement unanimous, yet discordant, as if the nerves of this social body that was " Mrs. Downey's " were being played upon every way at once. Each boarder seemed to be preparing for an experience that, whether agreeable or otherwise, would be disturbing to the last degree. The birds of passage raised their heads with a faint flutter. Miss Walker contemplated a chromo-lithograph with a dreamy air. Mr. Soper strove vainly to fix himself in an attitude of dignified detachment.

The boarding-house was about to suffer the tremendous invasion of a foreign element. For a moment it was united.

Mrs. Downey's face revealed a grave anxiety. She was evidently asking herself: " Was he, or was he not, in his vein? "

A glance at the object of his adoration decided the question for Mr. Spinks. Rickman was, thank goodness, *not* in his vein, in which state he was incomprehensible to anybody but Miss Roots. He was in that comparatively commonplace condition which rendered him accessible to Mr. Spinks.

" Ladies and gentlemen, allow me to introduce my friend, the lyte Mr. Ryzors. Jemima, show the deceased gentleman to his chair. Miss Walker, Mr. Ryzors. He is really 'appy to myke your acquaintance, Miss Walker, though at first sight he may not appear so. Wot you might be apt to mistyke for coldness is merely 'is intense reserve."

" Oh, dry up, Spinks."

No, Mr. Rickman was certainly not in his vein this evening. He made no apology whatever for his lateness. He ignored the commercial gentleman's " Good-evening, Rickman." As he slipped into his place between Miss Walker and Miss Roots he forgot his usual " Busy to-day at the Museum, Miss Roots? " A question that recognized her as a fellow worker in the fields of literature, thus lightening the obscurity that hid her labours there.

And for Miss Flossie's timid greeting (the lifting of her upper lip that just showed two dear little white teeth) he gave back a reluctant and embarrassed smile. He used to like sitting by Flossie because she was so pretty and so plump. He used to be sorry for her, because she worked so hard, and, though plump, was so pathetically anæmic and so shy. Critically considered, her body in spite of its plumpness, was a little too small for her head, and her features were a little too small for her face, but then they were so very correct, as correct as her demeanour and the way she did her hair. She had clusters and curls and loops and coils of hair, black as her eyes, which were so black that he couldn't tell the iris from the pupil. Not that Flossie had ever let him try. And now he had forgotten whether they were black or blue, forgotten everything about them and her. Flossie might be as correct as Flossie pleased, she simply didn't matter.

When she saw him smile she turned up her eyes to the chromo-lithograph again. The little clerk brought with her from the City an air of incorruptible propriety, assumed for purposes of self-protection, and at variance with her style of hair-dressing and the blueness and gaiety of her blouse. With all that it implied and took for granted, it used to strike him as pathetic. But now, he didn't find Flossie in the least pathetic.

He was waiting for the question which was bound to come.

It came from Spinks, and in a form more horrible than any that he had imagined.

"I say, Rickets, wot did you want all those shirts for down in Devonshire?"

Instead of replying Rickets blew his nose, making his pocket-handkerchief conceal as much of his face as possible. At that moment he caught Miss Bishop staring at him, and if there was one thing that Mr. Rickman disliked more than another it was being stared at. Particularly by Miss Bishop. Miss Bishop had red hair, a loose vivacious mouth, and her stare was grossly interrogative.

Flossie sent out a little winged look at him like a soft dark butterfly. It skimmed and hovered about him, and flitted, too ethereal to alight.

Miss Bishop, however, had no scruples, and put it to him point blank.

"Devonshire?" said Miss Bishop, "what were you doing down there?" She planted her elbows on the table and propped her chin on her finger-tips; her stare thus tilted was partly covered by her eyelids.

"If you really want," said Mr. Spinks, "to see that gentleman opposite, you'll have to take a telescope." The adoring youth conceived that it had been given to him alone

of the boarders to penetrate the mind of Rickman, that he
was the guardian of his mood, whose mission it was to protect him from the impertinent approaches of the rest.

"A telescope? Wot d'you mean?"

"Don't you think he's got a sort of a far-away look?
Especially about the mouth and nose?"

Whether it was from being stared at or for some other
reason, by this time Mr. Rickman had certainly become a little distant. He was not getting on well with
anybody or anything, not even with Mrs. Downey's excel-
lent dinner, nor yet with the claret, an extra ordered for
his private drinking, always to Mrs. Downey's secret trepidation. She gave a half-timid, half-tender look at him
and signalled to her ladies to withdraw. She herself remained behind, superintending the removal of the feast;
keeping a motherly eye, too, on the poor boy and his claret.
Ever since that one dreadful Sunday morning when she
had found him asleep in full evening dress upon his bedroom floor, Mrs. Downey was always expecting to see him
drop under the table. He had never done it yet, but there
was no knowing when he mightn't.

Whatever the extent of Mr. Rickman's alleged intemperance, his was not the vice of the solitary drinker, and to-
night the claret was nearly all drunk by Spinks and Soper.
It had the effect of waking in the commercial gentleman
the demon of sociability that slept.

What Mr. Soper wanted to know was whether Rickman
could recommend 'Armouth as a holiday resort? Could
he tell him of any first-class commercial hotel or boarding-house down there? To which Rickman replied that
he really couldn't tell him anything at all.

"Perhaps," said Mrs. Downey, peering over the edge
of the table-cloth she was helping to fold, "perhaps he has
his reasons."

The claret had made Mr. Soper not only sociable, but
jocose. "Reasons? That's a new name for 'em. If he
don't want more than one at a time, I wish he'd introduce
the rest of 'em to me."

"I daresay he would be very happy, if he thought you
would understand them, Mr. Soper."

"Understand 'em? Why, I don't suppose they talk
Greek?"

"Ryzors," said Spinks indignantly, "could give 'em points if they did. He speaks the language."

Mr. Soper replied that in that case perhaps Mr. Rickman would oblige him with the Greek for "crumby bits."

At the moment Mr. Rickman did not look like obliging Mr. Soper with anything. The provocation was certainly immense. Mr. Soper's voice inspired him with a fury of disgust. The muscles of his mouth twitched; the blood rushed visibly to his forehead; he stood looming over the table like a young pink thunder-god.

Mrs. Downey and Mr. Partridge retreated in some alarm. Mr. Soper, however, was one of those people who are not roused, but merely disconcerted, by the spectacle of passion. Mr. Soper said he supposed he could "make a 'armless remark." And still thirsting for companionship he pursued Mrs. Downey to the drawing-room. As he went, he fingered his little box of bon-bons as if it had been a talisman or charm.

Rickman poured himself out some claret, which he drank slowly, with closed eyelids, leaning back in his chair. "For God's sake, Spinks," he muttered; "don't speak to me."

"All right, old chappy, I won't." But he whispered, "I wouldn't go off just yet, Ryzors, if I were you" (by "going off," Mr. Spinks meant departure in a train of thought). "He'll be back in another minute."

He was back already, sociable, elated, smoking a cigar. Upstairs with the ladies he and his bon-bons had met with unprecedented success. Rickman opened his eyes.

"Ever try," said Mr. Soper, "a Flor di Dindigul? 'Ave one. You'll find the flavour very delicate and mild." He held it out, that Flor di Dindigul, as an olive branch to the tempestuous young man.

It was not accepted. It was not even seen.

Rickman rose to his feet. To his irritated vision the opposite wall seemed to heave and bulge forward, its chocolate design to become distended and to burst, spreading itself in blotches on the yellow ochre. On the face of the hideous welter swam the face of Mr. Soper, as it were bodiless and alone.

He drew in his breath with a slight shudder, pushed his chair back from the table, and strode out of the room.

Spinks looked after him sorrowfully.

" Why couldn't you leave him alone, Soper? You might see he didn't want to talk."

" How could I see wot he wanted? One minute 'e's as chatty and sociable—and the next he's up like three dozen of bottled stout. *It's wot I sy.* You can't dee-pend on 'im with any certainty."

That opinion was secretly shared by Miss Flossie Walker.

CHAPTER XXXVIII

RICKMAN, it seemed, was doomed to inspire that sense of agonizing uncertainty.

It was the second evening after his return. The Dinner was not going off well. Miss Walker was depressed, Mr. Spinks was not in his accustomed spirits, and Mrs. Downey had been going about with red eyes all day. Mr. Rickman had confided to her the deplorable state of his finances. And Mrs. Downey had said to herself she had known from the first that he would not be permanent.

He didn't want to be permanent. He desired to vanish, to disappear from the boarding-house and the boarders, and from Poppy Grace on the balcony next door; to get away from every face and every voice that he had known before he knew Lucia Harden's. Being convinced that he would never see her again, he wanted to be alone with his vivid and piercing memory of her. At first it was the pain that pierced. She had taken out her little two-edged sword and stabbed him. It wouldn't have mattered, he said, if the sword had been a true little sword, but it wasn't; it had snapt and left a nasty bit of steel inside him. Her last phrase was the touch that finished him. But the very sting of it created a healthy reaction. By his revolt against that solitary instance of her cruelty he had recovered his right to dwell upon her kindness. He dwelt upon it until at times he entered again into possession of the tender, beautiful, dominating dream. So intense was his hallucination, that as he walked alone in any southerly direction he still felt Muttersmoor on his right hand and Harcombe on his left, and he had waked in the morning to the sound of the sea beating upon Harmouth beach.

But these feelings visited him more rarely in the boarding-house than elsewhere. That was why he wanted to get away from it. The illusion was destroyed by these irrelevant persons of the dinner-table. Not that he noticed them much; but when he did it was to discover in them some quality that he had not observed before. He found imbecility in the manners of Spinks, coarseness and violence in the figures of Mrs. Downey and Miss Bishop, insipidity in the whole person of Miss Flossie Walker. And now, as he looked round the table, he wondered how it was he ever came there. After living for four weeks with Lucia Harden or the thought of her, he had a positive difficulty in recognizing even Spinks and Flossie as people he had once intimately known. Miss Roots alone, for some inscrutable reason, seemed familiar, in keeping with that divine experience to which the actual hour did violence. It was almost as if she understood.

A shrewdly sympathetic glance went out from a pair of hazel eyes set in a plain, clever, strenuous face. Miss Roots was glad, she said, to see him back again. He turned to her with the question that had never failed to flatter and delight. Was Miss Roots doing anything specially interesting now? But there was no interest in his tone.

Miss Roots looked up with a smile that would have been gay if it had not been so weary. Yes, she was collecting material for a book on Antimachus of Colophon. No, not her own book.

(At the mention of Antimachus of Colophon Mr. Soper folded his arms and frowned with implacable resentment. Mr. Soper was convinced that these subjects were introduced on purpose to exclude him from the conversation.)

Miss Roots, like Mr. Rickman, lived apart from the murmur of the boarding-house. She had raised a barrier of books in a bedroom six feet by nine, behind which she worked obscurely. She had never been known to converse until Mr. Rickman came. A sort of fluctuating friendship had sprung up between Mr. Rickman and Miss Roots. He had an odd feeling, half pity, half liking, for this humble servant of literature, doomed to its labour, ignorant of its delight. And yet Miss Roots had a heart which went out to the mad-cap journalist, wild with youth and the joy of letters. And now these things were coming back to her.

The sources of intellectual desire had been drying up with the blood in her cheeks; but when Rickman came they began to flow again. When Rickman talked as only he could talk, Miss Roots felt a faint fervour, a reminiscent thrill. She preened her poor little thoughts as if for pairing time, when soul fluttered to soul across the dinner-table. She knew that, intellectually speaking, she had been assigned to Rickman; for Mrs. Downey held that just as Mr. Rickman was the first to rouse Miss Roots to conversation, so Miss Roots alone had the power of drawing him out to the best advantage.

"Indeed?" said Rickman in a voice devoid of all intelligence.

Now if anything could have drawn Mr. Rickman out it was Antimachus of Colophon. Four weeks ago he would have been more interested in Antimachus than Miss Roots herself, he would have talked about him by the hour together. So that when he said nothing but "Indeed?" she perceived that something was the matter with him. But she also perceived that he was anxious to be talked to, therefore she talked on.

Miss Roots was right; though his mind was unable to take in a word she said to him, he listened, soothed by the singular refinement of her voice. It was a quality he had not noticed in it four weeks ago. Suddenly a word flashed out, dividing the evening with a line of light.

"So you've been staying in Harmouth?"

He started noticeably, and looked at her as if he had not heard. Miss Roots seemed unaware of having said anything specially luminous; she repeated her question with a smile.

"Why?" he asked. "Have you been there?"

"I've not only been there, I was born there."

He looked at her. Miss Roots had always been, to say the least of it, prosaic, and now it was as if poetry had dropped from her lips, as if she had said, "I too was born in Arcadia."

"I suppose," she said, "you saw that beautiful old house by the river?"

"Which beautiful old house by the river?"

"Court House. You see it from the bridge. You must have noticed it."

" Oh, yes, I know the one you mean."

" Did you happen to see or hear anything of the lady who lives in it? Miss Lucia Harden?"

" I—I must have seen her, but I can't exactly say. Do you know her?"

His words seemed to be torn from him in pieces, shaken by the violent beating of his heart.

" Know her?" said Miss Roots. " I lived five years with her. I taught her."

He looked at her again in wonder, in wonder and a sort of tenderness. For a second his heart had come to life again and leapt like a lunatic to his lips. Happily his wits were there before it. He stroked his upper lip, as if brushing away some wild phrase that sat there.

" Then I'm sure," he said, contriving a smile, " that Miss Harden is an exceedingly well educated lady."

Miss Roots' hazel eyes looked up at him intelligently; but as they met that unnatural smile of gallantry there was a queer compression of her shrewd and strenuous face. She changed the subject. He wondered if by any chance she knew; if she corresponded with Miss Harden; if Miss Harden had mentioned him in the days before her troubles came; if Miss Roots were trying to test him, to draw him out as she had never drawn him out before. No, it was not in the least likely that Miss Harden should have mentioned him; if she had, Miss Roots would have said so. She would never have set a trap for him; she was a kind and straightforward little lady. Her queer look meant nothing, it was only her way of dealing with a compliment.

The sweat on his forehead witnessed to the hot labour of his thought. He wondered whether anybody had observed it.

Mr. Soper had and drew his own conclusions.

" 'E's been at it again," said Mr. Soper, with significance. But nobody took any notice of him; and upstairs in the drawing-room that night his bon-bons failed to charm.

" I suppose you're pleased," said he, approaching his hostess, " now you've got Mr. Rickman back again?"

A deeper flush than the Dinner could account for was Mrs. Downey's sole reply.

" 'Is manners 'aven't improved since 'is residence in the country. I met 'im in the City to-day—wy, we were on the

same slab of pavement—and 'e went past and took no more
notice of *me* than if I'd been the Peabody statue."

" Depend upon it, he was full of something."

" Full of unsociability and conceit. And wot is 'e? Wot
is 'e? 'Is father keeps a bookshop."

" A very fine bookshop, too," said Miss Roots. It was
the first time that she had ever spoken of her own accord to
Mr. Soper.

" He may have come out lately, but you should have seen
the way 'e began, in a dirty little second-'and shop in the
City. A place," said Mr. Soper, " I wouldn't 'ave put my
nose into if I was paid. Crammed full of narsty, mangy,
'Olloway Street rubbish."

" Look here now," said Mr. Spinks, now scarlet with
fury, " you needn't throw his business in his face, for he's
chucked it."

" I don't think any the better of him for that."

" Don't you? Well, he won't worry himself into fits about
your opinion."

" 'Ad he got a new berth then, when he flung up the old
one? "

Now one thing Mrs. Downey, with all her indulgence, did
not permit, and that was any public allusion to her boarders'
affairs. She might not refuse to discuss them privately with
Miss Bramble or Miss Roots, but that was a very different
thing. Therefore she maintained a dignified silence.

" Well, then, I should like to know 'ow he's going to pay
'is way."

Before the grossness of this insinuation Mrs. Downey
abandoned her policy of silence.

" Some day," said Mrs. Downey, " Mr. Rickman will be
in a very different position to wot he is now. You mark
my words." (And nobody marked them but little Flossie
Walker.)

Two tears rolled down Mrs. Downey's face and mingled
with the tartan of her blouse. A murmur of sympathy went
round the room, and Mr. Soper perceived that the rest of
the company were sitting in an atmosphere of emotion from
which he was shut out.

" I beg of you, Mr. Soper, that you will let Mr. Rickman
be, for once this evening. Living together as we do, we all
ought," said Mrs. Downey, " to respect each other's feelings."

" Ah—feelings. Wot sort of respect does your young gentleman ever show to mine? Takes me up one day and cuts me dead the next."

" He wouldn't have dreamed of such a thing if he hadn't been worried in his mind. Mr. Rickman, Mr. Soper, is in trouble."

Mr. Soper was softened. " Is he? Well, really, I'm very sorry to hear it, very sorry, I'm sure."

" My fear is," said Mrs. Downey, controlling her voice with difficulty, " that he may be leaving us."

" If he does, Mrs. Downey, nobody will regret it more than I do."

" Well, I hope it won't come to that."

· Mrs. Downey did not consider it politic to add that she was prepared to make any sacrifice to prevent it. It was as well that Mr. Soper should realize the consequences of an inability to pay your way. She was not prepared to make any sacrifice for the sake of keeping *him*.

" But what," said Mrs. Downey to herself, " will the Dinner be without Mr. Rickman?"

The Dinner was, in her imagination, a function, a literary symposium. At the present moment, if you were to believe Mrs. Downey, no dinner-table in London could show such a gathering of remarkable people. But to none of these remarkable people did Mrs. Downey feel as she felt to Mr. Rickman, who was the most remarkable of them all. By her own statement she had enjoyed exceptional opportunities for studying the ways of genius. There was a room at Mrs. Downey's which she exhibited with pride as " Mr. Blenkinsop's room." Mr. Blenkinsop was a poet, and Mr. Rickman had succeeded him. If Mrs. Downey did not immediately recognize Mr. Rickman as a genius it was because he was so utterly unlike Mr. Blenkinsop. But she had felt from the first that, as she expressed it, " there was something about him," though what it was she couldn't really say. Only from the first she had had that feeling in her heart—" He will not be permanent." The joy she had in his youth and mystery was drenched with the pathos of mutability. Mrs. Downey rebelled against mutability's decree. " Perhaps," she said, " we might come to some arrangement."

All night long in her bedroom on the ground-floor Mrs. Downey lay awake considering what arrangement could be come to. This was but a discreet way of stating her previous determination to make any sacrifice if only she could keep him. The sacrifice which Mrs. Downey (towards the small hours of the morning) found herself contemplating amounted to no less than four shillings a week. Occupying his present bed-sitting room, he should remain for twenty-one shillings a week instead of twenty-five.

Unfortunately, at breakfast the next morning their evil genius prompted Mr. Spinks and Mr. Soper to display enormous appetites, and Mrs. Downey, to her everlasting shame, was herself tempted of the devil. A fall of four shillings a week, serious enough in itself, was not to be contemplated with gentlemen eating their heads off in that fashion. It would have to be made up in some way, to be taken out of somebody or something. She would—yes, she would take it out of them all round by taking it out of the Dinner. And yet when it came to the point, Mrs. Downey's soul recoiled from the immorality of this suggestion. There rose before her, as in a vision, the Dinner of the future, solid in essentials, but docked of its splendour, its character and its pride. No; that must not be. What the Dinner was now it must remain as long as there were eight boarders to eat it. If Mrs. Downey made any sacrifice she must make it pure. "On this condition," said Mrs. Downey by way of putting a business-like face on it, "on the condition of his permanence."

But it seemed that twenty-one shillings were more than Mr. Rickman could afford to pay.

Mrs. Downey spent another restless night, and again towards the small hours of the morning she decided on a plan. After breakfast she watched Mr. Soper out of the dining-room, closed the door behind him with offensive and elaborate precaution, and approached Mr. Rickman secretly. If he would promise not to tell the other gentlemen, she would let him have the third floor back for eighteen shillings.

Mr. Rickman stood by the door like one in great haste to be gone. He could not afford eighteen shillings either. He would stay where he was on the old terms for a fortnight, at the end of which time, he said firmly, he would be obliged to go. Mr. Rickman's blue eyes were dark and profound with the pathos of recent illness and suffering, so that he appeared to be touched by Mrs. Downey's kindness. But he

wasn't touched by it; no, not the least bit in the world. His
heart inside him was like a great lump of dried leather. Mrs.
Downey looked at him, sighed, and said no more. Things
were more serious with him than she had supposed.

Things were very serious indeed.

His absence at Harmouth had entailed consequences that
he had not foreseen. During those four weeks, owing to the
perturbation of his mind and the incessant demands on his
time, he had written nothing. True, while he was away his
poems had found a publisher; but he had nothing to expect
from them; it would be lucky if they paid their expenses.
On his return to town he found that his place on *The Planet*
had been filled up. At the most he could only reckon on
placing now and then, at infrequent intervals, an article or
a poem. The places would be few, for from the crowd of
popular magazines he was excluded by the very nature of
his genius. To make matters worse, he owed about thirty
pounds to Dicky Pilkington. The sum of two guineas, which
The Museion owed him for his sonnet, would, if he accepted
Mrs. Downey's last offer, keep him for exactly two weeks.
And afterwards? Afterwards, of course, he would have to
borrow another ten pounds from Dicky, hire some den at
a few shillings a week, and try his luck for as many months
as his money held out. Then there would be another " afterwards," but that need not concern him now.

The only thing that concerned him was the occult tie between him and Miss Roots. Up to the day fixed for his departure he was drawn by an irresistible fascination to Miss
Roots. His manner to her became marked by an extreme
gentleness and sympathy. Of course it was impossible to
believe that it was Miss Roots who lit the intellectual flame
that burnt in Lucia. Enough to know that she had sat with
her in the library and in the room where she made music;
that she had walked with her in the old green garden, and
on Harcombe Hill and Muttersmoor. Enough to sit beside
Miss Roots and know that all the time her heart was where
his was, and that if he were to speak of these things she
would kindle and understand. But he did not speak of them;
for from the way Miss Roots had referred to Lucia Harden
and to Court House, it was evident that she knew nothing of
what had happened to them, and he did not feel equal to
telling her. Lucia's pain was so great a part of his pain that

as yet he could not touch it. But though he never openly approached the subject of Harmouth, he was for ever skirting it, keeping it in sight.

He came very near to it one evening, when, finding himself alone with Miss Roots in the back drawing-room, he asked her how long it was since she had been in Devonshire. It seemed that it was no longer ago than last year. Only last year? It was still warm then, the link between her and the woman whom he loved. He found himself looking at Miss Roots, scanning the lines of her plain face as if it held for him some new and wonderful significance. For him that faced flamed transfigured, as in the moment when she had first spoken of Lucia. The thin lips which had seemed to him so utterly unattractive had touched Lucia's, and were baptized into her freshness and her charm; her eyes had looked into Lucia's, and carried something of their light. In her presence he drifted into a sort of mysticism peculiar to lovers, seeing the hand of a holy destiny in the chance that had seated him beside her. Though her shrewdness might divine his secret he felt that with her it would be safe.

As for his other companions of the dinner-table he was obliged to admit that they displayed an admirable delicacy. After Mrs. Downey's revelation not one of them had asked him what he had been doing those four weeks. Spinks had a theory, which he kept to himself. Old Rickets had been having a high old time. He had eloped with a bar-maid or an opera girl. For those four weeks, he had no doubt, Rickets had been gloriously, ruinously, on the loose. Mrs. Downey's speculations had taken the same turn. Mr. Rickman's extraordinary request that all his clean linen should be forwarded to him at once had set her mind working; it suggested a young man living in luxury beyond his means. Mrs. Downey's fancy kindled and blushed by turns as it followed him into a glorious or disreputable unknown. Whatever the adventures of those four weeks, she felt that they were responsible for his awful state of impecuniosity. And yet she desired to keep him. " There is something about him," said Mrs. Downey to Miss Roots, and paused searching for the illuminating word; " something that goes to your heart without 'is knowing it."

She had found it, the nameless, ineluctable charm.

And so for those last days the Dinner became a high

funereal ceremony, increasing in valedictory splendour that proclaimed unmistakably, "Mr. Rickman is going."

In a neighbouring street he had found a room, cheap and passably clean, and (failing a financial miracle worked on his behalf) he would move into it to-morrow. He was going, now that he would have given anything to stay.

In the dining-room after dinner Spinks with a dejected countenance sat guarding for the last time the sacred silence of Rickman. They had finished their coffee, when the door that let out the maid with empty cups let in Miss Bishop, Miss Bramble, and Miss Walker.

First came Miss Bishop; she advanced in a side-long and embarrassed manner, giggling, and her face for once was as red as her hair. She carried a little wooden box which with an unaccustomed shyness she asked him to accept. The sliding lid disclosed a dozen cedar pencils side by side, their points all ready sharpened, also a card with the inscription: "Mr. Rickman, with best wishes from Ada Bishop." At one corner was a date suggesting that the gift marked an epoch; at the other the letters P. T. O. The reverse displayed this legend, "If you ever want any typing done, I'll always do it for *you* at 6*d.* a thou. *Only don't let on.* Yours, A. B." Now Miss Bishop's usual charge was, as he knew, a shilling per thousand.

"Gentlemen," said she, explaining away her modest offering, "always like anything that saves them trouble." At this point Miss Bishop, torn by a supreme giggle, vanished violently from the scene.

Mr. Rickman smiled sadly, but his heart remained as before. He had not loved Miss Bishop.

Next came Miss Bramble with her gift mysteriously concealed in silver paper. "All brain-workers," said Miss Bramble, "suffered from cold feet." So she had just knitted him a pair of socks—"*bed*-socks" (in a whisper), "that would help to keep him warm." Her poor old eyes were scarlet, not so much from knitting the bed-socks, as from contemplating the terrible possibility of his needing them.

Under Mr. Rickman's waistcoat there was the least little ghost of a quiver. He had not loved Miss Bramble; but Miss Bramble had loved him. She had loved him because he was young, and because he had sometimes repeated to her the little dinner-table jests that she was too deaf to hear.

Last of the three, very grave and demure, came Flossie, and she, like her friend, carried her gift uncovered. She proffered it with her most becoming air of correctness and propriety. It was a cabinet photograph of herself in her best attitude, her best mood, and her best blue blouse. It was framed beautifully and appropriately in white silk, embroidered with blue forget-me-nots by Flossie's clever hands. She had sat up half the night to finish it. He took it gently from her and looked at it for what seemed to Flossie an excessively long time. He was trying to think of something particularly pretty and suitable to say. In his absorption he did not notice that he was alone with her, that as Flossie advanced Spinks and Soper had withdrawn.

" I don't know whether you'll care for it," said she. She was standing very close beside him, and her face under the gas-light looked pale and tender.

" Of course I'll care for it." He laid her gift on the table beside the others and stood contemplating them. She saw him smile. He was smiling at the bed-socks.

" You are all much too good to me, you know."

" Oh, Mr. Rickman, you've been so awfully good to me."

He looked round a little anxiously and perceived that they were alone.

" No, Flossie," he said, " I've not been good to any one. I'm not very good to myself. All the same, I'm not an utter brute; I shan't forget you."

Flossie's eyes had followed, almost jealously, the movement of his hand in putting down her gift; and they had rested there, fixed on her own portrait, and veiled by their large white lids. She now raised them suddenly, and over their black profundity there moved a curious golden glitter that flashed full on his face.

" You didn't remember me, much, last time you went away."

" I didn't remember anybody, Flossie; I had too much to think of."

It struck him that this was the first time she had looked him full in the face; but it did not strike him that it was also the first time that he had found himself alone in a room with her, though they had been together many times out of doors and in crowded theatres and concert halls. Her look conveyed some accusation that he at first failed to understand. And then there came into his mind the promise he had made to her at Easter, to take her to the play, the promise broken without apology or explanation. So she still resented it, did she? Poor little Flossie, she was so plump and pretty, and she had been so dependent on him for the small pleasures of her life.

"You're always thinking," said Flossie, and laughed.

"I'm sorry, Flossie; it's a disgusting habit, I own. I'll make up for it some day. We'll do a lot of theatres and—and things together, when my ship comes in."

"Thank you, Mr. Rickman," said she with a return to her old demeanour. "And now I suppose I'd better say good-night?"

She turned. They said good-night. He sprang to open the door for her. As she went through it, his heart, if it did not go with her, was touched, most palpably, unmistakably touched at seeing her go. He had not loved Flossie; but he might have loved her.

Mr. Soper, who had been waiting all the while on the stairs, walked in through the open door. He closed it secretly.

He laid his hand affectionately on Rickman's shoulder. "Rickman," he said solemnly, "while I 'ave the opportunity, I want to speak to you. If it should 'appen that a fiver would be useful to you, don't you hesitate to come to me."

"Oh, Soper, thanks most awfully. Really, no, I couldn't think of it."

"But I mean it. I really do. So don't you 'esitate; and there needn't be any hurry about repayment. That," said Mr. Soper, "is quite immaterial." Failing to extract from Rickman any distinct promise, he withdrew; but not before he had pressed upon his immediate acceptance a box of his favourites, the Flor di Dindigul.

By this time Rickman's heart was exceedingy uncomfortable inside him. He had hated Soper.

He thought it was all over, and he was glad to escape from these really very trying interviews to the quiet of his own room. There he found Spinks sitting on his bed waiting for him. Spinks had come to lay before him an offering and a scheme. The offering was no less than two dozen of gents' best all wool knitted hose, double-toed and

heeled. The scheme was for enabling Rickman thencefor-
ward to purchase all manner of retail haberdashery at whole-
sale prices by the simple method of impersonating Spinks.
At least in the long-run it amounted to that, and Rickman
had some difficulty in persuading Spinks that his scheme,
though in the last degree glorious and romantic, was, from
an ethical point of view, not strictly feasible.

" What a rum joker you are, Rickman. I never thought
of that. I wonder,"—he mused in an unconscious endeavour to restore the moral balance between him and Rickman,—" I wonder who'll put you to bed, old chappy, when
you're tight."

" Don't fret, Spinky. I'm almost afraid that I shall never
be tight again in this world."

" Oh, Gosh! " said Spinks, and sighed profoundly. Then,
with a slight recovery, " Do you mean you won't be able to
afford it? "

" You can put it that way, if you like."

In time Spinks left him and Rickman was alone. Just
as he was wondering whether or no he would pack his books
up before turning in, there was a soft rap at his door. He
said, " Come in " to the rap; and to himself he said, " Who
next? "

It was Mrs. Downey; she glanced round the room, looked
at Flossie's photograph with disapproval, and removed, not
without severity, Miss Bramble's bed-socks from a chair.
She had brought no gift; but she sat down heavily like a
woman who has carried a burden about with her all day,
and can carry it no farther. Her features were almost obliterated with emotion and glazed with tears that she made no
effort to remove.

" Mr. Rickman," she said, " do you really wish to go, or
do you not? "

He looked up surprised. " My dear Mrs. Downey, I
don't; believe me. Did I ever say I did? "

Her face grew brighter and rounder till the very glaze on
it made it shine like a great red sun. " Well, we'd all been
wondering, and some of us said one thing, and some another,
and I didn't know what to think. But if you want to stay
perhaps—we can come to some arrangement." It was the
concentrated phrase.

He shook his head.

" Come, I've been thinking it over. You won't be paying less than five shillings a week for your empty room, perhaps more? "

He would, he said, be paying six shillings.

" There now! And that, with your food, makes sixteen shillings at the very least."

" Well—it depends upon the food."

" I should think it *did* depend upon it." Mrs. Downey's face literally blazed with triumph. She said to herself, " I was right. Mr. Spinks said he'd take it out of his clothes. Miss Bramble said he'd take it out of his fire. *I* said he'd take it out of his dinner."

" Now," she continued, " if you didn't mind moving into the front attic—it's a good attic—for a time, I could let you 'ave that, *and* board you, for fifteen shillings a week, or for fourteen, I could, and welcome. As I seldom let that attic, it would be money in the pocket to me.

" Come," she went on well pleased. " I know all about it. Why, Mr. Blenkinsop, when he first started to write, he lived up there six months at a time. He had his ups, you may say, and his downs. One year in the attic and the next on the second floor, having his meals separate and his own apartments. Then up he'd go again quite cheerful, as regularly as the bills came round." Here Mrs. Downey entered at some length upon the history of the splendour and misery of Mr. Blenkinsop. " And that, I suppose," said Mrs. Downey, " is what it is to be a poet."

" In fact," said Rickman relating the incident afterwards to Miss Roots, " talk to Mrs. Downey of the Attic Bee and she will thoroughly understand the allusion."

After about half an hour's conversation she left him without having received any clear and definite acceptance of her proposal. That did not prevent her from announcing to the drawing-room that Mr. Rickman was not going after all.

At the hour of the last post a letter was pushed under his door. It was from Horace Jewdwine, asking him to dine with him at Hampstead the next evening. Nothing more, nothing less; but the sight of the signature made his brain reel for a second. He stood staring at it. From the adjoining room came sounds made by Spinks, dancing a jig of joy which brought up Mr. Soper raging from the floor below.

Jewdwine? Why, he had made up his mind that after the affair of the Harden library Jewdwine most certainly would have nothing more to do with him.

Jewdwine was another link. And at that thought his heart heaved and became alive again.

CHAPTER XXXIX

IN the act of death, as in everything else that he had ever done, Sir Frederick Harden had hit on the most inappropriate, the most inconvenient moment. The moment, that is to say, when Horace Jewdwine had been appointed editor of *The Museion,* when every minute of his day was taken up with forming his staff and thoroughly reorganizing the business of his paper. It was, besides, the long-desired moment, for which all his years at Oxford had been a training and a consecration; it was that supreme, that nuptial moment in which an ambitious man embraces for the first time his Opportunity.

The news of Lucia's trouble found him, as it were, in the ardours and preoccupations of the honeymoon.

It was characteristic of Jewdwine that in this courting of Opportunity there had been no violent pursuit, no dishevelment, no seizing by the hair. He had hung back, rather; he had waited, till he had given himself value, till Opportunity had come to him, with delicate and ceremonious approach. Still, his head had swum a little at her coming, so that in the contemplation of his golden bride he had for the time being lost sight of Lucia.

As for marrying his cousin, that was a question with which for the present he felt he really could not deal. No doubt it would crop up again later on to worry him.

Meanwhile he gave to Lucia every minute that he could spare from the allurements of his golden bride. For more than a fortnight her affairs had been weighing on him like a nightmare. But only like a nightmare, a thing that troubled him chiefly in the watches of the night, leaving his waking thoughts free to go about the business of the day, a thing against which he felt that it was impossible to contend. For Lucia's affairs had the vagueness, the confusion of a nightmare. Details no doubt there were; but they had disappeared in the immensity of the general effect. Being powerless to deal with them himself, he had sent down his own solicitor to assist in disentangling them. But as the full meaning of the disaster sank into him, he realized with a cold pang of disappointment that their marriage must now be indefinitely postponed.

To be sure, what had as yet passed between them hardly amounted to an understanding. All Jewdwine's understandings had been with himself. But the very fact that he was not prepared to act on such an understanding made him feel as responsible as if it actually existed. Being conscious of something rather more than cousinly tenderness in the past, he really could not be sure that he was not already irretrievably committed. Not that Lucia's manner had ever taken anything of the sort for granted. He had nothing to fear from her. But he had much (he told himself) to fear from his own conscience and his honour.

All this was the result of deliberate reflection. In the beginning of the trouble, at the first news of his uncle's death, **his** sympathy with Lucia had been free from any sordid anxiety for the future which he then conceived to be inseparably bound up with his own. Rickman's letter was the first intimation that anything had gone wrong. It was a shock none the less severe because it was not altogether a surprise. It was just like his uncle Frederick to raise money on the Harden library. The shock lay in Rickman's assumption that he, Jewdwine, was prepared, instantly, at ten days' notice, to redeem it. It was what he would have liked to do; what, if he had been a rich man, he infallibly would have done; what even now, with his limited resources, he might do if it were not for the risk. Rickman had assured him that there was no risk, had implied almost that it was an opportunity, a splendid investment for his money. He could see for himself that it was his chance of doing *the* beautiful thing for Lucia. Looking back upon it all afterwards, long afterwards, he found consolation in the thought that his first, or nearly his first, impulse had been generous.

At first, too, he had not given a thought to Rickman except as the medium, the unauthorized and somewhat curious medium, of a very startling communication. Enough that he was expected to produce at ten days' notice a sum which might be anything you pleased over one thousand two hundred pounds. It was not until he realized that he was seriously invited to contend with Rickman's in a private bid for the Harden library that he began to criticise Rickman's movement in the matter. Everything depended on Rickman's estimate of the risk, and Rickman was not infallible. In denying Rickman's infallibility he had not as yet committed himself to any harsh judgment of his friend. His first really unpleasant reflection was that Rickman's information was unsatisfactory, because vague; his next that Rickman was giving him precious little time for deliberation. He was excessively annoyed with Rickman upon both these heads, but chiefly upon the latter. He was being hurried; he might almost say that pressure was being put on him. And why?

It was at this point that he found himself drawn into that dangerous line, the attributing of motives.

He perceived in Rickman's suggestion a readiness, an eagerness to stand back and, as it were, pass on the Harden library. Rickman was a sharp fellow; he knew pretty well what he was about. Jewdwine's mind went back to the dawn of their acquaintance, and to a certain Florio Montaigne. Rickman had got the better of him over that Florio Montaigne. Hitherto, whenever Jewdwine had thought of that little transaction he had smiled in spite of himself; he really could not help admiring the smartness of a young man who had worsted him in a bargain. Jewdwine was a terror to all the second-hand booksellers in London and Oxford; he would waste so much of their good time in cheapening a book that it was hardly worth their while to sell it to him at double the price originally asked. The idea that he had paid five shillings for a book that he should have got for four and six would keep Jewdwine awake at night. And now his thought advanced by rapid steps in the direction unfavourable to Rickman. Rickman had driven a clever bargain over that Florio Montaigne; Rickman had cheated him, yes, cheated him infamously, over that Florio Montaigne. You could see a great deal through a very small hole, and a man who would cheat you over a Florio Montaigne would cheat you over a whole library if he got the chance. Not that there was any cheating in the second-hand book-trade; it was each man for himself and the Lord for us all.

The question was, what was young Rickman driving at?

And what was he, Jewdwine, being let in for now? He found himself unable to accept Rickman's alleged motive in all its grand simplicity. It was too simple and too grand to be entirely probable. If young Rickman was not infallible, he was an expert in his trade. He was not likely to be grossly mistaken in his valuation. If the Harden library would be worth four or five thousand pounds to Jewdwine it would be worth as much or more to Rickman's. Young Rickman being merely old Rickman's assistant, he could hardly be acting without his father's knowledge. If young Rickman honestly thought that the library was worth that sum, it was not likely that they would let the prize slip out of their hands. The thing was not in human nature.

The more he thought of it the more he was convinced that it was a put-up job. He strongly suspected that young Rickman, in the rashness of his youth, had proceeded farther than he cared to own, that Rickman's found themselves let in for a bad bargain, and were anxious to get out of it. Young Rickman had no doubt discovered that the great Harden library was not the prize they had always imagined it to be. Jewdwine remembered that there was no record, no proper catalogue, or if there ever had been, it had been mislaid or lost. He had a vision (unconsciously exaggerated) of the inconceivable disorder of the place when he had last visited it; and as he recalled those great gaps on the shelves it struck him that the library had been gutted. His uncle Frederick had not been altogether the fool he seemed to be; nothing was more likely than that he knew perfectly well the value of the volumes that were the unique glory of the collection, and had long ago turned them into ready money. The rest would be comparatively worthless.

He read Rickman's letter over again and had a moment of compunction. It seemed a very simple and straightforward letter. But then, Rickman was a very clever fellow, he had the gift of expression; and there was that Florio Montaigne. He wouldn't have suspected him if only his record had been pure.

So instead of committing himself by writing to Rickman, he had sent his solicitor down to look into these matters. A day or two later, in reply to his further inquiries, his solicitor assured him that there could be no doubt that the library was intact.

To Jewdwine in his present state of mind this information was upsetting. It not only compelled him to modify his opinion of Rickman after having formed it, but it threw him back on the agony and responsibility of decision. On the last morning of the term allowed him for reflection he received that hurried note from Rickman, who had flung all his emotions into one agonized line, " For God's sake wire me what you mean to do." The young poet, so careful of his prose style, had not perceived that what he had written was blank verse of the purest; which to Jewdwine in itself sufficiently revealed the disorder of his mind.

That *cri de cœur* rang in Jewdwine's brain for the next twenty-four hours. Then at the last moment he came forward with an offer of one thousand three hundred. The next day he heard from Lucia (what indeed he feared) that he had stepped in too late. The library was sold, to Isaac Rickman.

His dominant emotion was now anger; he was furious with Rickman for not having given him more time. He forgot his own delay, his fears and vacillations; he felt that he would have done this thing if he had only had more time. He had no doubt that Rickman had meant honestly by him; but he had blundered; he could and he should have given him more time. But gradually, as the certainty of his own generosity grew on him, his indignation cooled. Reinstated in his self-esteem he could afford to do justice to Rickman. What was more, now that the danger was over. he.saw his risk more clearly than ever. He had a vision of his brilliant future clouded by a debt of one thousand three hundred pounds impetuously raised on the unknown, of the Harden library hung like a mill-stone round his neck. He had no doubt that Rickman, in the very ardour of his honesty, had greatly exaggerated its value. And as he surveyed the probable consequences of his own superb impulse, he was almost grateful to Rickman for *not* having given him time to make a fool of himself. Thanks to Rickman, he had now all the credit of that reckless offer without the risk.

A week later he had a long letter from Lucia. She thanked him with much warmth and affection for his generosity; it was evident that it had touched her deeply. She assured him (as she had assured him before) that she

needed no help. The library had sold for twelve hundred
pounds, and two hundred had been handed over to her.
Mr. Pilkington was afraid that no further sum would be
forthcoming from the sale of the pictures and furniture,
which had been valued over rather than under their present
market price, and represented the bulk of the security.
Still, she hoped to sell Court House; it could not bring in
less than five thousand. That and a small part of her
capital would pay off all remaining debts. It was a weari-
some business; but Horace would be glad to hear that she
would come out of it not owing a farthing to anybody, and
would still have enough to live on.

Yes. Jewdwine had his pride. He was glad that his
disreputable uncle's affairs had not landed him in the Bankruptcy Court after all; but he had a movement of indignation on Lucia's account and of admiration for Lucia.

No more of herself or her affairs; the rest was concerned
with Rickman and his. "My dear Horace," she wrote,
"we must do something for this poor little friend of yours.
You were quite right about him. He is a genius; but
fortunately, or perhaps unfortunately, for himself, he is so
much else besides. To think that *he* of all people should be
entangled in our miserable business! He has got badly
hurt, too. First of all, it preyed on his mind till he worried
himself into nervous fever. Kitty Palliser, who saw him,
said he was nearly off his head. It seems he considered
his honour implicated. As it happens he has behaved
splendidly. He did everything in his power to prevent our
losing the library, or at any rate to keep it out of his father's
hands; and the mere fact that he failed doesn't lessen our
obligation. He has simply ruined his own prospects in the
attempt. Do you know, he tried to force his father to withdraw by threatening to leave their business if he didn't;
and he had to keep his word. The horrible thing is that I
actually owe him money—money which he won't take. He
had been working hard for three weeks on a catalogue for
me, and is insulted at the bare suggestion of payment. And
here he is—absolutely stranded; in debt, I believe, and without a farthing. What in the world am I to do?"

"Poor Lucy!" thought Jewdwine, "as if she hadn't
enough to bear without having Rickman on her shoulders."

"-It seems to me that as he has done all this for us, we

ought to stand by him. If you *could* do anything for him —couldn't you help him with some introductions? Or, better still, give him work, at any rate till he has found his feet? I'm sure you can count on his devotion——"

" Dear Lucy, she might be recommending me a valet."

" *Do* do something for him, and you will oblige me more than I can say."

That letter of Lucia's gave Jewdwine much matter for reflection and some pain. He had winced at the sale of Court House; it struck him as a personal blow. He had had a kind of tacit understanding with himself that, in that future which he had meant to share with Lucia, Court House would be the home of his retirement. Still, it must go. He had to live in town, and, if at the moment he could have afforded to marry a penniless Lucia, he could not have afforded two establishments.

As for the redemption of the Harden library he realized with a sharp pang that risk there had been none. He saw that what young Rickman had offered him was a unique and splendid opportunity, the opportunity of doing a beautiful thing for Lucia, and that without the smallest inconvenience to himself. And this opportunity had been missed. Just because he could not make up his mind about Rickman, could not see what Lucia had always seen, what he too saw now, that positively luminous sincerity of his. He saw it even now reluctantly—though he could never veer round again to his absurd theory of Rickman's dishonesty. He would have liked, if he could, to regard him as a culpable bungler; but even this consoling view was closed to him by Lucia. It was plain from her account that Rickman's task had been beyond human power. Jewdwine, therefore, was forced to the painful conclusion that for this loss to himself and Lucia he had nothing to blame but his own vacillation.

As for Rickman——

Lucia had taken a great deal of pains with that part of her subject, for she was determined to do justice to it. She was aware that it was open to her to take the ordinary practical view of Rickman as a culpable blunderer, who, by holding his tongue when he should have spoken, had involved her in the loss of much valuable property. To an ordinary practical woman the fact that this blunder had entailed such serious consequences to herself would have made any other theory impossible. But Lucia was not a woman who could be depended on for any ordinary practical view. Mere material issues could never confuse her estimate of spiritual values. To her, Rickman's conduct in that instance was a flaw in honour, and as such she had already sufficiently judged it. The significant thing was that he too should have so judged it; that he should have been capable of such profound suffering in the thought of it. And now, somehow, it didn't seem to her to count.

It simply disappeared in her final pure and luminous view of Rickman's character. What really counted was the alertness of his whole attitude to honour, his readiness to follow the voice of his own ultimate vision, to repudiate the unclean thing revealed in its uncleanliness; above all, what counted was his passionate sincerity. With her unerring instinct of selection Lucia had again seized on the essential. The triumph of Rickman's greater qualities appealed to her as a spectacle; it was not spoiled for her by the reflection that she personally had been more affected by his failure. If she showed her insight into Rickman's character by admitting the relative insignificance of that failure, she showed an equal insight into Jewdwine's by suppressing all mention of it now. For Horace would have regarded it as essential. It would have loomed large in his view by reason of its material consequences. Allowing for Horace's view she kept her portrait truer by omitting it.

And Jewdwine accepted her portrait as the true one. It appealed irresistibly to his artistic sense. He was by profession a connoisseur of things beautifully done. Rickman's behaviour, as described by Lucia, revived his earlier amused admiration for his young disciple. It was so like him. In its spontaneity, its unexpectedness, its—its colossal impertinence, it was pure Rickman.

Lucia had achieved a masterpiece of appreciation.

But what helped him in his almost joyous re-discovery of his Rickman was his perception that here (in doing justice to Rickman) lay his chance of rehabilitating himself. If he could not buy back the Harden library, he could at any rate redeem his own character. He did not hold himself responsible for Lucia's father's debts, but he was willing, not to say glad, to take up Lucia's. It was certainly most improper that she should be under any obligation to Rickman. In any case, Rickman's action concerned Lucia's family as much as Lucia; that is to say, it was his (Jewdwine's) affair. And personally he disliked indebtedness.

Another man might have handed Rickman a cheque for fifty pounds (the price of the catalogue *raisonné*) and washed his hands of him. But Jewdwine was incapable of that grossness.

He gave the matter a fortnight's delicate consideration. At the end of that time he had made up his mind not only to invite Rickman to contribute regularly to *The Museion* (a thing he would have done in any case) but to offer him, temporarily, the sub-editorship. Rash as this resolution seemed, Jewdwine had fenced himself carefully from any risk. The arrangement was not to be considered permanent until Rickman had proved himself both capable and steady —if then. In giving him any work at all on *The Museion* Jewdwine felt that he was stretching a point. It was a somewhat liberal rendering of his editorial programme.

The Museion was the one solitary literary journal that had the courage to profess openly a philosophy of criticism. Its philosophy might be obsolete, it might be fantastic, it might be altogether wrong; the point was that it was there. Its presence was a protest against the spirit of anarchy in the world of letters. The paper had lost influence lately owing to a certain rigidity in the methods of its late editor, also to an increasing dulness in its style. It was suffering, like all old things, from the unequal competition with insurgent youth. The proprietors were almost relieved when the death of its editor provided them with a suitable opportunity for giving it over into the hands of younger men. "We want new blood," said the proprietors. The difficulty was how to combine new blood with the old spirit, and Horace Jewdwine solved this problem, presenting the remarkable combination of an old head upon comparatively young shoulders. He was responsible, authoritative, inspired by a high and noble seriousness. He had taken his Aristotle with a high and noble seriousness; and in the same spirit he had approached his Kant, his Hegel and his Schopenhauer in succession. He was equipped with the most beautiful metaphysical theory of Art, and had himself written certain *Prolegomena to Æsthetics*.

Metaphysics had preyed on Jewdwine like a flame. He was consumed with a passion for unity. The unity which Nature only strives after, blindly, furiously, ineffectually; the unity barely reached by the serene and luminous processes of Thought—the artist achieves it with one stroke. In him, by the twin acts of vision and creation, the worlds of Nature and the Idea are made one. He leaps at a bound into the very heart of the Absolute. He alone can be said to have attained, and (this was the point which Jewdwine insisted on) attained only by the sacrifice of his individuality.

Thus Jewdwine in his *Prolegomena to Æsthetics*.

As that work could be regarded only as a brutal and terrific challenge to the intellect, the safer course was to praise it, and it was unanimously praised. Nobody was able to understand a word of it except the last chapter on "Individualism in Modern Art." But as criticism wisely concentrated itself on this, the only comprehensible portion of the book, Jewdwine (who otherwise would have perished in his own profundity) actually achieved some journalistic notoriety as a dealer in piquant paradox and vigorous personalities.

Jewdwine was ambitious. On the strength of his *Prolegomena* he had come up from Oxford with a remarkable reputation, which he had every inducement to cherish and to guard. He was therefore the best possible editor for such a review as *The Museion,* and such a review as *The Museion* was the best possible instrument of his ambition.

His aim was to preserve the tradition of the paper as pure as on the day when it was given into his hands.

He was a little doubtful as to how far young Rickman would lend himself to that.

However, as the fruit of Jewdwine's meditations, Rickman received a note inviting him to dine with the editor alone, at Hampstead. Jewdwine, whose health required pure air, had settled very comfortably in that high suburb. And, as his marriage seemed likely to remain long a matter for dubious reflection, he had arranged that his sister Edith should keep house for him. In inviting Rickman to dine at Hampstead his intention was distinctly friendly; at the same time he was careful to fix an evening when Miss Jewdwine would not be there. He was willing to help Rickman in every possible way short of introducing him to the ladies of his family.

But before dinner was ended he had to admit that this precaution was excessive. Rickman (barring certain dreadful possibilities of speech) was really by no means unpresentable. He was attired with perfect sanity. His methods at the dinner table, if at all unusual, erred on the side of restraint rather than of extravagance; he gave indications of a certain curious personal refinement; and in the matter of wine he was almost incredibly abstemious. It was the first time that Jewdwine had come to close quarters with his disciple, and with some surprise he saw himself going through the experience without a shock. Either he had been mistaken in Rickman, or Rickman had improved.

Shy he still was, but he had lost much of his old ungovernable nervousness, and gave Jewdwine the impression of an immense reserve. He seemed to have entered into some ennobling possession which raised him above the region of small confusions and excitements. His eye, when Jewdwine caught it, no longer struggled to escape; but it seemed to be held less by him than by its own controlling inner vision.

Jewdwine watched him narrowly. It never entered into his head that what he was watching was the effect of three weeks' intercourse with Lucia Harden. He attributed it to Rickman's deliverance from the shop. To be sure Rickman did not strike him as particularly happy, but this again he accounted for by the depressing state of his finances.

Neither of them made the most distant allusion to Lucia. Jewdwine was not aware of the extent of Rickman's acquaintance with his cousin, neither could he well have conceived it. And for Rickman it was not yet possible either to speak or to hear of Lucia without pain.

It was not until dinner was over, and Rickman was no longer eating Jewdwine's food, that they ventured on the unpleasant topic that lay before them, conspicuous, though untouched. Jewdwine felt that, as it was impossible to ignore what had passed between them since they had last met, the only thing was to refer to it as casually as might be.

"By the way, Rickman," he said, when they were alone

in his study, "you were quite right about that library. I only wish you could have let me know a little sooner."

"I wish I had," said Rickman, and his tone implied that he appreciated the painfulness of the subject.

There was a pause which Rickman broke by congratulating Jewdwine on his appointment. This he did with a very pretty diffidence and modesty, which smoothed over the awkwardness of the transition, if indeed it did not convey an adroit suggestion of the insignificance of all other affairs. The editor, still observing his unconscious candidate, was very favourably impressed. He laid before him the views and aims of *The Museion.*

Yes; he thought it had a future before it. He was going to make it the organ of philosophic criticism, as opposed to the mere personal view. It would, therefore, be unique. Yes; certainly it would also be unpopular. Heaven forbid that anything he was concerned in should be popular. It was sufficient that it should be impartial and incorruptible. Its tone was to be sober and scholarly, but militant. Rickman gathered that its staff were to be so many knights-errant defending the virtue of the English Language. No loose slip-shod journalistic phrase would be permitted in its columns. Its articles, besides being well reasoned, would be examples of the purity it preached. It was to set its face sternly against Democracy, Commercialism, and Decadence.

The disciple caught fire from the master's enthusiasm; he approved, aspired, exulted. His heart was big with belief in Jewdwine and his work. Being innocent himself of any sordid taint, he admired above all things what he called his friend's intellectual chastity. Jewdwine felt the truth of what Lucia had told him. He could count absolutely on Rickman's devotion. He arrived by well-constructed stages at the offer of the sub-editorship.

Rickman looked up with a curious uncomprehending stare. When he clearly understood the proposal that was being made to him, he flushed deeply and showed unmistakable signs of agitation.

"Do you think," said Jewdwine discreetly, "you'd care to try it for a time?"

"I don't know, I'm sure," said Rickman thoughtfully.

"Well, it's only an experiment. I'm not offering you anything permanent."

" Of course, that makes all the difference."

" It does ; if it isn't good enough——"

" You don't understand me. That's what would make it all right."

" Make what all right ? "

" My accepting—if you really only want a stop-gap."

" I see," said Jewdwine to himself, " the youth has tasted liberty, and he objects to being caught and caged."

" The question is," said Rickman, sinking into thought again, " whether you really want *me*."

" My dear fellow, why on earth should I say so if I didn't ? "

" N—no. Only I thought, after the mess I've made of things, that none of your family would ever care to have anything to do with me again." It was the nearest he had come to mentioning Lucia Harden, and the pain it cost him was visible on his face.

" My family," said Jewdwine with a stiff smile, " will *not* have anything to do with you. It has nothing to do with *The Museion*."

" In that case, I don't see why I shouldn't try it, if I can be of any use to you." From the calmness of his manner you would have supposed that salaried appointments hung on every lamp-post, ready to drop into the mouths of impecunious young men of letters.

" Thanks. Then we'll consider that settled for the present."

Impossible to suppose that Rickman was not properly grateful. Still, instead of thanking Jewdwine, he had made Jewdwine thank him. And he had done it quite unconsciously, without any lapse from his habitual sincerity, or the least change in his becoming attitude of modesty. Jewdwine considered that what Maddox had qualified as Rickman's colossal cheek was simply his colossal ignorance; not to say his insanely perverted view of the value of salaried appointments.

" Oh," said he, " I shall want you as a contributor, too. I don't know how you'll work in with the rest, but we shall see. I won't have any but picked men. The review has always stood high; but I want it to stand higher. It isn't a commercial speculation. There's no question of making it pay. It must keep up its independence whether it can afford it or not. We've been almost living on Vaughan's advertisements. All the same, I mean to slaughter those new men he's got hold of."

Rickman admired this reckless policy. It did not occur to him at the moment that Jewdwine was reader to a rival publisher.

" What," he said, " all of them at once ? "

" No—we shall work them off weekly, one at a time."

Rickman laughed. " One at a time? Then you allow them the merit of individuality ? "

" It isn't a merit; it's a vice, *the* vice of the age. It shrieks; it ramps. Individuality means slow disease in ethics and politics, but it's sudden death to art. When will you young men learn that art is self-restraint, not self-expansion? "

" Self-expansion—it seems an innocent impulse."

" If it were an impulse—but it isn't. It's a pose. A cold, conscious, systematic pose. So deadly artificial; and so futile, if they did but know. After all, the individual is born, not made."

" I believe you. "

" Yes; but he isn't born nowadays. He belongs to the ages of inspired innocence and inspired energy. We are not inspired; we are not energetic; we are not innocent. We're deliberate and languid and corrupt. And we can't reproduce by our vile mechanical process what only exists by the grace of Nature and of God. Look at the modern individual—for all their cant and rant, is there a more contemptible object on the face of this earth? Don't talk to me of individuality."

" It's given us one or two artists——"

" Artists? Yes, artists by the million; and no Art. To produce Art, the artist's individuality must conform to the Absolute."

Jewdwine in ninety-two was a man of enormous utterances and noble truths. With him all artistic achievements stood or fell according to the canons of the *Prolegomena to Æsthetics*. Therefore in ninety-two his conversation was not what you would call diverting. Yet it made you giddy; his ideas kept on circulating round and round the same icy, invisible pole. Rickman, in describing the interview afterwards, said he thought he had caught a cold in the head talking to Jewdwine; his intellect seemed to be sitting in a thorough draught.

"And if the artist has a non-conforming devil in him? If he's the sort of genius who can't and won't conform? Strikes me the poor old Absolute's got to climb down."

"If he's a genius—he generally isn't—he'll know that he'll express himself best by conforming. He isn't lost by it, but enlarged. Look at Greek art. There," said Jewdwine, a rapt and visionary air passing over his usually apathetic face, "the individual, the artist, is always subdued to the universal, the absolute beauty."

"And in modern art, I take it, the universal absolute beauty is subdued to the individual. That seems only fair. What you've got to reckon with is the man himself."

"Who wants the man himself? We want the thing itself—the reality, the pure object of art. Do any of your new men understand that?"

"We *want* it—some of us."

"Do you *understand* it?"

"Not I. Do you understand it yourself? Would you know it if you met it in the street?"

"It never is in the street."

"How do you know? You can't say where it is or what it is. You can't say anything about it at all. But while you're all trying to find out, the most unlikely person suddenly gets up and produces it. And *he* can't tell you where he got it. Though, if you ask him, ten to one he'll tell you he's been sitting on it all the time."

"Well," said Jewdwine, "tell me when you've 'sat on' anything yourself."

"I will." He rose to go, being anxious to avoid the suspicion of having pushed the question to a personal issue. It was only in reply to more searching inquiries that he mentioned (on the doorstep) that a book of his was coming out in the autumn.

"What, *Helen?*"

"No. *Saturnalia* and—a lot of things you haven't seen yet." It was a rapid nervous communication, made in the moment of withdrawing his hand from Jewdwine's.

"Who's your publisher?" called out Jewdwine.

Rickman laughed as the night received him. "Vaughan!" he shouted from the garden gate.

"Now, what on earth," said Jewdwine, "could have been his motive for not consulting me?" He had not got the clue to the hesitation and secrecy of the young man's behaviour. He did not know that there were three things which Rickman desired at any cost to keep pure—his genius, his friendship for Horace Jewdwine, and his love for Lucia Harden.

CHAPTER XL

THE end of May found Rickman still at Mrs. Downey's, established on the second floor in a glory that exceeded the glory of Mr. Blenkinsop. He had now not only a bed-room, but a study, furnished with a simplicity that had the effect of luxury, and lined from floor to ceiling with his books. Mrs. Downey had agreed that Mr. Rickman should, whenever the mysterious fancy took him, have his meals served to him in his own apartment after the high manner of Mr. Blenkinsop; and it was under protest that she accepted any compensation for the break thus made in the triumphal order of the Dinner.

Here then at last, he was absolutely alone and free. Feeling perhaps how nearly it had lost him, or impressed by the sudden change in his position, the boarding-house revered this privacy of Rickman's as a sacred thing. Not even Mr. Soper would have dared to violate his virgin leisure. The charm of it was unbroken, it was even heightened by the inaudible presence of Miss Roots in her den on the same floor. Miss Roots, indeed, was the tie that bound him to Mrs. Downey's; otherwise the dream of his affluence would have been chambers in Westminster or the Temple. For his income, in its leap from zero to a fluctuating two hundred a year, appeared to him as bound-less affluence. To be sure, Jewdwine had expressly stated that it would not be permanent, but this he had understood to be merely a delicate way of referring to his former im-perfect record of sobriety. And he had become rich not only in money, but in time. Rickman's had demanded an eight or even a ten hours' day; the office of *The Museion* claimed him but five hours of four days in the week. From five o'clock on Thursday evening till eleven on Monday morning, whatever work remained for him to do could be done in his own time and his own temper.

Much of the leisure time at his disposal he spent in endeavouring to follow the Harden library in its dispersion. He attended the great auctions in the hope of intercepting some treasure in its passage from Rickman's to the home of the collector. Once, in his father's absence, he bought a dozen volumes straight over the counter from his successor there. It was also about this time that Spinks and Soper appeared in the new character of book fanciers, buying according to Rickman's instructions and selling to him on commission, a transaction which filled these gentlemen with superb importance. Thus Rickman became possessed of about twenty or thirty volumes which he ranged behind a curtain, on a shelf apart. The collection, formed gradually, included nothing of any intrinsic value; such as it was he treasured it with a view to restoring it ultimately to Lucia Harden. He was considering whether with the means at his disposal he could procure a certain Aldine Dante of his memory, when the Harden library disappeared from the market as suddenly and mysteriously as it had come. No volume belonging to it could be bought for love or money; and none were displayed in the windows of Rickman's. Keith learnt nothing by his inquiries beyond the extent of his estrangement from his father. When he called at the shop his successor regretted that he was unable to give him any information. When he visited the suburban villa Isaac refused to see him. When he wrote Isaac never answered the letters. His stepmother in an unpleasant interview gave him to understand that the separation was final and complete.

He would have been more hurt by this rupture but for that other and abiding pain. The thought of Lucia Harden checked his enjoyment in the prospect of a now unimpeded career. Rickman was like some young athlete who walks on to the field stripped and strong for the race, but invisibly handicapped, having had the heart knocked out of him by some shameful incident outside the course. Apart from his own disgrace he was miserably anxious about Lucia herself, about her health, her happiness, her prospects; his misery being by no means lightened by his perception that these things were not exactly his concern.

He tried to picture her living as poor ladies live; he had seen them sometimes at Mrs. Downey's. He could not see her there, or rather, seeing her he could see nothing else; he perceived that surroundings and material accessories contributed nothing to his idea of her. Still, he knew nothing; and he had to accept his ignorance as part, and the worst part, of the separation that was his punishment. Many mixed feelings, shame and passion, delicacy and pride, restrained him from asking Jewdwine any question. Even if Jewdwine had not told him as much, he would have known that his acquaintance with Jewdwine's affairs would not involve acquaintance with Jewdwine's family. He had absolutely nothing to hope for from that connection.

And yet he hoped. The probabilities were that if Lucia did not make her home with her cousins, she would at any rate stay with them the greater part of the year. He was always walking up to Hampstead Heath on the chance of some day seeing her there. Sometimes he would pass by the front of Jewdwine's beautiful old brown house, and glance quickly through the delicate iron gate and up at the windows. But she was never there. Sometimes he would sit for hours on one of the seats under the elm tree at the back. There was a high walk there overlooking the West Heath and shaded by the elms and by Jewdwine's garden wall. The wall had a door in it that might some day open and let out the thing he longed for. Only it never did. There was nothing to hope for from Jewdwine's house.

At last his longing became intolerable, and one day, in the office, he made up his mind to approach Jewdwine himself. He had been telling him about the apparent check in the career of the Harden library, when he saw his opportunity and took it.

" By the way, can you tell me where your cousin is now ? "

" Miss Harden," said Jewdwine coldly, " is in Germany with Miss Palliser." He added, as if he evidently felt that some explanation was necessary (not on Rickman's account, but on his own), " She was to have come to us, but we were obliged to give her up to Miss Palliser, who is living alone."

" Alone ? "

" Yes. Mrs. Palliser is dead."

Rickman turned abruptly away to the window and stared into the street below. Jewdwine from his seat by the table

looked after him thoughtfully. He would have given a
good deal to know what was implied in the sudden turning of Rickman's back. What on earth did it matter to
Rickman if old Mrs. Palliser was dead or alive? What
could he be thinking of?

He was thinking of Kitty, who had shown him kindness;
of Kitty and the pleasant jests with which she used to cover
his embarrassment; of Kitty who had understood him at
the last. It was impossible not to feel some grief for the
grief of Lucia's friend; but he had no business to show it.
Therefore he had turned away.

And then he thought of Lucia; and in his heart he cursed
that other business which was his and yet not his; he cursed
the making of the catalogue; he cursed the great Harden
library which had brought them together and divided
them. But for that, his genius, a thing apart, might have
claimed her friendship for itself. As it was, his genius,
being after all bound up with his person, which suffered and
was ashamed, had (as far as Lucia was concerned) to accept
its humiliation and dismissal.

And all the time his genius, already vigorous enough in
all conscience, throve on his suffering as it had thriven on
his joy. In that summer of ninety-two Rickman's
Saturnalia were followed by *On Harcombe Hill,* and *The
Four Winds,* and that greatest poem of his lyric period, *The
Song of Confession.* Upon the young poet about town there
had descended, as it were out of heaven, a power hitherto
undreamed of and undivined. No rapture of the body was
ever so winged and flamed, or lost itself in such heights and
depths of music, as that cry of the passion of his soul.

CHAPTER XLI

MEANWHILE, of a Sunday evening, Miss Poppy Grace
wondered why Ricky-ticky never by any chance appeared upon his balcony. At last, coming home about ten
o'clock from one of his walks to Hampstead, he found
Poppy leaning out over *her* balcony most unmistakably on
the look-out.

" Come in and have some supper," said she.

" No thanks, I fancy it's a little late."

"Better late than never, when it's supper with *me*. Catch!" And Poppy, in defiance of all propriety, tossed her latch-key over the balcony. And somehow that latch-key had to be returned. He did not use it, but rang, with the intention of handing it to the servant; an intention divined and frustrated by Poppy, who opened the door to him herself.

"Don't go away," she said, "I've got something to tell you."

"Not now, I think——"

Her eyes were hideous to him in their great rings of paint and bistre.

"Why ever not? It'll only tyke a minute. Come in; there's nobody up there that matters."

And because he had no desire to be brutal or uncivil, he went up into the room he knew so well. It being summer, the folding doors were thrown wide open, and in the room beyond they came upon a large lady in a dirty tea-gown, eating lobster. For Poppy, now that she saw respectability departing from her, held out to it a pathetic little hand, and the tea-gown, pending an engagement as heavy matron on the provincial stage, was glad enough to play Propriety in Miss Grace's drawing-room. To-night Poppy made short work of Propriety. She waited with admirable patience while the large lady (whom she addressed affectionately as Tiny) followed up the last thin trail of mayonnaise; but when Tiny showed a disposition to toy with the intricacies of an empty claw, Poppy protested.

"Hurry up and clear out, there's a dear. I want to give Rickets his supper, and we haven't got a minute to spare."

And Tiny, who seemed to know her business, hurried up and cleared out.

But Rickets didn't want any supper, and Poppy was visibly abstracted and depressed. She mingled whipped cream with minute fragments of lobster, and finally fell to torturing a sandwich with a spoon; and all with an immense affectation of not having a minute to spare.

"Well, Ryzors," she said at last (and her accent jarred him horribly), "this is very strynge behyviour."

"Which?"

"Which? Do you know you haven't been near me for two months?"

He laughed uneasily. "I couldn't be near you when I was away."

"Never said you could. But what did you go away for?"

"Business."

"Too busy to write, I suppose?"

"Much too busy."

She rose, and with one hand on his shoulder steered him into the front room.

"Sit down," she said. "And don't look so sulky. I want to talk to you sensibly."

He sat down where he had sat that night two months ago, on the polar bear skin. She sat down too, with a sweeping, sidelong movement of her hips that drew her thin skirts close about her. She contemplated the effect a little dubiously, then with shy, nervous fingers loosened and shook out the folds. He leaned back, withdrawn as far as possible into the corner of the divan. The associations of the place were unspeakably loathsome to him.

"Look here, dear." In Poppy's world the term of endearment went for nothing; it was simply the stamp upon the current coin of comradeship. If only that had been the beginning and the end between them!

"I haven't a minute—but, I'm going to ask you something." Though Poppy hadn't a minute she was applying herself very leisurely to the making of cigarettes. "Don't go and get huffy at what I'm going to say. Do you happen to owe Dicky anything?"

"Why?"

"Tell you why afterwards. *Do* you owe him anything?"

"Oh, well—a certain amount. Why?"

"Why? Because I think he owes *you* something. And that's a grudge. It isn't my business, but if I were you, Rickets, I'd pay him orf and have done with him."

"Oh, that's all right. I'm safe enough."

"You? It's just you who isn't. Dicky's not a bad sort, in his way. All the same, he'd sell you up as soon as look at you. Unless,"—for a moment her bright eyes clouded charged with the melancholy meanings of the world,— "unless you happened to be an orf'ly pretty woman." She laid her right leg across her left knee and struck a vesta on the heel of her shoe.

" Then, of course, he'd sooner look at me."

Poppy puffed at her cigarette and threw the vesta into the grate with a dexterous jerk of her white forearm. " Look at you first. Sell you up—after." Then Poppy burst into song:

> "Oh, he is such a nice little boy,
>   When there's nothing you do to annoy;
>   But he's apt to stand aloof
>   If you arsk him for the oof,
>   And it's then that he looks coy.
>   Oh, he'll show the cloven hoof,
>   If you put him to the proof,
>   When you want him to hand you the boodle
> He's *not* such a nice little boy.

Yes, dicky, *I* see you!"

The canary, persuaded by Poppy's song that it was broad daylight, was awake and splashing in his bath. Again in Poppy's mind (how unnecessarily) he stood for the respectabilities and proprieties; he was an under-study for Tiny of the dirty tea-gown.

" Going? "

" Yes. I must go."

" Wait." She rose and held him by the collar of his coat, a lapel in each small hand. He grasped her wrists by an instinctive movement of self-preservation, and gently slackened her hold. She gave his coat a little shake. " What's the matter with you, Rickets? You're such a howling swell."

Her eyes twinkled in the old way, and he smiled in spite of himself.

" Say, I'm a little nuisance, Rickets, *say* I'm a little nuisance."

" You are a little nuisance."

" A d——d little nuisance."

" A d——d little nuisance."

" Ah, now you feel better, don't you? Poor Ricky-ticky, don't you be afraid. It's only a *little* nuisance. It'll never be a big one. It's done growing. That is, I won't rag you any more, if you'll tell me one thing—oh, what a whopper of a sigh! Promise me you'll pay Dicky off."

" All right. I'll pay him."

"To-morrow?"

"To-morrow, then. Don't, Poppy. I—I've got a sore

throat." For Poppy, standing on tip-toe, had made an effort to embrace him.

" I sy, if you blush like that, Rickets, you'll have a fit. Poor dear! *Did* I crumple his nice little stylish collar!"

He endured while she smoothed out an imaginary wrinkle. her head very much on one side. " You see, Ryzors, we've been such chums. Whatever happens, I want to be all right and straight with you."

" What should happen?"

" Oh, anything." Again there was that troubling of the bright shallows of her eyes. " You remember larst time you were here?" His shudder told her that he remembered well. " I *did* try to send you away, didn't I?"

" As far as I can remember, you did."

" What did you think I did it for?"

" I suppose, because you wanted me to go."

" Stupid! I did it because I wanted you to *stay.*" She looked into his eyes and the light went out of her own; among its paint and powder her audacity lay dead. It was as if she saw on his face the shadow of Lucia Harden, and knew that her hour had come.

She met it laughing. " Good-night, Ricky-ticky."

As he took her hand he muttered something about being " fearful sorry."

" Sorry?" Poppy conjured up a poor flickering ghost of her inimitable wink. " The champagne was bad, dear. Don't you worry."

When he had left her she flung herself face downwards on the divan. " Oh, dicky, will you hold your horrid little tongue?" But as she sobbed aloud, the canary, symbol of invincible Propriety, rocked on his perch and shook over her his piercing and exultant song.

Rickman was sorry for her, but the sight and touch of her were hateful to him. He took her advice, however. He had had good luck with some articles, and he called on Pilkington the next afternoon and paid him his thirty pounds with interest. Dicky was in a good humour and inclined to be communicative. He congratulated him on his present berth, and informed him that Rickman's was " going it." The old man had just raised four thousand on the Harden library, the only security that he, Dicky, would accept.

" I suppose," said Rickman simply, " you'd no idea of its value when you let him buy it ? "

Dicky stared through his eyeglass with his blue eyes immense and clear.

" My dear fellow, do you take me for a d——d fool? "

So that had been Dicky's little game? Trust Dicky.

And yet for the time being, held in the opposing grip of two firm cupidities, it was safe, the great Harden library, once the joy of scholars, loved with such high intellectual passion, and now the centre of so many hot schemes and rivalries and lusts. Now that the work of sacrilege was complete, housed at last in the Gin Palace of Art, it stood, useless in its desecrated beauty, cumbering the shelves whence no sale would remove it until either Rickman's or Pilkington let go. So far the Hardens were avenged.

CHAPTER XLII

MORE than once, after that night when Rickman dined with him, Jewdwine became the prey of many misgivings. He felt that in taking Rickman up he was assuming an immense responsibility. It might have been better, happier for Rickman, poor fellow, if after all he had left him in his decent obscurity ; but having dragged him out of it, he was in a manner answerable to the world for Rickman and Rickman for the world. Supposing Rickman disappointed the world? Supposing the world disappointed Rickman?

Jewdwine lived in hope, natural to a distinguished critic, of some day lighting up a genius. The glory of that find would go far to compensate him for his daily traffic with mediocrity. Genius was rarely to be seen, but Jewdwine felt that he would be the first to recognize it if he did see it ; the first to penetrate its many curious disguises ; the first to give it an introduction (if it wanted one) to his own superior world. And here was Rickman—manifestly in need of an introduction—a man who unquestionably had about him some of the marks by which a genius is identified ; and yet he left you terribly uncertain. He was the very incarnation of uncertainty. Jewdwine was perfectly willing to help the man if only he were sure of the genius. But was he sure? Had it really pleased the inscrutable divine thing to take up its abode in this otherwise rather impossible person?

Meanwhile Rickman seemed to be settling down fairly comfortably to the work of *The Museion;* and Jewdwine, having other things to think of, began to forget his existence. He was, in fact, rapidly realizing his dream. He had won for himself and his paper a position lonely and unique. The reputation of *The Museion* was out of all proportion to its circulation, but Jewdwine was making himself heard. As an editor and critic he was respected for his incorruptibility and for the purity of his passion for literature. His utterances were considered to carry authority and weight.

Just at first the weight was perhaps the more conspicuous quality of the two. Jewdwine could not be parted from his "Absolute." He had lived with it for years in Oxford, and he brought it up to town with him; it walked beside him on the London pavements and beckoned him incessantly into the vast inane. It cut a very majestic figure in his columns, till some irritable compositor docked it of its capital and compelled it to march with the rank and file of vulgar adjectives. Even thus degraded it ruled his paragraphs as it ruled his thoughts.

But lately the review seemed to be making efforts to redeem itself from the charge of heaviness. In certain of its columns there was a curious radiance and agitation, as of some winged and luminous creature struggling against obscurity; and it was felt that Jewdwine was binding in a pious tradition of dulness a spirit that would otherwise have danced and flown. Whether it was his own spirit or somebody else's did not definitely appear; but now and again it broke loose altogether, and then, when people complimented him on the brilliance of his appearance that week, he smiled inscrutably.

It was impossible to say how far Jewdwine's conscience approved of these outbursts of individuality. Certainly he did his best to restrain them, his desire being to give to his columns a distinguished unity of form. He saw himself the founder of a new and higher school of journalism, thus satisfying his undying tutorial instincts. He had chosen his staff from the most promising among the young band of disciples who thronged his lecture-room at

Oxford; men moulded on his methods, inspired by his ideals, drenched in his metaphysics; crude young men of uncontrollable enthusiasm, whose style awaited at his hands the final polishing.

He knew that he had done a risky thing in associating young Rickman with them in this high enterprise. But under all his doubts there lay a faith in the genius of his sub-editor, a faith the more fascinating because it was so far removed from any certainty. In giving Rickman his present post he conceived himself not only to be paying a debt of honour, but doing the best possible thing for *The Museion*. It was also, he considered, the best possible thing for Rickman. His work on the review would give him the discipline he most needed, the discipline he had never had. To be brought into line with an august tradition; to be caught up out of the slough of modern journalism into a rarer atmosphere; to breathe the eternal spirit of great literature (a spirit which according to Jewdwine did not blow altogether where it listed); to have his too exuberant individuality chastened and controlled, would be for Rickman an unspeakable benefit at this critical stage of his career.

The chastening and controlling were difficult. Rickman's phrases were frequently more powerful than polite. Like many young writers of violent imagination he was apt to be somewhat vividly erotic in his metaphors. And he had little ways that were very irritating to Jewdwine. He was wasteful with the office paper and with string; he would use penny stamps where half penny ones would have served his purpose; he had once permitted himself to differ with Jewdwine on a point of scholarship in the presence of the junior clerk. There were times when Jewdwine longed to turn him out and have done with him; and yet Rickman stayed on. When all was said and done there was a charm about him. Jewdwine, in fact, had proved the truth of Lucia's saying; he could rely absolutely on his devotion. He could not afford to let him go. Though Rickman tampered shamelessly with the traditions of the review, it could not be said that as yet he had injured its circulation. His contributions were noticed with approval in rival columns; and they had even been quoted by Continental critics, with whom *The Museion* passed as being the only British review that had the true interests of literature at heart.

But though Rickman helped to bring fame to *The Museion,* *The Museion* brought none to him. The identity of its contributors was merged into that of its editor, and those brilliant articles were never signed.

The spring of ninety-three, which found Jewdwine comfortably seated on the summit of his ambition, saw Rickman almost as obscure as in the spring of ninety-two. His poems had not yet appeared. Vaughan evidently regarded them as so many sensitive plants, and, fearing for them the boisterous seasons of autumn and spring, had kept them back till the coming May, when, as he expressed it, the market would be less crowded. This delay gave time to that erratic artist, Mordaunt Crawley, to complete the remarkable illustrations on which Vaughan relied chiefly for success. Vaughan had spared no expense, but naturally it was the artist and the printer, not the poet, whom he paid.

Rickman, however, had not thought of his *Saturnalia* as a source of revenue. It had been such a pleasure to write them that the wonder was he had not been called upon to pay for that. Happily for him he was by this time independent. As sub-editor and contributor to *The Museion,* he was drawing two small but regular incomes. He could also count on a third (smaller and more uncertain) from *The Planet,* where from the moment of his capture by Jewdwine he had been reinstated.

He found it easy enough to work for both. *The Planet* was poor, and it was out of sheer perversity that it indulged a disinterested passion for literature. In fact, Maddox and his men were trying to do with gaiety of heart what Jewdwine was doing with superb solemnity. But whenever Rickman mentioned Maddox to Jewdwine, Jewdwine would shrug his shoulders and say, " Maddox is not important "; and when he mentioned *The Museion* to Maddox, Maddox would correct him with a laugh, " The Museum, you mean," and refer to his fellow-contributors as " a respectable collection of meiocene fossils." Maddox had conceived a jealous and violent admiration for Savage Keith Rickman. " Rickman," he said, " you shall not go over body and soul to *The Museion.*" He regarded himself as the keeper and lover of Rickman's soul, and would not have been sorry to bring about a divorce between it and Jewdwine.

His irregular attentions were to save it from a suicidal devotion to a joyless consort. So that Rickman was torn between Maddox's enthusiasm for him and his own enthusiasm for Jewdwine.

That affection endured, being one with his impetuous and generous youth; while his genius, that thing alone and apart, escaped from Jewdwine. He knew that Jewdwine's incorruptibility left him nothing to expect in the way of approval and protection, and the knowledge did not greatly affect him. He preferred that his friend should remain incorruptible. That Jewdwine should greatly delight in his *Saturnalia* was more than he at any time expected. For there his muse, Modernity, had begun to turn her back resolutely on the masters and the models, to fling off the golden fetters of rhyme, gird up her draperies to her naked thighs, and step out with her great swinging stride on perilous paths of her own. To be sure there were other things which Jewdwine had not seen, on which he himself felt that he might rest a pretty secure claim to immortality.

Of his progress thither his friends had to accept Vaughan's announcements as the only intimation. Rickman had not called upon any of the Junior Journalists to smooth the way for him. He had not, in fact, called on any of them at all, but as April advanced he retreated more and more into a foolish privacy; and with the approaches of May he vanished. One night, however, some Junior Journalists caught him at the club, belated, eating supper. They afterwards recalled that he had then seemed to them possessed by a perfect demon of indiscretion; and when his book finally appeared on the first of May, it was felt that it could hardly have been produced under more unfavourable auspices. This reckless attitude was evidently unaffected (nobody had ever accused Rickman of affectation); and even Maddox pronounced it imprudent in the extreme. As for Jewdwine, it could not be accounted for by any motives known to him. His experience compelled him to take a somewhat cynical view of the literary character. Jewdwine, among his authors, was like a man insusceptible of passion, but aware of the fascinations that caused him to be pursued by the solicitations of the fair. He was flattered by the pursuit, but the pursuer inspired him with the liveliest contempt. It had not yet occurred to him that Rickman could have any delicacy in approaching him. Still less could he believe that Rickman could be indifferent to the fate of his book. His carelessness therefore did not strike him as entirely genuine. There could be no doubt however as to the genuineness of Rickman's surprise when he came upon Jewdwine in the office reading *Saturnalia*.

He smiled upon him, innocent and unconscious. "Ah!" he said, "so you're reading it? You won't like it."

Jewdwine crossed one leg over the other, and it was wonderful the amount of annoyance he managed to convey by the gesture. His face, too, wore a worried and uncertain look; so worried and so uncertain that Rickman was sorry for him. He felt he must make it easy for him.

"At any rate, you won't admire its personal appearance."

"I don't. What possessed you to give it to Vaughan?"

"Some devil, I think."

"You certainly might have done better."

"Perhaps. If I'd taken the trouble. But I didn't."

Jewdwine raised his eyebrows (whenever he did that Rickman thought of someone who used to raise her eyebrows, too, but with a difference).

"You see, it was last year. I let things slide."

Jewdwine looked as if he didn't see. "If you had come to me, I think I could have helped you."

"I didn't want to bother you. I knew you wouldn't care for the things."

"Well, frankly, I don't care very much for some of them. But I should have stretched a point to keep you clear of Crawley. I'm sorry he put temptation in your way."

"He didn't. They say I put temptation in his way. Horrid, isn't it, to think there's something in me that appeals to his diseased imagination?"

"It's a pity. And I don't know what I can do for you. You see you've identified yourself with a school I particularly abominate. It isn't a school. A school implies a master and some attempt at discipline. It should have a formula. Crawley has none."

"Oh, I don't know about that." He stood beside Jewdwine, who was gazing at the frontispiece. "Talk about absolute beauty, any fool can show you the beauty of a beautiful thing, or the ugliness of an ugly one; but it takes a clever beast like Crawley to show you beauty in anything so absolutely repulsive as that woman's face. Look at it! He's got hold of something. He's caught the lurking fascination, the—the leer of life."

Jewdwine made a gesture of disgust.

"Of course, it's no good as an illustration. I don't see life with a leer on its face. But he can draw. Look at the fellow's line. Did you ever see anything like the purity of it? It's a high and holy abstraction. By Jove! He's got *his* formula. Pure line remains pure however bestial the object it describes. I wish he'd draw it at illustrating *me*. But I suppose if he saw it that way he had to draw it that way."

Jewdwine turned over the pages gingerly, as if he feared to be polluted. He was at the moment profoundly sorry for Rickman in this marriage of his art with Mordaunt Crawley's. Whatever might be said of Rickman's radiant and impetuous genius it neither lurked nor leered; it was in no way represented by that strange and shameless figure, half Mænad, half modern courtesan, the face foreshortened, tilted back in the act of emptying a wine-cup.

"At any rate," said Rickman, "he hasn't lied. He's had the courage to be his filthy self."

"Still, the result isn't exactly a flattering portrait of your Muse."

"She *is* a caution. It's quite enough to make you and Hanson lump me with Letheby and that lot."

This touched Jewdwine in two sensitive places at once. He objected to being "lumped" with Hanson. He also felt that his generosity had been called in question. For a moment the truth that was in him looked out of his grave and earnest eyes.

"I do *not* lump you with Letheby or anybody. On the contrary, I think you stand by yourself. Quite one half of this book is great poetry."

"You really think that?"

"Yes," said Jewdwine solemnly; "I do think it. That's why I deplore the appearance of the other half. But if you *had* to publish, why couldn't you bring out your *Helen in Leuce?* It was far finer than anything you have here."

"Yes. Helen's all right *now*." His tone implied only

too plainly that she was not all right when Jewdwine had approved of her.

" Now? What on earth have you been doing to her? "

" Only putting a little life into her limbs. But Vaughan wouldn't have her at any price."

" My dear Rickman, you should have come to *me*. I hope to goodness Vaughan won't tempt you into any more *Saturnalia*."

" After all—what's wrong with them? "

Jewdwine leaned back, keenly alive to these stirrings of dissent; he withdrew, as it were, his protecting presence a foot or two farther. He spoke slowly and with emphasis.

" Excess," said he; " too much of everything. Too much force, too much fire, and too much smoke with your fire. In other words, too much temperament, too much Rickman."

" Too much Rickman? "

" Yes; far too much. It's nothing but a flaming orgy of individuality."

" And that's why it's all wrong? " He really wondered whether there might not be something in that view after all.

" It seems so to me. Look here, my dear fellow. Because a poet happens to have been drunk once or twice in his life it's no reason why he should write a poem called *Intoxication*. That sort of exhibition, you know, is scandalous."

Rickman hung his head. That one poem he would have given anything at the moment to recall. It *was* scandalous, if you came to think of it. Only in the joy of writing it he had not thought of it; that was all.

" It's simply astounding in a splendid scholar like you, Rickman. It's such an awful waste." He looked at him as he spoke, and his soul was in his eyes. It gave him a curious likeness to his cousin, and in that moment Rickman worshipped him. " Go back. Go back to your Virgil and your Homer and your Sophocles, and learn a little more restraint. There's nothing like them. They'll take you out of this ugly, weary, modern world where you and I, Rickman, had no business to be born."

" And yet," said Rickman, " there *are* modern poets."

" There are very few, and those not the greatest. By modern, I mean inspired by the modern spirit; and the modern spirit does not inspire great poetry. The greatest have been obliged to go back—back to primeval nature, back to the Middle Ages, back to Greece and Rome—but always back."

"I can't go back," said Rickman. "I mayn't know what I'm working for yet, but I believe I'm on the right road. How can I go back?"

"Why not? Milton went back to the Creation, and *he* was only born in the seventeenth century. You have had the unspeakable misfortune to be born in the nineteenth. You must live on your imagination—the world has nothing for you."

"I believe it *has* something for me, if I could only find it."

"Well, don't lose too much time in looking for it. Art's long and life's short, especially modern life; and that's the trouble."

Rickman shook his head. "No; that's not the trouble. It's the other way about. Life's infinite and art's one. And at first, you know, it's the infinity that staggers you." He flung himself into a chair opposite Jewdwine, planted his elbows on the table, and propped his chin on his hands. He looked as if he saw the infinity he spoke of. "I can't describe to you," he said, "what it is merely to be alive out there in the streets, on a sunny day, when the air's all fine watery gold, and goes dancing and singing into your head like dry champagne. I've given up alcohol. It isn't really necessary. I got as drunk as a lord the other day going over Hampstead Heath in a west wind" (he *looked* drunk at the mere thought of it). "Does it ever affect *you* in that *way?*"

Jewdwine smiled. The wind on Hampstead Heath had never affected him in that way.

"No. It isn't what you think. I used to go mad about women, just as I used to drink. I don't seem to care a rap about them now." But his eyes had a peculiar large and brilliant look, as if he saw the woman of his desire approaching him. His voice softened. "Don't you know when the world—all the divine maddening beauty of it—lies naked before your eyes, and you want to get hold of it—now—this minute, and instead it gets hold of you, and pulls you every way at once—don't you know? The thing's got a thousand faces, and two thousand arms, and ten thousand devils in it."

Jewdwine didn't know. How should he? He had a

horror of this forcing of the sensuous and passionate note.
The author of the *Prolegomena to Æsthetics* recoiled from
" too much temperament." He felt, moreover, the jealous
pang of the master who realizes that he has lost his hold.
This was not that Rickman who used to hang all flushed
and fervid on Jewdwine's words. He remembered how
once on an April day, a year ago, the disciple had turned at
the call of woman and of the world, the call of the Spring
in his heart and in his urgent blood.

And yet this was not that Rickman either.

" My dear Rickman, I don't understand. *Are* you talking about the world? Or the flesh? Or the devils?"

" All of them, if you like. And you can throw in the sun
and the moon and the stars, too. There are moments, Jewdwine, when I understand God. At any rate I know how he
felt the very day before creation. His world's all raw chaos
to me, and I've got to make my world out of it."

" I'm afraid I cannot help you *there.*"

As they parted he felt that perhaps he had failed to be
sufficiently sympathetic. " I'll do my best," said he, " to set
you right with the public."

Left alone, he stood staring earnestly at the chair where
Rickman had sat propping his chin in his hands. He seemed
to be contemplating his phantom; the phantom that had
begun to haunt him.

What had he let himself in for?

CHAPTER XLIII

THERE was one man who was sure, perfectly sure; and
that man was Maddox. He had read Rickman's book
before Jewdwine had seen it, and while Jewdwine was still
shaking his head over it in the office of *The Museion,*
its chances were being eagerly discussed in the office of *The
Planet.* Maddox was disgusted with the publishers, Stables
with the price, Rankin with the illustrations.

" It's all very well," said Rankin; " but those borrowed
plumes will have to be paid for."

" Borrowed plumes with a vengeance," said Maddox.
" Vaughan might just as well have turned him out tarred
and feathered as illustrated by Mordaunt Crawley. Mind

you, some of that tar will stick. It'll take him all his time to get it off."

"Did you see," said Stables, "that Hanson bracketed him with Letheby in this morning's *Courier?*"

"No, did he?" said Maddox; "I'm sorry for that. It's rough on little Rickman."

"It's what you must expect," said Rankin, "if you're illustrated by Crawley."

"It's what you must expect," said Stables, "if you go out of your way to offend people who can help you. You know he refused an introduction to Hanson the other day?"

"No!"

"Fact. And it was in his sublimest manner. He said he hadn't any use for Hanson. Hanson couldn't help him till he'd helped himself. I don't know whether any one was kind enough to tell that tale to Hanson."

"Hanson," said Maddox, "is too big a man to mind it if they did."

"Anyhow, he *hasn't* helped him."

"No," said Rankin; "but that's another story. Hanson was dining with Jewdwine, and Jewdwine was cracking up Rickman most extravagantly (for him). That was quite enough to make Hanson jump on him. He was bound to do it by way of asserting his independence."

"I wonder if Jewdwine calculated that that would be the natural effect."

"Oh, come, he's a subtle beast; but I don't suppose he's as subtle as all that."

"You'll find that all the reviews will follow Hanson like a flock of sheep."

"How about the *Literary Observer?* Mackinnon was friendly."

Maddox smiled. "He *was*. But our Ricky-ticky alienated Mackinnon on the very eve of publication."

"How?"

"By some awful jest. Something about Mackinnon's head and the dome of the British Museum."

"Well, if it was a joke, Mackinnon wouldn't see it."

"No, but he'd feel it, which would be a great deal worse. Our Ricky-ticky is devoid of common prudence."

"Our Ricky-ticky is a d——d fool," said Stables.

" Well," said Rankin, " I suppose he knows what he's about. He's got Jewdwine at his back."

Maddox shrugged his enormous shoulders. " Jewdwine? Jewdwine won't slate his own man, but he can't very well turn round and boom the set he always goes for. This," said Maddox, " is *my* deal. I shall sail in and discover Ricky-ticky."

" He's taking precious good care to hide himself. It's a thousand pities he ever got in with those wretched decadents."

" He isn't in with them."

" Well, he mayn't be exactly immersed, but the tide's caught him."

" The tide? You might be talking of the Atlantic."

" The stream then—' the stream of tendency that makes for '—muck."

" It isn't a stream, it's a filthy duck-pond in somebody's back yard. There's just enough water for the rest to drown in, but it isn't deep enough to float a man of Rickman's size. He's only got his feet wet, and that won't hurt him."

" There are things," said Rankin, " in *Saturnalia* that lend themselves to Crawley's treatment."

" And there are things in it that Crawley can't touch. And look at the later poems—*The Four Winds, On Harcombe Hill,* and *The Song of Confession.* Good God! It makes my blood boil to compare the man who wrote that with Letheby. *Letheby!* I could wring Vaughan's neck and Hanson's too. I should like to take their heads and knock them together. As for Letheby, I'll do for him. I'll smash him in one column, and I'll give Rickman his send-off in four."

(*The Planet* in those early days was liberal with its space.)

" After all," he added in a calmer tone, " he was right. We can't help him, except by taking a back seat and letting him speak for himself. I shall quote freely. *The Song of Confession* is the best answer to Hanson."

" It seems to me," said Stables, " you'll want a whole number at this rate."

" I shall want six columns, if I'm to do him any justice," said Maddox, rising. " Poor beggar, I expect he's a bit off colour. I shall go and look him up."

At eight that evening he went and looked him up. He

found him in his room tranquilly reading. Thinking of him as a man of genius who had courted failure and madly fooled away his chances, and seeing him sitting there, so detached, and so unconscious, Maddox was profoundly moved. He had come with cursing and with consolation, with sympathy, with prophecy, with voluble belief. But all he could say was, " It's all right, Rickman. It's great, my son, it's great."

All the same he did not conceal his doubts as to the sort of reception Rickman had to expect. That part of the business, he said, had been grossly mismanaged, and it was Rickman's own fault.

" Look here," he said, " what on earth possessed you to go and refuse that introduction to Hanson? Was it just your cheek, or the devil's own pride, or what? "

" Neither," said Rickman, in a tone that pathetically intimated that he was worn out. " I think it was chiefly my desire for peace and quiet. I'm writing some more poems, you see. I wouldn't have refused it at any other time."

" At any other time it wouldn't have mattered so much. You should be civil to the people who can help you."

" I rather distrust that sort of civility myself. I've seen too much of the dirty back stairs of Fleet Street. I've tumbled over the miserable people who sit on them all day long, and I don't mean anybody to tumble over me. When I've got my best trousers on I want to keep them clean."

" It's a mistake," said Maddox, " to wear your best trousers every day."

" Perhaps. But I mean to wear them."

" Wear them by all means. But you must make up your mind for a certain amount of wear and tear. In your case it will probably be tear."

" That's my look-out."

" Quite so. I wouldn't say anything if it was only Hanson you'd offended, but you shouldn't alienate your friends."

" My friends? "

" Yes. Why, oh, why, did you make that joke about Mackinnon's head? "

" We were all making jokes about Mackinnon's head."

" Yes; but we weren't all of us bringing out poems the next day. Your position, Ricky-ticky, was one of peculiar delicacy—and danger."

" What does it matter? " said Rickman wearily.   " I can trust my friends to speak the truth about me."

" Heaven bless you, Rickman, and may your spring suitings last for ever." He added, as Jewdwine had added, " Anyhow, *this* friend will do his level best for you."

At which Rickman's demon returned again. " Don't crack me up too much, Maddy. You might do me harm."

But before midnight Maddox burst into the office and flung himself on to his desk.

" Give me room! " he cried; " I mean to spread myself, to roll, to wallow, to wanton, to volupt! "

Before morning he had poured out his soul, in four columns of *The Planet,* the exuberant, irrepressible soul of the Celt. He did it in an hour and twenty minutes. As he said himself afterwards (relating his marvellous achievement) he was sustained by one continuous inspiration; his passionate pen paused neither for punctuation nor for thought. The thoughts, he said, were there. As the critical notices only appeared weekly, to pause would have entailed a delay of seven days, and he meant that his panegyric should appear the very next day after the article in the *Literary Observer,* as an answer to Hanson's damnable paragraph.

If Maddox was urged to these excesses by his contempt for Jewdwine's critical cowardice, Jewdwine was cooled by the spectacle of Maddox's intemperance. He had begun by feeling a little bitter towards Rickman on his own account. He was disappointed in him. Rickman had shown that he was indifferent to his opinion. That being so, Jewdwine might have been forgiven if he had had no very keen desire to help him. Still, he *had* desired to help him; but his desire had ceased after reading Maddox's review. There was no pleasure in helping him now, since he had allowed himself to be taken up and caressed so violently by other people. The clumsy hand of Maddox had brushed the first bloom from his Rickman, that once delightful youth. He was no longer Jewdwine's Rickman, his disciple, his discovery.

But though Jewdwine felt bitter, he was careful that no tinge of this personal feeling should appear in his review of Rickman's poems. It was exceedingly difficult for him to review them at all. He had to take an independent attitude, and most possible attitudes had been taken already. He could not ignore Rickman's deplorable connection with the Decadents; and yet he could not insist on it, for that was what Hanson and the rest had done. Rickman had got to stay there; he could not step in and pluck him out like a brand from the burning; for Maddox had just accomplished that heroic feat. He would say nothing that would lend counfenance to the extravagance of Maddox. There was really no room for fresh appreciation anywhere. He could not give blame where Hanson had given it; and Maddox had plastered every line with praise. He would have been the first to praise Rickman, provided that he *was* the first. Not that Jewdwine ever committed himself. As a critic his surest resource had always lain in understatement. If the swan was a goose, Jewdwine had as good as said so. If the goose proved a swan, Jewdwine had implied as much by his magnificent reserve. But this time the middle course was imposed on him less by conviction than necessity. He had to hold the balance true between Hanson and Maddox.

In his efforts to hold it true, he became more than ever academic and judicial. So judicial, so impartial was he in his opinion, that he really seemed to have no opinion at all; to be merely summing up the evidence and leaving the verdict to the incorruptible jury. Every sentence sounded as though it had been passed through a refrigerator. Not a hint or a sign that he had ever recognized in Rickman the possibility of greatness.

Now, if Rickman had not been connected with *The Museion,* the review would have done him neither harm nor good. As it was, it did him harm. It was naturally supposed that Jewdwine, so far from understating his admiration, had suppressed his bad opinion in the interests of friendship. Rickman's *Saturnalia* remained where Hanson had placed it, rather low in the ranks of young Decadence.

And then, just because he had suppressed the truth about him, because he felt that he had given Rickman some grounds for bitterness, Jewdwine began to feel more and more bitter himself.

If Rickman felt any bitterness he never showed it. He had only two thoughts on reading Jewdwine's articles. " It wouldn't have mattered except that *she* will see it "; and " I wouldn't have minded if it was what he really thought."

Maddox, rightly judging that Rickman would be suffering more in his affection than his vanity, called on him that afternoon and dragged him out for his usual Saturday walk. As if the thought of Jewdwine dominated their movements, they found themselves on the way to Hampstead. Maddox attempted consolation.

" It really doesn't matter much what Jewdwine says. These fellows come up from Oxford with wet towels round their heads to keep the metaphysics in. Jewdwine's muddled himself with the Absolute Beauty till he doesn't know a beautiful thing if you stick it under his nose."

" Possibly not; if you keep it farther off he might have a better chance. Trust him to know."

" Well, if he knows, he doesn't care."

" Oh, doesn't he. That's where Jewdwine's great. He cares for nothing else. He cares more than any man alive— in his heart."

" D——n his heart! I don't believe he has one."

" Would you oblige me by not talking about him any more?"

Maddox obliged him.

They tramped far into the country, returning at nightfall by the great road that crosses the high ground of the Heath. Rickman loved that road; for by night, or on a misty evening, it was possible to imagine some remote resemblance between it and the long straight ridge of Harcombe Hill.

They paused by common consent where the Heath drops suddenly from the edge of the road, opening out the view towards London. The hollow beneath them, filled by a thin fog, had become mysterious and immense.

" By the way," said Maddox, following an apparently irrelevant train of thought, " what has become of your friendship for Miss Poppy Grace?"

" It has gone," said Rickman, " where the old trousers go. Look there——"

Above them heaven seemed to hang low, bringing its stars nearer. A few clouds drifted across it, drenched in the blue of the night behind them, a grey-blue, watery and opaque. Below, sunk in a night greyer and deeper, were the lights of London. The ridge they stood on was like the rampart of another world hung between the stars which are the lights of poets, and the lights which are the stars of men. Under the stars Maddox chanted softly the last verses of the *Song of Confession* that Rickman had made.

"Oh, Ricky-ticky," he said, "you know everything. How did you know it?"

"Because I've been there."

"But—you didn't stay?"

"No—no. I didn't stay. I couldn't."

"I'm still there. And for the life of me I see no way out. It's like going round in the underground railway—a vicious circle. Since you're given to confession—own up. Don't you ever want to get back there?"

"Not yet. My way won't take me back if I only stick to it."

Under the stars he endeavoured to account for his extraordinary choosing of the way.

"I've three reasons for keeping straight. To begin with, I've got a conviction that I'll write something great if I don't go to the devil first. Then, there's Horace Jewdwine."

Maddox hardened his face; he had been told not to talk about Jewdwine, and he wasn't going to.

"If I go to the devil, he won't go with me. Say what you like, he's a saint compared with you and me. If he doesn't understand Songs of Confession, it's because he's never had anything to confess. The third reason—if I go to the devil—no, I can't tell you the third reason. It's also the reason why I wear my magnificent trousers. All the reasons amount to that. If I go to the devil I can't wear those trousers. Never, Maddox, believe me, never again."

Maddox smiled, and, unlike Maddox, he said one thing and thought another.

What he said was, "Your trousers, Ricky-ticky, are of too heavenly a pattern for this wicked world. They are such stuff as dreams are made of, and their little life——" He paused. What he thought was, "Your way, Ricky-ticky, is deuced hard for the likes of me. But I'll go with you as far as I can, my son."

Under the stars they looked into each other's faces and they knew themselves aright.

CHAPTER XLIV

JEWDWINE made up for the coldness of his published
utterances by the fervour of his secret counsel. His
advice to Rickman was, " Beware of the friendship of little
men."

This Rickman understood to be a reflection on Maddox's
position in the world of letters. He did not care a rap about
Maddox's position; but there were moments when it was
borne in upon him that Maddox was a bigger man even than
Horace Jewdwine, that his reckless manner poorly disguised
a deeper insight and a sounder judgment. His work on *The
Planet* proved it every day. And though for himself he
could have desired a somewhat discreeter champion, he had
the highest opinion of his friend's courage in standing up
for him when there was absolutely nothing to be gained
by it. He had every reason therefore to be attached to
Maddox.

But it was true enough that he knew too many little men;
men who were at home in that house of bondage from which
he was for ever longing to escape; men whom he had met
as he had described, sitting contentedly on the dirty back-
stairs of Fleet Street; men who, in rubbing shoulders with
each other in that crowded thoroughfare, had had to allow
for a great deal of what Maddox called wear and tear.
Those little men had remained invincibly, imperturbably
friendly. They knew perfectly well that he thought them
little men, and they delighted in their great man all the same,
more than ever, in fact, since his new suit of morals provided them with a subject of eternal jest. For Maddox was
but human, and he had found Rickman's phrase too pregnant
with humour to be lost. They were sometimes very funny,
those Junior Journalists, especially on a Saturday night. But
Rickman was not interested in the unseemly obstacle race
they dignified by the name of a career, and he did not care
to mix too freely with young men so little concerned about
removing the dirt and sweat of it. He clung to Maddox and
Rankin as the strongest and the cleanest of them all. But
even they had inspirations that left him cold, and they
thought many things large and important that were too small
for him to see. He would have died rather than let either of

them know what he was doing now. He saw with dismay that they suspected him of doing something, that their suspicions excited them most horribly, that they were watching him; and he had told Maddox that what he desired most was peace and quietness.

He found it in the Secret Chamber of the Muse, where he shut himself up when his work with them was done. In there, his days and nights were as the days and nights of God. There he forecast the schemes of dramas yet to be, dramas no longer neo-classic. And as his genius foresaw the approach of its maturity, it purified and emptied itself of the personal passion that obscures the dramatist's vision of the world. This it did in a sequence of Nine and Twenty Sonnets, a golden chain that bound Lucia's name to his whether she would or no. They recorded nine and twenty moments in the life of his passion, from the day of its birth up to the present hour, the hour of its purification.

For it was still young in him; though at this distance of time Lucia's image was no longer one and indivisible. He had come to think of her as two persons clothed mysteriously in the same garment of flesh. One carried that garment a little more conspicuously than the other; it was by her beauty that she pierced him with the pain of longing; and not by her beauty only, but by the marks of suffering that in his memory still obscured it. She came before him, and her tragic eyes reproached him with the intolerable pathos of her fate, making him suffer too, through his exceeding pity. And yet his longing had not been consumed by pity, but had mingled with it as flame in flame. Long after he had parted from her, his senses ached as they recalled the exquisite movements of her body. He had only to shut his eyes, and he was aware of the little ripple of her shoulders and the delicate swaying of her hips. To lie awake in the dark was to see her kneeling at his side, to feel the fragrance of her thick braid of hair flattened and warmed by her sleep, and the light touch of her hands as they covered him. And before that memory his shame still burnt deeper than his desire.

But this Lucia had no desire for him and no pity. Her countenance, seen even in dreams, expressed a calm but immutable repugnance. No wonder, for *she* was only acquainted with the pitiably inadequate sample of him introduced to her as Mr. Rickman of Rickman's. He was aware that she belonged exclusively not only to Jewdwine's class, but to Jewdwine himself in some way (a way unspeakably disagreeable to contemplate). If he was not to think of her as enduring the abominations of poverty, he must think of her as married to Jewdwine. Married to Jewdwine, she would make an end of his friendship as she had made an end of his peace of mind. There had been moments, at the first, when he had felt a fierce and unforgiving rage against her for the annoyance that she caused him.

But now, dividing the host of turbulent and tormenting memories, there appeared a different Lucia, an invincible but intimate presence that brought with it a sense of deliverance and consolation. It was Lucia herself that saved him from Lucia. Her eyes were full of discernment and of an infinite tenderness and compassion. They kindled in him the desire that fulfils itself in its own utterance.

That this Lucia was not wholly the creature of his imagination he was assured by his memory of certain passages in his life at Harmouth, a memory that had all the vividness and insistence of the other. It was the Lucia he had known before the other Lucia, the Lucia who had divined and would divine him still. In a way she was more real than the other, more real than flesh and blood, even as that part of him by which he apprehended her was more real than the rest. From her he was not and could not be divided; they belonged to each other, and by no possibility could he think of this Lucia as married to Jewdwine, or of his friendship for Jewdwine as in any way affected by her. He was hers by right of her perfect comprehension of him; for such comprehension was of the nature of possession. It was also an assurance of her forgiveness, if indeed she had anything to forgive. He had not wronged her; it was the other Lucia he had wronged. In all this he never once thought of her as his inspiration. She would not have desired him to think of her so, being both too humble and too proud to claim any part in the genius she divined. But she could not repudiate all connection with it, because it was in the moments when his genius was most dominant that he had this untroubled assurance of her presence.

And there in the Secret Chamber he bound her to him

by an indestructible chain, the chain of the Nine and Twenty Sonnets.

The question was what should he do with it now that it was made? To dedicate twenty-nine sonnets to Lucia was one thing, to print them was another. If it was inevitable that he should thus reveal himself after the manner of poets, it was also inevitable that she should regard a public declaration as an insult rather than an honour. And he himself shrank from exposing so sacred a thing to the pollution and violence of publicity. Therefore he took each sonnet as it was written, and hid it in a drawer. But he was not without prescience of their ultimate value, and after all this method of disposal seemed to him somehow unsatisfactory. So he determined that he would leave the manuscript to Lucia in his will, to be afterwards dealt with as she judged best, whether she chose to publish or to burn. In the former case the proceeds might be regarded as partial payment of a debt. And so two years passed and it was spring again.

CHAPTER XLV

THERE are many ways of achieving distinction, but few are more effectual than a steady habit of punctuality. By this you may shine even in the appalling gloom of the underground railway. Among all the women who wait every morning for the City trains at Gower Street Station, there was none more conspicuously punctual than Miss Flossie Walker. The early clerk who travelled citywards was always sure of seeing that little figure on the same spot at the same moment, provided he himself were punctual and kept a sharp look-out. This you may be sure he took good care to do. To look at Flossie once was to look again and yet again. And he was fortunate indeed if his route lay between Moorgate Street Station and the Bank, for then he had the pleasure of seeing her sharply threading her way among the traffic, if that can be said of anything so soft and round as Flossie.

If Flossie's figure was small and round, her face was somewhat large, a perfect oval moulded in the subtlest curves, smooth and white moreover, with a tinge of ivory sallow towards the roots of her black hair. Wonderful hair was Flossie's. In those days she parted it in the middle and waved it symmetrically on either side of her low forehead; she brought it over her ears, covering all but the tips and the delicate pink lobes; she coiled it at the back in an elaborate spiral and twisted it into innumerable little curls about the nape of her neck. Unfortunately that neck was rather short; but she wore low collars which made the most of it. And then Flossie's features were so very correct. She had a correct little nose, neither straight nor aquiline, but a distracting mixture of both, and a correct little mouth, so correct and so small that you wondered how it managed to display so many white teeth in one diminutive smile. Flossie's eyes were not as her mouth; they were large, full-lidded, long-lashed, and blacker than her hair. No wonder if the poor clerk who passed her on her ways to and fro in the City rejoiced as they looked up at him. She might be going to her work as he to his, but what with her bright eyes and her blue ribbons, she looked the very genius of holiday as she went.

At first she was a little subdued and awed by the Bank, and by her own position in it. But when this feeling wore off, the plump girl rolled into her place with a delicious abandonment. Flossie was one of fifty girls who sat, row after row, at long flat desks covered with green cloth. A soft monotonous light was reflected from the cream-coloured walls against which Flossie's head stood out with striking effect, like some modern study in black and morbid white. You would have picked her out among the fifty at once. Hers was the lightest of light labour, the delicate handling of thousands of cancelled notes—airy, insubstantial things, as it were the ghosts of bank-notes, released from the gross conditions of the currency. Towards the middle of the morning Flossie would be immersed in a pale agitated sea of bank-notes. The air would be full of light sounds, always the sharp brisk rustling of the notes, and now and then a human undertone, or towards lunch time, a breath that was like a sigh. A place to grow light-headed in if you began to think about it. Happily no thought was required beyond the intelligence that lives in sensitive finger-tips. It was almost mechanical labour, and for that Flossie had more than a taste, she had a positive genius. It was mechanical labour idealized and reduced to a fine art, an art in which the personality of the artist counted. The work displayed to perfection the prettiness of Flossie's hands, from the rapid play of her fingers in sifting, and their little fluttering, hovering movements in arranging, to the exquisitely soft touches of the palms when she gathered all her sheaves of notes into one sheaf, shaking, caressing, coaxing the rough edges into line. Flossie worked with the rhythm and precision of a machine; and yet humanly, self-consciously, almost coquettishly, as under the master's eye.

But all this was of yesterday. To-day Flossie was different. She was not quite so precise, so punctual as she had been. Something had gone wrong with the bright little mechanism. It worked erratically, now under protest, and now with spurts of terrifying activity. The fine fly-wheels of thought had set off whirring on their own account and had got mixed up with the rest of the machinery. Flossie had begun to philosophize, to annoy destiny with questions. There was time for that in the afternoon when the worst of the sorting was done. She was in the stage of doubt so attractive in philosophers and women, asking herself: Is knowledge possible? And if so, what do I know? She was aware that there are certain insurpassable limits to human knowledge; all the same, woman-like, she raised herself on tip-toe, and tried to peep over the boundaries. What did she know? She knew that somebody pitied her, because, poor little woman, she had to earn her living like man. Well, she would not have to do that if—if he—Yes, and if he didn't? And how was she to know? And yet, and yet she had an idea. Anybody may have an idea. Then the long desks became the green tables where Flossie gambled with fate; trying—trying—trying to force the invisible hand.

For with Flossie it was spring-time, too. Under the little clerk's correctness and demureness there ran and mingled with her blood the warm undercurrent of a dream. The dream had come to her many springs ago; and as Flossie grew plumper and rosier it grew plump and rosy too. To be married (to a person hitherto unspecified in fancy, whose features remained a blur or a blank), to be the mistress of a dear little house (the house stood out very clear in Flossie's fancy), and the mother of a dear little girl (a figure ever present to her, complete in socks and shoes and all the delicious details of its dress). Compared with that vision of Flossie's, no dream was ever so soft, so rosy and so young.

And now in the spring-time all her being moved softly under the current of the dream. Flossie's fancy did not associate it consciously with Keith Rickman (she would have blushed if the association had been made apparent to her) ; the spring did that for her, mingling with her blood.

Meanwhile, as Flossie dreamed, the same hour every week-day morning Rickman was awakened by the same sounds, the click of the door-latch in the bedroom overhead and the patter of the girl's feet on the stairs. He knew it was Miss Flossie Walker going down to early breakfast. And when he heard it he turned in his bed on the side farthest from the window and sighed. Such a deep unhappy sigh.

Lucia had delivered him from Lucia, but there were other troubles from which she could not save him. Not, in the warm spring days, from the newly awakened trouble of his youth ; not, in the sleepless summer nights, from the brief but recurrent tyranny of sense, and not from the incessant hunger of the heart. Though it was she who had created that hunger in him, it was not (at five and twenty) to be satisfied by the mere image of her, however vividly present to him. He was only five and twenty, and the spring had come with its piercing sweetness, its irresistible delicate lure, to the great stirring, melting, and unbinding of his manhood. He could be faithful to Lucia for ever in his soul ; but there were moments in this season when he was aware of a distinct cleavage between his soul and his senses.

It seemed to him that Miss Flossie Walker lay in wait for him in just those moments, with the secret but infallible instinct of the creatures whom the spring touches to its own uses. He could not blame her. Flossie was innocent, being but the unconscious handmaid of the spring.

It was not because Lucia was for ever absent and Flossie for ever on the spot. At first he was unaware of the danger that lurked for him in Flossie's ways, because his soul in its love for Lucia was so utterly secure. At first the sighs were all on Flossie's account ; poor Flossie, who had to be up so early while he settled himself for another luxurious slumber. At first he only pitied Flossie. He thought of her at odd moments as a poor little girl (rather pretty) who worked too hard and never had any fun to speak of; but the rest of the time he never thought of her at all.

And in the early days of their acquaintance, Miss Flossie Walker (then only an apprentice to a firm of type-writers in Holborn) was very much to be pitied. He could remember how she had come (a little while before that memorable Bank holiday) to Mrs. Downey's boarding-house, a plump but rather anæmic maiden, black haired, and demure. He had begun by talking to her at table, because she sat next to him, and he had ended, if there ever is an end to these things, by taking her to matinées, picture-galleries, restaurants, and the British Museum. The girl was so young, so confiding, and so obviously respectable, that he was careful to keep to the most guileless of middle-class entertainments. A few weeks of this existence brought shy smiles and a lively play of dimples on Flossie's face. She grew plumper still, less anæmic, though hardly less demure. A few months, and Flossie's beauty flowered and expanded, she began to dress as became it, entering into rivalry with Miss Ada Bishop, until it dawned on him that Flossie was really, in her own place and way, a very engaging little creature.

About this time Flossie's circumstances had improved as much as her appearance. Her father had been a clerk in the Bank of England, and on his death she obtained a post there as sorter. That position gave Flossie both dignity and independence; it meant light work and hours which brought hope with them every day towards three o'clock. Under these circumstances Flossie's beauty went on flowering and expanding, till she became more than ever a thing of danger and disaster.

Her intimacy with Mr. Rickman, which had lapsed lately, owing to his increasing passion for solitude and separation, revived suddenly in the spring of ninety-five. It happened in this manner. With the spring, Mrs. Downey's was once more agitated by the hope of the Bank holiday, and Mr. Spinks inquired of Rickman if he were going out of town for Easter. (Rickman was incautiously dining that evening at the general table.) But Rickman wasn't going out of town. He said he thought of going somewhere up the river. He had also thought, though he did not say so, that in fulfilment of an ancient promise he would take Miss Flossie to the play on Saturday afternoon. Yet when it came to the point he had some diffidence in asking her. She might not think it proper.

It was Mr. Soper who precipitated his resolve. He wanted to know if Rickman had made up a party for the River, and 'ad any companion?

No. He hadn't made up a party. Thanks, awfully. He was going by Himself.

Mr. Soper didn't think, now, that was a very enjoyable way of spendin' a Bank holiday.

He put it that if it was Rickman's intention to hire a row-boat, it wouldn't be at all a bad idea if he, Soper, and Mr. Spinks, say, were to join.

As Soper's incredible suggestion sank into him, the expression of Rickman's face was pitiable to see. It was then that casually, as if the idea had only just occurred to him, he wondered whether Miss Walker would by any chance care for a matinée ticket for the play? He was anxious to give his offer an uncertain and impromptu character, suggesting that Miss Walker must be torn between her many engagements, and have matinée tickets in large numbers up the sleeve of her charming blouse.

Flossie was so shy that when you spoke to her she never answered all at once; so shy that when she spoke to you she never turned her head to look at you, but left you to judge of the effect you made on her by the corners of her mouth and eyes. So now he had to look very carefully at her to see whether she was saying yes or no. Casually again (as if this course were not necessarily involved in acceptance) he inquired whether he might have the pleasure of taking her.

Miss Bishop looked another way. Her loose mouth hung desirous. (Miss Bishop's face was flagrantly frank, devoid of repose. None of these people had any repose about them except Flossie.) Flossie was dubious and demure. Was he quite sure it was a pleasure? He protested that in a world where few things were certain, that, at any rate, admitted of no doubt. Flossie deliberated whether this further step were or were not a departure from her ideal of propriety. And it was not until he showed signs of retracting his proposal that she intimated her consent. But, as for pleasure, if Flossie were pleased she did not allow it to appear. And although her heart beat excitedly under her blue blouse, it was on the side that was not next to Mr. Rickman.

Then Miss Roots began to talk of incomprehensible things excitedly. So excitedly, that she had, for the moment, quite a colour. And ·while they talked, all the other boarders turned in their places and watched Mr. Rickman as if he had been some wonderful enchanter; Mr. Soper alone emphasizing by an attitude his entire aloofness from the general interest.

And all the time Miss Roots was talking, Flossie, without saying a word, contrived to seize upon the disengaged portion of his mind. He wondered what she was thinking about.

She was thinking, first, that it really paid to put on your best blouse every evening. Next, that it wasn't worth while if he would keep on talking to the lady on his right. Then that she couldn't decide the point until she knew where he was going on Sunday.

That she never knew; but she went to the play with him on Saturday, and on many Saturdays after that. There was nobody so gay that spring as Flossie.

Coming fresh to Flossie after a long estrangement, Rickman couldn't recognize her from his old account of her as a poor little girl who worked too hard and never had any fun to speak of. In so describing her, no doubt he had been influenced by the melancholy of his earlier mood. But there were other reasons why he still insisted on regarding her in this pathetic light. It provided him with several very agreeable sensations, and the most agreeable of all was the voluptuous passion of pity. It kept him detached, always in the superior position of a benefactor. Benefactor, indeed! He was in a fair way of becoming Flossie's deity, her Providence, the mystic source of theatre-tickets and joy. No really brave man ever shrinks from the dangers of apotheosis, when the process involves no loss of personal dignity. And apart from the gratification of his natural healthy vanity, Rickman's heart was touched by the thought that the little thing turned to him instinctively for all her innocent pleasures.

Then all at once the innocent pleasures ceased. They ceased just as Flossie's palpitating heart told her that she was really making an impression on this singularly unimpressionable young man. She knew it by the sudden softening of his voice as he spoke to her, by the curious brilliant dilation of his eyes as they followed her about the room. For after much easy practice on Mr. Spinks she knew precisely by what movements and what glances she could best produce these interesting effects. And yet nothing could be farther from Flossie's fancy than flirtation. The little clerk was nothing if not practical, even under the tender impulse of her dream.

Flossie was determined that whatever else she failed in she would not fail in her woman's trade. She would have considered herself disgraced by such bankruptcy. Not that she feared it. Nature had started her with a sufficient capital of fascination, and at Mrs. Downey's she had, so to speak, established a connection. And now it seemed there had come a period of depression. It still rained tickets, more tickets than ever, but there was no Mr. Rickman to escort her to the concert or the play; Mr. Rickman always had another engagement, never specified. No Mr. Rickman to take her into the suburbs on a Sunday; Mr. Rickman was off, goodness knew where, scouring the country on his bicycle. No Mr. Rickman to talk to her at dinner; Mr. Rickman took all his meals in his own room now. For these and all other delinquencies his invariable excuse was that he was busy; and Flossie, mind you, was sharp enough to see through *that*.

No. Mr. Rickman had changed, suddenly, unaccountably, without a moment's warning. First of all, the other boarders noticed that he had become most frightfully irritable in his temper. He had not been over polite to any of them lately, but to her he was insufferably rude, most ungentlemanly, she called it. He would pretend not to see her if by any chance she looked his way, not to hear her if by any chance she spoke to him. Once (they were quite alone) he had broken off in the middle of an exciting conversation and rushed out of the room, out of the house. She saw him over the balcony railings, walking up and down the street like a lunatic, with his hands thrust down into his pockets and no hat on. And he was not only ungentlemanly, but positively unkind. If they met on the stairs (somehow they did this very often) he would draw himself up flat against the wall as if he was afraid of the frill of her dress touching him. If she came into the drawing-room he would walk out of it; or if he stayed, it was only to sit staring at her (poor innocent little Flossie, who was so pretty) with an ugly scowl on his face. There were times when poor innocent little Flossie said to herself that she positively believed he hated her. And she was so innocent that she couldn't think what she had done to make him hate her.

She was right about the hatred. An indignant anger was certainly what he felt when he first realized that she had power to make him feel at all. Her prettiness tormented him; therefore he hated her, and everything about her. He hated the sound of her little tongue upraised among the boarders, and of her little feet running up and down the stairs. He hated every glance of her black eyes and every attitude and movement of her plump little body. More than all he hated the touch of her soft arms as they stirred against him at the tightly packed dinner-table. Therefore he avoided the dinner-table, and the drawing-room; he avoided as far as possible the house, filled as it was with the disastrous presence. He fatigued himself with excesses of walking and cycling, in the hope that when he flung himself into his bed at midnight he would be too tired to feel. And sometimes he was.

At last poor Flossie, weary of conjecture, unbent so far as to seek counsel of Miss Bishop. For Miss Bishop gave you to understand that on the subject of " gentlemen " there was nothing that she did not know. It was a little humiliating, for only a month ago Flossie had said to her in strictest confidence, " I feel in my bones, Ada, that he's going to come forward this spring."

Ada laughed coarsely, but not unkindly, at the tale of her perplexity. Ada had every reason to be sympathetic; for, Mr. Rickman once securely attached, Mr. Spinks would be lonely, unappropriated, free. " Don't you worry," said she, " *he's* all right."

" All right? Can't you see how frightfully rude he is to me ? "

" I should think I did see it. A jolly lot you know about

gentlemen. You've nothing to go on when they're so ever-lastingly polite, but when they turn mad like that all of a sudden, you may be sure they're coming to the point. To tell you the truth, I didn't use to think you'd very much chance, Flossie; but when I saw him walk out of the room the other day, I said to myself, ' *She's* got 'im!'"

" I wish I knew. I don't want it hanging on for ever."

" It won't. If he doesn't propose in May, he will in June, when you've got a new dress and a new hat."

Flossie shook her head despairingly. " I wonder," said she, " what I'd really better do. I think sometimes I'd better go away."

" Well, sometimes that *does* fetch them; and then, again, sometimes it doesn't. It's risky. Some girls," she added reflectively, " try doing their hair another way; but I wouldn't, if I was you. That's risky, too. If they're really fond of you, as often as not it only puts them off."

" Then what *am* I to do?"

" If you take my advice," said Miss Bishop, " you'll not do anything. You'll just go on the same as before, as if you hadn't noticed anything out of the way."

And Flossie went on just the same as before, with the result that every morning Mr. Rickman sighed more and more heavily as he heard the early patter of those feet upon the floor.

CHAPTER XLVI

FLOSSIE had been working with one eye on the clock all afternoon. At the closing hour she went out into Lothbury with the other girls; but instead of going up Moorgate Street as usual, she turned out of Prince's Street to her right, and thence made her way westward as quickly as she could for the crowd. It was September, a day when it was good to be out of doors at that hour. The sunlight filtered into the dusty thoroughfare from the west; on her left the sprawling mounted legends over the shops were so many gold blazons on an endless field of grey; on her right, a little way ahead, the tall plane-tree in Wood Street hung out its green leaves over Cheapside like a signal. Thither Flossie was bound.

As she sidled out of the throng into the quiet little lane, Mr. Rickman came forward, raising his hat. He had been waiting under the plane-tree for twenty minutes, and was now beguiling his sylvan solitude with a cigarette. Two years had worked a considerable change in his appearance. His face had grown graver and clearer cut. He had lost his hectic look and had more the air of a man of the world than of a young poet about town. To Flossie's admiration and delight he wore an irreproachable frock-coat and shining linen; she interpreted these changes as corresponding with the improvement in his prospects, and judged that the profession of literature was answering fairly well.

They shook hands seriously, as if they attached importance to these trifles. "Am I dreadfully late?" she asked.

"Dreadfully." He smiled with one corner of his mouth, holding his cigarette firmly in the other, while he took from her the little cape she carried over her arm.

"I expect I've kept you waiting a good bit?" A keen observer of Flossie's face might have detected in it a faintly triumphant appreciation of the fact. "I'm awfully sorry. I got behind-hand and had to stay till I'd finished up."

"Never mind, Flossie, it don't matter. At any rate it's worth it." The words implied that Mr. Rickman's time was valuable, otherwise he would not have given it to Flossie. "Where shall we go, and what shall we do?"

"I don't much care."

"Shall we have tea somewhere while we're making up our minds?"

"Well—I wouldn't mind. I hadn't time to get any at the Bank."

"All right. Come along." And they plunged into Cheapside again, he breasting the stream, making a passage for her. They found a favourite confectioner's in St. Paul's Churchyard, where they had sometimes gone before. He noticed that she took her seat with rather a weary air.

"Floss, you must come for a walk on the Embankment. You look as if you didn't get out enough. Why will you go up and down in that abominable underground? You're awfully white, you know."

"I never had a red face."

"Then what's the matter?"

"Nothing. I shall be better when I've had my tea."

She had her tea, which after a proper protest on her part was paid for by Rickman. Then they turned into the cathedral gardens, where it was still pleasant under the trees. Thus approached from the north-east, the building rose up before them in detached incoherent masses, the curve of its greatest dome broken by the line of the north transept seen obliquely from below. It turned a forbidding face citywards, a face of sallow stone blackened by immemorial grime, while the north-west columns of the portico shone almost white against the nearer gloom.

" It's clever of it to look so beautiful," murmured Rickman, " when it's so infernally ugly." He stood for a few minutes, lost in admiration of its eccentricity. Thus interested, he was not aware that his own expression had grown somewhat abstracted, impersonal, and cold.

" I call that silly," said Flossie, looking at him out of the corner of her black eyes. Had he come there to pay attention—to the Cathedral?

" Do you? Why? "

" Because—I suppose you wouldn't say I was beautiful if I were—well, downright ugly? "

" I might, Flossie, if your ugliness was as characteristic, as suggestive as this."

Flossie shrugged her shoulders (not, he thought, a pretty action in a lady with so short a neck). To her St. Paul's was about as beautiful as the Bank and infinitely less " suggestive." Mr. Rickman interpreted her apathy as fatigue and looked about for a lonely seat. They found one under the angle of the transept.

" Let's sit down here," he said; " better not exert ourselves violently so soon after tea."

" For all the tea I've had, it wouldn't matter," said Flossie, as if resenting an ignoble implication. Rickman laughed a little uncomfortably and blushed. Perhaps she had hardly given him the right to concern himself with these intimate matters. Yet from the very first his feeling for Flossie had shown itself in minute cares for her physical well-being. They sat for a while in silence. A man passed them smoking; he turned his head to look back at the girl, and the flying ash from his cigarette lighted on her dress.

" Confound the brute! " said Rickman, trying to brush away the obnoxious powder with a touch which would have been more effectual if it had been less of a caress. She shivered slightly, and he put her cape gently about her shoulders. A curious garment, Flossie's cape, made of some thin grey-blue stuff, with gold braid on the collar, cheap, pretty, and a little vulgar.

" There's not much warmth in that thing," he said, feeling it with his fingers.

" I don't want to be warm, thank you, a day like this," she retorted, pushing back the cape. For, though it was no longer spring, Flossie's dream tugged at her heart-strings. There was a dull anger against him in her heart. At that moment Flossie could have fought savagely for her dream.

What could have made her so irritable, poor little girl? She didn't look well; or—perhaps it was her work. He was sorry for all women who worked. And Flossie—she was such an utter woman. That touch of exaggeration in the curves of her soft figure made her irresistibly, super-latively feminine. To be sure, as he had hinted in that unguarded moment, her beauty was of the kind that sug-gests nothing more interesting than itself. Yet there were times when it had power over him, when he was help-less and stupid before it. And now, as he leaned back looking at her, his intellect seemed to melt away gradually and merge in dreamy sense. They sat for a while, still without speaking; then he suddenly bent forward, gazing into her eyes.

" What is it, Flossie? Tell me."

Flossie turned away her face from the excited face approaching it.

" Tell me."

" It's nothing. Can't you see I'm only tired. I've 'ad a hard day."

" I thought you never had hard days at the Bank?"

" No. No more we do—not to speak of."

" Then it's something you don't like to speak of. I say—have the other women been worrying you?"

" No, I should think not indeed. Catch any one trying that on with me!"

" Then I can't see what it can be."

" I daresay you can't. You don't know what it is! It's not much, but it's the same thing day after day, day after day, till I'm sick and tired of it all! I don't see any end to it either."

"I'm so sorry, Floss," said Rickman in a queer thick voice. She had turned her face towards him now, and its expression was inscrutable—to him. To another man it would have said that it was all very well for him to be sorry; he could put a stop to it soon enough if he liked.

"Oh—you needn't be sorry."

"Why not? Do you think I don't care?"

Immense play of expression on Flossie's face. She bit her lip; and that meant that he might care no end, or he mightn't care a rap, how was she to know? She smiled a bitter smile as much as to say that she *didn't* know, neither did she greatly care. Then her lips quivered, which meant that if by any chance he did care, it was a cruel shame to leave a poor girl in the dark.

"Care? About the Bank?" she said at last. "You needn't. I shan't stand it much longer. I shall fling it up some of these days; see if I don't?"

"Would that be wise?"

"I don't know whether it's wise or not. I know I can't go on like this for ever."

"Yes, but would anything else be better, or even half as good? You didn't get much fun out of that last place, you know."

"Well, for all the fun I get out of that old Bank, I might as well be in a ladies' boarding school. If I thought it would end in anything—but it won't."

"How do you know? It may end in your marrying a big fat manager."

"Don't be silly."

"Supposing you knew it would end some day, not necessarily in marrying the manager, would you mind going on with it?"

She looked away from him, and tears formed under her eyelashes, the vague light tears that never fall. "There's no use my talking of flinging it up. I'm fixed there for good."

"Who knows?" said Rickman; and if Flossie's eyes had been candid they would have said, "You ought to know, if anybody does." Whatever they said, it made him shudder, with fear, with shame, but no, not with hatred. "Poor

Flossie," he said gently; and there was a pause during which Flossie looked more demure than ever after her little outburst. She had seen the look in his eyes that foreboded flight.

He rose abruptly. " Do you know, I'm awfully sorry, but I've got an appointment at half-past five to meet a fellow in Fleet Street."

The fellow was Maddox; but the appointment, he had made it that very minute, which was the twenty-fifth minute past five.

They went their ways; he to Fleet Street, and she home. Maddox did not turn up to the appointment and Rickman had to keep it with himself. As the result of the interview he determined to try the effect of a little timely absence. He did not attempt to conceal from himself that he was really most horribly afraid; his state of mind or rather body (for the disorder was purely physical) was such that he positively dared not remain in the same house with Flossie another day. What he needed was change of air and scene.

He approached Mrs. Downey with a shame-faced air, and a tale of how he was seedy and thought if he could get away for a week it would set him up. It seemed to him that Mrs. Downey's manner conveyed the most perfect comprehension of his condition. He did not care; he was brought so low that he could almost have confided in Mrs. Downey. " Mark my words," said the wise woman to the drawing-room. " He'll be back again before the week's up." And as usual, little Flossie marked them.

He walked out to Hampstead that very evening and engaged rooms there by the week, on the understanding that he might require them for a month or more. He did not certainly know how long the cure would take.

Hampstead is a charming and salubrious suburb, and Jewdwine was really very decent to him while he was there, but in four days he had had more of the cure than he wanted. Or was it that he didn't want to be cured? Anyway a week was enough to prove that the flight to Hampstead was a mistake. He had now an opportunity of observing Miss Flossie from a judicious distance, with the result that her image was seen through a tender wash of atmosphere at the precise moment when it acquired relief. He began to miss her morning greetings, the soft touch of her hand when they said good-night, and the voice that seemed to be always saying " How orf'ly good of you," " Thanks orf'ly, Mr. Rickman, I've had a lovely day." He hadn't given her many lovely days lately, poor little girl.

At the end of the week, coming up from Fleet Street, instead of making straight for the Hampstead Road as he ought to have done, he found himself turning aside in the direction of Tavistock Place. The excuse that he made to himself was that he wanted a book that he had left behind at Mrs. Downey's. Now it was not in the least likely that he had left it in the dining-room, nor yet in the drawing-room, but it was in those places that he thought of looking first. Not finding what he wanted, he went on dejectedly to the second floor, feeling that he must fulfil the quest that justified his presence. And there in his study, in, yes, *in* it, as far in as anybody could get, by the bookcase next the window, Flossie was sitting; and sitting (if you could believe it) on the floor; sitting and moving her hands along the shelves as familiarly as you please. Good Heavens! if she wasn't busy dusting his books!

Flossie didn't see him, for she had her back to the door; and he stood there on the threshold for a second, just looking at her. She wore a loose dark-blue overall, evidently intended to wrap her up and conceal her. But so far from concealing her, the overall, tucked in and smoothed out, and altogether adorably moulded by her crouching attitude, betrayed the full but tender outline of her body. Her face, all but the white curve of her cheek and forehead, was hidden from him, but he could see the ivory bistre at the nape of her bowed neck, with the delicate black tendrils of her curls clustering above it. Her throat, as she stooped over her task, was puckered and gathered, like some incredibly soft stuff, in little folds under her chin. He drew in his breath with a sighing sound which to Flossie was the first intimation of his presence.

To say that Flossie rose to her feet would be a misleading description of her method. She held on to the edge of a bookshelf by the tips of her fingers and drew herself up from the floor, slowly, as it were by some mysterious unfolding process, not ungraceful. She turned on him the wide half-mischievous, half-frightened eyes of a child caught, this time, in some superb enormity.

"Flossie," he said with an affectation of severity, "what *have* you been doing?"

She produced her duster gingerly. "You can see," said she, "only I didn't mean you to catch me at it." She knelt down by the fire-place and gave her duster a little flick up the chimney. "I never, never in all my life saw such a lot of dust. I can't think how you've gone on living with it."

He smiled. "No more can I, Flossie. I don't know how I did it."

"Well, you haven't got to do it, now. It's all perfectly sweet and clean."

"It's all perfectly sweet, I know that, dear." She turned towards the door, but not without a dissatisfied look back at the bookcase she had left. "Aren't you going to let me thank you?"

"You needn't. I was only helping Mrs. Downey."

"Ah——"

"She's been having a grand turnout while you were away."

"The deuce she has——"

"Oh, you needn't be frightened. Nobody's touched your precious books but me. I wouldn't let them."

"Why wouldn't you let them?"

"Be-cause—Oh, I say, it's six o'clock; are you going to stay?"

"Perhaps. Why?"

"Because I'd only one more shelf to dust and then I'd 'ave finished. I—I'm in rather a hurry."

"Why won't you stay and dust it now?"

"Well—you—know——" She took one step inside the room timidly, then another, and stood still.

"Is it me you're afraid of? I'll sit outside, on the stairs, if you'd rather."

"How silly." She removed an invisible atom of dust from a chair as she spoke; as much as to say she was inspired solely by the instinct of order.

The diminutive smile played about the corners of her mouth. "Miss Roots said I'd better not meddle with your books."

"Did she? Then Miss Roots is a beast."

" She seemed to think I didn't know how to dust them."

" Perhaps she's right. I say, suppose you let me see."

And Flossie, willingly cajoled, began again, and, as he saw with horror, on his hoarded relics of the Harden library. " No, Flossie," he said, with a queer change in his voice. " Not those." But Flossie's fingers moved along their tops with a delicacy born of the incessant manipulation of bank notes. All the same, she did do it wrong, for she dusted towards the backs instead of away from them. But he hadn't the heart to correct her. He watched a moment; then he pretended to be looking for the book he had pretended he wanted to find; then he sat down and pretended to write a letter whilst Flossie went on dusting, skilfully, delicately. She even managed to get through ten volumes of his own Bekker's Plato without damage to the beautiful but perishing Russia leather. That made it all the more singular that the back of the eleventh volume should come off suddenly with a rip.

She gave a little cry of dismay. He looked up, and she came to him holding the book in one hand and its back in the other. She really was a little frightened. " Look," she said, " I didn't think it would have gone and done like that."

" Oh, I say, Flossie——"

" I'm orf'ly sorry." Her mouth dropped, not unbecomingly; her eyes were so liquid that he could have sworn they had tears in them. She looked more than ever like an unhappy child, standing beside him in her long straight overall. " And I wouldn't let anybody look at them but me."

" Why wouldn't you? I've asked you that before, Flossie —why wouldn't you?" He took the book and its mutilated fragment from her, and held both her hands in his.

" Because I knew you were fond enough of *them*."

" And is there anything I wasn't fond enough of—do you think?"

" I don't think; I know."

" No, you know nothing, you know nothing at all about anything. What *did* you think?"

" I thought you hated me."

" Hated you?"

" Yes. Hated me like poison."

He put his arms about her, gathering her to him! He

drew her head down over his heart. "I hate you like this—and this—and this," he said, kissing in turn her forehead, her eyelids, and her mouth. He held her at arm's length and gazed at her, as if he wondered whether they were the same woman, the Flossie he had once known, and this Flossie that he had kissed. Then he led her to the sofa, and drew her down by his side, and held her hands to keep her there. And yet he felt that it was he who was being led; he who was being drawn, he who was being held—over the brink of the immeasurable, inexpirable folly. In all this his genius remained alone and apart, unmoved by anything he did or said, as if it knew that through it all the golden chain still held.

Her mouth quivered. "If you didn't hate me, why were you so rude to me, then?" was the first thing she said.

"Because I loved you when I didn't want to love you, and it was more than I could stand. And because—because I didn't know it. But *you* knew it," he said almost savagely. It seemed to him that his tongue refused the guidance of his brain.

"I'm sure I didn't know anything of the sort." Her mouth quivered again; but this time it was with a smile.

"Why not? Because I didn't say so in a lot of stupid words? You *are* literal. But surely you understood? Not just at first, of course; I didn't care a bit at first; I didn't care till long after."

"Long after what?" Flossie was thinking of Miss Poppy Grace on the balcony next door.

"Never mind what."

Flossie knew all about Miss Poppy Grace, and she didn't mind at all.

"Would I be here now if I didn't love you?" He still had to persuade himself that this was love. It seemed incredible.

"Rubbish—you know you only came to look at those silly old books," said Flossie, nodding contemptuously towards the bookcase.

"Did you imagine I was in love with them? And think of all the things we've done together. Didn't you know? Didn't you feel it coming on?"

"I know you've been orf'ly good—orf'ly. But as for anything else, I'm sure I *never* thought of it."

" Then think of it now. Or—does that mean that you don't care for me? "

There was an awful pause. Then Flossie said very indistinctly, so indistinctly that he had to lean his face to hers to catch the words, " No, of course it doesn't." Her voice cleared suddenly. " But if you didn't hate me, why did you go away? "

" I went away because I was ill."

" And are you any better? "

" Yes, I think I'm better. I think I'm nearly all right now. I might say I'll undertake never to be ill again, at least, not if you'll marry me."

At these words his genius turned and looked at him with eyes ominous and aghast. He had a vision of another woman kneeling beside a hearth as her hands tended a dying fire. And he hardly saw the woman at his side as he drew her to him and kissed her again because of the pain at his heart. And Flossie wondered why in that moment he did not look at her.

He was looking now. And as he looked his genius hid his face.

" You knew that was what I wanted? "

She shook her head slowly. " What does that mean? That you didn't know? Or that you won't? But you will, Flossie? "

As he drew her to him a second time the old terror woke in his heart; but only for a moment. For this time Flossie kissed him of her own accord, with a kiss, not passionate like his own, but sweet and fugitive. It was like a reminder of the transience of the thing he sought, a challenge rousing him to assert its immortality.

He put her from him, and stooped over his own outstretched arms and clasped hands; staring stupidly at the floor. When he spoke again it was hardly, incisively, as a man speaks the truth he hates. " Do you know what this means? It means waiting."

" Waiting? "

" Yes. I'm not a bit well off, you know; I couldn't give you the sort of home you ought to have just yet. I'd no business to say anything about it; but somehow I thought you'd rather know. And of course I've no business to ask you, but—will you wait? "

" Well—if we must, we must."

" And if it means working at that beastly Bank for another year, do you think you can keep it up so long? "

" I'll try to."

She leaned towards him, and they sat there, holding each other's hands, looking into each other's eyes, hearing nothing, feeling nothing, but the beating of their own riotous hearts.

It was love as nature loves to have it. It was also what men call honest love. But in the days when he had loved dishonestly, he had never slipped from Poppy Grace's side with such a sense of misery and solitude and shame.

CHAPTER XLVII

THE game was over and Flossie had won. She had forced Fate's hand, or rather, Mr. Rickman's. Not by any coarse, premeditated methods; Flossie was too subtly feminine for that. She had trusted rather to the inspiration of the moment, and when her beautiful womanly emotions gave her the opening she had simply followed it, that was all. And could anything have been more correct? She had not " given herself away " once by word or look. With true maidenly modesty she had hidden her own feelings until she was perfectly sure of Mr. Rickman's. There was nothing —nothing to make her feel ashamed when she looked back upon that day; a reflection from which she derived much consolation afterwards.

It gave her courage to fly downstairs to Mrs. Downey's private room where that lady sat doing her accounts, to lean over the back of Mrs. Downey's chair and to whisper into her ear, " I've been dusting Mr. Rickman's books. He caught me at it."

Mrs. Downey could not have shown more excitement if Flossie had told her that the kitchen boiler had burst. " Flossie! My goodness, whatever did he say? "

" He didn't mind one bit. Only—you won't tell him you told me not to touch them, will you, Mrs. Downey? " She brought her soft blushing cheek close to Mrs. Downey's and the warmth of it told her tale.

And Mrs. Downey promised not to tell, pardoning the

subterfuge for love's sake which excuses all. " Has he gone, Flossie?" she inquired anxiously.

" No. He's not going. He's come back for good."

" There! Didn't I say he would!"

" And what d'you think," said Flossie, sitting down and spreading her plump arm on the secretary all over the accounts. " He's done it. He did it up there."

Mrs. Downey stared, and Flossie nodded as much as to say " Fact!"

" You don't mean to say so?"

" Nobody's more surprised than myself."

The rest was kisses and congratulations, wholly magnanimous on Mrs. Downey's part; for the announcement of Flossie's engagement cost her one of the gayest, most desirable, and most remunerative of her brilliant circle. Mr. Spinks (regarded by himself and everybody else as permanent) gave notice and vanished from that hour, carrying with him the hopes of Miss Ada Bishop. Meanwhile Flossie (hitherto regarded from a merely decorative point of view) became a person of considerable importance in the boarding-house. It was not merely that she was an engaged young lady; for, as Miss Bishop pointed out to her with some natural asperity, anybody can be engaged; but she had now the privilege, denied to any other boarder, of going in and out of Mr. Rickman's study. She said that she went in to tidy it; but strange to say, the more Flossie tidied it the more hopeless it became. Mr. Rickman's study was never what you might call a really tidy room; but at any rate there had always been a certain repose about it. And now you could not well imagine a more unrestful place, a place more suggestive of hurry and disorder, of an utter lack of the leisure in which ideas ripen and grow great.

The table had become a troubled sea of primeval manuscript, where Mr. Rickman sat with his head in his hands, brooding over the face of the waters. He had once profanely said that God's world was a chaos he had got to work on. Now it was *his* world that was chaos. A tempestuous chaos, where things to be weltered in the wreck of things that were. Rickman's genius, like Nature, destroyed in order that it might create; yet it seemed to him that nowadays the destruction was out of all proportion to the creation. He sighed as he gazed at the piteous fragments that represented six months' labour; fragments that wept blood; the torn and mutilated limbs of living thoughts; with here and there huge torsos of blank verse, lopped and hewn in the omnipotent fury of a god at war with his world; mixed up with undeveloped and ethereal shapes, the embryos of dreams.

And yet it was not altogether the divine rage of the artist that had wrought this havoc. The confusion argued a power at war with itself rather than with its creations; the very vastness of it all suggested a deity tied as to time, but apparently unshackled as to space. That was it. There really wasn't as much time as there used to be. It was in his free evenings and on Sundays that his best thoughts came to him, the beautiful shy thoughts that must be delicately courted. And now his free evenings and his Sundays were given up to the courting of Flossie. And even on a weekday this was what would happen. He would rush home early from Fleet Street and settle down for two hours' work before dinner. Then a little timid knock would be heard at the door, and Flossie would come in bringing him a cup of tea. He couldn't just swill it down like a pig and send the dear little thing away. He *had* to let her sit and see him drink it, slowly, as if he thoroughly enjoyed it. Or he would come in (as on that blessed evening six months ago) and find Flossie dusting books; standing perhaps on two tottering hassocks and a chair, at an altitude perilous to so plump a person. And Flossie had to be lifted down from the hassocks and punished with hard kisses, and told not to do it again. And Flossie would do it again. So that a great deal of time was lost in this way. And with the touch of those soft little arms about his neck demoralization would set in for the evening.

And then there was Flossie's education to be attended to; and that took more time than anything. It meant that, as the November days drew in, he had to read or talk to Flossie as she sat in his arm-chair with her dear little feet on his fender, and her dear little hands mending his socks and shirts and things. They might have been married for years, only they weren't; that was what made it so exciting. Flossie's hands were always mending or making something (generally something to wear), and it was rather strange that it never occurred to such a busy person that other people might be busy too. He tried to break it to her. He told her (like a brute) that he thought all his things must be mended now, and that perhaps for another week he would be better without any tea. And Flossie (very naturally offended) didn't put her dear little nose in at his door for two weeks. And for all you could get through in that time it was hardly worth while offending her.

But he was very far wrong in supposing that Flossie never thought about his work. She had been thinking a great deal about it lately. One cold, bright Sunday morning in November she tapped at his door and walked in, dressed for the open air. " Aren't you coming for a walk," she said, " this lovely day? "

" Too busy." To signify his annoyance, or to keep himself from temptation, he bent closer over the article he was writing for *The Museion.* She came and stood beside him, watching him as he worked, still with his air of passionate preoccupation. Presently he found himself drawn against his will into the following conversation :

" How long does it take you to do one of those things? "

" It depends."

" Depends on what? "

" Oh, on the amount of trouble I take over it."

" And do they pay you any more for taking trouble? "

" No, Flossie. I'm sorry to say they frequently pay me less."

" Then why on earth do you do it? "

This question seemed to him so curious that it caused him to look up, beholding for the first time the plump figure clothed entirely in a new suit of brown, and wearing on its head a fascinating hat made of something that resembled fur. He tried to look at it with disapproval, while his mind dealt independently with the amazing question put to him.

" Well, Flossie, if you really care anything about style——"

" Style? " She stroked down the front of her jacket with a delicious movement of her little hands. "Don't you like it? "

He smiled. " I adore it. It makes you look like a dear little brown Beaver, as you are." " The Beaver " was only one of the many names he had for her; it was suggested irresistibly by her plumpness, her singularly practical intelligence, and her secretive ways.

"Then what do you mean by style?" asked the Beaver in a challenging tone that forced him to lay down his pen.

"What do I mean by style?" He explained, moved by the mad lust for mystification which seizes a man in the presence of adorable simplicity. "I don't mean anything in the least resembling a Beaver's coat (there really isn't any style about a Beaver's coat). And if you want me to say it's the clothing of your thoughts, I won't. The less clothing they have the better. It can't be treated as a Beaver treats its coats. You can put it on and off (I was putting it on when you came in and interrupted me); and you can mend it, and brush it up a bit; but you can't measure it, or make it to order, and when it wears out you can't get another where you got the first. Style isn't the clothing, it's the body of your thoughts, my Beaver; and in a slap-up, A 1 style, the style of the masters, *my* style, you can't tell the body from the soul."

"If you'd said you couldn't tell the body from the skirt it would sound like sense."

That remark was (for the Beaver) really so witty that he leaned back in his chair and laughed at it. But the Beaver was in no laughing humour. "Look here," she said, "you *say* that if you write those stylish things that take up such a lot of time, they only pay you less for them."

"Well?"

"Well, is it fair of you to go on writing them?"

"Fair of *me?* My dear child, why not?"

"Be-*cause,* if I buy stylish things I *have* to pay for them. And I've been buying them long enough, just to please you."

"I don't follow. But I suppose a Beaver has to reason backwards; because, you know, all its intelligence is in its tail."

"Gracious, Keith! You *are* a silly."

"I am not alone in my opinion. It's the opinion of some very eminent zoologists." He drew her gently on his knee; raised her veil and looked into her eyes. They were (as he had often had occasion to notice) of so deep and black a black that the iris was indistinguishable from the pupil, and this blackness limited the range of their expression. They could only tell you what Flossie was feeling, never what she was thinking; for thought requires a translucent medium, and the light of Flossie's eyes was all on the surface. On the other hand, the turns and movements of her body were always a sufficient indication of the attitude of her mind. At the present moment, sitting on Keith's knee, her pose was not one of pure complacency. But holding her there, little brown Beaver, his own unyielding virile body deliciously aware of the strange, incredible softness of hers, he wondered whether it were possible for him to feel anything but tender to a creature so strangely and pathetically made. Positively she seemed to melt and grow softer by sheer contact; and presently she smiled a sweet diminutive smile that didn't uncover more than two of her little white teeth.

" Oh, what a shame it is to treat a Beaver so! " said he.

" When are you going to take me for a nice walk? " said she. " Any time before Christmas? "

" Perhaps. But you mustn't build on it."

" I don't see that I can build on anything at this rate."

" I suppose a Beaver can't be happy unless it's always building? That's why some people say it hasn't any intelligence at all. They won't even allow that it can build. They think its architectural talent is all a delusion and a sham; because it builds in season and out of season. Keep it in your study, and it will make a moat round the hearth-rug with tobacco pouches and manuscripts and boots—whatever it can lay its hands on. It will even take the ideas out of a man's head, if it can't find anything better. Is there any logic in an animal that can do that? " And if Flossie did not understand the drift of these remarks at least she seemed to understand the kisses that punctuated them.

But before very long he obtained more light on the Beaver's logic, and owned that it was singularly sound. They managed to put in a great many nice walks between that Sunday and Christmas. Whenever he could spare time Rickman made a point of meeting Flossie at the end of her day's work. He generally waited at the corner where the long windowless wall of the Bank stretches along Prince's Street, iron and implacable. It was too cold now to sit under the shadow of St. Paul's. Sometimes they would walk home along Holborn, sometimes they would go down Ludgate Hill and thence on to the Embankment. It was certainly better for Flossie to be out of doors than in the dingy drawing-room in Tavistock Place. They could talk freely in the less crowded thoroughfares; and it was surprising the things they still found to say to each other all about nothing. Every trace of Flossie's depression had vanished; she walked with a brisk step, she chatted gaily, she laughed the happiest laughter at the poorest jokes. All was going well; and why, oh, why, could he not let well alone?

They were walking on the Embankment one day, and she, for such a correct little person, was mad with mirth, when he broke out. " Flossie, you little lunatic! You might be going to marry a stock-broker instead of a journalist."

" I'm going to marry a very rich man—for me."

" For you, darling? A devilish poor one, I'm afraid."

" Oh, don't! We've said enough about that."

" Yes, but I haven't told you everything. Do you know, I might have been fairly well off by now, if I'd only chosen."

Now there was no need whatever for him to make that revelation. He was driven to it by vanity. He wanted to make an impression. He wanted Flossie to see him in all his moral beauty.

" How was that? " she asked with interest.

" I can't tell you much about it. It was something to do with business. I got an offer of a thumping big partnership three years ago—and I refused it."

He had made an impression. Flossie turned on him a look of wonder, a look uncertain and inscrutable. " What did you do that for? "

" I did it because it was right. I didn't like the business."

" That's not quite the same thing, is it? "

" Not always. It happened to be in this case."

" Why, what sort of business was it? "

" It wasn't scavenging, and it wasn't burglary—exactly. It was—" he hesitated— " only the second-hand book-trade."

" I know—they make a lot of money that way."

" They make too much for my taste sometimes. Besides——"

" Besides what? " They had turned into an embrasure of the parapet to discuss this question. They stood close together looking over the river.

" It isn't my trade. I'm only a blooming journalist."

" You don't make so very much out of that, do you? Is that the reason why we have to wait? "

" I'm afraid so. But I hope I shall be something more than a journalist some day."

" You *like* writing, don't you? "

" Yes, Flossie ; I shouldn't be much good at it, if I didn't."

" I see." She was looking eastwards away from him, and her expression had changed; but it was still inscrutable. And yet by the turning of her head, he saw her mind moving towards a conclusion; but it was impossible to say whether she reached it by the slow process of induction, or by woman's rapid intuition. Anyhow she had reached it. Presently she spoke again. " Could you still get that thing, that partnership any time—if you tried? "

" Any time. But I'm not going to try."

She turned round abruptly with an air of almost fierce determination. " Well, if *I* get an offer of a good place, *I* shan't refuse it. I shall leave the Bank." She spoke as if so desperate a step would be followed by the instantaneous collapse of that institution.

He was surprised to find how uneasy this threat always made him. The proverbial safety of the Bank had impressed him in more ways than one. And Flossie's post there had other obvious advantages. It brought her into contact with women of a better class than her own, with small refinements, and conventions, which were not conspicuous at Mrs. Downey's.

" Let me implore you not to do that. Heaven knows, I hate you having to earn your own living at all, but I'd rather you did it that way than any other."

" Why, what difference would it make to you, I should like to know? "

" It makes all the difference if I know you're doing easy work, not slaving yourself to death as some girls do. It *is* an easy berth. And—and I like the look of those girls I saw you with to-day. They were nice. I'd rather think of you working with them than sitting in some horrible office like a man. Promise me you won't go looking out for anything else."

" All right. I promise."

" No, but—on your honour? "

" Honour bright. There! Anything for a quiet life."

They turned on to the street again. Rickman looked at his watch. " Look here, we're both late for dinner—supposing we go and dine somewhere and do a theatre after, eh? "

"Oh, no—we mustn't." All the same Flossie's eyes brightened, for she dearly loved the play.

"Why not?"

"Because I don't think perhaps you ought to."

"You mean I can't afford it?"

"Well——"

"Oh, I fancy even a journalist's income will run to that."

It did run to that and to a hansom afterwards, though Flossie protested, dragging at his arm.

"I'd rather walk," said she, "indeed I would."

"Nonsense. Come, bundle in."

"Please—please let me walk." He helped her in and closed the apron sharply. He was annoyed. That was the second time she had insisted on his poverty. He thought she had a little too much the air of preparing herself to be a poor man's wife. Of course it was pretty of her; but he thought it would have been prettier still if she had let it alone.

Now Flossie had never thought of him as a poor man before to-night; but somehow the idea of the good income he might have had and hadn't made him appear poor by comparison. She lay back in the hansom meditating. "If you could only write a play like that, Keith, what a lot of money you'd make."

"Shouldn't I? But then, you see, I couldn't write a play like that."

"Rubbish. I don't believe that author—what d'you call him?—is so very much cleverer than you."

"Thanks." He bowed ironically.

"Well, I mean it. And look how they clapped him—why, they made as much fuss about him as any of the actors. I say, wouldn't you like to hear them calling 'Author! Author!'? And then clapping!"

"H'm!"

"Oh, wouldn't you love it just; you needn't pretend! Look there, I declare I've split my glove." (That meant, as Flossie had calculated, a new pair that *she* should not have to pay for.)

"If *you* clapped me I would, Flossie. I should need all the consolation I could get if I'd written as bad a play."

"Well, if that was a bad play, I'd like to see a good one."

"I'll take you to a good one some day."

" Soon? "

" Well, I'm afraid not very soon." He smiled; for the play he thought of taking her to was not yet written; would never be written if many of his evenings were like this. But to Flossie, meditating, his words bore only one interpretation—that Keith was really very much worse off than she had taken him to be.

As they lingered on the doorstep in Tavistock Place, a young man approached them in a deprecating manner from the other side of the street, and took off his hat to Flossie.

" Hallo, Spinks! " said Rickman.

" That you, Razors? " said Spinks.

" It is. What are you doing here? "

" Oh, nothing. I was in the neighbourhood, and I thought I'd have a look at the old place."

" Come in, will you? (If they don't come, Flossie, I shall *have* to use my latch-key.")

" Not to-night, thanks, it's a bit too late. I'd better be going." But he did not go.

" I hope," said Flossie politely, " you're comfortable where you are now? "

" Oh, very comfortable, very comfortable indeed." Yet his voice had a melancholy sound, and under the gaslight his face (a face not specially designed for pathos) looked limp and utterly dejected.

" I think, Keith," said Flossie, " you'd better ring again." Ringing was a concession to propriety that Flossie insisted on and he approved. He rang again; and Mrs. Downey in a beautiful wrapper herself opened the door. At the sight of Spinks she gave a joyful exclamation and invited him into the hall. They left him there.

" What's up? " asked Rickman as they parted on his landing.

" Who with? Sidney? I can't tell you—really."

" I wonder why he left."

" I can't tell you that, either." They said good-night at the foot of the stairs, and she kissed him laughing. And the two men heard it echoing in their dreams, that mysterious laughter of woman, which is as the ripple over the face of the deep.

CHAPTER XLVIII

ISAAC RICKMAN stood in his front shop at the close of a slack winter day. He looked about him with a gaze uncheered by the contemplation of his plate-glass and mahogany; and as he looked he gathered his beard into a serious meditative hand, not as of old, but with a certain agitation in the gesture.

Isaac was suffering from depression; so was the book-trade. Every year the pulse of business beat more feebly, and in the present year, eighteen ninety-six, it was almost standing still. Isaac had seen the little booksellers one by one go under, but their failure put no heart into him; and now the wave of depression was swallowing him up too. He had not got the grip of the London book-trade; he would never build any more Gin Palaces of Art; he had not yet freed himself from the power of Pilkington; and, more than all his depression, the mortgage of the Harden Library weighed heavy on his soul. The Public in which he trusted had grown tricky; and he found that even capital and incomparable personal audacity are powerless against the malignity of events.

For his own part Isaac dated his decline from the hour of his son's defection. He had not been brought to this pass by any rashness in speculation, or by any flaw whatever in his original scheme. But his original scheme had taken for granted Keith's collaboration. He had calculated to a nicety what it would cost him to build up his fortunes; and all these calculations had been based on the union of his own borrowed capital with Keith's brilliant brains. And Keith with unimaginable perfidy had removed himself and his brilliant brains at the crisis of the start. Isaac thought he had estimated pretty accurately the value of his son's contribution; but it was only in the actual experiment of separation that he realized the difference it had made.

The immediate effect of the blow was to paralyze the second-hand department. As far as new books went Isaac was fairly safe. If the Public was tricky he was generally up to its tricks. But with second-hand books you never knew where you were, not unless you had made a special study of the subject. Owing to his defective education he had always been helpless in the second-hand shop; liable at any moment to be over-reached by one of those innocent, lantern-jawed student fellows who go poking their noses everywhere.

And in buying he was still more at a disadvantage. He had grown nervous in the auction-room; he never knew what to do there, and when he did it, it was generally wrong. He would let himself be outbidden where Keith would have carried all before him by a superb if reckless persistence.

But if business was at its worst in the second-hand department, in the front shop there was a sense of a sadder and more personal desolation. Rickman's was no longer sought after. It had ceased to be the rendezvous of affable young men from Fleet Street and the Temple. The customers who came nowadays were of another sort, and the tone of the business was changing for the worse. The spirit, that something illuminating, intimate, and immortal, had perished from the place.

At first Isaac had not been able to take its departure seriously. He had never really grasped the ground of that disagreement with his son; he had put it all down to " some nonsense about a woman "; and certain hints dropped by Pilkington supported him in that belief. Keith, he had said to himself, would come back when his belly pinched him. Every day he looked to see him crawling through the big swinging doors on that empty belly. When he did it, Isaac meant to take him back instantly, unquestioned, unreproved, and unreproached. His triumph would be so complete that he could afford that magnanimity. But Keith had not come back; he had never put his nose inside the shop from that day to this. He called to see his father now and again on a Sunday (for Isaac no longer refused to admit him into his house) ; and then, as if in obedience to the holy conventions that ruled in the little villa at Ilford in Essex, no allusion was made to the business that had driven them apart. In the same spirit Isaac sternly refrained from inquiring into the state of Keith's finances; but from his personal appearance he gathered that, if Keith returned to the shop, it would not be hunger that would send him there. And if the young man's manner had not suggested the unlikelihood of his return, a hint to that effect was conveyed by his clothes.

They were the symbols of prosperity, nay more, of a social advance that there could be no going back upon. Isaac had only to look at him to realize his separation. The thing was monstrous, incomprehensible, but certain. But it was in Keith's gaze (the gaze which he could never meet, so disturbing was it in its luminous sincerity) that he read the signs of a more profound and spiritual desertion.

Isaac stood pondering these things in the front shop, at the hour of closing. As he moved drearily away, the lights were turned out one by one behind him, the great iron shutters went up with a clang, and it was dark in Rickman's.

That evening, instead of hailing a Liverpool Street 'bus, he crossed the Strand and walked up Bow Street, and so into Bloomsbury. It was the first time for four years that he had called in Tavistock Place. He used to go up alone to the boarding-house drawing-room, and wait there till Keith appeared and took him into his bedroom on the second floor. Now his name brought an obsequious smile to the maid's face; she attended him upstairs and ushered him with ceremony into a luxurious library. Keith was writing at a table strewn with manuscripts, and he did not look up all at once. The lamp-light fell on his fair head and boyish face, and Isaac's heart yearned towards his son. He held out his hand and smiled after his fashion, but said no word.

The grip of the eager young hand gave him hope.

Keith drew up two chairs to the fire. The chairs were very deep, very large, very low, comfortable beyond Isaac's dreams of comfort. Keith lay back in his, graceful in his abandoned attitude; Isaac sat up very straight and stiff, crushing in his knees the soft felt hat that made him look for ever like a Methodist parson.

His eyes rested heavily on the littered table. " Well," he said, " how long have you been at it? "

" Oh, ever since nine in the morning—— "

(Longer hours than he had in the shop); "—and—I've two more hours to put through still." (And yet he had received him gladly.)

" It doesn't look quite as easy as making catalogues."

" It isn't."

Isaac had found the opening he desired. " I should think all this literary work was rather a 'eavy strain."

" It does make you feel a bit muzzy sometimes, when you're at it from morning to night."

" Is the game worth the candle? Is it worth it? Have you made your fortune at it? "

" Not yet."

" Well—I gave you three years."

Keith smiled. " What did you give me them for? To make my fortune in? "

" To learn common-sense in."

Keith laughed. " It wasn't enough for that. You should have given me three hundred, at the very least! "

The laugh was discouraging, and Isaac felt that he was on the wrong tack.

" I'd give you as many as you like, if I could afford to wait. But I consider I've waited long enough already."

" What were you waiting for? "

" For you to come back——"

Keith's face was radiant with innocent inquiry.

" To come back into the business."

The light of innocence died out of the face as suddenly as it had kindled.

" My dear father, I shall never come back. I thought I'd made that very clear to you."

" You never made it clear—your behaviour to me. Not but what I 'ad an idea, which perhaps I need not name. I've never asked what there was at the bottom of that foolish business, and I've never blamed you for it. If it made you act badly to me, I've reason to believe it kept you out of worse mischief."

Keith felt a queer tightening at the heart. He understood that his father was referring darkly to Lucia Harden. He was surprised to find that even this remote and shadowy allusion was more than he could bear. He must call him off that trail; and the best way of doing it was to announce his engagement.

" As you seem to be rather mixed, father, I ought to tell you that I'm engaged to be married. Have been for the last eighteen months."

" Married? " Isaac's face was tense with anxiety; for he could not tell what this news meant for him; whether it would remove his son farther from him, or bring him, beyond all expectation, near.

" May I ask who the lady is? Any of your fine friends in Devonshire?"

Keith was silent, tongue-tied with presentiment of the coming blow. It came.

" I needn't ask. It's that—that Miss 'Arden. *I've* heard of her."

" As it happens it's somebody you haven't heard of. You may have seen her, though—Miss Flossie Walker."

" No. I've never seen her, not to my knowledge. How long have you known her?"

" Ever since I came here. She's one of the boarders."

" Ah-h. Has she any means?"

" None."

Isaac's heart leapt high.

" Aren't you going to congratulate me?"

" How can I, when I haven't seen the lady?"

" You would, if you *had* seen her."

" And when is it to be? Like most young people, you're a bit impatient, I suppose?"

Keith betrayed the extremity of his impatience by a painful flush. This subject of his marriage was not to be approached without a certain shame.

" I suppose so; and like most young people we shall have to wait."

Isaac's eyes narrowed and blinked in the manner of a man uncertain of his focus; as it happened, he was just beginning to see.

" Ah—that's what's wearing you out, is it?"

" I'm beginning to get a bit sick of it, I own."

" What's she like to look at, this young lady? Is she pretty?"

" Very."

A queer hungry look came over the boy's face. Isaac had seen that look there once or twice before. His lips widened in a rigid smile; he had to moisten them before they would stretch. He was profoundly moved by Keith's disclosure, by the thought of that imperishable and untameable desire. It held for him the promise of his own continuance. It stirred in him the strange fury of his fatherhood, a fatherhood destructive and malign, that feeds on the life of children. As he looked at his son his sickly frame trembled before that embodiment of passion **and** vigour and immortal youth. He longed to possess himself of these things, of the superb young intellect, of the abounding life, to possess himself and live.

And he would possess them. Providence was on his side. Providence had guided him. He could not have chosen his moment better; he had come at a crisis in Keith's life. He knew the boy's nature; after all, he would be brought back to him by hunger, the invincible, implacable hunger of the flesh.

"Your mother was pretty. But she lost her looks before I could marry her. I had to wait for her; so I know what you're going through. But I fancy waiting comes harder on you than it did on me."

"It does," said Keith savagely. "Every day I think I'll marry to-morrow and risk it. But," he added in a gentler tone, "that might come hard on her."

"You *could* marry to-morrow, if you'd accept the proposal I came to make to you."

Keith gave a keen look at his father. He had been touched by the bent figure, the wasted face; the evident signs of sickness and suffering. He had resolved to be very tender with him. But not even pity could blind him to the detestable cunning of that move. It revolted him. He had not yet realized that the old man was fighting for his life.

"I'm not open to any proposals," he said coldly. "I've chosen my profession, and I mean to stick to it."

"That's all very well; but you should 'ave a solid standby, over and above."

"Literature doesn't leave much room for anything over and above."

"That's where you're making a mistake. Wot you want is variety of occupation. There's no reason why you shouldn't combine literature with a more profitable business."

"I can't make it combine with any business at all."

"Well, I can understand your being proud of your profession."

"Can you understand my profession being proud of me?" Isaac smiled. Yes, he could well understand it.

"And," said he, "I can understand your objection to the shop."

"I haven't any objection to the shop."

"Well—then there's no reason why we shouldn't come to an agreement. If I don't mind owning that I can't get on without your help, you might allow that you'd get on a bit better with mine."

"Why, *aren't* you getting on, father?"

"Well, considering that my second-'and business depended on you entirely—and that that's where the profits are to be made nowadays—— That's where I'm 'andicapped. I can't operate without knowledge; and from hour to hour I've never any security that I'm not being cheated."

Isaac would gladly have recalled that word. Keith met it with silence, a silence more significant than any speech; charged as it was with reminiscence and reproof.

"Now, what I propose——"

"Please don't propose anything. I—I—I can't do what you want."

Keith positively stammered in his nervous agitation.

"Wait till you hear what I want. I'm not going to ask you to make catalogues, or stand behind the counter, or," he added almost humbly, "to do anything a gentleman doesn't do." He looked round the room. The materials of the furnishing were cheap; but Keith had appeased his sense of beauty in the simplicity of the forms and the broad harmony of the colours. Isaac was impressed and a little disheartened by the refinement of his surroundings, a refinement that might be fatal to his enterprise. "You shall 'ave your own private room fitted up on the first floor, with a writing table, and a swivel chair. You needn't come into contact with customers at all. All I want is to 'ave you on the spot to refer to. I want you to give me the use of those brains of yours. Practically you'd be a sleeping partner; but we should 'alve profits from the first."

"Thanks—thanks" (his voice seemed to choke him)— "it's awfully good and—and generous of you. But I can't."

"Why not?"

"I've about fifteen reasons. One's enough. I don't like the business, and I won't have anything to do with it."

"You—don't—like—the business?" said Isaac, with the air of considering an entirely new proposition.

"No. I don't like it."

"I am going to raise the tone of the business. That's wot I want you for. To raise the tone of the business."

" I should have to raise the tone of the British public first."

" Well—an intelligent bookseller has a good deal of influence with customers; and you with your reputation, there's nothing you couldn't do. You could make the business anything you choose. In a few years we should be at the very head of the trade. I don't deny that the house has been going down. There's been considerable depression. Still, I should be in a very different position now, Keith, if you hadn't left me. And in the second-hand department— *your* department—there are still enormous—*enor*mous— profits to be made."

" That's precisely why I object to my department, as you call it. I don't approve of those enormous profits."

" Now look 'ere. Let's have a quiet talk. We never have 'ad, for you were always so violent. If you'd stated your objections to me in a quiet reasonable manner, there'd never have been any misunderstanding. Supposing you explain why you object to those profits."

" I object, because in nine cases out of ten they're got by trading on another person's ignorance."

" Of course they are. Why not? If he's ignorant, it's only fair he should pay for his ignorance; and if I'm an expert, it's fair I should get an expert's profits. It's all a question of buying and selling. He can't sell what he hasn't got; and I can't sell what I haven't got. Supposing I've got knowledge that he hasn't—if I can't make a profit out of *that,* what can I make a profit out of? "

" I can't say. My own experience of the business was unfortunate. It struck me, if you remember, that some of your profits meant uncommonly sharp practice."

" Talk of ignorance! Really, for a clever fellow, Keith, you talk a deal of folly. There's sharp practice in every trade—in your own trade, if it comes to that. Supposing you write a silly book, and some of your friends boom it high and low, and the Public buys it for a work of genius— well—aren't you making a profit out of other people's ignorance? Of course you are."

" I haven't made *much* profit that way—yet."

" Because you're unbusiness-like. Well. I'm perfectly willing to believe your objections are conscientious. But look at it another way. I'm a God-fearing, religious-minded man " (unconsciously he caressed his soft hat, the hat of a

Methodist parson, as he spoke), " is it likely I'd continue in any business I couldn't reconcile to my conscience?"

" I've no doubt you've reconciled it to your conscience. That's hardly a reason why I should reconcile it to mine."

" That means that you'll let me be ruined for want of a little advice which I'd 'ave paid you well for?"

" If my advice is all you want, you can have it any day for nothing."

" Wot you get for nothing is worth just about wot you get it for. No. Mine was a fair business proposal, and either you come into it or you stay out."

" Most decidedly I prefer—to stay out."

" Then," said Isaac suddenly, " I shall have to give up the shop."

" I'm most awfully sorry."

" There's no good your being sorry if you won't help me."

" I would help you—if I could."

" If you could!" He paused. Prudence plucked him by the sleeve, whispering that never while he lived must he breathe the word Insolvency; but a wilder instinct urged him to disclosure. " Why—it rests with you to keep me out of the Bankruptcy Court."

Keith said nothing. He had held out against the appeal to his appetites; it was harder to withstand this call on his finer feelings. But if the immediate effect of the news was to shock and distress him, the next instant he was struggling with a shameful reflection. For all his shame it was impossible not to suspect his father of some deeper, more complicated ruse.

Isaac sat very still, turning on his son a look of concentrated resentment. Keith's youth was hateful to him now; it withheld pitilessly, implacably, the life that it was in its hands to give. Meanwhile Keith wrestled with his suspicion and overcame it.

" Look here, father, I'll do what I can. I'll come round to-morrow and look into things for you, if that's any good."

The instant he had made the offer he was aware of its futility. It was not for his business capacity that he was valued; and he never had been permitted to interfere with the finances of the shop. The suggestion roused his father to a passion that partook of terror.

" Look into things? " He rose trembling. " You mind your own business. I can look into things myself. There'd 'ave been no need to look into them at all if you 'adn't robbed and deceived me. Robbed and deceived me, I said. You took your education—which *I* gave *you* to put into *my* business—you took it out of the business, and set up with it on your own account. And I tell you you might as well 'ave made off with a few thousands out of my till. Robbing's wot *you've* been guilty of, in the sight of God; and you can come and talk to me about your conscience. I don't understand your kind of conscience—Keith." There was still a touch of appeal in his utterance of his son's name.

" Perhaps not," said Keith sorrowfully. " I don't understand it myself."

He walked with his father to Holborn, silently, through the drizzling rain. He held an umbrella over him, while they waited, still silently, for the Liverpool Street omnibus. He noticed with some anxiety that the old man walked queerly, shuffling and trailing his left foot, that he had difficulty in mounting the step of the omnibus, and was got into his seat only after much heaving and harrying on the part of the conductor. His face and attitude, as he sank crouching into his seat, were those of a man returning from the funeral of his last hope.

And in Keith's heart there was sorrow, too, as for something dead and departed.

CHAPTER XLIX

IF, much to Rickman's regret, Flossie did not take kindly to Miss Roots, very soon after her engagement she discovered her bosom friend in Miss Ada Bishop. The friendship was not founded, as are so many feminine attachments, upon fantasy or caprice, but rested securely on the enduring commonplace. If Flossie respected Ada because of her knowledge of dress, and her remarkable insight into the ways of gentlemen, Ada admired Flossie because of the engagement, which, after all, was not (like some girls' engagements) an airy possibility or a fiction, but an accomplished fact.

This attachment, together with the firm possession of

Keith, helped to tide Flossie over the tedium of waiting. Only one thing was wanting to complete her happiness, and even that the thoughtful gods provided.

About six o'clock one evening, as Rickman was going out of the house, he was thrust violently back into the passage by some one coming in. It was young Spinks; and the luggage that he carried in his hand gave a frightful impetus to his entry. At the sight of Rickman he let go a hat-box, an umbrella and a portmanteau, and laid hold of him by both hands.

"Razors—what luck! I say, I've gone and done it. Chucked them—hooked it. Stood it eighteen months—couldn't stand it any longer. On my soul I couldn't. But it's all right—I'll explain."

"Explain what? To whom, you God-forsaken lunatic?"

"Sh—sh—sh! To you. For heaven's syke don't talk so loud. They'll hear you. You haven't got a train you want to catch, or an appointment, have you?"

"I haven't got a train, but I have got an appointment."

"You might spare a fellow five minutes, ten minutes, can't you? I shan't keep you more than ten at the outside. There's something I must tell you; but I can't do it here. And *not there!*" As Rickman opened the dining-room door Spinks drew back with a gesture of abhorrence. He then made a dash for the adjoining room; but retired precipitately backwards. "Oh, damn! That's somebody's bedroom, now. How could *I* tell?"

"Look here, if you're going to make an ass of yourself, you'd better come up to my room and do it quietly."

"Thanks, I've got a room somewhere; but I don't know which it is yet."

Rickman could only think that the youth had broken his habit of sobriety. He closed the study door discreetly, lit the lamp and took a good look at him. He fancied he caught a suggestion of melancholy in the corners of his mouth and the lines of his high angular nose. But there was no sign of intoxication in Sidney's clear grey eye, nor trace of wasting emotion in his smooth-shaven cheek. Under the searching lamplight he looked almost as fresh, as pink, as callow, as he had done four years ago. He dropped helplessly into a low chair. Rickman took a seat opposite him and waited. While not under the direct stimulus of nervous excitement, young Spinks had some difficulty in finding utterance. At last he spoke.

" I say, you must think I've acted in a very queer way."

" Queer isn't the word for it. It's astounding."

" D'you really think so? You mean I 'adn't any right— it—it wasn't fair to you—to come back as I've done? "

" Well, I don't know about its being very fair; it certainly wasn't very safe."

" Safe? Safe? Ah—I was afraid you'd think that. Won't you let me explain? "

" Certainly. I should like to know your reasons for running into me like a giddy locomotive."

" Well, but I can't explain anything if you go on rotting like that."

" All right. Only look sharp. I've got to meet a fellow in Baker Street at seven. If you'll get under way we might finish off the explanation outside, if you're going back that way."

" Going back. Oh, Lord—don't you know that I've come back here to stay. I've got a room——"

" Oh, that's the explanation, is it? "

" No, that's the thing I've got to explain. I thought you'd think I'd acted dishonourably in—in following her like this. But I couldn't stand it over there without her. I tried, but on my soul I couldn't. I shall be all right if I can only see her sometimes, at meals and—and so forth. I shan't say a word. I haven't said a word. I don't even think she knows; and if she did—— So it's perfectly safe, you know, Rickman, it's perfectly safe."

" Who doesn't know what? And if who did? " roared Rickman, overcome with laughter.

" Sh—sh—sh—Flossie. I mean—M—miss Walker."

Rickman stopped laughing and looked at young Spinks with something like compassion. " I say, old chap, what do you mean? "

" I mean that I should have gone off my chump if I'd hung on at that place. I couldn't get her out of my mind, not even in the shop. I used to lie awake at nights, thinking of her. And then, you know—I couldn't eat."

" In fact, you were pretty bad, were you? "

" Oh, well, I just chucked it up and came here. It's all right, Razors; you needn't mind. I never had a chance with her. She never gave me so much as a thought. Not a thought. It's the queerest thing. I couldn't tell you how I got into this state—I don't know myself. Only now she's engaged and so forth, you might think that—well, you might think"—young Spinks had evidently come to the most delicate and complicated part of his explanation. "Well, that I'd no right to go on getting into states. But when it doesn't make any difference to her, and it can't matter to you." He paused; but Rickman gathered that what he wished to plead was that in those circumstances he was clearly welcome to his "state." "I mean that if it's all up with me, you know, it's all right—I mean, it's safe enough —for you."

Poor Spinks became lost in the maze of his own beautiful sentiments. Adoration for Rickman (himself the soul of honour) struggled blindly with his passion for Flossie Walker. But the thought, which his brain had formed, which his tongue refused to utter, was that the hopelessness of his passion made it no disloyalty to his friend. "It can make no difference to her, my being here," he said simply.

"Nonsense, you've as much right to be here as I have."

"Yes, but under the circumstances, it mightn't have been perfectly fair to you. See?"

"My dear Spinky, it's perfectly fair to me; but is it— you won't mind me suggesting it—is it perfectly fair to yourself?"

Spinks sat silent for a minute, laying his hand upon the place of thought, as if trying to take that idea in. "Yes," he said deliberately. "That's all right. In fact, nothing else will do my business. It sounds queer; but that's the only way to get her out of my head. You see, when I see her I don't think about her; but when I don't see her I can't think of anything else."

Rickman was interested. It struck him that latterly he had been affected in precisely the opposite way. It was curious to compare young Sidney's sensations with his own. He forgot all about the man in Baker Street.

"I don't mean to say I shall ever get over it. When a man goes through this sort of business it leaves its mark on him somewhere." And indeed it seemed to have stamped an expression of permanent foolishness on Spinks's comely face.

Rickman smiled even while he sympathized. "Yes, I daresay. I'm sorry, old man; but if I were you I wouldn't be too down in the mouth. It's not worth it—I mean—after all, there are other things beside women in the world. It wouldn't be a bad place even if there weren't any women in it. Life is good," said the engaged man. "You had better dress for dinner." He could give no richer consolation without seeming to depreciate the unique value of Flossie. As for Spinks's present determination, he thought it decidedly risky for Spinks, but if Spinks enjoyed balancing himself in this way on the edge of perdition it was no business of his.

As it happened, the event seemed to prove that Spinks knew very well what he was about. The callow youth had evidently hit on the right treatment for his own disease. In one point, however, his modesty had deceived him. His presence was far from being a matter of indifference to Flossie. A rejected lover is useful in so many ways. It may be a triumph to make one man supremely happy; but the effect is considerably heightened if you have at the same time made another man supremely wretched. Flossie found that the spectacle of young Sidney's dejection restored all its first fresh piquancy to her engagement. At Tavistock Place he more than justified his existence. True, he did not remain depressed for very long, and there was something not altogether flattering in the high rebound of his elastic youth; but, as Miss Bishop was careful to point out, his joyous presence would have a most salutary effect in disturbing that prosaic sense of security in which gentlemen's affections have been known to sleep.

But Spinks was destined to serve the object of his infatuation in yet another way.

It was in the second spring after Rickman's engagement. Flossie and Ada were in the drawing-room one half hour before dinner, putting their heads together over a new fashion-book.

"Shouldn't wonder," said Miss Bishop, "if you saw me coming out in one of these Gloriana coats this spring. I shall get a fawn. Fawn's my colour."

"I must say I love blue. I think I'm almost mad about blue; any shade of blue, I don't care what it is. I know I can't go wrong about a colour. But then there's the style." Flossie's fingers turned over the pages with soft lingering touches, while her face expressed the gravest hesitation. " Keith likes me best in these stiff tailor-made things; but I can't bear them. I like more of a fancy style."

" I see you do," said Miss Bishop solemnly.

" Yes, that's because she's a bit of a fancy article herself," murmured a voice from the back drawing-room, where Mr. Spinks had concealed himself behind a curtain, and now listened with a voluptuous sense of unlawful initiation.

" I sy, we shall have to stop, if he *will* keep on listening that wy."

" Don't stop, please, Miss Ada. There, I've got my fingers in my ears. On my honour, I have. You can talk as many secrets as you like now. I can't hear a word."

The two girls dropped their voices to a low impassioned monotone.

" You've got to dress for somebody else besides yourself now—an engaged young lady."

" Oh, I don't know that he takes so much notice. But he's given me lots of things, besides my ring. I'm to have a real silver belt—a Russian—next birthday."

" I sy, he's orf'ly good to you, you know. Some gentlemen get so careless once they're sure of you. D'you know, we all think you acted so honourable, giving out your engagement as soon as it was on. When do you think you'll be married?"

" I can't say. I don't know yet. Never, I think, as long as I'm in that old Bank."

Even with his fingers in his ears, young Sidney heard that voice, and before he could stop himself he was listening again.

" Don't you like it?" said Miss Bishop.

" No. I hate it."

Spinks gave a cough; and Miss Bishop began reading to herself in ostentatious silence, till the provocations of the page grew irresistible.

" Look here, Floss," she said excitedly. " Look at *me*. ' Fawn will be the pree-vyling colour this year, and for morning wear a plain tailor-myde costume in palest fawn is, for 'er who can stand it, most undeniably *chic*.' " Hitherto

Miss Bishop had avoided that word (which she pronounced
" chick ") whenever she met it ; but now, in its thrilling
connection with the fawn-coloured costume, it was brought
home to her in a peculiarly personal manner, and she
pondered. " I wish I knew what that word meant. It's
always coming up in my magazine."

" I think," said Flossie, " it means something like smart.
Stylish, you know."

Young Sidney leapt suddenly from his seat. " Go it,
Flossie! Give us the French for a nice little cup er tea."

" Really, it's too bad we can't have a place to ourselves
where we can talk. I'm going." And as Miss Bishop went
she still pondered Flossie's rendering of the word *chic*.
Little did any of them know what grave issues were to hang
on it.

Then Mr. Spinks emerged from his hiding-place. " Miss
Walker," he said (he considered it more honourable to call
her Miss Walker now whenever he could think of it ; only
he couldn't always think), " I didn't know you knew the
French language."

" And why shouldn't I know it as well as other people? "

" I expect you know it a jolly sight better. Do you think
now, you could read and write it easily? "

" I might," said Flossie guardedly, " if I had a little practice."

" Because, if you could—You say you're tired of the
Bank? "

" I should think I *was* tired of it."

" Well, Flossie, do you know, a good typewriter girl
who can read and write French can get twice as much as
you're getting."

" How do you know? "

" Girl I know told me so. She's corresponding clerk for
a big firm of wine merchants in the City. She's going to
be married this autumn ; and if you looked sharp, you might
get her berth."

" In a wine-merchant's shop? Mr. Rickman wouldn't
hear of it."

" It isn't a shop, you know, it's an office. You ask him."

Flossie did not ask him ; she knew a trick worth two
of that. But not very long after Mr. Spinks had made his
suggestion, finding Keith very snug in his study one even-

ing, reading Anatole France, to his immense delight she whispered into his ear a little shy request that some day when he wasn't busy, he would help her a bit with her French. The lessons were arranged for then and there, at so many kisses an hour, payable by quarterly instalments, if desired. And for several evenings (sitting very close together, as persons must sit who are looking over the same book) they read, translating turn by turn, the delicious *Livre de Mon Ami,* until Flossie's interest was exhausted.

"Come, I'm not going on with any more of that stuff, so you needn't think it. I've no time to waste, if you have; and I haven't come across one word in that book yet that'll be any use to me."

"What a utilitarian Beaver!" He lay back in his chair laughing at her, as he might have laughed at the fascinating folly of a child.

"I'll tell you what it is, Mr. Savage; I'll get another French master, if you don't look out. Some one who'll teach me the way I want to learn."

"I'll teach you any way you like, Floss, on any system; if you'll only explain what you want. What's your idea?"

"My idea's this. How would it be if you and me were to write French letters to each other?"

"Rather! The Beaver's intelligence is going to its head. That's the way to learn, Floss; you'll get over the ground like winking. But you know—I shall have to raise my terms."

"All right. We'll see about that."

He was delighted with her idea. That Flossie should have an idea at all was something so deliciously new and surprising; and what could be more heartrending than these prodigious intellectual efforts, her evident fear that her limitations constituted a barrier between them? As if it mattered! As if he wanted a literary critic for his wife. And how brutally he had criticised *her*—as if it mattered! Still, in spite of his compunction, the French lessons were not altogether a success. There was too much disagreement and discussion about terms; for the master became more and more exorbitant in his charges as the days went on, and the pupil still complained that she was learning nothing. She was thoroughly dissatisfied with his method. He would break off at the most interesting, the most instructive point, and let loose his imagination in all sorts of ridiculous histories that followed from the idea of her being a Beaver; and when she desired him to tell her such simple things as the French for "Your esteemed favour to hand," "Cheque enclosed," "We have forwarded to you to-day as per invoice," he wanted to know what on earth a beaver had to do with invoices.

It was Spinks who explained the nature of the connection.

Poor Spinks, who had made the suggestion with an almost suicidally honourable intention, was, to his immense astonishment, merely sworn at for his interference. And when Flossie brought Keith his tea that evening she found him in a most ungentlemanly humour.

She waited demurely for a pause in the storm that raged round Spinks and his confounded wine-merchant. She cast a significant glance at the table strewn at that moment with the rough draft of Rickman's tragedy. (Flossie couldn't understand why he could never write a thing out clearly from the first, nor why she shouldn't write it for him at his dictation.)

"It's all very well, Keith," said she, "but if *you* can't do more, *I* must."

Before she left the room it was understood between them that Flossie would renounce her wine-merchant, and that they would be married, if possible, some time in the autumn. He felt curiously shaken by that interview.

He spent the evening reading over what he had written, vainly trying to recall his inspiration, to kindle himself anew at his own flame. Last night he had had more inspiration than he could do with; his ideas had come upon him with a rush, in a singing torrent of light. His mind had been then almost intolerably luminous; now, there was twilight on its high parts and darkness over the face of its deep. His ideas, arrested in mid-air, had been flung down into the deep; and from the farther shore he caught, as it were, the flutter of a gown and the light laughter of a fugitive Muse.

CHAPTER L

ONE day, four years after the publication of *Saturnalia*, Rickman received a letter in an unknown hand; a woman's hand, but with a familiar vivid signature, the signature that is to be seen beneath the portraits of Walter Fielding, the greatest among contemporary poets, the living god of Rickman's idolatry.

" Dear Sir," he wrote (or rather, some woman had written for him), " I came across your Poems the other day; by chance, I must confess, and not by choice. I have something to say to you about them, and I would therefore be glad if you could call on me here to-morrow. I say, call on me; for I am an old man, and you, if I am not mistaken, are a young one; and I say to-morrow, because the day after to-morrow I may not have that desire to see you which I feel to-day. Faithfully yours,

" WALTER FIELDING.

" P. S.—You had better come in time for lunch at one o'clock."

Rickman's hand trembled as he answered that letter. All evening he said to himself, " To-morrow I shall see Fielding "; and the beating of his heart kept him awake until the dawn of the wonderful day. And as he dressed he said to himself, " To-day I shall see Fielding." That he should see him was enough. He could hardly bear to think what Fielding had to say to him.

He had risen early, so as to go down into Surrey on his bicycle. About noon he struck into the long golden road that goes straight across the high moor where the great poet had built him a house. Inside his gates, a fork of the road sloped to the shore of a large lake fringed with the crimson heather. The house stood far back on a flat stretch of moor, that looked as if it had been cut with one sweep of a gigantic scythe from the sheltering pine-woods.

He saw Fielding far off, standing at the door of his house to welcome him. Fielding was seventy-five and he looked sixty. A strong, straight figure, not over tall nor over slender, wearing, sanely but loosely, the ordinary dress of an English gentleman. A head with strong straight features, masses of white hair that hid the summit of the forehead, a curling moustache and beard, close-clipped, showing the line of the mouth still red as in his youth. A head to be carved in silver or bronze, its edges bitten by time, like the edges of an antique bust or coin.

"So you've come, have you?" was his greeting which the grasp of his hand made friendly.

He took Rickman straight into his study where a lady sat writing at a table in the window.

"First of all," said he, "I must introduce you to Miss Gurney, who introduced you to me."

Miss Gurney rose and held out a slender feverish hand. She did not smile (her face narrowed so abruptly below her cheekbones that there was hardly room for a smile on it), but her eyes under their thick black brows turned on him an eager gaze.

Her eyes, he thought, were too piercing to be altogether friendly. He wondered whether it was the flame in them that had consumed her face and made it so white and small.

She made a few unremarkable remarks and turned again to her writing table.

"Yes, Gertrude, you may go."

Her sallow, nervous hands had already begun gathering up her work in preparation for the word that banished her. When it came she smiled (by some miracle), and went.

They had a little while to wait before luncheon. The poet offered whisky and soda, and could hardly conceal his surprise when it was refused.

"You must forgive me," he said presently, "for never having heard of you till yesterday. My secretary keeps these things from me as a rule. This time she allowed herself to be corrupted."

Rickman felt a sudden interest in Miss Gurney.

"Your poems were sent to her by a friend of hers, with the request—a most improper one—that I should read them. I had no intention of reading them; but I was pleased with the volume at first sight. It was exactly the right length."

"The right length?"

"Yes, small octavo; the very best length for making cigar lighters."

Rickman had heard of the sardonic, the cruel humour with which Fielding scathed his contemporaries; still, he could hardly have expected even him to deal such a violent and devilish blow. Though he flushed with the smart he bore himself bravely under it. After all, it was to see Fielding that he had come.

"I am proud," said he, "to have served so luminous a purpose."

His readiness seemed to have disarmed the formidable Fielding. He leaned back in his chair and looked at the young man a moment or two without speaking. Then the demon stirred in him again with a malignant twinkle of his keen eyes.

"You see I was determined to treat you honourably, as you came to me through a friend of Miss Gurney's. But for her, you would have gone where your contemporaries go—into the waste-paper basket. They serve no purpose—luminous or otherwise." He chuckled ominously. "I had the knife ready for you. But if you want to know why I paused in the deed of destruction, it was because I was fascinated, positively fascinated by the abominations of your illustrator. And so, before I knew what I was doing (or I assure you I would never have done it), I had read, actually read the lines which the creature quotes at the bottom of his foul frontispiece. Why he quoted them I do not know—they have no more to do with his obscenities than I have. And then—I read the poem they were taken from."

He paused. His pauses were deadly.

"You have one great merit in my eyes."

Rickman looked up with a courageous smile, prepared for another double-edged pleasantry more murderous than the last.

"You have not imitated me."

For one horrible moment Rickman was inspired to turn some phrase about the hopelessness of imitating the inimitable. He thought better of it; but not before the old man divined his flattering intention. He shook himself savagely in his chair.

"Don't—please don't say what you were going to say. If you knew how I loathe my imitators. I shouldn't have sent for you if you had been one of them."

His mind seemed to be diverted from his present victim

by some voluptuous and iniquitous reminiscence. Then he began again. " But you and your *Saturnalia*—Ah !"

He leant forward suddenly as he gave out the interjection like a growl.

" Do you know you're a very terrible young man ? What do you mean by setting my old cracked heart dancing to those detestable tunes ? I wish I'd never read the d——d things."

He threw himself back in his chair.

" No, no; you haven't learnt any of those tunes from me. My Muse wears a straighter and a longer petticoat; and I flatter myself she has the manners of an English gentlewoman."

Rickman blushed painfully this time. He had no reply to make to that.

" I didn't mean," Fielding went on, " to talk to you about your *Saturnalia*. But *On Harcombe Hill*, and *The Song of Confession*—those are great poems."

Rickman looked up, startled out of his self-possession by the unexpected words and the sudden curious vibration in the voice that uttered them. Yet he could hardly realize that Fielding was praising him.

" They moved me," said Fielding, " as nothing moves me now, except the Psalms of David. I have been a great poet, as poets go nowadays; but " (he smiled radiantly) " the painful conviction is forced upon me that you will be a greater. If you live. I wanted to tell you this, because nobody else is likely to find it out until you're dead. You may make up your mind to that, my friend."

" I had made up my mind to many things. But they don't matter—now."

Fielding ignored the compliment. " *Has* any one found it out? Except yourself?"

" Only one person."

" Man or woman?"

He thought of Maddox, that irresponsible person. " A man. And perhaps he hardly counts."

The old poet gave him a keen glance from his all-knowing eyes.

" There *is* one other person, who apparently doesn't count, either. Well, I think that was the luncheon bell."

On their way to the dining-room he remarked: " That's

another reason why I sent for you. Because I hear they've not been particularly kind to you. Don't suppose I'm going to pity you for that."

" I don't pity myself, sir."

" No—no—you don't. That's what I like about you," he added, taking his guest by the arm and steering him to his place.

At luncheon Miss Gurney took a prominent part in the conversation, which Rickman for her sake endeavoured to divert from the enthralling subject of himself. But his host (perceiving with evident amusement his modest intention) brought it up again.

" Don't imagine, for a moment," said he, " that Miss Gurney admires you. She hates young poets."

Miss Gurney smiled; but as Rickman saw, more in assent than in polite denial. Throughout the meal she had the air of merely tolerating his presence there because it humoured the great man's eccentricity. From time to time she looked at him with an interest in which he detected a certain fear. The fear, he gathered, was lest his coming should disturb, or in any way do harm to the object of her flagrant adoration.

After she had left the table Fielding reproached him for mixing water with his wine.

" In one way," said he, " you're a disappointment. I should have preferred to see you drink your wine like a man."

" Unfortunately," said Rickman, " it's not so easy to drink it like a man, if you've ever drunk it like a beast."

" Ah—h. You're an even more remarkable person than I thought you were," said the poet, rising abruptly from the table.

He proposed that they should take a walk in the garden, or rather on the moor; for the heather ran crimson to the poet's doors, and the young pines stood sentinel at his windows.

They walked slowly towards the lake. On their way there Fielding stopped and drew a deep breath, filling his lungs with the pure, sweet air.

" Ah! that's better." He looked round him. " After all, we're right, Rickman. It's the poets that shall judge the world; and if *we* say it's beautiful, it *is* beautiful. *And* good."

Happy Fielding, thought Rickman. Fielding had never suffered as he had suffered; *his* dream had never been divorced from reality. It seemed fitting to the younger poet that his god should inhabit these pure and lofty spaces, should walk thus on golden roads through a land of crimson, in an atmosphere of crystal calm. He would have liked to talk to Fielding of Fielding; but his awe restrained him.

Fielding's mind did not wander long from his companion. " Let me see," said he, " do you follow any trade or profession?" He added with a smile, " Besides your own?"

" I'm a journalist." Rickman mentioned his connection with *The Museion* and *The Planet*.

" Ah, I knew there was an unlucky star somewhere. Well, at any rate, you won't have to turn your Muse on to the streets to get a living. But a trade's better than a profession; and a craft's better than a trade. It doesn't monopolize the higher centres. I certainly had the impression that you had been in trade."

Rickman wondered who could have given it to him. Miss Gurney's friend, he supposed. But who was Miss Gurney's friend? A hope came to him that made his heart stand still. But he answered calmly.

" I was. I worked for two years in a second-hand bookshop as a bibliographical expert; and before that I stood behind the counter most of my time."

" Why did you leave it? You weren't ashamed of your trade?"

" Not of my trade, but of the way I had to follow it. I'm not ashamed of working for Mr. Horace Jewdwine."

He brought the name in awkwardly. In bringing it in at all he had some vague hope that it might lead Fielding to disclose the identity of the friend. Horace Jewdwine was a link; if his name were familiar to Fielding there would be no proof perhaps, but a strong presumption that what he hoped was true.

" He is a friend of yours?"

" Yes." His hope leapt high; but Fielding dashed it to the ground.

" I never heard of him. I see," he said, " you've got a conscience. Have you also got a wife?"

" Not yet—but——"

" Good. So young a man as you cannot afford to keep *both*. I am so old that I may be pardoned if I give you some advice. But why should I? You won't take it."

" I should like to hear it all the same, sir."

" Well, well, it's cheap enough. Whatever you do, don't fritter yourself away upon the sort of women it may be your misfortune to have met."

It was beautifully done, this first intimation of his consciousness of any difference between them; between Rickman, who had glorified a variety actress, and Walter Fielding, whose Muse had " always had the manners of an English gentlewoman." And to Rickman's heart, amid vivid images of Poppies and Flossies, the memory of Lucia Harden stirred like a dividing sword.

" That is my advice," said Fielding. " But you will not take it."

" These things," said Rickman, " are not always in our power."

In the silence which followed he put the question that was burning in him.

" May I ask who the friend was who told Miss Gurney about me? "

" You may ask Miss Gurney; but I do not think she'll tell you. It seems to be a secret, and Miss Gurney, strange to say, is a young woman who can keep a secret."

He led the way to a seat overlooking the lake, where they sat for awhile in silence, and Rickman found his thoughts roaming from his god.

Presently, Fielding rose and turned back to the house. Rickman felt that the slow footsteps were measuring now the moments that he had to be with him. He was glad that they were slow.

Fielding stopped at his house-door, and stood for a second gazing earnestly at the young man.

" When you write anything," he said, " you may always send it to me. But no more—please—no more *Saturnalia*."

" There won't be any more *Saturnalia*."

" Good. I do not ask you to come again to see me."

Rickman struggled for an answer, but could not think of anything better than, " It's enough for me to have seen you once," which was not at all what he had meant to **say**.

Fielding smiled faintly; his humour pleased, Rickman fancied, with the ambiguity of his shy speech.

" I'm afraid I've tired you, sir," he said impulsively.

" You have not tired me. I tire myself. But here is Miss Gurney; she will look after you and give you tea. "Geniality," he continued, "is not my strong point, as you may have perceived. And any unnatural effort of the kind fatigues me. My own fault."

" You have been very generous to me."

" Generous? There can't be any generosity between equals. Only a simple act of justice. It is you who have been good to me."

" I? To you?"

" Yes. You have satisfied my curiosity. I own that sometimes I have wanted to know what sort of voice will be singing after I am dead. And now I *do* know. Good-bye, and thank you."

He pressed his hand, turned abruptly and shuffled into the house. He was noticeably the worse for his walk, and Rickman felt that he had to answer for it to Miss Gurney.

" I'm afraid I've tired him. I hope I haven't done him harm."

Miss Gurney glanced sharply at him, turned, and disappeared through the study window. Her manner implied that if he had harmed Fielding she would make him feel it.

She came back still unsmiling. " No. You have not tired him."

" Then," said he, as he followed her into the drawing-room, " I am forgiven."

" Yes. But I did not say you had not done him harm." The lady paused in her amenities to pour out his tea.

" Miss Gurney," he said, as he took the cup from her, " can you tell me the name of the friend who sent my book to you?"

" No, I'm afraid I cannot."

" I see. After all, I am not forgiven?"

" I am not at all sure that you ought to be.

" I heard what he said to you," she went on almost fiercely. " That's why I hate young poets. He says there is only you to hate."

" So, of course, you hate me?"

"I think I do. I wish I had never heard of you. I wish he had never seen you. I hope you will never come again. I haven't looked at your poems that he praises so. He says they are beautiful. Very well, I shall hate them *because* they are beautiful. He says they have more life in them than his. Do you understand *now* why I hate them and you? He was young before you came here. You have made him feel that he is old, that he must die. I don't know what else he said to you. Shall I tell you what he said to me? He said that the world will forget him when it's listening to you."

"You misunderstood him." He thought that he understood her; but it puzzled him that, adoring Fielding as she did, she yet permitted herself to doubt.

"Do you suppose I thought that he grudged you your fame? Because he doesn't. But I do."

"You needn't. At present it only exists in his imagination."

"That's enough. If it exists there——"

"You mean, it will go down the ages?"

She nodded.

"And you don't want it to go?"

"Not unless his goes too, and goes farther."

"You need hardly be afraid."

"I'm *not* afraid. Only, he has always stood alone, so high that no one has touched him. I've always seen him that way, all my life—and I can't bear to see him any other way. I can't bear any one to touch him, or even to come anywhere near him."

"No one ever will touch him. Whoever comes after him, he will always stand alone. And," he added gently, "you will always see him so."

"Yes," she said, but in a voice that told him she was still unconsoled. "If I had seen him when he was young, I suppose I should always see him young. Not that I care about that so much. His youth is the part of him that interests me least; perhaps because it was never in any way a part of me."

He looked at her. Did she realize how far Fielding's youth, if report spoke truly, had belonged to, or in her own words, "been a part of" other women? Did she resent their part in him? He thought not. It was not so much that she was jealous of Fielding's youth, as that she shrank from any appearance of disloyalty to his age.

"And yet," she said, " I feel that no one has a right to be young when he is old. I hate young poets because they are young. I hate my own youth——"

Her youth? Yes, it was youth that leapt quivering in her tragic face, like a blown flame. Her body hardly counted except as fuel to the eager and incessant fire.

" Don't hate it," he said. " It is the most beautiful thing you have to give him."

"Ah—if I *could* give it him! "

He smiled. " You have given it him. He isn't old when he can inspire such devotion. He is to be envied."

He rose and held out his hand. As she took it, Miss Gurney's flame-like gaze rested on him a moment and grew soft.

" If you want to know, it was Lucia Harden who sent me your poems," said she. And he knew that for once Miss Gurney had betrayed a secret.

He wondered what had made her change her mind. He wondered whether Lucia had really made a secret of it. He wondered what the secret had to do with Fielding. And wondering, he went away, envying him the love that kept its own divine fire burning for him on his hearth.

CHAPTER LI

THERE were times when Rickman, harassed by his engagement, reviewed his literary position with dismay. Of success as men count success, he had none. He was recognized as a poet by perhaps a score of people; to a few hundreds he was a mere name in the literary papers; to the great mass of his fellow-countrymen he was not even a name. He had gone his own way and remained obscure; while his friends, Jewdwine and Maddox, had gone theirs and won for themselves solid reputations. As for Rankin (turned novelist) he had achieved celebrity. They had not been able to impart to him the secret of success. But the recognition, and something more than recognition, of the veteran poet consoled him for the years of failure, and he felt that he could go through many such on the strength of it.

The incident was so momentous that he was moved to speak of it to Jewdwine and to Maddox. As everything that interested him interested Maddox, he related it to Maddox in full; but with Jewdwine (such was his exceeding delicacy) he observed a certain modest reticence. Still there was no diminution in his engaging candour, his innocent assumption that Jewdwine would be as pleased and excited as Maddox and himself.

" He really seemed," said he, selecting from among Fielding's utterances, " to think the things were great."

Jewdwine raised his eyebrows. " My dear Rickman, I congratulate you." He paused for so long that his next remark, thoughtfully produced, seemed to have no reference to Rickman's communication. " Fielding is getting very old." If Rickman had been in a state of mind to attend carefully to Jewdwine's manner, he might have gathered that the incident had caused him some uneasiness.

It had indeed provided the editor of *The Museion* with much matter for disagreeable thought. As it happened (after months of grave deliberation), he had lately had occasion to form a very definite opinion as to the value of Rickman the journalist. He knew that Rickman the journalist had no more deadly enemy than Rickman the poet; and at that particular moment he did not greatly care to be reminded of his existence. Jewdwine's attitude to Rickman and his confidences were the result of a change in the attitude of *The Museion* and its proprietors. *The Museion* was on the eve of a revolution, and to Jewdwine as its editor Rickman the journalist had suddenly become invaluable.

The revolution itself was not altogether sudden. For many months the behaviour of *The Museion* had been a spectacle of great joy to the young men of its contemporary, *The Planet*. The spirit of competition had latterly seized upon that most severely academic of reviews, and it was now making desperate efforts to be popular. It was as if a middle-aged and absent-minded don, suddenly alive to the existence of athletic sports in his neighbourhood, should insist on entering himself for all the events, clothed, uniquely, if inappropriately, in cap and gown. He would be a very moving figure in the eyes of hilarious and immortal youth. And such a figure did *The Museion* in its latter days present. But the proprietors were going to change all that. *The Museion* was about to be withdrawn from circulation and reissued in a new form under the new title of *Metropolis.* As if aware of the shocking incongruity it was going to fling off its cap and gown. Whatever its staying power might be, its spirit and its outward appearance should henceforth in no way differ from those of other competitors in the race for money and position.

While the details of the change were being planned in the offices of *The Museion,* the burning question for the proprietors was this: would their editor, their great, their unique and lonely editor, be prepared to go with them? Or would he (and with him his brilliant and enthusiastic staff) insist on standing by the principles that had been the glory of the paper and its ruin? Mr. Jewdwine had shown himself fairly amenable so far, but would he be any use to them when it really came to the point?

To Jewdwine that point was the turning-point in his career. He had had to put that burning question to himself. Was he, after all, prepared to stand by his principles? It was pretty certain that if he did, his principles would not stand by him. Was there anything in them that *would* stand at all against the brutal pressure that was moulding literature at the present hour? No organ of philosophic criticism could (at the present hour) exist, unless created and maintained by Jewdwine single-handed and at vast expense. His position was becoming more unique and more lonely every day, quite intolerably lonely and unique. For Jewdwine after all was human. He longed for eminence, but not for such eminence as meant isolation. Isolation is not powerful; and even more than for eminence he longed for power. He longed for it with the passion of a weak will governed despotically by a strong intellect. It amounted to a positive obsession, the tyranny of a cold and sane idea. He knew perfectly well now what his position as editor of *The Museion* was worth. Compared with that great, that noble but solitary person, even Maddox had more power. But the editor of *Metropolis,* by a few trifling concessions to the spirit of modernity, would in a very short time carry all before him. He must then either run with the race or drop out of it altogether; and between these two courses, Jewdwine, with all his genius for hesitation, could not waver. After much deliberation he had consented (not without some show of condescension) to give his name and leadership to *Metropolis;* and he reaped the reward of his plasticity in a substantial addition to his income.

This great change in the organization of the review called for certain corresponding changes in its staff. And it was here that Rickman came in. He had been retained on *The Museion* partly in recognition of his brilliance, partly by way of satisfying the claims of Jewdwine's magnanimity. On *The Museion* he had not proved plastic either as sub-editor or as contributor. He did not fit in well with the traditions of the paper; for he was, to Jewdwine, modernity incarnate, the living spirit of revolt, to be bound down with difficulty by the editorial hand. Looking back on the record of the past four years Jewdwine marvelled how and why it was that he had kept him. A score of times he had been tempted to dismiss him after some fresh enormity; and a score of times Rickman had endeared himself by the seductive graces of his style. But Rickman on the staff of *Metropolis* was, Jewdwine considered, Rickman in the right place. Not only could he now be allowed to let loose his joyous individuality without prejudice to the principles of that paper (for the paper, strictly speaking, would have no principles) but he was indispensable if it was to preserve the distinction which its editor still desired. Jewdwine had no need of the poet; but of the journalistic side of Rickman he had endless need. It was a baser faculty, but his care must be to develop it, to train it, to handle it judiciously, until by handling he had made it pliable to all the uses of his paper. Jewdwine had a genius for licking young men into shape. He could hardly recognize that band of awkward and enthusiastic followers in his present highly disciplined and meritorious staff. None of them were like Rickman; none of them had done anything to rouse an uneasy suspicion of their genius. Still, none of them were precisely fitted for his present purpose. Rickman the poet, of course, you could not lick into shape. His shape, plastic only under the divine fire, was fashioned by the fingers of the god. But Rickman the journalist, once get him on to the right journal, would prove to be made of less unmanageable stuff. If he had not hitherto proved manageable, that was no doubt because hitherto he had been employed on the wrong journal.

And yet, when he came to discuss the change of programme with the different members of his staff (some of whom he was giving their dismissal), it was with Rickman (whom he proposed to retain) that he felt the most acute embarrassment. Rickman, although at the moment dining with Jewdwine, was so abominably direct.

" I see," he said, after listening to a lengthy exposition of the proprietors' view; " they want to popularize the thing."

Jewdwine winced perceptibly. "Well, hardly," said he. " In that case they would have been obliged to change their editor. We certainly want to draw a rather larger public than we have done; and to do that we must make *some* concessions to modernity. There's no doubt that the paper's interests have suffered from its tradition. We have been too exclusive, too detached. We can no longer afford to be detached. We propose to abandon the tradition in favour of—well—of a somewhat broader attitude." He looked keenly at Rickman, as if he defied him to put it any other way.

" I see. We've either got to take a more genial view of our contemporaries—or scoot."

" *You* may put it that way if you like. It simply means that if we are to appeal to a wider public, we must take a wider view. It's surely in the interests of the public, *and* of literature, that we should not narrow the influence of the paper any more than we can help. Not make the best criticism inaccessible." He continued to take the lofty and the noble view. The habit was inveterate. But his last remark started him on the way of self-justification. " Of course I couldn't go on with the paper if I hadn't come to see this for myself. The fact is, you cannot run a leading review on abstract principles."

Rickman forbore to smile at the fulfilment of his prophecy. Jewdwine's " Absolute " had been obliged to " climb down."

" Not," said Jewdwine, " if that review is really to lead public opinion."

" And certainly not," said Rickman, " if public opinion is to lead the review."

" In either case," said Jewdwine nobly, " the principles remain."

" Only they're not applied? "

" They are not applied. because there is nothing to apply

them to. In the present state of literature a review like *The Museion* has no reason for its existence."

"I don't know. It was a very useful protest against some forms of modernity."

"My dear fellow, modernity simply means democracy. And when once democracy has been forced on us there's no good protesting any longer."

"All the same, you'll go on protesting, you know."

"As a harmless private person, yes. As a critic I must accept a certain amount of defeat at the hands of the majority."

"But you don't happen to believe in the majority?"

"I do believe in it," said he bitterly. "I believe that it has destroyed criticism by destroying literature. A critic only exists through the existence of great men. And there are no great men nowadays; only a great number of little men."

"I see. Othello's occupation's gone."

"Not at all. Othello's occupation's only beginning. You can't criticise these people, but you must review them. And I assure you it means far more labour and a finer discrimination to pick out your little man from a crowd of little men than to recognize your great man when you see him."

"When you see him——"

"Ah yes—*when* I see him. But where is he? Show me," said Jewdwine, "one work of unmistakable genius published any time in the last five, the last ten years."

Rickman looked at him and said nothing. And to Jewdwine his silence was singularly uncomfortable. He would have been more uneasy still but for his conviction that the serenity in Rickman's eyes was reflected from the eyes of Fielding. Rickman, he thought, was rather too obviously elated at the great man's praise; and the exhibition of elation was unpleasant to him. Worse than all, he realized that Rickman, in spite of his serenity, was hurt. On the top of that came a miserable misgiving as to the worthiness of his own attitude to his friend.

As for Rickman, he had no feeling that he could have put into words, beyond owning in his heart that he was hurt. He had never before had any occasion for such a confession; he felt it to be humiliating both to Jewdwine and himself. Sometimes, in moments of depression he had suspected that it was Jewdwine's coldness that preserved his incorruptibility; but he had so sincere a desire for purity in their relations, that he had submitted without resentment to the freezing process that ensured it. He had in reserve his expectation of the day when, by some superlative achievement, he would take that soul, hitherto invincible, by storm. But now, in his inmost heart he owned that he was hurt.

Jewdwine changed the subject.

CHAPTER LII

WHEN Jewdwine changed the subject, it was to intimate that his friend might now expect a salary rising steadily with the fortunes of *Metropolis*.

That promise to marry Flossie in the autumn had made Rickman very uneasy on this head. The sources of his income had been hitherto uncertain; for *The Planet* might at any moment cease to be, and only indomitable hope could say that *The Museion* would be long for this world.

The amount of his income, too, depended on conditions which were, to some extent, beyond his own control. It had never sunk below a hundred and fifty, and had never risen above three hundred, even in the years when he wrote more articles than poems. Whereas, if he wrote more poems than articles, two hundred was the highest figure it had yet attained. And supposing the poems came and the articles didn't? For in these things he was in the hands of the god. Therefore he had long been a prey to devastating anxiety. But he hoped great things from the transformation of *The Museion*. It certainly promised him a larger and more certain revenue in the future, almost justifying his marriage in the autumn. It had been expressly understood that his promise to Flossie was to be fulfilled only if possible. But meanwhile he had got to make it possible, for Flossie (in spite of *her* promise) kept the terror of her wine-merchant perpetually dangling above his head. He had visited Messrs. Vassel & Hawkins' detestable establishment; and it made him shudder to think of his pretty Beaver shut up in a little mahogany cage, with her bright eyes peeping sad and shy through the brass netting, and her dear little nostrils sniffing the villainous alcoholic air.

But as the time approached and their marriage grew every day more certain and more near, the joy and excitement of the bridegroom were mingled with an inexplicable terror and misgiving. He had been disagreeably impressed by the manner of Flossie's insistence on his poverty. He had not missed the fine contempt conveyed by all her references to his profession, which she not unjustly regarded as the cause of the poverty. He was well aware that his genius was a heavy burden for so small a thing to bear; and his chivalry had determined that it should lie lightly on her lest it should crush or injure her. It was part of her engaging innocence that she knew nothing of the world in which his supremacy began and hers ended, that she had not even suspected its existence. If he had any illusions about her it was his own mind that created and controlled them. He delighted in them deliberately, as in a thing of his creating; seeing through them with that extraordinary lucidity of his, yet abandoning himself all the more. Flossie's weakness made him tender, her very faults amused him. As for his future, he could not conceive of his marriage as in any way affecting him as a poet and a man of letters. While the little suburban Eros lit his low flame upon the hearth, his genius would still stand apart, guarding with holy hands the immortal fire. For those two flames could never mingle. In that dream he saw himself travelling with ease and rapidity along two infinite lines that never touched and never diverged; a feat only possible given two Rickmans, not one Rickman. There used to be many more of him; it was something that he had reduced the quantity to two. And in dreams nothing is absurd, nothing impossible.

Pity that the conditions of waking life are so singularly limited. At first it had been only a simple question of time and space. Not that Flossie took up so very much space; and he owned that she left him plenty of time for the everyday work that paid. But where was that divine solitude? Where were those long days of nebulous conception? Where the days when he removed himself, as it were, and watched his full-orbed creations careering in the intellectual void? The days when Keith Rickman was as a god? He was hardly aware how fast they were vanishing already; and where would they be in two months' time? It was on his tragedy that he based his hopes for his future; the future in which Flossie had no part. He knew that the plea of art sounded weak before the inexorable claims of nature; he felt that something ought to be sacrificed to the supreme passion; but he couldn't give up his tragedy. He was consumed by two indomitable passions; and who was to say which of them was supreme? Still, tragedies in blank verse were a luxury; and Flossie had more than once pointed out to him he couldn't afford luxuries. He would sit up working on the tragedy till long past midnight; and when he woke in the morning his sense of guilt could not have been greater if he had been indulging in the most hateful orgies. But you can't burn even genius at both ends; and his paying work began to suffer. Jewdwine complained that it was not up to his usual level. Maddox had returned several articles. So at last he stuffed his tragedy into a drawer to wait there for a diviner hour. " That would have been a big expensive job," he said to himself. " I suppose it's possible to put as good work into the little things that pay; but I shall have to cut myself in pieces." That was what he was doing now; changing his gold into copper as fast as he could, so many pennies for one sovereign. Nobody was cheated. He knew that in his talent (his mere journalistic talent) there was a genius that no amount of journalism had as yet subdued. But he had an awful vision of the future, when he saw himself swallowed up body and soul in journalism. The gods were dead; but there were still men and columns.

That would be the inevitable surrender to reality. To have no part in the triumph of the poetic legions; but to march with the rank and file, to a detestable music not his own; a mere mercenary ingloriously fighting in a foreign cause.

To Jewdwine, Jewdwine once incorruptible, it seemed that Rickman was preparing himself very suitably for the new campaign. But Maddox mourned as he returned those articles; and when he heard of the approaching marriage which explained them he was frantic. He rushed up on Sunday afternoon, and marched Rickman out into the suburbs and on to a lonely place on Hampstead Heath. And there, for the space of one hour, with his arm linked in Rickman's, he wrestled with Rickman for his body and his soul. Jewdwine's cry had been, " Beware of the friendship of little men;" the burden of Maddox was, "Beware of the love of little women."

"That's all you know about it, Maddy. The love of great women absorbs you, dominates you. The little women leave you free."

Maddox groaned.

"A fat lot of freedom you'll get, Ricky, when you're married." Rickman looked straight before him to the deep blue hills of the west, as if freedom lay on the other side of them. "Good God," he said, "what am I to do? I must marry. I can't go back to Poppy Grace, and her sort."

"If that's all," said Maddox, "I don't see much difference. Except that marriage is worse. It lasts longer." Whereupon Rickman blushed, and said that wasn't all, and that Maddox was a brute. He would change his opinion when he knew Miss Walker.

Before very long he had an opportunity of changing it.

Rickman had been in error when he told Flossie that if she would consent to marry him he would never again be ill. For he was ill the first week in September, not two years after he had made that ill-considered statement. The Fielding episode, when the first fine stimulus was over, had left him miserable and restless. It was as if he had heard the sound of Lucia Harden's voice passing through the immeasurable darkness that divided them. And now he seemed to be suffering from something not unlike the nervous fever that had attacked him once before at Harmouth; complicated, this time, by a severe cold on the chest, caught by walking about through pouring rain in great agony of mind.

For Flossie (who may have felt latterly that she had chanced upon another season of depression in her woman's trade) that illness was a piece of amazing good luck, coming as it did at the moment of Keith's misgivings. It not only drew them together, just as they were drifting insensibly apart, but it revealed them to each other in a tenderer and serener light. There was a little hard spot in Flossie which was impervious to the subtler charm of Rickman when he was well. But Rickman ill and at her mercy, confined to the bed where (so long as Flossie waited on him) he lay very quietly with the sheet drawn tight up to his chin, in a state of touching dependence and humiliation, was a wholly different person from the stormy and incomprehensible Rick-

man who for more than two years had struggled so madly
in her toils. And if, to the eye of Mrs. Downey, Flossie
appeared untouched by the really heart-rending pathos
of his attitude in sleep; beholding unmoved his huddled
boyish form under the blankets, one half-naked arm laid
slack along the bed, the other thrust out straight into the
cold outside it; if she left Mrs. Downey to cover the poor
fellow up, wondering why on earth the girl could sit there
and never do it; if, when he woke, she missed the extreme
poignancy of appeal in the murmurs that followed her as
she went Beaver-like about her business in the room, it may
be that in that unaccustomed service the hidden prescient
motherhood in her was awakened and appeased (Flossie
being still under the dominion of her dream). As yet it
struggled blindly with her invincible propriety; a struggle
poor Rickman was made aware of by the half-averted manner of her approaches, the secrecy and hesitation of her
touch. But the little clerk undoubtedly found that patting
pillows, straightening coverlets, and making mustard plas-
ters, was an employment more satisfying to her nature than
the perpetual handling of bank notes. And to Rickman,
lying there with his hungry heart filled for the time quite
full with his own humility and gratitude, lying in a helplessness that had in it something soothing and agreeable,
feeling the soft, shy woman's hands about his bed, following
with affectionate, remorseful eyes her coming and going,
or watching as she sat patiently mending his socks, it came
with the freshness of a new discovery that she was, after all,
a very engaging little Beaver. He had never for one instant
glorified his love for her; he understood it too thoroughly.
It was love as Nature loves to have it; honest enough, too,
but of its kind singularly devoid of any inspiring quality.
Flossie had never moved him to the making of sonnets or
of songs. Moreover, he had discovered in her a certain
lack of tenderness, or of the outward signs of tenderness.
Not but what Flossie commanded all the foolish, endearing
language of young love; only she was apt to lavish it on
little details of attire, on furniture, on things seen in shop-
windows and passionately desired. But there was something
very transfiguring in the firelight of his bedroom hearth.
As he lay in it, enjoying the pure sweet foretaste of domestic
felicity, it was as if he saw more clearly into himself and her

and the life that would so soon make them one. If it was not the best life; he told himself that of its kind it would be very good. He had no doubt now that Flossie loved him. He was led to this certainty by the maternal quality in her present dealings with him, when perhaps it should have warned him rather that these cares were not for him.

Flossie had somewhat elaborated her dream. Bearing the fascinating name of Muriel Maud, it had grown softer and rosier than ever. She could not any longer deny its mysterious association with Keith Rickman, though she would have died rather than that Keith should have suspected it. And now as she sat mending Keith's socks her fancy all the time was busy fashioning delicious garments for her dream. Flossie never pursued her vision of Muriel Maud beyond the period of enchanting infancy; when it outgrew the tender folly of those garments it was dismissed from Flossie's fancy with unmaternal harshness. Therefore it appeared eternally innocent and young, mortal in a delicate immortality. In fact, viewing her life too in the light of the bedroom firelight, Flossie was herself deceived.

They were both blissfully unaware that Nature cares nothing about love, but was bent upon using them for the only end she does care about, the end that gives to love the illusion of its own eternity.

But Maddox saw through it in a minute. It was in the earlier stages of the poet's illness, and Maddox had happened to put his head into Rickman's room at the moment when Flossie, compelled by Mrs. Downey, was helping to put a stinging mustard plaster on his chest. They shrieked, and Maddox instantly withdrew.

He painted the scene afterwards for Rankin in the lurid and symbolic colours of his Celtic fancy. " Talk of Samson among the Philistines, it's nothing to Ricky-ticky in that d——d boarding-house. There was a woman on each side of his bed. They'd got him down on it; they were pinning the poor little chap in his blankets. I could just see Ricky-ticky's face between their shoulders; it was very red; and I shall never forget the expression on it, never. The agony, Rankin, the hopeless, unutterable agony."

" What were they doing to him? "

" I couldn't see properly. But I think they were cutting his hair off."

He declared later that he had distinctly heard the squeaking of that young Delilah's scissors. " We're not told whether Delilah was Samson's wife," said he. " But the Scriptures were never wrong on a point of human nature."

At which Rankin looked depressed; for he too was thinking of getting married; though, as Maddox reminded him for his comfort, not to Miss Flossie Walker.

" Is our Ricky-ticky," urged Rankin, " the man to show wisdom in choosing a wife? "

" He isn't the man to marry at all."

" Did you expect him to live like an anchorite, then? "

" I didn't expect anything. He might have lived as he liked, provided he didn't ruin himself as he's doing now."

And though Maddox now saw that young Delilah frequently, and always at her prettiest and her best, he did not change his opinion.

CHAPTER LIII

IT was now the third week in September, and the wedding was fixed for the twenty-fifth of October. Everything was fixed, even Flossie's ideas on the subject of her trousseau. There never was a little woman so unwavering in her choice of such things as clothes and furniture. To be married in ivory white, and to go away in powder blue; to have a drawing-room furnished in imitation rosewood and tapestry, and a dining-room in stamped velvet and black oak (imitation, too), had been Flossie's firm determination from the first. It saves endless time and contention when a young woman so absolutely knows her own mind.

Not but what she required approval and support in her decisions; otherwise she would have been hardly recognizable as a young woman. And for Rickman to go shopping with the Beaver in Tottenham Court Road, to follow her undeviating course through the furniture galleries, to note the infallible instinct by which she made for and seized upon the objects of her choice, to see the austerity with which she resisted the seductions of the salesman who sought to entangle her with a more expensive article, the calmness of her mind in dealing with the most intricate problems of measurement and price, was to be led a helpless captive in a triumph of practical ability. Ability, good Lord! was there ever anything like Flossie's grasp of all facts that can be expressed in figures? His brain reeled before the terrifying velocity of her mental arithmetic. What a little woman it was to do sums in the top of its head!

Not that she dragged him on the chain for ever. There were idyllic resting places, delicious, thrilling pauses in her progress; when she tried every chair in succession in the drawing-room suite; when she settled herself in the tapestry one, before the little rosewood tea-table (spread, for the heightening of the illusion, with a tea-service all complete); when she pretended to pour out tea, smiling over the teapot in the prettiest delight. With such a smile she would welcome him, with such a smile she would pour out his tea when he came back from Fleet Street to the home that was to be. (It did not occur to him that at the moment Flossie was only smiling at the teapot.) Though he stood aloof from the anticipatory scene, as he looked at her he grew positively weak with tenderness. In everything Flossie had her way. When they climbed (as they inevitably did) to the upper galleries he indeed offered some show of resistance when she insisted on choosing a terrible bedstead of brass with mother-o'-pearl ornaments. But to do him justice, it was sheer nervous terror which prompted the brutal remark that, "Really, mother-o'-pearl ornaments were more than he could stand"; for he melted and gave in at once at the sight of Flossie feeling the rosy down coverlet with her little hands. When their eyes met, Flossie's face was as rosy as the coverlet; so that the attendant spirit of commerce himself turned from them abashed. That there would, that there must be, such a moment Keith had had a horrible foreboding as he followed up the stairs.

Nobody could have been more happy than Flossie following the dream in Tottenham Court Road; and Rickman was happy because she was. Happy for a whole fortnight; and then for the first time they quarrelled.

And this was how it happened. They were going to live at Ealing; not because they liked it, but because the neighbourhood was cheap. Flossie had said, "When we're rich, we'll go to Kensington;" and he had answered with an odious flippancy, "Yes, and when we die we'll go to heaven;" but for the present, Flossie (wise Flossie who loved economy even more than Kensington) was content with Ealing. That

she was obliged to be content with it made her feel, naturally,
that she was entitled to gratification on every other point.
It was not over Ealing, then, that they quarrelled, but over
the choosing of the house. Flossie was all for a gay little
brand-new, red-brick villa, with nice clean white paint about
it, only two minutes from the tram; he for a little old-fash-
ioned brown-brick house with jasmine all over it, and a garden all grass and lilac bushes at the back. He said the garden
would be nice to sit in. She said, what was the good of sitting in a garden when you had to walk ever so far to the
tram? He retorted that walking was a reason for sitting;
and she that if it came to that they could sit in the house.
She wouldn't hear of the old brown house, nor he of the
brand-new villa. He was peculiarly sensitive to his surroundings.

" The villa," said he, " is a detestable little den."

" It isn't," said she, " it's got a lovely bay window in the
drawing-room, and a *dear* little balcony on the top."

" But there isn't a quiet place in it, dear, where I could
write."

" Oh, that's all you're thinking of——"

" Well, there isn't, really. Whereas here " (they were
going now through the little brown house), " there's a
jolly big room at the back, where you can see miles away
over the fields towards Harrow."

" Oh, you've got time to look out of the window, have
you, though you *are* so busy? "

" Never mind the window, let's look at the house. What's
wrong with it? "

" What's wrong with the house? It won't suit the furniture, that's what's wrong with it."

" You mean the furniture won't suit it? "

" The furniture's chosen and the house isn't. There's no
good going back on that."

" Look here, this is the room I meant." They had climbed
to the top of the little brown house, and Flossie had hardly
condescended to glance through the doors he had opened on
their way. He opened one now at the head of the stairs,
and this time she looked in.

" It would make all the difference to me, Floss," he said
humbly, " if I had a place like this when I want to get away
to write."

"When you want to get away from me, you mean."
Her lips shook; she looked round her with angry eyes, as
if jealous of the place, and all that he meant to do in it.

It was a large room, with a wide window looking on to
the garden and away across meadows and cornfields to
Harrow Hill with its thin church spire. The window was
guarded with iron bars. The wall-paper was designed in
little circles; and in each circle there were figures of little
boys and girls, absurd and gay. So many hundreds of little
figures, and so absurd and gay, that to sit in that room surrounded by them, to look at them and endeavour to count
them, was to go mad. But those figures fascinated Flossie.

"Oh, Lord, what a beastly wall-paper," said he.

"I think it's sweet," said she. And though she wasn't
going to let him have the house, she was ready to quarrel
with him again about the wall-paper. And then, in the
corner by the window they came upon a child's toy, a little
wooden horse, broken. He pointed it out to her, half-smil-
ing. "Some kiddy must have left that there."

"Of course," said she, "it's been a nursery. And, I
say, Keith, I think it must have *died*."

"How do you make that out?"

"It couldn't have been long here. Don't you see, the
wall-paper's all new." (He thought that was rather sharp
of her, the practical Beaver!) "And yet," she said con-
tinuing her train of induction; "it couldn't. If it had, they'd
never have left *that* here."

Ah, that was not sharp; it was something better. There
was, after all, about his Beaver a certain poetry and
tenderness.

She picked up the little wooden horse, and held it in her
hands, and adjusted its loosened mane, and mended its
broken legs, fitting the edges delicately with her clever
fingers. And it seemed to him that as she bent over the toy
her face grew soft again. When she lifted her head her
eyes rested on him, but without seeing him. Never had
Flossie had so poignant a vision of Muriel Maud.

He looked at her with a new wonder in his heart. For
the first time he was made aware of the change that two
years had worked in her. She had grown, he thought, finer
in growing firmer; her body in its maturity was acquiring a
strength and richness that had been wanting in its youth;

as if through that time of waiting it were being fashioned
for the end it waited for. But that was not all. She had
clothed herself unconsciously with poetry. She stood for a
moment transfigured before him; a woman with sweet eyes
beholding her desired destiny from far. Her soul (for a
moment) rose in her face like a star; a dim prophetic star
that trembled between darkness and dawn. He knew that
she saw herself now as the possible mother of his children.

The anger and the jealousy were over; and all of a sudden
she gave in.

" You can have the house, if you like, Keith."

" All right; I do like it. That's a dear little Beaver."

As he approached her her glance fled. " I didn't say **you**
could have the room. I want to keep it empty."

He put his arm round her and led her to the window.
" What do you want to keep it empty for, Flossie? "

Her poor little thoughts, surprised and dismayed, went
scurrying hither and thither, trying to hide their trail.

" Oh," she said, still looking away from him. " To store
things in." He drew her closer to him and kissed her
tenderly.

It seemed to him that a serene and happy light rested on
the garden, on the empty house, and on the empty room
that she had peopled already with her innocent dream. It
seemed to him that in that remote gaze of her woman's eyes,
abstracted from her lover, unconsciously desirous of the
end beyond desire, he saw revealed the mystery, the sanctity,
the purity of wedded love. And seeing it he forgave her
that momentary abstraction.

But the Beaver never dreamed; she was far too practical.
She was building, that was all.

CHAPTER LIV

THAT evening as they sat down to dinner, it might have
been noticed that Mrs. Downey's face was more flushed
and festal than it had been since the day was fixed for Mr.
Rickman's wedding and departure. She seated herself ex-
pansively, with a gay rustling of many frills, and smiled
well-pleased upon the arrangements of her table. From
these signs it was evident that Mrs. Downey was expecting

another boarder, a boarder of whom she had reason to be proud. Rickman noticed with dismay that the stranger's place was laid beside his own. He knew them so well, these eternal, restless birds of passage, draggled with their flight from one boarding-house to another. The only tolerable thing about them was that, being here to-day, they were gone to-morrow.

The new boarder was late, culpably late. But Mrs. Downey was proud of that too, as arguing that the poor bird of passage had stayed to smooth her ruffled plumage. Mrs. Downey approved of all persons who thus voluntarily acknowledged the high ceremonial character of the Dinner. She was glad that Mr. Rickman would appear to-night in full evening dress, to rush away in the middle of the meal, a splendour the more glorious, being brief. She was waiting for the delightful moment when she would explain to the visitor that the gentleman who had just left the room was Mr. Rickman, "the reviewer and dramatic critic." She would say it, as she had said it many times before, with the easy accomplished smile of the hostess familiar with celebrity.

But that moment never came. The very anticipation of it was lost in the thrill of the visitor's belated entrance. Yet nothing could have been quieter than the manner of it. She (for it *was* a lady) came into the room as if she had lived at Mrs. Downey's all her life, and knew her way already from the doorway to her chair. When she said, " I'm so sorry, I'm afraid I'm rather late," she seemed to be taking for granted their recognition of a familiar personal characteristic. Perhaps it was because she was so tall that her voice sounded like music dropt downward from a height.

There was a stir, a movement down each side of the table; it was subtle, like the flutter of light and wind, and sympathetic, answering to her footfall and the flowing rhythm of her gown. As it passed, Mrs. Downey's face became, if possible, more luminous, Miss Bramble's figure, if possible, more erect. A feeble flame flickered in Mr. Partridge's cheeks; Mr. Soper began feeling nervously in his pocket for the box of bon-bons, his talisman of success; while Mr. Spinks appeared as if endeavouring to assume a mental attitude not properly his own. Miss Bishop searched, double-chinned, for any crumbs that might have lodged in the bosom of her blouse; and Flossie, oh, Flossie became more demure, more correct, more absolutely the model of all propriety. Each was so occupied with him or her self that no one noticed the very remarkable behaviour of Mr. Rickman. He rose to his feet. He turned his back on Flossie. There was a look on his face as of a man seized with sudden terror, and about to fly.

In turning he found himself face to face with Lucia Harden.

He had the presence of mind to stand back and draw her chair from the table for her; so that his action appeared the natural movement of politeness.

Though she held out her hand by an instinct of recognition, there was a perceptible pause before she spoke. He had known that it was she before he saw her. She had to look at him twice to make quite sure.

And then, being sure, she smiled; not the slow, cold smile of politeness that dies downwards on the lips, but the swift smile of pleasure that leaps to the eyes and forehead.

"Mr. Rickman? I think I should have known you anywhere else; but I didn't expect to meet you here."

He looked at her courageously.

And as he looked there fell from him the past five years, the long estranging years of bitterness and misery and vain desire, and the years, still more estranging, of his madness and his folly; and not the thinnest phantom shadow of time divided him from the days of Harmouth. That moment of recognition annihilated all between; a lustre of his life swept away in one sweep of her eyelids, dropt fathom deep and forgotten in the gaze of her pure and tender eyes. It was not the Lucia of their last meeting; the tragic and terrible Lucia who had been so divided from him by her suffering and her grief. As she had appeared to him on that evening, the last of his brief, incredible happiness, when he sat with her alone in the drawing-room at Court House, and she had declared her belief in him, so she appeared to him now. The unforgetable movements of her face, the sweet curve of her mouth (the upper lip so soft and fine that it seemed to quiver delicately with the rhythm of her pulses and her breath), the turn of her head, the lifting of her eyebrows, told him that she had kept no memory of his part in the things that had happened after that.

And he too forgot. With Lucia sitting at his right hand, he forgot the woman sitting at his left; he forgot the house of bondage, and he forgot that other house where the wedding chamber yet waited for the bride.

"I should have known you anywhere." His eyes dropped and he said no more.

That act of recognition had only lasted a second; but it had made its mark. Over the dim, fluttering table was the hush of a profound astonishment. He neither saw nor felt it; nor did he hear Mrs. Downey scattering the silence with agitated apologies.

"You'll excuse us beginning, Miss Harden; but it's Mr. Rickman's night at the theatre."

Miss Harden looked at him again, lifting her eyebrows with that air of interested inquiry that he knew so well. And yet, beyond those first half dozen words he said nothing.

"Silly boy," said Mrs. Downey to herself, "why can't he say he's sorry he has to go. I'm sure I gave him his opportunity." She was annoyed at his rudeness.

Whether he were sorry or not, he went at his appointed time. He never knew how he got out of the room, nor how he had behaved before going. He had simply looked at her, held her hand and left her. And he had not said a word; or none at least that he could remember.

Miss Harden was, it seemed, the guest, or the ostensible guest, of Miss Roots. And Miss Roots enjoyed herself, delighting openly in the recovery of the friend she had lost sight of for so many years. But from Mrs. Downey's point of view the Dinner that night was not exactly a success. Mr. Rickman had behaved in an extraordinary manner. Mr. Soper and Miss Bishop had never looked so—well, so out of place and common. And she could see that Mr. Spinks had taken advantage of the general consternation to help himself outrageously to ginger.

Lucia took her friend aside when it was over. "You might have told me he was here," said she.

"My dear, I didn't know you knew him."

"Then, did he never——" Whatever Lucia was going to say she thought better of it.

She did not see him till the next night, after dinner, when he came to her as she was sitting in a corner of the back drawing-room alone. And as he came, she looked at him with a curiously intent yet baffled gaze, as if trying to fit a present impression to one past. And yet she could hardly have had any difficulty in recognizing him; for his face was unforgetable, unique; but she missed something in it which used to be familiar. And now she saw that what she had missed was the restless look of youth; the sensuous eagerness that had helped to make it so irregular. It had settled into the other look that she had found there more rarely; the look that strengthened and refined the mobile features, and brought them into harmony with the clean prominent lines of the chin and of the serious level brows. Of all his looks it was the one that she used to like best.

" So you've come back again? " he said.

" But I never was away."

" I thought you were abroad? "

" Who told you that? "

" I don't know. I suppose I must have dreamt it."

" I think you must. I've been in town for the last six weeks."

" In town? "

" Yes, if Hampstead's town. I've been staying with the Jewdwines. Didn't he tell you? "

" No, he never told me anything."

She was silent for a moment. " So *that's* why you never came to see me."

" To see you? I didn't know—and if I had I shouldn't have thought——" He hesitated.

" Of what? Of coming to see me? "

" No, that you would have cared for me to come."

" I think that's not a thing you ought to say. Of course I cared."

" Well, but I couldn't take that for granted, could I? "

" Couldn't you? Not after the messages I sent you? "

" But I never got any messages."

" Didn't you? " Her upper lip quivered; it was as if she winced at some thought that struck her like a blow. " Then my cousin must have forgotten to give them to you. Just like him; he is shockingly careless."

Now Rickman knew it was not just like him; Jewdwine was not careless, he was in all things painfully meticulous; and he never forgot.

" I don't think I can forgive him for that."

" You must forgive him. He is overwhelmed with work. And he isn't really as thoughtless as you might suppose. He has given me news of you regularly. You can't think how glad I was to hear you were getting on so well. As for the latest news of all——" She lifted her face and looked at him with her sweet kind eyes. " It *is* true that you are going to be married?"

" Quite true."

" I was so glad to hear that, too."

" Thanks." There was a slight spasm in his throat. That thick, difficult word stuck in it and choked him for the moment.

" I hope I shall meet your wife some day."

" You have met her." Lucia looked puzzled and he smiled, a little sadly for a bridegroom. " You sat next her at dinner. She's here somewhere."

Lucia turned her head to where Flossie was sitting by a table, sitting very upright, with her little air of strained propriety.

" Is it—is it that pretty lady? Do you think I might go up and speak to her? I would so like to know her."

" I'll bring her to you. There's rather a crowd just now in the other room."

He went to her, hardly knowing how he went. " Flossie," he said, " I want to introduce you to Miss Harden."

Flossie's eyes brightened with surprise and pleasure; for she had learnt from Mrs. Downey that the visitor was the daughter of Sir Frederick Harden; and Lucia's distinction subdued her from afar. Keith, being aware of nothing but Lucia, failed to perceive, as he otherwise might have done, that he had risen in Flossie's opinion by his evident intimacy with Miss Harden. She came blushing and smiling and a little awkward, steered by Keith. But for all her awkwardness she had never looked prettier than at that moment of her approach.

If Keith had wanted to know precisely where he stood in the order of Lucia's intimacies, he might have learnt it from her reception of Miss Walker. By it he might have measured, too, the height of her belief in him, the depth of her ignorance. She who had divined him was ready to take his unknown betrothed on trust; to credit her, not with vast intellect, perhaps (what did that matter?), but certainly with some rare and lovely quality of soul. He loved her; that was enough. Lucia deduced the quality from the love, not the love from the quality. His pretty lady must be lovable since he loved her. He had noticed long ago that Lucia's face had a way of growing more beautiful in the act of admiration; as if it actually absorbed the loveliness it loved to look upon. And now, as she made a place for Flossie at her side, it wore that look of wonder, ardent yet restrained, that look of shy and tentative delight with which five years ago she had approached his *Helen*. It was as if she had said to herself, " He always brought his best to show me. Five years ago he brought me his dream, to read and care for. Now he brings me the real thing, to read and care for too." She was evidently preparing to read Flossie as if she had been a new and beautiful poem.

He was unaware of all his; unaware of everything except the mingled beatitude and torture of the moment. He sat leaning forward, staring over his clasped hands at Lucia's feet, where he longed to fall down and worship. He heard her telling Flossie how glad she was to meet her; how unexpected was her finding of him here, after five years; how five years ago she had known him in Devonshire; and so on. But in his ears the music of her voice detached itself wholly from the meaning of her words. Thus he missed the assurance which, if he had only listened intelligently, they might have had for him; the assurance of an indestructible friendship that welcomed and enfolded his pretty lady for his sake.

But whatever her almost joyous acceptance of the pretty lady promised for the future, it could not be said that, conversationally, Lucia was getting on very fast with Flossie in the present; and Rickman's abstraction did not make things easier. Therefore she was a little relieved when Miss Roots joined them, and Rickman, startled into consciousness, got up and left the room. He feared that lady's sympathy and shrewdness. Nothing could be hidden from her clever eyes.

And now, perceiving that the conversation flagged, Miss Roots endeavoured to support it.

" Have you seen *Metropolis?* " she asked in her tired voice.

Lucia shook her head. " I don't know that I want to see it."

" You'd better not say so before Miss Walker."

" Oh, never mind me," said Miss Walker. " I haven't been yet. Is it good? "

" Some people seem to think so. It depends."

" Yes ; there's such a difference in the way they put them on the stage, too."

Miss Roots' face relaxed, and her fatigued intelligence awoke.

" Who's on in it? " asked Flossie, happy and unconscious ; and the spirit of mischief seized upon Miss Roots.

" I can't tell you. I'm not well posted in these things. But I think you'd better not ask Mr. Rickman to take you to see *Metropolis.*"

Flossie was mystified and a little indignant. If the play was so improper, why had Miss Roots taken for granted that she had seen it?

" That wasn't at all nice of her, was it? " said Lucia, smiling as Miss Roots went away. Her look was a healing touch laid on Flossie's wounded vanity. " That's the sort of little trap she used to lay for me."

" I suppose you mean she was rotting me. I always know when other people are rotting. But that's the worst of her ; you never can tell, and she makes you look so ignorant, doesn't she? "

" She makes me *feel* ignorant, but that's another thing."

" But whatever did she mean just now? "

" Just now she meant that you knew all about *Metropolis.*"

" Why should I? Do *you* know anything about it? "

" Not much ; though it is my cousin's paper. But as Mr. Rickman writes for it, you see——"

" Well, how was I to know that? He's always writing for something ; and he'd never think of coming to *me* every time. I never talk shop to him, and he never talks shop to me. Of course he told me that he'd got on to some better paying thing," she added, anxious to show that she was not shut out from the secrets of his heart ; " but when you said *Metropolis* I didn't take it in."

Lucia made no further attempt to converse. She said good-night and followed Sophie Roots to her tiny room.

" That was rather dreadful," she said to herself. " I wonder——" But if she did not linger long over her wondering, neither did she stop to find out why she was so passionately anxious to think well of the woman who was to be Keith Rickman's wife, and why it was such a relief to her to be angry with Sophie for teasing the poor child.

CHAPTER LV

HE asked himself how it was that he had had no premonition of the thing that was about to happen to him; that the supreme moment should have come upon him so casually and with so light a step; that he went to meet it in a mood so commonplace and unprepared? (Good Heavens! He remembered that he had been eating pea soup at the time, and wishing it were artichoke.)

Had he not known that she would come back again, and in just that way? Had he not looked for her coming five years ago? And what were five years, after all? How was it that he had heard no summons of the golden and reverberant hour?

And what was he going to do with it, or it with him, now that it had come? That was a question that he preferred to leave unanswered for the present.

It seemed that Lucia was going to stay for a week as Miss Roots' guest; and it was Mrs. Downey's hope that she would be with them for a much longer period on her own account. This hope Rickman judged to be altogether baseless; she would never be able to bear the place for more than a week. He inquired of Miss Roots early the next morning on this subject; and at the same time he found out from her what Lucia had been doing in the last five years. She had not been (as Jewdwine had allowed him to suppose) abroad all the time with Kitty Palliser. She had only lived with Miss Palliser in the holidays. The rest of the year, of the five years, she had been working for her living as music mistress in a Women's College somewhere in the south of England. To his gesture of horror Miss Roots replied that this was by no means the hideous destiny he conceived it to be.

" But—for *her!* " he exclaimed.

"And why not for her?" Miss Roots, B. A., retorted, stung by his undisguised repugnance. If Lucia *had* got her post merely by interest (which Miss Roots seemed to consider as something of a blot on her career) at the end of her first year she had the pick of the students waiting for her. Unfortunately Lucia had never been strong; and this summer her health had completely broken down.

At that he shuddered, and turned abruptly away. Miss Roots looked at him and wondered why. When he approached her again it was to offer her, with every delicacy and hesitation, the loan of his study for the time of Miss Harden's visit. This was not an easy thing to do; but he was helped by several inspirations. The room, he said, was simply standing empty all day. He had hardly any use for it now. He would be kept busy at the office up to the time of his marriage. And he thought it would be a little more comfortable for Miss Harden than the public drawing-room.

"I want," he said (lying with a certain splendour), "to pay some attention to her. You see, she's my editor's cousin——"

Miss Roots turned on him a large look that took him in, his monstrous mendacity and all. But she nodded as much as to say that the explanation passed.

"One hardly likes to think of her, you know, sitting in the same room with Soper."

"We all have to put up with Mr. Soper."

"Yes; but if she isn't strong, she ought to have some place where she can be alone and rest. Besides, it'll be nicer for *you*. You'll see a great deal more of her, you know, that way."

In the end the offer was accepted. For, as Miss Roots pointed out to her friend, it would give him far more pleasure to lend his room than to sit in it himself.

Certainly it gave him pleasure, a thrilling, subtle, and perfidious pleasure, every time that he thought of Lucia occupying his room. But before she could be allowed to enter, he caused it to be thoroughly cleansed, and purified as far as possible from the tobacco smoke that lingered in the curtains and the armchairs. He tidied it up with his own hands, removing or concealing the unlovelier signs of his presence and profession. He bought several cushions (silk and down) for the sofa, and a curtain for the door to keep out the draught, and a soft rug for Lucia's feet; also a tea-table, a brass kettle and a spirit lamp, and flowers in an expensive pot. He did things to them to make them look as if they had been some little time in use. He caused a wrinkle to appear in the smooth blue cheeks of the sofa cushions. He rubbed some of the youth off the edges of the tea-table. He made the brass kettle dance lightly on the floor, until, without injury to its essential beauty, it had acquired a look of experience. It was the deceit involved in these proceedings that gave him the first clear consciousness of guilt. He persuaded himself that all these articles would come in nicely for the little house at Ealing, then remembered that he had provided most of them already.

In doubt as to the propriety of these preparations, he again approached Miss Roots. " I say," said he, " you needn't tell her all these things are mine. I'm going to leave them here in case she wants to stay on afterwards. She won't have to pay so much then, you know." He hesitated. " Do you think that's a thing that can be done? "

" Oh, yes, it can be *done,*" she replied with an unmistakable emphasis.

" But I mayn't do it? Mayn't I? It's all right if she doesn't know, you know."

Miss Roots said nothing; but he gathered that she would not betray him, that she understood.

He could not explain matters half so clearly to himself. He might have wanted to lend his study to his friend's cousin; he certainly did want to lend it to Lucia for her own sake; but, besides these very proper and natural desires, he had other motives which would not bear too strict examination. Lucia, sitting in the same room with Mr. Soper, was not a spectacle that could be calmly contemplated; but he hoped that by providing her with a refuge from Mr. Soper he might induce her to stay till the moment of his own departure. And there was another selfish consideration. It was impossible to see her, to talk to her with any pleasure in the public drawing-room. Lucia could not come into his study as long as it was his; but if he gave it up to her and her friend, it was just possible that he might be permitted to call on her there. That she accepted him as a friend he could not any longer doubt. There were so many things that he had to say to her, such long arrears of explanation and understanding to make up. He could see that, unlike the Lucia he used to know, she had mis-understood him; indeed she had owned as much. And for this he had to thank Horace Jewdwine.

Jewdwine's behaviour gave him much matter for reflection, painful, but instructive. Jewdwine had not lied to him about Lucia's movements; but he had allowed him to remain in error. He had kept his cousin regularly posted in the news she had asked for, as concerning an unfortunate young man in whom they were both interested; but he had contrived that no sign of her solicitude should reach the object of it. It was as if he had been merely anxious to render an account of his stewardship; to assure her that the unfortunate young man was now prospering under his protection, was indeed doing so well that there was no occasion for Lucia to worry herself about him any more. Apparently he had even gone so far as to admit that there was friendship between Rickman and himself, while taking care that there should never be anything of the sort between Rickman and Lucia. He had constituted himself a way by which news of Rickman might reach Lucia; but he had sternly closed every path from Lucia to Rickman. That meant that Lucia might be depended upon; but that Rickman must be allowed no footing lest he should advance too far. In other words it meant that they acknowledged, and always would acknowledge, the genius while they judged it expedient to ignore the man.

But *she* had not always ignored him. Did it not rather mean, then, that Jewdwine would not trust her there; that, knowing her nature and how defenceless it lay before the impulses of its own kindness, he feared for her any personal communication with his friend? It did not occur to Rickman that what Jewdwine dreaded more than anything for Lucia was the influence of a unique and irresistible personal charm. As far as he could see, Jewdwine was merely desperately anxious to protect his kinswoman from what he considered an undesirable acquaintance. And five years ago his fears and his behaviour would have been justifiable; for Rickman owned that at that period he had not been fit to sit in the same room with Lucia Harden, far less, if it came to that, than poor Soper. But his life since he had known her was judged even by Jewdwine to be irreproachable. As Rickman understood the situation, he had been sacrificed to a prejudice, a convention, an ineradicable class-feeling on the part of the distinguished and fastidious don. It was not the class-feeling itself that he resented; he could have forgiven Jewdwine a sentiment over which he had apparently no control; he could have forgiven him anything, even his silence and his subterfuge, if he had only delivered Lucia's messages. That was an unpardonable cruelty. It was like holding back a cup of water from a man dying of thirst. He had consumed his heart with longing for some word or sign from her; he had tortured himself with his belief in her utter repudiation of him; and Jewdwine, who had proof of the contrary, had abandoned him to his belief. He could only think that, after taking him up so gently, Lucia had dropped him and left him where he fell. He owned that Jewdwine was not bound to tell him that Lucia had returned to England, or to provide against any false impression he might form as to her whereabouts; and it was not there, of course, that the cruelty came in. He could have borne the sense of physical separation if, instead of being forced to infer her indifference from her silence, he had known that her kind thoughts had returned to him continually; if he had known that whatever else had been taken from him, he had kept her friendship. Her friendship—it was little enough compared with what he wanted—but it had already done so much for him that he knew what he could have made of it, if he had only been certain that it was his. He could have lived those five years on the memory of her, as other men live on hope; sustained by the intangible but radiant presence, by inimitable, incommunicable ardours, by immaterial satisfactions and delights. If they had not destroyed all bodily longing, they would at least have made impossible its separation from her and transference to another woman. They would have saved him from this base concession to the folly of the flesh, this marriage which, as its hour approached, seemed to him more inevitable and more disastrous. Madness lay in the thought that his deliverance had been near him on the very day when he fixed that hour; and that at no time had it been very far away. No; not when two years ago he had stood hesitating on the edge of the inexpiable, immeasurable folly; the folly that had received, engulfed him now beyond deliverance and return. If only he had known; if he could have been sure of her friendship; if he could have seen her for one moment in many months, one hour in many years, the thing would never have begun; or, being begun, could never have been carried through.

Meanwhile the friendship remained. His being married could not make it less; and his being unmarried would certainly not have made it more. As there could be neither more or less of it, he ought to have been able to regard it as a simple, definite, solidly satisfactory thing. But he had no sooner realized that so much at least was his than he perceived that he had only the very vaguest notion as to the nature and extent of it. Of all human relations, friendship was the obscurest, the most uncertainly defined. At this point he remembered one fatal thing about her; it had always been her nature to give pleasure and be kind. The passion, he imagined, was indestructible; and with a temperament like that she might be ten times his friend without his knowing from one day to another how he really stood with her. And hitherto one means of judging had been altogether denied to him; he had never had an opportunity of observing her ways with other men.

This third evening he watched her jealously, testing her dealings with him by her behaviour to the boarders, and notably to Spinks and Soper. For Lucia, whether she was afraid of hurting the feelings of these people, or whether she hesitated to establish herself altogether in Mr. Rickman's study, had determined to spend the first hours after dinner in the drawing-room. Miss Roots protested against these weak concessions to the social order. " You'll never be able to stand them, dear," she said; " they're terrible."

But Lucia had her way. " You've stood them for five years," said she.

" Yes, but I've had my work, and I'm used to it; and in any case I'm not Miss Lucia Harden."

" Mr. Rickman stands them."

" Does he? You wouldn't say so if you'd known him for five years."

" I wonder why he stayed."

" Do you? Perhaps Miss Flossie could enlighten you."

" Of course. I was forgetting her."

" Don't forget her," said Miss Roots drily; " she's important."

Miss Roots went up to the study, and Lucia turned into the drawing-room. She owned to herself that what took her there was not so much an impulse of politeness as an irresistible desire to know what manner of people Keith Rickman had had to live among. In those evenings the scene had grown familiar to her; the long room with the three tall windows looking on the street; the Nottingham lace curtains tied with yellow sashes in the middle; the vivid blue-green painting of the wood-work, a bad match for the wall-paper; the oleographs and pier-glasses in their gilded frames; the carpet, with its monstrous, meaningless design in brown and amber; the table, secretary, and cabinet of walnut wood whose markings simulated some horrible discolouration of decay; the base company of chairs, and the villainous little maroon velvet ottoman, worn by the backs of many boarders; and beyond the blue-green folding doors the dim little chamber looking on a mews. And the boarders, growing familiar, too, to her sensitive impressionable brain; Miss Bramble, upright in her morning gown and poor little lace cap and collar; Mrs. Downey sitting, flushed and weary, in the most remote and most uncomfortable chair; Mr. Spinks reading the paper with an air of a man engaged in profound literary research; the two girls sitting together on the ottoman under the gaselier; Mr. Soper wandering uneasily among them, with his insignificant smile and his offerings of bon-bons; and Keith Rickman sitting apart, staring at his hands, or looking at Flossie with his blue, deep-set, profoundly pathetic eyes. For that pretty lady's sake, how he must have suffered in those five years.

Rickman, from his retreat in the back drawing-room, watched her ways. She was kind to Miss Bramble. She was kind to that old ruffian Partridge, whose neck he would willingly have wrung. She was kind, good heavens! yes, she was kind to Soper. When the commercial gentleman approached her with his infernal box of bon-bons, she took one. He could have murdered Soper. He was profoundly depressed by the spectacle of Lucia's ways. If she behaved like that to every one, what had he to go upon?

Nothing, nothing; it was just her way. And yet, he did not exactly see her sending messages to Soper.

He rose and opened the grand piano that stood in the back drawing-room. He went up to her (meeting with a nervous smile Flossie's inquiring look as he passed). He stood a moment with one arm on the chimney-piece, and waited, looking down at Lucia. Presently she raised her head and smiled, as surely she could never have smiled at Soper.

"Do you want me to play for you?" she said.

"That is exactly what I wanted." He drew the flattering inference that, while apparently absorbed in conversation with Miss Bramble, she had been aware of his presence in the background, and of every movement he had made.

"Well, I must ask our hostess first, mustn't I?"

She went to that lady and bent over her with her request.

If Lucia's aim was to give pleasure she had certainly achieved it. Mrs. Downey may or may not have loved music, but she was visibly excited at the prospect of hearing it. So were the boarders. They settled themselves solemnly in their seats. Spinks crushed his noisy newspaper into a ball and thrust it behind him; Miss Bramble put away her clicking needles; while Mr. Soper let himself sink into a chair with elaborate silence; one and all (with the exception of Mr. Partridge, who slept) they turned their faces, politely expectant, towards the inner room. It struck Lucia that in this the poor things were better mannered than many a more aristocratic audience.

Rickman lit the candles on the piano and seated himself beside her.

"I know what I have got to play," said she.

"What?"

"The Sonata Appassionata, isn't it?"

"Fancy your remembering!"

"Of course I remember. It isn't every one who cares for Beethoven. I'm afraid the others won't like it, though."

"They've got to like it," he said doggedly.

And Lucia, with her fatal passion for giving pleasure, played. And as the stream of music flowed through the half-lit room, it swept away all sense of his surroundings, all memory of the love and truth and honour pledged to his betrothed, and every little scruple of pity or of conscience. It bore down upon the barriers that stood between him and Lucia, and swept them away too. And the secret sources of his inspiration, sealed for so many months, were opened and flowed with the flowing of the stream; and over them the deep flood of his longing and his misery rose and broke and mingled with the tumult. And through it, and high above it all, it was as if his soul made music with her; turning the Sonata Appassionata into a singing of many voices, a symphony of many strings.

So lost was he that he failed to perceive the effect of her playing on the audience of the outer room. Flossie sat there, very quiet in her awe; Miss Bishop kept her loose mouth open, drinking in the sounds; Mr. Soper leaned forward breathing heavily in a stupid wonder; there, over the tops of the chairs, one up-standing ribbon on Miss Bramble's cap seemed to be beating time to the music all by itself; while Mrs. Downey flushed and swelled with pride at the astonishing capabilities of her piano. He did not notice either that, as Lucia played the tender opening bars of the Sonata, Mr. Partridge shook off the slumber that bound him in that hour; that, as she struck the thundering chords that signal the presto Finale, he raised his head like an old war-horse at the sound of the trumpet. He stared solemnly at Lucia as she came forward followed by Rickman; then he rose from his own consecrated chair, heavily but with a certain dignity suited to the moral grandeur of the act, and made a gesture of abdication.

" I was a professional myself once," said he. " My instrument was the flute."

There was no doubt about the spirit of Lucia's reception that night. Perhaps the finest appreciation of connoisseurs had never touched her more than did the praise of that simple audience. Rickman was the only one who did not thank her. For when her playing was over he had turned suddenly very cold, seized with a fierce shivering, the reaction from the tense fever of his nerves; and it was with difficulty that he controlled the chattering of his teeth. But before they parted for the night he asked if he might " call " some afternoon; his tone pointing the allusion to the arrangement that permitted this approach. " We can't talk very well here, can we?" he said.

She answered by inviting him and Miss Walker to tea

the next day. He was conscious of a base inward exultation when he heard poor Flossie say that she could only look in later for a little while. In October, work was heavy at the Bank, and the Beaver seldom got home till after tea-time. His conscience asked him sternly if he had reckoned on that too?

When to-morrow came, Miss Roots was busy also, and disappeared after tea. He had certainly reckoned on that disappearance.

There was a moment of embarrassment on his part when he found himself alone with Lucia in the room (his room) that he had made ready for her. He had done his work so thoroughly well that the place looked as if it had been ready for her since the beginning of time.

She was tired. He remembered how tired she used to be at Harmouth; and he noticed with a pang how little it took to tire her now. She leaned back in his chair, propped by the cushions he had chosen for her (chosen with a distinct provision of the beauty of the white face and dark hair against that particular shade of greenish blue). She had been reading one of his books; it lay in her lap. Her feet rested on his fender, they stretched out towards the warmth of his fire. If only it were permitted to him always to buy things for her; always to give her the rest she needed; always to care for her and keep her warm and well. He wondered how things had gone with her those five years. Had she been happy in that college in the south? Had they been kind to her, those women; or had they tortured her, as only women can torture women, in some devilish, subtle way? Or would overwork account for the failure of her strength? He thought he saw signs in her tender face of some obscure, deep-seated suffering of the delicate nerves. Well, anyhow she was resting now. And in looking at her he rested, too, from the labour of conscience and the trouble of desire. Heart and senses were made quiet by her mere presence. If his hands trembled as they waited on her, it was not with passion, but with some new feeling, indescribable and profound. For brought so near to him as this, so near as to create the illusion of possession, she became for him something too sacred for his hands to touch.

He could count on about half an hour of this illusion

before Flossie appeared. Afraid of losing one moment of it, he began instantly on the thing he had to say.

"All this time I've been waiting to thank you for your introduction to Fielding."

" Oh," she said eagerly, " what did he say? Tell me."

He told her. As she listened he could see how small a pleasure was enough to give life again to her tired face.

" I am so glad," she said in the low voice of sincerity; " so very glad." She paused. " That justifies my belief in you. Not that it needed any justification."

" I don't know. Your cousin, who is the best critic I know, would tell you that it did."

" My cousin—perhaps. But he *does* see that those poems are great. Only he's so made that I think no greatness reconciles him to—well, to little faults, if they are faults of taste."

" Did you find many faults of taste? "

She smiled. " I found some; but only in the younger poems. There were none—none at all—in the later ones. Which of course is what one might expect."

" It is, indeed. Did you look at the dates? Did you notice that all those later things were written either at Harmouth, or after? "

" I did."

" And didn't that strike you as significant? Didn't you draw any conclusions? "

" I drew the conclusion that—that the poet I knew had worked out his own salvation."

" Exactly—the poet you knew. Didn't it occur to you that he might never have done it, if you hadn't known him? "

He looked at her steadily. The colour on her face had deepened, but her eyes, as they met his, were grave and meditative. She seemed to be considering the precise meaning of his words before she answered.

" No, it didn't."

" What, never? Think. Don't you remember how you used to help me? "

She shook her head. " I only remember that I meant to have helped you. And I was very sorry because I couldn't. But I see now how absurd it was of me; and how unnecessary."

He knew that she was thinking now of her private secretary.

"It was beautiful of you. But, you know, it couldn't have happened. It was one of those beautiful things that never can happen."

"That's why I was so sorry. I thought it must look as if I hadn't meant it."

"But you did mean it. Nothing can alter that, can it?"

"No. You must take the will for the deed."

"I do. The will is the only thing that matters."

"Yes. But—it was absurd of me—but I thought you might have been counting on it?"

"Did I count on it? I suppose I did; though I knew it was impossible. You forget that I knew all the time it was impossible. It was only a beautiful idea."

"I'm sorry, then, that it had to remain an idea."

"Don't be sorry. Perhaps that's the only way it could remain beautiful. It wouldn't have done, you know. You only thought it could because you were so kind. It was all very well for me to work for you for three weeks or so. It would have been very different when you had me on your hands for a whole year at a stretch. And it's much better for me that it never came off than if I'd had to see you sorry for it afterwards."

"If I had been sorry, I should not have let you see it."

"I should have seen it, though, whether you let me or not. I always see these things."

"But I think, you know, that I wouldn't have been sorry."

"You would! You would! You couldn't have stood me."

"I think I could."

"What, a person with a villainous cockney accent? Who was capable of murdering the Queen's English any day in your drawing-room?"

"Oh, no; whatever you do you'll never do that."

"Well, I don't know. I'm not really to be trusted unless I've got a pen in my hand. I'm better than I used to be. I've struggled against it. Still, a man who has once murdered the Queen's English always feels, you know, as if he'd got the body under the sofa. It's like homicidal mania; the poor wretch may be cured, but he lives in terror of an attack returning. He knows it doesn't matter what he is or what he does; he may live like a saint or write like an archangel; but one aitch omitted from his conversation will wreck him at the last."

" You needn't be afraid; you never omit them."

" You mean I never omit them now. But I did five years ago. I couldn't help it. Everybody about me did it. The only difference between them and me was that I knew it, and they didn't."

" You *were* conscious of it, then?"

" Conscious? Do you know that for every lapse of the sort in your presence I suffered the torments of the damned? Do you suppose I didn't know how terrible I was?"

She shook her head, this time with disapproval. " You shouldn't say these things."

" Do you mean, I shouldn't say them, or shouldn't say them to you?"

" Well, I think you shouldn't say them to me. Don't you see that it sounds as if I had done or said something to make you feel like that."

" You? Good heavens! rather not! But whatever you said or did, I couldn't help knowing how you thought of me."

" And how was that?"

" Well, as half a poet, you know, and half a hair-dresser."

" That's funny; but it's another of the things you shouldn't say. Because you know it isn't true."

" I only say them because I want you to see how impossible it was."

" For me to help you?"

" Yes."

" I do see it. It *was* impossible—but not for any of the reasons you suppose. If it had been possible——"

" What then?"

" Then, perhaps, I needn't have felt so sorry and ashamed. You know I really *am* a little bit ashamed of having asked a great poet to be my private secretary."

It was thus that she extricated herself from the embarrassing position in which his clumsiness had placed her. For he saw what she meant when she told him that he should not say these things to her. He had made her feel that she ought to defend him from the charges he had brought against himself, when she knew them to be true, when her gentleness could only have spared him at the expense of her sincerity. How beautifully she had turned it off. He refrained from the obvious petty speeches. His eyes had answered her.

"If you knew that you *had* done something for me; not a little thing, but a great one——" He paused; and in the silence they heard the sound of Flossie's feet coming up the stair. He had only just time to finish his sentence—"Would it please you or annoy you?"

She answered hurriedly; for as she rose, Flossie was knocking at the door.

"It would please me more than I can say."

"Then," he said in a voice that was too low for Flossie to hear, "you *shall* know it."

CHAPTER LVI

IT was impossible that Rickman's intimacy with Miss Harden should pass unnoticed by the other boarders. But it was well understood by Miss Roots, by Flossie, and by all of them, that any attentions he paid to her were paid strictly to his editor's cousin. And if there was the least little shade of duplicity in this explanation, his conscience held him so far guiltless, seeing that he had adopted it more on Lucia's account than his own. Incidentally, however, he was not displeased that it had apparently satisfied Flossie.

But if Flossie felt no uneasiness at the approaches of Mr. Rickman and Miss Harden, the news that Lucia was staying under the same roof with the impossible young poet could hardly be received with complacency by her relations. It threw Edith Jewdwine into an agony of alarm. Horace as yet knew nothing about it, for he was abroad. Even Edith had heard nothing until her return from her autumn holiday in Wales, when a letter from Lucia informed her that she would be staying for the next week or two with Sophie Roots in Tavistock Place. Edith was utterly unprepared for her cousin's change of plans. She had not asked Lucia to go with her to Wales; for Lucia's last idea had been to spend September and October in Devonshire with Kitty Palliser. Edith, eager for her holiday, had not stopped to see whether the arrangements with Kitty were completed; and Lucia, aware of Edith's impatience, had omitted to mention that they were not. But what made Lucia's move so particularly trying to Edith was the circumstance that relations between them had latterly been a little strained; and when Edith searched her heart she found that for this unhappy tension it was she and not Lucia who had been to blame.

And now (while Lucia was resting calmly on Mr. Rickman's sofa), in the grave and beautiful drawing-room of the old brown house at Hampstead, a refined and fastidious little lady walked up and down in a state of high nervous excitement. That little lady bore in her slight way a remarkable resemblance to her brother Horace. It was Horace in petticoats, diminutive and dark. There was the same clearness, the same distinction of feature, the same supercilious forehead, the same quivering of the high-bred nose, the same drooping of the unhappy mouth. But the flame of Edith's small steel black eyes revealed a creature of more ardour and more energy.

At the moment Edith was visited with severe compunction; an intrusive uncomfortable feeling that she had never before been thus compelled to entertain. For looking back upon the past two years she perceived that her conduct as mistress of that drawing-room and house had not always been as fastidious and refined as she could wish. The house and the drawing-room were mainly the cause of it. Before Horace became editor of *The Museion,* Edith had been mistress of a minute establishment kept up with difficulty on a narrow income. In a drawing-room seventeen feet by twelve she received with difficulty a small circle of the cultured; ladies as refined and fastidious as herself, and (after superhuman efforts on the part of these ladies) occasionally a preoccupied and superlatively married man. From this position, compatible with her exclusiveness, but not with her temperament or her ambition, Edith found herself raised suddenly to a perfect eminence of culture and refinement as head of the great editor's house. She held a sort of salon, to which her brother's reputation attracted many figures if possible more distinguished than his own. She found herself the object of much flattering attention on the part of persons anxious to stand well with Horace Jewdwine. With a dignity positively marvellous in so small a woman, her head held high and made higher still by the raised roll of her black hair, Edith reigned for three years in that long drawing-room. She laid down the law grandiloquently to the young aspirants who thronged her court; she rewarded with superb compliments those who had achieved. Happily for Edith those gentlemen were masters of social legerdemain; and they conveyed their smiles up the sleeves of their dress-coats adroitly unperceived.

And then, in the very flower of her small dynasty, Lucia came. Lucia, with her music and her youth and her indestructible charm. And the little court, fickle by its every nature, went over bodily to Lucia. To Lucia who did not want it, who would much rather have been without it, but must needs encourage it, play to it, sympathize with it, just to satisfy that instinct of hers which was so fatal and so blind. And Horace, who, to Edith's great relief, had freed himself from this most undesirable attachment, who for three years had presented every appearance of judicious apathy, Horace, perceiving that men's eyes (and women's too) loved to follow and rest upon his cousin, discovering all over again on his own account the mysterious genius of her fascination, had ended by bowing down and worshipping too. His adoration was the more profound (and in Edith's shrewd opinion more dangerous), because he kept it to himself; because it pledged him to nothing in the eyes of Lucia and the world.

But the eyes of the world, especially of the journalistic world, are exceedingly sharp; and if Lucia had not been charming in herself those literary ladies and gentlemen would have found her so, as the lady whom Horace Jewdwine was presumably about to marry. It was Hanson, Hanson of the *Courier,* who sent the rumour round, *"La reine est morte, vive la reine."* The superb despotic Edith saw herself not only deserted, but deposed; left with neither court nor kingdom; declining from the palace of royalty to the cottage of the private gentlewoman, and maintaining her imperious refinement on a revenue absurdly disproportioned to that end. Not that as yet there had been any suggestion of Edith's abdication. As yet Lucia had only spent her winter holidays at Hampstead. But when, at the end of the present summer, Lucia suddenly and unexpectedly broke down and her salary ceased with her strength, it became a question of providing her with a home for three months at the very least. Even then, the revolution was delayed; for Horace had gone abroad in the autumn. But with every month that Edith remained in power she loved power more; and in her heart she had been considering how, without scandal to the world, or annoyance to Horace, or offence to Lucia, she could put her rival delicately aside. She had long been on the look-out for easy posts for Lucia, for posts in rich and aristocratic families in the provinces, or better still for ladies in want of charming travelling companions.

But now, better, a thousand times better, that Edith should have been forced to abdicate than that Lucia should have taken herself out of the way in this fashion; a fashion so hideously suggestive of social suicide; that she should be living, within four miles of her fastidious and refined relations, in a fifth-rate boarding-house inhabited by Goodness knows whom. If only that had been all! Of course it was intolerable to think of Lucia mixing with the sort of people whom nobody but Goodness ever does know; but, after all, she wouldn't mix with them; she hadn't had time to; and if she instantly removed from the place of contamination she might yet be presented to society again without spot or taint. But it was not all. Out of the many hundred base abodes of Bloomsbury Lucia had picked out the one house she ought to have avoided, the one address which for five years her cousin Horace had been endeavouring to conceal from her; it being the address of the one disreputable, the one impossible person of his acquaintance. Rickman had appeared, as strange people sometimes did, at Edith's court; an appearance easily explained and justified by the fact that he was a genius of whom Horace Jewdwine hoped great things. But he had never been suffered in that salon when Lucia had been there. Horace had taken untold pains, he had even lied frequently and elaborately, to prevent Lucia's encountering, were it only by accident, that one impossible person; and here she was living, actually living in the same house with him. Even if Rickman could be trusted to efface himself (which wasn't very likely; for if there is anything more irrepressible than a cockney vulgarian it is a poet; and Rickman was both!), could they, could anybody trust Lucia and her idiotic impulse to be kind? To be kind at any cost. She never calculated the cost of anything; which was another irritating reflection for Miss Jewdwine. Poor as she was, she thought nothing of paying twenty-five or thirty shillings for her board and a miserable lodging, when she might—she ought—to have been living with her relations free of all expense. But there was the sting, the unspeakable sting; for it meant that Lucia would do anything, pay anything, rather than stop another week in Hampstead. And Edith knew that it was she who had made Lucia feel like that; she who had driven her to this deplorable step. Not by anything done, or said, or even implied; but by things not done, things not said, things darkly or passionately thought. For Lucia, with her terrible gift of intuition, must somehow have known all the time what Edith hardly knew, what at least she would never have recognized if she had not observed the effect on Lucia. Edith had no patience with people who were so abominably sensitive. It was all nerves, nerves, nerves. Lucia was and always had been hopelessly neurotic. And if people were to be shaken and upset by every passing current of another person's thought, it was, Edith said to herself a little pathetically, rather hard upon the other person. Nobody can help their thoughts; and there was something positively indecent in the uncanny insight that divined them. All the same, Edith, confronted with the consequences of these movements of the unfettered brain, was stung with compunction and considerable shame. Horace would be furious when he knew; more furious with Edith than Lucia. Therefore Edith was furious with Sophia Roots, the cause of this disaster, who must have known that, even if Lucia was too weak-minded to refuse her most improper invitation, that invitation ought never to have been given.

Edith had her pride, the pride of all the Jewdwines and the Hardens; and her private grievances gave way before a family catastrophe. She did not want Lucia at Hampstead; but at all cost to herself Lucia must be brought back to her cousin's house before anybody knew that she had ever left it. It was even better that Horace should marry her than that they should risk the scandal of a mésalliance, or even a passing acquaintance with a man like Rickman. She would go and fetch Lucia now, this very evening.

She went as fast as a hansom could take her, and was shown up into Rickman's room, where she had the good luck to find Lucia alone. Lucia was too tired to go out very much; and at that moment of her cousin's entrance she was resting on Mr. Rickman's sofa. As the poor poet had been so careful to remove the more telling tokens of his occupation, Edith did not see that it was Mr. Rickman's room; and she was a little surprised to find Sophia Roots so comfortably, not to say luxuriously lodged.

She lost no time in delivering her soul, lest Sophia should pop in upon them.

" Lu-*chee*-a," she said with emphasis, " I think you ought to have told me."

" Told you what? "

" Why, that you hadn't anywhere to go to, instead of coming here."

" But I didn't come here because I hadn't anywhere to go to. I came because I wanted to see something of Sophie after all these years."

" You could have seen Sophie at Hampstead. I would have asked her to stay with you if I'd known you wanted her."

" That would have been very nice of you. But I'm afraid she wouldn't have come. You see she can't leave her work at the Museum—ever, poor thing."

" Oh. Then you don't see so much of Sophie after all? "

" Not as much as I should like. But I must be somewhere; and I'm perfectly happy here."

As she rose to make tea for Edith (at the poet's table, and with the poet's brass kettle), she looked, to Edith's critical eyes, most supiciously at home. Edith's eyes, alert for literature, roamed over the book-cases before they settled on the tea-pot (the poet's tea-pot) ; but it was the tea-pot that brought her to the point. Did Lucia mix with the other boarders after all?

" This isn't a bad room," she said. " I suppose you have all your meals up here? "

" Only tea and breakfast."

" But, my dear girl, where do you lunch and dine? "

" Downstairs, in the dining-room."

" With all the other boarders? "

Lucia smiled. " Yes, all of them. You see we can't very well turn any of them out."

" Really, Lucia, before you do things like this you might stop to consider how your friends must feel about it."

" Why should they feel anything? It's all right, Edith, really it is."

" Right for you to take your meals with these dreadful people? You can't say they're not dreadful, Lucia; for they are."

" They're not half so dreadful as you might suppose. In fact you've no idea how nice they can be, some of them. Indeed I don't know one of them that isn't kind and considerate and polite in some way. Yes, polite. They're all inconceivably polite. And do you know, they all want me to stay on; and I've half a mind to stay."

" Oh, no, my dear, you're not going to stay. I've come to carry you off the very minute we've finished tea. Sophia should have known better than to bring you here."

" Poor little Sophie. If she can stand it, I might."

" That doesn't follow at all. And if you can stand it, your relations can't. So make up your mind that you're going back with me."

" It's extremely kind of you; but I should hurt Sophie's feelings terribly if I went. Why should I go?"

" Because it isn't a fit place for you to be in. To begin with, I don't suppose they feed you properly."

" You can't say I look the worse for it."

No, certainly she couldn't; for Lucia looked better than she had done for many months. In the fine air of Hampstead she had been white and languid and depressed; here in Bloomsbury she had a faint colour, and in spite of her fatigue, looked almost vigorous. What was more, her face bore out her own account of herself. She had said she was perfectly happy, and she looked it.

A horrible idea occurred to Edith. But she did not mean to speak of Rickman till she had got Lucia safe at Hampstead.

" Besides," said Lucia simply, " I'm staying for the best of all possible reasons; because I want to."

" Well, if it's pleasant for you, you forget that it's anything but pleasant for Horace and me. Horace—if you care what he thinks—would be exceedingly annoyed if he knew about it."

" Isn't he just a little unreasonable?"

" He is not. Is it nice for him to know that you prefer living with these people to staying in his house? "

" What would he say if he knew that one of these people lent us this room? "

The words and the smile that accompanied them challenged Edith to speak; and speak she must. But she could not bring herself to utter the abominable name. "And was that on Sophie's account or yours? "

" On both our accounts; and it was beautifully done."

" Oh, if it was done beautifully there's no doubt on whose account it was done. I should have thought you were the last person, Lucia, to put yourself under such an obligation."

" There was no obligation. It was kinder to Mr. Rickman to take his room than refuse it, that was all."

Lucia had no difficulty whatever in bringing out the name. And that, if Edith's perceptions had not been dulled by horror, would have struck her as a favourable sign.

" Young Rickman! " Edith's astonishment was a master stroke in all that it ignored and in all that it implied of the impossibility of that person. " Your notions of kindness are more than I can understand. Whatever possessed you to take this room? If he'd offered it fifty times! "

" But it wasn't wanted."

Edith relaxed the tension of her indignant body and sank back in her chair (or rather, Mr. Rickman's chair) with an immense relief. " You mean he isn't in the house at present? "

" Oh, yes, he's in the house, I'm glad to say. Neither Sophie nor I could stand very much of the house without him."

That admission, instead of rousing Edith to renewed indignation, appeared to crush her. " Lucia," she murmured, " you are hopeless."

Another cup of tea, however, revived the spirit of remonstrance.

" I know you don't see it, Lucia, but you are laying yourself under an obligation of the worst sort; the sort that puts a woman more than anything in a man's power."

Lucia ignored the baser implication (so like Lucia). " I'm under so many obligations to Mr. Rickman already, that one more hardly counts." She hastened to appease the dumb distress now visible on her cousin's face. "I don't mean money obligations; though there's that, too— Horace knows all about it. I don't know if I can explain——" She laid her hands in her lap and looked at Edith and beyond her, with liquid and untroubled eyes; not seeing her, but seeing things very far off, invisible from Edith's point of view; which things she must endeavour, if possible, to make her see. "The kind of obligations I mean are so difficult to describe, because there's nothing to take hold of. Only, when you've once made a man believe in you and trust you, so that he comes to you ever afterwards expecting nothing but wonderful discernment, and irreproachable tact, and—and an almost impalpable delicacy of treatment, and you know that you failed in all these things just when he needed them most, you do feel some obligations. There's the obligation to make up for your blunders; the obligation to think about him in a certain way because no other way does justice to his idea of you; the obligation to show him the same consideration he showed to you; the obligation to take a simple kindness from him as he would have taken it from you——"

"My *dear* Lucia, you forget that a man may accept many things from a woman that she cannot possibly accept from him."

"Yes, but they are quite another set of things. They don't come into it at all. That's where you make the mistake, Edith. I've got—for my own sake—to behave to that man as finely as he behaved to me. I owe him a sort of spiritual redress. I always shall owe it him; but I'm doing something towards it now." She said to herself, "I am a fool to try to explain it to her. She'll never understand. I wish Kitty were here. She would have understood in a minute."

Edith did not understand. She thought that Lucia's perceptions in this matter were blunt, when they were only superlatively fine.

"All this," said she, "implies an amount of intimacy that I was not aware of."

"Intimacy? Yes, I suppose it *is* intimacy, of a sort."

"And how it could have happened with a man like that——"

" A man like what? "

" Well, my dear girl, a man that Horace wouldn't dream of allowing you to meet, even in his own house."

" Horace? You talk about my being under an obligation. It was he who helped to put me under it."

" And how? "

" By never delivering one of my messages to him; by letting him believe that I behaved horribly to him; that I sent him away and never gave him a thought—when he had been so magnificent. There were a thousand things I wanted to explain and set right; and I asked Horace for an opportunity and he never gave it me. He can't blame me if I take it now."

" If Horace did all these things, he did them for the best possible reasons. He knows rather more of this young man than you do, or could have any idea of. I don't know what he is now, but he was, at one time, thoroughly disreputable."

" Whatever *did* he do? "

" Do? He did everything. He drank; he ran after the worst sort of women—he mixes now with the lowest class of journalists in town; he lived for months, Horace says, with a horrid little actress in the next house to this."

Lucia's face quivered like a pale flame.

" I don't believe it. I don't believe it for a moment."

" It's absurd to say you don't believe what everybody knows, and what anybody here can tell you."

" I never heard a word against him here. Ask Sophie. She's known him for five years. Besides, *I* know him. That's enough."

" Lucy, when you once get hold of an idea you're blind to everything outside it."

" I take after my family in that. But no, I'm not blind. He may have gone wrong once, at some time—but never, no, I'm sure of it, since I knew him."

" Still, when a man has once lived that sort of life, the coarseness must remain."

" Coarseness? There isn't any refinement, any gentleness he isn't capable of. He's fine through and through. Stay and meet him, Edith, and see for yourself."

" I *have* met him."

" And yet you can't see? "

" I've seen all I want to see."

" Don't, Edith——"

There was a sound of feet running swiftly up the stair; the door of the adjoining room opened and shut, and a man's voice was heard singing. These sounds conveyed to Edith a frightful sense of the nearness and intimacy of the young man, and of the horror of Lucia's position. As she listened she held her cousin by her two hands in a dumb agony of entreaty.

"Horace is coming back," she whispered.

" No, Edith, it's no good. I'm going to stay till Kitty takes me."

Edith wondered whether, after all, Lucia was so very fastidious and refined; whether, indeed, in taking after her family, she did not take after the least estimable of the Hardens. There was a wild strain in them; their women had been known to do queer things, unaccountable, disagreeable, disreputable things; and Lucia was Sir Frederick's daughter. Somehow that young voice singing in the next room rubbed this impression into her. She stiffened and drew back.

" And am I to tell Horace, then, that you are happy here? "

"Yes. Tell him to come and see how happy I am."

" Very well."

As Edith opened the door to go, the voice in the next room stopped singing, and the young man became suddenly very still.

CHAPTER LVII

LUCIA lay back in her chair, wondering, not at Edith, but at herself. Her cousin's visit had been so far effectual that it had made her aware of the attitude of her own mind. If she had been told beforehand that she could be happy in a Bloomsbury boarding-house, or within any reasonable distance of such people as Miss Bishop and Mr. Soper, the thing would have appeared to her absurd. And yet it was so. She was happy among these dreadful people, as she had not been happy at Hampstead among the cultured and refined. But when she came to examine into the nature of this happiness she found that it contained no positive element; that it consisted mainly of relief, relief from the strain of an incessant anxiety and uncertainty. That the strain had been divided between her and Horace had only made it worse, for she had had the larger share of the anxiety, he of the uncertainty. Not that he was more uncertain than in the old days at Harmouth. He was less so. But she had never been anxious then. For after all they had understood each other; and apparently it was the understanding now that failed. Yet Horace had been right when he told himself that Lucia would never imply anything, infer anything, claim anything, take anything for granted on the sanction of that understanding. She would not have hurried by a look or word the slow movements of the love which somehow he had led her to believe in. Love between man and woman to her mind was a sort of genius; and genius, as she said long ago to poor Rickman, must always have about it a divine uncertainty. Yes, love too was the wind of the divine spirit blowing where it listeth, the kindling of the divine fire. She had waited for it patiently, reverently, not altogether humbly, but with a superb possession of her soul. Better to wait for years than rush to meet it, and so be tossed by the wind and shrivelled by the fire. Then, when the crash came five years ago, though she could hardly conceive it as altering her cousin's attitude, she knew that it must alter hers. The understanding had been partly a family affair; and her side of the family was now involved in debt and poverty and dishonour. When the debts were paid off, and the poverty reduced, and the honour redeemed, it would be time to reconsider the understanding. But, as it was just possible that Horace, if not exactly fascinated by her debts and all the rest of it, might feel that these very things bound him, challenged him in some sort to protection, Lucia withdrew herself from the reach of the chivalrous delivering arm. She took her stand, not quite outside the circle of the cousinly relation, but on the uttermost fringe and verge of it, where she entered more and more into her own possession. They met; they wrote long letters to each other all about art and literature and philosophy, those ancient unimpassioned themes; for, if Lucia assumed nothing herself she allowed Horace to assume that whatever interested him must necessarily interest her. In short, perceiving the horrible situation in which poor Horace had been left by that premature understanding, she did everything she could to help him out of it.

And she succeeded beyond her own or Horace's expectation.

After three years' hard work, when all the debts were paid, and she was independent, Lucia thought she might now trust herself to stay with Horace in his house at Hampstead. She had stayed there already with Edith when Horace was away, but that was different. And at first all was well; that is to say, there was no anxiety and no uncertainty. The calm and successful critic of *The Museion* knew his own mind; and Lucia said to herself that she knew hers. The understanding between them was perfect now. They were simply first cousins; each was the other's best friend; and they could never be anything else. She stood very much nearer to the heart of the circle, in the place where it was warm and comfortable and safe. If Horace could only have let her stay there, all would have been well still. But a mature Lucia, a Lucia entirely self-possessed, calm and successful, too, in her lesser way; a Lucia without any drawbacks, and almost to his mind as uncertain as himself; a Lucia who might be carried off any day before his eyes by some one of the many brilliant young men whom it was impossible not to introduce to her, proved fatally disturbing to Horace Jewdwine. And it was then that the anxiety and uncertainty began.

They were at their height in the sixth year, when Lucia broke down and came to Hampstead to recover. Fate (not Lucia, of course; you could not think such things about Lucia) seemed anxious to precipitate matters, and Jewdwine in his soul abhorred precipitancy. Edith, too, was secretly alarmed, and Lucia could read secrets. But it was to avoid, both a grossly pathetic appeal to the emotions and an appearance of collusion with the intrigues of Fate, that Lucia had feigned recovery and betaken herself to Sophie in Tavistock Place, before, and (this was subtlety again), well, before the return of Horace from his holiday. And if the awful reflection visited her that this step might prove to be a more importunate appeal than any, to be a positive forcing of his hand, Edith had dissipated it by showing very plainly that the appeal was to their pride and not their pity.

Lucia did not consider herself by any means an object of pity. She was happy. The absence of intolerable tension was enough to make her so. As for the society she was thrown with, after the war of incessant subtleties and uncertainties, there was something positively soothing in straightforward uninspired vulgarity. These people knew their own minds, if their minds were not worth knowing; and that was something. It seemed to her that her own mind was growing healthier every day; till, by the time Edith visited her, there was no need to feign recovery, for recovery had come. And with it had come many benign and salutary things; the old delicious joy of giving pleasure; a new sense of the redeeming and atoning pathos of the world; all manner of sweet compunctions and tender tolerances; the divine chance, she told herself, for all the charities in which she might have failed. There had come Sophie. And there had come, at last, in spite of everything, Keith Rickman.

As for Keith Rickman, her interest in him was not only a strong personal matter, but it had been part of the cool intellectual game she had played, for Horace's distraction and her own deception; a game which Horace, with his subterfuges and suppressions, had not played fair. But when, seeking to excuse him, she began to consider the possible motives of her cousin's behaviour, Lucia was profoundly disturbed.

It had come to this: if Horace had cared for her he might have had a right to interfere. But he did not care. Therefore, no interference, she vowed, should come between her and her friendship for the poet who had honoured her by trusting her. She could not help feeling a little bitter with Horace for the harm he had done her, or rather, might have done her in Keith Rickman's eyes.

For all that she had now to make amends.

CHAPTER LVIII

MEANWHILE the Beaver, like a sensible Beaver, went on calmly furnishing her house. She thoroughly approved of Keith's acquaintance with Miss Harden, as she approved of everything that gave importance to the man she was going to marry. If she had not yet given a thought to his work, except as a way (rather more uncertain and unsatisfactory than most ways) of making money, she thought a great deal of the consideration it brought him with that lady. She was prouder of Keith now than she ever had been before. But the Beaver was before all things a practical person; and she had perceived further that for Keith to make up to people like Miss Harden was one of the surest and quickest means of getting on. Hitherto she had been both distressed and annoyed by his backwardness in making up to anybody. And when Keith told her that he wanted to pay some attention to his editor's cousin, if she was a little surprised at his unusual display of smartness (for when had Keith been known to pay attention to any editors, let alone their cousins?), she accepted the explanation as entirely natural. She was wide awake now to the importance of *Metropolis* and Mr. Jewdwine. By all means, then, let him cultivate Mr. Jewdwine's cousin. And if there had been no Mr. Jewdwine in the case, Flossie would still have smiled on the acquaintance; for it meant social advancement, a step nearer Kensington. So nobody was more delighted than Flossie when Miss Harden invited Keith to tea in her own room; especially as she was always included in the invitation.

It was Miss Bishop, primed with all the resources of her science, who looked upon these advances with alarm. It struck Miss Bishop that Miss Harden and Mr. Rickman were going it pretty strong. She wouldn't have liked those goings on if she'd been Flossie. You might take it from her that gentlemen never knew their own minds when there were two to choose from; and Miss Bishop hadn't a doubt that it was a toss-up between Flossie and Miss Harden. Miss Harden would be willing enough; anybody could see that. Ladies don't keep on asking gentlemen to have tea with them alone in their rooms if they're not up to something.

It was not only Miss Bishop's fatal science that led her to these conclusions, but the still more fatal prescience of love. When Flossie was once securely married to Mr. Rickman the heart of Spinks would turn to her for consolation, that she knew. It was a matter of common experience that gentlemen's hearts were thus caught on the rebound. But if that Miss Harden carried off Rickman, there would be nothing left for Flossie but to marry Spinks, for the preservation of her trousseau and her dignity. Therefore Miss Bishop was more than ever set on Flossie's marrying Mr. Rickman.

They were turning over the trousseau, the trousseau which might play such a disastrous part in the final adjustment of Flossie's mind.

"Your dresses are orfully smart and that," said Ada; "and yet somehow they don't seem to do you justice. It would have been worth your while to go to a tip-top dressmaker, my dear. You'd have a better chance than that Miss Harden any day. No, I don't like you in that powder blue; I don't, really." Miss Bishop was nothing if not frank.

"I never go wrong about a colour," said Flossie passionately.

"No. It isn't the colour. It's the cut. It makes her look as if she 'ad a better figure than you; and that's nonsense. You've got a bust, and she hasn't. Gentlemen don't care to look at a girl who's as flat as two boards back and front. That's what I say, it's the cut that gives her her style."

"No, it isn't. It isn't her clothes at all; it's the way she carries them. She may look as if she was well-dressed, but she isn't."

"Anyhow I like that coat of hers better than yours."

"It hasn't got the new sleeves," said Flossie fondling her powder-blue.

It was this immobile complacency of hers, in the face of his own profound and sundering agitations, that stirred in Rickman the first stinging of remorse. For he could see that the poor Beaver, with her blind and ineradicable instinct, was going on building—you couldn't call them castles in the air—but houses such as Beavers build, houses of mud in running water. Her ceaseless winding in and out of shops, her mad and furious buying of furniture, her wild grasping at any loose articles that came in her way, from rugs to rolling-pins, appeared to him as so many futile efforts to construct a dam. Over and over again the insane impulse came on him to seize her little hands and stop her; to tell her that it was no good, that the absurd thing could never stand, that he alone knew the strength of the stream, its sources and its currents. But he hadn't the heart to tell her, and the Beaver went on constructing her dam, without knowing that it was a dam, because she was born with the passion thus to build.

She could not see that anything had happened, and Heaven forbid that he should let her see. He might abandon hope, but the Beaver he could not abandon. That was not to be thought of for an instant. He was too deeply pledged for that. Lest he should be in danger of forgetting, it was brought home to him a dozen times a day.

The very moment when Flossie was making that triumphant display of her wedding finery, he had caught a glimpse of her (iniquitously) as he passed her room on his way to Spinks's. She was standing, a jubilant little figure, in the line of the half-open door, shaking out and trailing before her some white, shiny, frilly thing, the sight of which made him shudder for the terror, and sigh for the pity of it. And the girls' laughter and the banging of the door as he went by, what was it but a reminder of the proprieties and decencies that bound him? A hint that he had pledged himself thrice over by that unlawful peep?

It seemed to him that was the beginning of many unlawful glimpses, discoveries of things he ought never to have seen. Was it that he was more quick to see? Or that Flossie was less careful than she had been? Or was it simply the result of living in this detestable boarding-house, where, morally speaking, the doors were never shut? Propinquity, that had brought them together, had done its best for Flossie and its worst. It had revealed too little and too much. He had only to forget her for a week, to come back and see her as she really was; to wonder what he had ever seen in her. Her very prettiness offended him. Her flagrantly feminine contours, once admired, now struck him as exaggerated, as an emphasis of the charm which is most subduing when subdued. As for her mind, good heavens! Had it taken him five years to discover that her mind was a *cul de sac?* When he came to think of it, he had to own that intellectually, conversationally even, he had advanced no farther with her than on the first day of their acquaintance. There was something compact and immovable about Flossie. In those five years he had never known her change or modify an opinion of people or of things. And yet Flossie was not stupid, or, if she were, her stupidity was a force; it had an invincible impetus and sweep, dragging the dead weight of character behind it. It was beginning to terrify him. In fact he was becoming painfully sensitive to everything she said or did. Her little tongue was neither sharp nor hard, and yet it hurt him every time it spoke. It did not always speak good grammar. Sometimes, in moments of flurry or excitement, an aspirate miscarried. Happily those moments were rare; for at bottom Flossie's temperament was singularly calm. Remembering his own past lapses, he felt that he was the last person to throw a stone at her; but that reflection did not prevent a shudder from going down his back every time it happened. And if her speech remained irreproachable, the offending strain ran through all her movements. He disliked the way she walked, and the way she sat down, the way she spread her skirts or gathered them, the way she carried her body and turned her head, the way her black eyes provoked a stare and then resented it, her changes of posture under observation, the perpetual movement of her hands that were always settling and resettling her hat, her hair, her veil; all the blushings and bridlings, the pruderies and impertinences of the pretty women of her class, he disliked them all. He more than disliked, he distrusted her air of over-strained propriety. He detected in it the first note of falseness in her character. In a thousand little things her instincts, her perceptions, were at fault.

This was disagreeably borne in upon him that first Saturday after Lucia's arrival, when he and Flossie were in the train going down to Ealing. The compartment was packed with City men (how he wished Flossie would turn her head and not her eyes if she must look at them!); and as they got in at Earl's Court, one of them, a polite person, gave up his seat to the lady. Flossie turned an unseeing eye on the polite person, and took his seat with a superb pretence of having found it herself after much search. And when Rickman said " Thanks " to the polite person her indignant glance informed him that she had expected support in her policy of repudiation.

" My dear Beaver," he said as he helped her on to the platform at Ealing, " when you take another person's seat the least you can do is to say thank you."

" I *never* speak to gentlemen in trains and 'buses. That's the way they always begin."

" Good Heavens, the poor man was only being civil."

" Thank you. I've gone about enough to know what 'is kind of civility means. I wasn't going to lay myself open to impertinence."

" I should have thought you'd gone about enough to know the difference."

Flossie said nothing. She was furious with him for his failure to defend her from the insulting advances of the City gentleman. But perhaps she would hardly have taken it so seriously, if it had not been significant to her of a still more intolerable desertion. Ada Bishop had said something to her just before they started, something that had been almost too much even for Flossie's complacency.

" I'm glad," she still heard Ada saying, " you're going to take him out all day. If I were you I shouldn't let him see too much of that Miss Harden."

There hadn't been much to take hold of in Ada's words, but Ada's manner had made them unmistakable; and from that moment a little worm had begun to gnaw at Flossie's heart.

And he, as he looked at her with that strange new sight of his that was already bringing sorrow to them both, he said to himself that he supposed it was her " going about," her sad acquaintance with unlovely manners, that had made her as she was. Only how was it that he had never noticed it before? Poor little girl; it was only last Saturday when they had come back from looking over the house at Ealing that, drawing upon all the appropriate resources of natural history, he had called her a little vesper Vole, because she lived in a bank and only came out of it in the evening. What Flossie called him that time didn't matter; it was her parsimony in the item of endearments that provoked him to excesses of the kind. And now the thought of those things made him furious; furious with himself;

furious with Fate for throwing Flossie in his way; furious
with Flossie for being there. And when he was ready to
damn her because she was a woman, he melted, and could
have wept because she was a Beaver. Poor little girl; one
day to be called a vesper Vole, the next to be forgotten
altogether, the next to be remembered after this fashion.

And so they went on silently together, Flossie in pain
because of the little worm gnawing at her heart, he thinking many things, sad and bitter and tender things, of the
woman walking by his side. From time to time she looked
at him as she had looked at those City gentlemen, not turning her head, but slewing the large dark of her eye into its
corner. Presently she spoke.

"You don't seem to have very much to say for yourself
to-day."

"To-day? I'm not given to talking very much at any
time."

"Oh, come, you don't seem to have any difficulty in
talking to Miss Harden. I've heard you. Wot a time you
did sit yesterday. And you were up there an hour or more
before I came, I know."

"Three-quarters of an hour, to be strictly accurate."

"Well, that was long enough, wasn't it?"

"Quite long enough for all I had to say."

Now that was playing into Flossie's hands, for it meant
that he had had nothing to say after her arrival. And she
was sharp enough to see it.

"That's all very well, Keith," said she, apparently ignoring her advantage, "but Ada says they'll be talking if she
keeps on asking you up there just when she's all by herself. It's not the thing to do. I wouldn't do it if it was
me, no more would Ada."

"My dear child, Miss Harden may do a great many
things that you and Ada mayn't. Because, you see, she
knows how to do them and you don't."

"Oh, well, if you're satisfied. But it isn't very nice for
for me to 'ave you talked about, just when we're going to be
married, is it?"

"I think you needn't mind Ada. Miss Harden knows
that I *have* to see her sometimes, and that I can't very well
see her in any other way. And I think you might know
it too."

" Oh, don't you go thinking I'm jealous. I know *you're* all right."

" If I'm all right, who's wrong? "

" Well—of course I understand what you want with *her;* but I can't see what she wants with you."

" You *little* fool. What should she want, except to help me? "

Flossie said nothing to that, for indeed her mind had not formulated any clear charge against Miss Harden. Keith had annoyed her and she wanted to punish him a little. She was also curious to see in what manner the chivalry that had deserted her would defend Miss Harden.

He stood still and looked at her with brilliant, angry eyes.

" You don't understand a great deal, Flossie; but there's one thing you *shall* understand—You are not to say these things about Miss Harden. Not that you'll do her any harm, mind, by saying them. Think for one minute who and what she is, and you'll see that the only person you are harming is yourself."

Flossie did think for a minute, and remembered that Lucia was the daughter of a baronet and the cousin of an editor; and she did see that this time she had gone a bit too far.

" And in injuring yourself, you know, you injure me," he said more gently. " I don't know whether that will appeal at all to you."

It did appeal to her in the sense in which her practical mind understood that injury.

" Do you really think she'll be able to help you to a good thing? "

He laughed aloud. " I think she'll help me to many good things. She has done that already."

" Oh, well then, I suppose it's all right."

Though he said it was all right he knew that it was all wrong; that she was all wrong too. He wondered again how it was that he had never noticed it before. It seemed to him now that he must always have seen it, and that he had struggled not to see it, as he was struggling now.

Struggle as he would, he knew that he was only putting off the inevitable surrender. Putting off the moment that must face him yet, at some turning of the stair or opening of a door, as they went from room to room of the house that, empty, had once seemed to him desirable, and now, littered with the solid irrevocable results of Flossie's furnishing, inspired him with detestation and despair. How could he ever live in it? He and his dream, the dream that Lucia had told him was divorced from reality? She had told him too that his trouble all lay there, and he remembered that then as now she had advised a reconcilation. But better a divorce than reconcilation with any of the realities that faced him now. Better even illusion than these infallible perceptions. Better to be decently, charitably blind where women are concerned, than to see them so; to see poor Flossie as she was, a reality divorced from any dream.

A foolish train of thought that. As if he were only a dreamer. As if it were a dream that had to do with it. As if his dream had not long ago loved, followed, and embraced a divine reality. As if it had ever fallen away after that one superb act of reconciliation.

He had done poor Flossie some injustice. She suffered in his eyes because she came short, not of the dream, but of the reality. To be placed beside Lucia Harden would have been a severe test for any woman; but for Flossie it was cruelty itself. He had never subjected her to that, not even in thought; for he felt that the comparison, cruel to one woman, was profanation to the other. It was only feminine Fate who could be so unkind as to put those two side by side, that he might look well, and measure his love for Flossie by his love for Lucia, seeing it, too, as it was. Maddox had not been far wrong there. For anything spiritual in that emotion, he might as well have gone back to Poppy Grace. Better; since between him and Flossie that gross tie, once formed, could not be broken. Better; since there had at least been no hypocrisy in his relations with the joyous Poppy. Better anything than this baseness skulking under the superstition of morality. If a man has no other feeling for an innocent woman than that, better that a millstone should be hanged about his neck than that he should offend by marrying her.

And yet there had been something finer and purer in this later love than in the first infatuation of his youth. On that day, seven days ago, the last day it had to live, he had been touched by something more sacred, more immortal than desire. There had been no illusion in the poetry that clothed the figure of a woman standing in an empty room, dearer to her than the bridal chamber; a woman whose face grew soft as her instinct outran the bridal terror and the bridal joy, divining beyond love the end that sanctifies it.

But beyond all that again he could see that, whereas the love of all other women had torn him asunder, the love of Lucia made him whole. Poppy had drawn him by his senses; Flossie by his senses and his heart; Lucia held him by his senses, his heart, his intellect, his will, by his spirit, by his genius, by the whole man. Long after his senses had renounced their part in her, the rest of him would cling to her, satisfied and appeased. And but for Flossie it would have been so even now. Though his senses had rest in Lucia's presence, their longing for her was reawakened, not only by the thought of his approaching marriage, but by the memory of that one moment when he had realized the mystery of it, the moment of poor Flossie's transfiguration, when he had seen through the thick material veil, deep into the spiritual heart of love. With Lucia the veil had been transparent from the first. It was not with her as it was with those women who must wait for the hour of motherhood to glorify them. Of those two years of his betrothal what was there that he would care to keep? Only one immortal moment, that yet knew of the mortality before and after it. While of the last seven days Lucia had made a whole heavenly procession of ascending hours, every moment winged with the immortal fire. Flying moments; but flame touched flame in flying, and they became one life.

But he was going to marry Flossie.

And she, the child that was to have borne the burden of his genius and his passion; poor little blameless victim of the imagination that glorifies desire, how would it be with her in this empty house, empty of the love she had looked for and would never find? How would it be with him? Had he pledged himself to a life of falsehood, and had he yet to know what torment awaited him at the hands of the avenging truth? Truth, as he had once defined it, was the soul of the fact. It was the fact that he was going to marry Flossie; but it was not the truth. Only love

could have given it a soul and made it true. If he was
bound to maintain that it had a soul when it hadn't, that
was where the falseness would come in.

Yet no. He might go mad by thinking about it, but
life after all was simpler than thought. Things righted
themselves when you left off thinking about them. He
would be unhappy; but that could only make Flossie unhappy if she cared for him. And in a year's time, when
he had left off thinking, she would have left off caring.
He had shrewdly divined that what Flossie chiefly wanted
was to have children; or if she did not want it, Nature
wanted it for her, which came to the same thing. As for
mating her to a man of genius, that was just Nature's
wanton extravagance. Maddox had once said that any
man would have done as well, perhaps better; Flossie
wouldn't care. Well, he would give her children, and she
would care for them. Indeed, he sincerely hoped that for
him she would not care. It would make things simpler.
Maddox, he remembered, had also said that she was the
sort of woman who would immolate her husband for
her children; whereas Poppy—but then, Maddox was a
beast.

It never occurred for a moment to him to throw Flossie
over. That, he had settled once for all, could not now be
done. Circumstances conspired to make the thing irrevocable. Her utter dependence on him, the fact that she
had no home but the one he offered her, no choice between
marriage and earning her own living in a way she hated,
the flagrant half-domestic intimacy in which they had
been living, more than all, the baseness of his past love,
and the inadequacy of his present feeling for her, both
calling on him to atone, all these things made a promise
of marriage as binding as the actual tie. Their engagement
might possibly have been broken off at any of its earlier
stages without profound dishonour. It was one thing to
jilt a girl within a decent interval of the first congratulations, another thing altogether to abandon her with her
trousseau on her hands. It had gone so far that his failure
at the last moment would be the grossest insult he could
offer her.

Gross indeed; yet not so gross but that he could think
of one still grosser—to let her marry him, when he had no

feeling to offer her but such indifference as marriage deepens to disgust, or such disgust as it tones down into indifference. Would he go on shuddering and wincing as he had shuddered and winced to-day? Passion, that might have condoned her failings, was out of the question; but would it be possible to keep up the decent appearance of respect?

And yet he was going to marry her.

That was impressed on him by Flossie's voice saying that if he wouldn't decide which of those two rooms was to be *their* room, she must. Because the men wanted to put up the bedstead.

It was an intimation that he was bound to her, not by any fine ties of feeling or of honour, but by a stout unbreakable chain of material facts. He looked out of the window. The vans were unloading in the street. It seemed to him that there was something almost grossly compromising in the wash-stand, dumped down there in the garden; and as the bedstead was being borne into the house in portions, reverentially, processionally, he surrendered before that supreme symbol of finality. As he made his bed, he must lie; even if it was a brass bed with mother-o'-pearl ornaments; and he refused to listen to the inner voice which suggested that the bed was not made yet, it was not even paid for, and that he would be a fool to lie on it. He turned sad eyes on the little woman so flushed and eager over her packages. He had committed himself more deeply with every purchase they had made that day. How carefully he had laboured at his own destruction.

He had gone so far with these absurd reflections, that when Flossie exclaimed, " There, after all I've forgotten the kitchen hammer," his nerves relaxed their tension, and he experienced a sense of momentary but divine release. And when she insisted on repairing her oversight as they went back, he felt that the kitchen hammer had clinched the matter; and that if only they had not bought it he might yet be free.

There was something in the Beaver's building after all.

CHAPTER LIX

H E did not appear that evening, not even to listen to
Lucia's music, for his misery was heavy upon him.
Mercifully, he was able to forget it for a while in attending
to the work that waited for him; an article for *The Planet*
to be written; proofs to correct and manuscripts to look
through for *Metropolis;* all neglected till the last possible
moment, which moment had now come. For once he
reaped the benefit of his reckless habits of postponement.

But four hours saw him through it; and midnight recalled him to his care. Instead of undressing he refilled
his lamp, made up his fire, and drew his chair to the hearth.
There was a question, put off, too, like his work, from hour
to hour, and silenced by the scuffling, meaningless movements of the day. It related to the promise he had made
to Lucia Harden at the end of their last interview. He
had then said to her that, since she desired it, she should
know what it was that she had done for him. Hitherto
he had determined that she should not know it yet; not
know it till death had removed from her his embarrassing,
preposterous personality. The gift of knowledge that she
might have refused from the man, she could then accept
from the poet. The only condition that honour, that
chivalry, insisted on was the removal of the man. But
there were other ways of getting rid of a man besides the
clumsy device of death. Might he not be considered to
have effaced himself sufficiently by marriage? As far as
Lucia was concerned he could see very little difference
between the two processes; in fact, marriage was, if anything, the safer. For the important thing was that she
should know somehow; that he should hand over his gift
to her before it was too late. And suppose—suppose he
should fail to remove himself in time? Beholding the
years as they now stretched before him, it seemed to him
that he would never die.

There was another consideration which concerned his
honour, not as a man, but as a poet. He knew what it was
in him to do. The nature of the gift was such that if he
brought it to her to-day she would know that he had given
her his best; if he kept it till to-morrow it would be his

best no longer. Besides, it was only a gift when you looked at it one way. He was giving her (as he believed) an immortal thing; but its very immortality gave it a certain material value. The thing might be sold for much, and its price might go far towards covering that debt he owed her, or it might be held by her as a sort of security. He could see that his marriage would be a hindrance to speedy payment on any other system.

He rose, unlocked a drawer, and took from it the manuscript of the nine and twenty sonnets and the sealed envelope that contained his testament concerning them. He had looked at them but once since he had put them away three years ago, and that was on the night of his engagement. Looking at them again he knew he was not mistaken in his judgment, when calmly, surely, and persistently he had thought of the thing as immortal. But according to another condition that his honour had laid down, its immortality depended upon her. At this point honour itself raised the question whether it was fair to throw on her the burden of so great a decision? She might hesitate to deny him so large a part of his immortality, and yet object to being so intimately, so personally bound up with it. He could see her delicate conscience straining under the choice.

But surely she knew him well enough to know that he had left her free? She would know that he could accept nothing from her pity, not even a portion of his immortality. She would trust his sincerity; for that at any rate had never failed her. And since what he had written he had written, she would see that unless he destroyed it with his own hands the decision as to publication must rest with her. It concerned her so intimately, so personally, that it could not be given to the world without her consent. Whether what he had written should have been written was another matter. If she thought not, if her refinement accused him of a sin against good taste, that would only make his problem simpler. Even if her accusation remained unspoken, he would know it, he would see it, through whatever web her tenderness wrapped round it. His genius would contend against her judgment, would not yield a point to her opinion, but his honour would take it as settling the question of publication. In no case should she be able to say or think that he had used his genius as a cover for a cowardly passion, or that by compelling her admiration he had taken advantage of her pride.

But would she say it or think it? Not she. He knew her. And if his knowledge had brought much misery, it brought consolation too. Where Lucia was concerned he had never been sustained by any personal conceit; he had never walked vainly in the illusion of her love. At that supreme point his imagination had utterly broken down; he had never won from it a moment's respite from his intolerable lucidity. There was a certain dignity about his despair, in that, of all the wonderful web of his dreams, he had made no fine cloak to cover it. It shivered and suffered in a noble nakedness, absolutely unashamed. But one thing he knew also, that if Lucia did not love him, she loved his genius. Even when lucidity made suffering unendurable, he had still the assurance that his genius would never suffer at her hands. For did she not know that God gives the heart of a poet to be as fuel to his genius, for ever consumed and inconsumable? That of all his passions his love is the nearest akin to the divine fire? She of all women would never deny him the eternal right to utterance.

Neither could she well find fault with the manner of it. He went through the sonnets again, trying to read them with her woman's eyes. There was nothing, nothing, not an image, not a word, that could offend. Here was no " flaming orgy of individuality." He had chosen purposely the consecrated form that pledged him to perfection, bound him to a magnificent restraint.

There still remained the scruple as to the propriety of choosing this precise moment for his gift. It was overridden by the invincible desire to give, the torturing curiosity to know how she would take it.

One more last scruple, easily disposed of. In all this there was no disloyalty to the woman he was going to make his wife. For the Sonnets belonged to the past in which she had no part, and to the future which concerned her even less.

The next day, then, at about five o'clock, the time at which Lucia had told him she would be free, he came to her, bringing his gift with him.

Lucia's face gladdened when she saw the manuscript in his hand; for though they had discussed very freely what he had done once, he had been rather sadly silent, she thought, as to what he was doing now. He had seemed to her anxious to avoid any question on the subject. She had wondered whether his genius had been much affected by his other work; and had been half afraid to ask lest she should learn that it was dead, destroyed by journalism. She had heard so much of the perils of that career, that she had begun to regret her part in helping him to it. So that her glance as it lighted on the gift was, he thought, propitious.

He drew up his chair near her (he had not to wait for any invitation to do that now), and she noticed the trembling of his hands as he spread the manuscript on his knees. He had always been nervous in approaching the subject of his poems, and she said to herself, " Has he not got over that ? "

Apparently he had not got over it; for he sat there for several perceptible moments sunk in the low chair beside her, saying nothing, only curling and uncurling the sheets with the same nervous movement of his hand. She came to his help smiling.

" What is it ?　New poems ? "

" No, I don't think I can call them new.　I wrote them four or five years ago."

He saw that some of the gladness died out of her face, and he wondered why.

" Were you going to read them to me ? "

" Good Heavens, no."　He laughed the short laugh she had heard once or twice before that always sounded like a sob.

" I don't want to read them to you.　I want to give them to you——"

" To read ? "　She held out her hand.

" Yes, to read, of course, but not now."

The hand was withdrawn, evidently with some distressing consciousness of its precipitancy.

" You said the other night that you would have been glad to know that you had done something for me; and somehow I believe you meant it."

" I did, indeed."

"If you read these things you will know. There's no other way in which I could tell you; for you will see that they are part of what you did for me."

"I don't understand."

"You will, though, when you've read them. That," he said meditatively, "is why I don't want you to read them now." But then it struck him that he had blundered, introducing a passionate personal revelation under the dangerous veil of mystery. He had not meant to say, ' "What you have done for me was to make me love you," but, "I have done a great thing, and what you did for me was to make me do it." For all that she should know, or he acknowledge, the passion was the means, not the end.

"I don't want to be cryptic, and perhaps I ought to explain a little. I meant that you'll see that they're the best things I've written, and that I should not have written them if it had not been for you. I don't know whether you'll forgive me for writing them, but I think you will. Because you'll understand that I had to."

"Have you published any of them?"

It seemed to him that the question was dictated by a sudden fear.

"Rather not. I want to talk to you about that later on, when you've read them."

"When will you want them back?"

"I don't want them back at all. I brought them for you to keep."

"To keep?"

"Yes, if you care for them."

"But this is the original manuscript?" She was most painfully aware of the value of the thing.

He smiled. "Yes, I couldn't give you a copy, because there isn't one."

"What a reckless person you are. I must make a copy, then, and keep that."

"That would spoil my pleasure and my gift, too. It's only valuable because it's unique."

"Whatever it is it's sure to be that."

"I don't mean in that way altogether——" He hesitated, for he had touched a part of his subject which had to be handled gently; and he was aware that in handling it at all he was courting rejection of the gift.

" And you are going to leave it with me now? "

" Yes."

She did not look up, but kept her eyes fixed on the sheets that lay in her lap, her hands lightly covering them. Was it possible that her finger-tips had caught the secret of the page beneath them, and that their delicate nerves had already carried it to her brain? Was she considering what she was to do?

" You will see that one page is left blank; I couldn't fill it up till I knew whether you would accept the dedication."

" I? " She looked up. She was no doubt surprised; but he thought he could read something in her look that was deeper and sweeter than surprise.

" If you could, it would give me great pleasure. It's the only acknowledgment I can make for all your kindness."

" Please, please don't talk of my kindness."

" I won't. If it were any other book, it might be merely a question of acknowledgment, but this book belongs to you."

" Are you quite sure—— " She was about to question his right to offer it, which was as good as questioning his honour, as good as assuming that—— She paused, horrified as she realized what it was that she had almost assumed. Kitty had often told her that she erred through excess of subtlety. It wouldn't have mattered with anybody less subtle than Keith Rickman; but he would see it all. He did.

" Quite sure that I oughtn't to offer it to anybody else? I am quite sure. It was written four years ago, before—before I knew anybody else. It has nothing to do with anybody else, it couldn't have been dedicated to anybody else. If you don't accept it—— "

" But I do." Her eagerness was the natural recoil from her hesitation. She was so anxious to atone for that shocking blunder she had made.

" I say, how you do take things on trust."

" Some things."

" But you mustn't. You can't accept the dedication of a book you haven't read. Do you know, now I come to think of it, you've always taken me on trust? Do you remember when first I came to you—it's more than five years ago—you took me on trust then?" (Their talk had a way of running to this refrain of " Do you remember? ") " Do you remember how you said, ' I must risk it? ' "

" Yes, I remember how I insisted on keeping you, and how very unwilling you were to be kept."

" Do you mind telling me what made you want to keep me? You didn't know me in the least, you know."

" I wanted to keep you *because* you didn't want to stay. I knew then that I could trust you. But I confess that most people might not have seen it in that way."

" Well, I can't let you take these sonnets on trust. For this time, your principle doesn't apply, you see. You can't say you're accepting this dedication because I don't want to give it to you." Though he laughed, he rose and backed towards the door, suddenly anxious to be gone.

" Isn't it enough that I want to accept it? "

He shook his head, still backing, and at the door he paused to speak. " You've accepted nothing—as yet."

" Of course," she said to herself, " it would have been wiser to have read them first. But I can trust him."

But as she was about to read them a knock, a familiar knock at the door interrupted her. " Kitty! "

She laid the manuscript hastily aside, well out of Kitty's roving sight. She had noticed how his hand had trembled as he brought it; she did not notice that her own shook a little in thus putting it away from her.

Kitty Palliser, up in town for a week, had come less on her own account than as an impetuous ambassador from the now frantic Edith. She too was prepared to move heaven and earth, if only she could snatch her Lucy from Tavistock Place. But her anxiety was not wholly on Lucia's account, as presently appeared.

" How can you stand it for a minute? " said she.

" I'm standing it very well, indeed."

" But what on earth do you find to do all day long, when," said Kitty severely, " you're *not* talking to young Rickman? "

" All day long I go out, or lie down and read, or talk to Sophie."

" And in the evenings? "

" In the evenings sometimes I make an old man happy by playing."

"And I expect you're making a young man unhappy by playing, too—a very dangerous game."

"Kitty, that young man is perfectly happy. He's going to be married."

"All the worse. Then you'll make a young woman unhappy as well. This little game would be dangerous enough with a man of your own set. It isn't fair to play it with him, Lucy, when you know the rules and he doesn't."

"I assure you, Kitty, he knows them as well as you or I do; better."

"I doubt it." Kitty's eyes roamed round the room (they had not lost their alert and hungry look), and they took in the situation at a glance. That move in the game would never have been made if he had known the rules. How could she let him make it?

"Really, Lucy, for a nice woman, you do the queerest things."

"And, really, Kitty, for a clever woman, you say the stupidest. You're getting like Edith."

"I am not like Edith. I only say stupid things. She thinks them. What's more, in thinking them she only thinks of herself and her precious family. I'm thinking of you, dear, and "—Kitty's voice grew soft—" and of him. You ought to think of him a little too."

"I do think of him. I've been thinking of him all the time."

"I know you have. But don't let him suffer because of the insanely beautiful way you have of thinking."

There was a pause, in which it was evident to Kitty that Lucia was thinking deeply, and beautifully too.

"Have I made him suffer? I'm afraid I did once. He was valuable, and I damaged him."

"Yes; and ever since you've been trying to put him together again; in your own way, not his. That's fatal."

Lucia shook her head, and followed her own train of thought. "Kitty, to be perfectly honest, I think—I'm not sure, but I think—from something he said to-day that you were right about him once. I mean about his beginning to care too much. I'm afraid it was so, at Harmouth, towards the end. But it isn't so any more. He tried to tell me just now. He did it beautifully; as if he knew that that would make me happier. At least I think that's what he meant.

He didn't say much, but I'm sure he was thinking about his marriage."

"Heaven help his wife then—if he got as far as that. I suppose you take a beautiful view of her, too? Drop it, for goodness' sake, drop it."

"Not I. It would mean dropping him. It's all right, Kitty. You don't know the ways of poets."

"Perhaps not. But I know the ways of men."

Though Kitty had not accomplished her mission she so far prevailed that she carried her Lucy off to dinner.

It was somewhere towards midnight, when all the house was quiet, that Lucia first looked into Keith Rickman's sonnets. She had been led to expect something in the nature of a personal revelation, and the first sonnet struck the key-note, gave her the clue.

> I asked the minist'ring priests who never tire
>   In love's high service, who behold their bliss
>   Through golden gloom of Love's dread mysteries,
> What heaven there be for earth's foregone desire?
>
> And they kept silence. But the gentle choir
>   Who sing Love's praises answered me, "There is
>   No voice to speak of these deep sanctities,
> For Love hath sealed his servants' lips with fire.
>
> "Yet in his faithfulness put thou thy faith,
>   Though he hath bound thee in the house of pain,
>   And given thy body to the scourging years,
>   And brought thee for thy thirst the drink of tears,
>   That sorrowing thou shouldst serve him unto death;
>   For when Love reigneth, all his saints shall reign."

She kindled and flamed, her whole being one inspired and burning sympathy. She knew what it was all about. She was on the track of a Poet's Progress in quest of the beloved Perfection, Beauty, and Truth in one. Of those nine and twenty sonnets she looked for a score that should make immortal the moments of triumph and of vision, the moments of rapture and fulfilment of the heart's desire. Her glance fell now on two lines that clearly pointed to the goal of those who travel on the divine way—

> —Elysian calm and passion with no stain
>   Of mortal tears, no touch of mortal pain—

She hoped he had reached it. And more than that she hoped. She was ignorant of what his life had been before he knew her; but the *Song of Confession* had made her realize that, besides this way where the poet went invincibly, there was another where the man desired to go, where, as they were so ready to tell her, he had not always gone. But that was before she knew him. She hoped (taking her beautiful view) that, in this gift of his, he had meant to give to her who understood him some hint or sign that he had come near it also, the way of Righteousness. She looked to find many sonnets dealing with these secret matters of the soul. Therefore she approached them fearlessly, since she knew what they were all about. And since, in that curious humility of the man that went so oddly with the poet's pride, he had so exaggerated his obligation, taking, as he said, the will for the deed, and making of her desire to serve him a service actually done; since his imagination had played round her for a moment as it played round all things, transforming, magnifying, glorifying, she might perhaps find one sonnet of dedication to her who had understood him.

But when she had read them all she saw, and could not help seeing, that the whole nine and twenty were one continuous dedication—and to her. If she had found what she looked for, she found also that a revelation had been made to her of things even more sacred, more personal; a revelation that was in its way unique. He had hidden nothing, kept back nothing, not one moment of that three-weeks' passion (for so she dated it). It was all laid before her as it had been; all its immortal splendour, and all its mortal suffering and its shame. Not a line (if she could have stayed to think of that), not a word that could offend her taste or hurt her pride. The thing was perfect. She understood why it had been shown to her. She understood that he wanted to tell her that he had loved her. She understood that he never would have told her if it had not been all over. It was because it was all over that he had brought her this, to show her how great a thing she had done for him, she who thought she had done nothing. As she locked the sonnets away in a safe place for the night, in her heart there was a great pride and a still greater thankfulness and joy. Joy because it was all over, pride because it had once been, and thankfulness because it had been given her to know.

And in his room behind the wall that separated them the poet walked up and down, tortured by suspense; and said to himself over and over again, " I wonder how she'll take it."

CHAPTER LX

THAT was on a Thursday. It had been arranged earlier in the week that Flossie and he were to dine with Lucia on Friday evening. On Saturday and Sunday the Beaver would be let loose, and would claim him for her own. He could not hope to see Lucia alone before Monday evening; his suspense, then, would have to endure for the better part of four days. He had nothing to hope for from Friday evening. Lucia's manner was too perfect to afford any clue as to how she had taken it. If she were offended she would hardly let him see it before Flossie and Miss Roots. If she accepted, there again the occasion forbade her to give any sign to one of her guests that should exclude the other two. Still, it was just possible that he might gather something from her silence.

But as it happened, he had not even that to go upon. Never had Lucia been less silent than on Friday night. Not that she talked more than usual, but that all her looks, all her gestures spoke. They spoke of her pleasure in the happiness of her friend; of tenderness to the little woman whom he loved (so little and he so great); of love that embraced them both, the great and the little, a large, understanding love that was light and warmth in one. For Lucia believed firmly that she understood. She had always desired him to be happy, to be reconciled to the beautiful and glorious world; she had tried to bring about that reconciliation; and she conceived herself to have failed. And now because the thing had been done so beautifully, so perfectly (if a little unexpectedly), by somebody else, because she was relieved of all anxiety and responsibility, Lucia was rejoicing with all her heart.

He had not been five minutes in the room before he saw it all. Lucia believed that it was all over, and was letting herself go, carried away by the spectacle of a supreme and triumphal happiness. She triumphed too. Her eyes when they looked at him seemed to be saying "Didn't I tell you so?"

He saw why they had been asked to dinner. The spirit of the bridal hour was upon her, and she had made a little feast to celebrate it. Like everything she did, it was simple and beautiful and exquisite of its kind. And yet it was not with that immaculate white linen cloth, spread on Keith's writing-table, strewn with slender green foliage and set out with delicate food and fruit and wine, nor with those white flowers, nor with those six shaded candles, that she had worked the joyous tender charm. These things, in her hands and in his eyes, became sacramental, symbolic of Lucia's soul with its pure thoughts and beautiful beliefs, its inspired and burning charities.

And the hero of this feast of happiness sat at her right hand, facing his little bride-elect, a miserable man consumed with anguish and remorse. He had never had so painful a sense of the pathos of his Beaver. For if anybody was happy it was she. Flossie was aware that it was her hour, and that high honour was being paid to her. Moreover, he could see for the moment that the worm had ceased to gnaw, and that she had become the almost affectionate thrall of the lady whose motto was *Invictus*. She had been forced (poor little girl) to anticipate her trousseau in order to attire herself fitly for the occasion, and was looking remarkably pretty in her way. She sat very upright, and all her demeanour was irreproachably modest, quiet, and demure. Nothing could have been more correct than her smile, frequent, but so diminutive that it just lifted her upper lip and no more. No insight, no foreboding troubled her. Her face, soft and golden white in the candle-light, expressed a shy and delicate content. For Flossie was a little materialist through and through. Her smooth and over feminine body seemed to have grown smoother and more feminine still under the touch of pleasure; all that was hard and immobile in her melting in the sense of well-being.

It was not merely that Flossie was on her good behaviour. His imagination (in league with his conscience) suggested that the poor child, divinely protected by the righteousness of her cause, was inspired to confound his judgment of her, to give no vantage ground to his disloyalty, to throw him defenceless on his own remorse. Or was it Lucia who inspired her? Lucia, whose loving spirit could create the thing it loved, whose sweetness was of so fine and piercing a quality that what it touched it penetrated. He could not tell, but he thanked Heaven that, at least for this hour which was hers, the little thing was happy. He, for his part, by unprecedented acts of subterfuge and hypocrisy, endeavoured to conceal his agony.

Miss Roots alone divined it. Beyond looking festive in a black silk gown and a kind of white satin waistcoat, that clever lady took a strained and awkward part in the rejoicing. He was inclined to think that the waistcoat committed her to severity, until he became aware that she was watching him with a furtive sympathy in the clever eyes that saw through his pitiful play. How was it that Lucia, she who once understood him, could not divine him too?

From this estranging mood he was roused by the innocent laughter of the Beaver. He was aware of certain thin and melancholy sounds that floated up from some room below. They struggled with the noises of the street, overcame, and rose, strident and triumphant, to invade the feast. They seemed to him in perfect keeping with the misery and insanity of the hour.

It was Mr. Partridge playing on his flute.

Miss Roots looked at Lucia. "That's you, Lucy. You've been talking to him about that flute. I suppose you told him you would love to hear him play it?"

"No, Sophie, I didn't tell him that." But Lucy looked a little guilty. The flute rose as if in passionate protest against her denial. It seemed to say "You did! You know you did!"

"I only said it was a pity he'd given it up, and I meant it. But oh!" and Lucy put her hands up to her ears, "I don't mean it any more."

"That comes," said Rickman, "of taking things on trust."

She smiled and shook her head. It was her first approach to a sign of reassurance.

"That's the sort of thing she's always doing. It doesn't matter for you, Lucy. You won't have to stay on and hear him."

"I don't know. I think I shall stay on. You see, Mr. Rickman, I can't part with this pretty room."

"Do you like it?"

"I like it very much indeed. You're all coming to dine with me here again some day."

"And you must come and dine with us, Miss Harden, when we've got settled." It was Flossie who spoke.

"I shall be delighted."

He looked up, surprised. He could not have believed the Beaver could have done it so prettily. He had not even realized that it could be done at all. It never occurred to him that his marriage could bring him nearer to Lucia Harden. He looked kindly at the Beaver and blessed her for that thought. And then a thought bolder than the Beaver's came to him. "I hope," he said, "you'll do more than that. You must come and stay with us in the summer. You shall sit out in a deck-chair in the garden all day. That's the way to get strong."

Then he remembered that she could do that just as well in some one else's garden up at Hampstead, and he looked shy and anxious as he added, "Will you come?"

"Of course I'll come," said she.

He saw her going through the house at Ealing and sitting in the little green garden with the lilac bushes about her all in flower. And at the thought of her coming he was profoundly moved. His eyes moistened, and under the table his knees shook violently with the agitation of his nerves. Miss Roots gave one queer little glance at him and another at Flossie, and the moment passed.

And Lucia had not divined it. No, not for a moment, not even in the moment of leave-taking. She was still holding Flossie's hand in hers when her eyes met his, kind eyes that were still saying almost triumphantly, "I told you so."

As she dropped Flossie's hand for his, she answered the question that he had not dared to ask. "I've read them," she said, and there was no diminution in her glad look.

"When may I see you?"

"To-morrow, can you? Any time after four?"

CHAPTER LXI

HE came into Lucia's presence with a sense of doing something voluntary and yet inevitable, something sanctioned and foreappointed; a sense of carrying on a thing already begun, of returning, through a door that had never been shut, to the life wherein alone he knew himself. And yet this life, measured by days and hours and counting their times of meeting only, ran hardly to six weeks.

Since times and places were of no account, he might have been coming, as he came five years ago, to hear her judgment on his neo-classic drama. Strange and great things had happened to his genius since that day. Between *Helen in Leuce* and the Nine and Twenty Sonnets there lay the newly discovered, heavenly countries of the soul.

" Well," he said, glancing at the poems, as he seated himself, " what do you think of them? Am I forgiven? Do you consent? "

" So many questions? They're all answered, aren't they, if I say I consent? "

" And do you? " There was acute anxiety in his voice and eyes. It struck her as painful that the man, whom she was beginning to look on as possibly the greatest poet of his age, should think it necessary to plead to her for such a little thing.

" I do indeed."

" Without reservations? "

" What reservations should there be? Of course I should only be glad—and proud—that you should do me so much honour. If I can't say very much about it, don't think I don't feel it. I feel it more than I can say."

" Do you really mean it? I was afraid that it might offend you; or that you'd think I oughtn't to have written the things; or at any rate that I'd no business to show them to you. And as for the dedication, I couldn't tell how you'd feel about that."

And she, having before her eyes the greatness of his genius, was troubled by the humility and hesitation of his approach. It recalled to her the ways of his pathetic youth, his youth that obscurity made wild and shy and unassured.

" I can't tell either," she replied, " I don't know whether I ought to feel proud or humble about it; but I think I feel both. You wanting to dedicate anything to me would have been enough to make me very proud. Even if it had been a little thing—but this thing is great. In some ways it seems to me the greatest thing you've done yet. I did think just at first that I ought perhaps to refuse because of that. And then I saw that, really, that was what made it easy for me to accept. It's so great that the dedication doesn't count."

" But it *does* count. It's the only thing that counts to me. You can't take it like that and separate it from the rest. Those sonnets would still be dedicated to you even if you refused to let me write your name before them. I want you to see that they *are* the dedication."

Lucia shook her head. She had seen it. She could see nothing else when she read them. How was it that the poet's bodily presence made her inclined to ignore the reference to herself; to take these poems dedicated to her as an event, not in her life or his, but in the history of literature?

" No," she said, " you must not look at them that way. If they were, it might be a reason for refusing. I know most people would think they'd less right to accept what wasn't really dedicated to them. But, you see, it's just because it isn't really dedicated to me that I can accept it."

" But it is——"

" No, not to me. You wouldn't be so great a poet if it were. I don't see myself here; but I see you, and your idea of me. It's—it's dedicated to that dream of yours. Didn't I tell you your dream was divorced from reality? "

" You told me it would be reconciled to it."

" And it is, isn't it? And the reality is worth all the dreams that ever were? "

He could have told her that so it appeared to those who are bound in the house of bondage; but that in Leuce, the country of deliverance, the dream and the reality are indivisible, being both divine. He could have told her that he had known as much five years ago; even before he knew her.

" After all," he said, " that's admitting that they *are* divided. And that, if you remember, was what I said, not what you said."

Lucia evaded the issue in a fashion truly feminine. " It

doesn't matter a bit what either of us said then, so long as *you* know now."

" There's one thing I don't know. I don't know how you really take it; or whether you will really understand. Just now I thought you did. But after all it seems you don't. You think when I wrote those things I didn't mean them; my imagination was only taking a rather more eccentric flight than usual. Isn't that so? "

" I can't forget that you are a poet. You won't let me forget it. I can't separate your genius from the rest of you."

" And I can't separate the rest of me from it. That makes the difference, you see." He was angry as he said that. He had wondered whether she would deal as tenderly with his passion as she had dealt with his dream; and she had dealt just as tenderly. But it was because she identified the passion with the dream. He had not been prepared for that view of it; and somehow it annoyed him. But for that, he would never have spoken as he now did. " When I wondered how you would take it I thought it might possibly strike you as something rather too real, almost offensively so. Do you know, I'd rather you'd taken it that way than that you should talk about my dreams. My *dreams.*" (It was shocking, the violent emphasis of disgust the poet, the dreamer, flung into that one word.) " As if I'd dreamed that I knew you. As if I'd dreamed that I cared for you. Would you rather think I dreamed it? You can if you like. Or would you rather think it was the most real thing that ever happened to me? So real that after it happened— *because* it happened—I left off being the sort of man and the sort of poet I was, and became another sort. So real and so strong that it saved me from one or two other things, uncommonly strong and real, that had got a pretty tight hold of me, too. Would you rather think that you'd really done this for me, or that I'd dreamed it all? "

She looked at his face, the unforgotten, unforgetable face, which when she first knew it had kindled and darkened so swiftly and inexplicably. She knew it now. She held the key to all its mysteries. It was the face that had turned to her five years ago with just that look; in the mouth and lifted chin that imperious impetuous determination to make her see; in the eyes that pathetic trust in her seeing. The same face; and yet it would have told her, if he had not,

that he was another man. No, not another man; but of all
the ways that were then open to him to take he had chosen
the noblest. And so, of all the expressions that in its youth
had played on that singularly expressive face, it was the
finest only that had become dominant. That face had never
lied to her. Why should he not plead for the sincerity of
his passion, since it was all over now? Was it possible that
there was some secret insincerity in her? How was it that
she had made him think that she desired to ignore, to repudiate her part in him? That she preferred a meaningless
compliment to the confession which was the highest honour
that could be paid to any woman? Was it because the
honour was so great that she was afraid to take it?

" Of course I would rather think it was really so."

" Then you must believe that I really cared for you; and
that it is only because I cared that it is really so."

" I do believe it. But I can't take it all to myself. Another person might have cared just as much, and it might
have done him harm—I would never have forgiven myself
if I had done you harm—I want you to see that it wasn't
anything in *me;* it was something in *you* that made the
difference."

~He smiled sadly. " You know it *does* sound as if you
wanted to keep out of it."

" Does it? If I had really been in it, do you think that I
wouldn't be glad and thankful? I am, even for the little that
I have done. If I *did* help you—that way—I helped some
one else too. At least I should like to think I did. I should
like to think that one reason why you care for your wife so
much is because you cared a little for me. There is that way
of looking at it." Then, lest she should seem to be seeking
some extraneous justification of a fact that in her heart she
abhorred, she added, " Every way I look at it I'm glad.
I'm glad that you cared. I'm glad because it's been, and
glad because it's over. For if it hadn't been over——"

" What were you going to say? "

" I was going to say that if it hadn't been over you
couldn't have given me these. I didn't say it; because it
would have sounded as if that were all I cared about. As
if I wouldn't have been almost as glad if you'd never written a line of them. Only in that case I should never have
known."

" No. You would never have known. As it is, when I wrote them I never meant to show them to you."

" Oh, but I think——"

" Of course you do. But I wasn't going to print them before you'd seen them. Do you know what I'd meant to do with them—what in fact I *did* do with them? I left them to you in my will with directions that they weren't to be published without your consent. It seems a rather unusual bequest, but you know I had a conceited hope that some time they might be valuable. I thought they might possibly go a little way towards paying my debt."

" Your debt? I don't understand." But the trembling of her mouth belied its words.

" Don't you? Don't you remember?"

" No, I don't. I never *have* remembered."

" Probably not. But you can hardly suppose that I've forgotten it."

" What has it to do with you, or me—or this?"

" Not much, perhaps; but still something, you'll admit."

" I admit nothing. I can't bear your ever having thought of it. I wish you hadn't told me. It spoils everything."

" Does it? Such a little thing? Surely a friend might be allowed to leave you a small legacy when he was decently dead? And it wasn't *his* fault, was it, if it paid a debt as well?"

The tears rose in her eyes to answer him.

" But you see I didn't leave it. I didn't wait for that. I was afraid that my being dead would put you in a more embarrassing position than if I'd been alive. You might have hated those poems and yet you might have shrunk from suppressing them for fear of wounding the immortal vanity of a blessed spirit. You might even have hesitated to inflict so great a loss on the literature of your country." He tried to speak lightly, as if it were merely a whimsical and extravagant notion that he should be reckoned among the poets. And yet in his heart he knew that it must be so. " There's nothing gross about the transaction; nothing that need offend either you or me."

" I can't—I can't——"

" Well," he said gently, fearing the appearance of grossness in pressing the question, " we can settle that afterwards, can't we? Meanwhile at all events the publication rests with you."

"The publication has nothing whatever to do with me— the dedication, *perhaps.*"

"You've accepted that. Still, you might object to your name appearing before the public with mine."

Lucia looked bewildered. She thought she had followed him in all his subtleties; but she had had difficulty in realizing that he was actually proposing to suppress his poems in deference to her scruples, if she had any. Some shadowy notion of his meaning was penetrating her now.

"My name," she said, "will mean nothing to the public."

"Then you consent?"

"Of course. It's absurd to talk about my consent. Besides, why should I mind now—when it is all over?"

He was silent for a moment. When he spoke again, it was by an effort, as if he unwillingly obeyed some superior constraint. "If it hadn't been all over would you have minded then? Would you have refused your consent?"

"To your publishing your own poems? How could I?"

"To the dedication, I mean. If it hadn't been all over, would you have given your consent to that?"

His anxiety had deepened to an agony which seemed to have made his face grow sharp and thin almost as she looked at him. She judged that this question was vital, and that the truth was required of her.

"No, not to that. You see, it's only because it's all over that I've consented now."

"I see; that's the condition? You would never have consented but for that."

"Why should we talk about that now?"

"I wanted to know the truth."

"Why should you? It's a truth that has nothing to do with things as they are, only with things as they might have been. Isn't it enough to be glad that they weren't, that it is all over, and that this is the end of it?"

Even as she said the words it struck her that there was something ominous in this reiteration.

"But it isn't all over. This isn't the end of it."

His voice was so low that she could hardly have heard it but for the intense vibration of the tones. There was a

pause in which they seemed still to be throbbing, but with
no meaning behind the passionate pulse of sound.

" I didn't mean to tell you. I know you'd rather think
it wasn't so. And I would have let you think it if it hadn't
been for what you told me—what I made you tell me."

" I don't understand. What did I tell you? "

" You told me the truth." He spoke with a sudden
savage energy. " How could I go on lying after that? "

She looked at him with that almost imperceptible twitch-
ing of her soft mouth which he knew to be a sign of suffering; and in her eyes there was pain and a vague terror.

" I might have gone on lying to the end if nothing had
depended on it. But if you tell me that you only give your
consent to a thing on one condition, and I know that I
can't possibly fulfil the condition, what am I to do? Say
nothing about it, and do what you would loathe me for
doing if you knew? "

Till now she had left the manuscript lying in her lap,
where unconsciously her hands covered it with a gentle
protecting touch. But as he spoke she took it up and put
it away from her with an irresistible impulse of rejection
He knew that he was answered.

" If I had," he said, " in one sense I should have done
you no wrong. All this would be nothing to the world
which would read these poems. But when I knew that
it made all the difference to *you*——"

She turned, as he had seen her turn once and only once
before, in reproach that was almost anger.

" To me? Do you suppose I'm thinking of myself? "

" Perhaps not. That doesn't prevent my thinking of
you. What was I to do? "

She did not answer him. Once before, he remembered,
when his honour was in difficulties, she had refused to help
it out, left it to struggle to the light; which was what it
did now.

" It would have been better to have said nothing and
done nothing."

He expected her to close instantly with that view of his
behaviour which honour had presented as the final one,
but this she did not do.

" If you had said nothing you might have done what
you liked."

" I see. It's my saying it that makes the difference? "

" That is *not* what I meant. I meant that you were free to publish what you have written. You are not free to say these things to me."

" For the life of me I don't know why I said them. It means perdition for my poems and for me. I knew that was all I had to gain by telling you the truth."

" But it *isn't* the truth. You know it isn't. You don't even think it is."

" And if it were, would it be so terrible to you to hear it? "

She did not answer. She only looked at him, as if by looking she could read the truth. For his face had never lied.

He persisted. " If it were true, what would you think of me? "

" I should think it most dishonourable of you to say so. But it isn't true."

He smiled. " Therefore it can't be dishonourable of me to say so."

" No, not that. You are not dishonourable; therefore it can't be true. Let us forget that you ever said it."

" But I can't forget that it's true any more than I can make it untrue. You think me dishonourable, because you think I've changed. But I haven't changed. It always was so, ever since I knew you; and that's more than five years ago now. I am dishonourable; but that's not where the dishonour comes in. *The* dishonourable thing would have been to have left off caring for you. But I never did leave off. There never was a minute when it wasn't true, nor a minute when I didn't think it. If I was sure of nothing else I was always sure of that. Where the dishonour came in was in caring for another woman, in another way."

" The dishonour would come in if you'd left off caring for her. And you haven't done that. It would come in a little now, I think, if you said that you didn't care. But you don't say it; you don't even think it. Shall I tell you the truth? You've let your genius get too strong a hold over you. You've let it get hold, too, of this feeling that you had for me. And now, though you know perfectly well—as well as I do—that it's all over, your genius is trying to persuade you that the feeling is still there when it isn't."

"That is not so, but you can say it is, if it makes you any happier."

"It does make me happier to think that it's your genius, not you, that says these things. For I can forgive your genius; but I couldn't have forgiven you."

At that moment he felt a savage jealousy of his genius, because she loved it. "And yet, you said a little while ago you couldn't separate the two."

"You have obliged me to separate them, to find an excuse for you. This ought not to have happened; but it could not have happened to a man who was not a poet."

All the time she was miserably aware that she was trying to defend herself with subtleties against the impact of a terrible reality. And because that reality must weigh more heavily on him than her, she was trying to defend him too, against himself, to force on him, against himself, her own subtilizing, justifying view.

But his subtlety was a match for hers. "Your cousin once did me the honour to say I was one-seventh part a poet, and upon my honour I prefer his estimate to yours."

"What is mine?"

"That I'm nothing but a poet. That there wasn't enough of me left over to make a man."

"That is not my estimate, and you know it. I think you so much a man that your heart will keep you right, even though your genius has led you very far astray."

"Is that all you know about it?"

"Well, I'm not sure that it is your genius, this time. I rather think it's your sense of honour. I believe you think that because you once cared for me you've got to go on caring, lest I should accuse you of being faithless to your dream." ("Surely," she said to herself, "I've made it easy for him now!")

But the word was too much for him. "For goodness' sake, don't talk to me any more about my dream. You may think any mortal thing you like about me, so long as you don't do that."

She smiled faintly, as if with an effort at forbearance.

"Very well, then, I won't talk about your dream. I'll say you were afraid lest I should think you had been faithless to *me*. It would never have occurred to you if you hadn't seen me again. It will not occur to you after I am gone. It will be all over by to-morrow."

"Why to-morrow?" He spoke stupidly. Fear had made him stupid. "Why to-morrow?"

"Because I am going to-morrow."

Then he knew that it was indeed all over. The door which had been open to him was about to close; and once closed it would never be open to him again.

"What *must* you think of me——"

"I think you have done very wrong, and that our talking about it only makes it worse. And so—I'm sorry, but I must ask you to leave me."

But he did not leave her. "And I must ask you to forgive me," he said gently.

"I? I have nothing to forgive. You haven't done anything to me. But I should never forgive you if I thought this foolishness could make one moment's difference to—to Flossie."

"It never has made any difference to her," he replied coldly, "or to my feeling for her. I never felt towards any woman as I feel towards you. It isn't the same thing at all. Heaven knows I thought I cared enough for her to marry her. But it seems I didn't. That's why I say it makes no difference to her. Nothing is altered by it. As far as Flossie is concerned, whether I marry her or not I shall have behaved abominably. I don't know which is the more dishonourable."

"Don't you?"

"No. I only know which I'm going to do."

She turned her head away. And that turning away was intolerable. It was the closing of the door.

"Is it so very terrible to you?" he said gently.

He could not see the tears in her eyes, but he heard them in her voice, and he knew that he had wounded her, not in her pride, but in her tenderness and honour—Lucia's honour.

"To me? I'm not thinking of myself—not of myself at all. How could I think of myself? I'm thinking of *her*." She turned to him and let her tears gather in her eyes unheeded. "Don't you see what you've done?"

Oh, yes; he saw very well what he had done. He had

taken the friendship she had given to him to last his life
and destroyed it in a moment, with his own hands. All
for the sake of a subtlety, a fantastic scruple, a question
asked, a thing said under some obscure compulsion. He
had been moved by he knew not what insane urgency of
honour. And whatever else he saw he did not see how
he could have done otherwise. The only alternative was
to say nothing, to do nothing. Supposing he had suppressed both his passion and the poems that immortalized
it, what would she have thought of him then? Would she
not have thought that he had either dedicated to her a thing
that he was afterwards ashamed of, or that he had meant
nothing by the dedication?

" Don't you see what you have done? " she said. " You've
made me wish I had never come here and that I'd never
seen you again. It was only the other night—the dear
little girl—she came up here and sat with me, and we had a
talk. We talked about you. She told me how she came to
know you, and how good you'd been to her and how long it
was before either of you knew. She told me things about
herself. She is very shy—very reserved; but she let me
see how much she cares—and how much you care. Think
what you must be to her. She has no father and no mother,
she has nobody but you. She told me that. And then—
she took me up to her room and showed me all her pretty
things. She was so happy—and how can I look at her
again? She would hate me if she knew; and I couldn't
blame her, poor child. She could never understand that it
was not my fault."

But as she said it her conscience rose in contradiction
and told her that it was her fault. Her fault in the very
beginning for drawing him into an intimacy that his youth
and inexperience made dangerous. Her fault for sacrificing, yes, sacrificing, him to that impulse to give pleasure
which had only meant giving pleasure to herself at his
expense. Her fault for endlessly refining on the facts of
life, till she lost all feeling of its simpler and more obvious
issues. Kitty had been right when she told her that she
treated men as if they were disembodied spirits. She had
trusted too much to her own subtlety. That was how all
her blunders had been made. If she had been cold as well
as subtle—but Lucia was capable of passionate indiscreet

things to be followed by torments of her pride. Her pride
had only made matters worse. It was her pride, in the
beginning, that had blinded her. Afterwards she had not
been quite so proud; neither, since Kitty had opened her
eyes, had she been so blind; but she had been ten times more
foolish. Her mind had refused to dwell upon Kitty's
dreadful suggestions, because they were dreadful. Unconscious of her sex, she had remained unconscious of her
power; she had trusted (unconsciously) to the power of
another woman for protection. Flossie had, so to speak, detached and absorbed the passionate part of Keith Rickman;
by which process the rest of him was left subtler and more
pure. She had thought she could really deal with him now
as a disembodied spirit. And so under the shelter of
his engagement she had, after her own manner, let herself go.

These thoughts swept through her brain like one thought,
as she contemplated the misery she had made. They
came with the surging of the blood in her cheeks, so swiftly
that she had no time to see that they hardly exhausted
the aspects of her case. And it was not her own case that
she was thinking of.

She turned to him pleading. "Don't you see that I
could never forgive myself if I thought that I had hurt
her? You are not going to make me so unhappy?"

"Do you mean, am I going to marry her?"

She said nothing; for she was conscious now, conscious
and ashamed of using a power that she had no right to
have; ashamed, too, of being forced to acknowledge the
truth of the thing she had so passionately denied.

"You needn't be afraid," he said. "Of course I am
going to marry her."

He turned away from her as he had turned away five
years ago, with the same hopeless sense of dishonour and
defeat. She called him back, as she had called him back
five years ago, and for the same purpose, of delivering a
final stab. Only that this time she knew it was a stab;
and her own heart felt the pain as she delivered it.

But the terrible thing had to be done. She had got to
return the manuscript, the gift that should never have been
given. She gathered the loosened sheets tenderly, like
things that she was grieved to part from. He admitted

that she was handling her sword with all gentleness so as to avoid as far as possible any suggestion of a thrust.

"You must take them back," she said. "I can't keep them—or—or have anything to do with them after what you told me. I should feel as if I'd taken what belonged to some one else."

As he took the sheets from her and pocketed them, she felt that again he was pocketing an insult as well as a stab.

But the victim was no longer an inexperienced youth. So he smiled valorously, as beseemed his manhood. "And yet," he murmured, "you say it isn't true."

She did not contradict him this time. And as he turned he heard behind him the closing of the door.

BOOK IV

THE MAN HIMSELF

CHAPTER LXII

AFTER all, the wedding did not take place on the twenty-fifth; for on the twentieth Keith was summoned to Ilford by a letter from his stepmother. Mrs. Rickman said she thought he ought to know (as if Keith were seeking to avoid the knowledge!) that his father had had a slight paralytic seizure. He had recovered, but it had left him very unsettled and depressed. He kept on for ever worrying to see Keith. Mrs. Rickman hoped (not without a touch of asperity) that Keith would lose no time in coming, as his father seemed so uneasy in his mind.

Very uneasy in his mind was Isaac, as upstairs in the big front bedroom (which, from its excess of glass and mahogany, bore a curious resemblance to the front shop) he lay, a strangely shrunken figure in the great bed. His face, once so reticent and regular, was drawn on one side, twisted into an oblique expression of abandonment and agony.

Keith was not prepared for the change; and he broke down completely as the poor right hand (which Isaac *would* use) opened and closed in a vain effort to clasp his. But Isaac was intolerant of sympathy, and at once rebuked all reference to his illness. Above the wreck of his austere face, his eyes, blood-shot as they were and hooded under their slack lids, defied you to notice any change in him.

"I sent for you," he said, "because I wanted to talk over a little business." His utterance was thick and uncertain; the act of speech showed the swollen tongue struggling in the distorted mouth.

"Oh, don't bother about business now, father," said Keith, trying hard to steady his voice.

His father gave an irritable glance, as if he were repelling an accusation of mortality, conveyed in the word " now."

" And why not now as well as any other time? "

Keith blew his nose hard and turned away.

" What's the matter with you? Do you suppose I'm ill? "

" Oh, no, of course not."

" No, I'm just lying here to rest and get up my strength again; God willing. But *in case* anything should happen to me, Keith, I want you to be clear as to how you stand."

" Oh, that's all right," said Keith cheerfully.

" It's not all right. It's not as I meant it to be. Between you and me, my big house hasn't come to much. I think if you'd stayed in it—well, we won't say any more about that. But Paternoster Row—now—that's sound. Mrs. Rickman always 'ad a fancy for the City 'ouse, and she's put money into it. You'll have your share that was settled on you when I married your poor mother. You stick to the City 'ouse, Keith, and it'll bring you in something some day. And the Name'll still go on." It was pathetic, his persistent clinging to the immortality of his name. Pathetic, too, his inability to see it otherwise than as blazoned for ever and ever over a shop-front. His son's fame (if he ever achieved it) was a mere subsidiary glory. " But Pilkington'll get the Strand 'ouse. Whatever I do I can't save it. I don't mind owning now, the Strand 'ouse was a mistake."

" A very great mistake."

" And Pilkington'll get the 'Arden library."

" You don't know. You may get rid of him—before that time."

Isaac seemed to be torn by his thoughts the more because they found no expression in his face that was bound, mouth, eye, and eyelid, in its own agony. Before *what* time? Before the day of his death, or the day of redemption? " The mortgage," he said, " 'as still three years to run. But I can't raise the money."

Keith was silent. He hardly liked to ask, though he would have given a great deal to know, the amount of the sum his father could not raise. A possibility, a splendid, undreamed of possibility, had risen up before him; but he turned away from it; it was infamous to entertain it, for it depended on his father's death. And yet for the life of him he could not help wondering whether the share which would ultimately come to him would by any chance cover that mortgage. To be any good it would have to come before the three years were up, though. He put the splendid horrible thought aside. He could not contemplate it. The wish was certainly not the father of that thought. But supposing the thought became the father of the wish?

"That reminds me," said Isaac, "that there was something else I 'ad to say to you."

He did not say it all at once. At the very thought of it his swollen tongue moved impotently without words. At last he got it out.

"I've been thinking it over—that affair of the library. And I've been led to see that what I did was wrong. Wrong, I mean, in the sight of God."

There was a sense he could not get rid of, in which it might still be considered superlatively right.

"And wot you did——"

"Oh, never mind what I did. *That's* all right."

"You did the righteous and Christian thing."

"Did I? I'm sure I don't know why I did it."

"Ah—if you'd done it for the love of God, there's no doubt it'd 'ave been more pleasing to 'im."

"Well, you know I didn't do it for the love—of God."

"You did it for the love of woman? I was right then, after all."

Isaac felt inexpressibly consoled by Keith's cheerful disclaimer of all credit. His manner did away with the solemnity of the occasion; but it certainly smoothed for him the painful path of confession.

"Well, yes. If it hadn't been for Miss Harden I don't suppose I should have done it at all."

He said it very simply; but not all the magnificent consolations of religion could have given Isaac greater peace. It was a little more even, the balance of righteousness between him and Keith. He had never sinned, as Keith had done, after the flesh. Of the deeds done in the body he would have but a very small account to render at the last.

"And you see, you haven't got anything for it out of *her*."

There was a certain satisfaction in his tone. He saw a

mark of the divine displeasure in Keith's failure to marry the woman he desired.

"And if I could only raise that money——"

He meant it—he meant it. The balance, held in God's hands, hung steady now.

"How much is it?" asked Keith; for he thought, "Perhaps he's only holding on to that share for my sake; and if he knew that I would give it up now, he might really——"

"Four thousand nine with the interest," said Isaac. "Do you think, Keith, it would have sold for five?"

"Well, yes, I think it very possibly might."

"Ah!" Isaac turned his face from his son. The sigh expressed a profound, an infinite repentance.

CHAPTER LXIII

ON the twenty-fifth Isaac Rickman lay dead in his villa at Ilford. Two days after Keith's visit he had been seized by a second and more terrible paralytic stroke; and from it he did not recover. The wedding was now indefinitely postponed till such time as Keith could have succeeded in winding up his father's affairs.

They proved rather less involved than he had expected. Isaac had escaped dying insolvent. Though a heavy mortgage delivered Rickman's in the Strand into Pilkington's possession, the City house was not only sound, as Isaac had said, but in a fairly flourishing condition. Some blind but wholly salutary instinct had made him hold on to that humbler and obscurer shop where first his fortunes had been made; and, with its immense patronage among the Nonconformist population, Rickman's in the City held a high and honourable position in the trade. The bulk of the profits had to go to the bookseller's widow as chief owner of the capital; still, the slender partnership settled on his son, if preserved intact and carefully manipulated, would yield in time a very comfortable addition to Keith's income. If Isaac had lived, his affairs (as far as he was concerned) would have been easily settled. But for his son and heir they proved most seriously complicated.

For Keith was heir, not only to his father's estate, but

to that very considerable debt of honour which Isaac had left unpaid. It seemed as if the Harden library, the symbol of a superb intellectual vanity, was doomed to be in eternal necessity of redemption. Until yesterday it had not occurred to Keith that it could be his destiny to redeem it. Yesterday he had refused to let his mind dally with that possibility; to-day it had become the most fitting subject of his contemplation.

The thing was more easily conceived than done. His literary income amounted, all told, to about three hundred and fifty a year, but its sources were not absolutely secure. *Metropolis* or *The Planet* might conceivably at any moment cease to be. And there was his marriage. It was put off; but only for a matter of weeks. He had only a hundred and fifty pounds in ready money; the rest had been swallowed up by the little house at Ealing. It was impossible to redeem the Harden library unless he parted with his patrimony; which was, after all, his only safe and imperishable source of income. Still, he had not the smallest hesitation on this head. Neither he nor Flossie had taken it into their calculations when they agreed to marry, and he was not going to consider it now.

The first step proved simple. Mrs. Rickman had no objection to buying him out. On the contrary, she was thankful to get rid of a most reckless and uncomfortable partner. But in the present state of the trade it was impossible to estimate his share at more than four thousand. That covered the principal; but Isaac had paid no interest for more than two years; and that interest Keith would have to pay. Though the four thousand was secure, and Pilkington had given him three years to raise the seven hundred and fifty in, it was not so easily done on an income of three hundred and fifty. Not easy in three years; and impossible in any number of years if he married. Possible only, yes, just possible, if his marriage were postponed until such time as he could have collected the money. Some brilliant stroke of luck might unexpectedly reduce the term; but three years must be allowed. *Metropolis* and *The Planet* were surely good for another three years. The other alternative, that of repudiating the obligation, never entered his head for an instant. He could not have touched a shilling of his father's money till this debt was cleared.

There could be no doubt as to what honour demanded of him. But how would Flossie take it? The worst of it was that he was bound (in honour again) to give her the option of breaking off their engagement, if she didn't care to wait. And after all that had passed between them it might not be so easy to persuade her that he was not glad of the excuse; for he himself was so lacking in conviction. Still she was very intelligent; and she would see that it wasn't his fault if their marriage had to be put off. The situation was inevitable and impersonal, and as such it was bound to be hard on somebody. He admitted that it was particularly hard on Flossie. It would have been harder still if Flossie had been out of work; but Flossie, with characteristic prudence, had held on to her post till the very eve of her wedding-day, and had contrived to return to it when she foresaw the necessity for delay. Otherwise he would have had to insist on providing for her until she was independent again; which would have complicated matters really most horribly. It was quite horrible enough to have to explain all this to Flossie. The last time he had explained things (for he had explained them) to Flossie the result had not been exactly happy. But then the things themselves had been very different, and he had had to admit with the utmost contrition that a woman could hardly have had more reasonable grounds for resentment. That was all over and done with now. In that explanation they had explained everything away. They had left no single thread of illusion hanging round the life they were to live together. They accepted themselves and each other as they were. And in the absence of any brighter prospect for either of them there was high wisdom in that acceptance.

If then there was a lack of rapture in his relations with Flossie, there would henceforth at any rate be calm. Her temperament was, he judged, essentially placid, not to say apathetic. There was a soft smoothness about the plump little lady that would be security against friction. She was not great at understanding; but, taking it all together, she was now in an infinitely better position for understanding him than she had been two weeks ago. Besides, it was after all a simple question of figures; and Flossie's attitude to figures was, unlike his own, singularly uninfluenced by passion. She would take the sensible, practical view.

The sensible, practical view was precisely what Flossie did take. But her capabilities of passion he had again misjudged.

He chose his moment with discretion, when time and place and Flossie's mood were most propitious. The time was Sunday evening, the place was the Regent's Park, Flossie's mood was gentle and demure. She had been very nice to him since his father's death, and had shown him many careful small attentions which, with his abiding sense of his own shortcomings towards her, he had found extremely touching. She seemed to him somehow a different woman, not perhaps so pretty as she had been, but nicer. He may have been the dupe of an illusory effect of toilette, for Flossie was in black. She had discussed the propriety of mourning with Miss Bishop, and wore it to-day for the first time with a pretty air of solemnity mingled with satisfaction in her own delicate intimation that she was one with her lover in his grief. She had not yet discovered that black was unbecoming to her, which would have been fatal to the mood.

The flowers were gay in the Broad Walk, Flossie tried to be gay too; and called on him to admire their beauty. They sat down together on a seat in the embrasure of a bed of chrysanthemums. Flossie was interested in everything, in the chrysanthemums, in the weather, and in the passersby. Most particularly interested, he noticed, in the family groups. Her black eyes, that glanced so restlessly at the men and so jealously at the women, sank softly on the children, happy and appeased. Poor Flossie. He had long ago divined her heart. He did his best to please her, he sat down when she told him to sit down, stared when she told him to stare, and relapsed into his now habitual attitude of dejection. A little girl toddled past him in play; stopped at his knees and touched them with her hand and rubbed her small body against them, chuckling with delight.

"The dear little mite," said Flossie; "she's taken quite a fancy to you, Keith." Her face was soft and shy under her black veil, and when she looked at him she blushed. He turned his head away. He could not meet that look in Flossie's eyes when he thought of what he had to say to her. He was going to put the joy of life a little farther from her; to delay her woman's tender ineradicable hope.

This was not the moment or the place to do it in. They rose and walked on, turning into the open Park. And there, sitting under a solitary tree by the path that goes towards St. John's Wood, he broke it to her gently.

"Flossie," he said, "I've something to tell you that you mayn't like to hear."

She made no sign of agitation beyond scraping a worn place in the grass with the tips of her little shoes. "Well," she said, with an admirable attempt at patience, "what is it *now?*"

"You mean you think it's been about enough already?"

"If it's really anything unpleasant, for goodness' sake let's have it out and get it over."

"Right, Flossie. I'm awfully sorry, but I'm afraid we shan't be able to marry for another two years, perhaps three."

"And why not?" Her black eyes darted a vindictive look at him under her soft veil.

"My father's death has made a difference to me."

Her lips tightened, and she drew a sharp but inaudible breath through her nostrils. He had been wrong in supposing that she had not looked for any improvement in his finances after his father's death. On the contrary, knowing of their reconciliation and deceived by the imposing appearance of Rickman's in the Strand, she had counted on a very substantial increase of income.

"Do you mean to say, Keith, he hasn't left you anything?"

He laughed softly—an unpleasant way he had in situations where most people would consider it only decent to keep grave.

"He *has* left me something. A bad debt."

"What have you got to do with his bad debts? Nobody can come down on you to pay them." She paused. A horrible thought had struck her. "*Can* they? You don't mean to say they can?"

He shook his head and struggled with his monstrous mirth.

"Keith! What 'ave you done? You surely haven't been backing any bills?"

He laughed outright this time, for the sheer misery of the thing.

"No; oh, dear me, no! Not in your sense, at least."

"There *isn't* any other sense. Either you did or you didn't; and I think you might tell me which."

"It's not quite so simple, dear. I didn't back his bills, d'you see, but I backed *him.*"

"Can they make you responsible? Have they got it down in black and white?"

"Nobody can make me responsible, except myself. It's what they call a debt of honour, Flossie. Those debts are not always down in black and white."

"Why can't you speak plain? I really can't think what you mean by that."

"Can't you? I'll endeavour to explain. A debt of honour, Beaver dear, is a debt that's got to be paid whoever else goes unpaid."

"A fine lot of honour about that," said she.

Was it possible to make the Beaver understand? He gave her a slight outline of the situation; and he really could not complain of any fault in the Beaver's intelligence. For, by dint of a masterly cross-examination, she possessed herself of all the details, even of those which he most desired to keep from her. After their last great explanation there had been more than a tacit agreement between them that the name of Lucia Harden was never to come up again in any future discussion; and that name he would not give. She, however, readily inferred it from his silence.

"You needn't tell me the lady's name," she said.

"I certainly needn't. The name has nothing whatever to do with it."

"Oh, hasn't it? You'll not make me believe that you'd 'ave taken it up this way for any one but her."

"Whether I would or wouldn't doesn't affect the point of honour."

"I don't see where it comes in there."

"If you don't, I can't make you see it."

"I said I didn't see where it comes in—*there.* I know what's honourable as well as you, though I daresay my notions wouldn't agree with yours."

"Upon my soul, I shouldn't wonder if they didn't!"

"Look here, Keith. Did you ever make Miss Harden any promise to pay her that money when your father died?"

"Of course I didn't. How could I? Do you suppose she'd have let me do anything of the sort?"

"I don't know what she wouldn't have let you do. Anyhow, you didn't make her any promise. Think of the promises and promises you've made to me."

"I do think of them. Have I broken one of them?"

"I don't say you have yet, but you want to."

"I don't wa—I won't break them. I'll keep every one of the blessed lot, if you'll only give me time."

"Give you time? I know what that means. It means that I'm to go back and earn my living. I can slave till I drop for all you care—while you go and throw away all that money on another woman. And I'm to give you time to do it in!"

"I won't ask you to wait for me. I'm perfectly willing to release you from your engagement, if you like. It seems only fair to you."

"You care a lot, don't you, about what's fair to me? I believe you'd take the bread out of my mouth to give it to her."

"I would, Flossie, if it was her bread. That money doesn't belong to you or me; it belongs to Miss Harden."

"It seems to me," said Flossie, "that everything belongs to her. I'm sure you've as good as told me so."

"I've certainly given you some right to think so. But that has nothing to do with it; and we agreed that we were going to let it alone, didn't we?"

"It wasn't me that brought it up again, it was you; and it's got everything to do with it. You wouldn't have behaved like this, and you wouldn't be sitting there talking about what's honourable, if it hadn't been for Miss Harden."

"That may very well be. But it doesn't mean what you think it does. It means that before I knew Miss Harden I didn't know or care very much about what's honourable. She taught me to care. I wasn't fit to speak to a decent woman before I knew her. She made me decent."

"Did she sit up half the night with you to do it?"

He made a gesture of miserable impatience.

"You needn't tell me. I can see her."

"You can't. She did it by simply being what she is. If I ever manage to do anything right it will be because of her, as you say. But it doesn't follow that it'll be for her. There's a great difference."

" I don't see it."

" You must try to see it. There's one thing I haven't told you about that confounded money. It was I who let her in for losing it. Isn't that enough to make me keen? "

" You always were keen where she was concerned."

" Look here, Flossie, I thought you were going to give up this sort of thing? "

" So I was when I thought you were going to give her up. It doesn't look like it."

" My dear child, how can I give up what I never had or could have? "

" Well then—are you going to give up your idea? "

" No, I am not. But you can either give *me* up or wait for me, as I said. But if you marry me, you must marry me and my idea too. You don't like my idea; but that's no reason why you shouldn't like me."

" You're not taking much pains to make me like you."

" I'm taking all the pains I know. But your liking or not liking me won't alter me a little bit. You'll have to take me as I am."

As she looked up at him she realized at last the indomitable nature of the man she had to deal with. And yet he was not unalterable, even on his own showing. She knew some one who had altered him out of all knowledge.

" Come," said she, " don't say you never change."

" I don't say it. You'll have to allow for that possibility, too."

" It seems to me I have to allow for a good many things."

" You have indeed."

" Well, are we going to sit here all night? "

" I'm ready."

They walked back in silence over the straight path that seemed as if it would never end. Flossie stopped half-way in it, stung by an idea.

" There's something you haven't thought of. What are you going to do with the house? And with all that furniture? "

" Let them to somebody. That's all right, Beaver. The house and the furniture can't run away."

" No, but they'll never be the same again."

Nothing would ever be the same again; that was clear. The flowers were still gay in the Broad Walk, and the children, though a little sleepier, were still adorable; but Flossie did not turn to look at them as she passed. Would she ever look at them, at anything, with pleasure again? He had made life very difficult, very cruel to this poor child, whom after all he had promised to protect and care for.

" I say, Beaver dear, it *is* hard luck on you."

The look and the tone would have softened most women, at least for the time being; but the Beaver remained implacable.

" I'll try to make it easier for you. I'll work like mad. I'll do anything to shorten the time."

" Shorten the time? You don't know how many years you're asking me to wait."

" I'm not asking you to wait. I'm asking you to choose."

" Do you want me to do it now?"

" No, certainly not." She was not indeed in a mood favourable to choice; and he would not influence her decision. It was mean to urge her to an arduous constancy; meaner still to precipitate her refusal. " You must think. You can, you know, when you give your mind to it."

She appeared to be giving her mind to it for the rest of the way home; and her silence left him also free to think it over. After all, what had he done? He had not asked her to wait, but what if he had? Many men have to ask as much of the woman who loves them. Some men have asked even more of the woman whom they love. That was the secret. He could have asked it with a clear conscience if he had but loved her.

CHAPTER LXIV

FLOSSIE was in no hurry about making up her mind. If Keith had asked her to give him time, it was only fair that he should give her time too, and since his mind was made up in any case, time could be no object to him. So days and weeks had passed on and she had conveyed to him no hint of her decision.

On that Sunday evening, in the seclusion of her bedroom, Flossie said to herself that she had made one great mistake. Prudence and foresight were all very well in their way, but this time she had blundered through excess of caution. In sticking to the post that made her independent she had broken her strongest line of defence. If only she had had the courage to relinquish it at the crucial moment, she would have stood a very much better chance in her contest with Keith. She could then have appealed to his pity, as she had done with such signal success two years ago, when the result of the appeal had been to bring him violently to the point. She was wise enough to know that in contending with a chivalrous man a woman's strongest defence is her defencelessness. Though she was unable to believe that pure abstract honour was or could be the sole supreme motive of Keith's behaviour, she felt that if she could have said to him, " I've thrown up a good situation to marry you," his chivalry would not have held out against that argument.

But Flossie never made mistakes. She was too consummate a diplomatist. Therefore, though appearances were against her, it was only reasonable to suppose that she had not really done so now, and that her original inspiration had been right. It was foresight so subtle, so advanced, that it outstripped the ordinary processes of calculation, and appeared afterwards as the mysterious leading of a profounder power, of the under-soul that presses the innocent intellect into the services of its own elemental instincts. The people who yield most obediently to this compulsion are said to have good luck.

Flossie's good luck, however, was not yet apparent either to herself or to her fellow-boarders at Tavistock Place. Not that she had enlarged on her trouble to any of them. The whole thing had been too profoundly humiliating for that. To say nothing of being engaged to a man who had shown so very little impatience to marry her, to have taken and furnished a house and be unable to live in it, to have received congratulations and wedding presents which had all proved premature, to know, and feel that everybody else knew, that her bedroom was at this moment lumbered up with a trousseau which, whether she wore it or put it by two years, would make her equally ridiculous, was really a very trying position for any young lady, and to Flossie, whose nature was most delicately sensitive to such considerations, it was torture. But, after all, these things were material and external; and the worst of Flossie's suffering was in her soul. Before the appearance of Miss Harden, the last two years had passed for Flossie in gorgeous triumphal procession through the boarding-house. She had been the invincible heroine of Mrs. Downey's for two years, she had dragged its young hero at her chariot wheels for two years, she had filled the heart of Ada Bishop with envy and the hearts of Mr. Soper and Mr. Spinks with jealousy and anguish for two years; and now she had all these people pitying her and looking down on her because she had been so queerly treated; and this was even more intolerable to poor Flossie. She knew perfectly well what every one of them was saying. She knew that Ada Bishop had thanked goodness she wasn't in her shoes; that Miss Bramble spoke of her persistently as "that poor young thing"; that Mrs. Downey didn't know which she pitied most, her or poor Mr. Rickman. He was poor Mr. Rickman, if you please, because he was considered to have entangled himself so inextricably with her. She knew that Miss Roots maintained that it was all her (Flossie's) own fault for holding Keith to his engagement; that Mr. Partridge had wondered why girls were in such a hurry to get married; and that Mr. Soper said she'd made a great mistake in ever taking up with a young fellow you could depend on with so little certainty. And the burden of it all was that Flossie had made a fool of herself and been made a fool of. So she was very bitter in her little heart against the man who was the cause of it all; and if she did not instantly throw Keith Rickman over, that was because Flossie was not really such a fool as for the moment she had been made to look.

But there was one person of the boarding-house whose opinion was as yet unknown to Flossie or to anybody else; it was doubtful indeed if it was known altogether to himself; for Mr. Spinks conceived that honour bound him to a superb reticence on the subject. He had followed with breathless anxiety every turn in the love affairs of Flossie and his friend. He could not deny that a base and secret exultation had possessed him on the amazing advent of Miss Harden; for love had made him preternaturally keen, and he was visited with mysterious intimations of the truth. He did not encourage these visitings. He had tried hard to persuade himself that he was glad for Flossie's sake when Miss Harden went away; when, whatever there had been between Rickets and the lady, it had come to nothing; when the wedding day remained fixed, immovably fixed. But he had not been glad at all. On the contrary he had suffered horribly, and had felt the subsequent delay as a cruel prolongation of his agony. In the irony of destiny, shortly before the fatal twenty-fifth, Mr. Spinks had been made partner in his uncle's business, and was now enjoying an income superior to Rickman's not only in amount but in security. If anything could have added to his dejection it was that. His one consolation hitherto had been that after all, if Rickman did marry Flossie, as *he* was not in a position to marry her, it came to the same thing in the long run. Now he saw himself cut off from that source of comfort by a solid four hundred a year with prospects of a rise. He could forego the obviously impossible; but in that rosy dawn of incarnation his dream appeared more than ever desirable. Whenever Mr. Spinks's imagination encountered the idea of marriage it had tried to look another way. Marriage remote and unattainable left Mr. Spinks's imagination in comparative peace; but brought within the bounds of possibility its appeal was simply maddening. And now, bringing it nearer still, so near that it was impossible to look another way, there came these disturbing suggestions of a misunderstanding between Rickman and his Beaver. The boarding-house knew nothing but that the wedding was put off because Rickman was in difficulties and could not afford to marry at the moment. Spinks would have accepted this explanation as sufficient if it had not been for the peculiar behaviour of Rickman, and the very mysterious and agitating change in Flossie's manner. Old Rickets had returned to his awful solitude. He absented himself entirely from the dinner-table. When you met him on the stairs he was incommunicative and gloomy; and whatever you asked him to do he was too busy to do it. His sole attention to poor Flossie was to take her for an occasional airing in the Park on Sunday afternoons. Spinks had come across them there walking sadly side by side. Flossie for propriety's sake would be making a little conversation as he went by;

but Rickman had always the shut mouth and steady eyes of invincible determination.

What was it that Razors was so determined about? To marry Flossie? Or not to marry her? That was the question which agitated poor Spinks from morning till night, or rather from night till morning. The worst of it was that the very nature of his woes compelled him as an honourable person to keep them to himself.

But there was no secret which could be long concealed from the eyes of that clever lady, Miss Roots; and she had contrived in the most delicate manner to convey to the unfortunate youth that he had her sympathy. Spinks, bound by his honour, had used no words in divulging his agony; but their unspoken confidences had gone so far that Miss Roots at last permitted herself to say that it might be as well to find out whether " it was on or off."

" But," said the miserable Spinks, " would that be fair to Rickman? "

" I think so," said the lady, with a smile that would have been sweet had it been rather less astute. " Mind you, I'm not in their secrets; but I believe you really needn't be afraid of that."

" Yes. But how in heaven's name am I to find out? I can't ask him, and I can't ask her."

" Why can't you ask them? "

Spinks was unable to say why; but his delicacy shrank from either course as in some subtle way unfair. Besides he distrusted Miss Root's counsel, for she had not been nice to Flossie.

" Oh, Lord," said Spinks, " what an orful mess I'm in! " He said it to himself; for he had resolved to talk no longer to Miss Roots.

He could have borne it better had not the terrible preoccupation of Rickman thrown Flossie on his hands. In common decency he had to talk to her at the dinner-table. But it was chivalry (surely) that drew him to her in the drawing-room afterwards. She had to be protected (poor Flossie) from the shrewdness of Miss Roots, the impertinence of Mr. Soper, and the painful sympathy of the other boarders. With the very best and noblest intentions in the world, Mr. Spinks descended nightly into that atmosphere of gloom, and there let loose his imperishable hilarity.

He was quite safe, he knew, as long as their relations could be kept upon a purely hilarious footing; but Flossie's manner intimated (what it had never intimated before) that she now realized and preferred the serious side of him; and there was no way by which the humorous Spinks was more profoundly flattered than in being taken seriously. Some nights they had the drawing-room to themselves, but for the harmless presence of Mr. Partridge dozing in his chair; and then, to see Flossie struggling to keep a polite little smile hovering on a mouth too tiny to support it; to see her give up the effort and suddenly become grave; to see her turn away to hide her gravity with all the precautions another woman takes to conceal her merriment; to see her sitting there, absolutely unmoved by the diverting behaviour of Mr. Partridge in his slumber, was profoundly agitating to Mr. Spinks.

"I'm sure," said Flossie one night (it was nearly three weeks after the scene with Rickman in the Park), "I'm sure I don't know why we're laughing so much. There's nothing to laugh at that I can see."

Spinks could have have replied in Byron's fashion that if he laughed 'twas that he might not weep, but he restrained himself; and all he said was, "I like to see you larf."

"Well, you can't say you've ever seen me cry."

"No, I haven't. I shouldn't like to see *that*, Flossie. And I shouldn't like to be the one that made you."

"Wouldn't you?"

Flossie put her pocket handkerchief to her little nose, and under the corner of it there peeped the tail-end of a lurking smile.

"No," said Spinks simply, "I wouldn't." He was thinking of Miss Roots. The theory of Rickman's bad behaviour had never entered his head. "What's more, I don't think any nice person would do it."

"Don't you?"

"No. Not any really nice person."

"It's generally," said Flossie, sweetly meditative, "the nicest person you know who can make you cry most. Not that *I'm* crying."

"No. But I can see that somebody's been annoying you, and I think I can guess pretty well who it is, too. Nothing would please me more than to 'ave five minutes' private conversation with that person." He was thinking of Miss Harden now.

"You mustn't dream of it. It wouldn't do, you know; it really wouldn't. Look here, promise me you'll never say a word."

"Well, it's safe enough to promise. There aren't many opportunities of meeting."

"No, that's the worst of it, there aren't now. Still, you might meet him any minute on the stairs, or anywhere. And if you go saying things you'll only make him angry."

"Oh it's a him, is it?" (*Now* he was thinking of Soper.) "*I* know. Don't say Soper's been making himself unpleasant."

"He's always unpleasant."

"Is he? By 'Eaven, if I catch him!"

"Do be quiet. It isn't Mr. Soper."

"Isn't it?"

"No. How could it be? You don't call Mr. Soper *nice*, do you?"

Spinks was really quiet for a moment. "I say, Flossie, have you and Rickets been 'aving a bit of a tiff?"

"What do you want to know that for? It's nothing to you."

"Well, it isn't just my curiosity. It's because I might be able to help you, Floss, if you didn't mind telling me what it was. I'm not a clever fellow, but there's no one in this house understands old Razors as well as I do."

"Then you must be pretty sharp, for I can't understand him at all. Has he been saying anything to you?"

"Oh, no, he wouldn't say anything. You don't talk about these things, you know."

"I thought he might—to you."

"Me? I'm the very last person he'd dream of talking to."

"I thought you were such friends."

"So we are. But you see he never talks about you to me, Flossie."

"Why ever not?"

"That's why. Because we're friends. Because he wouldn't think it fair——"

"Fair to who?"

"To me, of course."

"Why shouldn't it be fair to you?" Her eyes, close-lidded, were fixed upon the floor. As long as she looked at him, Spinks held himself well in hand; but the sudden withdrawing of those dangerous weapons threw him off his guard.

"Because he knows I—— Oh, hang it all, that's what I swore I wouldn't say."

"You haven't said it."

"No, but I've made you see it."

His handsome face stiffened with horror at his stupidity. To let fall the slightest hint of his feeling was, he felt, the last disloyalty to Rickman. He had a vague idea that he ought instantly to go. But instead of going he sat there, silent, fixing on his own enormity a mental stare so concentrated that it would have drawn Flossie's attention to it, if she had not seen it all the time.

"If there's anything to see," said she, "there's no reason why I shouldn't see it."

"P'raps not. There's every reason, though, why I should have held my silly tongue."

"Why, what difference does it make?"

"It doesn't make any difference to you, of course, and it can't make any difference—really—to him; but it's a downright dishonourable thing to do, and that makes a jolly lot of difference to me. You see, I haven't any business to go and feel like this."

"Oh, well, you can't help your feelings, can you?" she said softly. "Anybody may have feelings——"

"Yes, but a decent chap, you know, wouldn't let on that he had any—at least, not when the girl he—he—— You know what I mean, it's what I mustn't say—when she and the other fellow weren't hitting it off very well together."

"Oh, you think it might make a difference then?"

"No, I don't—not really. It's only the feeling I have about it, don't you see. It seems somehow so orf'ly mean. Razors wouldn't have done it if it had been me, you know."

"But it couldn't have been you."

"Of course it couldn't," said the miserable Spinks, with a weak spurt of anger; "that was only my way of putting it."

"What are you driving at? What ever did you think I said?"

"Never mind what you said. You're making me talk about it, and I said I wouldn't."

"When did you say that?"

" Ages ago—when Rickets first told me you—and he——"

" Oh, that? That was so long ago that it doesn't matter much now."

" Oh, doesn't it, though; it matters a jolly sight more. You said " (there was bitterness in his tone), " you said it couldn't have been me. As if I didn't know that."

" I didn't mean it couldn't have been you, not in that way. I only meant that you'd have—well, you'd have behaved very differently, if it had been you; and so I believed you would."

" You don't know how I'd 'ave behaved."

" I've a pretty good idea, though." She looked straight at him this time, and he grew strangely brave.

" Look here, Flossie," he said solemnly, " you know—as I've just let it out—that I'm most orf'ly gone on you. I don't suppose there's anything I wouldn't do for you, except —well, I really don't know what you're driving at, but if it's anything to do with Razors, I'd rather not hear about it, if you don't mind. It isn't fair, really. You see, it's putting me in such a 'orribly delicate position."

" I don't think you're very kind, Sidney. You don't think of me, or what sort of a position you put me in. I'm sure I wouldn't have said a word, only you asked me to tell you all about it; you needn't say you didn't."

" That was when I thought, p'raps, I could help you to patch it up. But if I can't, it's another matter."

" Patch it up? Do you think I'd let you try? I don't believe in patching things up, once they're—broken off."

" I say, Flossie, it hasn't come to that?"

" It couldn't come to anything else, the way it was going."

" Oh Lord!" Spinks buried a crimson face in his hands. If only he hadn't felt such a horrible exultation!

" I thought you knew. Isn't that what we've been talking about all the time?"

" I didn't understand. I only thought—*he* didn't tell me, mind you—I thought it was just put off because he couldn't afford to marry quite so soon."

" Don't you think three hundred a year is enough to marry on?"

" Well, I shouldn't care to marry on that myself; not if it wasn't regular. He's quite right, Flossie. You see, a man hasn't got only his wife to think of."

" No—I suppose he must think of himself a little too."

" Oh, well, no; if he's a decent chap, he thinks of his children."

Flossie's face was crimson, too, while her thoughts flew to that unfurnished room in the brown house at Ealing. She was losing sight of Keith Rickman; for behind Keith Rickman there was Sidney Spinks; and behind Sidney Spinks there was the indomitable Dream. She did not look at Spinks, therefore, but gazed steadily at the top of Mr. Partridge's head. With one word Spinks had destroyed the effect he had calculated on from his honourable reticence. Perhaps it was because Flossie's thoughts had flown so far that her voice seemed to come from somewhere a long way off, too.

" What would you think enough to marry on, then? "

" Well, I shouldn't care to do it much under four hundred myself," he said guardedly.

"And I suppose if you hadn't it you'd expect a girl to wait for you any time until you'd made it? "

" Well, of course I should, if we were engaged already. But I shouldn't ask any girl to marry me unless I could afford to keep her——"

" You wouldn't *ask,* but——"

" No, and I wouldn't let on that I cared for her either. I wouldn't let on under four hundred—certain."

"Oh," said Flossie very quietly. And Spinks was crushed under a sense of fresh disloyalty to Rickman. His defence of Rickman had been made to turn into a pleading for himself. " But Razors is different; he'll be making twice that in no time, you'll see. I shouldn't be afraid to ask any one if I was him."

Vainly the honourable youth sought to hide his splendour; Flossie had drawn from him all she needed now to know.

" Look here, Floss, you say it's broken off. Would you mind telling me was it you—or was it he who did it? " His tone expressed acute anxiety on this point, for in poor Spinks's code of honour it made all the difference. But he felt that this question was clearly answered, for the silence of Razors argued sufficiently that it was he.

" Well," said Flossie with a touch of maidenly dignity, " whichever it was, it wasn't likely to be Keith."

Spinks's face would have fallen, but for its immense

surprise. In this case Rickman ought, yes, he certainly ought, to have told him. It wasn't behaving quite straight, he considered, to keep it from the man who had the best right in the world to know, a fellow who had always acted straight with him. But perhaps, poor chap, he was only waiting a little on the chance of the Beaver changing her mind.

"Don't you think, Flossie, that if he tried hard he could bring it on again?"

"No, he couldn't. Never. Not if he tried from now till next year. Not if he went on his bended knees to me."

Spinks reflected that Rickman's knees didn't take kindly to bending. "Haven't you been a little, just a little hard on him? He's such a sensitive little chap. If I was a woman I don't think I could let him go like that. You might let him have another try."

Poor Spinks was so earnest, so sincere, so unaffectedly determined not to take advantage of the situation, that it dawned on Flossie that dignity must now yield a little to diplomacy. She was not making the best possible case for herself by representing the rupture as one-sided. "To tell you the truth, Sidney, he doesn't want to try. We've agreed about it. We've both of us found we'd made a great mistake——"

"I wish *I* could be as sure of that."

"Why, what difference could it make to you?" said Flossie, turning on him the large eyes of innocence, eyes so dark, so deep, that her thoughts were lost in them.

"It would make all the difference in the world, if I knew you weren't making a lot bigger mistake now." He rose. "I think, if you don't mind, I'll 'ave a few words with Rickets, after all. I think I'll go up and see him now."

There was no change in the expression of her eyes, but her eyelids quivered. "No, Sidney, don't. For goodness' sake, don't go and say anything."

"I'm not going to say anything. I only want to know——"

"I've told you everything—everything I can."

"Yes; but it's what you can't tell me that I want to know."

"Well, but do wait a bit. Don't you speak to him before

I see him. Because I don't want him to think I've given him away."

"I'll take good care he doesn't think that, Flossie. But I'm going to get this off my mind to-night."

"Well then, you must just take him a message from me. Say I've thought it over and that I've told you everything. Don't forget. I've told you everything, say. Mind you tell him that before you begin about anything else. Then he'll understand."

"All right. I'll tell him."

Her eyes followed him dubiously as he stumbled over Mr. Partridge's legs in his excited crossing of the room. She was by no means sure of her ambassador's discretion. His heart would make no blunder; but could she trust his head?

Up to this point Flossie had played her game with admirable skill. She had, without showing one card of her own, caused Spinks to reveal his entire hand. It was not until she had drawn from him the assurance of his imperishable devotion, together with the exact amount of his equally imperishable income, that she had committed herself to a really decisive move. She was perfectly well aware of its delicacy and danger. Not for worlds would she have had Spinks guess that Rickman was still waiting for her decision. And yet, if Spinks referred rashly and without any preparation to the breaking off of the engagement, Rickman's natural reply would be that this was the first he had heard of it. Therefore did she so manœuvre and contrive as to make Rickman suppose that Spinks was the accredited bearer of her ultimatum, while Spinks himself remained unaware that he was conveying the first intimation of it. It was an exceedingly risky thing to do. But Flossie, playing for high stakes, had calculated her risk to a nicety. She must make up her mind to lose something. As the game now stood, the moral approbation of Spinks was more valuable to her than the moral approbation of Rickman; and in venturing this final move she had reckoned that the moral approbation of Rickman was all she had to lose. Unless, of course, he chose to give her away.

But Rickman could be trusted not to give her away.

When Spinks presented himself in Rickman's study he

obtained admission in spite of the lateness of the hour.
The youth's solemn agitation was not to be gainsaid. He
first of all delivered himself of Flossie's message, faithfully,
word for word.

"Oh, so she's told you everything, has she? And what
did she tell you?"

"Why, that it was all over between you, broken off, you
know."

"And you've come to me to know if it's true, is that it?"

"Well, no, why should I? Of course it's true if she
says so."

Rickman reflected for a moment; the situation, he
perceived, was delicate in the extreme, delicate beyond
his power to deal with it. But the god did not forsake his
own, and inspiration came to him.

"You're right there, Spinky. Of course it's true if she
says so."

"She seemed to think you wouldn't mind her telling me.
She said you'd understand."

"Oh, yes, I think I understand. Did she tell you *she*
had broken it off?" (He was really anxious to know how
she had put it.)

"Yes, but she was most awfully nice about it. I made
out—I mean she gave me the impression—that she did it,
well, partly because she thought she wanted it off. But
that's just what I want to be sure about. Do you want it
off, or don't you?"

"Is that what she wants to know?"

"No. It's what I want to know. What's more, Rickets,
I think I've got a fair right to know it, too."

"What do you want me to say? That I don't want to
marry Miss Walker or that I do?"

Spinks's face flushed with the rosy dawn of an idea. It
was possible that Rickets didn't want to marry her, that
he was in need of protection, of deliverance. There was a
great deed that he, Spinks, could do for Rickets. His eyes
grew solemn as they beheld his destiny.

"Look here," said he, "I want you to tell me nothing
but the bally truth. It's the least you can do under the
circumstances. I don't want it for her, well—yes, I do; but
I want it for myself, too."

"All right, Spinky, you shall have the best truth I can

give you at such uncommonly short notice. I can't say I don't want to marry Miss Walker, because that wouldn't be very polite to the lady. But I can say I think she's shown most admirable judgment, and that I'm perfectly satisfied with her decision. I wouldn't have her go back on it for worlds. Will that satisfy you?"

" It would if I thought you really meant it."

" I do mean it, God forgive me. But that isn't her fault, poor little girl. The whole thing was the most infernal muddle and mistake."

"Ah, that was what she called it—a mistake." Spinks seemed to be clinging to and cherishing this word of charm.

" I'm glad for her sake that she found it out in time. I'm not the sort of a man a girl like Flossie ought to marry. I ought never to have asked her."

" Upon my soul, Rickets, I believe you're right there. That's not saying anything against you, or against her either."

" No. Certainly not against *her*. She's all right, Spinky——"

" I know, I know."

Still Spinks hesitated, restraining his ardent embrace of the truth presented to him, held back by some scruple of shy unbelieving modesty.

" Then you think, you really *do* think, that there isn't any reason why I shouldn't cut in?"

" No, heaven bless you; no reason in the world, as far as I'm concerned. For God's sake cut in and win; the sooner the better. Now, this minute, if you feel like it."

But still he lingered, for the worst was yet to come. He lingered, nursing a colossal scruple. Poor Spinks's honour was dear to him, because it was less the gift of nature than the supreme imitative effort of his adoring heart. He loved honour because Rickman loved it; just as he had loved Flossie for the same reason. These were the only ways in which he could imitate him; and like all imitators he exaggerated the master's manner.

" I say, I don't know what you'll think of me. I said I'd never let on to Flossie that I cared; and I didn't mean to, I didn't on my word. I don't know how it happened; but to-night we got talking—to tell you the truth I thought I was doing my best to get her to make it up with you——"

"Thanks; that was kind," said Rickman in a queer voice which put Spinks off a bit.

"I was really, Razors. I do believe I'd have died rather than let her know how I felt about her; but before I could say knife——"

"She got it out of you?"

"No, she didn't do anything of the sort. It was all me. Like a damn fool I let it out—some'ow."

Nothing could have been more demoralizing than the spectacle of Spinks's face as he delivered himself of his immense confession; so fantastically did it endeavour to chasten rapture with remorse. Rickman controlled himself the better to enjoy it; for Spinks, taken seriously, yielded an inexhaustible vein of purest comedy. "Oh, Spinky," he said with grave reproach, "how could you?"

"Well, I know it was a beastly dishonourable thing to do; but you see I was really most awkwardly situated."

"I daresay you were." It was all very well to laugh; but in spite of his amusement he sympathized with Spinky's delicacy. He also had found himself in awkward situations more than once.

"Still," continued Spinks with extreme dejection, "I can't think how I came to let it out."

That, and the dejection, was too much for Rickman's gravity.

"If you want the truth, Spinky, the pity was you ever kept it in." And his laughter, held in, piled up, monstrous, insane, ungovernable, broke forth, dispersing the last scruple that clouded the beatitude of Spinks.

CHAPTER LXV

OFTEN, after half a night spent in a vain striving to shape some immense idea into the form of beauty, he had turned the thing neck and crop out of his mind and gone to sleep on it. Whenever he did this he was sure to wake up and find it there waiting for him, full-formed and perfect as he had dreamed it and desired. It had happened so often that he had grown to trust this profounder inspiration of his sleep.

Hitherto it was only the problems of his heart that had

been thus divinely dealt with; he had been left to struggle hopelessly with the problems of his life; and of these Flossie was the most insoluble. And now that he had given up thinking of her, had abandoned her to her own mysterious workings, it too had been solved and in the same simple inevitable way. His contempt for Flossie's methods could not blind him to the beneficence of the result.

He wrote to her that night to the effect that he gladly and entirely acquiesced in her decision; but that he should have thought that he and not Mr. Spinks had been entitled to the first intimation of it. He had no doubt, however, that she had done the best and wisest thing. He forbore to add " for both of us." His chivalry still persisted in regarding Flossie as a deeply injured person. He had wronged her from the beginning. Had he not laid on her, first the burden of his passion, and yet again the double burden of his genius and his honour? A heavier load, that, and wholly unfitted for the poor little back that would have had to bear it. It never occurred to him that he had been in any way the victim of Flossie's powerful instincts. It was Maddox who said that Mr. Spinks had made himself immortal by his marriage; that he should be put on the Civil List for his services to literature.

Of Rickman's place in literature there could be no question for the next two or three years. He foresaw that the all-important thing was his place on *The Planet*, his place on *Metropolis*, his place (if he could find one) on any other paper. He had looked to journalism for the means to support a wife, and journalism alone could maintain him in his struggle with Pilkington. Whether Maddox was right or wrong in his opinion of the disastrous influence of Flossie, there could be no doubt that for the present Rickman's genius had no more formidable rival than his honour. If it is perdition to a great tragic dramatist when passion impels him to marry on three hundred a year, it can hardly be desirable that conscience should constrain him to raise seven hundred and fifty pounds in three years. Fate seemed bent in forcing him to live his tragedies rather than write them; but Rickman, free of Flossie, faced the desperate prospect with the old reckless spirit of his youth.

For the first year the prospect did not look so very desperate. He had found cheap rooms unfurnished in Torring-

ton Square, where the houses are smaller and less sumptuous than Mrs. Downey's. He had succeeded in letting
the little house in Ealing, where the abominable furniture
that had nearly cost so dear justified its existence by adding
a small sum to his income. He had benefited indirectly
by Rankin's greatness; for Rankin seldom contributed
anything to *The Planet* now beyond his lively column once
a week; and Rickman was frequently called on to fill his
place. *The Planet* was good for at least a solid hundred
a year; *Metropolis* (once it began to pay) for a solid two
hundred and fifty or more; other papers for small and
varying sums. When he totted it all up together he found
that he was affluent. He could reckon on a round four
hundred all told. In Torrington Square, by the practice
of a little ingenious economy, he could easily live on a
hundred and twenty-five; so that by the end of the first
year he should have saved the considerable sum of two
hundred and seventy-five pounds. At that rate, in three
years—no, in two years and a—well, in rather more than
two and a half years the thing would be done. By a little
extra exertion he might be able to reduce it to two years; to
one, perhaps, by a magnificent stroke of luck. Such luck, for
instance, as a stage success, a run of a hundred nights for
the tragedy whose First Act he was writing now.

That, of course, it would be madness to count on; but
he had some hopes from the sudden and extraordinary transformation of *The Museion.*

Sudden enough, to the uninitiated, seeing that in September, ninety-seven, the organ of philosophic criticism to all appearances died, and that in October it burst into life again
under a new cover and a new title, Jewdwine himself sounding the trump of resurrection. *The Museion's* old contributors knew it no more; or failed to recognize it in *Metropolis.*
On the tinted cover there was no trace of the familiar
symbolic head-piece, so suggestive of an Ionic frieze, but
the new title in the broadest, boldest, blackest of type, proclaimed its almost wanton repudiation of the old tradition.

Jewdwine's first " concession to modernity " was a long
leading review of the " Art of Herbert Rankin." Herbert
Rankin was so much amused with it that it kept him quiet
for at least three weeks in his playground of *The Planet.*
After such a handsome appreciation as that, he had to wait

a decent interval before "going for Jewdwine." When he remarked to Rickman that it would have been more to the purpose if Jewdwine had devoted his six columns to the Art of S. K. R., Rickman blushed and turned his head away, as if Rankin had been guilty of some gross indelicacy. He was still virginally sensitive where Jewdwine was concerned.

But, in a sense not intended by Rankin, Jewdwine was very much occupied, not to say perturbed, by the art of S. K. R. Not exactly to the exclusion of every other interest; for Rickman, looking in on the great editor one afternoon, found him almost enthusiastic over his "last discovery." A new poet, according to Jewdwine, had arisen in the person of an eminent Cabinet Minister, who in ninety-seven was beguiling the tedium of office with a very pretty playing on the pastoral pipe. Mr. Fulcher's *In Arcadia* lay on the editorial table, bound in white vellum, with the figure of the great God Pan, symbolizing Mr. Fulcher, on the cover. Jewdwine's attitude to Mr. Fulcher was for Jewdwine humble, not to say reverent. He intimated to Rickman that in Fulcher he had found what he had wanted.

Jewdwine in the early days of *Metropolis* wore the hungry look of a man who, having swallowed all his formulas, finds himself unnourished. "The soul," Jewdwine used to say (perverting Emerson) "is appeased by a formula"; and it was clear that his soul would never be appeased until it had found a new one. Those who now conversed intimately with Jewdwine were entertained no longer with the Absolute, but they heard a great deal about the "Return to Nature." Mr. Fulcher's pipings, therefore, were entirely in harmony with Jewdwine's change of mood.

But Rickman, who had once protested so vigorously against the Absolute, would not hear of the Return to Nature either. That cry was only a symptom of the inevitable sickness of the academic spirit, surfeited with its own philosophy. He shook his head mournfully over Mr. Fulcher. What looked to Jewdwine like simplicity seemed to him only a more intolerably sophisticated pose than any other.

"I prefer Mr. Fulcher in Downing Street to Mr. Fulcher in Arcadia. Mr. Fulcher," he said, "can no more return to Nature than he can enter a second time into his mother's womb and be born."

He walked up and down the little office excitedly, while

he drew for Jewdwine's benefit an unattractive picture of the poet as babe, drinking from the breasts of the bounteous mother. "You can't go for ever hanging on your mother's breasts; it isn't decent and it isn't manly. Return to Nature! It's only too easy to return, and stay. You'll do no good at all if you've never been there; but if you mean to grow up you must break loose and get away. The great mother is inclined to hug some of her children rather too tight, I fancy; and by Heaven! it's pretty tough work for some of them wriggling out of her arms."

He came to a sudden standstill, and turned on Jewdwine the sudden leaping light of the blue eyes that seemed to see through Jewdwine and beyond him. No formula could ever frame and hold for him that vision of his calling which had come to him five years ago on Harcombe Hill. He had conceived and sung of Nature, not as the indomitable parent, by turns tyrannous and kind, but as the virgin mystery, the shy and tender bride that waits in golden abysmal secrecy for the embrace of spirit, herself athirst for the passionate, immortal hour. He foresaw the supreme and indestructible union. He saw one eternal nature and a thousand forms of art, differing according to the virile soul. And what he saw he endeavoured to describe to Jewdwine. "That means, mind you, that your poet is a grown-up man and not a slobbering infant."

"Exactly. And Nature will be the mother of his art. As *I* said."

"As you didn't say—the mother *only*. There isn't any immaculate conception of truth. Don't you believe it for a moment."

Jewdwine retired into himself a moment to meditate on that telling word. He wondered what lay beyond it.

"And Art," continued Rickman, "is truth. Just because it isn't Nature."

"If you mean," said Jewdwine, seeking a formula, "that modern art is essentially subjective, I agree with you."

"I mean that really virile and original art—the art, I believe, of the future—must spring from the supreme surrender of Nature to the human soul."

"And do you honestly believe that the art of the future will be one bit more 'virile' than the art of the present day?"

"On the whole, I do."

" Well, I don't. I see nothing that makes for it. No art can hold out for ever against commercialism. The nineteenth century has been commercial enough in all conscience, bestially, brutally commercial; but its commercialism and brutality will be nothing to the commercialism and brutality of the twentieth. If these things are deadly to art now, they'll be ten times more deadly then. The mortality, among poets, my dear Rickman, will be something terrific."

" Not a bit of it. The next century, if I'm not mistaken, will see a pretty big flare up of a revolution; and the soul will come out on top. Robespierre and Martin Luther won't be in it, Jewdwine, with the poets of that school."

" I'm glad you feel able to take that view of it. I don't seem to see the poets of the twentieth century myself."

" I see them all right," said Rickman simply. " They won't be the poets of Nature, like the nineteenth century chaps; they'll be the poets of human nature—dramatic poets, to a man. Of course, it'll take a revolution to produce that sort."

" A revolution? A cataclysm, you mean."

" No. If you come to think of it, it's only the natural way a healthy poet grows. Look at Shakespeare. I believe, you know, that most poets would grow into dramatic poets if they lived long enough. Only sometimes they don't live; and sometimes they don't grow. Lyric poets are cases of arrested development, that's all."

Jewdwine listened with considerable amusement as his subordinate propounded to him this novel view. He wondered what literary enormity Rickman might be contemplating now. That he had something at the back of his mind was pretty evident. Jewdwine meant to lie low till, from that obscure region, Rickman, as was his wont, should have brought out his monster for inspection.

He produced it the next instant, blushingly, tenderly, yet with no diminution of his sublime belief.

" You see—you'll think it sheer lunacy, but—I've a sort of idea that if I'm to go on at all, myself, it must be on those lines. Modern poetic drama—it's that or nothing, you know."

Jewdwine's face said very plainly that he had no doubt whatever of the alternative. It also expressed a curious and indefinable relief.

" Modern poetic drama? So that's your modest ambition, is it?"

Rickman owned that indeed it was.

" My dear fellow, modern poetic drama is a contradiction in all its terms. There are only three schools of poetry possible—the classic, the romantic, and the natural. Art only exists by one of three principles, normal beauty, spiritual spontaneity, and vital mystery or charm. And none of these three is to be found in modern life." These were the laws he had laid down in the *Prolegomena to Æsthetics,* which Rickman, in the insolence of his genius, had defied. Somehow the life seemed to have departed from those stately propositions, but Jewdwine clung to them in a desperate effort to preserve his critical integrity. He was soothed by the sound of his own voice repeating them. He caught as it were an echo of the majestic harmonies that once floated through his lecture-room at Lazarus. " Besides," he went on, " where will you find your drama to begin with?"

" In modern men and women."

" But modern men and women are essentially undramatic, *and* unpoetic."

" Still, I must take them, because, you see, there's nothing else to take. There never was or will be. The men and women of Shakespeare's time were modern to him, you know. If they seem poetic to us, that's because a poet made them so; and he made them so because he saw that—essentially—they *were* so."

Jewdwine pushed out his lips in the manner of one unwillingly dubious.

" My dear Rickman, you have got to learn your limitations; or if not your limitations, the limitations made for you by the ridiculous and unlovely conditions of modern life."

" I have learnt them. After all, what am I to do? I *am* modern—modern as my hat," said Rickman, turning it in his hands. " I admit that my hat isn't even a fugitive form of the eternal and absolute beauty. It is, I'm afraid, horribly like everybody else's hat. In moments of profound insight I feel that *I* am horribly like everybody else. If it wasn't for that I should have no hope of achieving my modest ambition."

" I'm not saying anything against your modesty or your

ambition. I'm not defying you to write a modern blank verse play; but I defy anybody to act one."

" I know," said Rickman, " it's sad of course, but to the frivolous mind of a critic there always will be something ridiculous in the notion of blank verse spouted on the stage by a person in a frock-coat and a top-hat. But do you think you'd see that frock-coat and top-hat if once the great tragic passions got inside them?"

" Where *are* the great tragic passions?"

" They exist and are poetic."

" As survivals only. They are poetic, but not modern. We have the passions of the divorce-court and the Stock Exchange. They are modern, if you like, but not strikingly poetic."

" Well—even a stock-broker—if you insist on stock-brokers——"

" I don't. Take the people—take the women I know, the women you know. Is there—honestly, is there any poetry in them?"

" There is—heaps. Oceans of poetry. There always has been and will be. It's the poets, the great poets, that don't turn up to time."

" Well; I don't care how great a poet you may be, modern poetic drama is the path of perdition for you.

" I wish," he added with an unmistakable air of turning to a subject of real interest, " I wish I knew what to do with Fulcher."

" I don't know. I only know Mr. Fulcher's art hasn't much to do with Nature. I'm afraid it's the illegitimate offspring of Mr. Fulcher and some young shepherdess of Covent Garden."

" He seems to have proved himself pretty much at home in Arcadia."

" Don't you believe him. He's only at home in Downing Street. You'd better leave him there."

But Jewdwine did not leave him there. He exalted Mr. Fulcher to the seventh heaven in four and a half columns of *Metropolis*. With his journalistic scent for the alluring and the vivid phrase, he took everything notable that Rickman had said and adapted it to Mr. Fulcher, *In Arcadia* supplying a really golden opportunity for a critical essay on " Truth to Nature," wherein Mr. Fulcher learnt, to his immense bewilderment, that there is no immaculate conception of that truth; but that to Mr. Fulcher, as poet, belonged the exultation of paternity. Jewdwine quoted Coleridge to the effect that Mr. Fulcher only received what he was pleased to give, and that in Mr. Fulcher's life alone did Nature live. And when Rankin, falling on that article, asked Maddox what it meant, Maddox replied that it meant nothing except that Mr. Fulcher was a Cabinet Minister.

But within three months of the day on which Jewdwine had pronounced the modern poetic drama to be dead, Rickman had written the Fist Act of his tragedy, which proved it (as far as a First Act can prove anything) to be very much alive.

Jewdwine received the announcement of this achievement with every appearance of pleasure. He was indeed genuinely relieved to think that Rickman was thus harmlessly employed. The incessant successful production of *Saturnalia* would have been prejudicial to the interests of *The Museion;* a series of triumphant *Helens in Leuce* would have turned Rickman aside for ever from the columns of *Metropolis;* but Jewdwine told himself that he had nothing to fear from the rivalries of the modern Tragic Muse. Rickman the journalist would live; for Rickman the poet had set out on the path of perdition.

Nobody could say that it was Jewdwine who had encouraged him to take it.

CHAPTER LXVI

IN January, ninety-eight, *Metropolis* began to pay, and Rickman's hopes were justified. He was now a solid man, a man of income. For eighteen months he kept strictly within the limits he had allowed himself. His nature inclined him to a riotous and absurd expenditure, and for eighteen months he wrestled with and did violence to his nature. Each sum he saved stood for some triumph of ingenious abnegation, some miracle of self-restraint. And for eighteen months Dicky Pilkington, beholding the spectacle of his heroism, laid ten to one against his ultimate success. The thing, Dicky said, was impossible; he could never keep it up. But Rickman once abandoned to a persistent and passionate economy, there was no more hold-ing him in on that path than on any other. By the middle of the following year, out of an income of four hundred he had saved that sum.

He said to himself that the worst was over now. He had paid off more than half of his debt, and the remainder had still another fourteen months to run. Only fourteen months' passionate economy and the Harden library would be 'redeemed. As he saw himself within measurable distance of his end he was seized by an anxiety, an excitement that he had not been aware of at the start. The sight of the goal perturbed him; it suggested the failure that up to that moment he had not allowed himself to contemplate. Like an athlete he gathered himself together for the final spurt; and ninety-nine was a brilliant year for *The Planet,* made glorious by the poems, articles, and paragraphs showered on it by S. K. R. Maddox shook his head over some of them; but he took them all and boasted, as he well might, that *The Planet* published more Rickman—the real Rickman—in six months than *Metropolis* would do in as many years. He distinguished between Rickman's genius and his talent; provided he got his best work, anybody else was welcome to his second-best. By anybody else he meant Jewdwine.

Yet it was a nobler feeling than professional rivalry that made him abhor the poet's connection with *Metropolis;* for Maddox was if anything more jealous for Rickman's reputa-tion than for his own. From the very beginning he had never ceased to wonder at his unaccountable affection for Horace Jewdwine; the infatuation, for it amounted to infatuation, would have been comprehensible enough in any other man, but it was unaccountable in Rickman, who was wholly destitute of reverence for the sources of his income. Jewdwine of *The Museion* had been in Maddox's opin-ion a harmless philosophic crank; he had done nothing, absolutely nothing, for Rickman's genius; but Jewdwine of *Metropolis* was dangerous, for he encouraged Rickman's talent; and Rickman's talent would, he was afraid, be ulti-mately destructive to the higher power.

So Maddox prayed to heaven for promotion, that he might make Rickman independent of Jewdwine and his journal. There were many things that he had in his mind to do for him in the day of advancement. His eyes raked the horizon, sighting promotion from afar. And in the last two years, promotion had come very near to Maddox. There were quarters, influential quarters, where he was spoken of as a singularly original young man; and he had the knack of getting hold of singularly original young men; young men of originality too singular perhaps to make the paper pay. Still, though the orbit of *The Planet* was hardly so vast as Maddox had anticipated, as to its brilliance there could be no two opinions. In the year ninety-eight, the year that saw Rickman first struggling in the financier's toils, Maddox had delivered his paper from the power of Pilkington. Promotion played with Maddox; it hovered round him, touching him tentatively with the tips of its wings; he lured it by every innocent art within his power, but hitherto it had always settled on some less wild and wanton head.

At last it came, it kept on coming, from a quarter where, as he had every right to look for it, he had of course never dreamed of looking. Rankin's publishers, grown rich on the proceeds of Rankin's pen, were dissatisfied with their reader (the poor man had not discovered Rankin); on Rankin's advice they offered his post to Maddox (who had), and that at double his salary. They grew richer, and at a further hint from Rankin they made Maddox a director. In the same mad year they started a new monthly, and (Rankin again) appointed Maddox as their editor.

His opportunity had come. On the very night of this third appointment Maddox called on Rickman and proposed, on behalf of Rankin and Stables, to hand over to him the editorship of *The Planet*. For Stables, he said, was too dog lazy, and Rankin too grossly prosperous to have anything to do with it. He didn't think any of them would ever make a fortune out of it; but its editor's income would be at any rate secure. He omitted to mention that it would be practically secured out of his, Maddox's, own pocket.

"You may reckon," said he, "on three hundred and fifty." He named the sum modestly, humbly almost; not that he thought Rickman would be sorry to have that little addition to his income, but because he was always diffident in offering anything to Rickman, "when you thought of what he was"; and he found something startling, not to say upsetting, in the joy that leapt up in his young eyes. You never could tell how Ricky-ticky would take a thing;

but if he had known he was going to take it that way he would have written him a note. He wondered whether Ricky-ticky was in a tight corner, head over ears in debt or love. Did the young lunatic want to marry after that near shave he had two years ago? You wouldn't exactly refuse three hundred and fifty; but a beggar must be brought pretty low to be crumpled up in that way by the mere mention of the sum.

Maddox was not aware that no other combination of figures could have excited precisely those emotions; three hundred and fifty being the exact sum that Rickman needed for the accomplishment of his purpose. It brought his dream nearer to him by a year. A year? Why, it did more. He had only to ask and Maddox would advance the money. His dream was now, this moment, within his grasp.

And all he could say was, " I say, you know, this is awfully good of you."

"Good of you, Rickets, to take the thing off my hands. I can't very well run a monthly and a weekly with all my other jobs thrown in."

" The question is whether I can manage two weeklies and the other things."

" No, you can't. You're not built that way. But if you take *The Planet*, you can afford to chuck *Metropolis*. Tell you the truth, that's one reason why I want you to take it."

Some of the joy died out of Rickman's face.

" The other reason is, of course, that I can't think of a better man."

" It's awfully good of you to think of me at all. But why do you want me to chuck *Metropolis?*"

" Never mind why. I don't say *The Planet* is the best imaginable place for you, nor are you the best imaginable man for *The Planet;* but I really can't think of a better."

" No, but why——"

(" Confound him, why can't he leave it alone? I shall lose my temper in another minute," said Maddox to himself.) " The question is, would you like it? Because, if you wouldn't, don't imagine you've got to take it to oblige me."

" Of course I'd like it. There isn't anything I'd like so well."

" It's settled then."

It might have been, but Rickman turned on him again with his ungovernable " Why? "

" If you'd like it, Ricky, there's nothing more to be said. I know it isn't exactly a sumptuous berth for you, but it's a bit better salary."

" I'm not thinking of the salary. Oh, yes, I am, though ; God forgive me, I'm thinking of nothing else."

" Salary apart," said Maddox, with the least touch of resentment, " it's a better thing for you to edit *The Planet* than to sub-edit *Metropolis.*"

" Of course it is. Still, I should like to know why you want me to throw Jewdwine over."

" Hang Jewdwine. I said *Metropolis.*"

" I'm glad you admit the distinction."

" I *don't* admit it."

" Why do you want me to throw the thing over, then ? Do you mean that I can't work for you and Jewdwine at the same time ? "

" I never said anything about Jewdwine at all. But—if you will have it—I can't say I consider the connection desirable for the editor of *The Planet.*"

" I think I'm the best judge of that."

" I said—for the editor of *The Planet.*"

" For the editor of *The Planet* then, why not? "

" Ours is a poor but honest paper," said Maddox with his devilish twinkle.

" I don't see how I can very well be the editor of *The Planet* so long as it insists on shying a dead cat every week at the editor of *Metropolis.*"

" We have never mentioned the editor of *Metropolis.* Still—if you can induce Rankin to give up his little jest— the cat is certainly very dead by this time."

" He'll have to give it up if you make me editor."

" You'd better tell him so."

" I shall."

" All right, Rickets ; only wait till you *are* editor. Then you can put as much side on as you like."

" Good Heavens, did you ever see me put on side? "

" Well, I've seen you strike an attitude occasionally."

" All my attitudes put together hardly amount to side."

" They do, if they assume that they're going to affect the attitude of our paper."

"I didn't know it had one."

"It has a very decided attitude with regard to the ethics of reviewing; and whatever else you make it give up, it's not going to give up that. *The Planet,* Ricky, doesn't put on side. Side would be fatal to any freedom in the handling of dead cats. I wouldn't go so far as to say that it makes its moral being its prime care; but there are some abuses which it lives to expose, though the exposure doesn't help it much to live."

"Oh, I say, Maddy! That's what keeps you going. My poems would have sunk you long ago, if it hadn't been for your thrilling personalities."

"Personalities or no personalities, what I mean to rub into you is that *The Planet* is impartial; it's *the* only impartial review in this country. It has always reserved to itself an absolutely untrammelled hand in the shying of dead cats; and because a man happens to be a friend of the editor, it's no guarantee whatever that he won't have one slung at him the minute he deserves it. His only security is to perpetrate some crime so atrocious that we can't publish his name for fear of letting ourselves in for an action for libel. Your attitude to Mr. Jewdwine is naturally personal. Ours is not. I should have thought you'd have been the first to see that."

"I don't see what you've got against him, to begin with. I wish you'd tell me plainly what it is."

"If you will have it, it is simply this—he isn't honest."

"What the devil *do* you mean?"

"I mean what you mean when you say a woman isn't honest. As you've so often remarked, there's such a thing as intellectual chastity. Some people have it, and some have not. You have it, my dear Rickets, in perfection, not to say excess; but most of us manage to lose it more or less as we go on. It's a deuced hard thing, I can tell you, for any editor to keep; and Jewdwine, I'm afraid, has latterly been induced to part with it to a considerable, a very considerable extent. It's a thousand pities; for Jewdwine had the makings in him of a really fine critic. He might have been a classic if he'd died soon enough."

"He *is* a classic—he's the only man whose opinion's really worth having at this moment."

" Whom are we talking about? Jewdwine? Or the editor
of *Metropolis?*"

" I'm talking about Jewdwine. I happen to know him,
if you don't."

" And I'm talking about the other fellow whom you don't
happen to know a little bit. Nobody cares a tuppenny damn
about *his* opinion, except the fools who read it and the
knaves who buy it."

" And who do you imagine those people are? "

" Most of them are publishers, I believe. But a good few
are authors, I regret to say."

" Authors have cheek enough for most things; but I
should like to see one suggesting to Jewdwine that he should
sell him his opinion."

" My dear fellow, anybody may suggest it. That's what
he's there for, since he turned his opinion on to the streets.
Whether you get a pretty opinion or not depends on the
length of your purse."

" Why don't you call it bribery at once? "

" Because bribery's too harsh a term to apply to an editor,
mon semblable, mon frère; but in a woman, or a parliamen-
tary candidate, it might possibly be called corruption."

" Thanks. Well, you've made me a very generous offer,
Maddox, so generous that I'm glad you've explained yourself before I took it. For after that, you know, it would
have been rather awkward for me to have to tell you you're
a liar! "

" You consider me a liar, do you? " said Maddox in a
mild dispassionate voice.

" Certainly I do, when you say these things about Jewdwine."

" How about Rankin? He says them."

" Then Rankin's a liar, too! "

" And Stables? "

" *And* Stables—if he says them."

" My dear Rickman, everybody says them; only they
don't say them to you. We can't all be liars."

" There's a difference, I admit. Anybody who says them
is a liar; and anybody who says them to *me* is a d——d
liar! That's the difference."

Whereupon Maddox intimated (as honour indeed compelled him) that Rickman was the sort of young fool for

which there is no salvation. And by the time Rickman had replied with suitable hyperbole; and Maddox, because of the great love he bore to Rickman, had observed that if Rickman chose to cut his confused throat he might do so without its being a matter of permanent regret to Maddox; and Rickman, because of the great love he bore to Maddox, had suggested his immediate departure for perdition, it was pretty clearly understood that Rickman himself preferred to perish, everlastingly perish, rather than be connected even remotely with Maddox and his paper. And on that understanding they separated.

And when the door was closed between them, Rickman realized that his folly was even as Maddox had described it. In one night, and at a crisis of his finances, he had severed himself from a fairly permanent source of income; flung up the most desirable chance that had presented itself hitherto in his career; and quarrelled disgracefully and disagreeably with his best friend. He supposed the split was bound to come; but if he could only have staved it off for another year, till he had collected that seven hundred and fifty! There could be no doubt that that was what he ought to have done. He ought to have been prudent for Lucia's sake. And on the top of it all came the terrible reflection—Was it really worth it? Did he really believe in Jewdwine? Or had he sacrificed himself for an idea?

CHAPTER LXVII

RICKMAN could never be made to speak of the quarrel with Maddox. He merely mentioned to Jewdwine in the most casual manner that he had left *The Planet*. As for his grounds for that abrupt departure Jewdwine was entirely in the dark. It was Lucia that enlightened him.

For all things, even the deep things of journalism, sooner or later come to light. Rickman, before the quarrel, had given Miss Roots an introduction to the young men of *The Planet,* and its editor had taken kindly to Miss Roots. Maddox, it is true, did his best to keep the matter quiet, until in a moment of expansion he allowed that shrewd lady to lure him into confidences. Maddox tried to take it and present it philosophically. " It was bound to happen," he said;

" our Ricky-ticky is a bad hand at serving two masters,"
but as to which was God and which Mammon in this connection he modestly reserved his opinion. Jewdwine's name
was carefully avoided, but Miss Roots was left in no doubt
as to the subject of dispute.

She and Maddox were one in their inextinguishable
enthusiasm for their Rickman, for Rickman had the gift, the
rarest of all gifts, of uniting the hearts that loved him. If
Jewdwine had showed anything like a proper appreciation
of the poet, Maddox would have spared him now. So the
two looked at each other, with eyes that plumbed all the
depths of the unspoken and unspeakable, eyes that sent out
a twinkling flash of admiration as they agreed that it was
" just like Rickman." That phrase was for ever on the lips
of his admirers, a testimony to the fact that Rickman was
invariably true to himself.

He was being true to himself now in being true to Jewdwine, and it was in that form that the tale went round. " I
can't tell you all the ins and outs of it," wrote Miss Roots
to Lucia, " but he is paying for his loyalty to Mr. Jewdwine ; " and Lucia with equal pride in her cousin and her
friend, repeated it to Kitty Palliser, who repeated it to somebody else with the comment, " I'm not surprised to hear it ; "
and somebody else repeated it in a good many quarters without any comment at all. For everybody but Lucia understood that it spoke for itself.

And nobody understood it better than Jewdwine when
his cousin said, " You *will* be nice to him, Horace, won't
you? He is suffering for his loyalty to you." Lucia herself
had adopted a theory which she now set forth (reluctantly,
by reason of the horrible light it threw on human nature).
Mr. Maddox (whoever he might be) was of course jealous
of Horace. It was a shocking theory, but it was the only one
which made these complications clear to her.

But Jewdwine had no need of theories or explanations.
He understood. He knew that a certain prejudice, not to
say suspicion, attached to him. Ideas, not very favourable
to his character as a journalist, were in the air. And as his
mind (in this respect constitutionally susceptible) had seldom
been able to resist ideas in the air there were moments when
his own judgment wavered. He was beginning to suspect
himself.

He was not sure, and if he had been he would not have acted on that certainty; for he had never possessed the courage of his opinions. But it had come to this, that Jewdwine, the pure, the incorruptible, was actually uncertain whether he had or had not taken a bribe. As he lay awake in bed at four o'clock in the morning his conscience would suggest to him that he had done this thing; but at noon, in the office of *Metropolis,* his robust common sense, then like the sun, in the ascendant, boldly protested that he had done nothing of the sort. He had merely made certain not very unusual concessions to the interests of his journal. In doing so he had of course set aside his artistic conscience, an artistic conscience being a private luxury incompatible with the workings of a large corporate concern. He was bound to disregard it in loyalty to his employers and his public. They expected certain things of him and not others. It was different in the unexciting days of the old *Museion;* it would be different now if he could afford to run a paper of his own dedicated to the service of the Absolute. But Jewdwine was no longer the servant of the Absolute. He was the servant and the mouthpiece of a policy that in his heart he abhorred; irretrievably committed to a programme that was concerned with no absolute beyond the absolute necessity of increasing the circulation of *Metropolis.* Such a journal only existed on the assumption that its working expenses were covered by the advertisements of certain publishing houses. But if this necessity committed him to a more courteous attitude than he might otherwise have adopted towards the works issued by those houses, that was not saying that he was in their pay. He was, of course, in the pay of his own publishers, but so was every man who drew a salary under the same conditions; and if those gentlemen, finding their editor an even more competent person than they had at first perceived, were in the habit of increasing his salary in proportion to his competence, that was only the very correct and natural expression of their good opinion.

Whatever he had thought of himself at four o'clock in the morning, by four o'clock in the afternoon Jewdwine took an extremely lenient, not to say favourable view. Unfortunately he had not the courage of that opinion either. Therefore he was profoundly touched by this final instance of Rickman's devotion, and all that it argued of reckless and inspired belief. In the six months that followed he saw more of Rickman than he had seen in as many years. Whenever he had a slack evening he would ask him to dinner, and let him sit talking on far into the night. He was afraid of being left alone with that uncomfortable doubt, that torturing suspicion. Rickman brought with him an atmosphere charged with stimulating conviction, and in his presence Jewdwine breathed freely and unafraid. He felt himself no longer the ambiguous Jewdwine that he was, but the noble incorruptible Jewdwine that he had been. Up there in the privacy of his study Jewdwine let himself go; to that listener he was free to speak as a critic noble and incorruptible. But there were moments, painful for both men, when he would pause, gripped by his doubt, in the full swing of some high deliverance; when he looked at Rickman with a pathetic anxious gaze, as if uncertain whether he were not presuming too far on a character that he held only at the mercy of his friend's belief.

Though as yet he was not fully aware of the extent to which he relied on that belief, there could hardly have been a stronger tie than that which now bound him to his subordinate. He would have shrunk from loosing it, lest he should cut himself off from some pure source of immortality, lest he should break the last link between his soul and the sustaining and divine reality. It was as if through Rickman he remained attached to the beauty which he still loved and to the truth which he still darkly discerned.

In any case he could not have suffered him to go unrewarded. He owed that to himself, to the queer personal decency which he still managed to preserve after all his flounderings in the slough of journalism. It was intolerable to his pride that Rickman should be in any pecuniary embarrassment through his uncompromising devotion. He hardly knew whether he was the more pleased because Rickman had stuck to him or because he had thrown his other friends over. He had never quite forgiven him that divided fealty. He cared nothing for an allegiance that he had had to share with Maddox and his gang. But now that Rickman was once more exclusively, indisputably his, he was in honour bound to cherish and protect him. (Jewdwine was frequently visited by these wakenings of the feudal instinct that slept secretly in his blood.) If he could not make up to Rickman for the loss of the proposed editorship, he saw to it that he was kept well supplied with lucrative work on his own paper. As an even stronger proof of his esteem he allowed him for the first time a certain authority, and an unfettered hand.

For six months Rickman luxuriated in power and increase of leisure and of pay. If the pay was insufficient to cover all his losses, the leisure was invaluable; it enabled him to get on with his tragedy.

Now if Rickman had been prudent he would have finished his tragedy then and there and got it published in all haste. For there is no doubt that if any work of his had been given to the world any time within those six months, Jewdwine would have declared the faith that was in him. Whatever the merits of the work he would have celebrated its appearance by a sounding Feast of Trumpets in *Metropolis*. He would have done anything to strengthen the tie that attached him to the sources of his spiritual content. But Rickman was not prudent. He let the golden hours slip by, while he sat polishing up his blank verse as if he had all eternity before him.

Meanwhile he did all he could for Jewdwine. Jewdwine indeed could not have done a better thing for himself than in giving Rickman that free hand. In six months there was a marked improvement in the tone of *Metropolis* and the reputation of its editor, and, but for the unexpected which is always happening, Jewdwine might in the long run have emerged without a stain.

Nothing in fact could have been more utterly unforeseen, and yet, in reviewing all the steps which led to the ultimate catastrophe, Rickman said to himself that nothing would have been more consistent and inevitable. It came about first of all through a freak, a wanton freak of Fate, in the form of a beardless poet, a discovery, not of Jewdwine's nor of Rickman's, but of Miss Roots'. That Miss Roots could make a discovery clearly indicated the finger of fate. Miss Roots promptly asked Rickman to dinner and presented to him the discovery, beardless, breathless also and hectic, wearing an unclean shirt and a suit of frayed shoddy.

He came away from that dinner, that embarrassing, palpitating encounter, with a slender sheaf of verses in his pocket. It did not take him long to read them, nor to see (the unforeseen again!) that the verses would live longer than their maker. They were beardless, breathless, and hectic like the boy, but nobody could have been keener than Rickman to recognize the immortal adolescence, the swift panting of the pursuing god, the burning of the inextinguishable flame. He wrote a letter to him, several letters, out of the fulness of his heart. Then Maddox, to whom he had not spoken since the day of their falling out, came up to him at the Junior Journalists, shook his hand as if nothing had happened, and thanked him for his appreciation of young Paterson. He said that it had put new life into the boy. They made it up over young Paterson. And that was another step towards the inevitable conclusion.

The next step was that somebody who was paying for the boy's doctor's bills paid also for the publication of his poems. They arrived (this of course was only to be expected) at the office of *Metropolis* (the slender sheaf grown slenderer by some omissions which Rickman had advised). But it was Fate that contrived that they should arrive in the same week with a volume (by no means slender), a volume of Poems issued by the publisher of *Metropolis* and written by a friend (and an influential friend) of the editor. Therein were the last sweet pipings of the pastoral Fulcher. No other hand but Jewdwine's, as Jewdwine sorrowfully owned, could have done anything for this work, and he meant to have devoted a flattering article to it in the next number. But, in the arrangements of the unforeseen, it was further provided that Jewdwine should be disabled, at what he playfully called the " critical moment," by an attack of influenza. The two volumes, the slender and the stout, were forwarded to Rickman in the same parcel, and Jewdwine in a note discreetly worded threw himself and the poems of his influential friend on Rickman's mercy. Would Rickman deal with the big book? He would see for himself that it *was* a big book. He gave him as usual a perfectly free hand as to space, but he thought it might be well to mention that the book *was* to have had a two-page article all to itself. He drew Rickman's attention to the fact that it was published by So and So, and hoped that he might for once at least rely on his discretion. Perhaps as he was reviewing the work of a " brother bard " it would be better to keep the article anonymous.

There was nothing coarse about Jewdwine's methods. Through all his career he remained refined and fastidious, and his natural instincts forbade him to give a stronger hint. Unfortunately, in this instance, refinement had led him into a certain ambiguity of phrase!

On this ambiguity Rickman leapt, with a grin of diabolical delight. He may have had some dim idea that it would be his shelter in the day of rebuke; but all he could clearly think of, as he held the boy's frail palpitating volume in his hand, was that he had but that moment in which to praise him. This was his unique and perfect opportunity, the only sort of opportunity that he was not likely to let slip.

Quem Deus vult perdere prius dementat; and it really looked as if madness had come upon Rickman in the loneliness and intoxication of his power. With those two volumes of poetry before him, a small one by a rank outsider, unknown, unkempt, and unprotected; a boy from whom no more was to be expected, seeing that he was about to depart out of the world where editors are powerful; and one, a large, considerable volume by a person eminent already in that world and with many years of poetry and influence before him, he gave (reckless of all proportion) the two-page article to the slender volume and the paragraph to the stout. That was what he did—he, the sub-editor.

Of the paragraph the less said the better. As for the article it was such a song of jubilation as one poet sings over the genius of another; and nothing that he had ever done for *Metropolis* delighted him so much as the making of it. He sent the proofs to Jewdwine as usual with a note. " Here they are. I *think* I've been discreet. I've done what I could for Mr. Fulcher, but as you'll see, I've dealt nobly with young Paterson, as he deserves." As he heard nothing from Jewdwine, he could only suppose that the chief was satisfied, and he could not help reflecting with some complacency that no doubt old Maddox would be satisfied too.

The next thing that happened was that he was cut by Maddox at the Junior Journalists. (It was on a Saturday, and *Metropolis, the* number, had appeared the night before). Cut unmistakably, with a thrust from the blue eyes and an expressive turning of the enormous shoulders. A number once issued from his hands, Rickman never looked at it again if he could help it, and he never troubled to look at it now. He simply regarded Maddox's behaviour as unaccountable. In the hope of lighting on some explanation he called at Tavistock Place one Sunday afternoon, at a time when he was pretty sure of finding Miss Roots alone. He wanted to know, he said, what was the matter with Maddy. Apparently Miss Roots had something the matter with her too, for her only answer was to hand him stiffly a copy of *Metropolis* with the pages scored in blue pencil at his own article. He took it with a radiant and confiding smile, a smile that assumed such a thoroughly delightful understanding between him and Miss Roots that the little lady, who had evidently counted on a very different effect, was put to some intellectual confusion. She noticed that as he read the smile vanished and gave place, first to an expression of absolute bewilderment, and then to a furious flush, whether of shame or indignation she could not tell, but it looked (again to her confusion) uncommonly like both.

" I see," he said quietly, and laid the paper aside.

What he had seen was that, save for a few ingenious transpositions, the two reviews stood very much as he had written them. The only striking alteration was that Mr. Fulcher had got the article and young Paterson the paragraph.

" Oh, you see, do you? " said Miss Roots bitterly. " That's more than I do."

" I see there's been some astonishing mistake." For one moment he exonerated Jewdwine and embraced the wild hypothesis of a printer's error. He took back the accursed journal; as he held it his hand trembled uncontrollably. He glanced over the notices again. No. It was not after this fashion that the printers of the *Metropolis* were wont to err. He recognized the familiar hand of the censor, though it had never before accomplished such an incredible piece of editing as this.

And yet it was in strict accordance with the old tradition. The staff of *Metropolis* knew that before a line of theirs was printed it had to pass under their editor's reforming hand; that was the understood condition on which they wrote for him at all; it was the method by which Jewdwine maintained the unity of his empire. But in the case of Rickman he either forbore to exercise his privilege, or exercised it in such a manner as preserved the individuality of the poet's style. Like some imperial conqueror Jewdwine had absorbed the literary spirit of the man he conquered, and *Metropolis* bore the stamp of Rickman for all time. So now the style of the articles remained intact; they might have passed equally for the work of Rickman or of Jewdwine.

"I suppose," he said helplessly, "it is a little short."

"Short? You weren't bound to make it long; but there was no occasion to be so contemptuous."

"Contemptuous? Good God!"

"That's what it amounts to when you're so insufferably polite."

Oh, yes, he recognized it, the diabolical urbanity that had seemed the very choicest method of dealing with Mr. Fulcher.

"Politeness was not exactly all you led us to expect from you."

He passed his hand wearily over his forehead and his eyes. Miss Roots had a moment of compunction. She thought of all that he had done for her. He had delivered her from her labours in the Museum; he had introduced her to the young men of *The Planet,* and had made Maddox send her many books to review; he had lifted her from the obscurity that threatened to engulf her. And he had done more for her than this. He had given her back her youth and intellect; he had made her life a joy instead of a terror to her. But Miss Roots was just. The agony on his face would have melted her heart, but for another agony that she saw.

"If the poor boy knew that *you* had written that paragraph——"

"He needn't know unless some kind friend goes and tells him. It isn't signed."

"No. I don't wonder that you were ashamed to put your name to it."

He rose to go. She looked up at him with a queer little look, half penetrating and half pleading, and held out her hand.

"Well," she said, "what am I to say if he asks me if you wrote it? Can you deny it?"

"No," he said curtly, "I can't deny it."

"And you can't explain it?"

"No, and I can't explain it. Surely," he said with a horrible attempt at laughter, "it speaks for itself."

" It does indeed, Keith."

And Maddox, to whom Miss Roots related the substance of that interview, echoed her sentiment.

" It does indeed."

Of all that brilliant band of young men lured by journalism to ruin they looked on their Rickman as the most splendid, the most tragic.

CHAPTER LXVIII

UP till now it had never occurred to Rickman that his connection with *Metropolis* could directly damage him, still less that Jewdwine could personally inflict a blow. But the injury now done to him was monstrous and intolerable; Jewdwine had hurt him in a peculiarly delicate and shrinking place. Because his nature was not originally magnificent in virtue of another sort, it was before all things necessary that he should preserve his intellectual chastity. That quality went deeper than the intellect; it was one with a sense of honour so fine that a touch, impalpable to ordinary men, was felt by it as a laceration and a stain. He walked up to Hampstead that Sunday evening, taking the hill at a round swinging pace. Not all the ardour and enthusiasm of his youth had ever carried him there with such an impetus as did his burning indignation against Jewdwine. And as he went the spirit of youth, the spirit of young Paterson, went beside him and breathed upon the flame.

And yet he was the same man who only an hour ago had been defending Jewdwine's honour at the expense of his own; without a thought that in so defending it he was doing anything in the least quixotic or remarkable. He had done nothing. He had simply refrained at a critical moment from giving him away. Maddox was Jewdwine's enemy; and to have given Jewdwine away at that moment would have meant delivering him over to Maddox to destroy.

No; when he thought of it he could hardly say he had defended his friend's honour at the expense of his own; for Jewdwine's honour was Lucia's, and Lucia's was not Jewdwine's, but his, indistinguishably, inseparably his.

But though he was not going to give Jewdwine up to

Maddox, he was going to give him up. It might come to
the same thing. He could imagine that, to anybody who
chose to put two and two together, an open rupture would
give him away as completely as if he had accused him in so
many words. That, of course, he could not help. There
was a point beyond which his honour refused to identify
itself with Jewdwine's. He had never felt a moment's
hesitation upon that point. For in his heart he condemned
his friend far more severely than Maddox could have condemned anybody. He had a greater capacity for disgust
than Maddox. He would draw up, writhing, at trifles over
which Maddox would merely shrug his shoulders and pass
on. In this instance Maddox, whose Celtic soul grew
wanton at the prospect of a fight, would have fallen upon
Jewdwine with an infernal joy, but he would have been the
first to deprecate Rickman's decision as absurd. As for
Rankin or Stables, instead of flying into a passion, they
would, in similar circumstances, have sat still and smiled.

If it had not been for young Paterson, Rickman would
have smiled too, even if he had been unable to sit still; for
his vision of Fulcher pocketing the carefully selected praise
intended for Paterson was purely and supremely comic;
so delightful in fact, that he could have embraced Jewdwine
for providing it. But Paterson, who had looked to him as
to the giver of life or death, Paterson on his death-bed
taking Fulcher's paragraph to himself and wondering
whether it were indeed Rickman who had done this thing,
the thought of Paterson was too painful to be borne. Honour or no honour, it would be impossible for him to work
for Jewdwine after that.

He had got to make that clear to Jewdwine; and anything more unpleasant than the coming interview he could
not well conceive.

Unpleasantness, you would have said, was far from
Jewdwine's mind that Sunday evening. He himself suggested nothing of the sort. He was in his study, sitting in
an armchair, with a shawl over his knees, smoking a cigarette and looking more pathetically refined than ever after
his influenza, when Rickman burst in upon his peace. He
was so frankly glad to see him that his greeting alone was
enough to disarm prejudice. It seemed likely that he
would carry off the honours of the discussion by remaining

severely polite while Rickman grew more and more perturbed and heated. Rickman, however, gained at the out-
set by making straight for his point. As Jewdwine gave
him no opening he had to make one and make it as early
as possible, before the great man's amenities had time to
lure him from the track.

"I wish," said he abruptly, "you'd tell me what was
wrong with those reviews of mine, that you found it necessary to alter them?"

"The reviews? Oh, the reviews were all right—excel-
lent material—they only wanted a little editing."

"Do you mind telling me what you mean by editing?"

"*That* is the last point an editor is competent to explain."

"All the same I'd like to hear what you've got to say. I
think you'll admit that you owe me some explanation."

"My dear fellow—sit down, won't you?—I admit nothing of the sort."

Jewdwine no longer stood on his dignity, he lay back on
it, lounged on it, stretched all his graceful length upon it,
infinitely at ease. Time had mellowed his manners and
made them incomparably gentle and humane.

"You seem to think I took a liberty with your articles.
I didn't. I merely exercised an ancient editorial right. I
couldn't possibly have let them be printed as they stood.
Conceive my feelings if I'd had to sit next Mr. Fulcher at
dinner that evening. It might easily have happened. It's
all very well for you, Rickman, you're young and irresponsible, and you haven't got to sit next to Mr. Fulcher at dinner; but you'll own that it would have been rather an awkward situation for me?"

"I can forgive you Fulcher, but I can't forgive you
Paterson."

"And I could have forgiven you Paterson, but I
couldn't forgive you Fulcher. Do you see?"

He allowed a few moments for reflection, and continued:

"Of course, I understand your feelings. In fact I sympathize profoundly. As a rule I never dream of touching
anything with your signature; I've far too great a reverence for style."

"Style be d——d. For all I care you may cut up my
style till you can't tell it from Fulcher's. I object to your

transposing my meaning to suit your own. Honestly, Jewdwine, I'd rather write like Fulcher than write as you've made me appear to have written."

"My dear Rickman, that's where you make the mistake. You don't appear at all." He smiled with urbane tolerance of the error. "The editor, as you know, is solely responsible for unsigned reviews."

So far Jewdwine had come off well. He had always a tremendous advantage in his hereditary manners; however right you had been to start with, his imperturbable refinement put you grossly in the wrong. And at this point Rickman gave himself away.

"What's the good of that?" said he, "if young Paterson believes I wrote them?"

"Young Paterson isn't entitled to any belief in the matter."

"But—he knew."

There was a shade of genuine annoyance on Jewdwine's face.

"Oh, of course, if you've told him that you were the author. That's rather awkward for you, but it's hardly my fault. I'm sorry, Rickman, but you really *are* a little indiscreet."

"I wish I could explain your behaviour in the same way."

"Come, since you're so keen on explanations, how do you propose to explain your own? I gave you certain instructions, and what right had you to go beyond them, not to say against them?"

"What earthly right had you to make me say the exact opposite of what I did say? But I didn't go against your instructions. Here they are."

He produced them. "You'll see that you gave me a perfectly free hand as to space."

Jewdwine looked keenly at him. "You knew perfectly well what I meant. And you took advantage of—of a trifling ambiguity in my phrasing, to do—as you would say—the exact opposite. That was hardly what I expected of you."

As he spoke Jewdwine drew his shawl up about his waist, thus delicately drawing attention to his enfeebled state. The gesture seemed to convict Rickman of taking advantage, not only of his phrase, but of his influenza, behaviour superlatively base.

" I can give you a perfectly clear statement of the case. You carefully suppressed *my* friend and you boomed your own for all you were worth. Naturally, I reversed your judgment. Of course, if you had told me you wanted to do a little log-rolling on your own account, I should have been only too delighted—but I always understood that you disapproved of the practice."

" So I do. Paterson isn't a friend of mine."

" He's your friend's friend. I think Mr. Maddox might have been left to look after his own man."

Rickman rose hastily, as if he were no longer able to sit still and bear it.

" Jewdwine," he said, and his voice had the vibration which the master had once found so irresistible. " Have you read young Paterson's poems? "

" Yes. I've read them."

" And what is your honest—your private opinion of them? "

" I'm not a fool, Rickman. My private opinion of them is the same as yours."

" What an admission! "

" But," said Jewdwine suavely, " that's not the sort of opinion my public—the public that pays for *Metropolis*— pays to have."

" You mean it's the sort of opinion I'm paid to give."

" Well, broadly speaking—of course there are exceptions, and Paterson in other circumstances might have been one of them—that's very much what I do mean."

" Then—I'm awfully sorry, Jewdwine—but if that's so I can't go on working for *Metropolis*. I must give it up. In fact, that's really what I came to say."

Jewdwine too had risen with an air of relief, being anxious to end an interview which was becoming more uncomfortable than he cared for. He had stood, gazing under drooping eyelids at his disciple's feet. Nobody would have been more surprised than Jewdwine if you had suggested to him that he could have any feeling about looking anybody in the face. But at that last incredible, impossible speech of his he raised his eyes and fixed them on Rickman's for a moment.

In that moment many things were revealed to him.

He turned and stood with his back to Rickman, staring through the open window. All that he saw there, the quiet walled garden, the rows of elms on the terrace beside it, the dim green of the Heath, and the steep unscalable grey blue barrier of the sky, had taken on an unfamiliar aspect, as it were a tragic simplicity and vastness. For these things, once so restfully indifferent, had in a moment become the background of his spiritual agony, a scene where his soul appeared to him, standing out suddenly shelterless, naked and alone. No—if it *had* only been alone; but that was the peculiar horror of it. He could have borne it but for the presence of the other man who had called forth the appalling vision, and remained a spectator of it.

There was at least this much comfort for him in his pangs —he knew that a man of coarser fibre would neither have felt nor understood them. But it was impossible for Jewd-wine to do an ignoble thing and not suffer; it was the inner-most delicacy of his soul that made it writhe under the destiny he had thrust upon it.

And in the same instant he recognized and acknowl-edged the greatness of the man with whom he had to do, acknowledged, not grudgingly, nor in spite of him-self, but because of himself, because of that finer soul within his soul which spoke the truth in secret, being born to recognize great things and admire them. He wondered now how he could ever have mistaken Rick-man. He perceived the origin and significance of his attitude of disparagement, of doubt. It dated from a certain hot July afternoon eight years ago when he lay under a beech-tree in the garden of Court House and Lucia had insisted on talking about the poet, displaying an enthusiasm too ardent to be borne. He had meant well by Rickman, but Lucia's ardour had somehow put him off. Maddox's had had the same effect, though for a totally different reason, and so it had gone on. He had said to himself that if other people were going to take Rick-man that way he could no longer feel the same peculiar interest.

He turned back again.

" Do you really mean it? " said he.

" I'm afraid I do."

"You mean that you intend to give up reviewing for *Metropolis?*"

"I mean that after this I can't have anything more to do with it."

"He means," thought Jewdwine, "that he won't have anything more to do with me."

And Rickman saw that he was understood. He wondered how Jewdwine would take it.

He took it nobly. "Well," he said, "I'm sorry. But if you must go, you must. To tell the truth, my dear fellow, at this rate, you know, I couldn't afford to keep you. I wish I could. You're not the only thing I can't afford." He said it with a certain emotion not very successfully concealed beneath his smile. Rickman was about to go; but he detained him.

"Wait one minute. Do you mind telling me whether you've any regular sources of income besides *Metropolis?*"

"Well, not at the moment."

"And supposing—none arise?"

"I must risk it."

"You seem to have a positive mania for taking risks." Yes, that was Rickman all over, he found a brilliant joy in the excitement; he was in love with danger.

"Oh, well, sometimes, you know, you've *got* to take them."

Happy Rickman! The things that were so difficult and complicated to Jewdwine were so simple, so incontestable to him. "Some people, Rickman, would say you were a fool." He sighed, and the sigh was a tribute his envy paid to Rickman's foolishness. "I won't offer an opinion; the event will prove."

"It won't prove anything. Events never do. They merely happen."

"Well, if they happen wrong, and I can help you, you've only got to come to me."

Never in all his life had Jewdwine so nearly achieved the grace of humanity as in this offer of his help. He would have given anything if Rickman could have accepted it, but refusal was a foregone conclusion. And yet he offered it.

"Thanks—thanks awfully." It was Rickman who appeared nervous and ashamed. His mouth twitched; he held out his hand abruptly; he was desperately anxious to say good-night and get it over. It seemed to him that he had been six years taking leave of Jewdwine; each year had seen the departure of some quality he had known him by. He wanted to have done with it now for ever.

But Jewdwine would not see his hand. He turned away; paced the floor, swung back on a hesitating heel and approached him, smiling.

"You're not going to disappear altogether, are you? You'll turn up again, and let me know how you're getting on?"

To Rickman there was something tragic and retrospective in Jewdwine's smile. It had no joy in it, but an appeal, rather, to the memory of what he had been. He found it irresistible.

"Thanks. I shall get on all right; but I'll turn up again, sometime."

Jewdwine's smile parted with its pathos, its appeal. It conveyed a promise, an assurance that whatever else had perished in him his friendship was not dead.

For there were ways, apart from the ways of journalism, in which Jewdwine could be noble still. And still, as he watched Rickman's departing back, the back that he seemed doomed to know so well, he said to himself—

"He's magnificent, but I can't afford him."

CHAPTER LXIX

IN all this his history had only repeated itself. When six years ago he had turned his back on Rickman's he had made it inevitable that he should turn his back on Jewdwine now. On each occasion his behaviour had provoked the same melancholy admission, from Jewdwine—"He is magnificent, but I can't afford him"; from Isaac Rickman—"I can't afford to pay your price, my boy." The incredible thing was that Jewdwine should have been brought to say it. Jewdwine was changed; but Rickman was the same Rickman who had swung the shop door behind him, unmoved by the separation from his salary.

But, after all, he could only keep half of that rash vow he had made himself on the way to Hampstead. He must give up the Editor of *Metropolis;* but he could not give up Horace Jewdwine. It was not the first time he had been compelled to admit the distinction which Maddox for decency's sake had insisted on. When it came to the point, as now, he found himself insisting on it with even greater emphasis than Maddox. He knew that in his soul Jewdwine still loved and worshipped what was admirable, that in his soul he would have given anything to recall his injustice to young Paterson. But young Paterson was too great to have need either of Jewdwine or of him. Young Paterson had his genius to console him. His profounder pity was for the man who had inflicted such awful injuries on himself; the great man who had made himself mean; the spiritual person who had yielded to a material tyranny; the incorruptible person who had sold his soul, who only realized the value of his soul now that he had sold it.

And yet he knew that there could be nothing more sundering than such meanness, such corruptibility as Jewdwine's. Their friendship could never be the same. There was a certain relief in that. There could never be any hypocrisy, any illusion in their relations now. And nobody knew that better than Jewdwine. Well, the very fact that Jewdwine had still desired and chosen that sad-hearted, clear-eyed communion argued a certain greatness in him.

Therefore he resolved to spare him. It would cost him the friendship of better men than he; but that could not be helped. They must continue to think that he had sold, or at any rate lent himself at interest to Jewdwine. Honour debarred him from all explanation and defence, an honour so private and personal that it must remain unsuspected by the world. In the beginning he had made himself almost unpleasantly conspicuous by the purity of his literary morals; his innocence had been a hair-lifting spectacle even to honest journalists. And now the fame he would have among them was the fame of a literary prostitute, without a prostitute's wages.

On the contrary he would have to pay heavily for the spiritual luxury of that break with the editor of *Metropolis*. When he reached his comfortable room on the third floor in Torrington Square, he sat down by his writing-table, not to write, but to think. It was war-time, fatal to letters. Such terrors arose before him as must arise before a young man severed by his own rash act from the sources of his income. What a moment he had chosen for the deed, too! When money was of all things the thing he most passionately desired; when to his fancy the sum of a hundred and seventy-five pounds was the form that most nearly, most divinely presented the adored perfection; when, too, that enchanting figure was almost in his grasp. A few brief spasms of economy, and ten months of *Metropolis* would have seen him through.

And yet there was no bitterness in the dismay with which he contemplated his present forlorn and impecunious state. It was inevitable that he should sever himself from the sources of his income when they were found to be impure. Much more inevitable than that he should have cut off that untainted supply which six months ago would have flowed to him through Maddox. Common prudence had not restrained him from quarrelling with Maddox over a point of honour that was shadowy compared with this. It was hardly likely that it should have restrained him now. There were few things that he would not do for Lucia Harden, but not even for her sake could he have done otherwise than he had done. It was the least that honour could require of him, the very least.

His attitude to honour had in a manner changed. Eight years ago it had seemed to him the fantastic child of a preference for common honesty, coupled with a preposterous passion for Lucia Harden. He had indulged it as a man indulges the creature of fantasy and caprice, and had felt that he was thrusting a personal infatuation into a moral region where such extravagances are unknown. It belonged rather to the realm of imagination, being essentially a poet's honour, a winged and lyric creature, a creature altogether too radiant and delicate to do battle with the gross material world, a thing as mysterious and indomitable as his genius; a very embarrassing companion for a young journalist in his first start in life. And now he had grown so used to it that it seemed to him no longer mysterious and fantastic; obedience to it was as simple as the following of a natural impulse, a thing in no way conspicuous and superb. It was the men who knew nothing of such leadership who seemed to him separated from the order of the world. But to the friends who watched him Rickman's honour had been always an amazing spectacle. Like another genius, it had taken possession of him and led him through what Jewdwine had called the slough of journalism, so that he went with fine, fastidious feet, choosing the clean places in that difficult way. Like another genius, it had lured him, laughing and reckless, along paths perilous and impossible to other men. How glad he had been to follow that bright-eyed impetuous leader.

And this was where it had led him to, the radiant and delicate comrade of his youth. As he sat propping his chin up with his hands the face that confronted destiny had grown haggard in an hour.

He pulled himself together, and deliberately reviewed the situation. He had at that moment three and eight pence in his pocket, and, lying about somewhere in the table-drawer, there was part of last week's salary and a cheque for nine pounds, the price of a recent article. He could count on five pounds at Michaelmas, the quarterly rent of the furniture in the little house at Ealing. Added to these certain sums there was that unknown incalculable amount that he might yet receive for unsolicited contributions. He had made seventy-five pounds in this way last year. The casual earnings of ninety-nine were no security for nineteen hundred; still, invincible hopefulness fixed the probabilities at that figure.

But it was now January, and Dicky Pilkington's bill would be due in November. By successive triumphs of ingenious economy he had reduced that once appalling seven hundred and fifty to a hundred and seventy-five. He couldn't actually count on more than twenty-six pounds three and eight pence with which to meet the liability. And he had also to live for ten months before he met it. Even invincible Hope was nervous facing those formidable figures. It did indeed suggest the presence of a shadowy army in the rear, whole columns of figures marching invincibly to his aid. They were the sums that might, that ought to be obtained by a dramatic poet in the hour of his success. But Rickman had not been born over a bookseller's shop for nothing; and an austere hereditary voice reminded him that he couldn't really count on a penny from his tragedy. He couldn't even afford to write it. The thing was, economically speaking, a crime. It would of course be finished, as it had been begun, in defiance of economy, as of all other human pieties and laws, but it would be unreasonable to expect that any financial blessing could rest on it.

He had only got ten months to raise the money in. It would probably take him that time to find regular work, if he found it. There was not an editor in London to whom the initials S. K. R. conveyed the unique significance they did to Jewdwine, to Maddox, and to Rankin. He now thought with regret of the introductions he had refused in the insolence of his youth. To Hanson for instance. Hanson was a good sort, and he might have come in very handy now. A few other names passed before him, men whom it would be useless for him to approach. There was old Mackinnon, though, who was a good sort, too. He had long ago forgotten that ancient jest which compared his head with the dome of the Museum. He had been the most frequent entertainer of adventitious prose. Mackinnon might be good for something. He had half a mind to look him up. The thought of Mackinnon made him feel almost cheerful again.

Before he went to bed he put ten pounds into a tobacco-jar on an inaccessible shelf, keeping one pound three and eight pence for the expenses of the coming week. The next morning he looked Mackinnon up.

Now Mackinnon's head was so far unlike the dome of the Museum that it was by no means impervious to light; and where Mackinnon's interests were concerned it was positively limpid in its transparency. So that Mackinnon was not slow to perceive the advantages of an alliance with impecunious brilliance. The brilliance he was already familiar with, the impecuniosity he inferred from the more than usual offhandedness of Rickman's manner. The war had hit Mackinnon also; the affairs of the *Literary Observer* were not flourishing as Mackinnon could have wished; and he was meditating some reductions in his staff. He reflected that young men in Rickman's mood and Rickman's circumstances were sometimes willing to do the work of two journalists for a lower salary than he had been paying to one. And when he further learnt that Rickman had left *Metropolis*, he felt that, besides these solid advantages, a subtler satisfaction would be his. Jewdwine, corruptible or incorruptible, had not endeared himself to other editors, and even the sober Mackinnon was unable to resist the temptation of annexing the great man's great man. But the dome-like head, impenetrable in this, betrayed none of the thoughts that were going on inside it, and in the bargaining that followed it was concealed from Rickman that his connection with *Metropolis* had in any way increased his market value. He made the best terms he could; and the end of the interview found him retained on Mackinnon's staff as leader writer and dramatic critic at a salary of two pounds ten a week. Mackinnon had offered two pounds, Rickman had held out for three, and they split the difference. As the poet left the room Mackinnon turned to his desk with a smile of satisfaction that seemed to illuminate the dome. He had effected a considerable saving by that little transaction.

And for the poet it did not prove so bad a bargain after all. He had now more ample leisure; and for the first time in his journalistic career he knew what it was to be left mercifully, beneficently alone. He had cut himself off from all his friends; and though at times his heart suffered, his genius profited by the isolation. It was not until he had escaped from Jewdwine that he realized what that special deliverance meant for him. He could not well have encountered a more subtle and dangerous influence than that of the author of the *Prolegomena to Æsthetics.* Jewdwine had been hostile to his genius from the beginning, though he had cared for it, too, in his imperious way. He would have tamed the young, ungovernably ardent thing and wedded it to his own beautiful and passionless idea; an achievement which would have reflected some glory on Jewdwine as the matchmaker. But he had left off caring when he found that he had less to gain from Rickman's genius than from his talent, and had turned his attention to the protection and encouragement of the more profitable power. As that talent ran riot in the columns of *Metropolis,* Rickman himself was unaware how relentlessly it drew on the vitality that sustained his genius. It was Jewdwine's excuse that the vitality seemed inexhaustible.

Jewdwine, as he had once said, dreaded the divine fire. He would ultimately have subdued the flame by a persistent demand for brilliance of another kind. Even Maddox (who adored his Rickman) had not seen that his Rickman, his young divinity, must change and grow. He admired his immortal adolescence; he would have him young and lyrical for ever. He had discovered everything in him but the dramatic poet he was yet to be. Thus, through the very fervour of his superstition, Maddox had proved hostile, too. But in Mackinnon Rickman found no malign disturbing influence, no influence of any kind at all. No thought of capturing his genius or exploiting his talent had ever entered his dome-like head. Mackinnon, his mortal nature appeased by his victory over Jewdwine, and further gratified by the consciousness of having secured a good man cheap, made no exorbitant claims on his contributor. Let Rickman write what he would, Mackinnon knew he had got his money's worth.

Rickman squared himself nobly for the next round with fortune. And Dicky, in his attitude of enthusiastic but not uninterested spectator, cheered him on, secretly exultant. Dicky was now serenely sure of his odds. It was war-time; and Rickman could not hold out long after such an injury to his income.

But Rickman, unconquered, made matters even by reducing his expenditure. It was winter, and the severity of the weather would have ruined him in coal alone, had he not abandoned the superstition of a fire. With an oil-stove there was always some slight danger of asphyxia, but Rickman loved the piquancy of danger. By many such ingenious substitutions he effected so prodigious a saving that three-fifths or more of his salary went into the tobacco-jar, and thence into Dicky Pilkington's pocket. He rejoiced to see it go, so completely had he subdued the lust of spending, so ardently embraced the life of poverty; if it were poverty to live on a pound a week. Was it not rather wanton, inquitous extravagance to have allowed himself three times that amount? But for that his position at this moment would have been such that three months on the *Literary Observer* would have cleared him. As he stood, the remainder of his debt loomed monstrous under the shadow of next November.

And it was this moment (when he should have been turning his talents into ready money by unremitting journalism) that he chose for finishing his tragedy. If he could be said to have chosen it; for it was rather the Tragic Muse that had claimed him for her own. She knew her hour, the first young hour of his deliverance, when he had ceased from hungering and thirsting after life, and from the violence and stress of living, and was no more tormented by scruple and by passion; when the flaming orgy of his individuality no longer confused the pageant of the world. He had been judging by himself when he propounded the startling theory that lyric poets must grow into dramatic poets, if they grow at all. It was now, when his youth no longer sang aloud in him, that he heard the living voices of the men and women whom he made. Their flesh and blood no longer struggled violently for birth, no longer tortured the delicate tissue of the dream. His dreams themselves were brought forth incarnate, he being no longer at variance with himself, as in the days of neo-classic drama.

And so now, when he contemplated his poverty, he saw in it the dream-crowned head and austere countenance of an archangel destiny. In the absence of all visible and material comfort the invisible powers assumed their magnificent domination. He gave his evenings to Mackinnon and his mornings, his fresh, divine mornings, to the Tragic Muse, thus setting a blessed purifying interval of sleep between his talent and his genius. But through it all, while he slept and while he worked, and while he scribbled with a tenth part of his brain, mechanically filling in his columns of the *Literary Observer,* he felt that his genius, conscious of its hour, possessed him utterly. Not even for Lucia's sake could he resist the god who was so tyrannous and strong. In his heart he called on her to forgive him for writing unsalable tragedies, when he ought to have been making money for her. His heart kept on accusing him. " You would write tragedies if she were starving," it said. And the god, indignant at the interruption, answered it, " You wouldn't, you fool, you know you wouldn't. And she isn't starving. It's you who'll starve, if anybody does; so fire away." And he fired away; for hope, still invincible, told him that he could afford to do it, that he had in a drawer fifty pounds' worth of unpublished articles, works of the baser power, and that, war or no war, he could surely sell them. He could sell his furniture also; and if the worst came to the worst, he could sell his books (his own books, not Lucia's). Meanwhile he must get on with his tragedy. He could easily finish it in six weeks, and expiate the crime by months of journalism.

He did finish it in six weeks; and when spring came he began another; for the hand of the god was heavy upon him. This he knew was madness, though a madness divine and irresistible. In view of its continuance he called upon Mackinnon and inquired, whether at any time, if the occasion should arise, he could count upon an advance of salary. Mackinnon, solid, impenetrable, but benignant, replied that very possibly it might be so. This Rickman interpreted as a distinct encouragement to dally with the Tragic Muse. It was followed by a request from Mackinnon that Rickman on his part should oblige him with a few columns in advance. This he did. He was now, though he was blissfully unaware of it, the last man on the paper. In six months from the time of his joining its staff the *Literary Observer* ceased from observing, and Mackinnon retired suddenly into private life.

Dicky, who had watched with joy the decline of the *Literary Observer,* chuckled openly at its fall. He was sorry for old Razors, though. It was hard luck on him. Old Razors, in Dicky's opinion, was about done for now.

It might have seemed so to Rickman, but that the experience had sobered him. He rose from the embraces of the Tragic Muse. Yet dizzy with the august rapture, he resisted and defied the god. He thrust his tragedy from him into the hindmost obscurity of his table-drawer. Then he betook himself, in a mood more imperative than solicitous, to Hanson. Hanson, who had labelled him Decadent, and lumped him with Letheby. It was no matter now. Whatever Hanson thought of his genius, there could be but one opinion of his talent.

Hanson was genial and complimentary. He, like Mackinnon, knew his business too well to let Savage Keith Rickman slip through his fingers. Like Mackinnon he was pleased with the idea of securing a deserter from the insufferable Jewdwine. But the *Courier* was full up with war news and entirely contented with its staff. Hanson was only good for occasional contributions.

Rickman again overhauled his complicated accounts. By what seemed to him a series of miracles he had saved seventy-five pounds somehow during those six months with

Mackinnon; but how he was going to raise a hundred in four months he did not know. That was what he meant to try for, though. It was July; and he loved more than ever the green peace of Torrington Square, and the room associated with the first austere delights of poverty and the presence of the Tragic Muse. But he could forego even peace for four months. After much search in the secret places of Bloomsbury, he found an empty attic in Howland Street. The house was clean, decent, and quiet, for a wonder. Thither he removed himself and his belongings. He had parted with all but the absolutely essential, among which he reckoned all Lucia's books and a few of his own. He had stripped himself for this last round with Fortune. He would come out of it all right if he wrote nothing but articles, lived on ten shillings a week, and sold the articles; which meant that in the weeks when no articles were sold he must live on less. It meant, too, that he must make his own bed, sweep his own room, and cook his own meals when they were cooked at all; that to have clean linen he must pay the price of many meals, as he counted meals.

The attic was not a nice place in July and August. Though the house was quiet, there flowed through it in an incessant, suffocating, sickly stream, the untamed smells and noises of the street. For the sake of peace he took to working through the night and going to bed in the day-time; an eccentricity which caused him to be regarded with some suspicion by his neighbours. In spite of their apparent decency he had judged it expedient to keep his door locked, a lack of confidence that wounded them. The lodger in the garret next to his went so far as to signify by laughter her opinion of his unfriendly secrecy. Her own door was never shut, except when he shut it. This interference with her liberty she once violently resented, delivering herself of a jet of oratory that bore with far-fetched fancy on his parentage and profession. For her threshold was her vantage ground. Upon it she stood and waited, listening for the footsteps of her luck.

It was a marvel to him how, under these conditions, he could turn out the amount of work he did. For some nights were as noisy as the day. There was no sort of repose about his next door neighbour. At times she coughed all night, at times she sang. Or again, by sounds of sobbing, he gathered that the poor wretch was not prospering in her trade. Still, there were long and blessed intervals of peace when she roamed far afield; intervals which might or might not be prolonged by alcoholic stupor after her return. It may have been owing to these influences that he began to notice a decided deterioration in his prose. Hanson had returned his last article. He had worked poor Hanson's geniality for all it was worth, and he felt that in common prudence he must withdraw from the *Courier* for a season. Meanwhile his best prose, the articles he had by him, remained unpublished. In war-time there was no market for such wares.

It was now October, and he had paid off but fifteen pounds of the hundred he still owed. The lease of the little house at Ealing was out at Michaelmas; he had the five pounds provided every quarter by the furniture. He sold his furniture and the last of his books, but when Dicky's bill fell due in November he was still fifty pounds to the bad. The fact that he had already paid three thousand and thirty-five would not prevent the sale and disposal of part, and perhaps the most valuable part, of the Harden Library. In that event he would get the money, not the books, and it was the books, all the books, he wanted. He had persuaded himself that the actual redemption of the whole was the only legitimate means by which he could now approach Lucia Harden. The mere repayment of the money was a coarser and more difficult method. And now at the last moment the end, all but achieved, was as far from him as ever, supposing Dicky should refuse to renew his bill.

But Dicky did not refuse. He gave him another two months. No longer term could be conceded; but, yes, he would give him another two months. "Just for the almighty fun of the thing. If there's one thing I like to see," said Dicky, "it's pluck." Dicky was more than ever sure of his game. He argued rightly that Rickman would never have sold his books if he could have sold his articles or borrowed from a friend; that, as he had nothing else to sell or offer as security, his end was certain. But it was so glorious to see the little fellow fighting his luck. Dicky was willing to prolong the excitement for another two months.

For two months he fought it furiously.

He spent many hours of many days in trying to find work;

a difficult thing when a man has cut himself loose from all his friends. Strangers were not likely to consider his superior claims when the kind of work for which he was now applying could be done by anybody as well or better. He counted himself uncommonly happy if he got a stray book to review or a job at the Museum, or if Vaughan held out the promise of giving him some translation by and by.

The conditions under which he worked were now appalling. It was hard to say whether the attic was more terrible in summer, or in the winter that forced him to the intimate and abominable companionship of his oil-stove. Nor was that all. A new horror was added to his existence. He was aware that he had become an object of peculiar interest to the woman in the next room, that she waited for him, and stealthily watched his going out and his coming in. As he passed on the landing, two eyes, dull or feverish, marked him through the chink of the door that never closed. By some hideous instinct of her kind she divined the days when he was in luck. By another instinct she divined also his nature. His mystic apathy held her brute soul in awe; and she no longer revenged herself by furious and vindictive song. So he stayed on, for he owed rent, and removals were expensive.

He found also that there were limits to the advantages of too eccentric an asceticism in diet. No doubt the strange meals he prepared for himself on his oil-stove had proved stimulating by their very strangeness; but when the first shock and surprise of them had worn off he no longer obtained that agreeable result. Perhaps there was something cloying in so much milk and cocoa; he fancied he gained by diluting these rich foods with water. It certainly seemed to him that his veins were lighter and carried a swifter and more delicate current to his brain, that his thoughts now flowed with a remarkable fineness and lucidity. And then all of a sudden the charm stopped working. What food he ate ceased to nourish him. He grew drowsy by day, and had bad dreams at night. He had not yet reached the reconciling stage of nausea, but was forever tormented by a strong and healthy craving for a square meal. There was a poor devil on the floor below him whose state in comparison with his own was affluence. That man had a square meal every Sunday. Even she, the lady of the ever-open door, was better off than he; there was always, or nearly always, a market for her wares.

His sufferings would have been unendurable if any will but his own had imposed them on him in the beginning. Not that he could continue to regard his poverty as a destiny in any way angelic. It was because hitherto he had not known the real thing, because he had seen it from very far away, that it had worn for him that divine, benignant aspect. Now it was very near him; a sordid insufferable companion that dogged his elbow in the street, that sat with him by his fireless hearth, that lay beside him all night, a loathsome bedfellow, telling him a shameful, hopeless tale, and driving the blessed sleep away from him. There were times when he envied his neighbour her nirvana of gin and water; times when the gross steam of the stew prepared for the man below awoke in him acute, intolerable emotion; times when the spiritual will that dominated him, so far from being purified by abstinence, seemed merged in the will of the body made conspicuous and clamorous by hunger.

There were ways in which he might have satisfied it. He could have obtained a square meal any day from Mrs. Downey or the Spinkses; but now that the value of a square meal had increased so monstrously in imagination, his delicacy shrank from approaching his friends with conscious designs upon their hospitality. Spinks was always asking him to dine at his house in Camden Town; but he had refused because he would have had abominable suspicions of his own motives in accepting. Trust Flossie to find him out too. And latterly he had hidden himself from the eye of Spinks. There were moments now when he might have been tempted to borrow fifty pounds from Spinks and end it; but he could not bring himself to borrow from Flossie's husband. The last time he had dined with them he thought she had looked at him as if she were afraid he was going to borrow money. He knew it so well, that gleam of the black eyes, half subtle and half savage. For Flossie had realized her dream, and her little hand clung passionately to the purse that provided for Muriel Maud. He couldn't borrow from Spinky. From Jewdwine? Never. From Hanson? Hardly. From Vaughan? Possibly. Vaughan was considering the expediency of publishing his tragedy, and might be induced to advance him a little on account. Such possibilities visited him in the watches of the night, but dawn revealed their obvious futility. And yet he knew all the time he had only to go to Maddox for the money, and he would get it. To Maddox or to Rankin, Rankin whose books stood open on every bookstall, whose face, in its beautiful photogravure portrait, smiled so impenetrably, guarding the secret of success. But he could not go to them without giving them the explanation he was determined not to give. He knew what they thought of him, therefore he would not go to them. If they had known him better they would have come to him.

He was reminded of them now by seeing in *The Planet* an obituary notice of young Paterson. Paterson had been dying slowly all the year, and December finished him. Though Rickman had been expecting the news for months, the death accomplished affected him profoundly. And at the thought of the young poet whom he had seemed to have so greatly wronged, at the touch of grief and pity and divine regret, his own genius, defied and resisted, descended on him again out of heaven. It was as if the spirit of young Paterson, appeased and reconciled, had bequeathed to him its own immortal adolescence. He finished the poem in four nights, sitting in his great coat, with his legs wrapped in his blankets, and for the last two nights drinking gin and water to keep the blood beating in his head. In the morning he felt as if it were filled with some light and crackling and infinitely brittle substance, the ashes of a brain that had kindled, flamed, and burned itself away. It was the last onslaught of the god, the last mad flaring of the divine fire.

For now he could write no longer. His whole being revolted against the labour of capturing ideas, of setting words in their right order. The least effort produced some horrible sensation. Now it was of a plunging heart that suddenly reversed engines while his brain shivered with the shock; now of a little white wave that swamped his brain with one pulse of oblivion; now it was a sudden giving way of the floor of consciousness, through which his thoughts dropped downwards, headlong, into the abyss. He had great agony and distress in following their flight. At night, as he lay in bed, watching the feeble, automatic procession of ideas, he noticed that they arrived in an order that was not the order of sanity, that if he took note of the language they clothed themselves in, he found he was listening as it were to the gabble of idiocy or aphasia. At such moment he trembled for his reason.

At first these horrors would vanish in the brief brilliance that followed the act of eating; but before long, in the next stage of exhaustion, food induced nothing but a drunken drowsiness. He had once said, as an excuse for refusing wine, that he could get drunk on anything else as well. In these days he got dead drunk on oatmeal porridge, while he produced a perishing ecstasy on bread and milk. But of genuine intoxication the pennyworth of gin and water that sustained the immortal Elegy was his last excess.

He sent the poem to Hanson. Hanson made no sign. But about the middle of January Rankin, of all people, broke the silence that had bound them for a year and a half. Rankin did not know his address, even Hanson had forgotten it. The letter had been forwarded by one of Hanson's clerks.

"My dear Rickman," it said, "where are you? And what are you doing? I dined with Hanson the other night, and he showed me your Elegy. It's too long for *The Courier,* and he's sending it back to you with a string of compliments. If you have no other designs, can you let us have it for *The Planet?* For Paterson's sake it ought to appear at once. My dear fellow, I should like to tell you what I think of it, but I will only state my profound conviction that you have given poor Paterson the fame he should have had and couldn't get, any more than we could get it for him; and I, as his friend, thank you for this magnificent tribute to his genius. Will you do me the honour of dining with me on Sunday if you have nothing better to do? There are many things I should like to talk over with you, and my wife is anxious to make your acquaintance.

"Sincerely yours,

"HERBERT RANKIN.

"P. S.—Maddox is out of town at present, but you'll meet him if you come on Sunday. By the way, I saw your friend Jewdwine the other day. He explained at my request a certain matter which I own with great regret should never have required explanation."

So Jewdwine had explained. And why had not Rankin asked for the explanation sooner? Why had he had to ask for it at all? Still, it was decent of him to admit that he ought not to have required it.

He supposed that he must accept Rankin's invitation to dine. Except for his hunger, which made the prospect of dining so unique and great a thing, he had no reason for refusing. Rankin had reckoned on a scruple, and removed the ground of it. He knew that there was no approaching Rickman as long as there remained the shadow of an assumption that the explanation should have come from him.

The invitation had arrived just in time, before Rickman had sent the last salable remnants of his wardrobe to the place where his dress-suit had gone before. He would have to apologize to Mrs. Rankin for its absence, but his serge suit was still presentable, for he had preserved it with much care, and there was one clean unfrayed shirt in his drawer.

But when Sunday came, the first febrile excitement of anticipation was succeeded by the apathy of an immense fatigue, and at the back of it all a loathsome sense of the positive indecency of his going. It was hunger that was driving him, the importunate hunger of many months, apparent in his lean face and shrunken figure. And, after all, could any dinner be worth the pain of dressing for it? When at the last moment he discovered a loose button on his trousers he felt that there was no motive, no power on earth that could urge him to the task of securing it. And when it broke from its thread and fell, and hid itself under the skirting board in a sort of malignant frenzy, he took its behaviour as a sign that he would do well to forego that dinner at Rankin's. He had hardly acquiesced in this decision when reason reasserted itself and told him that everything depended on that dinner and that the dinner depended on the button; therefore, that in all God's universe there was nothing so important, so essential to him as that button. He went down on his knees and dislodged the button with a penknife, after an agonizing search. He sat feebly on the edge of his bed, and with many sad, weak blasphemies bowed himself to a miserable, ignominious struggle. All malign and adverse fortunes seemed to be concentrated in the rolling, slippery, ungovernable thing.

The final victory was his, such a victory as amounted to a resurgence of the spiritual will.

CHAPTER LXX

ALL things seemed to work together to create an evening of misunderstanding rather than of reconciliation. To begin with, he arrived at the Rankins' half an hour after the time appointed. Rankin lived in Sussex Square, which seemed to him an interminably long way off. The adventure with the trouser button, and a certain dizziness which precluded all swift and decided movement, would have been enough to make him late, even if he had not miscalculated the distance between Hyde Park and Bloomsbury.

He had also miscalculated the distance between Rankin the Junior Journalist and Rankin the celebrity. Rankin had achieved celebrity in a way he had not meant. There was a time when even Jewdwine was outdone by the young men of *The Planet* in honest contempt for the taste and judgment of the many; when it had been Rankin's task to pursue with indefatigable pleasantry the figures of popular renown. And now he was popular himself. The British public had given to him its fatal love.

At first he looked on himself as a man irretrievably disgraced. However proudly he might bear himself in the company of strangers, he approached his colleagues with the air of a man made absurd by unsolicited attention, persecuted and compromised to the last degree. The bosses of his ruddy face displayed all the quiverings and tortures and suffusions of a smiling shame. He was, however, compensated for the loss of personal dignity by a very substantial income. Not that at first he would admit the compensation. " Ricky," he would say in the voice of a man bowed and broken on the wheel of life, " you needn't envy me my thousands. They are the measure of my abasement." Yet he continued to abase himself. Nothing was more amazing than his versatility. The public could hardly keep up with the flight of Rankin's incarnations. Drawing-room comedy,

pathetic pastoral, fantastic adventure, slum idyll and medie-
val romance, it was all one to Rankin. An infallible instinct
told him which *genre* should be chosen at any given
moment; a secret tocsin sounded far-off the hour of his
success. And still the spirit of Rankin held itself aloof;
and underneath his many disguises he remained a junior
journalist. But latterly (since his marriage with a rich
City merchant's daughter) an insidious seriousness had
overtaken him; he began first to tolerate, then to respect,
then to revere the sources of his affluence. The old ironic
spirit was there to chastise him whenever he caught himself
doing it; but that spirit made discord with the elegant
respectability which was now the atmosphere of his home.

Rankin's drawing-room (where he was now waiting for
Rickman) was furnished with the utmost correctness in the
purest Chippendale, upholstered in silver and grey and
lemon and rose brocade; it had grey curtains, rose-lined,
with a design of true lovers' knots in silver; straight
draperies of delicate immaculate white muslin veiled the
window-panes; for the feet, an interminable stretch of grey
velvet carpet whose pattern lay on it like a soft shadow.
Globes of electric lights drooped clustering under volumi-
nously fluted shades. Rankin himself looked grossly out of
keeping with the scene. It was (and they both knew it)
simply the correct setting for his wife, who dominated it, a
young splendour of rose-pink and rose-white and jewelled
laces and gold.

Rickman, after many weeks' imprisonment between four
dirty yellow ochre walls, was bewildered with the space, the
colours, the perfumes, the illumination. He was suffering
from a curious and, it seemed to him, insane illusion, the
illusion of distance, the magnifying of the spaces he had got
to traverse, and, as he entered Mrs. Rankin's drawing-room,
the way from the threshold to the hearth rug stretched
before him as interminably as the way from Howland Street
to Sussex Square. But of any other distance he was blissfully unaware. Beside his vision of Lucia Harden, Mrs.
Herbert Rankin was an entirely insignificant person.

Now Rankin was a little afraid of the elegant lady his
wife. He had had to apologize to her many times for the
curious people he brought to the house, and he was anxious

that Rickman should make a good impression. He was also hungry, as hungry as a man can be who has three square meals every day of his life. Therefore he was annoyed with Rickman for being late.

But his annoyance vanished at the first sight of him. His handshake was significant of atonement and immutable affection. He introduced him almost fearlessly to his wife. He had been at some pains to impress upon her that she was about to entertain a much greater man than her husband, and that it would be very charming of her if she behaved accordingly. At this she pouted prettily, as became a bride, and he pointed out that, as Keith Rickman was a poet, his greatness was incommensurable with that of her husband, it left him undisturbed upon his eminence as the supreme master of prose. So that Mrs. Rankin smiled dimly and deferentially, as an elegant hostess must smile upon a poet who has kept her waiting. There were two other ladies there (Rankin's mother and sister from the provinces); their greeting conveyed a rustling and excited consciousness of the guest's distinction.

As Rankin's family retreated, Maddox heaved himself forward and grasped Rickman's hand without a word.

Rickman had no very clear idea of what happened in the brief pause before dinner. His first sensation was one of confused beatitude and warmth, of being received into an enfolding atmosphere of friendliness. He was sure it was friendliness that made Maddox pluck him by the arm and draw him down beside him on the sofa; and he was too tired to wonder why Maddy should think it necessary to whisper into his collar, " Steady, you'll be all right if you sit still, old man." The strange voices of the women confused him further, and standing made him giddy; he was glad to sit still in his corner, obliterated by Maddy's colossal shoulders.

It was friendliness, he knew, that made Rankin dispense with ceremony and pilot him through those never-ending spaces to the dining-room. And it must have been an exaggeration of the same feeling that made him (regardless of his wife's uplifted eyebrows) insist on placing the guest of the evening between Maddox and himself. It was later on, about the time when the wine went round, that

Rickman became aware of a change, of a subtle undefined hostility in the air. He wondered whether the Rankins were annoyed with him because of his inability to take a brilliant part in the conversation, or to finish any one thing that he took upon his plate. But for the life of him he couldn't help it. He was too tired to talk, and he had reached that stage of hunger when the desire to eat no longer brought with it the power of eating, when the masterpieces of Rankin's *chef* excited only terror and repugnance. He ate sparingly, as starving men must eat, and he drank more sparingly than he ate; for he feared the probable effect of unwonted stimulants. So that his glass appeared ever to be full.

The hostility was more Mrs. Herbert Rankin's attitude than that of her husband, but he noticed a melancholy change in Rankin. His geniality had vanished, or lingered only in the curl of his moustache. He was less amusing than of old. His conversation was no longer that of the light-hearted Junior Journalist flinging himself recklessly into the tide of talk; but whatever topic was started he turned it to himself. He was exceedingly indignant on the subject of the war, which he regarded more as a personal grievance than as a national calamity. No doubt it was his eminence that constituted him the centre of so vast a range.

" The worst of it is," said he, " whichever side beats it's destruction to royalties. I lost a clean thousand on Spion Kop, and I can tell you I didn't recover much on Mafeking, though I worked Tommy Atkins for all he was worth. This year my sales have dropped from fifty to thirty thousand. I can't stand many more of these reverses."

He paused, dubious between two *entrées*.

" If it's had that effect on *me,*" said the great man, " heaven only knows what it's done to other people. How about you, Rickman ? "

" Oh, I'm all right, thanks." The war had ruined him, but his ruin was not the point of view from which he had yet seriously regarded it. He was frankly disgusted with his old friend's tone.

" If it goes on much longer, I shall be obliged," said Rankin solemnly, " to go out to the seat of war."

Rickman felt a momentary glow. He was exhilarated by the idea of Rankin at the seat of war. He said he could see Rankin sitting on it.

Rankin laughed, for he was not wholly dead to the humour of his own celebrity; but there was a faint silken rustle at the head of the table, subtle and hostile, like the stirring of a snake. Mrs. Herbert Rankin bent her fine flat brows towards the poet, with a look ominous and intent. The look was lost upon Rickman and he wondered why Maddox pressed his foot.

" Have you written anything on the war, Mr. Rickman? " she asked.

" No; I haven't written anything on the war."

She looked at him almost contemptuously, as at a fool who had neglected an opportunity.

" What do you generally write on, then? "

Rickman looked up with a piteous smile. He was beginning to feel very miserable and weary, and he longed to get up and go. It seemed to him that there was no end to that dinner; no end to the pitiless ingenuity of Rankin's *chef*. And he always had hated being stared at.

" I don't—generally—write—on anything," he said.

" Your last poem is an exception to your rule then? "

" It is. I wrote most of *that* on gin and water," said Rickman desperately.

Rankin had tugged all the geniality out of his moustache, and his face was full of anxiety and gloom. Maddox tried hard not to snigger. He was not fond of Mrs. Herbert Rankin.

And Rankin's *chef* continued to send forth his swift and fair creations.

Rickman felt his forehead grow cold and damp. He leaned back and wiped it with his handkerchief. A glance passed between Maddox and Rankin. But old Mrs. Rankin looked at him, and the motherhood stirred in her heart.

" Won't you change places with me? I expect you're feeling that fire too much at your back."

Maddox plucked his sleeve. " Better stay where you are," he whispered.

Rickman rose instantly to his feet. The horrible conviction was growing on him that he was going to faint, to faint or to be ignominiously ill. That came sometimes of starving, by some irony of Nature.

"Don't, Maddy—I think perhaps——"

Surely he was going to faint.

Maddox jumped up and held him as he staggered from the room.

Rankin looked at his wife and his wife looked at Rankin.

"He may be a very great poet," said she, "but I hope you'll never ask him to dine here again."

"Never. I can promise you," said Rankin.

The mother had a kinder voice. "I think the poor fellow was feeling ill from that fire."

"Well he might, too," said Rankin with all the bitterness that became the husband of elegant respectability.

"Go and make him lie down, and be sure and keep his head lower than his feet," said Rankin's mother.

"I shouldn't be surprised if Ricky's head were considerably lower than his feet already," said Rankin. And when he said it the bosses of his face grew genial again, as the old coarse Junior Journalistic humour possessed itself of the situation. And he went out sniggering and cursing by turns under his moustache.

Rankin's mother was right. Rickman was feeling very ill indeed. Without knowing how he got there he found himself lying on a bed in Rankin's dressing-room. Maddox and Rankin were with him. Maddox had taken off his boots and loosened his collar for him, and was now standing over him contemplating the effect.

"That's all very well," said Maddox, "but how the dickens am I to get him home? Especially as we don't know his address."

"Ask him."

"I'm afraid our Ricky-ticky's hardly in a state to give very reliable information."

"Sixty-five Howland Street," said Rickman faintly, and the two smiled.

"It was Torrington Square, but I forget the number."

"Sixty-five Howland Street," repeated Rickman with an effort to be distinct.

Maddox shook his head. Rickman had sunk low enough, but it was incredible to them that he should have sunk as low as Howland Street. His insistence on that address they regarded as a pleasantry peculiar to his state. "It's perfectly hopeless," said Maddox. "I don't see anything for it, Rankin, but to let him stay where he is."

At that Rickman roused himself from his stupor. "If you'd only stop jawing and give me some brandy, I could go."

"Oh, my aunt!" said Rankin, dallying with his despair. "It isn't half a bad idea. Try it."

They tried it. Maddox raised the poet's head and Rankin poured the brandy into him. Rankin's hand was gentle, but there was a sternness about Maddox and his ministrations. And as the brandy brought the blood back to his brain Rickman sat up on Rankin's bed, murmuring apologies that would have drawn pity from the nether millstone. But there was no sign of the tenderness that had warmed him when he came. He could see that they were anxious to get him out of the house. Since they had been so keen on reconciliation, whence this change to hostility and disapproval? Oh, of course, he remembered; he had been ill (outrageously ill) in Rankin's dressing-room. Perhaps it wasn't very nice of him; still he didn't do it for his own amusement, and Rankin might have been as ill as he liked in *his* dressing-room, if he had had one. Even admitting that the nature of his calamity was such as to place him beyond the pale of human sympathy, he thought that Rankin might have borne himself with a somewhat better grace. And why Maddox should have taken that preposterous tone——

Maddox explained himself as they left Sussex Square. Rickman did not at first take in the explanation. He was thinking how he could best circumvent Maddox's obvious intention of hailing a hansom and putting him into it. He didn't want to confess that he hadn't a shilling in his pocket.

Coppers anybody may be short of, and presently he meant to borrow twopence for a 'bus. Later on he would have to ask for a loan of fifty pounds; for you can borrow pounds and you can borrow pennies, but not shillings. Not at any rate if you are starving.

"If I were you, Ricky," Maddox was saying, "I should

go straight to bed when you get home. You'll be all right in the morning."

" I'm all right now. I can't think what bowled me over."

" Ricky, the prevarication is unworthy of you. Without humbug, I think you might keep off it a bit before you dine with people. It doesn't matter about us, you know, but it's hardly the sort of thing Mrs. Rankin's been accustomed to."

" Mrs. Rankin?"

" Well, yes, I said Mrs. Rankin; but it's not about her I care—it's about you. Of course you'll tell me to mind my own business, but I wish—I wish to goodness you'd give it up. Altogether. You did once, why not again? Believe me, the game isn't worth the candle." And he said to himself, noting the sharp line of his friend's haggard figure, " It's killing him."

" I see," said Rickman slowly. In an instant he saw it all; the monstrous and abominable suspicion that had rested upon him all the evening. It explained everything. He saw, too, how every movement of his own had lent itself to the intolerable inference. It was so complete, so satisfactory, so comprehensive, that he could not wonder that they had found no escape from it. He could find none himself. There was no way by which he could establish the fact of his sobriety; for it is the very nature of such accusations to feed upon defence. Denial, whether humorous or indignant, would but condemn him more. The very plausibility of the imputation acted on him as a despotic suggestion. He began to feel that he must have been drunk at Rankin's; that he was drunk now while he was talking to Maddox. And to have told the truth, to have said, " Maddy, I'm starving. I haven't had a square meal for four months," would have sounded too like a beggar's whine. Whatever he let out later on, it would be mean to spring all that on Maddox now, covering him with confusion and remorse.

He laughed softly, aware that his very laugh would be used as evidence against him. " I see. So you all thought I'd been drinking?"

" Well—if you'll forgive my saying so——"

" Oh, I forgive you. It was a very natural supposition."

" I think you'll have to apologize to the Rankins."

" I think the Rankins 'll have to apologize to me."

With every foolish word he was more hopelessly immersed.

He insisted on parting with Maddox at the Marble Arch. After all, he had not borrowed that fifty pounds nor yet that twopence. Luckily, Rankin's brandy enabled him to walk back with less difficulty than he came. It had also warmed him, so that he did not find out all at once that he had left his overcoat at Rankin's. He could not go back for it. He could never present himself at that house again.

It was a frosty night, with a bitter wind rising in the east and blowing up Oxford Street. His attic under the icicled tiles was dark and narrow as the grave. And on the other side of the thin wall a Hunger, more infernal and malignant than his own, waited stealthily for its prey.

CHAPTER LXXI

IT was five o'clock, and Dicky Pilkington was at his ease stretched before the fire in a low chair in the drawing-room of the flat he now habitually shared with Poppy Grace. It was beatitude to lie there with his legs nicely toasting, to have his tea (which he did not drink) poured out for him by the most popular little variety actress in London, and to know that she had found in him her master. This evening, his intellect in play under many genial influences, Dicky was once more raising the pæan of Finance. Under some piquant provocation, too; for Poppy had just informed him that she " didn't fancy his business."

" Now, look here," said Dicky, " you call yourself an artist. Well—this business of mine isn't a business, it's an art. Think of the delicacy we 'ave to use. To know to a hair's breadth how far you can go with a man, to know when to give him his head with the snaffle and when to draw him in with the curb. It's a feelin' your way all along. Why, I knew a fellow, a broker—an uncommonly clever chap he was, too—ruined just for want of a little tact. He was too precipitate, began hauling his man up just when he ought to have let him go. He'd no imagination, that fellow. (Don't you go eating too much cake, Popsie, or you'll make your little nose red.) I don't know any other

profession gives you such a grip of life and such a feelin'
of power. You've got some young devil plungin' about,
kickin' up his heels all over the shop, say. He thinks he's
got the whole place to break his neck in; and you know the
exact minute by your watch that you can bring him in
grovellin' on your office floor. It's the iron 'and in the velvet
glove," said Dicky.

"I know what you're driving at, and I call it a beastly
shame."

"No, it isn't. I shouldn't wonder if old Rickets paid up
all right, after all."

"And if he doesn't?"

"If he doesn't. Well——"

"I say, though, think wot a lot he's paid you. Can't
you let him go?"

Dicky shook his head and smiled softly as at some interior
vision.

"You'll ruin him for a dirty fifty pounds?"

"I won't ruin him. And it isn't for the money, it's for
the game. I like," said Dicky, "to see a man play in first-
class style. But I don't blame him if he hasn't got style so
long as he's got pluck. In fact, I don't know that of the
two I wouldn't rather have pluck. I've seen a good many
men play this game, but I've never seen any one who came
up to old Razors for pluck *and* style. It's a treat to see him.
Do you suppose I'm going to cut in now and spoil it all by
giving him points? That would take all the gilt off the
gingerbread. And do you suppose he'd let me? Not he;
he's spreading the gilt on thick, and he'd see me d——d
first."

Dicky smoked with half-closed eyes fixed on the fire, in
speechless admiration. He felt that he was encouraging
the display of high heroism by watching it. He singled out
a beautiful writhing flame, spat at it, and continued: "No,
I'll take good care that Rickets doesn't starve. But I'm
going to stand by and see him finish fair. If you like,
Popsie, you can back him to win. I don't care if he *does*
win. It would be worth it for what I've got out of him."

By what he had got out of him Dicky meant, not three
thousand seven hundred and odd pounds, but a spectacle
beyond all comparison exciting and sublime. For that he

was prepared to abandon any further advantage that might be wrung from the Harden library by a successful manipulation of the sales.

Poppy did not back Rickman to win; but she determined to call on him at his rooms, and leave a little note with a cheque and a request that he would pay Dicky and have done with him. "You'd better owe it to me than to him, old chappy," thus she wrote in the kindness and impropriety of her heart. But Rickman never got that little note.

CHAPTER LXXII

OF all the consequences of that terrible dinner at Rankin's there was none that Rickman resented more than the loss of his overcoat. As he lay between his blankets he still felt all the lashings of the east wind around his shivering body. He was awake all that night, and the morning found him feverish with terror of the illness that might overtake him before he attained his end. He stayed in bed all day to prevent it, and because of his weakness, and for warmth.

But the next day there came a mild and merciful thaw, a tenderness of heaven that was felt even under the tiles in Howland Street. And the morning of that day brought a thing that in all his dreams he had not yet dreamed of, a letter from Lucia.

He read it kneeling on the floor of his garret, supporting himself by the edge of the table. It was only a few lines in praise of the Elegy (which had appeared in *The Planet* the week before) and a postscript that told him she would be staying at Court House with Miss Palliser till the summer.

He knelt there a long time with his head bowed upon his arms. His brain failed him when he tried to write an answer, and he put the letter into his breast-pocket, where it lay like a loving hand against his heart. And yet there was not a word of love in it.

The old indomitable hope rose in his heart again and he forced himself to eat and drink, that he might have strength for the things he had to do. That night he did not sleep, but lay wrapt in his beatific passion. His longing was so intense that it created a vision of the thing it longed for. It seemed to him that he heard Lucia's soft foot-fall about his bed, that she came and sat beside his pillow, that she bowed her head upon his breast, and that her long hair drifted over him. For the beating of his own heart gave him the sense of a presence beside him all night long, as he lay with his right arm flung across his own starved body, guarding her letter, the letter that had not a word of love in it.

In the morning he discovered that another letter had lain on his table under Lucia's. It was from Dicky Pilkington, reminding him that it wanted but seven days to the thirtieth. Dicky said nothing about any willingness to renew the bill. What did it matter? Dicky would renew it, Dicky must renew it; he felt that there was force in him to compel Dicky to renew it. He went out and bought a paper with the price of a meal of milk (he couldn't pawn his good clothes; their assistance was too valuable in interviews with possible employers). He found the advertisement of an Exeter bookseller in want of a foreman and expert cataloguer at a salary of ninety pounds. He answered it by return. In the list of his credentials he mentioned that he had catalogued the Harden library (a feat, as he knew, sufficient to constitute him a celebrity in the eyes of the Exeter man). He added that if the bookseller felt inclined to consider his application he would be obliged by a wire, as he had several other situations in view.

The bookseller wired, engaging him for six months. The same day came a cheque for ten pounds from *The Planet,* the honorarium for the Elegy. He sent the ten pounds to Dicky at once (by way of showing what he could do) with a curt note informing him of his appointment and requesting a renewal for three months, by which time his salary would cover the remainder still owing.

Feeling that no further intellectual efforts were now required of him he went out to feed on the fresh air. As he crossed the landing an odour of hot pottage came to meet him. Through the ever-open door he caught a glimpse of a woman's form, throned, as it were, above clouds of curling steam. A voice went out, hoarse with a supreme emotion.

" Come in, you there, and 'ave a snack, wontcher? " it said.

" No, thank you," he answered.

" Garn then. I'll snack yer for a ——y fool! "

And from the peaceableness of the reply he gathered that this time the lady was not soliciting patronage but conferring it.

He was no longer hungry, no longer weighed upon by his exhausted body. A great restlessness had seized it, a desire to walk, to walk on and on without stopping. The young day had lured him into the Regent's Park. So gentle was the weather that, but for the bare branches and blanched sky, it might have been a day in Spring. As he walked he experienced sensations of indescribable delicacy and lightness, he saw ahead of him pellucid golden vistas of metaphysical splendour, he skimmed over fields of elastic air with the ease and ecstasy of a blessed spirit.

When he came in he found that the experience prolonged itself through the early night, even when he lay motionless on his bed staring at the wall. And as he stared it seemed to him that there passed upon the wall clouds upon clouds of exquisite and evanescent colour, and that strange forms appeared and moved upon the clouds. He saw a shoal of fishes (they *were* fishes, radiant, iridescent, gorgeous fishes, with the tails of peacocks) ; they swam round and round the room just under the cornice, an ever-revolving, ever-floating frieze. He was immensely interested in these decorative hallucinations. His brain seemed to be lifted up, to be iridescent also, to swim round and round with the swimming fishes.

He woke late in the morning, with a violent sore throat and pain in all his body. He was too giddy to sit up and help himself, but he knocked weakly on the thin wall. His neighbour roused herself at the faint summons and appeared. She stood at the foot of the bed with her hands on her hips and contemplated him for a moment. He tried to speak, but his tongue seemed to be stuck burning to the roof of his mouth. He pointed to his throat.

" Yes, I dessay," said she. " I said you'd get somefing and you've got it." So saying she disappeared into her own apartment.

As he saw her go despair shook him. He thought that he was abandoned. But presently she returned, bringing

a cup of hot tea with a dash of gin in it from her own
breakfast.

"I'd a seen to you afore ef you'd let me," she said.
"You tyke it from me, young man, wot you want is a good
hot lining to your belly. I'd 'ave given it to you ef you'd a
let me. I'm a lydy as tykes her dinner reg'ler, I am. No,
you don't!" This, as he turned away his head in protest.
She however secured it firmly with one filthy hand, while
with the other she held the reeking cup to his lips. She had
put it to her own first to test the heat and quality of the
brew. Yet he was grateful. He had some difficulty in
swallowing; and from time to time she wiped his mouth
with her villainous apron; and he was grateful still, having
passed beyond disgust.

She perceived the gratitude. "Garn," said she, "wot's a
cup er tea? I'd seen to yer afore ef you'd 'a' let me."

She continued her ministrations; she brought coal in her
own scuttle, and after immense pains she lighted a fire in
the wretched grate. Then she smoothed his bed-clothes till
they were covered with her smutty trail. She would have
gone for a doctor then and there, but difficulty arose. For
doctors meant hospitals, and the man below threatened to
sell his lodger's "sticks" if rent were not forthcoming.
She cast her eyes about in search of pawnable articles.
They fell upon his clothes. She took up his shirt and
examined it carefully, appraising the sleeve links and the
studs. But when she touched the coat, the coat that had
Lucia's letter in the breast-pocket, Rickman turned in his
bed and made agonizing signs, struggling with the voice that
perished in his burning·throat.

"Wot's the good," she said, "of a suit when yer can't
wear it? As I told you wot you wa—— No, the's no
sorter use your making fyces at me. And you keep
your ——y legs in, or I'll——" The propositions that followed were murmured in a hoarse but crooning tone, such
as a mother might have used to soothe a fractious child.
She went away, carrying the clothes with her, and turned
out the pockets in her den.

On her return she sent the man below to fetch the doctor.
But the man below fell in with boon companions on the way,
and no doctor came. All that night the woman watched

by Rickman's bedside, heedless of her luck. She kept life in him by feeding him with warm milk and gin, a teaspoonful at a time. Rickman, aware of footsteps in the room, fancied himself back again in Rankin's dressing-room. The whole scene of that evening floated before him all night long. He had a sense of presences hostile and offended, of being irretrievably disgraced. In the recurring nightmare he saw Lucia Harden instead of Mrs. Rankin. So persistently did he see her that when he woke he could not shake off the impression that she had been actually, if unaccountably, present, a spectator of his uttermost disgrace. He could never look her in the face again. No, for he was disgraced; absolutely, irredeemably, atrociously disgraced. Beyond all possibility of explanation and defence; though he sometimes caught himself explaining and pleading against those offended phantoms of his brain. Why should he suffer so? Just because of his inability to deal with Rankin's never-ending dinner, or to pay a debt of millions, many millions of figures that climbed up the wall. He was not sure which of these two obligations was laid upon him.

He became by turns delirious and drowsy, and the woman fetched a doctor early the next day. He found enteric and blood-poisoning also, of which Rickman's illness at the Rankins' must have been the first warning symptoms.

" He'll have to go to the hospital; but you'd better send word to his friends."

" 'E ain't got no friends. And *I* dunno 'oo 'e is."

The doctor said to himself, " Gone under," and looked round him for a clue. He examined a postcard from Spinks, and a parcel (containing an overcoat) from Rankin, with the novelist's name and address inside the wrapper. The poet's name was familiar to the doctor, who read *Metropolis.* He first of all made arrangements for removing his patient to the hospital. Then in his uncertainty he telegraphed to Jewdwine, to Rankin, and to Spinks.

The news of Rickman's illness was thus spread rapidly among his friends. It brought Spinks that afternoon, and Flossie, the poor Beaver dragged to Howland Street by her husband to see what her woman's hands could do. They entered upon a scene of indescribable confusion and clangour. Poppy Grace, arrived on her errand (for which she had attired herself in a red dress and ermine tippet), had mounted guard over the unconscious poet.

"Ricky," cried Poppy, bending over him, "won't you speak to me? It's Poppy, dear. Don't you know me?"

"No, 'e don't know yer, so you needn't arsk 'im."

Poppy placed her minute figure defiantly between Rickman and her rival of the open door. She had exhausted her emotions in those wild cries, and was prepared to enjoy the moment which produced in her the hallucination of self-conscious virtue.

The woman, voluble and fierce, began to describe Miss Grace's character in powerful but somewhat exaggerated language, appealing to the new-comers to vindicate her accuracy. Poppy seated herself on the bed and held a pocket-handkerchief to her virtuous nose. It was the dumb and dignified rebuke of Propriety in an ermine tippet, to Vice made manifest in the infamy of rags. The Beaver retreated in terror on to the landing, where she stood clutching the little basket of jellies and things which she had brought, as if she feared that it might be torn from her in the violence of the scene. Spinks, convulsed with anguish by the sight of his friend lying there unconscious, could only offer an inarticulate expostulation. It was the signal for the woman to burst into passionate self-defence.

"I ain't took nothing 'cept wot the boss 'e myde me. 'Go fer a doctor?' ses 'e. 'No, you don't. I don't 'ave no ——y doctor messing round 'ere an' cartin' 'im orf to the 'orspital afore 'e's paid 'is rent.' Ses 'e, 'I'm——'"

The entrance of Maddox and Rankin checked the hideous flow. They were followed by the porters of the hospital and the nurse in charge. Her presence commanded instantaneous calm.

"There are far too many people in this room," said she. Her expelling glance fell first on Poppy, throned on the bed, then on the convulsive Spinks. She turned more gently to Rankin, in whose mouth she saw remonstrance, and to Maddox, in whose eyes she had read despair. "It will really be better for him to take him to the hospital."

"No," cried Spinks, darting in again from the landing, "take him to my house 45 Dalmeny Av——" But the Beaver plucked him by the sleeve; for she thought of Muriel Maud.

" No, no, take him to mine, 87 Sussex Square," said Rankin, and he insisted. But in the end he suffered himself to be over-ruled; for he thought darkly of his wife.

" I'd give half my popularity if I could save him," he said to Maddox.

" Half your popularity won't save him, nor yet the whole of it," said Maddox savagely. In that moment they hated themselves and each other for the wrong they had done him. Their hearts smote them as they thought of the brutalities of Sunday night.

The woman still held her ground in the centre of the room, where she stood scowling at the nurse as she busied herself about the bed.

" I'd seen to 'im ef 'e'd 'a' let me," she reiterated.

Maddox dealt with her. He flicked a sovereign on to the table. " Look here," said he, " suppose you take that and go out quietly."

There was a momentary glitter in her eyes, but her fingers hesitated.

" I didn' fink 'e 'ad no frien's wen I come in." It was her way of intimating that what she had done she had not done for money.

" All right, take it."

She drew out a filthy grey flannel bag from the bosom of her gown and slipped the gold into it. And still she hesitated. She could not understand why so large a sum was offered for such slight services as she had rendered. It must have been for—— Another thought stirred in her brute brain.

They were raising Rickman in his bed before taking him away. His shoulders were supported on the nurse's arm, his head dropped on her breast. The posture revealed all the weakness of his slender body. The woman turned. And as she looked at the helpless figure she was visited by a dim sense of something strange and beautiful and pure, something (his helplessness perhaps) that was outraged by her presence, and called for vindication.

" 'E never 'ad no truck with me," she said. It struck Maddox that the denial had a sublimity and pathos of its own. She dropped the bag into her lean bosom and went out.

And the porters wrapped him in his blankets, and laid

him on a stretcher, and carried him out; past Maddox and Rankin, who turned their heads away; past Flossie, who shrank a little from the blankets, but cried softly to see him go; and past the woman standing on her threshold. And in that manner he passed Horace Jewdwine coming up the stair, too late. And all that Jewdwine could do was to stand back and let him pass.

It was Jewdwine's fear that made him uncover, as in the presence of the dead.

CHAPTER LXXIII

WHEN Rankin, Maddox, and Jewdwine stood alone in the garret whence they had seen Rickman carried away from them, remorse drove all hope of his recovery from their hearts. They learnt some of the truth about him from the woman in the next room, a keen observer of human nature. Jewdwine and Rankin, when they too had paid her for her services, were glad to escape from the intolerable scene. Maddox stayed behind, collecting what he could only think of as Rickman's literary remains.

He found in the table drawer three unpublished articles, a few poems, and the First Act of the second and unfinished tragedy, saved by its obscure position at the back of the drawer. The woman owned to having lit the fire with the rest. Maddox cursed and groaned as he thought of that destruction. He knew that many poems which followed *Saturnalia* had remained unpublished. Had they too been taken to light the fire? He turned the garret upside down in search of the missing manuscripts. At last in a cupboard he came upon a leather bag. It was locked and he could find no key, but he wrenched it open with the poker. It contained many manuscripts; among them the Nine and Twenty Sonnets, and the testament concerning them. He read the Sonnets, but not the other document, which was in a sealed envelope. He found also a bundle of Dicky Pilkington's receipts and his last letter threatening foreclosure. And when he had packed up the books (Lucia's books) and redeemed Rickman's clothes from the pawn-shop, he took all these things away with him for safety.

There was little he could do for Rickman, but he promised himself the pleasure of settling Dicky's claim. But even that satisfaction was denied him. For Dicky had just renewed his bill for a nominal three months. Nominal only. Dicky had in view a magnificent renunciation, and he flatly refused to treat with Maddox or anybody else. He was completely satisfied with his conclusion; it meant that Rickman, for all his style and pluck, had lost the game and that he, Pilkington, had done the handsome thing, as he could do it when the fancy took him. For Dicky's heart had been touched by the tale that Poppy told him, and it melted altogether when he went and saw for himself poor Ricky lying in his cot in the North-Western Hospital. He had a great deal of nice feeling about him after all, had Dicky.

Terrible days followed Rickman's removal to the hospital; days when his friends seemed justified in their sad conviction; days when the doctors gave up hope; days when he would relapse after some brief recovery; days when he kept them all in agonizing suspense.

But Rickman did not die. As they said, it was not in him to take that exquisitely mean revenge. It was not in him to truckle to the tradition that ordains that unfortunate young poets shall starve in garrets and die in hospitals. He had always been an upsetter of conventions, and a law unto himself. So there came a day, about the middle of March, when he astonished them all by appearing among them suddenly in Maddox's rooms, less haggard than he had been that night when he sat starving at Rankin's dinnertable.

And as he came back to them, to Jewdwine, to Maddox, and to Rankin, they each could say no more to him than they had said five years ago. "What a fool you were, Rickman. Why didn't you come to *me?*" But when the others had left, Maddox put his hands on Rickman's shoulders and they looked each other in the face.

"I say, Ricky, what did you do it for?"

But that was more than Rickman could explain, even to Maddox.

They had all contended which should receive him when he came out of hospital; but it was settled that for the present he should remain with Maddox in his rooms. There Dicky, absolutely prepared to do the handsome thing, called upon him at an early date. Dicky had promised himself some exquisite sensations in the moment of magnanimity; but the moment never came. Rickman remained firm in his determination that every shilling of the debt should be paid, and paid by him; it was more than covered by the money Maddox advanced for his literary remains. Dicky had to own that the plucky little fellow had won his game, but he added, " You couldn't have done it, Razors, if I hadn't given you points."

The great thing was that he had done it, and that the Harden library was his, was Lucia's. It only remained to tell her, and to hand it over to her. He had long ago provided for this difficult affair. He wrote, as he had planned to write, with a judicious hardness, brevity, and restraint. He told her that he desired to see her on some business connected with the Harden library, in which he was endeavouring to carry out as far as possible his father's last wishes. He asked to be allowed to call on her some afternoon in the following week. He thanked her for her letter without further reference, and remained—" sincerely "? No, " faithfully " hers.

He told Maddox that he thought of going down to Devonshire to recruit.

CHAPTER LXXIV

LUCIA was suffering from the disagreeable strain of a divided mind. To begin with she was not altogether pleased with Mr. Rickman. He had taken no notice of the friendly little letter she had written about the Elegy, her evident intention being to give him pleasure. She had written it on impulse, carried away by her ardent admiration. That was another of those passionate indiscreet things, which were followed by torments of her pride. And the torments had followed. His two months' silence had reproved her ardour, had intimated to her that he was in no mood to enter in at the door which she had closed to him three years ago. She took it that he had regarded her poor little olive branch as an audacity. And now that he *had* written there was not a word about the subject of her letter. He had only written because business compelled him, and his tone was not only cold, but positively austere.

But, she reflected, business after all did not compel him to come down and see her. Having reached this point she became aware that her heart was beating most uncomfortably at the bare idea of seeing him. For the first time this anticipation inspired her with anxiety and fear. Until their last meeting in Tavistock Place there had been in all their intercourse something intangible and rare, something that, though on her part it had lacked the warmth of love, she had acknowledged to be finer than any friendship. That beautiful, intangible quality had perished in the stress of their final meeting. And even if it came to life again it could never be the same, or so she thought. She had perceived how much its permanence had depended on external barriers, on the social gulf, and on the dividing presence of another woman. She could not separate him from his genius; and his genius had long ago overleapt the social gulf. And now, without poor Flossie, without the safeguard of his engagement, she felt herself insecure and shelterless. More than ever since he had overleapt that barrier too.

But though Lucia had found out all these things, she had not yet found out why it was that she had been so glad to hear that Keith Rickman was going to be married, nor why she had been so passionately eager to keep him to his engagement. In any case she could not have borne to be the cause of unhappiness to another woman; and that motive was so natural that it served for all.

As things had turned out, if he had married, that, she had understood, would have been such a closing of the door as would have shut him out for ever. And now that he was knocking at the door again, now that there was no reason why, once opened, it should not remain open, she began to be afraid of what might enter in with him. She made up her mind that she would not let him in. So she sat down and wrote a cold little note to say that she was afraid she would not be able to see him next week. Could he not explain the business in writing? She took that letter to the post herself. And as each step brought her nearer to the inevitable act, the conviction grew on her that this conduct of hers was cowardly, and unworthy both of him and of herself. A refusal to see him was a confession of fear, and fear assumed the existence of the very thing that his letter had

ignored. It was absurd, too, if he had come to see that his
feeling for her was (as she persisted in believing it to be) a
piece of poetic folly, an illusion of the literary imagination.
She turned back and tore up that cold little note, and wrote
another that said she would be very glad to see him any day
next week, except Friday. There was no reason why she
should have excepted Friday; but it sounded more business-
like somehow.

She did not take Kitty into her confidence, and in this she
failed to perceive the significance of her own secrecy. She
told herself that there was no need to ask Kitty's advice,
because she knew perfectly well already what Kitty's advice
would be.

He came on Tuesday. Monday was too early for his
self-respect, Wednesday too late for his impatience. He
had looked to find everything altered in and about Court
House; and he saw, almost with surprise, the same April
flowers growing in the green garden, and the same beech-
tree dreaming on the lawn. He recognized the black rifts
in its trunk and the shining sweep of its branches overhead. The door was opened by Robert, and Robert remembered him. There was a shade more gravity in the affectionate welcome, but then Robert was nine years older. He
was shown into the drawing-room, and it, too, was much
as he had left it nine years ago.

Kitty Palliser was there; she rose to meet him with her
irrepressible friendliness, undiminished by nine years. There
was nothing cold and business-like about Kitty.

"Will you tell Miss Harden?" said she to the detached,
retreating Robert. Then she held out her hand. "I am
very glad to see you." But a wave of compassion rather
than of gladness swept over her face as she looked at him.
She made him sit down, and gave him tea. There was a
marked gentleness in all her movements, unlike the hilarious
lady she used to be.

The minutes went by and Lucia did not appear. He
could not attend to what Kitty was saying. His eyes were
fixed on the door that looked as if it were never going to
open. Kitty seemed to bear tenderly with his abstraction.
Once he glanced round the room, recognizing familiar
objects. He had expected, after Dicky's descent on Court
House, to find nothing recognizable in it. Kitty was telling

him how an uncle of hers had lent them the house for a year, how he had bought it furnished, and how, but for the dismantled library and portrait gallery, it was pretty much as it had been in Miss Harden's time. So unchanged was it and its atmosphere that Rickman felt himself in the presence of a destiny no less unchanging and familiar. He had come on business, as he had done nine years ago; and he felt that the events of that time must in some way repeat themselves, that when he was alone with Lucia he would say to her such things as he had said before, that there would be differences, misunderstandings, as before, and that his second coming would end in misery and separation like the first. It seemed to him that Kitty, kind Kitty, had the same perception and foreboding. Thus he interpreted her very evident compassion. She meant to console him.

"Robert remembers you," said she.

"That's very clever of Robert," said he.

"No, it's only his faithfulness. What a funny thing faithfulness is. Robert won't allow any one but Miss Harden to be mistress here. My people are interlopers, abominations of desolation. He can barely be civil to their friends. But to hers—he is as you see him. It's a good thing for me I'm her friend, or he wouldn't let me sit here and pour out tea for you."

He thought over the speech. It admitted an encouraging interpretation. But Miss Palliser may have been more consoling than she had meant.

She rattled on in the kindness of her heart. He was grateful for her presence; it calmed his agitation and prepared him to meet Lucia with composure when she came. But Lucia did not come; and he began to have a horrible fear that at the last moment she would fail him. He refused the second cup that Kitty pressed on him, and she looked at him compassionately again. He was so used to his appearance that he had forgotten how it might strike other people. He was conscious only of Kitty's efforts to fill up agreeably these moments of suspense.

At last it ended. Lucia was in the doorway. At the sight of her his body shook and the strength in his limbs seemed to dissolve and flow downwards to the floor. His eyes never left her as she came to him with her rhythmic, unembarrassed motion. She greeted him as if they had met the other day; but as she took his hand she looked down at it, startled by its slenderness. He was glad that she seated herself on his right, for he felt that the violence of his heart must be audible through his emaciated ribs.

Kitty made some trivial remark, and Lucia turned to her as if her whole soul hung upon Kitty's words. Her absorption gave him time to recover himself. (It did not occur to him that that was what she had turned away for.) Her turning enabled him to look at her. He noticed that she seemed in better health than when he had seen her last, and that in sign of it her beauty was stronger, more vivid, and more defined.

They said little to each other. But when Kitty had left them they drew in their chairs to the hearth with something of the glad consent of those for whom the long-desired moment has arrived. He felt that old sense of annihilated time, of return to a state that had never really lapsed; and it struck him that she, too, had that feeling. It was she who spoke first.

" Before you begin your business, tell me about yourself."

" There isn't anything to tell."

She looked as if she rather doubted the truth of that statement.

" If you don't mind, I'd rather begin about the business and get it over."

" Why, is it—is it at all unpleasant? "

He smiled. " Not in the least, not in the very least. It's about the library."

" I thought we'd agreed that that was all over and done with long ago? "

" Well, you see, it hasn't anything to do with *us*. My father——"

" Don't let us go back to that."

" I'm sorry, but we must—a little. You know my father and I had a difference of opinion? "

" I know—I know."

" Well, in the end he owned that I was right. That was when he was dying."

He wished she would not look at him; for he could not look at her. He was endeavouring to make his tale appear in the last degree natural and convincing. Up till now he had told nothing but the truth, but as he was about to enter on the path of perjury he became embarrassed by the intentness of her gaze.

"You were with him?" she asked.

"Yes." He paused a moment to command a superior kind of calm. That pause wrecked him, for it gave her also time for thought. "He wanted either to pay you the money that you should have had, or to hand over the library; and I thought——"

"But the library was sold?"

He explained the matter of the mortgage carefully, but with an amount of technical detail meant to impose and mystify.

"Then how," she asked, "was the library redeemed?"

He repudiated an expression so charged with moral and emotional significance. He desired to lead her gently away from a line of thought that if pursued would give her intelligence the clue. "You can't call it redeemed. Nobody redeemed it. The debt, of course, had to be paid out of my father's estate."

"In which case the library became yours?"

He smiled involuntarily, for she had him there, and she knew it.

"It became nothing of the sort, and if it had I could hardly go against my father's wishes by holding on to it."

"Can't you see that it's equally impossible for me to take it?"

"Why? Try and think of it as a simple matter of business."

He spoke like a tired man, straining after a polite endurance of her feminine persistence and refining fantasy. "It hasn't anything to do with you or me."

Thus did he turn against her the argument with which she had crushed him in another such dispute nine years ago.

"I am more business-like than you are. I remember perfectly well that your father paid more than a thousand pounds for those books in the beginning."

"That needn't trouble you. It has been virtually deducted. I'm sorry to say a few very valuable books were sold before the mortgage and could not be recovered."

He had given himself away by that word "recovered."

Her eyes searched him through and through to find his falsehood, as they had searched him once before to find his truth. " It is very, very good of you," she said.

" Of *me?* Am *I* bothering you? Don't think of me except as my father's executor."

" Did you know that he wanted you to do this, or did you only think it? Was it really his express wish? "

He looked her in the face and lied, boldly and freely. " It was. Absolutely."

And as she met that look, so luminously, so superlatively sincere, she knew that he had lied. "All the same," said she, " I can't take it. Don't think it unfriendly of me. It isn't. In fact, don't you see it's just because we have been—we are—friends that I must refuse it? I can't take advantage of that——" She was going to say " feeling," but thought better of it.

"And don't you see by refusing you are compelling me to be dishonourable? If you were really my friend you would think more of my honour than of your own scruples. Or is that asking too much? " He felt that he had scored in this game of keen intelligences.

" No. But it would be wrong of me to let your honour be influenced by our friendship."

" Don't think of our friendship, then. It's all pure business, as brutally impersonal as you like."

" If I could only see it that way."

" I should have thought it was quite transparently and innocently clear." He had scored again. For now he had taxed her with stupidity. " If I could persuade you that it came from my father, you wouldn't mind. You mind because you think it comes from me. Isn't that so? "

She was silent, and he knew.

" How can I persuade you? I can only repeat that I've absolutely nothing to do with it." There was but little friendliness about him now. His whole manner was full of weariness and irritation. " Why should you imagine that I had? "

" Because it would have been so very like you."

" Then I must be lying abominably. Is that so very like me? "

" I have heard you do it before—once—twice—magnificently."

" When ? "

" About this time nine years ago."

He remembered. The wonder was that she should have remembered too.

" I daresay. But what possible motive could I have for lying now ? "

He had scored heavily this time. Far too heavily. There was a flame in Lucia's face which did not come from the glow of the fire, a flame that ran over her neck and forehead to the fine tips of her ears. For she thought, supposing all the time he had been telling her the simple truth? Why should she have raised the question? Why should she have taken for granted that any personal interest should have led him to do this thing? And in wondering she was ashamed. He saw her confusion, and attributed it to another cause.

" I'm only asking you to keep the two things distinct, as I do—as I must do," he said gently.

" I'll think about it, and let you know to-morrow."

" But I'm going to-night."

" Oh, no, I can't let you do that. You must stay over the night. Your room is ready for you."

He protested; she insisted; and in the end she had her way, as he meant to have his way to-morrow.

He stayed, and all that evening they were very kind to him. Kitty talked gaily throughout dinner; and afterwards Lucia played to him while he rested, propped up with great cushions (she had insisted on the cushions), in her chair. Kitty, his hostess, drew back, and seemed to leave these things to Lucia as her right. He knew it was Lucia, and not Kitty, who ran up to his room to see that all was comfortable and that his fire burnt well. In everything she said and did there was a peculiar gentleness and care. It was on the same lines as Kitty's compassion, only more poignant and intense. It was, he thought, as if she knew that it was for the last time, that of all these pleasant things to-morrow would see the end. Was it kind of her to let him know what her tenderness could be, when to-morrow must end it all? For he had no notion of the fear evoked by his appearance, the fear that was in both their hearts. He did not know why they looked at him with those kind glances, nor why Lucia told him that Robert was close at hand if he should want anything in the night. He slept in the room

that had once been Lucia's, the room above the library,
looking to the western hills. He did not know that they
had given it him because it was a good room to be ill and to
get well in.

Lucia and Kitty sat up late that night over the fire, and
they talked of him.

Kitty began it. "*Do* you remember," said she, " the
things we used to say about him?"

" Oh, don't, Kitty! I do."

" You needn't mind; it was only I who said them."

" Yes, you said them; but I thought them."

Then she told Kitty what had brought him there and the
story that he had told her. "And, Kitty, all the time I knew
he lied."

" Probably. You must take it, Lucy, all the same."

" How can I take it, when I know it comes out of his own
poor little waistcoat pocket?"

" You would, if you cared enough about him."

" No. It's just *because* I care that I can't."

" You do care, then?"

" Yes, of course I do."

" But not in the same way as *he* cares, Lucy."

Kitty's words sounded like a statement rather than a
question, so they passed unanswered.

" It's all right, Kitty. It's all over, at last. He doesn't
care a bit now, not a bit."

" Oh, doesn't he! How can you be so idiotic? All over?
I assure you it's only just begun."

Lucia turned her head away.

" Lucy, what are you going to do with him?"

Lucia smiled sadly. That was the question she had asked
Horace ten years ago, making him responsible. And now
the responsibility had been laid on her. "Kitty, did you
notice how thin he is? He looks as if he'd just come
through some awful illness. But I can't ask him about it."

" Rather not. You don't know whether he's had it, or
whether he's going to have it."

" I wonder if you'd mind asking him to stay a week or
two? It might help him to get strong."

" I doubt it."

" I don't. I think it's just what he wants. Oh, Kitty,
could you—would you, if I wanted it, too?"

" You needn't ask. But what earthly good can it do?"

" If he got strong here it would be so nice to think we sent him away well. And if he's going to be ill I could look after him——"

Her use of " we " and " I " did not pass unnoticed by the observant Kitty.

" And then?"

Lucia's face, which had been overcast with care, was now radiant. " Then I should have done something for him besides making him miserable. Will you ask him, Kitty?"

" You're a fool, Lucy, and I'm another. But I'll ask him. To-morrow, though; not to-day."

She waited to see what to-morrow would bring forth, for she was certain it would bring forth something.

It brought forth glorious weather after the east wind, a warm languid day, half spring, half summer. Lucia and Kitty seemed bent on putting all idea of business out of their guest's head. In the morning they drove about the country. In the afternoon they all sat out in the south square under the windows of the morning-room, while Lucia talked to him about his tragedies. Kitty still held her invitation in reserve.

At last she left them to themselves. It was Lucia who first returned to the subject of dispute. She had some sewing in her lap which gave her the advantage of being able to talk in a calm, detached manner and without looking up. He sat near her, watching with delight the quiet movements of her hands.

" I've been thinking over what you said yesterday," said she. " I can't do what you want; but I can suggest a compromise. You seem determined on restitution. Have you forgotten that you once offered it me in another form?"

" You refused it in that form—then."

" I wouldn't refuse it now. If you could be content with that."

" Do you remember why you refused it?"

She did not answer, but a faint flush told him that she had not forgotten.

" The same objection—the same reason for objecting— holds good now."

" Not quite. I should not be wronging any one else."

" You mean the Beaver, who dotes upon immortal verse?"

She smiled a little sadly. " Yes; there's no Beaver in the question now."

" You shall have the sonnets in any case. I brought them for you in place of the *Aurea Legenda,* and the Neapolitan Horace and——"

She lay back in her chair and closed her eyes, as if she could shut out sound with sight. " Please—please. If you go on talking about it we shall both be very tired. Don't you feel as if you'd like some tea?" She was bringing out all her feminine reserves to conquer him. But he was not going to be conquered this time. He could afford to wait; for he also had reserves.

" I'm so sorry," he said humbly, " I won't bore you any more till after tea."

And Lucia knew it was an armistice only and not peace.

At tea-time Kitty perceived that the moment was not yet propitious for her invitation. She was not even sure that it would ever come. Nor would it; for Rickman knew that his only chance lay in their imminent parting, in the last hour that must be his.

He was counting on it when the steady, resistless flow of a stream of callers cut short his calculations. It flowed between him and Lucia. They could only exchange amused or helpless glances across it now and then. At last he found a moment and approached her.

" I wanted to give you those things before I go."

" Very well. We'll go into the house in one minute."

He waited. She made a sign that said, " Come," and he followed her. She avoided the morning-room that looked on the courtyard with its throng of callers; hesitated, and opened the door into the library. He ran upstairs to fetch the manuscript, and joined her there. But for the empty bookshelves this room, too, was as he had left it.

Lucia was sitting in a window seat. He came to her and gave the poems into her open hands, and she thanked him.

" Nonsense. It's good of you to take them. But that doesn't release you from your obligations."

She laid the manuscript on the window-seat, protected by her hand. He sat there facing her, and for a moment neither spoke.

" I haven't very much time," he said at last. " I've got to catch the seven-forty."

"You haven't. We don't want you to go like this. Now you're here you must stay a fortnight at the very least."

He hung his head. He did not want her to see how immense was the temptation. He murmured some half-audible, agitated thanks, but his refusal was made quite plain. He could not give up the advantage he had counted on. "I'm afraid I must bore you again a little now. I've only got an hour."

"Don't spoil it, then. See how beautiful it is."

She rose and threw open the lattice, and they stood together for a moment looking out. It was about an hour before sunset, an April sunset, the golden consummation of the wedding of heaven and earth. He felt a delicate vibration in the air, the last tender resonance of the nuptial song. This April was not the April of the streets where the great wooing of the world goes on with violence and clangour; for the city is earth turned to stone and yields herself struggling and unwilling to the invasion of the sky. Here all the beautiful deep-bosomed land lay still, breathless in her escape from the wind to the sun. Up the western valley the earth gave all her greenness naked to the light; but the hills were dim with the divine approaches of her mystical union, washed by the undivided streams of blue and purple air that flowed to the thin spiritual verge, where earth is caught up and withdrawn behind heaven's inmost veil.

The hour was beautiful, as she had said. Its beauty had clothed itself with immortality in light; yet there was in it such mortal tenderness as drew his heart after it and melted his will in longing. He turned from the window and looked at her with all his trouble in his eyes.

Lucia saw that her words had saddened him, and she sat still, devising some comfort for him in her heart.

"I don't think," he said at last, "you quite know what you are doing. I'm going to tell you something that I didn't mean to tell you. When I said I'd had nothing to do with all this, it wasn't altogether true."

"So I supposed," she murmured.

"There was a—a certain amount of trouble and difficulty about it——"

"And what did that mean?"

"It only meant that I had to work rather hard to put it right. I liked it, so you needn't think anything of that. But if you persist in your refusal all my hard work goes for nothing." He was so powerless against her tender obstinacy that he had determined to appeal to her tenderness alone. " There were about three years of it, the best three years out of my life; and you are going to fling them away and make them useless. All for a little wretched scruple. This is the only argument that will appeal to you; or I wouldn't have mentioned it."

" The best years out of your life—why were they the best?"

" Because they were the first in which I was free."

She thought of the time nine years ago when she had taken from him three days, the only days when he was free, and how she had tried to make restitution and had failed. "And whatever else I refuse," she said, " I've taken *them?* I can't get out of that?"

" No. If you want to be very cruel you can say I'd no business to lay you under the obligation, but you can't get out of it."

She looked away. Did she want to be very cruel? Did she want to get out of it? Might it not rather be happiness to be in it, immersed in it? Lost in it, with all her scruples and all her pride?

His voice broke and trembled into passion. " And what is it that I'm asking you to take? Something that isn't mine and *is* yours; something that it would be dishonourable of me to keep. But if it *was* mine, it would be a little thing compared with what I wanted to give you, and you wouldn't have."

Her hands in her distress had fallen to their old unconscious trick of stroking and caressing the thing they held, the one thing that he had given her, that she had not refused. His eyes followed her movements. She looked up and saw the jealous hunger in them.

She saw too, through his loose thin suit, that the lines of his body were sharper than ever. His face was more than ever serious and clean cut; his eyes were more than ever sunk under the shadow of his brows, darkening their blue. He was refined almost to emaciation. And she saw other things. As he sat there, with one leg crooked over the other, his wrists stretched out, his hands clasped, nursing his knee, she noticed that his cuffs, though clean, were frayed; that his coat was worn in places; that his boots were patched and broken at the sole. He changed his attitude suddenly when he became aware of her gaze. She did not know why she had not noticed these details before, nor why she noticed them now. Perhaps she would not have seen them but for that attempt to hide them which revealed their significance. She said to herself, " He is poor; and yet he has done this." And the love that had been so long hidden, sheltered, and protected by her pity, came forth, and knew itself as love. And she forgot his greatness, and remembered only those pitiful human things in which he had need of her. So she surrendered.

" I will take everything—on one condition. That you will give me—what you said just now I wouldn't have." The eyes that she lifted to his were full of tears.

For one moment he did not understand. Very slowly he realized that the thing he had dreamed and despaired of, that he dared not ask for, was being divinely offered to him as a free gift. There was no moment, not even in that night of his madness, in this room nine years ago, nor in that other night in Howland Street, when he had desired it as he desired it now.

Her tears hung on the curved lashes of her eyes, and spilt themselves, and fell one by one on to the pages of the manuscript. He heard them fall.

Before he let himself be carried away by the sweep of her impulse and his own passion, he saw that, not honour, but common decency forbade him to take advantage of a moment's inspired tenderness. He had already made a slight appeal *ad misericordiam;* but that was for her sake, not his own. He realized most completely his impossible position. He had no income, and he had damaged his health so seriously that it might be long enough before he could make one; and these facts he could not possibly mention. She suspected him of poverty; but the smallest hint of his real state would have roused her infallible instinct of divination. He had felt, as her eyes rested on his emaciated body, that they could see the course of its sufferings, its starvation. He meant that she should never know what things had happened to him in Howland Street. His chivalry revolted against the brutality of capturing her tender heart by such a lacerating haul on its compassion.

All this swept through him between the falling of her tears. Last of all came the thought of what he was giving up. Was it possible that she cared for him?

It could not be. The illusion lasted only for an instant. Yet while it lasted the insane longing seized him to take her at her word and risk the consequences. For she would find out afterwards that she had never loved him; and she would disguise her feelings and he would see through her disguise. He would know. There could never be any disguise, any illusion between her and him. But at least he could take her in his arms and hold her now, while her tears fell; she would be his for this moment that was now.

He searched her face to see if indeed there had been any illusion. Through the tears that veiled her eyes he could not see whether it were love or pity that still shone in them; but because of the tears he thought it must be pity.

She went on. "You said I had taken the best years of your life. I would like to give you all of mine, instead, such as it is—if you'll take it."

She said it quietly, so quietly that he thought that she had spoken so only because she did not love him.

"How can I take it—now, in this way?"

(Her tears stopped falling suddenly.)

"I admit that I made a gross appeal to your pity."

"My pity?"

"Yes, your pity." His words were curt and hard because of the terrible restraint he had to put upon himself. "I did it because it was the best argument. Otherwise it would have been abominable of me to have said those things."

"I wasn't thinking of anything you said, only of what you've done."

"I haven't done much. But tell me the truth. Whether would you rather I had done it for your sake, or for mere honour's sake?"

"I would rather you had done it for honour's sake." She said it out bravely, though she knew that it was the profounder confession of her feeling. He, however, was unable to take it that way.

"I thought so," he said. "Well, that *is* why I did it."

"I see. I wanted to know the truth; and now I know it."

"You don't know half of it——" His passion leapt to his

tongue under the torture, but he held it down. He paused, knowing that this moment in which he stood was of those moments which have the spirit and power of eternity, and that it was his to save or destroy it. So admirable indeed was his control that it had taken their own significance from his words, and she read into them another meaning. Her face was white with terror because of the thing she had said; but she still looked at him without flinching. She hardly realized that he was going, that he was trying to say good-bye.

"I will take the books—if you can keep them for me a little while."

Some perfect instinct told her that this was the only way of atonement for her error. He thanked her as if they had been speaking of a trifling thing.

She rose, holding the manuscript loosely in her clasped hands, and he half thought that she was going to give it back to him. He took it from her and threw it on the window-seat, and held her hands together for an instant in his own. He looked down at them, longing to stoop and kiss them, but forbore, because of his great love for her, and let them go. He went out quickly. He had sufficient self-command to find Kitty and thank her and take his leave.

As the door closed on him Lucia heard herself calling him back, with what intention she hardly knew, unless it were to return his poems. "Keith," she said softly, "Keith." But even to her own senses it was less a name than a sound that began in a sob and ended in a sigh.

Kitty found her standing in the window-place where he had left her. "Has anything happened?" she asked.

"I asked him to marry me, Kitty, and he wouldn't. That was all."

"Are you sure you did, dear? From the look of him I should have said it was the other way about."

CHAPTER LXXV

I DON'T know what to think of it, Kitty. What do you think?"

"I think you have been playing with fire, dear. With

the divine fire. It's the most dangerous of all, and you've got your little. fingers burnt."

" Like Horace. He once said the burnt critic dreads the divine fire. I'm not a critic."

" That you most certainly are not."

" Still I used to understand him; and now I can't. I can't make it out at all."

" There's only one thing," said Kitty, musing till an inspiration came. " You haven't seen him for more than three years, and you can't tell what may have happened in between. He *may* have got entangled with another woman."

Kitty would not have hazarded this conjecture if she had not believed it plausible. But she dwelt on it with a beneficent intention. No other theory, she opined, would so effectually turn and rout the invading idea of Keith Rickman.

Kitty was for once mistaken in her judgment, not having all the evidence before her. The details which would have thrown light on the situation were just those which Lucia preferred to keep to herself. All that the benevolent Kitty had achieved was to fill her friend's mind with a new torment. Lucia had dreaded Rickman's coming; she had lost all sense of security in his presence. Still, she had understood him. And now she felt that her very understanding was at fault; that something troubled the fine light she had always viewed him in. Was it possible that she had never really understood?

Close upon Kitty's words there came back to her the things that Edith had said of him, that Horace had hinted; things that he had confessed to her himself. Was it possible that he was still that sort of man, the sort that she had vowed she would never marry? He was not bad; she could not think of him as bad; but was he good? Was he like her cousin Horace? No, certainly there was not the smallest resemblance between him and Horace. With Horace she had always felt—in one way—absolutely secure. If she had ever been uncertain, it had not been with this obscure, inexplicable dread.

How was it that she had never felt it before? Never felt it in the first weeks of their acquaintance, when, day after day and evening after evening, she had sat working with him, here, alone? When he had appeared to her in the first flush of his exuberant youth, transparent as glass, incapable of reservation or disguise? It was in those days (he had told her) that he had not been—good. And yet her own vision of him had never been purer, her divination subtler than then. Even in that last week, after her terrible enlightenment at Cannes, when she was ready to suspect every man, even Horace, she had never suspected him. And in the second period of their friendship, when his character was ripened and full-grown, when she had lived under the same roof with him, she had never had a misgiving or a doubt. And now there was no end to her doubt. She could not tell which was the instinct she should trust, or whether she were better able to judge him then or now. What had become of her calm and lucid insight? Of the sympathy in which they had once stood each transparent to the other?

For that was the worst of it: that he no longer understood her, and that she had given him cause for misunderstanding (this thought was beginning to keep her awake at night). She had made it impossible for him to respect her any more. He had his ideas of what a woman should and should not do, and he had been horrified at finding her so like, and oh, so unlike, other women (here Lucia's mood rose from misery to anger). She had thought him finer, subtler than that; but he had judged her as he judged such women. And she had brought that judgment on herself.

In an ecstasy of shame she recalled the various episodes of their acquaintance, from the time when she had first engaged him to work for her (against his will) to the present intolerable moment. There rose before her in an awful vision that night when she found him sleeping in the library; when she had stayed and risked the chances of his waking. Well, he could not think any the worse of her for that; because he had not waked. But she had risked it. The more she thought of it the more she saw what she had risked. He would always think of her as a woman who did risky things. Edith had said she had put herself in his power. She remembered how she had come between him and the woman whom he would have married but for her; how she had invited him to sit with her when the Beaver was away. He had liked it, but he must have had his own

opinion of her all the same. That was another of the risky
things. And of course he had taken advantage of it.
That was the very worst of all. He had loved her in his
way; she had been one of a series. Flossie had come before
her. And before Flossie? All that was fine in him had
turned against Flossie because of the feeling she had inspired. And it had turned against her.

For now, when he had got over it, had forgotten that he
had ever had that feeling, when all he wanted was to go his
own way and let her go hers, she had tried to force herself
upon him (Lucia was unaware of her violent distortion
of the facts). He had come with his simple, honourable
desire for reparation; and she had committed *the* unpardonable blunder—she had mistaken his intentions. And for
the monument and crown of her dishonour, she, Lucia
Harden, had proposed to him and been rejected.

Her misery endured (with some merciful intermissions)
for three weeks. Then Horace Jewdwine wrote and invited
himself down for the first week-end in May.

" *Can* he come, Kitty? " she asked wearily.

" Of course he can, dear, if you want him."

" I don't want him; but I don't mind his coming."

Kitty said to herself, " He has an inkling; Edith has
been saying things; and it has brought him to the point."
Otherwise she could not account for such an abrupt adventure on the part of the deliberate Horace. It was a Wednesday; and he proposed to come on Friday. He came on
Friday. Kitty's observation was on the alert; but it could
detect nothing that first evening beyond a marked improvement in Horace Jewdwine. With Lucia he was sympathetic,
deferential, charming. He also laid himself out, a little
elaborately, to be agreeable to Kitty.

In the morning he approached Lucia with a gift, brought
for her birthday (" I thought," said Lucia, " he had forgotten that I ever had a birthday "). It was an early copy
of Rickman's tragedy *The Triumph of Life,* just published.
His keen eyes watched her handling it.

" He suspects," thought Kitty, " and he's testing her."
But Lucia's equanimity survived. "Am I to read it now? "
" As you like."

She carried the book up to her own room and did not
appear till lunch-time. In her absence Horace seemed a

little uneasy; but he went on making himself agreeable to Kitty. "He must be pretty desperate," thought she, "if he thinks it worth while." Apparently he did think it worth while, though he allowed no sign of desperation to appear. Lucia, equally discreet, avoided ostentatious privacy. They sat out all the afternoon under the beech-trees while she read, flaunting *The Triumph of Life* in his very eyes. He watched every movement of her face that changed, as it were, to the cadence of the verse. It was always so, he remembered, when she was strongly moved. At last she finished and he smiled.

"You like your birthday present?"

"Very much. But, Horace, he has done what you said was impossible."

"Anybody would have said it was impossible. Modern drama in blank verse, you know——"

"Yes. It ought to have been all wrong. But because he's both a great poet and a great dramatist, it's all right, you see. Look," she said, pointing to a passage that she dared not read. "Those are human voices. Could anything be simpler and more natural? But it's blank verse, because it couldn't be more perfectly expressed in prose."

"Yes, yes. I wonder how he does it."

"It would have been impossible to anybody else."

"It remains impossible. If it's ever played, it will be played because of Rickman's stage-craft and inimitable technique, not because of his blank verse."

She put the book down, took up her work, and said no more. Horace seemed to have found his answer and be satisfied. "A fool," thought Kitty; "but he shall have his chance." So she left them alone together that evening.

But Jewdwine was very far from being satisfied, either with Lucia or himself. Lucia had refused to play to him yesterday because she had a headache; she had refused to walk with him to-day because she was tired; and to-night she would not sit up to talk to him because she had another headache. That evening he had all but succumbed to a terrible temptation. It was so long since he had been alone with Lucia, and there was something in her face, her dress, her attitude, that appealed to the authority on Æsthetics. He found himself wondering how it would be if he got up and kissed her. But just then Lucia leaned back in her chair, and there was that tired look in her face which he had come to dread. He thought better of it. If he had kissed her his sense of propriety would have obliged him to propose to her and marry her.

He almost wished he had yielded to that temptation, done that desperate deed. It would have at least settled the question once for all.

For Jewdwine had found himself a third time at the turning of the ways. He knew where he was; but not where he was going. It had happened with Jewdwine as it had with Isaac Rickman; as it happens to every man bent on serving two masters. He had forbidden his right hand all knowledge of his left. He lived in two separate worlds. In one, lit by the high, pure light of the idea, he stood comparatively alone, cheered in his intellectual solitude by the enthusiasm of his disciples. For in the minds of a few innocent young men Horace Jewdwine's reputation remained immortal; and these made a point of visiting the Master in his house at Hampstead. He allowed the souls of these innocent young men to appear before him in an undress; for them he still kept his lamp well trimmed, handing on the sacred, imperishable flame. Some suffered no painful disenchantment for their pilgrimage; and when the world that knew Jewdwine imparted to them its wisdom they smiled the mystic smile of the initiated. But many had become shaken in their faith. One of these, having achieved a little celebrity, without (as he discovered to his immense astonishment) any public assistance from the Master, had gone to Rickman and asked him diffidently for the truth about Jewdwine. Rickman had assured him that the person in the study, the inspired and inspiring person with the superhuman insight, who knew your thoughts before you had time to round your sentence, the person who in that sacred incommunicable privacy had praised your work, he was the real Jewdwine. " But," he had added, " everybody can't afford to be himself." And this had been Jewdwine's own confession and defence.

But now he had gone down into Devonshire, as Rickman had once gone before him, to find himself. He had returned to Lucia as to his own purer soul. That night Jewdwine sat up face to face with himself and all his doubts; his problem being far more complicated than before.

Three years ago it might have been very simply stated. Was he or was he not going to marry his cousin Lucia? But now, while personal inclination urged him to marry her, prudence argued that he would do better to marry a certain cousin of Mr. Fulcher's. His own cousin had neither money nor position. Mr. Fulcher's cousin had both. Once married to Miss Fulcher he could buy back Court House, if the Pallisers would give it up. The Cabinet Minister's cousin was in love with him, whereas he was well aware that his own cousin was not.

But then he had never greatly desired her to be so.

Jewdwine had neither respect nor longing for Miss Fulcher's passionate love. To his fragile temperament there was something infinitely more alluring in Lucia's virginal apathy. Her indifference (which he confused with her innocence) fascinated him; her reluctance was as a challenge to his languid blood. He was equally fascinated by her indifference to the income and position that were his. He admired that immaculate purity the more because he was not himself in these ways particularly pure. He loved money and position for their own sakes and hated himself for loving them. He would have liked to have been strong enough to despise these things, as Lucia had always despised them. But he did not desire that she should go on despising them, any more than he desired that her indifference should survive the marriage ceremony. He pictured with satisfaction her gradual yielding to the modest luxury he had to offer her, just as he pictured the exquisite delaying dawn of her wifely ardour.

The truth was he had lived too long with Edith. The instincts of his nature cried out (as far as anything so well-regulated could be said to cry out), in the most refined of accents for a wife, for children, and a home. He had his dreams of the holy, faithful spouse, a spouse with great dog-like eyes and tender breast, fit pillow for the head of a headachy, literary man. Lucia had dog-like eyes, and of her tenderness he had never had a doubt. He had never forgotton that hot June day, the year before he left Oxford, when he lay in the hammock in the green garden, and Lucia ministered to him. Before that there was a blessed Long Vacation when he had over-read himself into a nervous breakdown, and Lucia had soothed his headaches with the touch of her gentle hands. For the sake of that touch he would then have borne the worst headache man ever had.

And now it seemed that it was Lucia that was always having headaches. He had, in fact, begun to entertain the very gravest anxiety about her health. Her face and figure had grown thin; they were becoming less and less like the face and figure of the ideal spouse. Poor Lucia's arms offered no reliable support for a tired man.

To his annoyance Jewdwine found that he had to breakfast alone with his hostess, because of Lucia's headache.

"Lucia doesn't seem very strong," he said to Kitty sternly, as if it had been Kitty's fault. "Don't you see it?"

"I have seen it for some considerable time."

"She wants rousing."

And Jewdwine, who was himself feeling the need of exercise, roused her by taking her for a walk up Harcombe Hill. Half-way up she turned a white face to him, smiling sweetly, sat down on the hillside, and bent her head upon her knees. He sat beside her and waited for her recovery with punctilious patience. His face wore an expression of agonized concern. But she could see that the concern was not there altogether on her account.

"Don't be frightened, Horace, you won't have to carry me home."

He helped her to her feet, not ungently, and was very considerate in accommodating his pace to hers, and in reassuring her when she apologized for having spoilt his morning. And then it was that she thought that Keith Rickman, of his gentleness and his innumerable acts of kindness and of care; and she said to herself, "*He* would not be impatient with me if I were ill."

She rested in her room that afternoon and Kitty sat with her. Kitty could not stand, she said, more than a certain amount of Horace Jewdwine.

"Lucia," she asked suddenly, "if Horace Jewdwine had asked you to marry him five years ago would you have had him?"

"I don't know. I don't really know. He's a good man."

"You mean his morals are irreproachable. It's quite easy to have irreproachable morals if you have the temperament of an iceberg that has never broken loose from its

Pole. Now I call Keith Rickman a saint, because he could so easily have been the other thing."

Lucia did not respond; and Kitty left her.

Kitty's question had set her thinking. Would she have married Horace if he had asked her five years ago? Why not? Between Horace and her there was the bond of kindred and of caste. He was a scholar; he had, or he once had, a beautiful mind full of noble thoughts of the kind she most admired. With Horace she would have felt safe from many things. All his ideas and feelings, all his movements could be relied on with an absolute assurance of their propriety. Horace would never do or say anything that could offend her feminine taste. In his love (she had been certain) there would never be anything painful, passionate, disturbing. She had dreamed of a love which should be a great calm light rather than a flame. There was no sort of flame about Horace. *Was* Horace a good man? Yes. That is to say, he was a moral man. He would have come to her clean in body and in soul. She had vowed she would never marry a certain kind of man. And yet that was the kind of man Keith Rickman had been.

She had further demanded in her husband the finish of the ages. Who was more finished than Horace? Who more consummately, irreproachably refined? And yet her heart had grown more tender over Keith Rickman and his solecisms. And now it beat faster at the very thought of him, after Horace Jewdwine.

For Horace's coming had brought her understanding of Keith Rickman and herself. She knew now what had troubled her once clear vision of him. It was when she had loved him least that she had divined him best. Hers was not the facile heart that believes because it desires. It desired because it believed; and now it doubted because its belief was set so high.

And, knowing that she loved him, she thought of that last day when he had left her, and how he had taken her hands in his and looked at them, and she remembered, and wondered, and had hope.

Then it occurred to her that Horace would be leaving early the next morning, and that she really ought to go down to the drawing-room and talk to him.

Again by Kitty's mercy he had been given another chance.

He was softened by a mood of valediction mingled with remorse. He was even inclined to be a little sentimental. Lucia, because her vision was indifferent, therefore untroubled, could not but perceive the change in him. His manner had in it something of benediction and something of entreaty; his spirit brooded over, caressed and flattered hers. He deplored the necessity for his departure. "*Et ego in Arcadia,*" he quoted.

"But you'll go away to-morrow and become more—more Metropolitan than ever."

"Ah, Lucia, can't you leave my poor rag alone? Do you really think so badly of it?"

"Well, I was prouder of my cousin when he had *The Museion.*"

"I didn't ask you what you thought of *me*. Perhaps I'm not very proud of myself."

"I don't suppose it satisfies your ambition—I should be sorry if it did."

"My *ambition?* What do you think it was?"

"It was, wasn't it, to be a great critic?"

"It depends on what you call great."

"Well, you came very near it once."

"When?"

"When you were editor of *The Museion.*"

He smiled sadly. "The editor of *The Museion,* Lucia, was a very little man with a very big conceit of himself. I admit he made himself pretty conspicuous. So does every leader of a forlorn hope."

"Still he led it. What does the editor of *Metropolis* lead?"

"Public opinion, dear. He has—although you mightn't think it—considerable power."

Lucia was silent.

"He can make—or kill—a reputation in twenty-four hours."

"Does that satisfy your ambition?"

"Yes. It satisfies my ambition. But it doesn't satisfy me."

"I was afraid it didn't."

"You needn't be afraid, dear; for you know perfectly well what would."

"Do I know? Do you know yourself, Horace?"

"Yes, Lucia," he said gently; "after ten years. You may not be proud of your cousin——"

"I used to be proud of him always—or nearly always."

"When were you proud of him?"

"When he was himself; when he was sincere."

"I ought to be very proud of *my* cousin; for she is pitilessly sincere."

"Horace——"

"It is so, dear. Never mind, you needn't be proud of me, if you'll only care——"

"I have always cared."

"Or is it—nearly always?"

"Well—nearly always."

"You're right. I *am* insincere. I was insincere when I said you needn't be proud of me. I want you, I mean you to be."

"Do you mean to give up *Metropolis,* then?"

"Well, no. That's asking rather too much."

"I know it is."

"Do you hate it so much, Lucia? I wish you didn't."

"I have hated it so much, Horace, that I once wished I had been a rich woman, that you might be——" She was going to say "an honourable man."

"What's wrong with it? It's a better paper than the old one. There are better men on it, and it's editor's a better man."

"Is he?"

"Yes. He's a simpler, humbler person, and—I should have thought—more possible to like."

In her heart Lucia admitted that it was so. There was a charm about this later Horace Jewdwine which was wanting in that high spirit that had essayed to move the earth. He had come down from the chilly altitudes to mix with men; he had shed the superstition of omnipotence, he was aware of his own weakness and humanized by it. The man was soiled but softened by his traffic with the world. There was, moreover, an indescribable pathos in the contrast presented by the remains of the old self, its loftiness, its lucidity, and the vulgarity with which he had wrapped it round. Jewdwine's intellectual splendour had never been so impressive as now, when it showed thus tarnished and obscured.

"At any rate," he went on, "he is infinitely less absurd.

He knows his limitations. Also his mistakes. He tried to turn the republic of letters into a limited monarchy. Now he has surrendered to the omnipotence of facts."

"You mean he has lowered his standard?"

"My dear girl, what am I to do with my standard? Look at the rabble that are writing. I can't compare Tompkins with Shakespeare, or Brown with Sophocles. I'm lucky if I can make out that Tompkins has surpassed Brown this year, as Brown surpassed Tompkins last year; in other words, that Tompkins has surpassed himself."

"And so you go on, looking lower and lower."

"N-n-no, Lucia. I don't look lower; I look closer. I see that there is something to be said for Tompkins after all. I find subtler and subtler shades of distinction between him and Brown. I become more just, more discriminating, more humane."

"I know how fine your work is, and that's just the pity of it. You might have been a great critic if you hadn't wasted yourself on little things and little men."

"If a really big man came along, do you think I should look at him? But he doesn't come. I've waited for him ten years, Lucia, and he hasn't come."

"Oh, Horace——"

"He hasn't. Show me a big man, and I'll fall down and worship him. Only show him me."

"That's your business, isn't it, not mine? Still, I can show you one, not very far off—in fact very near."

"Too near for us to judge him, perhaps. Who is he?"

"If I'm not mistaken, he's a sort of friend of yours."

"Keith Rickman? Oh——"

"Do you remember the day we first talked about him?"

He did indeed. He remembered how unwilling he had been to talk about him; and he was still more unwilling now. He wanted, and Lucia knew that he wanted, to talk about himself.

"It's ten years ago," she said. "Have you been waiting all this time to see him?"

He coloured. "I saw him before you did, Lucia. I saw him a very long way off. I was the first to see."

"Were you? Then—oh, Horace, if you saw all those years ago why haven't you said so?"

"I have said so, many times."

" Whom have you said it to? "

" To you, for one. To every one, I think, who knows him. They'll bear me out."

" The people who know him? What was the good of that? You should have said it to the people who don't know him—to the world."

" You mean I should have posed as a prophet? "

" I mean that what you said you might have written."

" Ah, *litera scripta manet*. It isn't safe to prophesy. Remember, I saw him a very long way off. Nobody had a notion there was anybody there."

" You could have given them a notion."

" I couldn't. The world, Lucia, is not like you or me. It has no imagination. It wouldn't have seen, and it wouldn't have believed. I should have been a voice crying in the wilderness; a voice and nothing behind it. And as I said, prophecy is a dangerous game. In the first place, there is always a chance that your prediction may be wrong; and the world, my dear cousin, has a nasty way of stoning its prophets even when they're right."

" Oh, I thought it provided them with bread and butter, plenty of butter."

" It does, on the condition that they shall prophesy buttery things. When it comes to hard things, if they ask for bread the world retaliates and offers them a stone. And that stone, I need not tell you, has no butter on it."

" I see. You were afraid. You haven't the courage of your opinion."

" And I haven't much opinion of my courage. I own to being afraid."

" Afraid to do your duty as a critic and as a friend? "

" My first duty is to the public—*my* public; not to my friends. Savage Keith Rickman may be a very great poet —I think he is—but if my public doesn't want to hear about Savage Keith Rickman, I can't insist on their hearing, can I? "

" No, Horace, after all you've told me, I don't believe you can."

" Mind you, it takes courage, of a sort, to own it."

" I'm to admit your frankness, am I? You say you're afraid. But you said just now you had such power."

" If I had taken your advice and devoted myself to the

rôle of Vates I should have lost my power. Nobody would have listened to me. I began that way, by preaching over people's heads. *The Museion* was a pulpit in the air. I stood in that pulpit for five years, spouting literary transcendentalism. Nobody listened. When I condescended to come down and talk about what people could understand, then everybody listened. It wouldn't have done Rickman any good if I'd pestered people with him. But when the time comes I shall speak out."

" I dare say, when the time comes—it will come too—when he has made his name with no thanks to you, then you'll be the first to say ' I told you so.' It would have been a greater thing to have helped him when he needed it."

" I did help him. He wouldn't be writing now if it wasn't for me."

" Do you see much of him? "

" Not much. It isn't my fault," he added in answer to her reproachful eyes. " He's shut himself up with Maddox in a stuffy little house at Ealing."

" Does that mean that he's very badly off? "

" Well, no ; I shouldn't say so. He's got an editorship. But he isn't the sort that's made for getting on. In many things he is a fool."

" I admire his folly more than some people's wisdom."

From the look in Lucia's eyes Jewdwine was aware that his cousin no longer adored him. Did she adore Rickman?

" You're a little hard on me, I think. After all, I was the first to help him."

"*And* the last. Are you quite sure you helped him? How do you know you didn't hinder him? You kept him for years turning out inferior work for you, when he might have been giving us his best."

" He might—if he'd been alive to it."

" I'm only thinking of what you might have done. The sort of thing you've done for other people—Mr. Fulcher, for instance."

Jewdwine blushed as he had never blushed before. He was not given to that form of self-betrayal.

" You said just now you could either kill a book in twenty-four hours, or make it—did you say?—immortal."

" I might have said I could keep it alive another twenty-four hours."

"You know the reputations you have made for people."

"I do know them. I've made enough of them to know. The reputations I've made will not last. The only kind that does last is the kind that makes itself. Do you seriously suppose a man like Rickman needs my help? I am a journalist, and the world that journalists are compelled to live in is very poor and small. He's in another place altogether. I couldn't dream of treating him as I treat, say, Rankin or Fulcher. The best service I could do him was to leave him alone—to keep off and give him room."

"Room to stand in?"

"No. Room to grow in, room to fight in——"

"Room to measure his length in when he falls?"

"If you like. Rickman's length will cover a considerable area."

Lucia looked at her cousin with genuine admiration. How clever, how amazingly clever he was! She knew and he knew that he had failed in generosity to Rickman; that he had been a more than cautious critic and a callous friend. She had been prepared to be nice to him if they had kept Rickman out of their conversation; but as the subject had arisen she had meant to give Horace a terribly bad quarter of an hour; she had meant to turn him inside out and make him feel very mean and pitiful and small. And somehow it hadn't come off. Instead of diminishing, as he should have done, Horace had worked himself gradually up to her height, had caught flame from her flame, and now he was consuming her with her own fire. It was she who had taken the view most degrading to the man she admired; she who would have dragged her poet down to earth and put him on a level with Rankin and Fulcher and such people. Horace would have her believe that his own outlook was the clearer and more heavenly; that he understood Rickman better; that he saw that side of him that faced eternity.

His humility, too, was pathetic and disarmed her indignation. At the same time he made it appear that this was a lifting of the veil, a glimpse of the true Jewdwine, the soul of him in its naked simplicity and sincerity. And she was left uncertain whether it were not so.

"Even so," she said gently; "think of all you will have missed."

"Missed, Lucia?"

"Yes, missed. I think, to have believed in any one's greatness—the greatness of a great poet—to have been allowed to hold in your hands the pure, priceless thing, before the world had touched it—to have seen what nobody else saw—to feel that, through your first glorious sight of him, he belonged to you as he never could belong to the world, that he was your own—that would be something to have lived for. It would be greatness of a kind."

He bowed his head as it were in an attitude as humble and reverent as her own. " And yet," he said, " the world does sometimes see its poet and believe in him."

" It does—when he works miracles."

" Some day he will work his miracle."

" And when the world runs after him you will follow."

" I shall not be very far behind."

CHAPTER LXXVI

HE wondered how it was that Lucia had seen what he could not see. As far as he understood his own attitude to Rickman, he had begun by being uncertain whether he saw or not; but he had quite honestly desired to see. Yet he had not seen; not because he was incapable of seeing, but because there had come a time when he had no longer desired to see; and from not desiring to see he had gone on till he had ended by not seeing. Then, because he had not seen, he had persuaded himself that there was nothing to see. And now, in that last sudden flaming of Lucia's ardour, he saw what he had missed.

They parted amicably, with a promise on Lucia's part that she would stay with Edith in the summer.

By the time he returned to town he was very sure of what he saw. It had become a platitude to say that Keith Rickman was a great poet after the publication of *The Triumph of Life*. The interesting, the burning question was whether he were not, if anything, a greater dramatist. By the time Lucia came to Hampstead that point also had been settled, when the play had been actually running for three weeks. Its success was only sufficient to establish his position and no more. He himself required no more; but his friends still waited anxiously for what they regarded as the crucial test, the introduction of the new dramatist to a picked audience in Paris in the autumn.

Lucia had come up with Kitty Palliser to see the great play. She looked wretchedly ill. Withdrawn as far as possible into the darkness of the box, she sat through the tremendous Third Act apparently without a sign of interest or emotion. Kitty watched her anxiously from time to time. She wondered whether she were over-tired or over-wrought, or whether she had expected something different and were disappointed with Keith's tragedy. Kitty herself wept openly and unashamed. But to Lucia, who knew that tragedy by heart, it was as if she were a mere spectator of a life she herself had once lived passionately and profoundly. With every word and gesture of the actors she felt that there passed from her possession something of Keith Rickman's genius, something sacred, intangible, and infinitely dear; that the triumphant movement of the drama swept between him and her, remorselessly dividing them. She was realizing for the first time that henceforth he would belong to the world and not to her. And yet the reiterated applause sounded to her absurd and meaningless. Why were these people insisting on what she had known so well, had seen so long beforehand?

She was glad that Horace was not with her. But when he came out of his study to greet them on their return she turned aside into the room and called him to her. It was then that she triumphed.

" Well, Horace, he has worked his miracle."

" I always said he would."

" You doubted—once."

" Once, perhaps, Lucia. But now, like you, I believe."

" Like me? I never doubted. I believed without a miracle."

She leaned against the chimney-piece, and he saw that she was trembling. She turned to him a face white with trouble and anxiety.

" Where is he, Horace? "

" He's still with Maddox. You needn't worry, Lucy; if he scores a success like this in Paris that will mean magnificence." There was something unspeakably offensive to her in her cousin's tone. He did not perceive the disgust in her averted profile. He puzzled her. One moment he seemed to be worshipping humbly with her at the inner shrine, the next he forced her to suspect the sincerity of his conversion. She could see that now his spirit bowed basely before the possibility of the great poet's material success.

"You'll meet him if you stay till next week, Lucy. He'll be dining here on the tenth."

Again the tone, the manner, hurt her. Horace could not conceal his pride in the intimacy he had once repudiated. He so obviously exulted in the thought that some of Rickman's celebrity, his immortality, perhaps, must through that intimacy light upon him. For her own part she felt that she could not face Keith Rickman and his celebrity. His immortality she had always faced; but his celebrity—no. It rose up before her, crushing the tender hope that still grew among her memories. She said to herself that she was as bad as Horace in attaching importance to it; she was so sure that Keith would attach none to it himself. Yet nothing should induce her to stay for that dinner on the tenth; if it were only that she shrank from the spectacle of Horace's abasement.

Something of this feeling was apparent in the manner of her refusal; and Jewdwine caught the note of disaffection. He was not sure whether he still loved his cousin, but he could not bear that his self-love should thus perish through her bad opinion. It was in something of his old imperial mood that he approached her the next morning with the proofs of his great article on "Keith Rickman and the Modern Drama." There the author of the *Prolegomena to Æsthetics*, the apostle of the Absolute, the opponent of Individualism, had made his recantation. He touched with melancholy irony on the rise and fall of schools; and declared, as Rickman had declared before him, that "in modern art what we have to reckon with is the Man Himself." That utterance, he flattered himself, was not unbecoming in the critic who could call himself Keith Rickman's friend. For Rickman had been his discovery in the beginning; only he had lost sight of him in between.

He was immensely solemn over it. "I think that is what I should have said."

"Yes, Horace; it is what you should have said long ago, when he needed it; but not now."

He turned from her and shut himself up in his study with his article, his eulogy of Rickman. He had had pleasure in writing it, but the reading was intolerable pain. He knew that Lucia saw both it and him with the cold eye of the Absolute. There was no softening, no condonement in her gaze; and none in his bitter judgment of himself. Up till now there had been moments in which he persuaded himself that he was justified in his changes of attitude. If his conscience joined with his enemies in calling him a time-server, what did it mean but that in every situation he had served his time? He had grown opulent in experience, espousing all the fascinating forms of truth. And did not the illuminated, the supremely philosophic mood consist in just this openness, this receptivity, this infinite adaptability, in short? Why should he, any more than Rickman, be bound by the laws laid down in the *Prolegomena to Æsthetics?* The *Prolegomena to Æsthetics* was not a work that one could set aside with any levity; still, in constructing it he had been building a lighthouse for the spirit, not a prison.

But now he became the prey of a sharper, more agonizing insight, an insight that oscillated between insufferable forms of doubt. Was it possible that he, the author of the *Prolegomena,* had ceased to care about the Truth? Or was it that the philosophy of the Absolute had never taken any enormous hold on him? He had desired to be consistent as he was incorruptible. Did his consistency amount to this, that he, the incorruptible, had been from first to last the slave of whatever opinion was dominant in his world? Loyal only to whatever theory best served his own ungovernable egoism? In Oxford he had cut a very imposing figure by his philosophic attitude. In London he had found that the same attitude rendered him unusual, not to say ridiculous. Had the Absolute abandoned him, or had he abandoned the Absolute, when it no longer ministered to his personal prestige? Jewdwine was aware that, however it was, his case exemplified the inevitable collapse of a soul nourished mainly upon formulas. Yet behind that moral wreckage there remained the far-off source of spiritual illumination, the inner soul that judged him, as it judged all things, holding the pellucid, immaterial view. Its vision had never been bound, even by the *Prolegomena*. If he had trusted it he might have been numbered among those incorruptible spirits that preserve the immortal purity of letters. As it was, that supreme intelligence was only a light by which he saw clearly his own damnation.

CHAPTER LXXVII

MEANWHILE the Junior Journalists found amusement in discussing whether the great dramatist were Maddox's discovery or Jewdwine's. With the readers of *Metropolis* he passed as Jewdwine's—which was all that Jewdwine wanted. With the earnest aspiring public, striving to admire Keith Rickman because they had been told they ought to, he passed as their own. The few who had known him from the first knew also that poets like Rickman are never discovered until they discover themselves. Maddox, whom much worship had made humble, gave up the absurd pretension. Enough that he lived, and was known to live, with Rickman as his friend.

They shared that little house at Ealing, which Rickman, in the ardour of his self-immolation, had once destined for the young Delilah, his bride. It had now become a temple in which Maddox served with all the religious passion of his half-Celtic soul.

The poet had trusted the honour and the judgment of his friend so far as to appoint him his literary executor. Thus Maddox became possessed of the secret of the Sonnets. And here a heavy strain was put upon his judgment and his honour. Maddox had guessed that there was a power in Rickman's life more terrible than Jewdwine, who after all had never really touched him. There was, Maddox had always known, a woman somewhere. A thousand terrors beset the devotee when he noticed that, since fame had lighted upon Rickman, the divinity had again begun to furnish this part (the holy part) of the temple in a manner unmistakably suggestive of mortality. Maddox shuddered as he thought of the probable destination of that upper chamber which was the holiest of all. And now this terror had become a certainty. The woman existed; he knew her name; she was a cousin of the detestable Jewdwine;

the Sonnets could never be given to the world as long as she withheld her consent, and apparently she did withhold it. More than this had not been revealed to Maddox, and it was in vain that he tried to penetrate the mystery.

His efforts were not the most delicate imaginable. One evening, sitting with Rickman in that upper chamber, he entered on the subject thus:

" Seen anything of the Spinkses lately? "

" I called there last Saturday."

" How is the divine Flossie? "

" Flourishing. At least there's another baby. By the way, Maddy, you were grossly wrong about her there. The Beaver is absolutely devoid of the maternal instinct. She's decent to the baby, but she's positively brutal to Muriel Maud. How Spinky—— He protests and there are horrid scenes; but through them all I believe the poor chap's in love with her."

" Curious illusion."

Curious indeed. It had seemed incredible to Rickman when he had seen the Beaver pushing her first-born from her knee.

" Good heavens, Rickman, what a deliverance for you."

" I wonder if he's happy."

" Can't say; but possibly he holds his own. You see, Spinky's position is essentially sound. My theory is——"

But Rickman had no desire for a theory of marriage as propounded by Maddox. He had always considered that in these matters Maddox was a brute.

Maddox drew his own conclusions from the disgusted protest. He remembered how once, when he had warned Rickman of the love of little women, Rickman had said it was the great women who were dangerous. The lady to whom he had entrusted the immortality of his Sonnets would be one of these. As the guardian of that immortality Maddox conceived it was his duty to call on the lady and prevail on her to give them up. Under all his loyalty he had the audacity of the journalist who sticks at nothing for his own glorious end.

There was after all a certain simplicity about Maddox. He considered himself admirably equipped by nature for this delicate mission. He was, besides, familiar with what he called the " society woman," and he believed that he knew how to deal with her. Maddox always had the air of being able to push his way anywhere by the aid of his mighty shoulders. He sent in his card without a misgiving.

Lucia knew that Maddox was a friend of Keith Rickman's, and she received him with a courtesy that would have disarmed a man less singularly determined. It was only when he had stated his extraordinary purpose that her manner became such that (so he described it afterwards) it would have " set a worm's back up." And Maddox was no worm.

It was a little while before Lucia realized that this rather overpowering visitor was requesting her to " give up " certain sonnets of Keith Rickman's, written in ninety-three.

" I don't quite understand. Are you asking me to give you the manuscript or to give my consent to its publication? "

" Well—both. I *have* to ask you because he never would do it himself."

" Why should he not? "

" Oh, well, you know his ridiculous notions of honour."

" I do indeed. I daresay some people would consider them ridiculous."

It was this speech, Maddox confessed, that first set his back up. He was irritated more by the calm assumption of proprietorship in Rickman than by the implied criticism of himself.

" Do you mind telling me," she continued, still imperturbably, " how you came to know anything about it? "

Maddox stiffened. " I am Mr. Rickman's oldest and most intimate friend, and he has done me the honour to make me his literary executor."

" Did he also give you leave to settle his affairs beforehand? "

Maddox shrugged his shoulders by way of reply.

" If he did not," said Lucia, " there's nothing more to be said."

" Pardon me, there is a great deal more to be said. I don't know whether you have any personal reason for objecting——"

She coloured and was silent.

" If it's pride, I should have thought most women would have been prouder——" (A look from Lucia warned him that he would do well to refrain from thinking.) "Oh, well, for all I know, you might have fifty good reasons. The question is, are you justified in sacrificing a work of genius to any mere personal feeling?"

He had her there, and she knew it. She was silently considering the question. Three years ago she would have had no personal feeling in the matter beyond pride in the simple dedication. Now that personal feeling had come in and had concentrated itself upon that work of genius, and made it a thing so sacred and so dear to her, she shrank with horror from the vision of publicity. Besides, it was all of Keith Rickman that was left to her. His other works were everybody's property; therefore she clung the more desperately to that one which, as he had said, belonged to nobody but her. And Mr. Maddox had no right to question her. Instead of answering him she moved her chair a little farther from him and from the light.

Now, Maddox had the coldness as well as the passion of the Celt. He was not touched by Lucia's beauty, nor yet by the signs of illness or fatigue manifest in her face and all her movements. Her manner irritated him; it seemed the feminine counterpart of her cousin's insufferable apathy. He felt helpless before her immobility. But he meant to carry his point—by brute force, if necessary.

But not yet. "I'm not asking you to give up a mere copy of verses. The Sonnets are unique—even for Rickman; and for one solitary lady to insist on suppressing them— well, you know, it's a large order."

This time, she indeed showed some signs of animation. "How do you know they are unique? Did he show you them?"

"No, he did not. I found them among his papers when he was in hospital."

"In hospital?" She sat up and looked at him steadily and without emotion.

"Yes; I had to overhaul his things—we thought he was dying—and the Sonnets——"

"Never mind the Sonnets now, please. Tell me about his illness. What was it?"

Again that air of imperious proprietorship! "Enteric," he said bluntly—"and some other things."

"Where was he before he they took him to the hospital?"

" He was—if you want to know—in a garret in a back street off Tottenham Court Road."

" What was he doing there? "

" To the best of my belief, he was starving. Do you find the room too close? "

" No, no. Go on."

Maddox went on. He was enjoying the sensation he was creating. He went on happily, piling up the agony. Since she would have it he was not reticent of detail. He related the story of the Rankins' dinner. He described with diabolically graphic touches the garret in Howland Street. " We thought he'd been drinking, you know, and all the time he was starving."

" He was starving——" she repeated slowly to herself.

" He was not doing it because he was a poet. It seems he had to pay some debt, or thought he had. The poor chap talked about it when he was delirious. Oh—let *me* open that window."

" Thank you. You say he was delirious. Were you with him then? "

Maddox leapt to his conclusion. Miss Lucia Harden had something to conceal. He gathered it from her suddenly changed attitude, from her interrogation, from her faintness and from the throbbing terror in her voice. *That* was why she desired the suppression of the Sonnets.

" Were you with him? " she repeated.

" No. God forgive me! "

" Nobody was with him—before they took him to the hospital? "

" Nobody, my dear lady, whom you would call anybody. He owes his life to the charity of a drunken prostitute."

She was woman, the eternal, predestined enemy of Rickman's genius. Therefore he had determined not to spare her, but to smite her with words like sledge-hammers.

And to judge by the look of her he had succeeded. She had turned away from him to the open window. She made no sign of suffering, but for the troubled rising and falling of her breast. He saw in her a woman mortally smitten; but smitten, he imagined, in her vanity.

" Have I persuaded you," he said quietly, " to give up those Sonnets? "

"You shall have a copy. If Mr. Rickman wants the original he must come for it himself."

"Thanks." Maddox had ceased to be truculent, having gained his end. His blue eyes twinkled with their old infantile devilry. "Thanks. It's awfully nice of you. But—couldn't you make it seem a little more spontaneous? You see, I don't want Rickman to know I had to ask you for them." He had a dim perception of inconsistency in his judgment of the lady; since all along he had been trusting her generosity to shelter his indiscretion.

Lucia smiled even in her anguish. "That I can well imagine. The copy shall be sent to him."

And Maddox considered himself dismissed. He wondered why she called him back to ask for the number of that house in Howland Street. That afternoon she dragged herself there, that she might torture her eyes because they had not seen and her heart because it had not felt.

CHAPTER LXXVIII

AT Jewdwine's heart there was trouble and in his mind perfect peace. For he knew his own mind at last, though he was still a little indefinite as to the exact condition of his heart.

Three days after Maddox's extraordinary disclosures Lucia had become most obviously and inconsiderately ill; and had given her cousin Edith a great deal of trouble as well as a severe fright, till Kitty, also frightened, had carried her off to Devonshire out of the house of the Jewdwines. To Horace the working of events was on the whole beneficent. Lucia's change of attitude, her illness, her abrupt departure, though too unpleasant for his fastidious mind to dwell upon, had committed that mind irretrievably to the path of prudence.

So prudent was he, that of his saner matrimonial project the world in general took no note. Secure of the affections of Miss Fulcher, he had propitiated rumour by the fiction of his engagement to Lucia. Rumour, adding a touch of certainty to the story, had handed it on to Rickman by way of Maddox and Miss Roots. He thereupon left off beautifying his house at Ealing, and agreed with Maddox that, after

Paris in November, they should go on to Italy together, and
that he would winter there for his health.

But by November there came more rumours, rumours of
the breaking off of the engagement; rumours of some mysterious illness of Lucia's as the cause. They reached Rickman in the week before the date fixed for the production of
The Triumph of Life in Paris. He was paying a farewell
call on Miss Roots, who became inscrutable at the mention
of Lucia's name. He accused her with violence of keeping
the truth from him, and implored her with pathos to tell it
him at once. But Miss Roots had no truth, no certain truth
to tell; there were only rumours. Miss Roots knew nothing but that Lucia had been lying on her back for
months; she conjectured that possibly there might be
something the matter with her spine. Her mother had
been delicate, and Sir Frederick, well, the less said about
Sir Frederick the better. Rickman retreated, followed by
Miss Roots. As for an engagement, she was not aware that
there ever had been one; there was once, she admitted half-
way downstairs, an understanding, probably misunderstood.
He had better ask Horace Jewdwine straight out. "But,"
she assured him from the door-step, "it would take an
earthquake to get the truth out of *him*."

He flung himself into a hansom, and was one with the
driver in imprecation at the never-ending, ever-increasing
gradient of the hill. The delay, however, enabled him to
find Jewdwine at home and alone. He was aware that the
interview presented difficulties, but none deterred him.

Jewdwine, questioned as to his engagement, betrayed no
surprise; for with Rickman the unusual was to be expected.
He might not have condescended to answer Rickman, his
obscure disciple, but he felt that some concession must be
made to the illustrious dramatist.

There had been, he admitted, an understanding between him and Miss Harden. It hardly amounted to an
engagement; and it had been cancelled on the score of
health.

"Of *her* health?"

The compression of Jewdwine's lips intimated that the
great poet had sinned (not for the first time) against convention.

"She *is* ill, then?"

"I said on the score of health. We're first cousins, and it is not always considered advisable——"

"I see. Then that's all over."

"At any rate I'm not going to take any risks."

Rickman pondered that saying for a while. "Do you mean you're not going to let her take any risks?"

Jewdwine said nothing, but endeavoured to express by his manner a certain distaste for the conversation.

("Or does he mean," thought Rickman, "that he won't risk having a delicate wife on his hands?")

"It's not as if I didn't know," he persisted. "I know she—she lies on her back and can't move. Is it her spine?"

"No."

"Or her heart?"

"Not to my knowledge."

"Is it something worse?"

Jewdwine was silent.

And in the silence Rickman's mind wandered free among all imaginable horrors and forebodings. At last, out of the silence, there appeared to him one more terrible than the rest. He saw what Jewdwine must have meant. He gathered it, not from anything he had said, but from what he refused to say, from the sternness of his face, from his hesitations, his reserves. Jewdwine had created the horror for him as vividly as if he had shaped it into words.

"You needn't tell me what it is. Do you mind telling me whether it's curable or not?"

"My *dear* Rickman, if I knew why you are asking all these questions——"

"They must seem extraordinary. And my reason for asking them is more extraordinary still."

They measured each other with their eyes. "Then, I think," said Jewdwine quietly, "I must ask you for your reason."

"The reason is that if you're not going to marry her I am."

"That," said Jewdwine, "is by no means certain. There is not a single member of her family living except my sister and myself. Therefore I consider myself responsible. If I were her father or her brother I would not give my consent to her marrying, and I don't give it now."

"Oh. And why not?"

" For many reasons. Those that applied in my own case are sufficient."

" You only said there was a risk, and that you weren't going to take it. Now, I mean to take it. You see, those fools of doctors may be mistaken. But whether they're mistaken or not, I shall marry her just the same."

" The risk, you see, involves her happiness; and judging by what I know of your temperament——"

" What do you know about my temperament?"

" You know perfectly well what I know about it."

" I know. You don't approve of my morals. I don't altogether blame you, considering that since I knew Miss Harden I very nearly married some one else. My code is so different from yours that I should have considered marrying that woman a lapse from virtue. So the intention may count against me, if you like."

" Look here, Rickman, that is not altogether what I mean. Neither of us is fit to marry Miss Harden—and *I* have given her up." He said it with the sublime assurance of Jewdwine, the moral man.

" Does it—does her illness—make all that difference? It makes none to me."

" Oh, well—all right—if you think you can make her happy."

" My dear Jewdwine, I don't think, I know." He smiled that smile that Jewdwine had seen once or twice before. " It may be arrogant to suppose that I'll succeed where better men might fail; still——" He rose and drew himself up to all his slender height—" in some impossible things I have succeeded."

" They are not the same things."

" No; but in both, you see, it all depends upon the man." With that he left him.

As Rickman's back turned on him, Jewdwine perceived his own final error. As once before, in judging the genius, he had reckoned without the man, so now, in judging the man he had reckoned without the genius.

This horrid truth came home to him in his solitude. In the interminable watches of the night Jewdwine acknowledged himself a failure; and a failure for which there was no possible excuse. He had had every conceivable advantage that a man could have. He had been born free; free from all sociable disabilities; free from pecuniary embarrassment; free from the passions that beset ordinary men. And he had sold himself into slavery. He had opinions; he was packed full of opinions, valuable opinions; but he had never had the courage of them. He had always been a slave to other people's opinions. Rickman had been born in slavery, and he had freed himself. When Rickman stood before him, superb in his self-mastery, he had felt himself conquered by this man, whom, as a man, he had despised. Rickman's errors had been the errors of one who risks everything, who never deliberates or counts the cost. And in their repeated rivalries he had won because he had risked everything, when he, Jewdwine, had lost because he would risk nothing.

He had lost ever since the beginning. He had meant to discover this great genius; to befriend him; to protect him with his praise; eventually to climb on his shoulders into fame. And he had not discovered him; and as for climbing on his shoulders, he had been shaken off with one shrug of them. There had been risk in passing judgment on young Rickman, and he had not taken the risk. Therefore he had failed as a critic. He had waited to found an incorruptible review. It had been a risky proceeding, and he had not taken the risk. His paper was a venal paper, sold like himself to the public he despised. Of all that had ever appeared in it, nothing would live, nothing but a few immortal trifles, signed S. K. R. He had failed pretty extensively as an editor. Last of all he wanted to marry his cousin Lucia; but there was risk in marrying her, and he would not take the risk, and Rickman would marry her. He had failed most miserably as a man.

With that Jewdwine turned on his pillow, and consoled himself by thinking of Miss Fulcher and her love.

CHAPTER LXXIX

LUCIA had been lying still all afternoon on her couch in the drawing-room; so still that Kitty thought she had been sleeping. But Kitty was mistaken.

"Kitty, it's past five, isn't it?"

"Yes, dear; a quarter past."

" It'll be all over by this time to-morrow. Do you think he'll be very terrible ? "

" No, dear. I think he'll be very kind and very gentle."

" Not if he thinks I'm shamming."

" He won't think that." (" I wish he could," said Kitty to herself.)

They were waiting for the visit of Sir Wilfrid Spence. The Harmouth doctor had desired a higher light on the mysterious illness that kept Lucia lying for ever on her back. It might have been explained, he said, if she had suffered lately some deep mental or moral shock; but Lucia had not confessed to either, and in the absence of any mental cause it would be as well, said the Harmouth doctor, to look for a physical one. The fear at the back of the Harmouth doctor's mind was sufficiently revealed by his choice of the specialist, Sir Wilfrid Spence.

" *Do* you think I'm shamming, Kitty? Sometimes I think I am, and sometimes I'm not quite sure. You know, if you think about your spine long enough you can imagine that it's very queer. But I haven't been thinking about my spine. It doesn't interest me. Dr. Robson would have told me if he thought I was shamming, because I asked him to. There's one thing makes me think it isn't fancy. I keep on wanting to do things. I want—you don't know how I want to go to the top of Harcombe Hill. And my ridiculous legs won't let me. And all the while, Kitty, I want to play. It's such a long time since I made my pretty music."

A long time indeed, as Kitty was thinking sadly. Lucia had not made her pretty music since that night, six months ago, when she had played to please Keith Rickman.

" Things keep on singing in my head, and I want to play them. It stands to reason that I would if I could. But I *can't*. Oh, how I do talk about myself! Kitty, there must be a fine, a heavy fine, of sixpence, every time I talk about myself."

" I shouldn't make much by it," said Kitty.

Lucia closed her eyes, and Kitty went on with the manuscript she was copying. After a silence of twenty minutes Lucia opened her eyes again. They rested longingly on Kitty at her work.

" Kitty," she said, " do you know, I sometimes think it

would be better to sell those books. I can't bear to do it when he gave them to me. But I do believe I ought to. The worst of it is I should have to ask him to do it for me."

"Don't do anything in a hurry, dear. Wait and see," said Kitty cheerfully.

It seemed to Lucia that there was nothing to wait for now. She wondered why Kitty said that, and whether it meant that they thought her worse than they liked to say, and whether that was why Sir Wilfrid Spence was coming?

"Kitty," she said again, "I want you to promise me something. Supposing—it's very unlikely—but supposing after all I were to go and die——"

"I won't suppose anything of the sort. People don't go and die of nervous exhaustion. You'll probably do it fifty years hence, but that is just the reason why I won't have you harrowing my feelings this way now."

"I know I've had such piles of sympathy for my nervous exhaustion that it's horrid of me to try and get more for dying, too. I only meant, if I did do it, quite unexpectedly, of something else—you wouldn't tell him, would you?"

"Well, dear, of course I won't mention it if you wish me not to—but he'd be sure to see it in the papers."

"Kitty—you know what I mean. He couldn't see *that* in the papers. He couldn't see it anywhere unless you told him. And if you did, it might make him very uncomfortable, you know."

Poor Kitty, trying to be cheerful under the shadow of Sir Wilfrid Spence, was tortured by this conversation. She had half a mind to say, "You don't seem to think how uncomfortable you're making *me*." But she forbore. Any remark of that sort would rouse Lucia to efforts penitential in their motive, and more painful to bear than this pitiful outburst, the first in many months of patience and reserve. She remembered how Lucia had once nursed her through a long illness in Dresden. It had not been, as Kitty expressed it, "a pretty illness," and she had been distinctly irritable in her convalescence; but Lucy had been all tenderness, had never betrayed impatience by any look or word.

"I shouldn't mind anything, if only I'd been with him when *he* was ill. But perhaps he'd rather I hadn't been there. I think it's that, you know, that I really cannot bear."

Kitty would have turned to comfort her but for the timely entrance of Robert. He brought a letter for Lucia which Kitty welcomed as an agreeable distraction. It was from Horace Jewdwine. " Any news ? " she asked presently.

" Yes. What *do* you think ? He's going to Paris to-morrow. Then he's going on to Italy—to Alassio, with Mr. Maddox."

" Horace Jewdwine and Mr. Maddox ? What next ? "

" It isn't Horace that's going." She gave the letter to Kitty because she had shrunk lately from speaking of Keith Rickman by his name.

" That's a very different tale," said Kitty.

" I'm so glad he's going. That was what he always wanted to do. Do you remember how I asked him to be my private secretary ? Now I'm his private secretary ; which is as it should be."

" You mean *I* am."

" Yes. Do you think you could hurry up so that he'll get them before he goes ? Poor Kitty—I can't bear your having all these things to do for me."

" Why not ? You'd do them for me, if it was I, not you."

" I wish it were you. I mean I wish I were doing things for you. But you haven't done them all, Kitty. I did some. I forget how many."

" You did three, darling."

" Only three ? And there are nine and twenty. Still, he'll see that I began them. Kitty—do you think he'll wonder and guess why I left off ? "

" Oh, no, he isn't as clever as all that."

" You mustn't tell him. You're writing the letter, dear, now, aren't you ? You mustn't say a word about my illness. Only tell him I'm so glad to hear he's going to Alassio with Mr. Maddox."

" I don't think any the better of him for that. Fancy going to Italy with that brute of a man ! "

" He wasn't really a brute. He only said those things because he cared for him. You can't blame him for that."

" I don't blame him for that. I blame him for being a most appalling bounder."

" Do you mind not talking about him any more ? "

" No, dear, I don't a bit."

Lucia lay very quiet for some time before she spoke again. " They can't say now I sacrificed his genius to my pride. You *will* catch the post, won't you? What a plague I am, but if they're posted before seven he'll get them in the morning and he'll have time to write. Perhaps he won't be starting till the afternoon."

In the morning she again betrayed her mind's preoccupation. " He must have got them by now. Kitty, did you hear how the wind blew in the night? He'll have an awful crossing."

" Well, then, let's hope he won't be very ill; but he isn't going by the Bay of Biscay, dear."

The wind blew furiously all morning, and when it dropped a little towards evening it was followed by a pelting rain.

" He's at Dover now."

" In a mackintosh," said Kitty by way of consolation. But Lucia, uncomforted, lay still, listening to the rain. It danced like a thousand devils on the gravel of the courtyard. Suddenly she sat up, raising herself by her hands.

" Kitty ! " she cried. " He's coming. He is, really. By the terrace. Can't you hear? "

Kitty heard nothing but the rain dancing on the courtyard. And the terrace led into it by the other wing. It was impossible that Lucia could have heard footsteps there.

" But I *know,* Kitty, I know. It's his walk. And he always came that way."

She slipped her feet swiftly on to the floor, and to Kitty's amazement sat up unsupported. Kitty in terror ran to her and put her arm round her, but Lucia freed herself gently from her grasp. She was trembling in all her body. Kitty herself heard footsteps in the courtyard now. They stopped suddenly and the door-bell rang.

" Do go to him, Kitty—and tell him. And send him here to me."

Kitty went, and found Keith Rickman standing in the hall. Her instinct told her that Lucia must be obeyed. And as she sent him in to her, she saw through the open door that Lucia rose to her feet, and came to him, and never swayed till his arms held her.

She clung to him and he drew her closer and lifted her

and carried her to her couch, murmuring things inarticulate yet so plain that even she could not misunderstand.

" I thought you were going to Paris? " she said.

" I'm not. I'm here."

She sat up and laid her hands about him, feeling his shoulders and his sleeves.

" How wet your coat is."

He kissed her, and she held her face against his that was cold with the wind and the rain ; she took his hands and tried to warm them in her own, piteously forgetful of herself, as if it were he, not she, who needed tenderness.

" Lucy—are you very ill, darling? "

" No. I am very, very well."

He thought it was one of those things that people say when they mean that death is well. He gathered her to him as if he could hold her back from death. She looked smiling into his face.

" Keith," she said, " you *didn't* have a mackintosh. You must go away at once to Robert and get dry."

" Not now, Lucy. Let me stay."

" How long can you stay? "

" As long as ever you'll let me."

" Till you go to Italy? "

" Very well. Till I go to Italy."

" When are you going? "

" Not till you're well enough to go with me."

" How did you know I was ill? "

" Because I saw that Kitty had had to finish what your dear little hands had begun."

" Ah—you should have had them sooner——"

" Why should I have had them at all? Do you think I would have published them before I knew I had dedicated them to my wife? "

" Keith—dear—you mustn't talk about that yet."

She hid her face on his shoulder ; he lifted it and looked at it as if it could have told him what he had to know. It told him nothing ; it had not changed enough for that. It was like a beautiful picture blurred, and the sweeter for the blurring.

He laid his hand over her heart. At his touch it leapt and throbbed violently, suggesting a new terror.

"Darling, how fast your heart beats. Am I doing it harm?"

"No, it doesn't mind."

"But am I tiring it?"

"No, no, you're resting it."

She lay still a long time without speaking, till at last he carried her upstairs and delivered her into Kitty's care. At the open door of her room he saw a nurse in uniform standing ready to receive her. Her presence there was ominous of the unutterable things he feared.

"Kitty," said Lucia, when they were alone. "It looks as if I had been shamming after all. What do you think of me?"

"I think perhaps Sir Wilfrid Spence needn't come down to-morrow."

"Perhaps not. And yet it would be better to know. If there really is anything wrong I couldn't let him marry me. It would be awful. I want to be sure, Kitty, for his sake."

Kitty felt sure enough; and her certainty grew when Lucia came down the next morning. But she was unable to impart her certainty to Keith. The most he could do was to hide his anxiety from Lucia. It wanted but a day to the coming of the great specialist; and for that day they made such a brave show of happiness that they deceived both Kitty and themselves. Kitty, firm in her conviction, left them to themselves that afternoon while she went into Harmouth to announce to Lucia's doctor the miracle of her recovery.

When she had left the house a great peace fell on them. They had so much to say to each other, and so little time to say it in, when to-morrow might cut short their happiness. But Lucia was sorry for Kitty.

"Poor Kitty," said she, "she's going to marry her cousin Charlie Palliser. But that won't be the same."

"The same as what?"

"The same as my marrying you. Oh, Keith, that's one of the things I said we weren't to say. Do you know, once Kitty was angry with me. She said I was playing with fire—the divine fire. Ought I to have been afraid of it? Just a little bit in awe?"

"What? Of the divine fire? I gave it you, dearest, to play with—or to warm your little hands by."

" And now you've given it me to keep, to put my hands round it—so—and take care of it and see that it never goes out. I can do that, can't I, whatever happens?"

There was always that refrain: Whatever happens.

" I keep forgetting it doesn't really belong to me; it belongs to everybody, to the whole world. I believe I'm jealous."

" Of the British public? It doesn't really love me, Lucy, nor I it."

" Whether it does or not, you *do* remember that I loved you first—before anybody ever knew?"

" I do indeed."

" It *is* a shame to be so glad because Kitty is away."

Yet she continued to rejoice in the happiness that came of their solitude. It was Keith, not Kitty, who arranged her cushions for her and covered her feet; Keith, not Kitty, who poured out tea for her, and brought it her, and sat beside her afterwards, leaning over her and stroking her soft hair, as Kitty loved to do.

" Lucy," he said suddenly, " can you stand living with me in a horrid little house in a suburb?"

" I should love it. Dear little house."

" Maddox is in it now; but we'll turn him out. You don't know Maddox?"

She shuddered, and he drew the rug in closer about her.

" It's such a tiny house, Lucy; it would all go into this room."

" This room," said Lucy, " is much too large."

' There's only room for you and me in it."

" All the better, so long as there's room for me."

" And the walls are all lath and plaster. When Maddox is in another room I can hear him breathing."

" And when I'm in another room I shall hear you breathing; and then I shall know you're alive when I'm afraid you're not. I'm glad the walls are all lath and plaster."

" But it isn't a pretty house, Lucy."

" It will be a pretty house when I'm in it," said she, and was admitted to have had the best of the argument.

" Then, if you really don't mind, we shan't have to wait. Not a week, if you're ready to come to me."

But Lucia's face was sad. " Keith—darling—don't make plans till we know what Sir Wilfrid Spence says."

"I shall, whatever he says. But I suppose I must consult him before I take you to Alassio."

For still at his heart, under all its happiness, there lay that annihilating doubt; the doubt and fear that had been sown there by Horace Jewdwine. He could see for himself that one of his terrors was baseless; but there remained that other more terrible possibility. None of them had dared to put it into words; but it was implied, reiterated, in the name of Sir Wilfrid Spence. He had moreover a feeling that this happiness of his was too perfect, that it must be taken away from him.

He confided his trouble to Kitty that night, sitting up over the drawing-room fire. Lucia's doctor had come and gone.

"What did he say, Kitty?"

"He says there's no need for Sir Wilfrid Spence to see her at all. He is going to wire to him not to come."

He gave a sigh of relief. Then his eyes clouded.

"No. He must come. I'd rather he came."

"But why? He isn't a nerve specialist."

He shuddered. "I know. That's why I must have him. I can't trust these local men."

"It will be horribly expensive, Keith. And it's throwing money away. Dr. Robson said so."

"That's my affair."

"Oh, well, as for that, it was all arranged for."

"Nobody has any right to arrange for it but me."

"Much better arrange for a good time at Alassio."

"No. I want to be absolutely certain. You tell me she's perfectly well, and that doctor of yours swears she is, and I think it; and yet I can't believe it. I daren't."

"That's because you're not feeling very well yourself."

"I know that in some ways she is getting stronger every minute; but, you see, I can't help thinking what that other man said."

"What other man?"

"Well, the Jewdwines' doctor."

"What did *he* say?"

"Nothing. It was Jewdwine. He told me—well—that was why their engagement was broken off. Because she wasn't strong enough to marry."

Kitty's eyes blazed. "He told you *that?*"

" Not exactly. He couldn't, you know. I only thought their doctor must have told him—something terrible."

" I don't suppose he told him anything of the sort."

" Oh, well, you know, he didn't say so. But he let me think it."

" Yes. I know exactly how it was done. He wouldn't say anything he oughtn't to. But he'd let you think it. It was just his awful selfishness. He thought there was an off-chance of poor Lucy being a sort of nervous invalid, and he wouldn't risk the bother of it. But as for their engagement, there never was any. That was another of the things he let you think. I suppose he cared for Lucy as much as he could care for anybody; but the fact is he wants to marry another woman, and he couldn't bear to see her married to another man."

" Oh, I say, you know——"

" It sounds incredible. But you don't know how utterly I distrust that man. He's false through and through. There's nothing sound in him except his intellect. I wish you'd never known him. He's been the cause of all your— your suffering, and Lucy's too. You might have been married long ago if it hadn't been for him."

" No, Kitty. I don't think that."

" You might, really. If he hadn't been in the way she would have known that she cared for you, and let you know it, too. But nothing that he ever did or didn't do comes up to this."

" The truth is, Kitty, he thinks I'm rather a bad lot, you know."

" My dear Keith, he thinks that if *he* doesn't marry Lucy he'd rather you didn't. He certainly hit on the most effectual means of preventing it."

" Oh, did he! He doesn't know me. I shall marry her whatever Sir Wilfrid Spence says. If she's ill, all the more reason why I should look after her. I'm only afraid lest—lest——"

She knew what he thought and could not say—lest it should not be for very long.

" There are some things," he said quietly, " that *can't* be taken away from me."

Kitty was silent; for she knew what things they were.

" You can trust her to me, Kitty?"

" I can indeed."

And so on Sunday the great man came down.

It was over in half an hour. That half-hour Keith spent in pacing up and down the library, the place of so many dear and tender and triumphant memories. They sharpened his vision of Lucy doomed, of her sweet body delivered over to the torture.

He did not hear Kitty come in till she laid her hand upon his arm. He turned as if at the touch of destiny.

" Don't, Keith, for goodness' sake. It's all right. Only— he wants to see you."

Sir Wilfrid Spence stood in the morning-room alone. He looked very grave and grim. He had a manner, a celebrated manner that had accomplished miracles by its tremendous moral effect. It had helped to set him on his eminence and he was not going to sacrifice it now. He fixed his gaze on the poet as he entered, and held him under it for the space of half a minute without speaking.

He seemed, this master of the secrets of the body, to be invading despotically the province of the soul. It struck Rickman that the great specialist was passing judgment on him, to see whether in all things he were worthy of his destiny. The gaze thus prolonged became more than he could bear.

" Do you mind telling me at once what's wrong with her ? "

" There isn't anything wrong with her. What fool ever told you that there was? She has been made ill with grief."

Lucia herself came to him there and led him back into the library. They sat together in the window-seat, held silent for a little while by the passing of that shadow of their fear.

" Keith," she said at last, " is it true that you loved me when you were with me, here, ever so long ago? "

He answered her.

" And when you came to me and I was horrid to you, and when I sent you away? And when I never wrote to you, and Horace made you think I'd forgotten you? Did you love me then? "

" Yes, more than I did before, Lucy."

"But—Keith—you didn't love me when you were loving somebody else?"

"I did, more than ever then. That happened because I loved you."

"I can understand all the rest; but I can't understand that."

"I think I'd rather you didn't understand it, darling."

She sighed, puzzled over it, and gave it up. "But you didn't love me when you—when I—when you wouldn't have me?"

He answered her; but not with words.

"And now," said she, "you're going to Paris to-morrow."

"Perhaps."

"You must. Perhaps they'll be calling for you."

"And perhaps I shan't be there. Do you know, Lucy, you've got violets growing among the roots of your hair?"

"I know you're going to Paris to-morrow, to please me."

"Perhaps. And after that we're going to Alassio, and after that to Florence and Rome; all the places where your private secretary——"

"And when," said she, "is my private secretary going to take me home?"

"If his play succeeds, dear, he won't have to take you to that horrid house of his."

"Won't he? But I like it best of all."

"Why, Lucy?"

"Oh, for such a foolish reason. Because he's been in it."

"I'm afraid, darling, some of the houses he's been in——"

At that she fell to a sudden breathless sobbing, as if the life that had come back to her had spent itself again.

In his happiness he had forgotten Howland Street; or if he thought of it at all he thought of it as an enchanted spot, the stage that had brought him nearest to the place of his delight.

"Lucy, Lucy, how did you know? I never meant you to."

"Some one told me. And I—I went to see it."

"Good God!"

"I saw your room, the room they carried you out of. If I'd only known! My darling, why didn't you come to me then? Why didn't you? I had plenty. Why didn't you send for me?"

"How could I?"

"You could, you could——"

"But, sweetest, I didn't even know where you were."

"Wherever I was I would have come to you. I would have taken you away."

"It was worth it, Lucy. If it hadn't been for that, I shouldn't be here now. Looking back it seems positively glorious. And whatever it was I'd go through years of it for one hour with you here. One of those hours, even, when you didn't love me."

"I've always loved you, all my life long. Only I didn't know it was you.. Do you remember my telling you that your dream was divorced from reality? It wasn't true. That was what was wrong with me."

"I'm afraid I wasn't always very faithful to my dream."

"Because your dream wasn't always faithful to you. And yet it *was* faithful."

"Lucy, do you remember the things I told you? Can you forgive me for being what I was?"

"It was before I knew you."

"Yes, but after? That was worse; it was the worst thing I ever did; because I *had* known you."

She wondered why he asked forgiveness of her now, of all moments; and as she wondered the light dawned on her.

"I forgive you everything. It was my fault. I should have been there, and I wasn't."

Then he knew that, after all, she had understood. Her love was in her eyes, in their light and in their darkness. They gathered many flames of love into that tender, tragic gaze, all pitying, half maternal. Those eyes had never held for him the sad secrets of mortality. Love in them looked upon things invisible, incorruptible; divining, even as it revealed, the ultimate mystery. He saw that in her womanhood Nature was made holy, penetrated by the spirit and the fire of God. He knelt down and laid his face against her shoulder, and her arm, caressing, held him there, as if it were she who sheltered and protected.

"Keith," she whispered, "did you mean to marry me before you came this time, or after?"

" Before, oh, before."

" You thought—that terrible thing had happened to me? You thought you would always have me dragging on you? And yet you came? It made no difference. You came."

" I came because I wanted to take care of you, Lucy. I wanted nothing else. That was all."

Lucia's understanding was complete.

" I knew you were like that," said she; " I always knew it."

She bent towards his hidden face and raised it to her own.

THE END

S H A K E S P E A R E

ten Brink's Five Lectures on Shakespeare

Translated by JULIA FRANKLIN.

12mo, gilt top, $1.25.

Contents : The Poet and the Man ; The Chronology of Shakespeare's Works ; Shakespeare as Dramatist, as Comic Poet, as Tragic Writer.

" No single volume on the great dramatist is, in our judgment, superior in value to this modest but extremely able work."—*Outlook*.

" In the technical minutiæ that are the delight of so many German scholars our author does not indulge, limited as he is, in point of time, to five short hours ; fair-minded criticism he does present, even where one might understand prejudice, as in his comparison of Shakespeare, a romanticist of a Teutonic race, with Molière, a Frenchman and a classicist."—Mrs. Josephine M. Carter in the *Journal of Pedagogy*.

Brooke's Lectures on Shakespeare

By STOPFORD A. BROOKE.

An interpretation of the methods of Shakespeare as an artist by the well-known writer on English literary history. Each play considered (the list includes *Midsummer Night's Dream, Winter's Tale, Merchant of Venice, As You Like It, Richard II., Richard III., Macbeth, Tempest, Romeo and Juliet, Coriolanus*) is not so much analyzed as "appreciated" in a thoroughly sympathetic spirit and genial style. This volume will be followed by others similar in character from the hand of the same distinguished critic.

Henry Holt and Company

Publishers   (IV, '05)   New York